Index?

Indexed
3-30-54

D1420961

stories

BRITISH AND AMERICAN

JACK BARRY LUDWIG · W. RICHARD POIRIER

WILLIAMS COLLEGE

HOUGHTON MIFFLIN COMPANY

BOSTON · NEW YORK · CHICAGO · DALLAS · ATLANTA · SAN FRANCISCO

The Riverside Press Cambridge

This anthology has been designed for courses in Introduction to Literature, Freshman English, Critical Reading, the Short Story, Modern Fiction, and Creative Writing. With these courses in mind, the editors have selected stories for their artistic merit and their readability. The stories vary greatly in degree of complexity, but each is sufficiently interesting to stimulate sustained discussion.

The arrangement of the material in this volume involves consideration of historical developments and relative complexity. A particular feature of this anthology is that it allows students to deal with pairs of stories by a number of important writers. Section One includes stories of the nineteenth century; Section Two is devoted to the best and most famous British and American writers in the short story, most of whose work appears between the 1920's and the 1940's; in Section Three there are eight stories by young writers of the 40's and 50's, some of whose stories have never before appeared in a college anthology.

Chronology is not the most important consideration in the order of stories within the sections. Historically, the book is organized around the development of the short story from an explicit, narrated form, represented here by Goldsmith's "The Disabled Soldier," through Melville's "Bartleby," with its characteristics of modernity, to the more implicit and dramatic stories of Sections Two and Three. Within each section chronology has been ignored and the stories arranged roughly in order of complexity.

At the end of Section Two, this arrangement is temporarily disrupted in order to present as a group pairs of stories by E. M. Forster, D. H. Lawrence, Eudora Welty, and James Joyce. These pairs may profitably be used in class in a number of ways: to show how an understanding of one story can help in analyzing another by the same author: to show how the techniques of a particular writer, D. H. Lawrence for example, differ from story to story because of varying intentions. The two stories by Joyce, "The Dead" and "The Sisters," introduce the further problem of intentionally related stories. At this point the teacher may wish to discuss the emergence in modern fiction, in Anderson's *Winesburg, Ohio;* Faulkner's *Go Down, Moses;* Eudora Welty's *The Golden Apples* as well as in Joyce's *Dubliners,* of a separate form, connected short stories, somewhere between the short story and the novel.

Though the editors have a definite point of view, they have made no attempt to impose it on the students: for only two of the thirty stories in the anthology is any critical comment provided. Since the number of stories in the first section is necessarily small, and since the characteristics of these stories are discussed generally in the Introduction, analyses appear only in Section Two ("The Sisters" and "The Dead") and Section Three ("Under the Sky"). In the Introduction as well as in the analyses, the editors have tried to avoid special jargon and have tried to suggest some of the approaches which they have found useful in the classroom. The emphasis throughout is on the quality of the stories, the importance of the authors, and the freedom of the teacher in using this anthology as he sees fit.

Jack Barry Ludwig
W. Richard Poirier

contents

v

Section Three · a second generation

Notes on the Authors   499

introduction

During the twentieth century the short story has come of age: from a form of art which was once largely diversional it has become as serious in its purposes as the contemporary poem or novel. One aspect of this development has been the refinement of literary techniques. From the explicit, narrator's tale, represented in this book by Oliver Goldsmith's "The Disabled Soldier," the short story has developed through innovations by writers like Melville, Hawthorne, and Hardy, to what it is now — an implicit, highly dramatic form represented in the stories of Sections Two and Three by Joyce, E. M. Forster, Hemingway, Katherine Anne Porter, and J. F. Powers.

In a traditional tale like Goldsmith's, the narrator provided a frame whose purpose it was to tell the reader exactly what the story meant and how he was to feel about it. In a modern story like Conrad Aiken's "Strange Moonlight," on the other hand, no explicit effort is made to hamstring the reader: neither the dialogue of the characters nor the narration of the author pretends to interpret the story fully. The drama, the language and its rhythm, the symbols, and the tonality of the story are all as important as dialogue or narration; the story is organic in the sense that all elements in it are coordinated and none exists independently of the others. Because the story operates organically, each part of it sustaining and enriching every other part, it is in a sense independent of the author. He leaves it to speak for itself: having created the world of the work of art, he sits, in the words of Joyce, "paring his fingernails," allowing the reader to experience the wonders of discovery without a guidebook.

The twentieth century short story writer changed his attitude not only toward his reader and his material but also toward the ordering of that material. All the techniques of the art of fiction were put at the disposal of the commanding idea that the whole work of art was larger than the sum of its parts, that the work of art was an organic unity, that it was like a jigsaw puzzle: leave out a piece or fit one in improperly and daylight will show, the daylight of the real world which destroys the self-sufficient world of the work of art. Having this organic view of his material, the modern writer saw to it that everything in the story became not merely an end but a means to an end; and this held true of character, setting, and style alike. The piece could not take precedence over the completed picture.

In the analysis of the picture one may use methods similar to those used with a highly sophisticated modern poem. But once one has subjected the part, the "piece in the jigsaw puzzle," the means — whether it is metaphor, symbol, character, rhythm, or tableau — to the closest scrutiny, one must replace it in its proper setting, the organic whole, "the picture made from all the pieces," the end. If the reader keeps this relationship of means to ends in mind while reading through the stories in this book — and good twentieth century fiction in general — he will profit greatly from the use of the analytic method. He will see, for example, that what appeared at first as merely a decorative phrase — an end in itself — if taken in the context of a story like Katherine Anne Porter's "Flowering Judas," and analyzed that way, may prove to be part of the metaphoric pattern which pulls together the meaning of the entire story.

Such emphasis on the organic nature of the short story is profitable only if the reader is willing to analyze the parts, the particular literary effects which contribute to the whole. Style, for instance, the kind of language an author uses and the rhythm of his language, may be a means of objectifying an attitude or suggesting a feeling which is important to the story. The careful reader should be aware of the possibilities of parody through which his attitude toward certain characters and situations may be influenced. Language in the short story is delicately balanced. When the author disturbs the balance by dissociating language from its context (for instance, when a cultured man so loses the sense of who he is that in his attempt at some kind of communication he falls back wholly on the language of cliché), he does so to point up the character's dissociation from his world — his context. In the same way, rhythm goes beyond its sound values in the total story; for purposes of tonality and meaning it may be used to communicate a sense of excitement ("The Rocking-Horse Winner") or death (the description of the snow falling at the end of "The Dead") or comedy (the mock-epic movement of "On Stony Ground").

Considering the uses of language and rhythm in the modern story, it is little wonder that the reader who tries to skim through, hoping that the ending will clarify what he has ignored and tell him what he has not tried to understand, can miss the meaning entirely. This kind of superficial reading may serve well enough for many stories in the popular magazines. The structure of such stories, like the structure of the traditional tale, has a geometric analogy in the line which is not complete till the pencil is raised from the paper. It is linear in construction, and the story as a whole is dependent on the final stroke which is the ending. From this linear concept of structure, the modern writer has turned to a spatial one. Regardless of where the last piece fits in the modern story, the important thing is the picture as a whole. The so-called "trick ending," so important in the works of 'Saki,' O. Henry, Somerset Maugham, becomes a means to an end in stories like Elizabeth Bowen's "The Cat Jumps," Jean Stafford's "The Nemesis," E. M. Forster's "The Celestial Omnibus," and Angus Wilson's "Mummy to the Rescue." For example, in Miss Bowen's story the ending comes as a final touch to the mounting panic of the sophisticates who, through their denial of fear, have rejected all human warmth and reduced life to a series of sociological abstractions.

As with language, rhythm, and structure, so with character, setting, symbol, and tableau. It is no longer enough, to use nineteenth century terminology, that the characters be "memorable," the situations "real," or the settings "convincing." They may be all these, but each must earn its place in the structure and total effect of the

story. In fact, the characters in a modern story are often deliberately made "unmemorable," their personality pathetically weak,
their intellect insufficient to master the problems which beset them.
The very point of some of the stories in this volume is that the situation is so much larger than the character that he is rendered inde-
cisive and inarticulate except through violence.

Indeed, the question in twentieth century fiction often becomes
not merely "is or isn't this character memorable?" but "is this character involved in a situation which is memorable?" Even more important is an extension of this question: "What meaning is the
author dramatizing through this situation?" Charlie Wales in "Babylon Revisited" may or may not be a "memorable" character, but the
situation in which he finds himself is far more important to the
meaning and tonality of the story than the question of his "stature."
Similarly, in Joyce's "The Dead," Sansom's "On Stony Ground,"
and even Conrad's "The Heart of Darkness," the central character
or characters become only one term in a complex, one piece in a picture, one means to an end; they themselves are not fully aware of
the meaning of what happens to them — much less of the meanings
and tonalities which emerge from the whole story.

The kind of characters we have been discussing largely account
for the prominence of violence in modern fiction. And the use of
violence illustrates the difference in fictional techniques between
means and ends. Distinctions should be made between the "shock-
effect" violence of pulp fiction and the more complex violence of
serious modern literature. When it is merely a stock device for
shaking up the reader or bringing the story to its climax, violence
produces the melodramatic tone of much nineteenth century fiction. Such violence is often inadequate to the complexities of the
plot it is supposed to resolve. Violence in most modern stories is
not an escape from complexity, but a sign of the difficult relationship between the individual and his society. Violence is characteristic of modern fiction because of the contemporary concern with
the problem of self-identification. The world of much contemporary fiction is one in which man can no longer accept the abstract
definitions imposed upon him by society. His attempt to assert his
concrete awareness of self is invariably violent because within the
forms of society he would be permitted no other means of self-
articulation. Steve's assault on Max in Eudora Welty's "Keela, the
Outcast Indian Maiden" is necessary to dramatize his frustrated at-

tempt to assert his sense of personal guilt in a world of callous and uncompromising indifference. In such stories, violence is not separable from intellectual content.

When one analyzes the modern story for its intellectual content and its tonality, consideration should be given to the function of symbol. Both character and setting operate, at times, as symbols. A character in a story can be what he actually is — a drab and inconspicuous citizen like Bartleby — and at the same time symbolize a dilemma which is recognizably universal. Setting, or one property in a setting, can also carry more than literal meaning in the short story. A monument may be a thing of stone, a horse, a man, but it may also symbolize, say, the past and an attitude toward the past. The representational, as in modern art generally, is not an end in itself but a means to an end. Whether or not the description of the monument is "good" is a valid question but not a final one. The final question would entail placing the monument in the totality of the story and seeing it as a means to an end, not as an end in itself.

Another aspect of the modern story closely associated with symbolism is *tableau*, pictorial arrangement of characters or their gestures which gives added meaning to what is being dramatized. The handling of the children by Marion and Lincoln Peters during the climax of "Babylon Revisited," their act of drawing away from Charlie and to themselves both their own children and Charlie's daughter, serves to underline Charlie's isolation both from family life and the world of love, all he has left to give meaning to his existence. The reader of the modern short story must always be awake to the dramatic possibilities of tableau: he must try to visualize the action and movement of the characters as though he were reading a play.

The different parts of a story — tableau, setting, symbol, character, structure, and style — yield to rigorous and sensitive analysis. Yet any list of these "parts" is by its very nature incomplete because the modern story is always more than all these things combined. As we have said, the whole of a work of art, because of the organic nature of the world it creates, is always larger than the sum of its parts. That is why analysis can go only so far, and why the careful reader of these stories, while paying attention to the pieces in the jigsaw puzzle, must never lose sight of the assembled picture as a whole.

ONE

toward the dramatic

the disabled soldier

No observation is more common, and at the same time more true, than that one half of the world are ignorant how the other half lives. The misfortunes of the great are held up to engage our attention; are enlarged upon in tones of declamation; and the world is called upon to gaze at the noble sufferers: the great, under the pressure of calamity, are conscious of several others sympathising with their distress; and have, at once, the comfort of admiration and pity.

There is nothing magnanimous in bearing misfortunes with fortitude, when the whole world is looking on: men in such circumstances will act bravely even from motives of vanity: but he who, in the vale of obscurity, can brave adversity; who without friends to encourage, acquaintances to pity, or even without hope to alleviate his misfortunes, can behave with tranquillity and indifference, is truly great: whether peasant or courtier, he deserves admiration, and should be held up for our imitation and respect.

While the slightest inconveniences of the great are magnified into calamities; while tragedy mouths out their sufferings in all the strains of eloquence, the miseries of the poor are entirely disregarded; and yet some of the lower ranks of people undergo more real hardships in one day, than those of a more exalted station suffer in their whole lives. It is inconceivable what difficulties the meanest of our common sailors and soldiers endure without murmuring or regret; without passionately declaiming against providence, or calling their fellows to be gazers of their intrepidity. Every day is to them a day of misery, and yet they entertain their hard fate without repining.

With what indignation do I hear an Ovid, a Cicero, or a Rabutin complain of their misfortunes and hardships, whose greatest calamity was that of being unable to visit a certain spot of earth, to which they had foolishly attached an idea of happiness. Their distresses were pleasures, compared to what many of the adventuring poor every day endure without murmuring. They ate, drank, and slept; they had slaves to attend them, and were sure of subsistence for life; while many of their fellow creatures are obliged to wander without a friend to comfort or assist them, and even without shelter from the severity of the season.

I have been led into these reflections from accidentally meeting, some days ago, a poor fellow, whom I knew when a boy, dressed in a sailor's jacket, and begging at one of the outlets of the town, with a wooden leg. I knew him to have been honest and industrious when in the country, and was curious to learn what had reduced him to his present situation. Wherefore, after giving him what I thought proper, I desired to know the history of his life and misfortunes, and the manner in which he was reduced to his present distress. The disabled soldier, for such he was, though dressed in a sailor's habit, scratching his head, and leaning on his crutch, put himself into an attitude to comply with my request, and gave me his history as follows:

"As for my misfortunes, master, I can't pretend to have gone through any more than other folks; for, except the loss of my limb, and my being obliged to beg, I don't know any reason, thank Heaven, that I have to complain. There is Bill Tibbs, of our regiment, he has lost both his legs, and an eye to boot; but, thank Heaven, it is not so bad with me yet.

"I was born in Shropshire; my father was a labourer, and died when I was five years old, so I was put upon the parish. As he had been a wandering sort of man, the parishioners were not able to tell to what parish I belonged, or where I was born, so they sent me to another parish, and that parish sent me to a third. I thought in my heart, they kept sending me about so long, that they would not let me be born in any parish at all; but at last, however, they fixed me. I had some disposition to be a scholar, and was resolved at least to know my letters: but the master of the workhouse put me to business as soon as I was able to handle a mallet; and here I lived an easy kind of life for five years. I only wrought ten hours in the day, and had my meat and drink provided for my labour. It was true I was not suffered to stir out of the house, for fear, as they said, I should run away; but what of that? I had the liberty of the whole house, and the yard before the door, and that was enough for me. I was then bound out to a farmer, where I was up both early and late; but I ate and drank well; and liked my business well enough, till he died, when I was obliged to provide for myself; so I was resolved to go seek my fortune.

"In this manner I went from town to town, worked when I could get employment, and starved when I could get none; when, happening one day to go through a field belonging to a justice of the peace, I spied a hare crossing the path just before me; and I believe the devil put it into my head to fling my stick at it. Well, what will you have on't? I killed the hare, and was bringing it away, when the justice himself met me; he called me a poacher and a villain, and collaring me, desired I would give an account of myself. I fell upon my knees, begged his worship's pardon, and began to give a full account of all that I knew of my breed, seed, and generation; but though I gave a very true account, the justice said I could give no account; so I was indicted at the sessions, found guilty of being poor, and sent up to London to Newgate, in order to be transported as a vagabond.

"People may say this and that of being in jail, but, for my part, I found Newgate as agreeable a place as ever I was in in all my life. I had my belly full to eat and drink, and did no work at all. This kind of life was too good to last forever; so I was taken out of prison, after five months, put on board of ship, and sent off, with two hundred more, to the plantations. We had but an indifferent passage, for being all confined to the hold, more than a hun-

dred of our people died for want of sweet air; and those that remained were sickly enough, God knows. When we came ashore
we were sold to the planters, and I was bound for seven years more.
As I was no scholar, for I did not know my letters, I was obliged
to work among the negroes; and I served out my time, as in duty
bound to do.

"When my time was expired, I worked my passage home, and
glad I was to see old England again, because I loved my country. I
was afraid, however, that I should be indicted for a vagabond once
more, so did not much care to go down into the country, but kept
about the town, and did little jobs when I could get them.

"I was very happy in this manner for some time till one evening,
coming home from work, two men knocked me down, and then
desired me to stand. They belonged to a press-gang. I was carried
before the justice, and as I could give no account of myself, I had
my choice left, whether to go on board a man-of-war, or list for a
soldier. I chose the latter, and in this post of a gentleman, I served
two campaigns in Flanders, was at the battles of Val and Fontenoy,
and received but one wound through the breast here; but the doctor of our regiment soon made me well again.

"When the peace came on I was discharged; and as I could not
work, because my wound was sometimes troublesome, I listed for
a landman in the East India Company's service. I have fought the
French in six pitched battles; and I verily believe that if I could
read or write, our captain would have made me a corporal. But it
was not my good fortune to have any promotion, for I soon fell
sick, and so got leave to return home again with forty pounds in my
pocket. This was at the beginning of the present war, and I hoped
to be set on shore, and to have the pleasure of spending my money;
but the Government wanted men, and so I was pressed for a sailor,
before ever I could set foot on shore.

"The boatswain found me, as he said, an obstinate fellow: he
swore he knew that I understood my business well, but that I
shammed Abraham, to be idle; but God knows, I knew nothing of
sea-business, and he beat me without considering what he was
about. I had still, however, my forty pounds, and that was some
comfort to me under every beating; and the money I might have
had to this day, but that our ship was taken by the French, and so
I lost all.

"Our crew was carried into Brest, and many of them died, because they were not used to live in a jail; but, for my part, it was nothing to me, for I was seasoned. One night, as I was asleep on the bed of boards, with a warm blanket about me, for I always loved to lie well, I was awakened by the boatswain, who had a dark lantern in his hand. 'Jack,' says he to me, 'will you knock out the French sentry's brains?' 'I don't care,' says I, striving to keep myself awake, 'if I lend a hand.' 'Then follow me,' says he, 'and I hope we shall do business.' So up I got, and tied my blanket, which was all the clothes I had, about my middle, and went with him to fight the Frenchman. I hate the French, because they are all slaves, and wear wooden shoes.

"Though we had no arms, one Englishman is able to beat five French at any time; so we went down to the door where both sentries were posted, and rushing upon them, seized their arms in a moment, and knocked them down. From thence nine of us ran together to the quay, and seizing the first boat we met, got out of the harbour and put to sea. We had not been here three days before we were taken up by the Dorset privateer, who were glad of so many good hands; and we consented to run our chance. However, we had not as much luck as we expected. In three days we fell in with the *Pompadour* privateer of forty guns, while we had but twenty-three, so to it we went, yard-arm and yard-arm. The fight lasted three hours, and I verily believe we should have taken the Frenchman, had we but some more men left behind; but unfortunately we lost all our men just as we were going to get the victory.

"I was once more in the power of the French, and I believe it would have gone hard with me had I been brought back to Brest; but by good fortune we were retaken by the *Viper*. I had almost forgotten to tell you, that in that engagement, I was wounded in two places: I lost four fingers off the left hand, and my leg was shot off. If I had had the good fortune to have lost my leg and the use of my hand on board a king's ship, and not aboard a privateer, I should have been entitled to clothing and maintenance during the rest of my life; but that was not my chance: one man is born with a silver spoon in his mouth, and another with a wooden ladle. However, blessed be God, I enjoy good health, and will for ever love liberty and old England. Liberty, property, and old England, for ever, huzza!"

Thus saying, he limped off, leaving me in admiration at his intrepidity and content; nor could I avoid acknowledging, that an habitual acquaintance with misery serves better than philosophy to teach us to despise it.

THOMAS HARDY

absent-mindedness in a parish choir

It happened on Sunday after Christmas — the last Sunday they
ever played in Longpuddle church gallery, as it turned out,
though they didn't know it then. As you may know, sir, the players formed a very good band — almost as good as the Mellstock
parish players that were led by the Dewys; and that's saying a great
deal. There was Nicholas Puddingcome, the leader, with the first
fiddle; there was Timothy Thomas, the bass-viol man; John Biles,
the tenor fiddler; Dan'l Hornhead, with the serpent; Robert Dowdle,
with the clarionet; and Mr. Nicks, with the oboe — all sound and
powerful musicians, and strong-winded men — they that blowed.
For that reason they were very much in demand Christmas week
for little reels and dancing-parties; for they could turn a jig or a
hornpipe out of hand as well as ever they could turn out a psalm,
and perhaps better, not to speak irreverent. In short, one half-hour

9

they could be playing a Christmas carol in the squire's hall to the
ladies and gentlemen, and drinking tay and coffee with 'em as
modest as saints; and the next, at the Tinker's Arms, blazing away
like wild horses with the 'Dashing White Sergeant' to nine couple
of dancers and more, and swallowing rum-and-cider hot as flame.

Well, this Christmas they'd been out to one rattling randy after
another every night, and had got next to no sleep at all. Then came
the Sunday after Christmas, their fatal day. 'Twas so mortal cold
that year that they could hardly sit in the gallery; for though the
congregation down in the body of the church had a stove to keep
off the frost, the players in the gallery had nothing at all. So
Nicholas said at morning service, when 'twas freezing an inch an
hour, 'Please the Lord I won't stand this numbing weather no
longer; this afternoon we'll have something in our insides to make
us warm if it cost a king's ransom.'

So he brought a gallon of hot brandy and beer, ready mixed,
to church with him in the afternoon, and by keeping the jar well
wrapped up in Timothy Thomas's bass-viol bag it kept drinkably
warm till they wanted it, which was just a thimbleful in the
Absolution, and another after the Creed, and the remainder at the
beginning o' the sermon. When they'd had the last pull they felt
quite comfortable and warm, and as the sermon went on — most
unfortunately for 'em it was a long one that afternoon — they fell
asleep, every man jack of 'em; and there they slept on as sound as
rocks.

'Twas a very dark afternoon, and by the end of the sermon all
you could see of the inside of the church were the pa'son's two
candles alongside of him in the pulpit, and his spaking face behind
'em. The sermon being ended at last, the pa'son gie'd out the
Evening Hymn. But no choir set about sounding up the tune, and
the people began to turn their heads to learn the reason why, and
then Levi Limpet, a boy who sat in the gallery, nudged Timothy
and Nicholas, and said, 'Begin! begin!'

'Hey, what?' says Nicholas, starting up; and the church being
so dark and his head so muddled he thought he was at the party
they had played at all the night before, and away he went, bow
and fiddle, at 'The Devil among the Tailors,' the favorite jig of
our neighborhood at that time. The rest of the band, being in the
same state of mind and nothing doubting, followed their leader
with all their strength, according to custom. They poured out that

there tune till the lower bass notes of 'The Devil among the Tailors' made the cobwebs in the roof shiver like ghosts; then Nicholas,
seeing nobody moved, shouted out as he scraped (in his usual commanding way at dances when the folk didn't know the figures),
'Top couples cross hands! And when I make the fiddle squeak at
the end, every man kiss his pardner under the mistletoe!'

The boy Levi was so frightened that he bolted down the gallery
stairs and out homeward like lightning. The pa'son's hair fairly
stood on end when he heard the evil tune raging through the
church; and thinking the choir had gone crazy, he held up his hand
and said: 'Stop, stop, stop! Stop, stop! What's this?' But they didn't
hear 'n for the noise of their own playing, and the more he called
the louder they played.

Then the folks came out of their pews, wondering down to the
ground, and saying: 'What do they mean by such wickedness? We
shall be consumed like Sodom and Gomorrah!'

Then the squire came out of his pew lined wi' green baize,
where lots of lords and ladies visiting at the house were worship-
ping along with him, and went and stood in front of the gallery,
and shook his fist in the musicians' faces, saying, 'What! In this reverent edifice! What!'

And at last they heard 'n through their playing, and stopped.

'Never such an insulting, disgraceful thing — never!' says the
squire, who couldn't rule his passion.

'Never!' says the pa'son, who had come down and stood beside
him.

'Not if the angels of Heaven,' says the squire, (he was a wick-
edish man, the squire was, though now for once he happened to
be on the Lord's side)— 'not if the angels of Heaven come down,'
he says, 'shall one of you villanous players ever sound a note in
this church again; for the insult to me, and my family, and my visitors, and God Almighty, that you've a-perpetrated this afternoon!'

Then the unfortunate church band came to their senses, and
remembered where they were; and 'twas a sight to see Nicholas
Puddingcome and Timothy Thomas and John Biles creep down
the gallery stairs with their fiddles under their arms, and poor Dan'l
Hornhead with his serpent, and Robert Dowdle with his clarionet,
all looking as little as ninepins; and out they went. The pa'son
might have forgi'ed 'em when he learned the truth o't, but the
squire would not. That very week he sent for a barrel-organ that

would play two-and-twenty new psalm tunes, so exact and particular that, however sinful inclined you was, you could play
nothing but psalm tunes whatsoever. He had a really respectable
man to turn the winch, as I said, and the old players played no
more.

NATHANIEL HAWTHORNE

wakefield

In some old magazine or newspaper, I recollect a story, told as truth, of a man — let us call him Wakefield — who absented himself for a long time from his wife. The fact, thus abstractedly stated, is not very uncommon, nor — without a proper distinction of circumstances — to be condemned either as naughty or nonsensical. Howbeit, this, though far from the most aggravated, is perhaps the strangest instance on record of marital delinquency; and, moreover, as remarkable a freak as may be found in the whole list of human oddities. The wedded couple lived in London. The man, under pretence of going a journey, took lodgings in the next street to his own house, and there, unheard of by his wife or friends, and without the shadow of a reason for such self-banishment, dwelt upwards of twenty years. During that period, he beheld his home every day, and frequently the forlorn Mrs. Wakefield. And after so great a gap in his matrimonial felicity

— when his death was reckoned certain, his estate settled, his name dismissed from memory, and his wife, long, long ago, resigned to her autumnal widowhood — he entered the door one evening, quietly, as from a day's absence, and became a loving spouse till death.

This outline is all that I remember. But the incident, though of the purest originality, unexampled, and probably never to be repeated, is one, I think, which appeals to the generous sympathies of mankind. We know, each for himself, that none of us would perpetrate such a folly, yet feel as if some other might. To my own contemplations, at least, it has often recurred, always exciting wonder, but with a sense that the story must be true and a conception of its hero's character. Whenever any subject so forcibly affects the mind, time is well spent in thinking of it. If the reader choose, let him do his own meditation; or if he prefer to ramble with me through the twenty years of Wakefield's vagary, I bid him welcome; trusting that there will be a pervading spirit and a moral, even should we fail to find them, done up neatly, and condensed into the final sentence. Thought has always its efficacy, and every striking incident its moral.

What sort of a man was Wakefield? We are free to shape out our own idea, and call it by his name. He was now in the meridian of life; his matrimonial affections, never violent, were sobered into a calm, habitual sentiment; of all husbands, he was likely to be the most constant, because a certain sluggishness would keep his heart at rest, wherever it might be placed. He was intellectual, but not actively so; his mind occupied itself in long and lazy musings, that tended to no purpose, or had not vigour to attain it; his thoughts were seldom so energetic as to seize hold of words. Imagination, in the proper meaning of the term, made no part of Wakefield's gifts. With a cold, but not depraved nor wandering heart, and a mind never feverish with riotous thoughts, nor perplexed with originality, who could have anticipated that our friend would entitle himself to a foremost place among the doers of eccentric deeds? Had his acquaintances been asked, who was the man in London, the surest to perform nothing to-day which should be remembered on the morrow, they would have thought of Wakefield. Only the wife of his bosom might have hesitated. She, without having analysed his character, was partly aware of a quiet selfishness, that had rusted into his inactive mind, — of a peculiar sort of vanity, the most uneasy attribute about him, — of a disposition to craft, which had seldom produced more positive effects than the keeping of petty secrets, hardly worth revealing, — and, lastly, of what she called a little strangeness, sometimes, in the good man. This latter quality is indefinable, and perhaps non-existent.

Let us now imagine Wakefield bidding adieu to his wife. It is the dusk of an October evening. His equipment is a drab great-coat, a hat covered with an oil-cloth, top-boots, an umbrella in one hand and a small portmanteau in the other. He has informed Mrs. Wakefield that he is to take the night coach into the country. She would fain inquire the length of his journey, its object, and the probable time of his return; but, indulgent to his harmless love of mystery, interrogates him only by a look. He tells her not to expect him positively by the return coach, not to be alarmed should he tarry three or four days; but, at all events, to look for him at supper on Friday evening. Wakefield himself, be it considered, has no suspicion of what is before him. He holds out his hand; she gives her own, and meets his parting kiss, in the matter-of-course way of a ten years' matrimony; and forth goes the middle-aged Mr. Wakefield, almost resolved to perplex his good lady by a whole week's absence. After the door has closed behind him, she perceives it thrust partly open, and a vision of her husband's face, through the aperture, smiling on her, and gone in a moment. For the time, this little incident is dismissed without a thought. But, long afterwards, when she has been more years a widow than a wife, that smile recurs, and flickers across all her reminiscences of Wakefield's visage. In her many musings, she surrounds the original smile with a multitude of fantasies, which make it strange and awful; as, for instance, if she imagines him in a coffin, that parting look is frozen on his pale features; or, if she dreams of him in heaven, still his blessed spirit wears a quiet and crafty smile. Yet, for its sake, when all others have given him up for dead, she sometimes doubts whether she is a widow.

But our business is with the husband. We must hurry after him, along the street, ere he lose his individuality, and melt into the great mass of London life. It would be vain searching for him there. Let us follow close at his heels, therefore, until, after several superfluous turns and doublings, we find him comfortably established by the fireside of a small apartment, previously bespoken. He is in the next street to his own, and at his journey's end. He can scarcely trust his good fortune in having got thither unperceived, — recollecting that, at one time, he was delayed by the throng, in the very focus of a lighted lantern; and, again, there were footsteps, that seemed to tread behind his own, distinct from the multitudinous tramp around him; and, anon, he heard a voice shouting afar, and fancied that it called his name. Doubtless, a dozen busybodies had been watching him, and told his wife the whole affair. Poor Wakefield! Little knowest thou thine own insignificance in this great world! No mortal eye but mine has traced thee. Go quietly to thy bed, foolish man; and, on the morrow, if thou wilt be wise, get thee home to good Mrs. Wakefield, and tell her the truth. Remove not thyself, even for a little week, from thy place in her chaste bosom. Were she, for a single moment, to deem thee dead, or lost, or lastingly divided from her, thou wouldest be woefully conscious of a change in thy true wife forever after. It is perilous to make a chasm in human affections; not that they gape so long and wide, but so quickly close again!

Almost repenting of his frolic, or whatever it may be termed, Wakefield lies down betimes, and starting from his first nap, spreads forth his arms into the wide and solitary waste of the unaccustomed bed. "No," — thinks he, gathering the bedclothes about him, — "I will not sleep alone another night."

In the morning, he rises earlier than usual, and sets himself to consider what he really means to do. Such are his loose and rambling modes of thought that he has taken this very singular step, with the consciousness of a purpose, indeed, but without being able to define it sufficiently for his own contemplation. The vagueness of the project, and the convulsive effort with which he plunges into the execution of it, are equally characteristic of a feeble-minded man. Wakefield sifts his ideas, however, as minutely as he may, and finds himself curious to know the progress of matters at home — how his exemplary wife will endure her widowhood of a week; and, briefly, how the little sphere of creatures and circumstances, in which he was a central object, will be affected by his removal. A morbid vanity, therefore, lies nearest the bottom of the affair. But, how is he to attain his ends? Not, certainly, by keeping close in this comfortable lodging, where, though he slept and woke in the next street to his home, he is as effectually abroad, as if the stage-coach had been whirling him away all night. Yet, should he reappear, the whole project is knocked on the head. His poor brains being hopelessly puzzled with this dilemma, he at length ventures out, partly resolving to cross the head of the street, and send one hasty glance towards his forsaken domicile. Habit — for he is a man of habits — takes him by the hand, and guides him, wholly unaware to his own door, where, just at the critical moment, he is aroused by the scraping of his foot upon the step. Wakefield! whither are you going?

At that instant, his fate was turning on the pivot. Little dreaming of the doom to which his first backward step devotes him, he hurries away, breathless with agitation hitherto unfelt, and hardly dares turn his head, at the distant corner. Can it be that nobody caught sight of him? Will not the whole household — the decent Mrs. Wakefield, the smart maid-servant, and the dirty little footboy — raise a hue and cry, through London streets, in pursuit of their fugitive lord and master? Wonderful escape! He gathers courage to pause and look homeward, but is perplexed with a sense of change about the familiar edifice, such as affects us all, when, after a separation of months or years, we again see some hill or lake, or work of art, with which we were friends of old. In ordinary cases, this indescribable impression is caused by the comparison and contrast between our imperfect reminiscences and the reality. In Wakefield, the magic of a single night has wrought a similar transformation, because, in that brief period, a great moral change has been effected. But this is a secret from himself. Before leaving the spot, he catches a far and momentary glimpse of his wife, passing athwart the front window, with her face turned towards the head of the street. The crafty nincompoop takes to his heels, scared with the idea, that, among a thousand such atoms of mortality, her eye must have detected him. Right glad is his heart, though his brain be somewhat dizzy, when he finds himself by the coalfire of his lodgings.

So much for the commencement of this long whim-wham. After the initial conception, and the stirring up of the man's sluggish temperament to put it in practice, the whole matter evolves itself in a natural train. We may suppose him, as the result of deep deliberation, buying a new wig, of reddish hair, and selecting sundry garments, in a fashion unlike his customary suit of brown, from a Jew's old-clothes bag. It is accomplished. Wakefield is another man. The new system being now established, a retrograde movement to the old would be almost as difficult as the step that placed

him in his unparalleled position. Furthermore, he is rendered obstinate by a sulkiness, occasionally incident to his temper, and brought
on, at present, by the inadequate sensation which he conceives to
have been produced in the bosom of Mrs. Wakefield. He will not
go back until she be frightened half to death. Well; twice or thrice
has she passed before his sight, each time with a heavier step, a
paler cheek, and more anxious brow; and in the third week of his
non-appearance, he detects a portent of evil entering the house, in
the guise of an apothecary. Next day, the knocker is muffled. Towards nightfall comes the chariot of a physician, and deposits its
big-wigged and solemn burden at Wakefield's door, whence, after
a quarter of an hour's visit, he emerges, perchance the herald of
a funeral. Dear woman! Will she die? By this time, Wakefield is
excited to something like energy of feeling, but still lingers away
from his wife's bedside, pleading with his conscience, that she must
not be disturbed at such a juncture. If aught else restrains him,
he does not know it. In the course of a few weeks, she gradually
recovers; the crisis is over; her heart is sad, perhaps, but quiet; and,
let him return soon or late, it will never be feverish for him again.
Such ideas glimmer through the mist of Wakefield's mind, and
render him indistinctly conscious that an almost impassable gulf
divides his hired apartment from his former home. "It is but in
the next street!" he sometimes says. Fool! it is in another world.
Hitherto, he has put off his return from one particular day to another; henceforward, he leaves the precise time undetermined. Not
to-morrow, — probably next week, — pretty soon. Poor man! The
dead have nearly as much chance of revisiting their earthly homes,
as the self-banished Wakefield.

Would that I had a folio to write, instead of an article of a dozen
pages! Then might I exemplify how an influence, beyond our control, lays its strong hand on every deed which we do, and weaves
its consequences into an iron tissue of necessity. Wakefield is spellbound. We must leave him, for ten years or so, to haunt around
his house, without once crossing the threshold, and to be faithful
to his wife, with all the affection of which his heart is capable,
while he is slowly fading out of hers. Long since, it must be
remarked, he has lost the perception of singularity in his conduct.

Now for a scene! Amid the throng of a London street, we distinguish a man, now waxing elderly, with a few characteristics to
attract careless observers, yet bearing, in his whole aspect, the

handwriting of no common fate, for such as have the skill to read it. He is meagre; his low and narrow forehead is deeply wrinkled; his eyes, small and lustreless, sometimes wander apprehensively about him, but oftener seem to look inward. He bends his head, and moves with an indescribable obliquity of gait, as if unwilling to display his full front to the world. Watch him, long enough to see what we have described, and you will allow, that circumstances — which often produce remarkable men from nature's ordinary handiwork — have produced one such here. Next, leaving him to sidle along the footwalk, cast your eyes in the opposite direction, where a portly female, considerably in the wane of life, with a prayer-book in her hand, is proceeding to yonder church. She has the placid mien of settled widowhood. Her regrets have either died away, or have become so essential to her heart, that they would be poorly exchanged for joy. Just as the lean man and well-conditioned woman are passing, a slight obstruction occurs, and brings these two figures directly in contact. Their hands touch; the pressure of the crowd forces her bosom against his shoulder; they stand, face to face, staring into each other's eyes. After a ten years' separation, thus Wakefield meets his wife!

The throng eddies away, and carries them asunder. The sober widow, resuming her former pace, proceeds to church, but pauses in the portal, and throws a perplexed glance along the street. She passes in, however, opening her prayer-book as she goes. And the man! with so wild a face, that busy and selfish London stands to gaze after him, he hurries to his lodgings, bolts the door, and throws himself upon the bed. The latent feelings of years break out; his feeble mind acquires a brief energy from their strength; all the miserable strangeness of his life is revealed to him at a glance: and he cries out, passionately, "Wakefield! Wakefield! You are mad!"

Perhaps he was so. The singularity of his situation must have so moulded him to himself, that, considered in regard to his fellow-creatures and the business of life, he could not be said to possess his right mind. He had contrived, or rather he had happened, to dissever himself from the world, — to vanish, — to give up his place and privileges with living men, without being admitted among the dead. The life of a hermit is nowise parallel to his. He was in the bustle of the city, as of old; but the crowd swept by, and saw him not; he was, we may figuratively say, always beside his wife, and at his hearth, yet must never feel the warmth of the one, nor the affection of the other. It was Wakefield's unprecedented fate, to retain his original share of human sympathies, and to be still involved in human interests, while he had lost his reciprocal influence on them. It would be a most curious speculation, to trace out the effect of such circumstances on his heart and intellect, separately, and in unison. Yet, changed as he was, he would seldom be conscious of it, but deem himself the same man as ever; glimpses of the truth, indeed, would come, but only for the moment; and still he would keep saying, "I shall soon go back!" nor reflect that he had been saying so for twenty years.

I conceive, also, that these twenty years would appear, in the retrospect, scarcely longer than the week to which Wakefield had at first limited his absence. He would look on the affair as no more than an interlude in the main business of life. When, after a little while more, he should deem it time to re-enter his parlour, his wife would clap her hands for joy, on beholding the middle-aged Mr. Wakefield. Alas, what a mistake! Would Time but await the close of our favourite follies, we should be young men, all of us, and till Doomsday.

One evening, in the twentieth year since he vanished, Wakefield is taking his customary walk towards the dwelling which he still calls his own. It is a gusty night of autumn, with frequent showers, that patter down upon the pavement, and are gone, before a man can put up his umbrella. Pausing near the house, Wakefield discerns, through the parlour windows of the second floor, the red glow, and the glimmer and fitful flash of a comfortable fire. On the ceiling appears a grotesque shadow of good Mrs. Wakefield. The cap, the nose and chin, and the broad waist form an admirable caricature, which dances, moreover, with the up-flickering and down-sinking blaze, almost too merrily for the shade of an elderly widow. At this instant, a shower chances to fall, and is driven, by the unmannerly gust, full into Wakefield's face and bosom. He is quite penetrated with its autumnal chill. Shall he stand, wet and shivering here, when his own hearth has a good fire to warm him, and his own wife will run to fetch the gray coat and small clothes, which doubtless she has kept carefully in the closet of their bedchamber? No! Wakefield is no such fool. He ascends the steps, — heavily! — for twenty years have stiffened his legs, since he came down, — but he knows it not. Stay, Wakefield! Would you go to the sole home that is left you? Then step into your grave! The door opens. As he passes in, we have a parting glimpse of his visage, and recognize the crafty smile, which was the precursor of the little joke that he has ever since been playing off at his wife's expense. How unmercifully has he quizzed the poor woman! Well, a good night's rest to Wakefield!

This happy event — supposing it to be such — could only have occurred at an unpremeditated moment. We will not follow our friend across the threshold. He has left us much food for thought, a portion of which shall lend its wisdom to a moral, and be shaped into a figure. Amid the seeming confusion of our mysterious world, individuals are so nicely adjusted to a system, and systems to one another, and to a whole, that, by stepping aside for a moment, a man exposes himself to a fearful risk of losing his place for ever. Like Wakefield, he may become, as it were, the Outcast of the Universe.

HERMAN MELVILLE

bartleby the scrivener: a story of wall street

I am a rather elderly man. The nature of my avocations, for the last thirty years, has brought me into more than ordinary contact with what would seem an interesting and somewhat singular set of men, of whom, as yet, nothing, that I know of, has ever been written — I mean, the law-copyists, or scriveners. I have known very many of them, professionally and privately, and, if I pleased, could relate divers histories, at which good-natured gentlemen might smile, and sentimental souls might weep. But I waive the biographies of all other scriveners, for a few passages in the life of Bartleby, who was a scrivener, the strangest I ever saw, or heard of. While, of other law-copyists, I might write the complete life, of Bartleby nothing of that sort can be done. I believe that no materials exist, for a full and satisfactory biography of this man. It is

22

an irreparable loss to literature. Bartleby was one of those beings of whom nothing is ascertainable, except from the original sources, and, in his case, those are very small. What my own astonished eyes saw of Bartleby, *that* is all I know of him, except, indeed, one vague report, which will appear in the sequel.

Ere introducing the scrivener, as he first appeared to me, it is fit I make some mention of myself, my *employés*, my business, my chambers, and general surroundings; because some such description is indispensable to an adequate understanding of the chief character about to be presented. Imprimis: I am a man who, from his youth upwards, has been filled with a profound conviction that the easiest way of life is the best. Hence, though I belong to a profession proverbially energetic and nervous, even to turbulence, at times, yet nothing of that sort have I ever suffered to invade my peace. I am one of those unambitious lawyers who never address a jury, or in any way draw down public applause; but, in the cool tranquillity of a snug retreat, do a snug business among rich men's bonds, and mortgages, and title-deeds. All who know me, consider me an eminently *safe* man. The late John Jacob Astor, a personage little given to poetic enthusiasm, had no hesitation in pronouncing my first grand point to be prudence; my next, method. I do not speak it in vanity, but simply record the fact, that I was not unemployed in my profession by the late John Jacob Astor; a name which, I admit, I love to repeat; for it hath a rounded and orbicular sound to it, and rings like unto bullion. I will freely add, that I was not insensible to the late John Jacob Astor's good opinion.

Some time prior to the period at which this little history begins, my avocations had been largely increased. The good old office, now extinct in the State of New York, of a Master in Chancery, had been conferred upon me. It was not a very arduous office, but very pleasantly remunerative. I seldom lose my temper; much more seldom indulge in dangerous indignation at wrongs and outrages; but I must be permitted to be rash here and declare, that I consider the sudden and violent abrogation of the office of Master in Chancery, by the new Constitution, as a —— premature act; inasmuch as I had counted upon a life-lease of the profits, whereas I only received those of a few short years. But this is by the way.

My chambers were up stairs, at No. —— Wall Street. At one end, they looked upon the white wall of the interior of a spacious skylight shaft, penetrating the building from top to bottom.

This view might have been considered rather tame than otherwise, deficient in what landscape painters call "life." But, if so, the view from the other end of my chambers offered, at least, a contrast, if nothing more. In that direction, my windows commanded an unobstructed view of a lofty brick wall, black by age and everlasting shade; which wall required no spy-glass to bring out its lurking beauties, but, for the benefit of all near-sighted spectators, was pushed up to within ten feet of my window-panes. Owing to the great height of the surrounding buildings, and my chambers being on the second floor, the interval between this wall and mine not a little resembled a huge square cistern.

At the period just preceding the advent of Bartleby, I had two persons as copyists in my employment, and a promising lad as an office-boy. First, Turkey; second, Nippers; third, Ginger Nut. These may seem names, the like of which are not usually found in the Directory. In truth, they were nicknames, mutually conferred upon each other by my three clerks, and were deemed expressive of their respective persons or characters. Turkey was a short, pursy Englishman, of about my own age — that is, somewhere not far from sixty. In the morning, one might say, his face was of a fine florid hue, but after twelve o'clock, meridian — his dinner hour — it blazed like a grate full of Christmas coals; and continued blazing — but, as it were, with a gradual wane — till six o'clock, P.M., or thereabouts; after which, I saw no more of the proprietor of the face, which, gaining its meridian with the sun, seemed to set with it, to rise, culminate, and decline the following day, with the like regularity and undiminished glory. There are many singular coincidences I have known in the course of my life, not the least among which was the fact, that, exactly when Turkey displayed his fullest beams from his red and radiant countenance, just then, too, at that critical moment, began the daily period when I considered his business capacities as seriously disturbed for the remainder of the twenty-four hours. Not that he was absolutely idle, or averse to business then; far from it. The difficulty was, he was apt to be altogether too energetic. There was a strange, inflamed, flurried, flighty recklessness of activity about him. He would be incautious in dipping his pen into his inkstand. All his blots upon my documents were dropped there after twelve o'clock, meridian. Indeed, not only would he be reckless, and sadly given to making blots in the afternoon, but, some days, he went further, and was rather noisy. At such times, too, his face flamed with augmented blazonry, as if cannel coal had been heaped on anthracite. He made an unpleasant racket with his chair; spilled his sand-box; in mending his pens, impatiently split them all to pieces, and threw them on the floor in a sudden passion; stood up, and leaned over his table, boxing his papers about in a most indecorous manner, very sad to behold in an elderly man like him. Nevertheless, as he was in many ways a most valuable person to me, and all the time before twelve o'clock, meridian, was the quickest, steadiest creature, too, accomplishing a great deal of work in a style not easily to be matched — for these reasons, I was willing to overlook his eccentricities, though indeed, occasionally, I remonstrated with him. I did this very gently, however, because, though the civilest, nay, the blandest and most reverential of men in the morning, yet, in the afternoon, he was disposed, upon provocation, to be slightly rash with his tongue — in fact, insolent. Now, valuing his morning services as I did, and resolved not to lose them — yet, at the same time, made uncomfortable by his inflamed ways after twelve o'clock — and being a man of peace, unwillingly by my admonitions to call forth unseemly retorts from him, I took upon me, one Saturday noon (he was always worse on Saturdays) to hint to him, very kindly, that, perhaps, now that he was growing old, it might be well to abridge his labors; in short, he need not come to my chambers after twelve o'clock, but, dinner over, had best go home to his lodgings, and rest himself till tea-time. But no; he insisted upon his afternoon devotions. His countenance became intolerably fervid, as he oratorically assured me — gesticulating with a long ruler at the other end of the room — that if his services in the morning were useful, how indispensable, then, in the afternoon?

"With submission, sir," said Turkey, on this occasion, "I consider myself your right-hand man. In the morning I but marshal and deploy my columns; but in the afternoon I put myself at their head, and gallantly charge the foe, thus" — and he made a violent thrust with the ruler.

"But the blots, Turkey," intimated I.

"True; but, with submission, sir, behold these hairs! I am getting old. Surely, sir, a blot or two of a warm afternoon is not to be severely urged against gray hairs. Old age — even if it blot the page — is honorable. With submission, sir, we *both* are getting old."

This appeal to my fellow-feeling was hardly to be resisted. At all events, I saw that go he would not. So, I made up my mind to let him stay, resolving, nevertheless, to see to it that, during the afternoon, he had to do with my less important papers.

Nippers, the second on my list, was a whiskered, sallow, and, upon the whole, rather piratical-looking young man, of about five-and-twenty. I always deemed him the victim of two evil powers — ambition and indigestion. The ambition was evinced by a certain impatience of the duties of a mere copyist, an unwarrantable usurpation of strictly professional affairs, such as the original drawing up of legal documents. The indigestion seemed betokened in an occasional nervous testiness and grinning irritability, causing the teeth to audibly grind together over mistakes committed in copying; unnecessary maledictions, hissed, rather than spoken, in the heat of business; and especially by a continual discontent with the height of the table where he worked. Though of a very ingenious mechanical turn, Nippers could never get this table to suit him. He put chips under it, blocks of various sorts, bits of pasteboard, and at last went so far as to attempt an exquisite adjustment, by final pieces of folded blotting-paper. But no invention would answer. If, for the sake of easing his back, he brought the table-lid at a sharp angle well up towards his chin, and wrote there like a man using the steep roof of a Dutch house for his desk, then he declared that it stopped the circulation in his arms. If now he lowered the table to his waistbands, and stooped over it in writing, then there was a sore aching in his back. In short, the truth of the matter was, Nippers knew not what he wanted. Or, if he wanted anything, it was to be rid of a scrivener's table altogether. Among the manifestations of his diseased ambition was a fondness he had for receiving visits from certain ambiguous-looking fellows in seedy coats, whom he called his clients. Indeed, I was aware that not only was he, at times, considerable of a ward-politician, but he occasionally did a little business at the Justices' courts, and was not unknown on the steps of the Tombs. I have good reason to believe, however, that one individual who called upon him at my chambers, and who, with a grand air, he insisted was his client, was no other than a dun, and the alleged title-deed, a bill. But, with all his failings, and the annoyances he caused me, Nippers, like his compatriot Turkey, was a very useful man to me; wrote a neat, swift hand; and, when he chose, was not deficient in a gentlemanly sort of deportment. Added to this, he always dressed in a gentlemanly sort of way; and so, incidentally, reflected credit upon my chambers. Whereas, with respect to Turkey, I had much ado to keep him from being a reproach to me. His clothes were apt to look oily, and smell of eating-houses. He wore his pantaloons very loose and baggy in summer. His coats were execrable; his hat not to be handled. But while the hat was a thing of indifference to me, inasmuch as his natural civility and deference, as a dependent Englishman, always led him to doff it the moment he entered the room, yet his coat was another matter. Concerning his coats, I reasoned with him; but with no effect. The truth was, I suppose, that a man with so small an income could not afford to sport such a lustrous face and a lustrous coat at one and the same time. As Nippers once observed, Turkey's money went chiefly for red ink. One winter day, I presented Turkey with a highly respectable-looking coat of my own — a padded gray coat, of a most comfortable warmth, and which buttoned straight up from the knee to the neck. I thought Turkey would appreciate the favor, and abate his rashness and obstreperousness of afternoons. But no; I verily believe that buttoning himself up in so downy and blanket-like a coat had a pernicious effect upon him — upon the same principle that too much oats are bad for horses. In fact, precisely as a rash, restive horse is said to feel his oats, so Turkey felt his coat. It made him insolent. He was a man whom prosperity harmed.

Though, concerning the self-indulgent habits of Turkey, I had my own private surmises, yet, touching Nippers, I was well persuaded that, whatever might be his faults in other respects, he was, at least, a temperate young man. But, indeed, nature herself seemed to have been his vintner, and, at his birth, charged him so thoroughly with an irritable, brandy-like disposition, that all subsequent potations were needless. When I consider how, amid the stillness of my chambers, Nippers would sometimes impatiently rise from his seat, and stooping over his table, spread his arms wide apart, seize the whole desk, and move it, and jerk it, with a grim, grinding motion on the floor, as if the table were a perverse voluntary agent, intent on thwarting and vexing him, I plainly perceive that, for Nippers, brandy-and-water were altogether superfluous.

It was fortunate for me that, owing to its peculiar cause — indigestion — the irritability and consequent nervousness of Nippers were mainly observable in the morning, while in the afternoon he was comparatively mild. So that, Turkey's paroxysms only coming on about twelve o'clock, I never had to do with their eccentricities at one time. Their fits relieved each other, like guards. When Nippers's was on, Turkey's was off; and *vice versa*. This was a good natural arrangement, under the circumstances.

Ginger Nut, the third on my list, was a lad, some twelve years old. His father was a carman, ambitious of seeing his son on the bench instead of a cart, before he died. So he sent him to my office, as student at law, errand-boy, cleaner and sweeper, at the rate of one dollar a week. He had a little desk to himself, but he did not use it much. Upon inspection, the drawer exhibited a great array of the shells of various sorts of nuts. Indeed, to this quick-witted youth, the whole noble science of the law was contained in a nut-shell. Not the least among the employments of Ginger Nut, as well as one which he discharged with the most alacrity, was his duty as cake and apple purveyor for Turkey and Nippers. Copying law-papers being proverbially a dry, husky sort of business, my two scriveners were fain to moisten their mouths very often with Spitzenbergs, to be had at the numerous stalls nigh the Custom House and Post Office. Also, they sent Ginger Nut very frequently for that peculiar cake — small, flat, round, and very spicy — after which he had been named by them. Of a cold morning, when business was but dull, Turkey would gobble up scores of these cakes, as if they were mere wafers — indeed, they sell them at the rate of six or eight for a penny — the scrape of his pen blending with the crunching of the crisp particles in his mouth. Of all the fiery afternoon blunders and flurried rashnesses of Turkey, was his once moistening a ginger-cake between his lips, and clapping it on to a mortgage, for a seal. I came within an ace of dismissing him then. But he mollified me by making an oriental bow, and saying —

"With submission, sir, it was generous of me to find you in stationery on my own account."

Now my original business — that of a conveyancer and title hunter, and drawer-up of recondite documents of all sorts — was considerably increased by receiving the Master's office. There was now great work for scriveners. Not only must I push the clerks already with me, but I must have additional help.

In answer to my advertisement, a motionless young man one

morning stood upon my office threshold, the door being open, for it was summer. I can see that figure now — pallidly neat, pitiably respectable, incurably forlorn! It was Bartleby.

After a few words touching his qualifications, I engaged him, glad to have among my corps of copyists a man of so singularly sedate an aspect, which I thought might operate beneficially upon the flighty temper of Turkey, and the fiery one of Nippers.

I should have stated before that ground-glass folding-doors divided my premises into two parts, one of which was occupied by my scriveners, the other by myself. Accordingly to my humor, I threw open these doors, or closed them. I resolved to assign Bartleby a corner by the folding-doors, but on my side of them, so as to have this quiet man within easy call, in case any trifling thing was to be done. I placed his desk close up to a small side-window in that part of the room, a window which originally had afforded a lateral view of certain grimy backyards and bricks, but which, owing to subsequent erections, commanded at present no view at all, though it gave some light. Within three feet of the panes was a wall, and the light came down from far above, between two lofty buildings, as from a very small opening in a dome. Still further to a satisfactory arrangement, I procured a high green folding screen, which might entirely isolate Bartleby from my sight, though not remove him from my voice. And thus, in a manner, privacy and society were conjoined.

At first, Bartleby did an extraordinary quantity of writing. As if long famishing for something to copy, he seemed to gorge himself on my documents. There was no pause for digestion. He ran a day and night line, copying by sunlight and by candle-light. I should have been quite delighted with his application, had he been cheerfully industrious. But he wrote on silently, palely, mechanically.

It is, of course, an indispensable part of a scrivener's business to verify the accuracy of his copy, word by word. Where there are two or more scriveners in an office, they assist each other in this examination, one reading from the copy, the other holding the original. It is a very dull, wearisome, and lethargic affair. I can readily imagine that, to some sanguine temperaments, it would be altogether intolerable. For example, I cannot credit that the mettlesome poet, Byron, would have contentedly sat down with Bartleby to examine a law document of, say five hundred pages, closely written in a crimpy hand.

Now and then, in the haste of business, it had been my habit to assist in comparing some brief document myself, calling Turkey or Nippers for this purpose. One object I had, in placing Bartleby so handy to me behind the screen, was, to avail myself of his services on such trivial occasions. It was on the third day, I think, of his being with me, and before any necessity had arisen for having his own writing examined, that, being much hurried to complete a small affair I had in hand, I abruptly called to Bartleby. In my haste and natural expectancy of instant compliance, I sat with my head bent over the original on my desk, and my right hand sideways, and somewhat nervously extended with the copy, so that, immediately upon emerging from his retreat, Bartleby might snatch it and proceed to business without the least delay.

In this very attitude did I sit when I called to him, rapidly stating what it was I wanted him to do — namely, to examine a small paper with me. Imagine my surprise, nay, my consternation, when, without moving from his privacy, Bartleby, in a singularly mild, firm voice, replied, "I would prefer not to."

I sat awhile in perfect silence, rallying my stunned faculties. Immediately it occurred to me that my ears had deceived me, or Bartleby had entirely misunderstood my meaning. I repeated my request in the clearest tone I could assume; but in quite as clear a one came the previous reply, "I would prefer not to."

"Prefer not to," echoed I, rising in high excitement, and crossing the room with a stride. "What do you mean? Are you moonstruck? I want you to help me compare this sheet here — take it," and I thrust it towards him.

"I would prefer not to," said he.

I looked at him steadfastly. His face was leanly composed; his gray eye dimly calm. Not a wrinkle of agitation rippled him. Had there been the least uneasiness, anger, impatience or impertinence in his manner; in other words, had there been anything ordinarily human about him, doubtless I should have violently dismissed him from the premises. But as it was, I should have as soon thought of turning my pale plaster-of-paris bust of Cicero out of doors. I stood gazing at him awhile, as he went on with his own writing, and then reseated myself at my desk. This is very strange, thought I. What had one best do? But my business hurried me. I concluded to forget the matter for the present, reserving it for my future leisure. So, calling Nippers from the other room, the paper was speedily examined.

A few days after this, Bartleby concluded four lengthy documents, being quadruplicates of a week's testimony taken before me in my High Court of Chancery. It became necessary to examine them. It was an important suit, and great accuracy was imperative. Having all things arranged, I called Turkey, Nippers and Ginger Nut, from the next room, meaning to place the four copies in the hands of my four clerks, while I should read from the original. Accordingly, Turkey, Nippers, and Ginger Nut had taken their seats in a row, each with his document in his hand, when I called to Bartleby to join this interesting group.

"Bartleby! quick, I am waiting."

I heard a slow scrape of his chair legs on the uncarpeted floor, and soon he appeared standing at the entrance of his hermitage.

"What is wanted?" said he, mildly.

"The copies, the copies," said I, hurriedly. "We are going to examine them. There" — and I held towards him the fourth quadruplicate.

"I would prefer not to," he said, and gently disappeared behind the screen.

For a few moments I was turned into a pillar of salt, standing at the head of my seated column of clerks. Recovering myself, I advanced towards the screen, and demanded the reason for such extraordinary conduct.

"*Why* do you refuse?"

"I would prefer not to."

With any other man I should have flown outright into a dreadful passion, scorned all further words, and thrust him ignominiously from my presence. But there was something about Bartleby that not only strangely disarmed me, but, in a wonderful manner, touched and disconcerted me. I began to reason with him.

"These are your own copies we are about to examine. It is labor saving to you, because one examination will answer for your four papers. It is common usage. Every copyist is bound to help examine his copy. Is it not so? Will you not speak? Answer!"

"I prefer not to," he replied in a flute-like tone. It seemed to me that, while I had been addressing him, he carefully revolved every statement that I made; fully comprehended the meaning;

could not gainsay the irresistible conclusion; but, at the same time, some paramount consideration prevailed with him to reply as he did.

"You are decided, then, not to comply with my request — a request made according to common usage and common sense?"

He briefly gave me to understand, that on that point my judgment was sound. Yes: his decision was irreversible.

It is not seldom the case that, when a man is browbeaten in some unprecedented and violently unreasonable way, he begins to stagger in his own plainest faith. He begins, as it were, vaguely to surmise that, wonderful as it may be, all the justice and all the reason is on the other side. Accordingly, if any disinterested persons are present, he turns to them for some reinforcement for his own faltering mind.

"Turkey," I said, "what do you think of this? Am I not right?"

"With submission, sir," said Turkey, in his blandest tone, "I think that you are."

"Nippers," said I, "what do *you* think of it?"

"I think I should kick him out of the office."

(The reader of nice perceptions will here perceive that, it being morning, Turkey's answer is couched in polite and tranquil terms, but Nippers replies in ill-tempered ones. Or, to repeat a previous sentence, Nippers's ugly mood was on duty, and Turkey's off.)

"Ginger Nut," said I, willing to enlist the smallest suffrage in my behalf, "what do *you* think of it?"

"I think, sir, he's a little *luny*," replied Ginger Nut, with a grin.

"You hear what they say," said I, turning towards the screen, "come forth and do your duty."

But he vouchsafed no reply. I pondered a moment in sore perplexity. But once more business hurried me. I determined again to postpone the consideration of this dilemma to my future leisure. With a little trouble we made out to examine the papers without Bartleby, though at every page or two Turkey deferentially dropped his opinion, that this proceeding was quite out of the common; while Nippers, twitching in his chair with a dyspeptic nervousness, ground out, between his set teeth, occasional hissing maledictions against the stubborn oaf behind the screen. And for his (Nippers's) part, this was the first and the last time he would do another man's business without pay.

Meanwhile Bartleby sat in his hermitage, oblivious to everything but his own peculiar business there.

Some days passed, the scrivener being employed upon another lengthy work. His late remarkable conduct led me to regard his ways narrowly. I observed that he never went to dinner; indeed, that he never went anywhere. As yet I had never, of my personal knowledge, known him to be outside of my office. He was a perpetual sentry in the corner. At about eleven o'clock though, in the morning, I noticed that Ginger Nut would advance toward the opening in Bartleby's screen, as if silently beckoned thither by a gesture invisible to me where I sat. The boy would then leave the office, jingling a few pence, and reappear with a handful of ginger-nuts, which he delivered in the hermitage, receiving two of the cakes for his trouble.

He lives, then, on ginger-nuts, thought I; never eats a dinner, properly speaking; he must be a vegetarian, then; but no; he never eats even vegetables, he eats nothing but ginger-nuts. My mind then ran on in reveries concerning the probable effects upon the human constitution of living entirely on ginger-nuts. Ginger-nuts are so called, because they contain ginger as one of their peculiar constituents, and the final flavoring one. Now, what was ginger? A hot, spicy thing. Was Bartleby hot and spicy? Not at all. Ginger, then, had no effect upon Bartleby. Probably he preferred it should have none.

Nothing so aggravates an earnest person as a passive resistance. If the individual so resisted be of a not inhumane temper, and the resisting one perfectly harmless in his passivity, then, in the better moods of the former, he will endeavor charitably to construe to his imagination what proves impossible to be solved by his judgment. Even so, for the most part, I regarded Bartleby and his ways. Poor fellow! thought I, he means no mischief; it is plain he intends no insolence; his aspect sufficiently evinces that his eccentricities are involuntary. He is useful to me. I can get along with him. If I turn him away, the chances are he will fall in with some less indulgent employer, and then he will be rudely treated, and perhaps driven forth miserably to starve. Yes. Here I can cheaply purchase a delicious self-approval. To befriend Bartleby; to humor him in his strange wilfulness, will cost me little or nothing, while I lay up in my soul what will eventually prove a sweet morsel for my conscience. But this mood was not invariable with me. The passiveness of Bartleby sometimes irritated me. I felt strangely goaded on to encounter him in new opposition — to elicit some angry spark from him answerable to my own. But, indeed, I might as well have essayed to strike fire with my knuckles against a bit of Windsor soap. But one afternoon the evil impulse in me mastered me, and the following little scene ensued:

"Bartleby," said I, "when those papers are all copied, I will compare them with you."

"I would prefer not to."

"How? Surely you do not mean to persist in that mulish vagary?"

No answer.

I threw open the folding-doors near by, and, turning upon Turkey and Nippers, exclaimed:

"Bartleby a second time says, he won't examine his papers. What do you think of it, Turkey?"

It was afternoon, be it remembered. Turkey sat glowing like a brass boiler; his bald head steaming; his hands reeling among his blotted papers.

"Think of it?" roared Turkey. "I think I'll just step behind his screen, and black his eyes for him!"

So saying, Turkey rose to his feet and threw his arms into a pugilistic position. He was hurrying away to make good his promise, when I detained him, alarmed at the effect of incautiously rousing Turkey's combativeness after dinner.

"Sit down, Turkey," said I, "and hear what Nippers has to say. What do you think of it, Nippers? Would I not be justified in immediately dismissing Bartleby?"

"Excuse me, that is for you to decide, sir. I think his conduct quite unusual, and, indeed, unjust, as regards Turkey and myself. But it may only be a passing whim."

"Ah," exclaimed I, "you have strangely changed your mind, then — you speak very gently of him now."

"All beer," cried Turkey; "gentleness is effects of beer — Nippers and I dined together to-day. You see how gentle *I* am, sir. Shall I go and black his eyes?"

"You refer to Bartleby, I suppose. No, not to-day, Turkey," I replied; "pray, put up your fists."

I closed the doors, and again advanced towards Bartleby. I felt additional incentives tempting me to my fate. I burned to be rebelled against again. I remembered that Bartleby never left the office.

"Bartleby," said I, "Ginger Nut is away; just step around to the Post Office, won't you?" (it was but a three minutes' walk) "and see if there is anything for me."

"I would prefer not to."

"You *will* not?"

"I *prefer* not."

I staggered to my desk, and sat there in a deep study. My blind inveteracy returned. Was there any other thing in which I could procure myself to be ignominiously repulsed by this lean, penniless wight? — my hired clerk? What added thing is there, perfectly reasonable, that he will be sure to refuse to do?

"Bartleby!"

No answer.

"Bartleby," in a louder tone.

No answer.

"Bartleby," I roared.

Like a very ghost, agreeably to the laws of magical invocation, at the third summons, he appeared at the entrance of his hermitage.

"Go to the next room, and tell Nippers to come to me."

"I prefer not to," he respectfully and slowly said, and mildly disappeared.

"Very good, Bartleby," said I, in a quiet sort of serenely-severe self-possessed tone, intimating the unalterable purpose of some terrible retribution very close at hand. At the moment I half intended something of the kind. But upon the whole, as it was drawing towards my dinner-hour, I thought it best to put on my hat and walk home for the day, suffering much from perplexity and distress of mind.

Shall I acknowledge it? The conclusion of this whole business was, that it soon became a fixed fact of my chambers, that a pale young scrivener, by the name of Bartleby, had a desk there; that he copied for me at the usual rate of four cents a folio (one hundred words); but he was permanently exempt from examining the work done by him, that duty being transferred to Turkey and Nippers, out of compliment, doubtless, to their superior acuteness; moreover, said Bartleby was never, on any account, to be dispatched on the most trivial errand of any sort; and that even if entreated to take upon him such a matter, it was generally understood that he would "prefer not to" — in other words, that he would refuse point-blank.

As days passed on, I became considerably reconciled to Bartleby. His steadiness, his freedom from all dissipation, his incessant industry (except when he chose to throw himself into a standing revery behind his screen), his great stillness, his unalterableness of demeanor under all circumstances, made him a valuable acquisition. One prime thing was this — *he was always there* — first in the morning, continually through the day, and the last at night. I had a singular confidence in his honesty. I felt my most precious papers perfectly safe in his hands. Sometimes, to be sure, I could not, for the very soul of me, avoid falling into sudden spasmodic passions with him. For it was exceeding difficult to bear in mind all the time those strange peculiarities, privileges, and unheard-of exemptions, forming the tacit stipulations on Bartleby's part under which he remained in my office. Now and then, in the eagerness of dispatching pressing business, I would inadvertently summon Bartleby, in a short, rapid tone, to put his finger, say, on the incipient tie of a bit of red tape with which I was about compressing some papers. Of course, from behind the screen the usual answer, "I prefer not to," was sure to come; and then, how could a human creature, with the common infirmities of our nature, refrain from bitterly exclaiming upon such perverseness — such unreasonableness? However, every added repulse of this sort which I received only tended to lessen the probability of my repeating the inadvertence.

Here it must be said, that, according to the custom of most legal gentlemen occupying chambers in densely-populated law buildings, there were several keys to my door. One was kept by a woman residing in the attic, which person weekly scrubbed and daily swept and dusted my apartments. Another was kept by Turkey for convenience sake. The third I sometimes carried in my own pocket. The fourth I knew not who had.

Now, one Sunday morning I happened to go to Trinity Church, to hear a celebrated preacher, and finding myself rather early on the ground I thought I would walk round to my chambers for a while. Luckily I had my key with me; but upon applying it to the lock, I found it resisted by something inserted from the inside. Quite surprised, I called out; when to my consternation a key was turned from within; and thrusting his lean visage at me, and holding the door ajar, the apparition of Bartleby appeared, in his shirt-sleeves, and otherwise in a strangely tattered deshabille, saying quietly that he was sorry, but he was deeply engaged just then, and — preferred not admitting me at present. In a brief word or two, he moreover added, that perhaps I had better walk round the block two or three times, and by that time he would probably have concluded his affairs.

Now, the utterly unsurmised appearance of Bartleby, tenanting my law-chambers of a Sunday morning, with his cadaverously gentlemanly *nonchalance*, yet withal firm and self-possessed, had such a strange effect upon me, that incontinently I slunk away from my own door, and did as desired. But not without sundry twinges of impotent rebellion against the mild effrontery of this unaccountable scrivener. Indeed, it was his wonderful mildness chiefly, which not only disarmed me, but unmanned me, as it were. For I consider that one, for the time, is a sort of unmanned when he tranquilly permits his hired clerk to dictate to him, and order him away from his own premises. Furthermore, I was full of uneasiness as to what Bartleby could possibly be doing in my office in his shirt-sleeves, and in an otherwise dismantled condition of a Sunday morning. Was anything amiss going on? Nay, that was out of the question. It was not to be thought of for a moment that Bartleby was an immoral person. But what could he be doing there? — copying? Nay again, whatever might be his eccentricities, Bartleby was an eminently decorous person. He would be the last man to sit down to his desk in any state approaching to nudity. Besides, it was Sunday; and there was something about Bartleby that forbade the supposition that he would by any secular occupation violate the proprieties of the day.

Nevertheless, my mind was not pacified; and full of a restless curiosity, at last I returned to the door. Without hindrance I inserted my key, opened it, and entered. Bartleby was not to be seen. I looked round anxiously, peeped behind his screen; but it was very plain that he was gone. Upon more closely examining the place, I surmised that for an indefinite period Bartleby must have ate, dressed, and slept in my office, and that too without plate, mirror, or bed. The cushioned seat of a rickety old sofa in one corner bore the faint impress of a lean, reclining form. Rolled away under his desk, I found a blanket; under the empty grate, a blacking box and brush; on a chair, a tin basin, with soap and a ragged towel; in a newspaper a few crumbs of ginger-nuts and a morsel of cheese. Yes, thought I, it is evident enough that Bartleby has been making his home here, keeping bachelor's hall all by himself. Immediately then the thought came sweeping across me, what miserable friendlessness and loneliness are here revealed! His poverty is great; but his solitude, how horrible! Think of it. Of a Sunday, Wall Street is deserted as Petra; and every night of every day it is an emptiness. This building, too, which of week-days hums with industry and life, at nightfall echoes with sheer vacancy, and all through Sunday is forlorn. And here Bartleby makes his home; sole spectator of a solitude which he has seen all populous — a sort of innocent and transformed Marius brooding among the ruins of Carthage!

For the first time in my life a feeling of overpowering stinging melancholy seized me. Before, I had never experienced aught but a not unpleasing sadness. The bond of a common humanity now drew me irresistibly to gloom. A fraternal melancholy! For both I and Bartleby were sons of Adam. I remembered the bright silks and sparkling faces I had seen that day, in gala trim, swan-like sailing down the Mississippi of Broadway; and I contrasted them with the pallid copyist, and thought to myself, Ah, happiness courts the light, so we deem the world is gay; but misery hides aloof, so we deem that misery there is none. These sad fancyings — chimeras, doubtless, of a sick and silly brain — led on to other and more special thoughts, concerning the eccentricities of Bartleby. Presentiments of strange discoveries hovered round me. The scrivener's pale form appeared to me laid out, among uncaring strangers, in its shivering winding-sheet.

Suddenly I was attracted by Bartleby's closed desk, the key in open sight left in the lock.

I mean no mischief, seek the gratification of no heartless curiosity, thought I; besides, the desk is mine, and its contents, too, so I will make bold to look within. Everything was methodically arranged, the papers smoothly placed. The pigeon-holes were deep, and removing the files of documents, I groped into their recesses. Presently I felt something there, and dragged it out. It was an old bandanna handkerchief, heavy and knotted. I opened it, and saw it was a saving's bank.

I now recalled all the quiet mysteries which I had noted in the man. I remembered that he never spoke but to answer; that, though at intervals he had considerable time to himself, yet I had never seen him reading — no, not even a newspaper; that for long periods he would stand looking out, at his pale window behind the screen, upon the dead brick wall; I was quite sure he never visited any refectory or eating-house; while his pale face clearly indicated that he never drank beer like Turkey, or tea and coffee even, like other men; that he never went anywhere in particular that I could learn; never went out for a walk, unless, indeed, that was the case at present; that he had declined telling who he was, or whence he came, or whether he had any relatives in the world; that though so thin and pale, he never complained of ill-health. And more than all, I remembered a certain unconscious air of pallid — how shall I call it? — of pallid haughtiness, say, or rather an austere reserve about him, which had positively awed me into my tame compliance with his eccentricities, when I had feared to ask him to do the slightest incidental thing for me, even though I might know, from his long-continued motionlessness, that behind his screen he must be standing in one of those dead-wall reveries of his.

Revolving all these things, and coupling them with the recently discovered fact, that he made my office his constant abiding place and home, and not forgetful of his morbid moodiness; revolving all these things, a prudential feeling began to steal over me. My first emotions had been those of pure melancholy and sincerest pity; but just in proportion as the forlornness of Bartleby grew and grew to my imagination, did that same melancholy merge into fear, that pity into repulsion. So true it is, and so terrible, too, that up to a certain point the thought or sight of misery enlists our best affections; but, in certain special cases, beyond that point it does not. They err who would assert that invariably this is owing to the inherent selfishness of the human heart. It rather proceeds from a certain hopelessness of remedying excessive and organic ill. To a sensitive being, pity is not seldom pain. And when at last it is perceived that such pity cannot lead to effectual succor, common sense bids the soul be rid of it. What I saw that morning persuaded me that the scrivener was the victim of innate and incurable disorder. I might give alms to his body; but his body did not pain him; it was his soul that suffered, and his soul I could not reach.

I did not accomplish the purpose of going to Trinity Church that morning. Somehow, the things I had seen disqualified me for the time from church-going. I walked homeward, thinking what I would do with Bartleby. Finally, I resolved upon this — I would put certain calm questions to him the next morning, touching his history, etc., and if he declined to answer them openly and unreservedly (and I supposed he would prefer not), then to give him a twenty dollar bill over and above whatever I might owe him, and tell him his services were no longer required; but that if in any other way I could assist him, I would be happy to do so, especially if he desired to return to his native place, wherever that might be, I would willingly help to defray the expenses. Moreover, if, after reaching home, he found himself at any time in want of aid, a letter from him would be sure of a reply.

The next morning came.

"Bartleby," said I, gently calling to him behind his screen.

No reply.

"Bartleby," said I, in a still gentler tone, "come here; I am not going to ask you to do anything you would prefer not to do — I simply wish to speak to you."

Upon this he noiselessly slid into view.

"Will you tell me, Bartleby, where you were born?"

"I would prefer not to."

"Will you tell me *anything* about yourself?"

"I would prefer not to."

"But what reasonable objection can you have to speak to me? I feel friendly towards you."

He did not look at me while I spoke, but kept his glance fixed upon my bust of Cicero, which, as I then sat, was directly behind me, some six inches above my head.

"What is your answer, Bartleby?" said I, after waiting a considerable time for a reply, during which his countenance remained immovable, only there was the faintest conceivable tremor of the white attenuated mouth.

"At present I prefer to give no answer," he said, and retired into his hermitage.

It was rather weak in me I confess, but his manner, on this occasion, nettled me. Not only did there seem to lurk in it a certain calm disdain, but his perverseness seemed ungrateful, considering the undeniable good usage and indulgence he had received from me.

Again I sat ruminating what I should do. Mortified as I was at his behavior, and resolved as I had been to dismiss him when I entered my office, nevertheless I strangely felt something superstitious knocking at my heart, and forbidding me to carry out my purpose, and denouncing me for a villain if I dared to breathe one bitter word against this forlornest of mankind. At last, familiarly drawing my chair behind his screen, I sat down and said: "Bartleby, never mind, then, about revealing your history; but let me entreat you, as a friend, to comply as far as may be with the usages of this office. Say now, you will help to examine papers to-morrow or next day: in short, say now, that in a day or two you will begin to be a little reasonable: — say so, Bartleby."

"At present I would prefer not to be a little reasonable," was his mildly cadaverous reply.

Just then the folding-doors opened, and Nippers approached. He seemed suffering from an unusually bad night's rest, induced by severer indigestion than common. He overheard those final words of Bartleby.

"*Prefer not*, eh?" gritted Nippers — "I'd *prefer* him, if I were you, sir," addressing me — "I'd *prefer* him; I'd give him preferences, the stubborn mule! What is it, sir, pray, that he *prefers* not to do now?"

Bartleby moved not a limb.

"Mr. Nippers," said I, "I'd prefer that you would withdraw for the present."

Somehow, of late, I had got into the way of involuntarily using this word "prefer" upon all sorts of not exactly suitable occasions. And I trembled to think that my contact with the scrivener had already and seriously affected me in a mental way. And what further and deeper aberration might it not yet produce? This apprehension had not been without efficacy in determining me to summary measures.

As Nippers, looking very sour and sulky, was departing, Turkey blandly and deferentially approached.

"With submission, sir," said he, "yesterday I was thinking about Bartleby here, and I think that if he would but prefer to take a quart of good ale every day, it would do much towards mending him, and enabling him to assist in examining his papers."

"So you have got the word, too," said I, slightly excited.

"With submission, what word, sir?" asked Turkey, respectfully crowding himself into the contracted space behind the screen, and by so doing, making me jostle the scrivener. "What word, sir?"

"I would prefer to be left alone here," said Bartleby, as if offended at being mobbed in his privacy.

"*That's* the word, Turkey," said I — "*that's* it."

"Oh, *prefer?* oh yes — queer word. I never use it myself. But, sir, as I was saying, if he would but prefer — "

"Turkey," interrupted I, "you will please withdraw."

"Oh certainly, sir, if you prefer that I should."

As he opened the folding-door to retire, Nippers at his desk caught a glimpse of me, and asked whether I would prefer to have a certain paper copied on blue paper or white. He did not in the least roguishly accent the word "prefer." It was plain that it involuntarily rolled from his tongue. I thought to myself, surely I must get rid of a demented man, who already has in some degree turned the tongues, if not the heads of myself and clerks. But I thought it prudent not to break the dismission at once.

The next day I noticed that Bartleby did nothing but stand at his window in his dead-wall revery. Upon asking him why he did not write, he said that he had decided upon doing no more writing.

"Why, how now? what next?" exclaimed I, "do no more writing?"

"No more."

"And what is the reason?"

"Do you not see the reason for yourself?" he indifferently replied.

I looked steadfastly at him, and perceived that his eyes looked dull and glazed. Instantly it occurred to me, that his unexampled diligence in copying by his dim window for the first few weeks of his stay with me might have temporarily impaired his vision.

I was touched. I said something in condolence with him. I hinted that of course he did wisely in abstaining from writing for a while; and urged him to embrace that opportunity of taking wholesome exercise in the open air. This, however, he did not do. A few days after this, my other clerks being absent, and being in a great hurry to dispatch certain letters by the mail, I thought that, having nothing else earthly to do, Bartleby would surely be less inflexible than usual, and carry these letters to the post-office. But he blankly declined. So, much to my inconvenience, I went myself.

Still added days went by. Whether Bartleby's eyes improved or not, I could not say. To all appearance, I thought they did. But when I asked him if they did, he vouchsafed no answer. At all events, he would do no copying. At last, in reply to my urgings, he informed me that he had permanently given up copying.

"What!" exclaimed I; "suppose your eyes should get entirely well — better than ever before — would you not copy then?"

"I have given up copying," he answered, and slid aside.

He remained as ever, a fixture in my chamber. Nay — if that were possible — he became still more of a fixture than before. What was to be done? He would do nothing in the office; why should he stay there? In plain fact, he had now become a millstone to me, not only useless as a necklace, but afflictive to bear. Yet I was sorry for him. I speak less than truth when I say that, on his own account, he occasioned me uneasiness. If he would but have named a single relative or friend, I would instantly have written, and urged their taking the poor fellow away to some convenient retreat. But he seemed alone, absolutely alone in the universe. A bit of wreck in the mid-Atlantic. At length, necessities connected with my business tyrannized over all other considerations. Decently as I could, I told Bartleby that in six days' time he must unconditionally leave the office. I warned him to take measures, in the interval, for procuring some other abode. I offered to assist him in this endeavor, if he himself would but take the first step towards a removal. "And when you finally quit me, Bartleby," added I, "I shall see that you go not away entirely unprovided. Six days from this hour, remember."

At the expiration of that period, I peeped behind the screen, and lo! Bartleby was there.

I buttoned up my coat, balanced myself; advanced slowly towards him, touched his shoulder, and said, "The time has come; you must quit this place; I am sorry for you; here is money; but you must go."

"I would prefer not," he replied, with his back still towards me.

"You *must*."

He remained silent.

Now I had an unbounded confidence in this man's common honesty. He had frequently restored to me sixpences and shillings carelessly dropped upon the floor, for I am apt to be very reckless in such shirt-button affairs. The proceeding, then, which followed will not be deemed extraordinary.

"Bartleby," said I, "I owe you twelve dollars on account; here are thirty-two; the odd twenty are yours — Will you take it?" and I handed the bills towards him.

But he made no motion.

"I will leave them here, then," putting them under a weight on the table. Then taking my hat and cane and going to the door, I tranquilly turned and added — "After you have removed your things from these offices, Bartleby, you will of course lock the door — since every one is now gone for the day but you — and if you please, slip your key underneath the mat, so that I may have it in the morning. I shall not see you again; so good-bye to you. If, hereafter, in your new place of abode, I can be of any service to you, do not fail to advise me by letter. Good-bye, Bartleby, and fare you well."

But he answered not a word; like the last column of some ruined temple, he remained standing mute and solitary in the middle of the otherwise deserted room.

As I walked home in a pensive mood, my vanity got the better of my pity. I could not but highly plume myself on my masterly management in getting rid of Bartleby. Masterly I call it, and such it must appear to any dispassionate thinker. The beauty of my procedure seemed to consist in its perfect quietness. There was no vulgar bullying, no bravado of any sort, no choleric hectoring, and striding to and fro across the apartment, jerking out vehement commands for Bartleby to bundle himself off with his beggarly traps. Nothing of the kind. Without loudly bidding Bartleby depart — as an inferior genius might have done — I *assumed* the ground that depart he must; and upon that assumption built all I had to say. The more I thought over my procedure, the more I was charmed with it. Nevertheless, next morning, upon awakening, I had my doubts — I had somehow slept off the fumes of vanity. One of the coolest and wisest hours a man has, is just after he awakes in the morning. My procedure seemed as sagacious as ever — but only in theory. How it would prove in practice — there was the rub. It was truly a beautiful thought to have assumed Bartleby's departure; but, after all, that assumption was simply my own, and none of Bartleby's. The great point was, not whether I had assumed that he would quit me, but whether he would prefer so to do. He was more a man of preferences than assumptions.

After breakfast, I walked down town, arguing the probabilities *pro* and *con*. One moment I thought it would prove a miserable failure, and Bartleby would be found all alive at my office as usual; the next moment it seemed certain that I should find his chair empty. And so I kept veering about. At the corner of Broadway and Canal Street, I saw quite an excited group of people standing in earnest conversation.

"I'll take odds he doesn't," said a voice as I passed.

"Doesn't go? — done!" said I, "put up your money."

I was instinctively putting my hand in my pocket to produce my own, when I remembered that this was an election day. The words I had overheard bore no reference to Bartleby, but to the success or non-success of some candidate for the mayoralty. In my intent frame of mind, I had, as it were, imagined that all Broadway shared in my excitement, and were debating the same question with me. I passed on, very thankful that the uproar of the street screened my momentary absent-mindedness.

As I had intended, I was earlier than usual at my office door. I stood listening for a moment. All was still. He must be gone. I tried the knob. The door was locked. Yes, my procedure had worked to a charm; he indeed must be vanished. Yet a certain melancholy mixed with this: I was almost sorry for my brilliant success. I was fumbling under the door mat for the key, which Bartleby was to have left there for me, when accidentally my knee knocked against a panel, producing a summoning sound, and in response a voice came to me from within — "Not yet; I am occupied."

It was Bartleby.

I was thunderstruck. For an instant I stood like the man who, pipe in mouth, was killed one cloudless afternoon long ago in Virginia, by summer lightning; at his own warm open window he was killed, and remained leaning out there upon the dreamy afternoon, till some one touched him, when he fell.

"Not gone!" I murmured at last. But again obeying that wondrous ascendancy which the inscrutable scrivener had over me, and from which ascendancy, for all my chafing, I could not completely escape, I slowly went down stairs and out into the street, and while walking round the block, considered what I should next do in this unheard-of perplexity. Turn the man out by an actual thrusting I could not; to drive him away by calling him hard names would not do; calling in the police was an unpleasant idea; and yet, permit him to enjoy his cadaverous triumph over me — this, too, I could not think of. What was to be done? or, if nothing could be done, was there anything further that I could *assume* in the matter? Yes, as before I had prospectively assumed that Bartleby would depart, so now I might retrospectively assume that departed he was. In the legitimate carrying out of this assumption, I might enter my office in a great hurry, and pretending not to see Bartleby at all, walk straight against him as if he were air. Such a proceeding would in a singular degree have the appearance of a home-thrust. It was hardly possible that Bartleby could withstand such an application of the doctrine of assumptions. But upon second thoughts the success of the plan seemed rather dubious. I resolved to argue the matter over with him again.

"Bartleby," said I, entering the office, with a quietly severe expression, "I am seriously displeased. I am pained, Bartleby. I had thought better of you. I had imagined you of such a gentlemanly organization, that in any delicate dilemma a slight hint would suffice — in short, an assumption. But it appears I am deceived. Why," I added, unaffectedly starting, "you have not even touched that money yet," pointing to it, just where I had left it the evening previous.

He answered nothing.

"Will you, or will you not, quit me?" I now demanded in a sudden passion, advancing close to him.

"I would prefer *not* to quit you," he replied, gently emphasizing the *not*.

"What earthly right have you to stay here? Do you pay any rent? Do you pay my taxes? Or is this property yours?"

He answered nothing.

"Are you ready to go on and write now? Are your eyes recovered? Could you copy a small paper for me this morning? or help examine a few lines? or step round to the post-office? In a word, will you do anything at all, to give a coloring to your refusal to depart the premises?"

He silently retired into his hermitage.

I was now in such a state of nervous resentment that I thought it but prudent to check myself at present from further demonstrations. Bartleby and I were alone. I remembered the tragedy of the unfortunate Adams and the still more unfortunate Colt in the solitary office of the latter; and how poor Colt, being dreadfully incensed by Adams, and imprudently permitting himself to get wildly excited, was at unawares hurried into his fatal act — an act which certainly no man could possibly deplore more than the actor himself. Often it had occurred to me in my ponderings upon the subject that had that altercation taken place in the public street, or at a private residence, it would not have terminated as it did. It was the circumstance of being alone in a solitary office, up stairs, of a building entirely unhallowed by humanizing domestic associations — an uncarpeted office, doubtless, of a dusty, haggard sort of appearance — this it must have been, which greatly helped to enhance the irritable desperation of the hapless Colt.

But when this old Adam of resentment rose in me and tempted me concerning Bartleby, I grappled him and threw him. How? Why, simply by recalling the divine injunction: "A new commandment give I unto you, that ye love one another." Yes, this it was that saved me. Aside from higher considerations, charity often operates as a vastly wise and prudent principle — a great safeguard to its possessor. Men have committed murder for jealousy's sake, and anger's sake, and hatred's sake, and selfishness' sake, and spiritual pride's sake; but no man, that ever I heard of, ever committed a diabolical murder for sweet charity's sake. Mere self-interest, then, if no better motive can be enlisted, should, especially with high-tempered men, prompt all beings to charity and philanthropy. At any rate, upon the occasion in question, I strove to drown my exasperated feelings towards the scrivener by benevolently construing his conduct. Poor fellow, poor fellow! thought I, he don't mean anything; and besides, he has seen hard times, and ought to be indulged.

I endeavored, also, immediately to occupy myself, and at the same time to comfort my despondency. I tried to fancy, that in the course of the morning, at such time as might prove agreeable to him, Bartleby, of his own free accord, would emerge from his hermitage and take up some decided line of march in the direction of the door. But no. Half-past twelve o'clock came; Turkey began to glow in the face, overturn his inkstand, and become generally obstreperous; Nippers abated down into quietude and courtesy; Ginger Nut munched his noon apple; and Bartleby remained standing at his window in one of his profoundest dead-wall reveries. Will it be credited? Ought I to acknowledge it? That afternoon I left the office without saying one further word to him.

Some days now passed, during which, at leisure intervals I looked a little into "Edwards on the Will," and "Priestley on Necessity." Under the circumstances, those books induced a salutary feeling. Gradually I slid into the persuasion that these troubles of mine, touching the scrivener, had been all predestinated from eternity, and Bartleby was billeted upon me for some mysterious purpose of an all-wise Providence, which it was not for a mere mortal like me to fathom. Yes, Bartleby, stay there behind your screen, thought I; I shall persecute you no more; you are harmless and noiseless as any of these old chairs; in short, I never feel so private as when I know you are here. At last I see it, I feel it; I penetrate to the pre-destinated purpose of my life. I am content. Others may have loftier parts to enact; but my mission in this world, Bartleby, is to furnish you with office-room for such period as you may see fit to remain.

I believe that this wise and blessed frame of mind would have continued with me, had it not been for the unsolicited and uncharitable remarks obtruded upon me by my professional friends who visited the rooms. But thus it often is, that the constant friction of illiberal minds wears out at last the best resolves of the more generous. Though to be sure, when I reflected upon it, it was not strange that people entering my office should be struck by the peculiar aspect of the unaccountable Bartleby, and so be tempted to throw out some sinister observations concerning him. Sometimes an attorney, having business with me, and calling at my office, and finding no one but the scrivener there, would undertake to obtain some sort of precise information from him touching my where-abouts; but without heeding his idle talk, Bartleby would remain standing immovable in the middle of the room. So after contem-plating him in that position for a time, the attorney would depart, no wiser than he came.

Also, when a reference was going on, and the room full of law-yers and witnesses, and business driving fast, some deeply-occupied legal gentleman present, seeing Bartleby wholly unemployed, would request him to run round to his (the legal gentleman's) office and fetch some papers for him. Thereupon, Bartleby would tranquilly decline, and yet remain idle as before. Then the lawyer would give a great stare, and turn to me. And what could I say? At last I was made aware that all through the circle of my professional acquaint-ance, a whisper of wonder was running round, having reference to the strange creature I kept at my office. This worried me very much. And as the idea came upon me of his possibly turning out a long-lived man, and keep occupying my chambers, and denying my authority; and perplexing my visitors; and scandalizing my pro-fessional reputation; and casting a general gloom over the premises;

keeping soul and body together to the last upon his savings (for doubtless he spent but half a dime a day), and in the end perhaps outlive me, and claim possession of my office by right of his perpetual occupancy: as all these dark anticipations crowded upon me more and more, and my friends continually intruded their relentless remarks upon the apparition in my room; a great change was wrought in me. I resolved to gather all my faculties together, and forever rid me of this intolerable incubus.

Ere revolving any complicated project, however, adapted to this end, I first simply suggested to Bartleby the propriety of his permanent departure. In a calm and serious tone, I commended the idea to his careful and mature consideration. But, having taken three days to meditate upon it, he apprised me, that his original determination remained the same; in short, that he still preferred to abide with me.

What shall I do? I now said to myself, buttoning up my coat to the last button. What shall I do? what ought I to do? what does conscience say I *should* do with this man, or, rather, ghost. Rid myself of him, I must; go, he shall. But how? You will not thrust him, the poor, pale, passive mortal — you will not thrust such a helpless creature out of your door? you will not dishonor yourself by such cruelty? No, I will not, I cannot do that. Rather would I let him live and die here, and then mason up his remains in the wall. What, then, will you do? For all your coaxing, he will not budge. Bribes he leaves under your own paper-weight on your table; in short, it is quite plain that he prefers to cling to you.

Then something severe, something unusual must be done. What! surely you will not have him collared by a constable, and commit his innocent pallor to the common jail? And upon what ground could you procure such a thing to be done? — a vagrant, is he? What! he a vagrant, a wanderer, who refuses to budge? It is because he will *not* be a vagrant, then, that you seek to count him *as* a vagrant. That is too absurd. No visible means of support: there I have him. Wrong again: for indubitably he *does* support himself, and that is the only unanswerable proof that any man can show of his possessing the means so to do. No more, then. Since he will not quit me, I must quit him. I will change my offices; I will move elsewhere, and give him fair notice, that if I find him on my new premises I will then proceed against him as a common trespasser.

Acting accordingly, next day I thus addressed him: "I find these chambers too far from the City Hall; the air is unwholesome. In a word, I propose to remove my offices next week, and shall no longer require your services. I tell you this now, in order that you may seek another place."

He made no reply, and nothing more was said.

On the appointed day I engaged carts and men, proceeded to my chambers, and, having but little furniture, everything was removed in a few hours. Throughout, the scrivener remained standing behind the screen, which I directed to be removed the last thing. It was withdrawn; and, being folded up like a huge folio, left him the motionless occupant of a naked room. I stood in the entry watching him a moment, while something from within me upbraided me.

I re-entered, with my hand in my pocket — and — and my heart in my mouth.

"Good-bye, Bartleby; I am going — good-bye, and God some way bless you; and take that," slipping something in his hand. But it dropped upon the floor, and then — strange to say — I tore myself from him whom I had so longed to be rid of.

Established in my new quarters, for a day or two I kept the door locked, and started at every footfall in the passages. When I returned to my rooms, after any little absence, I would pause at the threshold for an instant, and attentively listen, ere applying my key. But these fears were needless. Bartleby never came nigh me.

I thought all was going well, when a perturbed-looking stranger visited me, inquiring whether I was the person who had recently occupied rooms at No. — Wall Street.

Full of forebodings, I replied that I was.

"Then, sir," said the stranger, who proved a lawyer, "you are responsible for the man you left there. He refuses to do any copying; he refuses to do anything; he says he prefers not to; and he refuses to quit the premises."

"I am very sorry, sir," said I, with assumed tranquillity, but an inward tremor, "but, really, the man you allude to is nothing to me — he is no relation or apprentice of mine, that you should hold me responsible for him."

"In mercy's name, who is he?"

"I certainly cannot inform you. I know nothing about him. Formerly I employed him as a copyist; but he has done nothing for me now for some time past."

"I shall settle him, then — good morning, sir."

Several days passed, and I heard nothing more; and, though I often felt a charitable prompting to call at the place and see poor Bartleby, yet a certain squeamishness, of I know not what, withheld me.

All is over with him, by this time, thought I, at last, when, through another week, no further intelligence reached me. But, coming to my room the day after, I found several persons waiting at my door in a high state of nervous excitement.

"That's the man — here he comes," cried the foremost one, whom I recognized as the lawyer who had previously called upon me alone.

"You must take him away, sir, at once," cried a portly person among them, advancing upon me, and whom I knew to be the land-lord of No. — Wall Street. "These gentlemen, my tenants, cannot stand it any longer; Mr. B——," pointing to the lawyer, "has turned him out of his room, and he now persists in haunting the building generally, sitting upon the banisters of the stairs by day, and sleeping in the entry by night. Everybody is concerned; clients are leaving the offices; some fears are entertained of a mob; something you must do, and that without delay."

Aghast at this torrent, I fell back before it, and would fain have locked myself in my new quarters. In vain I persisted that Bartleby was nothing to me — no more than to any one else. In vain — I was the last person known to have anything to do with him, and they held me to the terrible account. Fearful, then, of being exposed in the papers (as one person present obscurely threatened), I considered the matter, and, at length, said, that if the lawyer would give me a confidential interview with the scrivener, in his (the lawyer's) own room, I would, that afternoon, strive my best to rid them of the nuisance they complained of.

Going up stairs to my old haunt, there was Bartleby silently sitting upon the banister at the landing.

"What are you doing here, Bartleby?" said I.

"Sitting upon the banister," he mildly replied.

I motioned him into the lawyer's room, who then left us.

"Bartleby," said I, "are you aware that you are the cause of great tribulation to me, by persisting in occupying the entry after being dismissed from the office?"

No answer.

"Now one of two things must take place. Either you must do

something, or something must be done to you. Now what sort of business would you like to engage in? Would you like to re-engage in copying for some one?"

"No; I would prefer not to make any change."

"Would you like a clerkship in a dry-goods store?"

"There is too much confinement about that. No, I would not like a clerkship; but I am not particular."

"Too much confinement," I cried, "why, you keep yourself confined all the time!"

"I would prefer not to take a clerkship," he rejoined, as if to settle that little item at once.

"How would a bar-tender's business suit you? There is no trying of the eye-sight in that."

"I would not like it at all; though, as I said before, I am not particular."

His unwonted wordiness inspirited me. I returned to the charge.

"Well, then, would you like to travel through the country collecting bills for the merchants? That would improve your health."

"No, I would prefer to be doing something else."

"How, then, would going as a companion to Europe, to entertain some young gentleman with your conversation — how would that suit you?"

"Not at all. It does not strike me that there is anything definite about that. I like to be stationary. But I am not particular."

"Stationary you shall be, then," I cried, now losing all patience, and, for the first time in all my exasperating connection with him, fairly flying into a passion. "If you do not go away from these premises before night, I shall feel bound — indeed, I *am* bound — to — to — to quit the premises myself!" I rather absurdly concluded, knowing not with what possible threat to try to frighten his immobility into compliance. Despairing of all further efforts, I was precipitately leaving him, when a final thought occurred to me — one which had not been wholly unindulged before.

"Bartleby," said I, in the kindest tone I could assume under such exciting circumstances, "will you go home with me now — not to my office, but my dwelling — and remain there till we can conclude upon some convenient arrangement for you at our leisure? Come, let us start now, right away."

"No: at present I would prefer not to make any change at all."

I answered nothing; but, effectually dodging every one by the suddenness and rapidity of my flight, rushed from the building, ran up Wall Street towards Broadway, and, jumping into the first omnibus, was soon removed from pursuit. As soon as tranquillity returned, I distinctly perceived that I had now done all that I possibly could, both in respect to the demands of the landlord and his tenants, and with regard to my own desire and sense of duty, to benefit Bartleby, and shield him from rude persecution. I now strove to be entirely care-free and quiescent; and my conscience justified me in the attempt; though, indeed, it was not so successful as I could have wished. So fearful was I of being again hunted out by the incensed landlord and his exasperated tenants, that, surrendering my business to Nippers, for a few days, I drove about the upper part of the town and through the suburbs, in my rockaway; crossed over to Jersey City and Hoboken, and paid fugitive visits to Manhattanville and Astoria. In fact, I almost lived in my rockaway for the time.

When again I entered my office, lo, a note from the landlord lay upon the desk. I opened it with trembling hands. It informed me that the writer had sent to the police, and had Bartleby removed to the Tombs as a vagrant. Moreover, since I knew more about him than any one else, he wished me to appear at that place, and make a suitable statement of the facts. These tidings had a conflicting effect upon me. At first I was indignant; but, at last, almost approved. The landlord's energetic, summary disposition, had led him to adopt a procedure which I do not think I would have decided upon myself; and yet, as a last resort, under such peculiar circumstances, it seemed the only plan.

As I afterwards learned, the poor scrivener, when told that he must be conducted to the Tombs, offered not the slightest obstacle, but, in his pale, unmoving way, silently acquiesced.

Some of the compassionate and curious by-standers joined the party; and headed by one of the constables arm-in-arm with Bartleby, the silent procession filed its way through all the noise, and heat, and joy of the roaring thoroughfares at noon.

The same day I received the note, I went to the Tombs, or, to speak more properly, the Halls of Justice. Seeking the right officer, I stated the purpose of my call, and was informed that the individual I described was, indeed, within. I then assured the functionary that Bartleby was a perfectly honest man, and greatly to be compassionated, however unaccountably eccentric. I narrated all

I knew, and closed by suggesting the idea of letting him remain in as indulgent confinement as possible, till something less harsh might be done — though, indeed, I hardly knew what. At all events, if nothing else could be decided upon, the alms-house must receive him. I then begged to have an interview.

Being under no disgraceful charge, and quite serene and harmless in all his ways, they had permitted him freely to wander about the prison, and, especially, in the inclosed grass-platted yards thereof. And so I found him there, standing all alone in the quietest of the yards, his face towards a high wall, while all around, from the narrow slits of the jail windows, I thought I saw peering out upon him the eyes of murderers and thieves.

"Bartleby!"

"I know you," he said, without looking round — "and I want nothing to say to you."

"It was not I that brought you here, Bartleby," said I, keenly pained at his implied suspicion. "And to you, this should not be so vile a place. Nothing reproachful attaches to you by being here. And see, it is not so sad a place as one might think. Look, there is the sky, and here is the grass."

"I know where I am," he replied, but would say nothing more, and so I left him.

As I entered the corridor again, a broad meat-like man, in an apron, accosted me, and, jerking his thumb over his shoulder, said — "Is that your friend?"

"Yes."

"Does he want to starve? If he does, let him live on the prison fare, that's all."

"Who are you?" asked I, not knowing what to make of such an unofficially speaking person in such a place.

"I am the grub-man. Such gentlemen as have friends here, hire me to provide them with something good to eat."

"Is this so?" said I, turning to the turnkey.

He said it was.

"Well, then," said I, slipping some silver into the grub-man's hands (for so they called him), "I want you to give particular attention to my friend there; let him have the best dinner you can get. And you must be as polite to him as possible."

"Introduce me, will you?" said the grub-man, looking at me with an expression which seemed to say he was all impatience for an opportunity to give a specimen of his breeding.

Thinking it would prove of benefit to the scrivener, I acquiesced; and, asking the grub-man his name, went up with him to Bartleby.

"Bartleby, this is a friend; you will find him very useful to you."

"Your sarvant, sir, your sarvant," said the grub-man, making a low salutation behind his apron. "Hope you find it pleasant here, sir; nice grounds — cool apartments — hope you'll stay with us some time — try to make it agreeable. What will you have for dinner to-day?"

"I prefer not to dine to-day," said Bartleby, turning away. "It would disagree with me; I am unused to dinners." So saying, he slowly moved to the other side of the inclosure, and took up a position fronting the dead-wall.

"How's this?" said the grub-man, addressing me with a stare of astonishment. "He's odd, ain't he?"

"I think he is a little deranged," said I, sadly.

"Deranged? deranged is it? Well, now, upon my word, I thought that friend of yourn was a gentleman forger; they are always pale and genteel-like, them forgers. I can't help pity 'em — can't help it, sir. Did you know Monroe Edwards?" he added, touchingly, and paused. Then, laying his hand piteously on my shoulder, sighed, "he died of consumption at Sing-Sing. So you weren't acquainted with Monroe?"

"No, I was never socially acquainted with any forgers. But I cannot stop longer. Look to my friend yonder. You will not lose by it. I will see you again."

Some few days after this, I again obtained admission to the Tombs, and went through the corridors in quest of Bartleby; but without finding him.

"I saw him coming from his cell not long ago," said a turnkey, "may be he's gone to loiter in the yards."

So I went in that direction.

"Are you looking for the silent man?" said another turnkey, passing me. "Yonder he lies — sleeping in the yard there. 'Tis not twenty minutes since I saw him lie down."

The yard was entirely quiet. It was not accessible to the common prisoners. The surrounding walls, of amazing thickness, kept off all sounds behind them. The Egyptian character of the masonry

weighed upon me with its gloom. But a soft imprisoned turf grew
under foot. The heart of the eternal pyramids, it seemed, wherein,
by some strange magic, through the clefts, grass-seed, dropped by
birds, had sprung.

Strangely huddled at the base of the wall, his knees drawn up,
and lying on his side, his head touching the cold stones, I saw the
wasted Bartleby. But nothing stirred. I paused; then went close up
to him; stooped over, and saw that his dim eyes were open; otherwise he seemed profoundly sleeping. Something prompted me to
touch him. I felt his hand, when a tingling shiver ran up my arm
and down my spine to my feet.

The round face of the grub-man peered upon me now. "His
dinner is ready. Won't he dine to-day, either? Or does he live
without dining?"

"Lives without dining," said I, and closed the eyes.

"Eh! — He's asleep, ain't he?"

"With kings and counselors," murmured I.

*   *   *

There would seem little need for proceeding further in this
history. Imagination will readily supply the meagre recital of poor
Bartleby's interment. But, ere parting with the reader, let me say,
that if this little narrative has sufficiently interested him, to awaken
curiosity as to who Bartleby was, and what manner of life he led
prior to the present narrator's making his acquaintance, I can only
reply, that in such curiosity I fully share, but am wholly unable
to gratify it. Yet here I hardly know whether I should divulge one
little item of rumor, which came to my ear a few months after the
scrivener's decease. Upon what basis it rested, I could never as-
certain; and hence, how true it is I cannot now tell. But, inasmuch
as this vague report has not been without a certain suggestive interest to me, however sad, it may prove the same with some others;
and so I will briefly mention it. The report was this: that Bartleby
had been a subordinate clerk in the Dead Letter Office at Washing-
ton, from which he had been suddenly removed by a change in the
administration. When I think over this rumor, hardly can I express
the emotions which seize me. Dead letters! does it not sound like
dead men? Conceive a man by nature and misfortune prone to a
pallid hopelessness, can any business seem more fitted to heighten it
than that of continually handling these dead letters, and assorting

them for the flames? For by the cart-load they are annually burned. Sometimes from out the folded paper the pale clerk takes a ring — the finger it was meant for, perhaps, moulders in the grave; a bank-note sent in swiftest charity — he whom it would relieve, nor eats nor hungers any more; pardon for those who died despairing; hope for those who died unhoping; good tidings for those who died stifled by unrelieved calamities. On errands of life, these letters speed to death.

Ah, Bartleby! Ah, humanity!

TWO

a mature art form

SHERWOOD ANDERSON

i want to know why

We got up at four in the morning, that first day in the east. On the evening before we had climbed off a freight train at the edge of town, and with the true instinct of Kentucky boys had found our way across town and to the race track and the stables at once. Then we knew we were all right. Hanley Turner right away found a nigger we knew. It was Bildad Johnson who in the winter works at Ed Becker's livery barn in our home town, Beckersville. Bildad is a good cook as almost all our niggers are and of course he, like everyone in our part of Kentucky who is anyone at all, likes the horses. In the spring Bildad begins to scratch around. A nigger from our country can flatter and wheedle anyone into letting him do most anything he wants. Bildad wheedles the stable men and the trainers from the horse farms in our country around Lexington. The trainers come into town in the evening to stand around and talk and maybe get into a poker game. Bildad gets in with them. He is always doing little favors and telling about things to eat, chicken browned in a pan, and how is the best way to cook sweet potatoes and corn bread. It makes your mouth water to hear him. When the racing season comes on and the horses go to the races and there is all the talk on the streets in the evenings about the new colts, and everyone says when they are going over to Lexington or to the spring meeting at Churchill Downs or to Latinia, and the horsemen that have been down to New Orleans or maybe at the winter meeting at Havana in Cuba come home to spend a week before they start out again, at such a time when everything talked about in Beckersville is just horses and nothing else and the outfits start out and horse racing is in every breath of air you breathe, Bildad shows up with a job as cook for some outfit. Often when I think about it, his always going all season to the races and working in the livery barn in the winter where horses are and where men like to come and talk about horses, I wish I was a nigger. It's a foolish thing to say, but that's the way I am about being around horses, just crazy. I can't help it.

Well, I must tell you about what we did and let you in on what I'm talking about. Four of us boys from Beckersville, all whites and sons of men who live in Beckersville regular, made up our minds we were going to the races, not just to Lexington or Louisville, I don't mean, but to the big eastern track we were always hearing our Beckersville men talk about, to Saratoga. We were all pretty young then. I was just turned fifteen and I was the oldest of the four. It was my scheme. I admit that and I talked the others into trying it. There was Hanley Turner and Henry Rieback and Tom Tumberton and myself. I had thirty-seven dollars I had earned during the winter working nights and Saturdays in Enoch Myer's grocery. Henry Rieback had eleven dollars and the others, Hanley and Tom, had only a dollar or two each. We fixed it all up and laid low until the Kentucky spring meetings were over and some of our men, the sportiest ones, the ones we envied the most, had cut out — then we cut out too.

I won't tell you the trouble we had beating our way on freights and all. We went through Cleveland and Buffalo and other cities and saw Niagara Falls. We bought things there, souvenirs and spoons and cards and shells with pictures of the falls on them for our sisters and mothers, but thought we had better not send any of the things home. We didn't want to put the folks on our trail and maybe be nabbed.

We got into Saratoga as I said at night and went to the track. Bildad fed us up. He showed us a place to sleep in hay over a shed and promised to keep still. Niggers are all right about things like that. They won't squeal on you. Often a white man you might meet, when you had run away from home like that, might appear to be all right and give you a quarter or a half dollar or something, and then go right and give you away. White men will do that, but not a nigger. You can trust them. They are squarer with kids. I don't know why.

At the Saratoga meeting that year there were a lot of men from home. Dave Williams and Arthur Mulford and Jerry Myers and others. Then there was a lot from Louisville and Lexington Henry Rieback knew but I didn't. They were professional gamblers and Henry Rieback's father is one too. He is what is called a sheet writer and goes away most of the year to tracks. In the winter when he is home in Beckersville he don't stay there much but goes away to cities and deals faro. He is a nice man and generous, is always sending Henry presents, a bicycle and a gold watch and a boy scout suit of clothes and things like that.

My own father is a lawyer. He's all right, but don't make much money and can't buy me things and anyway I'm getting so old now I don't expect it. He never said nothing to me against Henry, but Hanley Turner and Tom Tumberton's fathers did. They said to their boys that money so come by is no good and they didn't want their boys brought up to hear gamblers' talk and be thinking about such things and maybe embrace them.

That's all right and I guess the men know what they are talking about, but I don't see what it's got to do with Henry or with horses either. That's what I'm writing this story about. I'm puzzled. I'm getting to be a man and want to think straight and be O. K., and there's something I saw at the race meeting at the eastern track I can't figure out.

I can't help it, I'm crazy about thoroughbred horses. I've always been that way. When I was ten years old and saw I was going to be big and couldn't be a rider I was so sorry I nearly died. Harry Hellinfinger in Beckersville, whose father is Postmaster, is grown up and too lazy to work, but likes to stand around in the street and get up jokes on boys like sending them to a hardware store for a gimlet to bore square holes and other jokes like that. He played one on me. He told me that if I would eat a half a cigar I would be stunted and not grow any more and maybe could be a rider. I did it. When father wasn't looking I took a cigar out of his pocket and gagged it down some way. It made me awful sick and the doctor had to be sent for, and then it did no good. I kept right on growing. It was a joke. When I told what I had done and why most fathers would have whipped me but mine didn't.

Well, I didn't get stunted and didn't die. It serves Harry Hellinfinger right. Then I made up my mind I would like to be a stable boy, but had to give that up too. Mostly niggers do that work and I knew father wouldn't let me go into it. No use to ask him.

If you've never been crazy about thoroughbreds it's because you've never been around where they are much and don't know any better. They're beautiful. There isn't anything so lovely and clean and full of spunk and honest and everything as some race horses. On the big horse farms that are all around our town Beckersville there are tracks and the horses run in the early morning. More than a thousand times I've got out of bed before daylight and walked two or three miles to the tracks. Mother wouldn't of let me go but father always says, "Let him alone." So I got some bread out of the bread box and some butter and jam, gobbled it and lit out.

At the tracks you sit on the fence with men, whites and niggers, and they chew tobacco and talk, and then the colts are brought out. It's early and the grass is covered with shiny dew and in another field a man is plowing and they are frying things in a shed where the track niggers sleep, and you know how a nigger can giggle and laugh and say things that make you laugh. A white man can't do it and some niggers can't but a track nigger can every time.

And so the colts are brought out and some are just galloped by stable boys, but almost every morning on a big track owned by a rich man who lives maybe in New York, there are always, nearly every morning, a few colts and some of the old race horses and geldings and mares that are cut loose.

It brings a lump up into my throat when a horse runs. I don't mean all horses but some. I can pick them nearly every time. It's in my blood like in the blood of race-track niggers and trainers.

Even when they just go slop-jogging along with a little nigger on their backs I can tell a winner. If my throat hurts and it's hard for me to swallow, that's him. He'll run like Sam Hill when you let him out. If he don't win every time it'll be a wonder and because they've got him in a pocket behind another or he was pulled or got off bad at the post or something. If I wanted to be a gambler like Henry Rieback's father I could get rich. I know I could and Henry says so too. All I would have to do is to wait 'til that hurt comes when I see a horse and then bet every cent. That's what I would do if I wanted to be a gambler, but I don't.

When you're at the tracks in the morning — not the race-tracks but the training tracks around Beckersville — you don't see a horse, the kind I've been talking about, very often, but it's nice anyway. Any thoroughbred, that is sired right and out of a good mare and trained by a man that knows how, can run. If he couldn't what would he be there for and not pulling a plow?

Well, out of the stables they come and the boys are on their backs and it's lovely to be there. You hunch down on top of the fence and itch inside you. Over in the sheds the niggers giggle and sing. Bacon is being fried and coffee made. Everything smells lovely. Nothing smells better than coffee and manure and horses and niggers and bacon frying and pipes being smoked out of doors on a morning like that. It just gets you, that's what it does.

But about Saratoga. We was there six days and not a soul from home seen us and everything came off just as we wanted it to, fine weather and horses and races and all. We beat our way home and Bildad gave us a basket with fried chicken and bread and other eatables in, and I had eighteen dollars when we got back to Beckersville. Mother jawed and cried but Pop didn't say much. I told everything we done except one thing. I did and saw that alone. That's what I'm writing about. It got me upset. I think about it at night. Here it is.

At Saratoga we laid up nights in the hay in the shed Bildad had showed us and ate with the niggers early and at night when the race people had all gone away. The men from home stayed mostly in the grandstand and betting field, and didn't come out around the places where the horses are kept except to the paddocks just before a race when the horses are saddled. At Saratoga they don't have paddocks under an open shed as at Lexington and Churchill Downs and other tracks down in our country, but saddle the horses right out in an open place under trees on a lawn as smooth and nice as Banker Bohon's front yard here in Beckersville. It's lovely. The horses are sweaty and nervous and shine and the men come out and smoke cigars and look at them and the trainers are there and the owners, and your heart thumps so you can hardly breathe.

Then the bugle blows for post and the boys that ride come running out with their silk clothes on and you run to get a place by the fence with the niggers.

I always am wanting to be a trainer or owner, and at the risk of being seen and caught and sent home I went to the paddocks before every race. The other boys didn't but I did.

We got to Saratoga on a Friday and on Wednesday the next week the big Mullford Handicap was to be run. Middlestride was in it and Sunstreak. The weather was fine and the track fast. I couldn't sleep the night before.

What had happened was that both these horses are the kind it makes my throat hurt to see. Middlestride is long and looks awkward and is a gelding. He belongs to Joe Thompson, a little owner from home who only has a half dozen horses. The Mullford Handicap is for a mile and Middlestride 'can't untrack fast. He goes away slow and is always way back at the half, then he begins to run and if the race is a mile and a quarter he'll just eat up everything and get there.

Sunstreak is different. He is a stallion and nervous and belongs on the biggest farm we've got in our country, the Van Riddle place that belongs to Mr. Van Riddle of New York. Sunstreak is like a girl you think about sometimes but never see. He is hard all over and lovely too. When you look at his head you want to kiss him. He is trained by Jerry Tillford who knows me and has been good to me lots of times, lets me walk into a horse's stall to look at him close and other things. There isn't anything as sweet as that horse. He stands at the post quiet and not letting on, but he is just burning up inside. Then when the barrier goes up he is off like his name, Sunstreak. It makes you ache to see him. It hurts you. He just lays down and runs like a bird dog. There can't anything I ever see run like him except Middlestride when he gets untracked and stretches himself.

Gee! I ached to see that race and those two horses run, ached and dreaded it too. I didn't want to see either of our horses beaten. We had never sent a pair like that to the races before. Old men in

Beckersville said so and the niggers said so. It was a fact.

Before the race I went over to the paddocks to see. I looked a last look at Middlestride, who isn't such a much standing in a paddock that way, then I went to see Sunstreak.

It was his day. I knew when I see him. I forgot all about being seen myself and walked right up. All the men from Beckersville were there and no one noticed me except Jerry Tillford. He saw me and something happened. I'll tell you about that.

I was standing looking at that horse and aching. In some way, I can't tell how, I knew just how Sunstreak felt inside. He was quiet and letting the niggers rub his legs and Mr. Van Riddle himself put the saddle on, but he was just a raging torrent inside. He was like the water in the river at Niagara Falls just before it goes plunk down. That horse wasn't thinking about running. He don't have to think about that. He was just thinking about holding himself back 'til the time for the running came. I knew that. I could just in a way see right inside him. He was going to do some awful running and I knew it. He wasn't bragging or letting on much or prancing or making a fuss, but just waiting. I knew it and Jerry Tillford his trainer knew. I looked up and then that man and I looked into each other's eyes. Something happened to me. I guess I loved the man as much as I did the horse because he knew what I knew. Seemed to me there wasn't anything in the world but that man and the horse and me. I cried and Jerry Tillford had a shine in his eyes. Then I came away to the fence to wait for the race. The horse was better than me, more steadier, and now I know better than Jerry. He was the quietest and he had to do the running.

Sunstreak ran first of course and he busted the world's record for a mile. I've seen that if I never see anything more. Everything came out just as I expected. Middlestride got left at the post and was way back and closed up to be second, just as I knew he would. He'll get a world's record too some day. They can't skin the Beckersville country on horses.

I watched the race calm because I knew what would happen. I was sure. Hanley Turner and Henry Rieback and Tom Tumberton were all more excited than me.

A funny thing had happened to me. I was thinking about Jerry Tillford the trainer and how happy he was all through the race. I liked him that afternoon even more than I ever liked my own father. I almost forgot the horses thinking that way about him. It was because of what I had seen in his eyes as he stood in the paddocks beside Sunstreak before the race started. I knew he had been watching and working with Sunstreak since the horse was a baby colt, had taught him to run and be patient and when to let himself out and not to quit, never. I knew that for him it was like a mother seeing her child do something brave or wonderful. It was the first time I ever felt for a man like that.

After the race that night I cut out from Tom and Hanley and Henry. I wanted to be by myself and I wanted to be near Jerry Tillford if I could work it. Here is what happened.

The track in Saratoga is near the edge of town. It is all polished up and trees around, the evergreen kind, and grass and everything painted and nice. If you go past the track you get to a hard road made of asphalt for automobiles, and if you go along this for a few miles there is a road turns off to a little rummy looking farm house set in a yard.

That night after the race I went along that road because I had seen Jerry and some other men go that way in an automobile. I didn't expect to find them. I walked for a ways and then sat down by a fence to think. It was the direction they went in. I wanted to be as near Jerry as I could. I felt close to him. Pretty soon I went up the side road — I don't know why — and came to the rummy farm house. I was just lonesome to see Jerry, like wanting to see your father at night when you were a young kid. Just then an automobile came along and turned in. Jerry was in it and Henry Rieback's father, and Arthur Bedford from home, and Dave Williams and two other men I didn't know. They got out of the car and went into the house, all but Henry Rieback's father who quarreled with them and said he wouldn't go. It was only about nine o'clock, but they were all drunk and the rummy looking farm house was a place for bad women to stay in. That's what it was. I crept up along a fence and looked through a window and saw.

It's what gives me the fantods. I can't make it out. The women in the house were all ugly mean-looking women, not nice to look at or be near. They were homely too, except one who was tall and looked a little like the gelding Middlestride, but not clean like him, but with a hard ugly mouth. She had red hair. I saw everything plain. I got up by an old rose bush by an open window and looked. The women had on loose dresses and sat around in chairs. The

men came in and some sat on the women's laps. The place smelled
rotten and there was rotten talk, the kind a kid hears around a
livery stable in a town like Beckersville in the winter but don't
ever expect to hear talked when there are women around. It was
rotten. A nigger wouldn't go into such a place.

I looked at Jerry Tillford. I've told you how I had been feeling
about him on account of his knowing what was going on inside of
Sunstreak in the minute before he went to the post for the race in
which he made a world's record.

Jerry bragged in that bad woman house as I know Sunstreak
wouldn't never have bragged. He said that he made that horse, that
it was him that won the race and made the record. He lied and
bragged like a fool. I never heard such silly talk.

And then, what do you suppose he did! He looked at the woman
in there, the one that was lean and hard-mouthed and looked a
little like the gelding Middlestride, but not clean like him, and his
eyes began to shine just as they did when he looked at me and at
Sunstreak in the paddocks at the track in the afternoon. I stood
there by the window — gee! — but I wished I hadn't gone away
from the tracks, but had stayed with the boys and the niggers and
the horses. The tall rotten looking woman was between us just as
Sunstreak was in the paddocks in the afternoon.

Then, all of a sudden, I began to hate that man. I wanted to
scream and rush in the room and kill him. I never had such a
feeling before. I was so mad clean through that I cried and my
fists were doubled up so my finger nails cut my hands.

And Jerry's eyes kept shining and he waved back and forth,
and then he went and kissed that woman and I crept away and
went back to the tracks and to bed and didn't sleep hardly any,
and then next day I got the other kids to start home with me
and never told them anything I seen.

I been thinking about it ever since. I can't make it out. Spring
has come again and I'm nearly sixteen and go to the tracks mornings same as always, and I see Sunstreak and Middlestride and a
new colt named Strident I'll bet will lay them all out, but no one
thinks so but me and two or three niggers.

But things are different. At the tracks the air don't taste as good
or smell as good. It's because a man like Jerry Tillford, who knows
what he does, could see a horse like Sunstreak run, and kiss a woman

like that the same day. I can't make it out. Darn him, what did he want to do like that for? I keep thinking about it and it spoils looking at horses and smelling things and hearing niggers laugh and everything. Sometimes I'm so mad about it I want to fight someone. It gives me the fantods. What did he do it for? I want to know why.

WILLIAM FAULKNER

spotted horses

Yes, sir. Flem Snopes has filled that whole country full of spotted horses. You can hear folks running them all day and all night, whooping and hollering, and the horses running back and forth across them little wooden bridges ever now and then kind of like thunder. Here I was this morning pretty near half way to town, with the team ambling along and me setting in the buckboard about half asleep, when all of a sudden something come swurging up outen the bushes and jumped the road clean, without touching hoof to it. It flew right over my team big as a billboard and flying through the air like a hawk. It taken me thirty minutes to stop my team and untangle the harness and the buckboard and hitch them up again.

That Flem Snopes. I be dog if he ain't a case, now. One morn-

ing about ten years ago the boys was just getting settled down on
Varner's porch for a little talk and tobacco, when here come Flem
out from behind the counter, with his coat off and his hair all
parted, like he might have been clerking for Varner for ten years
already. Folks all knowed him; it was a big family of them about
five miles down the bottom. That year, at least. Share-cropping.
They never stayed on any place over a year. Then they would
move on to another place, with the chap or maybe the twins of
that year's litter. It was a regular nest of them. But Flem. The rest
of them stayed tenant farmers, moving ever year, but here come
Flem one day, walking out from behind Jody Varner's counter
like he owned it. And he wasn't there but a year or two before
folks knowed that if him and Jody was both still in that store in
ten years more it would be Jody clerking for Flem Snopes. Why,
that fellow could make a nickel where it wasn't but four cents to
begin with. He skun me in two trades myself, and the fellow that
can do that, I just hope he'll get rich before I do; that's all.

All right. So here Flem was, clerking at Varner's, making a nickel
here and there and not telling nobody about it. No, sir. Folks never
knowed when Flem got the better of somebody lessen the fellow
he beat told it. He'd just set there in the store-chair, chewing his
tobacco and keeping his own business to hisself, until about a week
later we'd find out it was somebody else's business he was keeping to hisself — provided the fellow he trimmed was mad enough
to tell it. That's Flem.

We give him ten years to own ever thing Jody Varner had. But
he never waited no ten years. I reckon you-all know that gal of
Uncle Billy Varner's, the youngest one; Eula. Jody's sister. Ever
Sunday ever yellow-wheeled buggy and curried riding horse in
that country would be hitched to Bill Varner's fence, and the young
bucks setting on the porch, swarming around Eula like bees around
a honey pot. One of these here kind of big, soft-looking gals that
could giggle richer than plowed new-ground. Wouldn't none of
them leave before the others, and so they would set there on the
porch until time to go home, with some of them with nine and
ten miles to ride and then get up tomorrow and go back to the
field. So they would all leave together and they would ride in a
clump down to the creek ford and hitch them curried horses and
yellow-wheeled buggies and get out and fight one another. Then
they would get in the buggies again and go on home.

Well, one day about a year ago, one of them yellow-wheeled buggies and one of them curried saddle-horses quit this country. We heard they was heading for Texas. The next day Uncle Billy and Eula and Flem come into town in Uncle Bill's surrey, and when they come back, Flem and Eula was married. And on the next day we heard that two more of them yellow-wheeled buggies had left the country. They mought have gone to Texas, too. It's a big place.

Anyway, about a month after the wedding, Flem and Eula went to Texas, too. They was gone pretty near a year. Then one day last month, Eula come back, with a baby. We figured up, and we decided that it was as well-growed a three-months-old baby as we ever see. It can already pull up on a chair. I reckon Texas makes big men quick, being a big place. Anyway, if it keeps on like it started, it'll be chewing tobacco and voting time it's eight years old.

And so last Friday here come Flem himself. He was on a wagon with another fellow. The other fellow had one of these two-gallon hats and a ivory-handled pistol and a box of gingersnaps sticking out of his hind pocket, and tied to the tail-gate of the wagon was about two dozen of them Texas ponies, hitched to one another with barbed wire. They was colored like parrots and they was quiet as doves, and ere a one of them would kill you quick as a rattlesnake. Nere a one of them had two eyes the same color, and nere a one of them had ever see a bridle, I reckon; and when that Texas man got down offen the wagon and walked up to them to show how gentle they was, one of them cut his vest clean offen him, same as with a razor.

Flem had done already disappeared; he had went on to see his wife, I reckon, and to see if that ere baby had done gone on to the field to help Uncle Billy plow, maybe. It was the Texas man that taken the horses on to Mrs. Littlejohn's lot. He had a little trouble at first, when they come to the gate, because they hadn't never see a fence before, and when he finally got them in and taken a pair of wire cutters and unhitched them and got them into the barn and poured some shell corn into the trough, they durn nigh tore down the barn. I reckon they thought that shell corn was bugs, maybe. So he left them in the lot and he announced that the auction would begin at sunup tomorrow.

That night we was setting on Mrs. Littlejohn's porch. You-all mind the moon was nigh full that night, and we could watch them

spotted varmints swirling along the fence and back and forth across
the lot same as minnows in a pond. And then now and then they
would all kind of huddle up against the barn and rest themselves by
biting and kicking one another. We would hear a squeal, and then
a set of hoofs would go Bam! against the barn, like a pistol. It
sounded just like a fellow with a pistol, in a nest of cattymounts,
taking his time.

II

It wasn't ere a man knowed yet if Flem owned them things or
not. They just knowed one thing: that they wasn't never going to
know for sho if Flem did or not, or if maybe he didn't just get on
that wagon at the edge of town, for the ride or not. Even Eck
Snopes didn't know, Flem's own cousin. But wasn't nobody surprised at that. We knowed that Flem would skin Eck quick as he
would ere a one of us.

They was there by sunup next morning, some of them come
twelve and sixteen miles, with seed-money tied up in tobacco sacks
in their overalls, standing along the fence, when the Texas man
come out of Mrs. Littlejohn's after breakfast and clumb onto the
gate post with that ere white pistol butt sticking outen his hind
pocket. He taken a new box of gingersnaps outen his pocket and
bit the end offen it like a cigar and spit out the paper, and said the
auction was open. And still they was coming up in wagons and a
horse- and mule-back and hitching the teams across the road and
coming to the fence. Flem wasn't nowhere in sight.

But he couldn't get them started. He begun to work on Eck,
because Eck holp him last night to get them into the barn and feed
them that shell corn. Eck got out just in time. He come outen that
barn like a chip on the crest of a busted dam of water, and clumb
into the wagon just in time.

He was working on Eck when Henry Armstid come up in his
wagon. Eck was saying he was skeered to bid on one of them,
because he might get it, and the Texas man says, 'Them ponies?
Them little horses?' He clumb down offen the gate post and went
toward the horses. They broke and run, and him following them,
kind of chirping to them, with his hand out like he was fixing to
catch a fly, until he got three or four of them cornered. Then he

jumped into them, and then we couldn't see nothing for a while because of the dust. It was a big cloud of it, and them blare-eyed, spotted things swoaring outen it twenty foot to a jump, in forty directions without counting up. Then the dust settled and there they was, that Texas man and the horse. He had its head twisted clean around like a owl's head. Its legs was braced and it was trembling like a new bride and groaning like a saw mill, and him holding its head wrung clean around on its neck so it was snuffing sky. 'Look it over,' he says, with his heels dug too and that white pistol sticking outen his pocket and his neck swole up like a spreading adder's until you could just tell what he was saying, cussing the horse and talking to us all at once: 'Look him over, the fiddle-headed son of fourteen fathers. Try him, buy him; you will get the best —' Then it was all dust again, and we couldn't see nothing but spotted hide and mane, and that ere Texas man's boot-heels like a couple of walnuts on two strings, and after a while that two-gallon hat come sailing out like a fat old hen crossing a fence.

When the dust settled again, he was just getting outen the far fence corner, brushing himself off. He come and got his hat and brushed it off and come and clumb onto the gate post again. He was breathing hard. The hammer-head horse was still running round and round the lot like a merry-go-round at a fair. That was when Henry Armstid come shoving up to the gate in them patched overalls and one of them dangle-armed shirts of hisn. Hadn't nobody noticed him until then. We was all watching the Texas man and the horses. Even Mrs. Littlejohn; she had done come out and built a fire under the washpot in her back yard, and she would stand at the fence a while and then go back into the house and come out again with a arm full of wash and stand at the fence again. Well, here come Henry shoving up, and then we see Mrs. Armstid right behind him, in that ere faded wrapper and sunbonnet and them tennis shoes. 'Git on back to that wagon,' Henry says.

'Henry,' she says.

'Here, boys,' the Texas man says; 'make room for missus to git up and see. Come on Henry,' he says; 'here's your chance to buy that saddle-horse missus has been wanting. What about ten dollars, Henry?'

'Henry,' Mrs. Armstid says. She put her hand on Henry's arm. Henry knocked her hand down.

'Git on back to that wagon, like I told you,' he says.

Mrs. Armstid never moved. She stood behind Henry, with her hands rolled into her dress, not looking at nothing. 'He hain't no more despair than to buy one of them things,' she says. 'And us not five dollars ahead of the pore house, he hain't no more despair.' It was the truth, too. They ain't never made more than a bare living offen that place of theirs, and them with four chaps and the very clothes they wears she earns by weaving by the firelight at night when Henry's asleep.

'Shut your mouth and git on back to that wagon,' Henry says. 'Do you want I taken a wagon stake to you here in the big road?'

Well, that Texas man taken one look at her. Then he begun on Eck again; like Henry wasn't even there. But Eck was skeered. 'I can git me a snapping turtle or a water moccasin for nothing. I ain't going to buy none.'

So the Texas man said he would give Eck a horse. 'To start the auction, and because you holp me last night. If you'll start the bidding on the next horse,' he says, 'I'll give you that fiddle-head horse.'

I wish you could have seen them, standing there with their seed-money in their pockets, watching that Texas man give Eck Snopes a live horse, all fixed to call him a fool if he taken it or not. Finally Eck says he'll take it. 'Only I just starts the bidding,' he says. 'I don't have to buy the next one lessen I ain't overtopped.' The Texas man said all right, and Eck bid a dollar on the next one, with Henry Armstid standing there with his mouth already open, watching Eck and the Texas man like a mad-dog or something. 'A dollar,' Eck says.

The Texas man looked at Eck. His mouth was already open too, like he had started to say something and what he was going to say had up and died on him. 'A dollar? You mean, *one* dollar, Eck?'

'Durn it,' Eck says; 'two dollars, then.'

Well, sir, I wish you could a seen that Texas man. He taken out that gingersnap box and held it up and looked into it, careful, like it might have been a diamond ring in it, or a spider. Then he throwed it away and wiped his face with a bandanna. 'Well,' he says. 'Well. Two dollars. Two dollars. Is your pulse all right, Eck?' he says. 'Do you have ager-sweats at night, maybe?' he says. 'Well,' he says, 'I got to take it. But are you boys going to stand there and see Eck get two horses at a dollar a head?'

That done it. I be dog if he wasn't nigh as smart at Flem Snopes.

He hadn't no more than got the words outen his mouth before here was Henry Armstid, waving his hand. 'Three dollars,' Henry says. Mrs. Armstid tried to hold him again. He knocked her hand off, shoving up to the gate post.

'Mister,' Mrs. Armstid says, 'we got chaps in the house and not corn to feed the stock. We got five dollars I earned my chaps a-weaving after dark, and him snoring in the bed. And he hain't no more despair.'

'Henry bids three dollars,' the Texas man says. 'Raise him a dollar, Eck, and the horse is yours.'

'Henry,' Mrs. Armstid says.

'Raise him, Eck,' the Texas man says.

'Four dollars,' Eck says.

'Five dollars,' Henry says, shaking his fist. He shoved up right under the gate post. Mrs. Armstid was looking at the Texas man too.

'Mister,' she says, 'if you take that five dollars I earned my chaps a-weaving for one of them things, it'll be a curse onto you and yourn during all the time of man.'

But it wasn't no stopping Henry. He had shoved up, waving his fist at the Texas man. He opened it; the money was in nickels and quarters, and one dollar bill that looked like a cow's cud. 'Five dollars,' he says. 'And the man that raises it'll have to beat my head off, or I'll beat his'n.'

'All right,' the Texas man says. 'Five dollars is bid. But don't you shake your hand at me.'

III

It taken till nigh sundown before the last one was sold. He got them hotted up once and the bidding got up to seven dollars and a quarter, but most of them went around three or four dollars, him setting on the gate post and picking the horses out one at a time by mouth-word, and Mrs. Littlejohn pumping up and down at the tub and stopping and coming to the fence for a while and going back to the tub again. She had done got done too, and the wash was hung on the line in the back yard, and we could smell supper cooking. Finally they was all sold; he swapped the last two and the wagon for a buckboard.

We was all kind of tired, but Henry Armstid looked more like a mad-dog than ever. When he bought, Mrs. Armstid had went back to the wagon, setting in it behind them two rabbit-sized, bone-pore mules, and the wagon itself looking like it would fall all to pieces soon as the mules moved. Henry hadn't even waited to pull it outen the road; it was still in the middle of the road and her setting in it, not looking at nothing, ever since this morning.

Henry was right up against the gate. He went up to the Texas man. 'I bought a horse and I paid cash,' Henry says. 'And yet you expect me to stand around here until they are all sold before I can get my horse. I'm going to take my horse outen that lot.'

The Texas man looked at Henry. He talked like he might have been asking for a cup of coffee at the table. 'Take your horse,' he says.

Then Henry quit looking at the Texas man. He begun to swallow, holding onto the gate. 'Ain't you going to help me?' he says.

'It ain't my horse,' the Texas man says.

Henry never looked at the Texas man again, he never looked at nobody. 'Who'll help me catch my horse?' he says. Never nobody said nothing. 'Bring the plowline,' Henry says. Mrs. Armstid got outen the wagon and brought the plowline. The Texas man got down offen the post. The woman made to pass him, carrying the rope.

'Don't you go in there, missus,' the Texas man says.

Henry opened the gate. He didn't look back. 'Come on here,' he says.

'Don't you go in there, missus,' the Texas man says.

Mrs. Armstid wasn't looking at nobody, neither, with her hands across her middle, holding the rope. 'I reckon I better,' she says. Her and Henry went into the lot. The horses broke and run. Henry and Mrs. Armstid followed.

'Get him into the corner,' Henry says. They got Henry's horse cornered finally, and Henry taken the rope, but Mrs. Armstid let the horse get out. They hemmed it up again, but Mrs. Armstid let it get out again, and Henry turned and hit her with the rope. 'Why didn't you head him back?' Henry says. He hit her again. 'Why didn't you?' It was about that time I looked around and see Flem Snopes standing there.

It was the Texas man that done something. He moved fast for a big man. He caught the rope before Henry could hit the third

time, and Henry whirled and made like he would jump at the
Texas man. But he never jumped. The Texas man went and taken
Henry's arm and led him outen the lot. Mrs. Armstid come behind
them and the Texas man taken some money outen his pocket and
he give it into Mrs. Armstid's hand. 'Get him into the wagon and
take him on home,' the Texas man says, like he might have been
telling them he enjoyed his supper.

Then here come Flem. 'What's that for Buck?' Flem says.

'Thinks he bought one of them ponies,' the Texas man says.
'Get him on away, missus.'

But Henry wouldn't go. 'Give him back that money,' he says. 'I
bought that horse and I aim to have him if I have to shoot him.'

And there was Flem, standing there with his hands in his pockets,
chewing, like he had just happened to be passing.

'You take your money and I take my horse,' Henry says. 'Give
it back to him,' he says to Mrs. Armstid.

'You don't own no horse of mine,' the Texas man says. 'Get him
on home, missus.'

Then Henry seen Flem. 'You got something to do with these
horses,' he says. 'I bought one. Here's the money for it.' He taken
the bill outen Mrs. Armstid's hand. He offered it to Flem. 'I bought
one. Ask him. Here's the money,' he says, giving the bill to Flem.

When Flem taken the money, the Texas man dropped the rope
he had snatched outen Henry's hand. He had done sent Eck
Snopes's boy up to the store for another box of gingersnaps, and he
taken the box outen his pocket and looked into it. It was empty
and he dropped it on the ground. 'Mr. Snopes will have your
money for you tomorrow,' he says to Mrs. Armstid. 'You can get
it from him tomorrow. He don't own no horse. You get him into
the wagon and get him on home.' Mrs. Armstid went back to the
wagon and got in. 'Where's that ere buckboard I bought?' the
Texas man says. It was after sundown then. And then Mrs. Littlejohn come out on the porch and rung the supper bell.

IV

I come on in and et supper. Mrs. Littlejohn would bring in a
pan of bread or something, then she would go out to the porch a
minute and come back and tell us. The Texas man had hitched his

team to the buckboard he had swapped them last two horses for, and him and Flem had gone, and then she told that the rest of them that never had ropes had went back to the store with I. O. Snopes to get some ropes, and wasn't nobody at the gate but Henry Armstid, and Mrs. Armstid setting in the wagon in the road, and Eck Snopes and that boy of hisn. 'I don't care how many of them fool men gets killed by them things,' Mrs. Littlejohn says, 'but I ain't going to let Eck Snopes take that boy into that lot again.' So she went down to the gate, but she come back without the boy or Eck neither.

'It ain't no need to worry about that boy,' I says. 'He's charmed.' He was right behind Eck last night when Eck went to help feed them. The whole drove of them jumped clean over that boy's head and never touched him. It was Eck that touched him. Eck snatched him into the wagon and taken a rope and frailed the tar outen him.

So I had done et and went to my room and was undressing, long as I had a long trip to make next day; I was trying to sell a machine to Mrs. Bundren up past Whiteleaf; when Henry Armstid opened that gate and went in by hisself. They couldn't make him wait for the balance of them to get back with their ropes. Eck Snopes said he tried to make Henry wait, but Henry wouldn't do it. Eck said Henry walked right up to them and that when they broke, they run clean over Henry like a hay-mow breaking down. Eck said he snatched that boy of hisn out of the way just in time and that them things went through that gate like a creek flood and into the wagons and teams hitched side the road, busting wagon tongues and snapping harness like it was fishing-line, with Mrs. Armstid still setting in their wagon in the middle of it like something carved outen wood. Then they scattered, wild horses and tame mules with pieces of harness and single trees dangling offen them, both ways up and down the road.

'There goes ourn, paw!' Eck says his boy said. 'There it goes, into Mrs. Littlejohn's house.' Eck says it run right up the steps and into the house like a boarder late for supper. I reckon so. Anyway, I was in my room, in my underclothes, with one sock on and one sock in my hand, leaning out the window when the commotion busted out, when I heard something run into the melodeon in the hall; it sounded like a railroad engine. Then the door to my room come sailing in like when you throw a tin bucket top into the wind and I looked over my shoulder and see something that looked like a fourteen-foot pinwheel a-blaring its eyes at me. It had to blare them fast, because I was already done jumped out the window.

I reckon it was anxious, too. I reckon it hadn't never seen barbed wire or shell corn before, but I know it hadn't never seen under-clothes before, or maybe it was a sewing-machine agent it hadn't never seen. Anyway, it whirled and turned to run back up the hall and outen the house, when it met Eck Snopes and that boy just coming in, carrying a rope. It swirled again and run down the hall and out the back door just in time to meet Mrs. Littlejohn. She had just gathered up the clothes she had washed, and she was com-ing onto the back porch with a armful of washing in one hand and a scrubbing-board in the other, when the horse skidded up to her, trying to stop and swirl again. It never taken Mrs. Littlejohn no time a-tall.

'Git outen here, you son of a bitch,' she says. She hit it across the face with the scrubbing-board; that ere scrubbing-board split as neat as ere a axe could have done it, and when the horse swirled to run back up the hall, she hit it again with what was left of the scrubbing-board, not on the head this time. 'And stay out,' she says.

Eck and that boy was half-way down the hall by this time. I reckon that horse looked like a pinwheel to Eck too. 'Git to hell outen here, Ad!' Eck says. Only there wasn't time. Eck dropped flat on his face, but the boy never moved. The boy was about a yard tall maybe, in overalls just like Eck's; that horse swoared over his head without touching a hair. I saw that, because I was just coming back up the front steps, still carrying that ere sock and still in my underclothes, when the horse come onto the porch again. It taken one look at me and swirled again and run to the end of the porch and jumped the banisters and the lot fence like a hen-hawk and lit in the lot running and went out the gate again and jumped eight or ten upside-down wagons and went on down the road. It was a full moon then. Mrs. Armstid was still setting in the wagon like she had done been carved outen wood and left there and forgot.

That horse. It ain't never missed a lick. It was going about forty miles a hour when it come to the bridge over the creek. It would have had a clear road, but it so happened that Vernon Tull was already using the bridge when it got there. He was coming back from town; he hadn't heard about the auction; him and his wife and three daughters and Mrs. Tull's aunt, all setting in chairs in the wagon bed, and all asleep, including the mules. They waked up when the horse hit the bridge one time, but Tull said the first he knew was when the mules tried to turn the wagon around in the middle of the bridge and he seen that spotted varmint run right twixt the mules and run up the wagon tongue like a squirrel. He said he just had time to hit it across the face with his whip-stock, because about that time the mules turned the wagon around on that ere one-way bridge and that horse clumb across onto the bridge again and went on, with Vernon standing up in the wagon and kicking at it.

Tull said the mules turned in the harness and clumb back into the wagon too, with Tull trying to beat them out again, with the reins wrapped around his wrist. After that he says all he seen was overturned chairs and womenfolks' legs and white drawers shining in the moonlight, and his mules and that spotted horse going on up the road like a ghost.

The mules jerked Tull outen the wagon and drug him a spell on the bridge before the reins broke. They thought at first that he was dead, and while they was kneeling around him, picking the bridge splinters outen him, here come Eck and that boy, still carrying the rope. They was running and breathing a little hard. 'Where'd he go?' Eck says.

V

I went back and got my pants and shirt and shoes on just in time to go and help get Henry Armstid outen the trash in the lot. I be dog if he didn't look like he was dead, with his head hanging back and his teeth showing in the moonlight, and a little rim of white under his eye-lids. We could still hear them horses, here and there; hadn't none of them got more than four — five miles away yet, not knowing the country, I reckon. So we could hear them and folks yelling now and then: 'Whooey. Head him!'

We toted Henry into Mrs. Littlejohn's. She was in the hall; she hadn't put down the armful of clothes. She taken one look at us, and she laid down the busted scrubbing-board and taken up the lamp and opened a empty door. 'Bring him in here,' she says.

We toted him in and laid him on the bed. Mrs. Littlejohn set the lamp on the dresser, still carrying the clothes. 'I'll declare, you men,' she says. Our shadows was way up the wall, tiptoeing too;

we could hear ourselves breathing. 'Better get his wife,' Mrs. Little-john says. She went out, carrying the clothes.

'I reckon we had,' Quick says. 'Go get her, somebody.'

'Whyn't you go?' Winterbottom says.

'Let Ernest git her,' Durley says. 'He lives neighbors with them.'

Ernest went to fetch her. I be dog if Henry didn't look like he was dead. Mrs. Littlejohn come back, with a kettle and some towels. She went to work on Henry, and then Mrs. Armstid and Ernest come in. Mrs. Armstid come to the foot of the bed and stood there, with her hands rolled into her apron, watching what Mrs. Littlejohn was doing, I reckon.

'You men get outen the way,' Mrs. Littlejohn says. 'Git outside,' she says. 'See if you can't find something else to play with that will kill some more of you.'

'Is he dead?' Winterbottom says.

'It ain't your fault if he ain't,' Mrs. Littlejohn says. 'Go tell Will Varner to come up here. I reckon a man ain't so different from a mule, come long come short. Except maybe a mule's got more sense.'

We went to get Uncle Billy. It was a full moon. We could hear them, now and then, four miles away: 'Whooey. Head him.' The country was full of them, one on every wooden bridge in the land, running across it like thunder: 'Whooey. There he goes. Head him.'

We hadn't got far before Henry begun to scream. I reckon Mrs. Littlejohn's water had brung him to; anyway, he wasn't dead. We went on to Uncle Billy's. The house was dark. We called to him, and after a while the window opened and Uncle Billy put his head out, peart as a peckerwood, listening. 'Are they still trying to catch them durn rabbits?' he says.

He come down, with his britches on over his nightshirt and his suspenders dangling, carrying his horse-doctoring grip. 'Yes, sir,' he says, cocking his head like a woodpecker; 'they're still a-trying.'

We could hear Henry before we reached Mrs. Littlejohn's. He was going Ah-Ah-Ah. We stopped in the yard. Uncle Billy went on in. We could hear Henry. We stood in the yard, hearing them on the bridges, this-a-way and that: 'Whooey. Whooey.'

'Eck Snopes ought to caught hisn,' Ernest says.

'Looks like he ought,' Winterbottom said.

Henry was going Ah-Ah-Ah steady in the house; then he begun

to scream. 'Uncle Billy's started,' Quick said. We looked into the hall. We could see the light where the door was. Then Mrs. Littlejohn come out.

'Will needs some help,' she says. 'You, Ernest. You'll do.' Ernest went into the house.

'Hear them?' Quick said. 'That one was on Four Mile bridge.' We could hear them; it sounded like thunder a long way off; it didn't last long:

'Whooey.'

We could hear Henry: 'Ah-Ah-Ah-Ah-Ah.'

'They are both started now,' Winterbottom says. 'Ernest too.'

That was early in the night. Which was a good thing, because it taken a long night for folks to chase them things right and for Henry to lay there and holler, being as Uncle Billy never had none of this here chloryfoam to set Henry's leg with. So it was considerate in Flem to get them started early. And what do you reckon Flem's comment was?

That's right. Nothing. Because he wasn't there. Hadn't nobody see him since that Texas man left.

VI

That was Saturday night. I reckon Mrs. Armstid got home about daylight, to see about the chaps. I don't know where they thought her and Henry was. But lucky the oldest one was a gal, about twelve, big enough to take care of the little ones. Which she did for the next two days. Mrs. Armstid would nurse Henry all night and work in the kitchen for hern and Henry's keep, and in the afternoon she would drive home (it was about four miles) to see to the chaps. She would cook up a pot of victuals and leave it on the stove, and the gal would bar the house and keep the little ones quiet. I would hear Mrs. Littlejohn and Mrs. Armstid talking in the kitchen. 'How are the chaps making out?' Mrs. Littlejohn says.

'All right,' Mrs. Armstid says.

'Don't they git skeered at night?' Mrs. Littlejohn says.

'Ina May bars the door when I leave,' Mrs. Armstid says. 'She's got the axe in bed with her. I reckon she can make out.'

I reckon they did. And I reckon Mrs. Armstid was waiting for Flem to come back to town; hadn't nobody seen him until this

morning; to get her money the Texas man said Flem was keeping
for her. Sho. I reckon she was.

Anyway, I heard Mrs. Armstid and Mrs. Littlejohn talking in the
kitchen this morning while I was eating breakfast. Mrs. Littlejohn
had just told Mrs. Armstid that Flem was in town. 'You can ask
him for that five dollars,' Mrs. Littlejohn says.

'You reckon he'll give it to me?' Mrs. Armstid says.

Mrs. Littlejohn was washing dishes, washing them like a man,
like they was made out of iron. 'No,' she says. 'But asking him
won't do no hurt. It might shame him. I don't reckon it will, but
it might.'

'If he wouldn't give it back, it ain't no use to ask,' Mrs. Armstid
says.

'Suit yourself,' Mrs. Littlejohn says. 'It's your money.'

I could hear the dishes.

'Do you reckon he might give it back to me?' Mrs. Armstid says.
'That Texas man said he would. He said I could get it from Mr.
Snopes later.'

'Then go and ask him for it,' Mrs. Littlejohn says.

I could hear the dishes.

'He won't give it back to me,' Mrs. Armstid says.

'All right,' Mrs. Littlejohn says. 'Don't ask him for it, then.'

I could hear the dishes; Mrs. Armstid was helping. 'You don't
reckon he would, do you?' she says. Mrs. Littlejohn never said
nothing. It sounded like she was throwing the dishes at one another.
'Maybe I better go and talk to Henry about it,' Mrs. Armstid says.

'I would,' Mrs. Littlejohn says. I be dog if it didn't sound like
she had two plates in her hands, beating them together. 'Then
Henry can buy another five-dollar horse with it. Maybe he'll
buy one next time that will out and out kill him. If I thought that,
I'd give you back the money, myself.'

'I reckon I better talk to him first,' Mrs. Armstid said. Then it
sounded like Mrs. Littlejohn taken up all the dishes and throwed
them at the cook-stove, and I come away.

That was this morning. I had been up to Bundren's and back,
and I thought that things would have kind of settled down. So after
breakfast, I went up to the store. And there was Flem, setting in
the store chair and whittling, like he might not have ever moved
since he come to clerk for Jody Varner. I. O. was leaning in the
door, in his shirt sleeves and with his hair parted too, same as Flem

was before he turned the clerking job over to I. O. It's a funny thing about them Snopes: they all looks alike, yet there ain't ere a two of them that claims brothers. They're always just cousins, like Flem and Eck and Flem and I. O. Eck was there too, squatting against the wall, him and that boy, eating cheese and crackers outen a sack; they told me that Eck hadn't been home a-tall. And that Lon Quick hadn't got back to town, even. He followed his horse clean down to Samson's Bridge, with a wagon and a camp outfit. Eck finally caught one of hisn. It run into a blind lane at Freeman's and Eck and the boy taken and tied their rope across the end of the lane, about three foot high. The horse come to the end of the lane and whirled and run back without ever stopping. Eck says it never seen the rope a-tall. He says it looked just like one of these here Christmas pinwheels. 'Didn't it try to run again?' I says.

'No,' Eck says, eating a bite of cheese offen his knife blade. 'Just kicked some.'

'Kicked some?' I says.

'It broke its neck,' Eck says.

Well, they was squatting there, about six of them, talking, talking at Flem; never nobody knowed yet if Flem had ere a interest in them horses or not. So finally I come right out and asked him. 'Flem's done skun all of us so much,' I says, 'that we're proud of him. Come on, Flem,' I says, 'how much did you and that Texas man make offen them horses? You can tell us. Ain't nobody here but Eck that bought one of them; the others ain't got back to town yet, and Eck's your own cousin; he'll be proud to hear, too. How much did you-all make?'

They was all whittling, not looking at Flem, making like they was studying. But you could a heard a pin drop. And I. O. He had been rubbing his back up and down on the door, but he stopped now, watching Flem like a pointing dog. Flem finished cutting the sliver offen his stick. He spit across the porch, into the road. 'Twarn't none of my horses,' he says.

I. O. cackled, like a hen, slapping his legs with both hands. 'You boys might just as well quit trying to get ahead of Flem,' he said.

Well, about that time I see Mrs. Armstid come outen Mrs. Littlejohn's gate, coming up the road. I never said nothing. I says, 'Well, if a man can't take care of himself in a trade, he can't blame the man that trims him.'

Flem never said nothing, trimming at the stick. He hadn't seen
Mrs. Armstid. 'Yes, sir,' I says. 'A fellow like Henry Armstid ain't
got nobody but hisself to blame.'

'Course he ain't,' I. O. says. He ain't seen her, either. 'Henry
Armstid's a born fool. Always is been. If Flem hadn't a got his
money, somebody else would.'

We looked at Flem. He never moved. Mrs. Armstid come on
up the road.

'That's right,' I says. 'But come to think of it, Henry never
bought no horse.' We looked at Flem; you could a heard a match
drop. 'That Texas man told her to get that five dollars back from
Flem next day. I reckon Flem's done already taken that money to
Mrs. Littlejohn's and give it to Mrs. Armstid.'

We watched Flem. I. O. quit rubbing his back against the door
again. After a while Flem raised his head and spit across the porch,
into the dust. I. O. cackled, just like a hen. 'Ain't he a beating fellow, now?' I. O. says.

Mrs. Armstid was getting closer, so I kept on talking, watching
to see if Flem would look up and see her. But he never looked up.
I went on talking about Tull, about how he was going to sue Flem,
and Flem setting there, whittling his stick, not saying nothing else
after he said they wasn't none of his horses.

Then I. O. happened to look around. He seen Mrs. Armstid.
'Pssst!' he says. Flem looked up. 'Here she comes!' I. O. says. 'Go
out the back. I'll tell her you done went in to town today.'

But Flem never moved. He just set there, whittling, and we
watched Mrs. Armstid come up onto the porch, in that ere faded
sunbonnet and wrapper and them tennis shoes that made a kind of
hissing noise on the porch. She come onto the porch and stopped,
her hands rolled into her dress in front, not looking at nothing.

'He said Saturday,' she says, 'that he wouldn't sell Henry no
horse. He said I could get the money from you.'

Flem looked up. The knife never stopped. It went on trimming
off a sliver same as if he was watching it. 'He taken that money off
with him when he left,' Flem says.

Mrs. Armstid never looked at nothing. We never looked at her,
neither, except that boy of Eck's. He had a half-et cracker in his
hand, watching her, chewing.

'He said Henry hadn't bought no horse,' Mrs. Armstid says. 'He
said for me to get the money from you today.'

'I reckon he forgot about it,' Flem said. 'He taken that money off with him Saturday.' He whittled again. I. O. kept on rubbing his back, slow. He licked his lips. After a while the woman looked up the road, where it went on up the hill, toward the graveyard. She looked up that way for a while, with that boy of Eck's watching her and I. O. rubbing his back slow against the door. Then she turned back toward the steps.

'I reckon it's time to get dinner started,' she says.

'How's Henry this morning, Mrs. Armstid?' Winterbottom says.

She looked at Winterbottom; she almost stopped. 'He's resting, I thank you kindly,' she says.

Flem got up, outen the chair, putting his knife away. He spit across the porch. 'Wait a minute, Mrs. Armstid,' he says. She stopped again. She didn't look at him. Flem went on into the store, with I. O. done quit rubbing his back now, with his head craned after Flem, and Mrs. Armstid standing there with her hands rolled into her dress, not looking at nothing. A wagon come up the road and passed; it was Freeman, on the way to town. Then Flem come out again, with I. O. still watching him. Flem had one of these little striped sacks of Jody Varner's candy; I bet he still owes Jody that nickel, too. He put the sack into Mrs. Armstid's hand, like he would have put it into a hollow stump. He spit again across the porch. 'A little sweetening for the chaps,' he says.

'You're right kind,' Mrs. Armstid says. She held the sack of candy in her hand, not looking at nothing. Eck's boy was watching the sack, the half-et cracker in his hand; he wasn't chewing now. He watched Mrs. Armstid roll the sack into her apron. 'I reckon I better get on back and help with dinner,' she says. She turned and went back across the porch. Flem set down in the chair again and opened his knife. He spit across the porch again, past Mrs. Armstid where she hadn't went down the steps yet. Then she went on, in that ere sunbonnet and wrapper all the same color, back down the road toward Mrs. Littlejohn's. You couldn't see her dress move, like a natural woman walking. She looked like a old snag still standing up and moving along on a high water. We watched her turn in at Mrs. Littlejohn's and go outen sight. Flem was whittling. I. O. begun to rub his back on the door. Then he begun to cackle, just like a durn hen.

'You boys might just as well quit trying,' I. O. says. 'You can't

git ahead of Flem. You can't touch him. Ain't he a sight, now?'
I be dog if he ain't. If I had brung a herd of wild cattymounts
into town and sold them to my neighbors and kinfolks, they would
have lynched me. Yes, sir.

WALTER VAN TILBURG CLARK

the wind and the snow of winter

I t was near sunset when Mike Braneen came onto the last pitch of the old wagon road which had led into Gold Rock from the east since the Comstock days. The road was just two ruts in the hard earth, with sagebrush growing between them, and was full of steep pitches and sharp turns. From the summit it descended even more steeply into Gold Rock, in a series of short switchbacks down the slope of the canyon. There was a paved highway on the other side of the pass now, but Mike never used that. Cars coming from behind made him uneasy, so that he couldn't follow his own thoughts long, but had to keep turning around every few minutes, to see that his burro, Annie, was staying out on the shoulder of the road, where she would be safe. Mike didn't like cars anyway, and on the old road he could forget about them and feel more like himself. He could forget about Annie too, except when the light, quick tapping of her hoofs behind him stopped. Even then he didn't really break his thoughts. It was more as if the tapping were another sound from his own inner machinery, and when it stopped he stopped too, and turned around to see what she was doing. When he began to walk ahead at the same slow, unvarying pace, his arms scarcely swinging at all, his body bent a little forward from the waist, he would not be aware that there had been any interruption of the memory or the story that was going on in his head. Mike did not like to have his stories interrupted except by an idea of his own, something to do with his prospecting, or the arrival of his story at an actual memory which warmed him to closer recollection or led into a new and more attractive story.

An intense, golden light, almost liquid, fanned out from the peaks above him and reached eastward under the gray sky, and the snow which occasionally swarmed across this light was fine and dry. Such little squalls had been going on all day, and still there was nothing like real snow down, but only a fine powder which the wind swept along until it caught under the brush, leaving the ground bare. Yet Mike Braneen was not deceived. This was not just a flurrying day; it was the beginning of winter. If not tonight, then tomorrow, or the next day, the snow would begin which shut off the mountains, so that a man might as well be on a great plain for all he could see, perhaps even the snow which blinded a man at once and blanketed the desert in an hour. Fifty-two years in this country had made Mike Braneen sure about such things, although he didn't give much thought to them, but only to what he had to do because of them. Three nights before he had been awakened by a change in the wind. It was no longer a wind born in the near mountains, cold with night and altitude, but a wind from far places, full of a damp chill which got through his blankets and into his bones. The stars had still been clear and close above the dark humps of the mountains, and overhead the constellations had moved slowly in full panoply, unbroken by any invisible lower darkness; yet he had lain there half awake for a few minutes, hearing the new wind beat the brush around him, hearing Annie stirring restlessly and thumping in her hobble. He had thought drowsily, "Smells like winter this time," and then, "It's held off a long time this year, pretty near the end of December." Then he had gone back to sleep, mildly happy because the change meant he would be going back to Gold Rock. Gold Rock was the other half of Mike Braneen's life. When the smell of winter came he always started back for Gold Rock. From March or April until the smell of winter he wandered slowly about among the mountains, anywhere between the White Pines and the Virginias, with only his burro for company. Then there would come the change, and they would head back for Gold Rock.

Mike had traveled with a good many burros during that time, eighteen or twenty, he thought, although he was not sure. He could not remember them all, but only those he had had first, when he was a young man and always thought most about seeing women when he got back to Gold Rock, or those with something queer about them, like Baldy, who'd had a great pale patch, like a bald spot, on one side of his belly, or those who'd had something queer happen to them, like Maria. He could remember just how it had been that night. He could remember it as if it were last night. It had been in Hamilton. He had felt unhappy, because he could remember Hamilton when the whole hollow was full of people and buildings, and everything was new and active. He had gone to sleep in the hollow shell of the Wells Fargo Building, hearing an old iron shutter banging against the wall in the wind. In the morning Maria had been gone. He had followed the scuffing track she made on account of her loose hobble, and it had led far up the old snow-gullied road to Treasure Hill, and then ended at one of the black shafts that opened like mouths right at the edge of the road. A man remembered a thing like that. There weren't many burros that foolish. But burros with nothing particular about them were hard to remember — especially those he'd had in the last twenty years or so, when he had gradually stopped feeling so personal about them and had begun to call all the jennies Annie and all the burros Jack.

The clicking of the little hoofs behind him stopped, and Mike stopped too, and turned around. Annie was pulling at a line of yellow grass along the edge of the road.

"Come on, Maria," Mike said patiently. The burro at once stopped pulling at the dead grass and came on up toward him, her small black nose working, the ends of the grass standing out on each side of it like whiskers. Mike began to climb again, ahead of her.

It was a long time since he had been caught by a winter, too. He could not remember how long. All the beginnings ran together in his mind, as if they were all the beginning of one winter so far back that he had almost forgotten it. He could still remember clearly, though, the winter he had stayed out on purpose, clear into January. He had been a young man then, thirty-five or forty or forty-five, somewhere in there. He would have to stop and try to bring back a whole string of memories about what had happened just before, in order to remember just how old he had been, and it wasn't worth the trouble. Besides, sometimes even that system didn't work. It would lead him into an old camp where he had been a number of times, and the dates would get mixed up. It was impossible to remember any other way, because all his comings and goings had been so much alike. He had been young, anyhow, and not much afraid of anything except running out of water in the wrong place; not even afraid of the winter. He had stayed out because he'd thought he had a good thing, and he had wanted to prove it. He could remember how it felt to be out in the clear winter weather on the mountains, the piñon trees and the junipers weighted down with feathery snow, and making sharp blue shadows on the white slopes. The hills had made blue shadows on one another too, and in the still air his pick had made the beginning of a sound like a bell's. He knew he had been young, because he could remember taking a day off now and then, just to go tramping around those hills, up and down the white and through the blue shadows, on a kind of holiday. He had pretended to his common sense that he was seriously prospecting, and had carried his hammer and even his drill along, but he had really just been gallivanting, playing colt. Maybe he had been even younger than thirty-five, though he could still be stirred a little, for that matter, by the memory of the kind of weather which had sent him gallivanting. High-blue weather, he called it. There were two kinds of high-blue weather, besides the winter kind, which didn't set him off very often, spring and fall. In the spring it would have a soft, puffy wind and soft, puffy white clouds which made separate shadows that traveled silently across hills that looked soft too. In the fall it would be still, and there would be no clouds at all in the blue, but there would be something in the golden air and the soft, steady sunlight on the mountains that made a man as uneasy as the spring blowing, though in a different way, more sad and not so excited. In the spring high-blue a man had been likely to think about women he had slept with, or wanted to sleep with, or imaginary women made up with the help of newspaper pictures of actresses or young society matrons, or of the old oil paintings in the Lucky Boy Saloon, which showed pale, almost naked women against dark, sumptuous backgrounds — women with long hair or braided hair, calm, virtuous faces, small hands and feet, and ponderous limbs, breasts, and buttocks. In the fall high-blue, though it had been much longer since he had seen a woman, or heard a woman's voice, he was more likely to think about old friends, men, or places he had heard about, or places he hadn't seen for a long time. He himself thought most often about Goldfield the way he had last seen it in the summer in 1912. That was as far south as Mike had ever been in Nevada. Since then he had never been south of Tonopah. When the high-blue weather was past, though, and the season worked toward winter, he began to think about Gold Rock. There were only three or four winters out of the fifty-two when he hadn't gone home to Gold Rock, to his old room at Mrs. Wright's, up on Fourth Street, and to his meals in the dining room at the International House, and to the Lucky Boy, where he could talk to Tom Connover and his other friends, and play cards, or have a drink to hold in his hand while he sat and remembered.

This journey had seemed a little different from most, though. It had started the same as usual, but as he had come across the two vast valleys, and through the pass in the low range between them, he hadn't felt quite the same. He'd felt younger and more awake, it seemed to him, and yet, in a way, older too, suddenly older. He had been sure that there was plenty of time, and yet he had been a little afraid of getting caught in the storm. He had kept looking ahead to see if the mountains on the horizon were still clearly outlined, or if they had been cut off by a lowering of the clouds. He had thought more than once how bad it would be to get caught out there when the real snow began, and he had been disturbed by the first flakes. It had seemed hard to him to have to walk so far too. He had kept thinking about distance. Also the snowy cold had searched out the regions of his body where old injuries had healed. He had taken off his left mitten a good many times, to blow on the fingers which had been frosted the year he was sixty-three, so that now it didn't take much cold to turn them white and stiffen them. The queer tingling, partly like an itch and partly like a pain, in the patch on his back that had been burned in that old powder blast was sharper than he could remember its ever having been before. The rheumatism in his joints, which was so old a companion that it usually made him feel no more than tight-knit and stiff, and the place where his leg had been broken and torn when that ladder broke in '97 ached, and had a pulse he could count. All this made him believe that he was walking more slowly than usual, although nothing, probably not even a deliberate attempt, could actually have changed his pace. Sometimes he even thought, with a moment of fear, that he was getting tired.

On the other hand, he felt unusually clear and strong in his mind. He remembered things with a clarity which was like living them again — nearly all of them events from many years back, from the time when he had been really active and fearless and every burro had had its own name. Some of these events, like the night he had spent in Eureka with the little brown-haired whore, a night in the fall in 1888 or '89, somewhere in there, he had not once thought of for years. Now he could remember even her name. Armandy, she had called herself: a funny name. They all picked names for their business, of course, romantic names like Cecily or Rosamunde or Belle or Claire, or hard names like Diamond Gert or Horseshoe Sal, or names that were pinned on them, like Indian Kate or Roman Mary, but Armandy was different.

He could remember Armandy as if he were with her now, not the way she had behaved in bed; he couldn't remember anything particular about that. In fact he couldn't be sure that he remembered anything about that at all. There were others he could remember more clearly for the way they had behaved in bed, women he had been with more often. He had been with Armandy only that one night. He remembered little things about being with her, things that made it seem good to think of being with her again. Armandy had a room upstairs in a hotel. They could hear a piano playing in a club across the street. He could hear the tune, and it was one he knew, although he didn't know its name. It was a gay tune that went on and on the same, but still it sounded sad when you heard it through the hotel window, with the lights from the bars and hotels shining on the street, and the people coming and going through the lights, and then, beyond the lights, the darkness where the mountains were. Armandy wore a white silk dress with a high waist, and a locket on a gold chain. The dress made her look very brown and like a young girl. She used a white powder on her face, that smelled like violets, but this could not hide her brownness. The locket was heart-shaped, and it opened to show a cameo of a man's hand holding a woman's hand very gently, just their fingers laid out long together, and the thumbs holding, the way they were sometimes on tombstones. There were two little gold initials on each hand, but Armandy would never tell what they stood for, or even if the locket was really her own. He stood in the window, looking down at the club from which the piano music was coming, and Armandy stood beside him, with her shoulder against his arm, and a glass of wine in her hand. He could see the toe of her white satin slippers showing from under the edge of her skirt. Her big hat, loaded with black and white plumes, lay on the dresser behind them. His own leather coat, with the sheepskin lining, lay across the foot of the bed. It was a big bed, with a knobby brass foot and head. There was one oil lamp burning in the chandelier in the middle of the room. Armandy was soft-spoken, gentle, and a little fearful, always looking at him to see what he was thinking. He stood with his arms folded. His arms felt big and strong upon his heavily muscled chest. He stood there, pretending to be in no hurry, but really thinking eagerly about what he would do with Armandy, who had something about her which tempted him to be cruel. He stood there, with his chin down into his heavy, dark beard, and watched a man come riding down the middle of the street from the west. The horse was a fine black, which lifted its head and feet with pride. The man sat very straight, with a high rein, and something about his clothes and hat made him appear to be in uniform, although it wasn't a uniform he was wearing. The man also saluted friends upon the sidewalks like an officer, bending his head just slightly, and touching his hat instead of lifting it. Mike Braneen asked Armandy who the man was, and then felt angry because she could tell him, and because he was an important man who owned a mine that was in bonanza. He mocked the airs with which the man rode, and his princely greetings. He mocked the man cleverly, and Armandy laughed and repeated what he said, and made him drink a little of her wine as a reward. Mike had been drinking whisky, and he did not like wine anyway, but this was not the moment in which to refuse such an invitation.

Old Mike remembered all this, which had been completely forgotten for years. He could not remember what he and Armandy had said, but he remembered everything else, and he felt very lonesome for Armandy, and for the room with the red, figured carpet and the brass chandelier with oil lamps in it, and the open window with the long tune coming up through it, and the young summer night outside on the mountains. This loneliness was so much more intense than his familiar loneliness that it made him feel very young. Memories like this had come up again and again during these three days. It was like beginning life over again. It had tricked him into thinking, more than once, "Next summer I'll make the strike, and this time I'll put it into something safe for the rest of my life, and stop this fool wandering around while I've still got some time left" — a way of thinking which he had really stopped a long time before.

It was getting darker rapidly in the pass. When the gust of wind brought the snow against Mike's face so hard that he noticed the flakes felt larger, he looked up. The light was still there, although the fire was dying out of it, and the snow swarmed across it more thickly. Mike remembered God. He did not think anything exact. He did not think about his own relationship to God. He merely felt the idea as a comforting presence. He'd always had a feeling about God whenever he looked at a sunset, especially a sunset which came through under a stormy sky. It had been the strongest feeling left in him until these memories like the one about Armandy had begun. Even in this last pass his strange fear of the storm had come on him again a couple of times, but now that he had looked at the light and thought of God it was gone. In a few minutes he would come to the summit and look down into his lighted city. He felt happily hurried by this anticipation.

He would take the burro down and stable her in John Hammersmith's shed, where he always kept her. He would spread fresh straw for her, and see that the shed was tight against the wind and snow, and get a measure of grain for her from John. Then he would go up to Mrs. Wright's house at the top of Fourth Street, and leave his things in the same room he always had, the one in front, which looked down over the roofs and chimneys of his city, and across at the east wall of the canyon, from which the sun rose late. He would trim his beard with Mrs. Wright's shears, and shave the upper part of his cheeks. He would bathe out of the blue bowl and pitcher, and wipe himself with the towel with yellow flowers on it, and dress in the good dark suit and the good black shoes with the gleaming box toes, and the good black hat which he had left in the chest in his room. In this way he would perform the ceremony which ended the life of the desert and began the life of Gold

Rock. Then he would go down to the International House, and greet Arthur Morris in the gleaming bar, and go into the dining room and eat the best supper they had, with fresh meat and vegetables, and new-made pie, and two cups of hot clear coffee. He would be served by the plump blond waitress who always joked with him, and gave him many little extra things with his first supper, including the drink which Arthur Morris always sent in from the bar.

At this point Mike Braneen stumbled in his mind, and his anticipation wavered. He could not be sure that the plump blond waitress would serve him. For a moment he saw her in a long skirt, and the dining room of the International House, behind her, had potted palms standing in the corners, and was full of the laughter and loud, manly talk of many customers who wore high vests and mustaches and beards. These men leaned back from tables covered with empty dishes. They patted their tight vests and lighted expensive cigars. He knew all their faces. If he were to walk down the aisle between the tables on his side they would all speak to him. But he also seemed to remember the dining room with only a few tables, with oilcloth on them instead of linen, and with moody young men sitting at them in their work clothes — strangers who worked for the highway department, or were just passing through, or talked mining in terms which he did not understand or which made him angry.

No, it would not be the plump blond waitress. He did not know who it would be. It didn't matter. After supper he would go up Canyon Street under the arcade to the Lucky Boy Saloon, and there it would be the same as ever. There would be the laurel wreaths on the frosted glass panels of the doors, and the old sign upon the window, the sign that was older than Tom Connover, almost as old as Mike Braneen himself. He would open the door and see the bottles and the white women in the paintings, and the card table in the back corner and the big stove and chairs along the wall. Tom would look around from his place behind the bar. "Well, now," he would roar, "look who's here, boys. Now will you believe it's winter?" he would roar at them.

Some of them would be the younger men, of course, and there might even be a few strangers, but this would only add to the dignity of his reception, and there would also be his friends. There would be Henry Bray with the gray walrus mustache, and Mark

Wilton and Pat Gallagher. They would all welcome him loudly.

"Mike, how are you, anyway?" Tom would roar, leaning across the bar to shake hands with his big, heavy, soft hand with the diamond ring on it. "And what'll it be, Mike? The same?" he'd ask, as if Mike had been in there no longer ago than the night before.

Mike would play that game too. "The same," he would say.

Then he would really be back in Gold Rock; never mind the plump blond waitress.

Mike came to the summit of the old road and stopped and looked down. For a moment he felt lost again, as he had when he'd thought about the plump blond waitress. He had expected Canyon Street to look much brighter. He had expected a lot of orange windows close together on the other side of the canyon. Instead there were only a few scattered lights across the darkness and they were white. They made no communal glow upon the steep slope, but gave out only single white needles of light, which pierced the darkness secretly and lonesomely, as if nothing could ever pass from one house to another over there. Canyon Street was very dark too. There it went, the street he loved, steeply down into the bottom of the canyon, and down its length there were only the few street lights, more than a block apart, swinging in the wind and darting about that cold, small light. The snow whirled and swooped under the nearest street light below.

"You are getting to be an old fool," Mike Braneen said out loud to himself, and felt better. This was the way Gold Rock was now, of course, and he loved it all the better. It was a place that grew old with a man, that was going to die sometime too. There could be an understanding with it.

He worked his way slowly down into Canyon Street, with Annie slipping and checking behind him. Slowly, with the blown snow behind them, they came to the first built-up block and passed the first dim light showing through a smudged window under the arcade. They passed the dark places after it, and the second light. Then Mike Braneen stopped in the middle of the street, and Annie stopped beside him, pulling her rump in and turning her head away from the snow. A highway truck, coming down from the head of the canyon, had to get way over onto the wrong side of the street to pass them. The driver leaned out as he went by, and yelled, "Pull over, Pop. You're in town now."

Mike Braneen didn't hear him. He was staring at the Lucky Boy.

The Lucky Boy was dark, and there were boards nailed across the big window that had shown the sign. At last Mike went over onto the boardwalk to look more closely. Annie followed him, but stopped at the edge of the walk and scratched her neck against a post of the arcade. There was the other sign, hanging crossways under the arcade, and even in that gloom Mike could see that it said Lucky Boy and had a Jack of Diamonds painted on it. There was no mistake. The Lucky Boy sign, and others like it under the arcade, creaked and rattled in the wind.

There were footsteps coming along the boards. The boards sounded hollow, and sometimes one of them rattled. Mike Braneen looked down slowly from the sign and peered at the approaching figure. It was a man wearing a sheepskin coat with the collar turned up around his head. He was walking quickly, like a man who knew where he was going, and why, and where he had been. Mike almost let him pass. Then he spoke.

"Say, fella —"

He even reached out a hand as if to catch hold of the man's sleeve, though he didn't touch it. The man stopped and asked, impatiently, "Yeah?" and Mike let the hand down again slowly.

"Well, what is it?" the man asked.

"I don't want anything," Mike said. "I got plenty."

"Okay, okay," the man said. "What's the matter?"

Mike moved his hand toward the Lucky Boy. "It's closed," he said.

"I see it is, Dad," the man said. He laughed a little. He didn't seem to be in quite so much of a hurry now.

"How long has it been closed?" Mike asked.

"Since about June, I guess," the man said. "Old Tom Connover, the guy that ran it, died last June."

Mike waited for a moment. "Tom died?" he asked.

"Yup. I guess he'd just kept it open out of love of the place anyway. There hasn't been any real business for years. Nobody cared to keep it open after him."

The man started to move on, but then he waited, peering, trying to see Mike better.

"This June?" Mike asked finally.

"Yup. This last June."

"Oh," Mike said. Then he just stood there. He wasn't thinking anything. There didn't seem to be anything to think.

"You knew him?" the man asked.

"Thirty years," Mike said. "No, more'n that," he said, and started to figure out how long he had known Tom Connover, but lost it, and said, as if it would do just as well, "He was a lot younger than I am, though."

"Hey," said the man, coming closer, and peering again. "You're Mike Braneen, aren't you?"

"Yes," Mike said.

"Gee, I didn't recognize you at first. I'm sorry."

"That's all right," Mike said. He didn't know who the man was, or what he was sorry about.

He turned his head slowly and looked out into the street. The snow was coming down heavily now. The street was all white. He saw Annie with her head and shoulders in under the arcade, but the snow settling on her rump.

"Well, I guess I'd better get Molly under cover," he said. He moved toward the burro a step, but then halted.

"Say, fella — "

The man had started on, but he turned back. He had to wait for Mike to speak.

"I guess this about Tom's mixed me up."

"Sure," the man said. "It's tough, an old friend like that."

"Where do I turn up to get to Mrs. Wright's place?"

"Mrs. Wright?"

"Mrs. William Wright," Mike said. "Her husband used to be a foreman in the Aztec. Got killed in the fire."

"Oh," the man said. He didn't say anything more, but just stood there, looking at the shadowy bulk of old Mike.

"She's not dead too, is she?" Mike asked slowly.

"Yeah, I'm afraid she is, Mr. Braneen," the man said. "Look," he said more cheerfully. "It's Mrs. Branley's house you want right now, isn't it? Place where you stayed last winter?"

Finally Mike said, "Yeah. Yeah, I guess it is."

"I'm going up that way. I'll walk up with you," the man said.

After they had started Mike thought that he ought to take the burro down to John Hammersmith's first, but he was afraid to ask about it. They walked on down Canyon Street, with Annie walking along beside them in the gutter. At the first side street they turned right and began to climb the steep hill toward another of the little street lights dancing over a crossing. There was no sidewalk here, and Annie followed right at their heels. That one street light was the only light showing up ahead.

When they were halfway up to the light Mike asked, "She die this summer too?"

The man turned his body half around, so that he could hear inside his collar.

"What?"

"Did she die this summer too?"

"Who?"

"Mrs. Wright," Mike said.

The man looked at him, trying to see his face as they came up toward the light. Then he turned back again, and his voice was muffled by the collar.

"No, she died quite a while ago, Mr. Braneen."

"Oh," Mike said finally.

They came up onto the crossing under the light, and the snow-laden wind whirled around them again. They passed under the light, and their three lengthening shadows before them were obscured by the innumerable tiny shadows of the flakes.

ERNEST HEMINGWAY

in another country

In the fall the war was always there, but we did not go to it any-
more. It was cold in the fall in Milan and the dark came very
early. Then the electric lights came on, and it was pleasant along
the streets looking in the windows. There was much game hanging outside the shops, and the snow powdered in the fur of the
foxes and the wind blew their tails. The deer hung stiff and heavy
and empty, and small birds blew in the wind and the wind turned
their feathers. It was a cold fall and the wind came down from the
mountains.

We were all at the hospital every afternoon, and there were different ways of walking across the town through the dusk to the
hospital. Two of the ways were alongside canals, but they were

long. Always, though, you crossed a bridge across a canal to enter
the hospital. There was a choice of three bridges. On one of them
a woman sold roasted chestnuts. It was warm, standing in front of
her charcoal fire, and the chestnuts were warm afterward in your
pocket. The hospital was very old and very beautiful, and you
entered through a gate and walked across a courtyard and out a gate
on the other side. There were usually funerals starting from the
courtyard. Beyond the old hospital were the new brick pavilions,
and there we met every afternoon and were all very polite and interested in what was the matter, and sat in the machines that were
to make so much difference.

The doctor came up to the machine where I was sitting and said:
"What did you like best to do before the war? Did you practice a
sport?"

I said: "Yes, football."

"Good," he said. "You will be able to play football again better
than ever."

My knee did not bend and the leg dropped straight from the
knee to the ankle without a calf, and the machine was to bend the
knee and make it move as in riding a tricycle. But it did not bend
yet, and instead the machine lurched when it came to the bending
part. The doctor said: "That will all pass. You are a fortunate
young man. You will play football again like a champion."

In the next machine was a major who had a little hand like a
baby's. He winked at me when the doctor examined his hand,
which was between two leather straps that bounced up and down
and flapped the stiff fingers, and said: "And will I too play football,
captain-doctor?" He had been a very great fencer, and before the
war the greatest fencer in Italy.

The doctor went to his office in a back room and brought a
photograph which showed a hand that had been withered almost as
small as the major's, before it had taken a machine course, and after
was a little larger. The major held the photograph with his good
hand and looked at it very carefully. "A wound?" he asked.

"An industrial accident," the doctor said.

"Very interesting, very interesting," the major said, and handed
it back to the doctor.

"You have confidence?"

"No," said the major.

There were three boys who came each day who were about the

same age I was. They were all three from Milan, and one of them was to be a lawyer, and one was to be a painter, and one had intended to be a soldier, and after we were finished with the machines, sometimes we walked back together to the Café Cova, which was next door to the Scala. We walked the short way through the communist quarter because we were four together. The people hated us because we were officers, and from a wineshop someone called out, "A basso gli ufficiali!" as we passed. Another boy who walked with us sometimes and made us five wore a black silk handkerchief across his face because he had no nose then and his face was to be rebuilt. He had gone out to the front from the military academy and been wounded within an hour after he had gone into the front line for the first time. They rebuilt his face, but he came from a very old family and they could never get the nose exactly right. He went to South America and worked in a bank. But this was a long time ago, and then we did not any of us know how it was going to be afterward. We only knew then that there was always the war, but that we were not going to it any more.

We all had the same medals, except the boy with the black silk bandage across his face, and he had not been at the front long enough to get any medals. The tall boy with a very pale face who was to be a lawyer had been a lieutenant of Arditi and had three medals of the sort we each had only one of. He had lived a very long time with death and was a little detached. We were all a little detached, and there was nothing that held us together except that we met every afternoon at the hospital. Although, as we walked to the Cova through the tough part of town, walking in the dark, with light and singing coming out of the wine-shops, and sometimes having to walk into the street when the men and women would crowd together on the sidewalk so that we would have had to jostle them to get by, we felt held together by there being something that had happened that they, the people who disliked us, did not understand.

We ourselves all understood the Cova, where it was rich and warm and not too brightly lighted, and noisy and smoky at certain hours, and there were always girls at the tables and the illustrated papers on a rack on the wall. The girls at the Cova were very patriotic, and I found that the most patriotic people in Italy were the café girls — and I believe they are still patriotic.

The boys at first were very polite about my medals and asked me what I had done to get them. I showed them the papers, which were written in very beautiful language and full of *fratellanza* and *abnegazione*, but which really said, with the adjectives removed, that I had been given the medals because I was an American. After that their manner changed a little toward me, although I was their friend against outsiders. I was a friend, but I was never really one of them after they had read the citations, because it had been different with them and they had done very different things to get their medals. I had been wounded, it was true; but we all knew that being wounded, after all, was really an accident. I was never ashamed of the ribbons, though, and sometimes, after the cocktail hour, I would imagine myself having done all the things they had done to get their medals; but walking home at night through the empty streets with the cold wind and all the shops closed, trying to keep near the street lights, I knew that I would never have done such things, and I was very much afraid to die, and often lay in bed at night by myself, afraid to die and wondering how I would be when I went back to the front again.

The three with the medals were like hunting-hawks; and I was not a hawk, although I might seem a hawk to those who had never hunted; they, the three, knew better and so we drifted apart. But I stayed good friends with the boy who had been wounded his first day at the front, because he would never know now how he would have turned out; so he could never be accepted either, and I liked him because I thought perhaps he would not have turned out to be a hawk either.

The major, who had been the great fencer, did not believe in bravery, and spent much time while we sat in the machines correcting my grammar. He had complimented me on how I spoke Italian, and we talked together very easily. One day I had said that Italian seemed such an easy language to me that I could not take a great interest in it; everything was so easy to say. "Ah, yes," the major said. "Why, then, do you not take up the use of grammar?" So we took up the use of grammar, and soon Italian was such a difficult language that I was afraid to talk to him until I had the grammar straight in my mind.

The major came very regularly to the hospital. I do not think he ever missed a day, although I am sure he did not believe in the machines. There was a time when none of us believed in the machines, and one day the major said it was all nonsense. The machines were new then and it was we who were to prove them. It was an idiotic idea, he said, "a theory, like another." I had not learned my grammar, and he said I was a stupid impossible disgrace, and he was a fool to have bothered with me. He was a small man and he sat straight up in his chair with his right hand thrust into the machine and looked straight ahead at the wall while the straps thumped up and down with his fingers in them.

"What will you do when the war is over if it is over?" he asked me. "Speak grammatically!"

"I will go to the States."

"Are you married?"

"No, but I hope to be."

"The more of a fool you are," he said. He seemed very angry "A man must not marry."

"Why, Signor Maggiore?"

"Don't call me 'Signor Maggiore.' "

"Why must not a man marry?"

"He cannot marry. He cannot marry," he said angrily. "If he is to lose everything, he should not place himself in a position to lose that. He should not place himself in a position to lose. He should find things he cannot lose."

He spoke very angrily and bitterly, and looked straight ahead while he talked.

"But why should he necessarily lose it?"

"He'll lose it," the major said. He was looking at the wall. Then he looked down at the machine and jerked his little hand out from between the straps and slapped it hard against his thigh. "He'll lose it," he almost shouted. "Don't argue with me!" Then he called to the attendant who ran the machines. "Come and turn this damned thing off."

He went back into the other room for the light treatment and the massage. Then I heard him ask the doctor if he might use his telephone and he shut the door. When he came back into the room, I was sitting in another machine. He was wearing his cape and had his cap on, and he came directly toward my machine and put his arm on my shoulder.

"I am so sorry," he said, and patted me on the shoulder with his good hand. "I would not be rude. My wife has just died. You must forgive me."

"Oh —" I said, feeling sick for him. "I am *so* sorry."

He stood there biting his lower lip. "It is very difficult," he said. "I cannot resign myself."

He looked straight past me and out through the window. Then he began to cry. "I am utterly unable to resign myself," he said and choked. And then crying, his head up looking at nothing, carrying himself straight and soldierly, with tears on both his cheeks and biting his lips, he walked past the machines and out the door.

The doctor told me that the major's wife, who was very young and whom he had not married until he was definitely invalided out of the war, had died of pneumonia. She had been sick only a few days. No one expected her to die. The major did not come to the hospital for three days. Then he came at the usual hour, wearing a black band on the sleeve of his uniform. When he came back, there were large framed photographs around the wall, of all sorts of wounds before and after they had been cured by the machines. In front of the machine the major used were three photographs of hands like his that were completely restored. I do not know where the doctor got them. I always understood we were the first to use the machines. The photographs did not make much difference to the major because he only looked out of the window.

the other margaret

Mark Jennings stood the picture up on the wide counter and he and Stephen Elwin stepped back and looked at it. It was one of Rouault's kings. A person looking at it for the first time might find it repellent, even brutal or cruel. It was full of rude blacks that might seem barbarically untidy.

But the two men knew the picture well. They looked at it in silence. The admiration they were sharing made a community between them which at their age was rare, for they had both passed forty. Jennings waited for Elwin to speak first — they were friends but Elwin was the customer. Besides, the frame had been designed by Jennings and in buying a reproduced picture the frame is of great importance, accounting for more than half the cost. Elwin

"The Other Margaret" by Lionel Trilling. Reprinted by permission of the author from *The Partisan Review*, Fall, 1945.

had bought the picture some weeks before but he was seeing it framed for the first time.

Elwin said, "The frame is very good, Mark. It's perfect." He was a rather tall man with an attractive, competent face. He touched the frame curiously with the tip of his forefinger.

Jennings replied in a judicious tone, as if it were not his own good taste but that of a very gifted apprentice of his. "*I* think so," he said. And he too touched the frame, but intimately, rubbing briskly up and down one moulding with an artisan's possessive thumb, putting an unneeded last touch. He explained what considerations of color and proportion made the frame right for the picture. He spoke as if these were simple rules anyone might find in a book.

The king, blackbearded and crowned, faced in profile to the left. He had a fierce quality that had modulated, but not softened, to authority. One could feel of him — it was the reason why Elwin had bought the picture — that he had passed beyond ordinary matters of personality and was worthy of the crown he was wearing. Yet he was human and tragic. He was not unlike the sculptured kings of Chartres. In his right hand he held a spray of flowers.

"Is he a favorite of yours?" Elwin said. He did not know whether he meant the king or the king's painter. Indeed, as he asked the question, it seemed to him that he had assumed that the painter was this archaic personage himself. He had never imagined the painter painting the canvas with a brush. It was the beginning of a new thought about the picture.

Jennings answered with a modified version of the Latin gesture of esteem, a single decisive shake of his lifted hand, thumb and forefinger touching in a circle.

Elwin acknowledged the answer with a nod but said nothing. He did not want Jennings' admiration, even though he had asked for it. Jennings would naturally give as much admiration to most of the fine pictures in fine reproduction with which his shop was filled. At that moment, Elwin was not interested in admiration or in art. But he liked what Jennings said next.

"It will give you a lot of satisfaction," Jennings said. It was exactly as if he had just sold Elwin a suit or a pair of shoes.

Elwin said, "Yes," a little hesitatingly, only politely agreeing, not committing himself in the matter of his money's worth until it should be proved.

From behind the partition that made Jennings' little office they had been hearing a man talking on the telephone. Now the conversation ended and a young soldier, a second lieutenant, came out into the shop. Jennings said to him, "Did the call get through?" and the young man said, "Oh yes, after some difficulty. It was eighty-five cents. Let me pay you for it." "Oh nonsense," said Jennings, and took him by the arm and quickly introduced him to Elwin as a cousin of his wife's. The young man offered Elwin the hand that had been reaching into his pocket and said, "I'm glad to meet you, sir."

He said it very nicely, with the niceness that new young officers are likely to have. Pleased with themselves, they are certain that everyone will be nice to them. This young man's gold bar did a good deal for him, did perhaps more than rank ought to have to do for a man. He was not really much of a person. Yet Elwin, meeting him, felt the familiar emotion in which he could not distinguish guilt from envy. He knew it well, knew how to control it and it did not diminish, not much, the sense of holiday he was having. The holiday was made by his leaving his office a little early. He published scientific books in a small but successful way and the war had made a great pressure of work for him, but he had left his office early when Jennings phoned that the picture was back from the framer's.

The young lieutenant was looking at the picture. He so clearly did not like it that Jennings said quickly, "Mr. Elwin's just bought it."

The lieutenant regarded the picture thoughtfully. "Very nice," he said, with an enthusiastic and insincere shake of his head. He did not want to spoil things for Jennings by undermining the confidence of the customer. Elwin looked from the king to the lieutenant and back to the king. It was perfectly polite, only as if he had looked at the young man to hear his opinion more clearly and then had examined again the thing they were talking about.

But Jennings understood the movement of Elwin's glance, for when the lieutenant had shaken hands and left the shop, Jennings said stoutly, "He's a good kid."

"Yes he is," Elwin said serenely.

"It's funny seeing him an officer. He used to be against anything like that. But he was glad to go — he said he did not want to miss sharing the experience of his generation."

"A lot of them say that." Elwin had heard it often from the young men, the clever ones. Someone had started it and all the young men with the semi-political views said it. Their reasons for saying it were various. Elwin liked some of the reasons and disliked others, but whether he liked the reasons or not, he never heard the phrase without a twinge of envy. Now it comforted him to think that this man with the black beard and the flower had done his fighting without any remarks about experience and generations.

The idea of age and death did not present itself to Elwin in any horrifying way. It had first come to him in the form of a sentence from one of Hazlitt's essays. The sentence was, "No young man believes he shall ever die," and the words had come to him suddenly from the past, part of an elaborate recollection of a scene at high-school. When he looked up the quotation, he found that he had remembered it with perfect accuracy, down to that very *shall* which struck his modern ear as odd and even ungrammatical. The memory had begun with the winter sunlight coming through the dirty windows of the classroom. Then there was the color, texture and smell of varnished wood. But these details were only pointing to the teacher himself and what he was saying. He was a Mr. Baxter, a heron-like man, esteemed as brilliant and eccentric, what some students called "a real person." Suddenly Mr. Baxter in a loud voice had uttered that sentence of Hazlitt's. He held the book in his hand but did not read from it. "No young man believes he shall ever die," he said, just as if he had thought of it himself.

It had been very startling to hear him say that, and this effect was of course just what the teacher wanted. It was the opening sentence of an essay called "On the Feeling of Immortality in Youth," and to Baxter it was important that the class should see what a bold and captivating way it was to begin an essay, how it was exactly as if someone had suddenly said the words, not written them after thought.

The chalky familiar classroom had been glorified by this moment of Mr. Baxter's. So many things had been said in the room, but here was one thing that had been said which was true. It was true in two ways. For Mr. Baxter it was true that no *young* man believes he shall ever die, but Mr. Baxter was not exactly a young man. For Stephen Elwin it was true that he would never die — he was scarcely even a young man yet, still only a boy. Between the student and the teacher the great difference was that the student would never die. Stephen Elwin had pitied Mr. Baxter and had been proud of himself. And mixed with the boy's feeling of immortality was a boy's pleasure at being involved with ideas which were not only solemn but complicated, for Mr. Baxter's mortality should have denied, but actually did not deny, the immortality that Stephen felt.

The Hazlitt sentence, once it had been remembered, had not left Elwin. Every now and then, sometimes just as he was falling asleep, sometimes just as he was waking up, sometimes right in the middle of anything at all, the sentence and the full awareness of what it meant would come to him. It felt like an internal explosion. It was not, however, an explosion of force but rather an explosion of light. It was not without pain but it was not wholly painful.

With the picture neatly wrapped in heavy brown paper, Elwin walked down Madison Avenue. It was still early. On a sudden impulse he walked west at 60th Street. Usually he came home by taxi, but this evening he thought of the Fifth Avenue bus, for some reason remembering that it was officially called a "coach" and that his father had spoken of it so, and had sometimes even referred to it as a "stage." The "coach" that he signaled was of the old kind, open wooden deck, platform at the rear, stairs connecting platform and deck with a big architectural curve. He saw it with surprise and affection. He had supposed that this model of bus had long been out of service and as he hailed it his mind sought for and found a word long unused. "DeDion," he said, pleased at having found it. "DeDion Bouton."

He pronounced it *Deedeeon*, the way he and his friends had said it in 1917 when they had discussed the fine and powerful motors from Europe that were then being used for the buses. Some of them had been Fiats, but the most powerful of all were said to be the DeDions from France. No one knew the authority for this superlative judgment, but boys finding a pleasure in firm opinions did not care. Elwin remembered the special note in his friends' voices as they spoke of the DeDions. They talked about the great Mediterranean motors with a respect that was not only technical but historical. There had never been more than a few of the DeDions in America. Even in 1917 they were no longer being imported and the boys thought of them as old and rare.

Elwin took his seat inside the bus, at the rear. As suddenly as the name DeDion, it came to him how the open deck had once been a deck indeed — how, as sometimes the only passenger braving the weather up there, he had been the captain of the adventure, facing into the cold wind, even into the snow or rain, stoic, assailed but unmoved by the elements, inhaling health, fortitude and growth, for he had a boy's certainty that the more he endured, the stronger he would become. And when he had learned to board the bus and alight from it while it was still moving — "board" and "alight" were words the company used in its notices — how far advanced in life he had felt. So many landmarks of Elwin's boyhood in the city had vanished but this shabby bus had endured since the days when it had taken him daily to school.

At 82nd Street the bus stopped for a red light. A boy stood at the curb near the iron stanchion that bore the bus-stop sign. He clutched something in his hand. It must have been a coin, for he said to the conductor, "Mister, how much does it cost to ride on this bus?"

Elwin could not be sure of the boy's age, but he was perhaps twelve, Elwin's own age when he had been touched by his friends' elegiac discussions of the DeDions. The boy was not alone, he had a friend with him, and to see this friend, clearly a follower, was to understand the quality of the chief. The subaltern was a boy like any other, but the face of his leader was alight with the power of mind and a great urgency. Perhaps he was only late and in a hurry, but in any case the urgency illuminated his remarkable face.

The conductor did not answer the question.

"Mister," the boy said again, "how much does it cost to ride on this bus?"

His friend stood by, sharing passively in the question but saying nothing. They did not dare "board" until they knew whether or not their resources were sufficient.

The boy was dressed sturdily enough, perhaps for a boy of his age he was even well dressed. But he had been on the town or in the park most of the afternoon, or perhaps he had been one of those boys who, half in awe, half in rowdy levity, troop incessantly through the Egyptian rooms of the Museum, repeatedly entering and emerging from and entering again the narrow slits of the grave vaults. His knickerbockers were sliding at the knees and his effort to control a drop at his nose further compromised but by no means destroyed his dignity. He had the clear cheeks and well-shaped head of a carefully reared child, but he seemed too far from home at this hour quite to be the child of very careful parents. There was an air about him which suggested that he had learned to expect at least a little resistance from the world and that he was ready to meet it.

The conductor did not reply to the second question. He had taken a large black wallet of imitation leather from some cranny of the rear platform and was making marks with a pencil on the cardboard trip-sheet it contained. He was an old man.

"Mister," said the boy again, and his voice, though tense, was reasonable. It was the very spirit of reasonableness. "Mister, how much does it cost to ride on this bus? A nickel or a dime?"

The conductor elaborately lifted his eyes from his record. He looked at the boy not hostilely nor yet quite facetiously, but with a certain quiet air of settled satisfaction. "What do you want to know for?" he said.

Elwin wanted to lower the window to tell the boy it was a dime. But he had waited too long. The conductor put his hand on the bell-button and gave the driver the signal. The light changed and the bus began to move.

"Mister!" the boy shouted. He may have been late to his supper but it was not this urgency that made his voice go up so loud and high. "For God's sake, mister!"

He of course did not bring in God by way of appeal. There was no longer any hope of his getting an answer. It was rather an expostulation with the unreasonable, the most passionate thing imaginable. Elwin looked back and saw the boy's hatred still following the conductor and, naturally, not only the conductor but the whole bus.

The conductor had now the modest look of a person who has just delivered a rebuke which was not only deserved but witty.

Well, Elwin thought, he is an old man and his pride is somewhere involved. Perhaps it was only that he could not at the moment bring himself to answer a question.

But he believed that in the past it could not have happened. When he was a boy the conductor might have said, "What do you want to know for?" — boys must always be teased a little by men. But the teasing would have stopped in time for him to board the bus. The bus was peculiarly safe. The people who rode in it and paid a dime after they had taken their seats were known to be nicer than the people who rode in the subway for a nickel which they paid before admission. It was the first public conveyance to which "nervous" parents entrusted their children — the conductors were known for their almost paternal kindness. For example, if you found on your trip to school that you had forgotten your money, the conductor would not fail to quiet the fear of authority that clutched your guilty heart. But this old man had outlived his fatherhood, which had once extended to all the bus-world of children. His own sons and daughters by now would have grown and gone and given him the usual causes for bitterness.

The old man's foolish triumph was something that must be understood. Elwin tried to know the weariness and sense of final loss that moved the old conductor to stand on that small dignity of his. He at once brought into consideration the conditions of life of the old man, especially the lack of all the advantages that he himself had had — the gentle rearing and the good education that made a man like Stephen Elwin answerable for all his actions. It had long been the habit of Elwin's mind to raise considerations of just this sort whenever he had reason to be annoyed with anyone who was not more powerful than himself.

But now, strangely, although the habit was in force, it did not check his anger. It was bewildering that he should feel anger at a poor ignorant man, a working man. It was the first time in his life that he had ever felt so. It shamed him. And he was the more bewildered and ashamed when he understood, as he did, that he was just as angry at the boy as at the old man. He was seeing the boy full grown and the self-pity and hatred taking root beside the urgency and power. The conductor and the boy were links in the great chain of the world's rage.

Clearly it was an unreasoning thing to feel. It was not what a wise man would feel. At this time in his life Stephen Elwin had the wish to be wise. He had never known a wise man. The very word sounded like something in a tale read to children. But the occasion for courage had passed. By courage Elwin meant something very simple, an unbending resistance of spirit under extreme physical difficulties. It was a boy's notion, but it had stayed with Elwin through most of his life, through his business and his pleasure, and nothing that he had ever done had given him the proof that he wanted. And now that the chance for that was gone — he was forty-one years old — it seemed to him that perhaps to be wise was almost as manly a thing as to be brave.

Two wars had passed Elwin by. For one he was too young, for

the other too old, though by no means, of course, old. Had it not
been for the war, and the consideration of age it so ruthlessly raised,
the recollection of the sentence from Hazlitt would no doubt have
been delayed by several years, and so too would the impulse to
which it had given rise, the desire to have "wisdom." More and
more in the last few months, Elwin had been able to experience the
sensation of being wise, for it was indeed a sensation, a feeling of
stamina, poise and illumination.

He was puzzled and unhappy as he "alighted" from the bus at
92nd Street. It seemed to him a great failure that his knowledge of
death and his having reached the years of wisdom — they were the
same thing — had not prevented him from feeling anger at an old
man and a boy. It then occurred to him to think that perhaps he
had felt his anger not in despite of wisdom but because of it. It
was a disturbing, even a horrifying, fancy. Yet as he walked the
two blocks to his home, he could not help recurring to it, with
what was, as he had to see, a certain gratification.

In his pleasant living-room, in his comfortable chair, Stephen
Elwin watched his daughter as she mixed the drink he usually had
before dinner. She was thirteen. About a month ago she had made
this her job, almost her duty, and she performed it with an unspeakable seriousness. She measured out the whiskey and poured it
into the tumbler. With the ice-tongs she reached the ice gently
into the bottom of the glass so that there would not be the least
splash of whiskey. She opened the bottle of soda. Holding up the
glass for her father's inspection, she poured the soda slowly, ready
to stop at her father's word. Elwin cried "Whoa!" and at the word
he thought that his daughter had reached the stage of her growth
where she did indeed look like a well-bred pony.

Now Margaret was searching for the stirring-spoon. But she had
forgotten to put it on the tray with all the other paraphernalia and
she gave a little cry of vexation and went to fetch it. Elwin did
not tell her not to bother, that it did not matter if the drink was
not stirred. He understood that this business had to proceed with
a ceremonial completeness.

Margaret returned with the stirring-spoon. She stirred the highball and the soda foamed up. She waited until it subsided, meanwhile shaking the spoon dry over the glass with three precise little
shakes. She handed her father the drink and put a coaster on the
table by his chair. She watched while he took his first sip. He had

taken the whole responsibility for the proportion of soda to whiskey. Still, she wanted to be told that she had made the drink just
right. Elwin said, "Fine. Just right," and Margaret tried not to
show the absurd pleasure she felt.

For this ritual of Margaret's there were, as Elwin guessed, several
motives. The honor of her home required that her father not make
his own highball in the pantry and bring it out to drink in his chair,
not after she had begun to take notice that in the homes of some
of her schoolmates, every evening and not only at dinner-parties,
a servant brought in, quite as a matter of course, a large tray of
drinking equipment. But Margaret had other reasons than snobbish-
ness — Elwin thought that she needed to establish a "custom," not
only for now but for the future, against the time when she could
say to her children, "And every night before dinner it was the *custom* in our family for me to make my father a drink." He supposed that this ritual of the drink was Margaret's first traffic with
the future. It seemed to him that to know a thing like this about
his daughter was one of the products of what could be called wisdom and he thought with irony but also with pleasure of his becoming a dim but necessary figure in Margaret's story of the past.

"I bought a picture today," Elwin said.

Margaret cocked an eye at him, as if to say, "Are you on the
loose again?" She said, "What is it? Did you bring it home?"

"Oh, just a reproduction, a Rouault."

"Rouault?" She said. She shook her head decisively. "Don't
know him." It quite settled Rouault for the moment.

"Don't know him?"

"Never heard of him."

"Well, take a look at it — it's over there."

She untied the string and took off the paper and sat there on the
big hassock, her feet far out in front of her, holding the great king
at arm's length. It was to Elwin strange and funny, this confron-
tation of the black, calm, tragic king and this blonde child in her
sweater and skirt, in her moccasin shoes. She became abstracted and
withdrawn in her scrutiny of the picture. Then Elwin, seeing the
breadth and brightness of her brow, the steady intelligence of her
gaze, understood that there was really no comic disproportion.
What was funny was the equality. The young lieutenant had been
quite neutralized by the picture. Even Mark Jennings had been a
little diminished by it. But Margaret, with her grave, luminous

brow, was able to meet it head on. And not in agreement either. "You don't like it?" Elwin said.

She looked from the picture to him and said, "I don't think so." She said it softly but it was pretty positive. She herself painted and she was in a very simple relation to pictures. She rose and placed the picture on the sofa as if to give it another chance in a different position and a better light. She stood at a distance and looked at it and Elwin stood behind her to get the same view of it that she had. He put his hand on her shoulder. After a moment she looked up at him and smiled. "I don't really *like* it," she said. The modulation of her voice was not apology, but simply a gesture of making room for another opinion. She did not think it was important whether she liked or disliked the picture. It said something to her that was not in her experience or that she did not want in her experience. Liking the picture would have given her pleasure. She got no pleasure from not liking it. It seemed to Elwin that in the little shake of her head, in her tone and smile, there was a quality, really monumental, by which he could explain his anger at the old conductor and the boy and forgive himself for having had it.

When Lucy Elwin came in, her face was flushed from the stove and she had a look of triumphant anticipation. She shamelessly communicated this to her family. "It's going to be ve-ry good," she said, not as if she were promising them a fine dinner, rather as if she were threatening them with a grim fate. She meant that her dinner was going to be so very good that if they did not extravagantly admire it, if they merely took it for granted, they would be made to feel sorry. "It will be ready in about ten minutes," she said. "Are you very hungry?"

"Just enough," Elwin said. "Are you tired?" For his wife had stretched out in the armchair and put back her head. She slouched with her long legs at full length, her skirt a little disordered, one ankle laid on the other. Her eyes being closed made her complicated face look simple and she seemed young and self-indulgent, like a girl who escapes from the embarrassment of herself into a broody trance. It was an attitude that had lately become frequent with Margaret.

Lucy Elwin said, "Yes, a little tired. But really, you know, I'd almost rather do the work myself than have that Margaret around."

She spoke with her eyes still closed, and so she did not see her daughter stiffen. But Elwin did. He knew that it was not because

Margaret thought that her mother meant her but because of the
feelings she had for the other Margaret, the maid. The other Margaret, as so often, had not come to work that day.

Margaret had mixed a drink for her mother and now she was
standing beside Lucy's chair, waiting with exaggerated patience for
Lucy to open her eyes. She said, "Here's your drink, mother!"

She said it as if she had waited quite long enough, using the
lumpish, martyred, unsuccessful irony of thirteen, her eyebrows
very weary, the expression of her mouth very dry. Lucy opened
her eyes and sat up straight in her chair. She took the drink from
Margaret and smiled. "Thank you, dear," she said. For the moment it was as if Margaret were the mother, full of rectitude and
manners, and Lucy the careless daughter.

That Lucy was being careless even her husband felt. No one
could say of their Negro maid, the other Margaret, that she was a
pleasant person. Even Elwin would have to admit to a sense of
strain in her presence. But surely Lucy took too passionate a notice
of her. Elwin felt that this was not in keeping with his wife's nature.
But no, that was really not so. It was often disquieting to Elwin,
the willingness that Lucy had to get angry even with simple people
when she thought they were not behaving well. And lately she had
been full of stories about the nasty and insulted temper that was
being shown by the people one daily dealt with. Only yesterday,
for example, there had been her story of the soda-fountain man who
made a point of mopping and puttering and changing the position of
pieces of pie and only after he had shown his indifference and independence would take your order. Elwin had to balance against the
notice his wife took of such things the deep, literal, almost childish
way she spoke of them, the innocence of her passion. But this particular story of the soda-fountain clerk had really distressed him,
actually embarrassing him for Lucy, and he had pointed out to her
how frequent such stories had become. She had simply stared at
him, the fact was so very clear. "Why, it's the war," she said.
"People are just much meaner since the war." And when his rebuke
had moved on to the matter of the maid Margaret, Lucy had said in
the most matter-of-fact way, "Why, she just hates us." And she
had shocked Elwin by giving, just like any middle-class housewife,
a list of all the precious things Margaret had broken. "And observe," Lucy had said, "that never once has she broken anything

cheap or ordinary, only the things I've pointed out to her that needed care."

Elwin had to admit that the list made a case. Still, even if the number of the green Wedgwood coffee cups had been much diminished, cups for which Elwin himself had a special fondness, and even if the Persian bowl had been dropped and the glass urn they had brought from Sweden had been cracked in the sink, they must surely not talk of such things. The very costliness of the objects which proved Margaret's animosity, the very affection which the Elwins felt for them, made the whole situation impossible to consider.

Lucy must indeed have been unaware of how deeply her husband resisted her carelessness in these matters and of what her daughter was now feeling. Otherwise she would not have begun her story, her eyes narrowing in anger at the recollection, "Oh, such a rotten thing happened on the way home on the bus."

It was Elwin who had had the thing happen on the bus, not quite "rotten" but sufficiently disturbing, and he was startled, as if his wife's consciousness had in some way become mixed up with his own in a clairvoyant experience. And this feeling was not diminished as Lucy told her story about a young woman who had asked the conductor a question. It was a simple, ordinary question, Lucy said, about what street one transferred at. The conductor at first had not answered, and then, when he came around again and the question was asked again, he had looked at the young woman — "looked her straight in the face," Lucy said — and had replied in a loud voice, "Vot deed you shay?"

"*Mother!*" cried Margaret. Her voice was all absolute childish horror.

Elwin at once saw what was happening, but Lucy, absorbed in what she had experienced, only said mildly, "What's the matter, dear?"

"Mother!" Margaret grieved, "you mustn't do that." Her face was quite aghast and she was standing stiff with actual fright.

"Why, do what, Margaret?" said Lucy. She was troubled for her daughter but entirely bewildered.

"Make fun of — fun of — " But Margaret could not say it.

"Of Jews?" said Elwin in a loud, firm, downright voice.

Margaret nodded miserably. Elwin said with enough sharpness,

"Margaret, whatever makes you think that Lucy is making fun of Jews? She is simply repeating —— "

"Oh," Margaret cried, her face a silly little moon of gratitude and relief. "Oh," she said happily, "what the woman said to the conductor!"

"No, Margaret. How absurd!" Lucy cried. "*Not* what the woman said to the conductor. What the conductor said to the woman."

Margaret just sat there glowering with silence and anger.

Elwin said to Margaret with a pedagogic clearness and patience, "The conductor was making fun of the woman for being Jewish."

"Not at all," Lucy said, beginning to be a little tried by so much misunderstanding. "Not at all, she wasn't Jewish at all. He was insulting her by pretending that she was Jewish."

Margaret had only one question to ask. "The *conductor?*" she cried with desperate emphasis.

And when Lucy said that it was indeed the conductor, Margaret said nothing, but shrugged her shoulders in an elaborate way and made with her hands a large grimace of despairing incomprehension. She was dismissing the grownups by this pantomime, appealing beyond all their sad nonsense to her own world of sure right reason. In that world one knew where one was, one knew that to say things about Jews was bad and that working men were good. And *therefore*.

Elwin, whose awareness was all aroused, wondered in tender amusement what his daughter would have felt if she had known that her gesture, which she had drawn from the large available stock of the folk-culture of children, had originally been a satiric mimicry of a puzzled shrugging Jew. The Margaret who stood there in sullenness was so very different from the Margaret who, only a few minutes before, had looked at the picture with him and had seemed, almost, to be teaching him something. Now he had to teach her. "That isn't a very pretty gesture," he said. "And what, please, is so difficult about Lucy's story? Don't you believe it?"

A mistake, as he saw at once. Margaret was standing there trapped — no, she did not believe it, but she did not dare say so. Elwin corrected himself and gave her her chance. "Do you think Lucy didn't hear right?"

Margaret nodded eagerly, humbly glad to take the way out that was being offered her.

"We studied the transit system," she said by way of explanation. "We made a study of it." She stopped. Elwin knew how her argument ran, but she herself was not entirely sure of it. She said tentatively, by way of a beginning, "They are underpaid."

Lucy was being really irresponsible, Elwin thought, for she said in an abstracted tone, as if she were musing on the early clues of an interesting scientific generalization, "They hate *women* — it's women they're always rude to. Never the men." Margaret's face flushed, and her eyes darkened at this new expression of her mother's moral obtuseness, and Elwin felt a quick impatience with his daughter's sensitivity — it seemed suddenly to have taken on a pedantic air. But he was annoyed with Lucy too, who ought surely be more aware of what her daughter was feeling. No doubt he was the more annoyed because his own incident of the bus was untold and would remain untold. But it was Lucy who saved the situation she had created. She suddenly remembered the kitchen. She hurried out, then came back, caught Margaret by the arm in a bustle of haste and said, "Come and hurl the salad." This was a famous new joke in the family. Elwin had made it, Margaret loved it. It had reference to a "tossed green salad" on a pretentious restaurant menu. Of the salad, when it was served to them in all its wiltedness, Elwin had said that apparently it needed to be more than tossed, it needed to be hurled.

And so all at once the family was restored, a family with a family joke. Margaret stood there grinning in the embarrassment of the voluptuous pleasure she felt at happiness returned. But she must have been very angry with her mother, for she came back and pulled Elwin's head down and whispered into his ear where he would be able to find and inspect the presents she had for Lucy's birthday next week.

He was to look for two things. In the top left-hand drawer of Margaret's desk he would find the "bought present" and on the shelf in the clothes closet he would find the "made present." The bought present was a wallet, a beautiful green wallet, so clearly expensive that Elwin understood why his daughter had had to tease him for money to supplement her savings, and so adult in its expensiveness that he had to understand how inexorably she was growing up.

The made present was also green, a green lamb, large enough to have to be held in two hands, with black feet and wide black eyes.

The eyes stared out with a great charming question to the world, expressing the comic grace of the lamb's awkwardness. Elwin wondered if Margaret had been at all aware of how much the lamb was a self-portrait. When Elwin, some two years before, had listened to his daughter playing her first full piece on the recorder, he had thought that nothing could be more wonderful than the impervious gravity of her face as her eyes focussed on the bell of the instrument and on the music-book while she blew her tune in a daze of concentration; yet only a few months later, when she had progressed so far as to be up to airs from Mozart, she had been able, in the very midst of a roulade, with her fingers moving fast, to glance up at him with a twinkling, sidelong look, her mouth puckering in a smile as she kept her lips pursed, amused by the music, amused by the frank excess of its ornamentation and by her own virtuosity. For Elwin the smile was the expression of gay and conscious life, of life innocently aware of itself and fond of itself, and, although there was something painful in having to make the admission, it was even more endearing than Margaret's earlier gravity. Life aware of itself seemed so much more life.

His daughter's room was full of life. His own old microscope stood on Margaret's desk and around it was a litter of slides and of the various objects from which she had been cutting sections, a prune and a dried apricot, a sliver of wood, a piece of cheese and what seemed to be a cockroach. There were tools for carving wood and for cutting linoleum blocks. The books were beginning to be too many for the small bookshelf, starting with *The Little Family* and going on to his own soiled copy of *The Light That Failed* that Margaret had unearthed. There was her easel and on one wall was a print of Picasso's trapeze people in flight, like fierce flames, and on another wall one of Benton's righteous stylizations, both at home, knowing nothing of their antagonism to each other. The dolls were no longer so much to the fore as they once were, but they were still about, and so was the elaborate doll's house which contained in precise miniature, accumulated over years, almost every object of daily living, tiny skillets, lamps, cups, kettles, packaged groceries. Surrounded by all that his daughter made and did and read, Elwin could not understand how she found the time. And then, on the thought of what time could be to a child, there came to him with more painful illumination than usual, the recurrent sentence. "No young man believes he shall ever die." And he stood contemplating the room with a kind of desolation of love for it.

Margaret burst in suddenly as if she were running away from something — as indeed she was, for her eyes blazed with the anger she was fleeing. She flung herself on the bed, ignoring her father's presence.

"Margaret, what's the matter?" Elwin said.

But she did not answer.

"Margaret!" There was the note of discipline in his voice. "Tell me what the matter is."

She was not crying, but her face, when she lifted it from the pillow, was red and swollen. "It's mother," she said. "The way she talked to Margaret."

"To Margaret? Has Margaret come?"

"Yes, she came." The tone implied: through flood and fire. "And mother — oh!" She broke off and shook her head in a rather histrionic expression of how impossible it was to tell what her mother had done.

"What did she say that was so terrible?"

"She said — she said, 'Look here ——'" But Margaret could not go on.

Lucy strode into the room with quite as much impulse as Margaret had and with eyes blazing quite as fiercely as her daughter's. "Look here, Margaret," she said. "I've quite enough trouble with that Margaret without your nonsense. Nobody is being exploited in this house and nobody is being bullied and I'm not going to have you making situations about nothing. I'm sure your Miss Hoxie is very sweet and nice, but you seem to have got your ideas from her all mixed up. You weren't that way about Millie when she was with us. As a matter of fact," Lucy said with remorseless irony, "you were often not at all nice to her."

Margaret had not heard the end of Lucy's speech. At the mention of Miss Hoxie in the tone that Lucy had used — "your Miss Hoxie" — at the sacred name of her teacher blasphemously uttered, she looked at her mother with the horror of seeing her now in her true terrible colors. The last bond between them had snapped at this attack upon her heart's best loyalty.

But Lucy was taking no account of finer feelings. She closed the door and said firmly, "Now look here, the simple fact is that that Margaret is a thoroughly disagreeable person, a nasty, mean person."

"Oh, she is not," Margaret wailed. And then, despite all her passion, the simple fact broke in upon her irresistibly. Elwin's heart quite melted as he saw her confront the fact and struggle with it. For the fact was as Lucy had stated it, and he himself at that moment had to realize it. And it was wonderful to see that Margaret's mind, whatever the inclination of her will, was unable to resist a fact. But the mind that had momentarily deserted her will, came quickly again to its help. "She's not responsible," she said desperately. "It's not her fault. She couldn't help it. Society —— " But at that big word she halted, unable to handle it. "We can't blame her," she said defiantly but a little lamely.

At that moment Lucy saw the green clay lamb that Elwin was still holding. She rushed to it and took it and cried, "Margaret, is this yours? I've never seen it, why didn't you show it to me?"

It was, of course, a decided point for Margaret that her birthday surprise was spoiled. She sat there looking dry and indifferent amid the ruins of family custom. Elwin said, "It's a birthday present for you, Lucy. You weren't supposed to see it," and their glances met briefly. He had been a little treacherous, for he could have managed to put the lamb out of sight, but some craftiness, not entirely conscious, had suggested its usefulness for peace.

"It's so *lovely*," Lucy said. "Is it really for me?"

Margaret had to acknowledge that it was, but with an elaborate ungraciousness from her bruised and empty heart. Her mother might have the gift, meaningless as it now was. But Lucy was in a flood of thanks and praise impossible to withstand — it was lovely, she said, to have a gift in advance of her birthday, it was something she had always wanted as a child and had never been able to induce her parents to allow, that she should have one, just one, of her presents before the others, and the lamb itself was simply beautiful, quite the nicest thing Margaret had ever made. "Oh, I love it," she said, stroking its face and then its rump. "Why darling!" she cried, "it looks exactly like you!" And Margaret had to submit to the child's pain at seeing the eminence of grief and grievance swept away. But at last, carried beyond the vacant moment when the forgiving and forgiven feeling had not yet come, she sat there in an embarrassed glow, beaming shyly as her mother kissed her and said quietly and finally, "Thank you."

When they were in the dining-room, all three of them feeling chastened and purged, Lucy said, "I must have it here by my place." And she put the lamb by her at the table, touching its cheek affectionately.

The dinner that Lucy had cooked was served by the other Margaret. She was a tall, rather light colored girl, with a genteel manner and eyebrows that were now kept very high. As she presented the casserole to Lucy, she looked far off into a distance and stood a little too far away for convenience. Lucy sat there with the serving spoon and fork in her hand and then said, "Come a little closer, Margaret." Margaret Elwin sat rigid, watching. Margaret the maid edged a little closer and continued her gaze. She moved to serve Elwin but Lucy said, "It's Margaret you serve next." Her tone was a little dry. Margaret Elwin flushed and looked mortified. It had been a matter of some satisfaction that she was now of an age to be served at table just after her mother, but she hated to have a point made of it if Margaret objected, and Margaret did seem to object and would not accept the reassuring smile that was being offered her over the casserole.

In the interval between the serving of the casserole and the serving of the salad that had once that evening made the family peace, Margaret held her parents with a stern and desperate eye. But she was unable to suppress a glance her mother sent to her father, a glance that had in it a touch of mild triumph. And her father did not this time fortify himself against it. The odds were terribly against her and she looked from one to the other and said in an intense whisper, "It's not her fault. She's not responsible."

"Why not?" Elwin asked.

It was his voice that made the question baffling to Margaret. She did not answer, or try to. It was not merely that the question was, for the moment, beyond her powers. Nor was it that she was puzzled because her father had seemed to change sides. But she was touched by the sense, so little formulated, so fleeting as scarcely to establish itself in her memory, that something other than the question, or the problem itself, was involved here. She barely perceived, yet she did perceive, her mother's quick glance at her father under lowered lids. It was something more than a glance of surprise. Neither Margaret nor Lucy, of course, knew anything about the sentence from Hazlitt. But this was one of the moments when the sentence had occurred to Elwin and with it the explosion of light. And his wife and daughter had heard the event in his voice. For Elwin an illumination, but a dark illumination, was thrown around the matter that concerned them. It seemed to him — not suddenly, for it had been advancing in his mind for some hours now — that in the aspect of his knowledge of death, all men were equal in their responsibility. The two bus conductors, Lucy's and his own, the boy with his face contorted in rational rage against the injustice he suffered, Margaret the maid with her genteel malice — all of them, quite as much as he himself, bore their own blame. Exemption was not given by age or youth, or sex, or color, or condition of life. It was the sense of this that made his voice so strange at his own dinner-table, as if it came not merely from another place but another time.

"Why not?" he said again. "Why not, Margaret?"

Margaret looked at her father's face and tried to answer. She seriously marshalled her thoughts and, as always, the sight of his daughter actually thinking touched Elwin profoundly. "It's because — because society didn't give her a chance," she said slowly. "She has a handicap. Because she's colored. She has to struggle so hard — against prejudice. It's so *hard* for her."

"It's true," Elwin said. "It's very hard for her. But it's hard for Millie too." Millie had been with the Elwins for nearly seven years. Some months ago she had left them to nurse a dying sister in the South.

Margaret of course knew what her father meant, that Millie, despite "society," was warm and good and capable. Her answer was quick, too quick. "Oh, Millie has a slave-psychology," she said loftily.

Really, Elwin thought, Miss Hoxie went too far. He felt a kind of disgust that a child should have been given such a phrase to use. It was a good school, he approved of its theory; but it must not give Margaret such things to say. He wondered if Margaret had submitted the question of Millie to Miss Hoxie. If she had, and if this was the answer she had been given, his daughter had been, yes, corrupted. He said, "You should not say such things about Millie. She is a good loyal person and you haven't any right to say she is not."

"Loyal!" said Margaret in triumph. "Loyal!"

"Why yes. To her sister in Alabama, Margaret, just as much as to us. Is it what you call slave-psychology to be loyal to your own sister?"

But Margaret was not to be put down. She kept in mind the main point, which was not Millie but the other Margaret.

"I notice," she said defiantly, "that when Millie sends you parts of the money you lent her, you take it all right."

Poor child, she had fumbled, and Elwin laid his hand on hers on the table. "But Margaret! Of course I do," he said. "If I didn't, wouldn't that be slave-psychology? Millie would feel very lowered if I didn't take it."

"But she can't afford it," Margaret insisted.

"No, she can't afford it."

"Well then!" and she confronted the oppressor in her father.

"But she can't afford not to. She needs it for her pride. She needs to think of herself as a person who pays her debts, as a responsible person."

"I wonder," Lucy said, "I wonder how Millie is. Poor thing!" She was not being irrelevant. She was successful in bringing her husband up short. Yes, all that his "wisdom" had done was to lead him to defeat his daughter in argument. And defeat made Margaret stupid and obstinate. She said, "Well, anyway, it's not Margaret's fault," and sat sulking.

Had he been truly the wise man he wanted to be, he would have been able to explain, to Margaret and himself, the nature of the double truth. As much as Margaret, he believed that "society is responsible." He believed the other truth too. He felt rather tired, as if the little debate with Margaret had been more momentous than he understood. Yet wisdom, a small measure of it, did seem to come. It came suddenly, as no doubt was the way of moments of wisdom, and he perceived what stupidly he had not understood earlier, that it was not the other Margaret but herself that his Margaret was grieving for, that in her foolish and passionate argument, with the foolish phrases derived from the admired Miss Hoxie, she was defending herself from her own impending responsibility. Poor thing, she saw it moving toward her through the air at a great rate, and she did not want it. Naturally enough, she did not want it. And he, for what reason he did not know, was forcing it upon her.

He understood why Lucy, when they had risen from the table, made quiet haste to put her arm around Margaret's shoulders as they went into the living-room.

They were sitting in the living-room, a rather silent family for the moment, when the other Margaret stood in the doorway. "You may as well know," she said, "that I'm through here." And she added, "I've had enough."

There was a little cry, as of horror, from Margaret. She looked at her parents with a bitter and tragic triumph. Lucy said shortly, "Very well, Margaret. Just finish up and I'll pay you." The quick acceptance took the maid aback. Angrier than before, she turned abruptly back into the dining-room.

For the third time that evening, Margaret Elwin sat in wretched isolation. Her father did not watch her, but he knew what she felt. She had been told *she* might go, never to return. She saw the great and frightening world before her. It was after all possible so to offend her parents that this expulsion would follow. Elwin rose to get a cigarette from the table near the sofa on which Margaret sat and he passed his hand over her bright hair. The picture of the king with the flower in his hand was in the other corner of the sofa.

It was as Elwin's hand was on his daughter's head that they heard the crash, and Elwin felt under his hand how Margaret's body experienced a kind of convulsion. He turned and saw Lucy already at the door of the dining-room, while there on the floor, in many pieces, as if it had fallen with force, lay the smashed green lamb, more white clay showing than green glaze. Lucy stooped down to the fragments, examining them, delicately turning them over one by one, as if already estimating the possibility of mending.

The maid Margaret stood there, a napkin in her hand clutched to her breast. All the genteel contempt had left her face. She looked only frightened, as if something was now, at last, going to be done to her. For her, almost more than for his own Margaret, Elwin felt sad. He said, "It's all right, Margaret. Don't worry, it's all right." It was a foolish and weak thing to say. It was not all right, and Lucy was still crouching, heartbroken, over the pieces. But he had had to say it, weak and foolish as it was.

"Ah, darling, don't feel too bad," Lucy said to her daughter as she came back into the living-room, tenderly holding the smashed thing in her hand.

But Margaret did not answer or even hear. She was staring into the dining-room with wide, fixed eyes. "She meant to do it," she said. "She *meant* to do it."

"Oh, no," Lucy said in her most matter-of-fact voice. "Oh, no, dear. It was just an accident."

"She meant to do it, she meant to do it." And then Margaret said, "I *saw* her." She alone had been facing into the dining-room and could have seen. "I saw her — with the napkin. She made a movement," and Margaret made a movement, "like this . . ."

Over her head her parents' eyes met. They knew that they could only offer the feeble lying of parents to a child. But they were determined to continue. "Oh, no," Elwin said, "it just happened." And he wondered if the king, within his line of vision as he stood there trying to comfort his daughter, would ever return to the old, fine, tragic power, for at the moment he seemed only quaint, extravagant and beside the point.

"She meant to. She didn't like me. She hated me," and the great sobs began to come. But Elwin knew that it was not because the other Margaret hated her that his Margaret wept, but because she had with her own eyes seen the actual possibility of what she herself might do, the insupportable fact of her own moral life. She was weeping bitterly now, her whole body shaking with the deepest of sobs, and she found refuge in a corner of the sofa, hiding her head from her parents. She had drawn up her knees, making herself as tight and inaccessible as she could, and Elwin, to comfort her, sat on what little space she allowed him on the sofa beside her, stroking her burrowing head and her heaving back, quite unable, whatever he might have hoped and wanted, to give her any better help than that.

ELIZABETH BOWEN

the cat jumps

After the Bentley murder, Rose Hill stood empty two years. Lawns mounted to meadows; white paint peeled from the balconies; the sun, looking more constantly, less fearfully in than sightseers' eyes through the naked windows, bleached the floral wallpapers. The week after the execution, Harold Bentley's legatees had placed the house on the books of the principal agents, London and local. But though sunny, up to date and convenient, though so delightfully situate over the Thames valley (above flood level), within easy reach of a golf-course, Rose Hill, while frequently viewed, remained unpurchased. Dreadful associations apart, the privacy of the place had been violated; with its terraced garden, lily-pond, and pergola cheerfully rose-encrusted, the public had

been made too familiar. On the domestic scene, too many eyes had
burnt the impress of their horror. Moreover, that pearly bathroom,
that bedroom with wide outlook over a loop of the Thames . . .
"*The Rose Hill Horror*": headlines flashed up at the very sound of
the name. "Oh, *no*, dear!" many wives had exclaimed, drawing
their husbands hurriedly from the gate. "Come away!" they had
urged, crumpling the agent's order to view as though the house
were advancing upon them. And husbands came away — with a
backward glance at the garage. Funny to think a chap who was
hanged had kept his car there.

The Harold Wrights, however, were not deterred. They had
light, bright, shadowless, thoroughly disinfected minds. They believed that they disbelieved in most things but were unprejudiced;
they enjoyed frank discussions. They dreaded nothing but inhibitions: they had no inhibitions. They were pious agnostics, earnest
for social reform; they explained everything to their children and
were annoyed to find their children could not sleep at nights because they thought there was a complex under the bed. They knew
all crime to be pathological, and read their murders only in scientific books. They had Vita glass put into all their windows. No
family, in fact, could have been more unlike the mistaken Harold
Bentleys.

Rose Hill, from the first glance, suited the Wrights admirably.
They were in search of a cheerful week-end house with a nice
atmosphere, where their friends could join them for frank discussions, and their own and their friends' children "run wild" during
the summer months. Harold Wright, who had a good head, got the
agent to knock six hundred off the quoted price of the house. "That
unfortunate affair," he murmured. Jocelyn commended his inspiration. Otherwise, they did not give the Bentleys another thought.

The Wrights had the floral wallpapers all stripped off and the
walls cream-washed; they removed some disagreeably thick pink
shades from the electricity, and had the paint renewed inside and
out. (The front of the house was bracketed over with balconies,
like an overmantel.) Their bedroom mantelpiece, stained by the
late Mrs. Bentley's cosmetics, had to be scrubbed with chemicals.
Also, they had removed from the rock-garden Mrs. Bentley's little
dog's memorial tablet, with a quotation on it from "Indian Love
Lyrics." Jocelyn Wright, looking into the unfortunate bath, *the*
bath, so square and opulent, with its surround of nacreous tiles, said,

laughing lightly, she supposed anyone *else* would have had that bath changed. "Not that that would be possible," she added; "the bath's built in . . . I've always wanted a built-in bath."

Harold and Jocelyn turned from the bath to look down at the cheerful river shimmering under a spring haze. All the way down the slope cherry-trees were in blossom. Life should be simplified for the Wrights; they were fortunate in their mentality.

After an experimental week-end, without guests or children, only one thing troubled them: a resolute stuffiness, upstairs and down — due, presumably, to the house's having been so long shut up — a smell of unsavory habitation, of rich cigarette-smoke stale in the folds of unaired curtains, of scent spilled on unbrushed carpets; an alcoholic smell — persistent in their perhaps too sensitive nostrils after days of airing, doors and windows open, in rooms drenched thoroughly with sun and wind. They told each other it came from the parquet; they didn't like it, somehow. They had the parquet taken up — at great expense — and put down plain oak floors.

In their practical way the Wrights now set out to expel, live out, live down, almost (had the word had place in their vocabulary) to "lay" the Bentleys. Deferred by trouble over the parquet, their occupation of Rose Hill (which should have dated from mid-April) did not begin till the end of May. Throughout a week, Jocelyn had motored from town daily, so that the final installation of themselves and the children was able to coincide with their first week-end party — they asked down five of their friends to warm the house.

That first Friday, everything was auspicious; afternoon sky blue as the garden irises; later, a full moon pendant over the river; a night so warm that, after midnight, their enlightened friends, in pyjamas, could run on the blanched lawns in a state of high though rational excitement. Jane, Jacob and Janet, their admirably spaced-out children, kept awake by the moonlight, hailed their elders out of the nursery skylight. Jocelyn waved to them: they never had been repressed.

The girl Muriel Barker was found looking up the terraces at the house, a shade doubtfully. "You know," she said, "I do rather wonder they don't feel . . . *sometimes* . . . you know what I mean?"

"No," replied her companion, a young scientist.

Muriel sighed. "No one would mind if it had been just a short sharp shooting. But, it was so . . . prolonged. It went on all over the house. Do you remember?" she said timidly.

"No," replied Mr. Carteret, "it didn't interest me."

"Oh, nor me either!" agreed Muriel quickly, but added: "How he must have hated her! . . ."

The scientist, sleepy, yawned frankly and referred her to Krafft-Ebing. But Muriel went to bed with *Alice in Wonderland*; she went to sleep with the lights on. She was not, as Jocelyn realized later, the sort of girl to have asked at all.

Next morning was overcast; in the afternoon it rained, suddenly and heavily — interrupting, for some, tennis, for others, a pleasant discussion, in a punt, on marriage under the Soviet. Defeated, they all rushed in. Jocelyn went round from room to room, shutting tightly the rain-lashed casements along the front of the house. These continued to rattle; the balconies creaked. An early dusk set in; an oppressive, almost visible moisture, up from the darkening river, pressed on the panes like a presence and slid through the house. The party gathered in the library, round an expansive but thinly burning fire. Harold circulated photographs of modern architecture; they discussed these tendencies. Then Mrs. Monkhouse, sniffing, exclaimed: "Who uses 'Trèfle Incarnat'?"

"Now *whoever* would ——" her hostess began scornfully. Then from the hall came a howl, a scuffle, a thin shriek. They sat too still; in the dusky library Mr. Carteret laughed out loud. Harold Wright, indignantly throwing open the door, revealed Jane and Jacob rolling at the foot of the stairs, biting each other, their faces dark with uninhibited passion. Bumping alternate heads against the foot of the banisters, they shrieked in concert.

"Extraordinary," said Harold; "they've never done that before. They have always understood each other so well."

"I wouldn't do that," advised Jocelyn, raising her voice slightly; "you'll hurt your teeth. Other teeth won't grow at once, you know."

"You should let them find that out for themselves," disapproved Edward Carteret, taking up the *New Statesman*. Harold, in perplexity, shut the door on his children, who soon stunned each other to silence.

Meanwhile, Sara and Talbot Monkhouse, Muriel Barker and Theodora Smith had drawn together over the fire in a tight little knot. Their voices twanged with excitement. By that shock just now, something seemed to have been released. Even Carteret gave them half his attention. They were discussing *crime passionel*.

"Of course, if that's what they really *want* to discuss . . ." thought Jocelyn. But it did seem unfortunate. Partly from an innocent desire to annoy her visitors, partly because the room felt awful — you would have thought fifty people had been there for a week — she went across and opened one of the windows, admitting a pounce of damp wind. They all turned, startled to hear rain crash on the lead of an upstairs balcony. Muriel's voice was left in forlorn solo: "Dragged herself . . . whining 'Harold' . . ."

Harold Wright looked remarkably conscious. Jocelyn said brightly, "Whatever *are* you talking about?" But unfortunately, Harold, on almost the same breath, suggested: "Let's leave that family alone, shall we?" Their friends all felt that they might not be asked again. Though they did feel, plaintively, that they had been being natural. However, they disowned Muriel, who, getting up abruptly, said she thought she'd like to go for a walk in the rain before dinner. Nobody accompanied her.

Later, overtaking Mrs. Monkhouse on the stairs, Muriel confided: absolutely, she could not stand Edward Carteret. She could hardly bear to be in the room with him. He seemed so . . . cruel. Cold-blooded? No, she meant cruel. Sara Monkhouse, going into Jocelyn's room for a chat (at her entrance Jocelyn started violently), told Jocelyn that Muriel could not stand Edward, could hardly bear to be in a room with him. "Pity," said Jocelyn, "I had thought they might do for each other." Jocelyn and Sara agreed that Muriel was unrealized: what she ought to have was a baby. But when Sara, dressing, told Talbot Monkhouse that Muriel could not stand Edward, and Talbot said Muriel was unrealized, Sara was furious. The Monkhouses, who never did quarrel, quarrelled bitterly, and were late for dinner. They would have been later if the meal itself had not been delayed by an outburst of sex-antagonism between the nice Jacksons, a couple imported from London to run the house. Mrs. Jackson, putting everything in the oven, had locked herself into her room.

"Curious," said Harold, "the Jacksons' relations to each other always seemed so modern. They have the most intelligent discussions."

Theodora said she had been re-reading Shakespeare — this brought them point-blank up against Othello. Harold, with titanic force, wrenched round the conversation to relativity: about this no one seemed to have anything to say but Edward Carteret. And Muriel, who by some mischance had again been placed beside him, sat deathly, turning down her dark-rimmed eyes. In fact, on the intelligent, sharp-featured faces all round the table, something — perhaps simply a clearness — seemed to be lacking, as though these were wax faces for one fatal instant exposed to a furnace. Voices came out from some dark interiority; in each conversational interchange a mutual vote of no confidence was implicit. You would have said that each personality had been attacked by some kind of decomposition.

"No moon to-night," complained Sara Monkhouse. Never mind, they would have a cosy evening; they would play paper games, Jocelyn promised.

"If you can see," said Harold. "Something seems to be going wrong with the light."

Did Harold think so? They had all noticed the light seemed to be losing quality, as though a film, smoke-like, were creeping over the bulbs. The light, thinning, darkening, seemed to contract round each lamp into a blurred aura. They had noticed, but, each with a proper dread of his own subjectivity, had not spoken.

"Funny stuff," Harold said, "electricity."

Mr. Carteret could not agree with him.

Though it was late, though they yawned and would not play paper games, they were reluctant to go to bed. You would have supposed a delightful evening. Jocelyn was not gratified.

The library stools, rugs and divans were strewn with Krafft-Ebing, Freud, Forel, Weiniger, and the heterosexual volume of Havelock Ellis. (Harold had thought it right to install his reference library; his friends hated to discuss without basis.) The volumes were pressed open with paper-knives and small pieces of modern statuary; stooping from one to another, purposeful as a bee, Edward Carteret read extracts aloud to Harold, to Talbot Monkhouse and to Theodora Smith, who stitched *gros point* with resolution. At the far end of the library, under the sallow drip from a group of electric candles, Mrs. Monkhouse and Miss Barker shared an ottoman, spines pressed rigid against the wall. Tensely one spoke, one listened.

"And these," thought Jocelyn, leaning back with her eyes shut between the two groups, "are the friends I liked to have in my life. Pellucid, sane . . ."

It was remarkable how much Muriel knew. Sara, very much shocked, edged up till their thighs touched. You would have thought the Harold Bentleys had been Muriel's relatives. Surely, Sara attempted, in one's large, bright world one did not think of these things? Practically, they did not exist! Surely Muriel should not. . . . But Muriel looked at her strangely.

"Did you know," she said, "that one of Mrs. Bentley's hands was found in the library?"

Sara, smiling a little awkwardly, licked her lip. "Oh," she said.

"But the fingers were in the dining-room. He began there."

"Why isn't he in Broadmoor?"

"That defence failed. He didn't really subscribe to it. He said, having done what he wanted was worth anything."

"Oh!"

"Yes, he was nearly lynched. . . . She dragged herself upstairs. She couldn't lock any doors — naturally. One maid — her maid — got shut into the house with them; he'd sent all the others away. For a long time everything seemed so quiet; the maid crept out and saw Harold Bentley sitting half-way upstairs, finishing a cigarette. All the lights were full on. He nodded to her and dropped the cigarette through the banisters. Then she saw the . . . state of the hall. He went upstairs after Mrs. Bentley, saying: 'Lucinda!' He looked into room after room, whistling; then he said, 'Here we are,' and shut a door after him.

"The maid fainted. When she came to, it was still going on, up-stairs. . . . Harold Bentley had locked all the garden doors; there were locks even on the french windows. The maid couldn't get out. Everything she touched was . . . sticky. At last she broke a pane and got through. As she ran down the garden — the lights were on all over the house — she saw Harold Bentley moving about in the bathroom. She fell right over the edge of a terrace and one of the tradesmen picked her up next day.

"Doesn't it seem odd, Sara, to think of Jocelyn in that bath?"

Finishing her recital, Muriel turned on Sara an ecstatic and brooding look that made her almost beautiful. Sara fumbled with a cigarette; match after match failed her. "Muriel, you ought to see a specialist."

Muriel held out her hand for a cigarette. "He put her heart in her hat-box. He said it belonged in there."

"You had no right to come here. It was most unfair on Jocelyn. Most . . . indelicate."

Muriel, to whom the word was, properly, unfamiliar, eyed incredulously Sara's lips.

"How dared you come?"

"I thought I might like it. I thought I ought to fulfill myself. I'd never had any experience of these things."

"*Muriel! . . .*"

"Besides, I wanted to meet Edward Carteret. Several people said we were made for each other. Now, of course, I shall never marry. Look what comes of it . . . I must say, Sara, I wouldn't be you or Jocelyn. Shut up all night with a man all alone — I don't know how you dare sleep. I've arranged to sleep with Theodora, and we shall barricade the door. I noticed something about Edward Carteret the moment I arrived: a kind of insane glitter. He is utterly pathological. He's got instruments in his room, in that black bag. Yes, I looked. Did you notice the way he went on and on about cutting up that cat, and the way Talbot and Harold listened?"

Sara, looking furtively round the room, saw Mr. Carteret making passes over the head of Theodora Smith with a paperknife. Both appeared to laugh heartily, but in silence.

"Here we are," said Harold, showing his teeth, smiling.

He stood over Muriel with a siphon in one hand, glass in the other.

At this point Jocelyn, rising, said she for one, intended to go to bed.

Jocelyn's bedroom curtains swelled a little over the noisy window. The room was stuffy and insupportable, so that she did not know where to turn. The house, fingered outwardly by the wind that dragged unceasingly past the walls, was, within, a solid silence: silence heavy as flesh. Jocelyn dropped her wrap to the floor, then watched how its feathered edges crept a little — a draught came in under her bathroom door.

Jocelyn turned in despair and hostility from the strained, pale woman looking at her from her oblong glass. She said aloud: "There *is* no fear"; then within herself heard this taken up: "But the death fear, that one is not there to relate! If the spirit, dismembered in agony, dies before the body! If the spirit, in the whole knowledge of its dissolution, drags from chamber to chamber, drops from plane to plane of awareness (as from knife to knife down an oubliette) shedding, receiving agony! Till, long afterwards, death, with its little pain is established in the indifferent body." There was no comfort: death (now at every turn and instant claiming her) was in its every possible manifestation violent death: ultimately, she was to be given up to terror.

Undressing, shocked by the iteration of her reflected movements, she flung a towel over the glass. With what desperate eyes of appeal, at Sara's door, she and Sara had looked at each other, clung with their looks — and parted. She could have sworn she heard Sara's bolt slide softly to. But what then, subsequently, of Talbot? And what — she eyed her own bolt, so bright (and for the late Mrs. Bentley so ineffective) — what of Harold?

"It's atavistic!" she said aloud, in the dark-lit room, and, kicking her slippers away, got into bed. She took *Erewhon* from the rack, but lay rigid, listening. As though snatched by a movement, the towel slipped from the mirror beyond her bed-end. She faced the two eyes of an animal in extremity, eyes black, mindless. The clock struck two: she had been waiting an hour.

On the floor her feathered wrap shivered again all over. She heard the other door of the bathroom very stealthily open, then shut. Harold moved in softly, heavily, knocked against the side of the bath and stood still. He was quietly whistling.

"Why didn't I understand? He must always have hated me. It's to-night he's been waiting for. . . . *He wanted this house.* His look, as we went upstairs . . ."

She shrieked: "Harold!"

Harold, so softly whistling, remained behind the imperturbable door, remained quite still. . . . "He's *listening* for me. . . ." One pin-point of hope at the tunnel-end: to get to Sara, to Theodora, to Muriel. Unmasked, incautious, with a long tearing sound of displaced air, Jocelyn leapt from the bed to the door.

But her door had been locked from the outside.

With a strange rueful smile, like an actress, Jocelyn, skirting the foot of the two beds, approached the door of the bathroom. "At least I have still . . . my feet." For some time, the heavy body of Mrs. Bentley, tenacious of life, had been dragging itself

from room to room. *"Harold!"* she said to the silence, face close
to the door.

The door opened on Harold, looking more dreadfully at her
than she had imagined. With a quick, vague movement he roused
himself from his meditation. Therein he had assumed the entire
burden of Harold Bentley. Forces he did not know of assembling
darkly, he had faced for untold ages the imperturbable door to his
wife's room. She would be there, densely, smotheringly there. She
lay like a great cat, always over the mouth of his life.

The Harolds, superimposed on each other, stood searching the
bedroom strangely. Taking a step forward, shutting the door behind him:

"Here we are," said Harold.

Jocelyn went down heavily. Harold watched.

Harold Wright was appalled. Jocelyn had fainted: Jocelyn never
had fainted before. He shook, he fanned, he applied restoratives.
His perplexed thoughts fled to Sara — oh, Sara certainly. "Hi!" he
cried, "Sara!" and successively fled from each to each of the locked
passage doors. There was no way out.

Across the passage a door throbbed to the maniac-drumming of
Sara Monkhouse. She had been locked in. For Talbot, agonized
with solicitude, it was equally impossible to emerge from his dressing-room. Further down the passage Edward Carteret, interested
by this nocturnal manifestation, wrenched and rattled his door-
handle in vain.

Muriel, on her way through the house to Theodora's bedroom,
had turned all the keys on the outside, impartially. She did not
know which door might be Edward Carteret's. Muriel was a woman
who took no chances.

babylon revisited

And where's Mr. Campbell?" Charlie asked.

"Gone to Switzerland. Mr. Campbell's a pretty sick man, Mr. Wales."

"I'm sorry to hear that. And George Hardt?" Charlie inquired.

"Back in America, gone to work."

"And where is the Snow Bird?"

"He was in here last week. Anyway, his friend, Mr. Schaeffer, is in Paris."

Two familiar names from the long list of a year and a half ago. Charlie scribbled an address in his notebook and tore out the page.

"If you see Mr. Schaeffer, give him this," he said. "It's my brother-in-law's address. I haven't settled on a hotel yet."

He was not really disappointed to find Paris was so empty. But the stillness in the Ritz bar was strange and portentous. It was not an American bar any more — he felt polite in it, and not as if he owned it. It had gone back into France. He felt the stillness from the moment he got out of the taxi and saw the doorman, usually in a frenzy of activity at this hour, gossiping with a *chasseur* by the servants' entrance.

Passing through the corridor, he heard only a single, bored voice in the once-glamorous women's room. When he turned into the bar he travelled the twenty feet of green carpet with his eyes fixed straight ahead by old habit; and then, with his foot firmly on the rail, he turned and surveyed the room, encountering only a single pair of eyes that fluttered up from a newspaper in the corner. Charlie asked for the head barman, Paul, who in the latter days of the bull market had come to work in his own custom-built car — disembarking, however, with due nicety at the nearest corner. But Paul was at his country house today and Alix giving him information.

"No, no more," Charlie said, "I'm going slow these days."

Alix congratulated him: "You were going pretty strong a couple of years ago."

"I'll stick to it all right," Charlie assured him. "I've stuck to it for over a year and a half now."

"How do you find conditions in America?"

"I haven't been to America for months. I'm in business in Prague, representing a couple of concerns there. They don't know about me down there."

Alix smiled.

"Remember the night of George Hardt's bachelor dinner here?" said Charlie. "By the way, what's become of Claude Fessenden?"

Alix lowered his voice confidentially: "He's in Paris, but he doesn't come here any more. Paul doesn't allow it. He ran up a bill of thirty thousand francs, charging all his drinks and his lunches, and usually his dinner, for more than a year. And when Paul finally told him he had to pay, he gave him a bad check."

Alix shook his head sadly.

"I don't understand it, such a dandy fellow. Now he's all bloated up — " He made a plump apple of his hands.

Charlie watched a group of strident queens installing themselves in a corner.

"Nothing affects them," he thought. "Stocks rise and fall, people loaf or work, but they go on forever." The place oppressed him. He called for the dice and shook with Alix for the drink.

"Here for long, Mr. Wales?"

"I'm here for four or five days to see my little girl."

"Oh-h! You have a little girl?"

Outside, the fire-red, gas-blue, ghost-green signs shone smokily through the tranquil rain. It was late afternoon and the streets were in movement; the *bistros* gleamed. At the corner of the Boulevard des Capucines he took a taxi. The Place de la Concorde moved by in pink majesty; they crossed the logical Seine, and Charlie felt the sudden provincial quality of the Left Bank.

Charlie directed his taxi to the Avenue de l'Opera, which was out of his way. But he wanted to see the blue hour spread over the magnificent façade, and imagine that the cab horns, playing endlessly the first few bars of *Le Plus que Lent*, were the trumpets of the Second Empire. They were closing the iron grill in front of Brentano's Book-store, and people were already at dinner behind the trim little bourgeois hedge of Duval's. He had never eaten at a really cheap restaurant in Paris. Five-course dinner, four francs fifty, eighteen cents, wine included. For some odd reason he wished that he had.

As they rolled on to the Left Bank and he felt its sudden provincialism, he thought, "I spoiled this city for myself. I didn't realize it, but the days came along one after another, and then two years were gone, and everything was gone, and I was gone."

He was thirty-five, and good to look at. The Irish mobility of his face was sobered by a deep wrinkle between his eyes. As he rang his brother-in-law's bell in the Rue Palatine, the wrinkle deepened till it pulled down his brows; he felt a cramping sensation in his belly. From behind the maid who opened the door darted a lovely little girl of nine who shrieked "Daddy!" and flew up, struggling like a fish, into his arms. She pulled his head around by one ear and set her cheek against his.

"My old pie," he said.

"Oh, daddy, daddy, daddy, daddy, dads, dads, dads!"

She drew him into the salon, where the family waited, a boy and girl his daughter's age, his sister-in-law and her husband. He greeted Marion with his voice pitched carefully to avoid either feigned enthusiasm or dislike, but her response was more frankly tepid, though she minimized her expression of unalterable distrust by directing her regard toward his child. The two men clasped hands in a friendly way and Lincoln Peters rested his for a moment on Charlie's shoulder.

The room was warm and comfortably American. The three children moved intimately about, playing through the yellow oblongs that led to other rooms; the cheer of six o'clock spoke in the eager smacks of the fire and the sounds of French activity in the kitchen. But Charlie did not relax; his heart sat up rigidly in his body and he drew confidence from his daughter, who from time to time came close to him, holding in her arms the doll he had brought.

"Really extremely well," he declared in answer to Lincoln's question. "There's a lot of business there that isn't moving at all, but we're doing even better than ever. In fact, damn well. I'm bringing my sister over from America next month to keep house for me. My income last year was bigger than it was when I had money. You see, the Czechs — "

His boasting was for a specific purpose; but after a moment, seeing a faint restiveness in Lincoln's eye, he changed the subject:

"Those are fine children of yours, well brought up, good manners."

"We think Honoria's a great little girl too."

Marion Peters came back from the kitchen. She was a tall woman with worried eyes, who had once possessed a fresh American loveliness. Charlie had never been sensitive to it and was always surprised when people spoke of how pretty she had been. From the first there had been an instinctive antipathy between them.

"Well, how do you find Honoria?" she asked.

"Wonderful. I was astonished how much she's grown in ten months. All the children are looking well."

"We haven't had a doctor for a year. How do you like being back in Paris?"

"It seems very funny to see so few Americans around."

"I'm delighted," Marion said vehemently. "Now at least you can go into a store without their assuming you're a millionaire. We've suffered like everybody, but on the whole it's a good deal pleasanter."

"But it was nice while it lasted," Charlie said. "We were a sort of royalty, almost infallible, with a sort of magic around us. In the bar this afternoon" — he stumbled, seeing his mistake — "there wasn't a man I knew."

She looked at him keenly. "I should think you'd have had enough of bars."

"I only stayed a minute. I take one drink every afternoon, and no more."

"Don't you want a cocktail before dinner?" Lincoln asked.

"I take only one drink every afternoon, and I've had that."

"I hope you keep to it," said Marion.

Her dislike was evident in the coldness with which she spoke, but Charlie only smiled; he had larger plans. Her very aggressiveness gave him an advantage, and he knew enough to wait. He wanted them to initiate the discussion of what they knew had brought him to Paris.

At dinner he couldn't decide whether Honoria was most like him or her mother. Fortunate if she didn't combine the traits of both that had brought them to disaster. A great wave of protectiveness went over him. He thought he knew what to do for her. He believed in character; he wanted to jump back a whole generation and trust in character again as the eternally valuable element. Everything else wore out.

He left soon after dinner, but not to go home. He was curious to see Paris by night with clearer and more judicious eyes than those of other days. He bought a *strapontin* for the Casino and watched Josephine Baker go through her chocolate arabesques.

After an hour he left and strolled toward Montmartre, up the Rue Pigalle into the Place Blanche. The rain had stopped and there were a few people in evening clothes disembarking from taxis in front of cabarets, and *cocottes* prowling singly or in pairs, and many Negroes. He passed a lighted door from which issued music, and stopped with the sense of familiarity; it was Bricktop's, where he had parted with so many hours and so much money. A few doors farther on he found another ancient rendezvous and incautiously put his head inside. Immediately an eager orchestra burst into sound, a pair of professional dancers leaped to their feet and a maître d'hôtel swooped toward him, crying, "Crowd just arriving, sir!" But he withdrew quickly.

"You have to be damn drunk," he thought.

Zelli's was closed, the bleak and sinister cheap hotels surrounding it were dark; up in the Rue Blanche there was more light and a local, colloquial French crowd. The Poet's Cave had disappeared, but the two great mouths of the Café of Heaven and the Café of Hell still yawned — even devoured, as he watched, the meagre contents of a tourist bus — a German, a Japanese, and an American couple who glanced at him with frightened eyes.

So much for the effort and ingenuity of Montmartre. All the catering to vice and waste was on an utterly childish scale, and he suddenly realized the meaning of the word "dissipate" — to dissipate into thin air; to make nothing out of something. In the little hours of the night every move from place to place was an enormous human jump, an increase of paying for the privilege of slower and slower motion.

He remembered thousand-franc notes given to an orchestra for playing a single number, hundred-franc notes tossed to a doorman for calling a cab.

But it hadn't been given for nothing.

It had been given, even the most wildly squandered sum, as an offering to destiny that he might not remember the things most worth remembering, the things that now he would always remember — his child taken from his control, his wife escaped to a grave in Vermont.

In the glare of a *brasserie* a woman spoke to him. He bought her some eggs and coffee, and then, eluding her encouraging stare, gave her a twenty-franc note and took a taxi to his hotel.

II

He woke upon a fine fall day — football weather. The depression of yesterday was gone and he liked the people on the streets. At noon he sat opposite Honoria at Le Grand Vatel, the only restaurant he could think of not reminiscent of champagne dinners and long luncheons that began at two and ended in a blurred and vague twilight.

"Now, how about vegetables? Oughtn't you to have some vegetables?"

"Well, yes."

"Here's *épinards* and *chou-fleur* and carrots and *haricots*."

"I'd like *chou-fleur*."

"Wouldn't you like to have two vegetables?"

"I usually only have one at lunch."

The waiter was pretending to be inordinately fond of children. *"Qu'elle est mignonne, la petite! Elle parle exactement comme une française."*

"How about dessert? Shall we wait and see?"

The waiter disappeared. Honoria looked at her father expectantly.

"What are we going to do?"

"First, we're going to that toy store in the Rue Saint-Honoré and buy you anything you like. And then we're going to the vaudeville at the Empire."

She hesitated. "I like it about the vaudeville, but not the toy store."

"Why not?"

"Well, you brought me this doll." She had it with her. "And I've got lots of things. And we're not rich any more, are we?"

"We never were. But today you are to have anything you want."

"All right," she agreed resignedly.

When there had been her mother and a French nurse he had been inclined to be strict; now he extended himself, reached out for a new tolerance; he must be both parents to her and not shut any of her out of communication.

"I want to get to know you," he said gravely. "First let me introduce myself. My name is Charles J. Wales, of Prague."

"Oh, daddy!" her voice cracked with laughter.

"And who are you, please?" he persisted, and she accepted a rôle immediately: "Honoria Wales, Rue Palatine, Paris."

"Married or single?"

"No, not married. Single."

He indicated the doll. "But I see you have a child, madame."

Unwilling to disinherit it, she took it to her heart and thought quickly: "Yes, I've been married, but I'm not married now. My husband is dead."

He went on quickly, "And the child's name?"

"Simone. That's after my best friend at school."

"I'm very pleased that you're doing so well at school."

"I'm third this month," she boasted. "Elsie" — that was her cousin — "is only about eighteenth, and Richard is about at the bottom."

"You like Richard and Elsie, don't you?"

"Oh, yes, I like Richard quite well and I like her all right."

Cautiously and casually he asked: "And Aunt Marion and Uncle Lincoln — which do you like best?"

"Oh, Uncle Lincoln, I guess."

He was increasingly aware of her presence. As they came in, a murmur of ". . . adorable" followed them, and now the people at the next table bent all their silences upon her, staring as if she were something no more conscious than a flower.

"Why don't I live with you?" she asked suddenly. "Because mamma's dead?"

"You must stay here and learn more French. It would have been hard for daddy to take care of you so well."

"I don't really need much taking care of any more. I do everything for myself."

Going out of the restaurant, a man and a woman unexpectedly hailed him.

"Well, the old Wales!"

"Hello there, Lorraine. . . . Dunc."

Sudden ghosts out of the past: Duncan Schaeffer, a friend from college. Lorraine Quarrles, a lovely, pale blonde of thirty; one of a crowd who had helped them make months into days in the lavish times of three years ago.

"My husband couldn't come this year," she said, in answer to his question. "We're poor as hell. So he gave me two hundred a month and told me I could do my worst on that. . . . This your little girl?"

"What about coming back and sitting down?" Duncan asked.

"Can't do it." He was glad for an excuse. As always, he felt Lorraine's passionate, provocative attraction, but his own rhythm was different now.

"Well, how about dinner?" she asked.

"I'm not free. Give me your address and let me call you."

"Charlie, I believe you're sober," she said judicially. "I honestly believe he's sober, Dunc. Pinch him and see if he's sober."

Charlie indicated Honoria with his head. They both laughed.

"What's your address?" said Duncan sceptically.

He hesitated, unwilling to give the name of his hotel.

"I'm not settled yet. I'd better call you. We're going to see the vaudeville at the Empire."

"There! That's what I want to do," Lorraine said. "I want to see some clowns and acrobats and jugglers. That's just what we'll do, Dunc."

"We've got to do an errand first," said Charlie. "Perhaps we'll see you there."

"All right, you snob. . . . Good-by, beautiful little girl."

"Good-by."

Honoria bobbed politely.

Somehow, an unwelcome encounter. They liked him because he was functioning, because he was serious; they wanted to see him, because he was stronger than they were now, because they wanted to draw a certain sustenance from his strength.

At the Empire, Honoria proudly refused to sit upon her father's folded coat. She was already an individual with a code of her own, and Charlie was more and more absorbed by the desire of putting a little of himself into her before she crystallized utterly. It was hopeless to try to know her in so short a time.

Between the acts they came upon Duncan and Lorraine in the lobby where the band was playing.

"Have a drink?"

"All right, but not up at the bar. We'll take a table."

"The perfect father."

Listening abstractedly to Lorraine, Charlie watched Honoria's eyes leave their table, and he followed them wistfully about the room, wondering what they saw. He met her glance and she smiled.

"I liked that lemonade," she said.

What had she said? What had he expected? Going home in a taxi afterward, he pulled her over until her head rested against his chest.

"Darling, do you ever think about your mother?"

"Yes, sometimes," she answered vaguely.

"I don't want you to forget her. Have you got a picture of her?"

"Yes, I think so. Anyhow, Aunt Marion has. Why don't you want me to forget her?"

"She loved you very much."

"I loved her too."

They were silent for a moment.

"Daddy, I want to come and live with you," she said suddenly.

His heart leaped; he had wanted it to come like this.

"Aren't you perfectly happy?"

"Yes, but I love you better than anybody. And you love me better than anybody, don't you, now that mummy's dead?"

"Of course I do. But you won't always like me best, honey. You'll grow up and meet somebody your own age and go marry him and forget you ever had a daddy."

"Yes, that's true," she agreed tranquilly.

He didn't go in. He was coming back at nine o'clock and he wanted to keep himself fresh and new for the thing he must say then.

"When you're safe inside, just show yourself in that window."

"All right. Good-by, dads, dads, dads, dads."

He waited in the dark street until she appeared, all warm and glowing, in the window above and kissed her fingers out into the night.

III

They were waiting. Marion sat behind the coffee service in a dignified black dinner dress that just faintly suggested mourning. Lincoln was walking up and down with the animation of one who had already been talking. They were as anxious as he was to get into the question. He opened it almost immediately:

"I suppose you know what I want to see you about — why I really came to Paris."

Marion played with the black stars on her necklace and frowned.

"I'm awfully anxious to have a home," he continued. "And I'm awfully anxious to have Honoria in it. I appreciate your taking in Honoria for her mother's sake, but things have changed now" — he hesitated and then continued more forcibly — "changed radically with me, and I want to ask you to reconsider the matter. It would be silly for me to deny that about three years ago I was acting badly —"

Marion looked up at him with hard eyes.

" — but all that's over. As I told you, I haven't had more than a drink a day for over a year, and I take that drink deliberately, so that the idea of alcohol won't get too big in my imagination. You see the idea?"

"No," said Marion succinctly.

"It's a sort of stint I set myself. It keeps the matter in proportion."

"I get you," said Lincoln. "You don't want to admit it's got any attraction for you."

"Something like that. Sometimes I forget and don't take it. But I try to take it. Anyhow, I couldn't afford to drink in my position. The people I represent are more than satisfied with what I've done, and I'm bringing my sister over from Burlington to keep house for me, and I want awfully to have Honoria too. You know that even when her mother and I weren't getting along well we never let anything that happened touch Honoria. I know she's fond of me and I know I'm able to take care of her and — well, there you are. How do you feel about it?"

He knew that now he would have to take a beating. It would last an hour or two hours, and it would be difficult, but if he modulated his inevitable resentment to the chastened attitude of the reformed sinner, he might win his point in the end.

Keep your temper, he told himself. You don't want to be justified. You want Honoria.

Lincoln spoke first: "We've been talking it over ever since we got your letter last month. We're happy to have Honoria here. She's a dear little thing, and we're glad to be able to help her, but of course that isn't the question — "

Marion interrupted suddenly. "How long are you going to stay sober, Charlie?" she asked.

"Permanently, I hope."

"How can anybody count on that?"

"You know I never did drink heavily until I gave up business and came over here with nothing to do. Then Helen and I began to run around with — "

"Please leave Helen out of it. I can't bear to hear you talk about her like that."

He stared at her grimly; he had never been certain how fond of each other the sisters were in life.

"My drinking only lasted about a year and a half — from the time we came over until I — collapsed."

"It was time enough."

"It was time enough," he agreed.

"My duty is entirely to Helen," she said. "I try to think what she would have wanted me to do. Frankly, from the night you did that terrible thing you haven't really existed for me. I can't help that. She was my sister."

"Yes."

"When she was dying she asked me to look out for Honoria. If you hadn't been in a sanitarium then, it might have helped matters."

He had no answer.

"I'll never in my life be able to forget the morning when Helen knocked at my door, soaked to the skin and shivering, and said you'd locked her out."

Charlie gripped the sides of the chair. This was more difficult than he expected; he wanted to launch out into a long expostulation and explanation, but he only said: "The night I locked her out —" and she interrupted, "I don't feel up to going over that again."

After a moment's silence Lincoln said: "We're getting off the subject. You want Marion to set aside her legal guardianship and give you Honoria. I think the main point for her is whether she has confidence in you or not."

"I don't blame Marion," Charlie said slowly, "but I think she can have entire confidence in me. I had a good record up to three years ago. Of course, it's within human possibilities I might go wrong any time. But if we wait much longer I'll lose Honoria's childhood and my chance for a home." He shook his head, "I'll simply lose her, don't you see?"

"Yes, I see," said Lincoln.

"Why didn't you think of all this before?" Marion asked.

"I suppose I did, from time to time, but Helen and I were getting along badly. When I consented to the guardianship, I was flat on my back in a sanitarium and the market had cleaned me out. I knew I'd acted badly, and I thought if it would bring any peace to Helen, I'd agree to anything. But now it's different. I'm functioning, I'm behaving damn well, so far as —"

"Please don't swear at me," Marion said.

He looked at her, startled. With each remark the force of her dislike became more and more apparent. She had built up all her fear of life into one wall and faced it toward him. This trivial reproof was possibly the result of some trouble with the cook several hours before. Charlie became increasingly alarmed at leaving Honoria in this atmosphere of hostility against himself; sooner or later it would come out, in a word here, a shake of the head there, and some of that distrust would be irrevocably implanted in Honoria. But he pulled his temper down out of his face and shut it up inside him; he had won a point, for Lincoln realized the absurdity of Marion's remark and asked her lightly since when she had objected to the word "damn."

"Another thing," Charlie said: "I'm able to give her certain advantages now. I'm going to take a French governess to Prague with me. I've got a lease on a new apartment — "

He stopped, realizing that he was blundering. They couldn't be expected to accept with equanimity the fact that his income was again twice as large as their own.

"I suppose you can give her more luxuries than we can," said Marion. "When you were throwing away money we were living along watching every ten francs. . . . I suppose you'll start doing it again."

"Oh, no," he said. "I've learned. I worked hard for ten years, you know — until I got lucky in the market, like so many people. Terribly lucky. It didn't seem any use working any more, so I quit. It won't happen again."

There was a long silence. All of them felt their nerves straining, and for the first time in a year Charlie wanted a drink. He was sure now that Lincoln Peters wanted him to have his child.

Marion shuddered suddenly; part of her saw that Charlie's feet were planted on the earth now, and her own maternal feeling recognized the naturalness of his desire; but she had lived for a long time with a prejudice — a prejudice founded on a curious disbelief in her sister's happiness, and which, in the shock of one terrible night, had turned to hatred for him. It had all happened at a point in her life where the discouragement of ill health and adverse circumstances made it necessary for her to believe in tangible villainy and a tangible villain.

"I can't help what I think!" she cried out suddenly. "How much you were responsible for Helen's death, I don't know. It's something you'll have to square with your own conscience."

An electric current of agony surged through him; for a moment he was almost on his feet, an unuttered sound echoing in his throat. He hung on to himself for a moment, another moment.

"Hold on there," said Lincoln uncomfortably. "I never thought you were responsible for that."

"Helen died of heart trouble," Charlie said dully.

"Yes, heart trouble." Marion spoke as if the phrase had another meaning for her.

Then, in the flatness that followed her outburst, she saw him plainly and she knew he had somehow arrived at control over the situation. Glancing at her husband, she found no help from him, and as abruptly as if it were a matter of no importance, she threw up the sponge.

"Do what you like!" she cried, springing up from her chair. "She's your child. I'm not the person to stand in your way. I think if it were my child I'd rather see her — " She managed to check herself. "You two decide it. I can't stand this. I'm sick. I'm going to bed."

She hurried from the room; after a moment Lincoln said:

"This has been a hard day for her. You know how strongly she feels — " His voice was almost apologetic: "When a woman gets an idea in her head."

"Of course."

"It's going to be all right. I think she sees now that you — can provide for the child, and so we can't very well stand in your way or Honoria's way."

"Thank you, Lincoln."

"I'd better go along and see how she is."

"I'm going."

He was still trembling when he reached the street, but a walk down the Rue Bonaparte to the quais set him up, and as he crossed the Seine, fresh and new by the quai lamps, he felt exultant. But back in his room he couldn't sleep. The image of Helen haunted him. Helen whom he had loved so until they had senselessly begun to abuse each other's love, tear it into shreds. On that terrible February night that Marion remembered so vividly, a slow quarrel had gone on for hours. There was a scene at the Florida, and then he attempted to take her home, and then she kissed young Webb at a table; after that there was what she had hysterically said. When he arrived home alone he turned the key in the lock in wild anger. How could he know she would arrive an hour later alone, that there would be a snowstorm in which she wandered about in slippers, too confused to find a taxi? Then the aftermath, her escaping pneumonia by a miracle, and all the attendant horror. They were "reconciled," but that was the beginning of the end, and Marion, who had seen with her own eyes and who imagined it to be one of many scenes from her sister's martyrdom, never forgot.

Going over it again brought Helen nearer, and in the white, soft light that steals upon half sleep near morning he found himself talking to her again. She said that he was perfectly right about Honoria and that she wanted Honoria to be with him. She said she was glad he was being good and doing better. She said a lot of other things — very friendly things — but she was in a swing in a white dress, and swinging faster and faster all the time, so that at the end he could not hear clearly all that she said.

IV

He woke up feeling happy. The door of the world was open again. He made plans, vistas, futures for Honoria and himself, but suddenly he grew sad, remembering all the plans he and Helen had made. She had not planned to die. The present was the thing — work to do and someone to love. But not to love too much, for he knew the injury that a father can do to a daughter or a mother to a son by attaching them too closely: afterward, out in the world, the child would seek in the marriage partner the same blind tenderness and, failing probably to find it, turn against love and life.

It was another bright, crisp day. He called Lincoln Peters at the bank where he worked and asked if he could count on taking Honoria when he left for Prague. Lincoln agreed that there was no reason for delay. One thing — the legal guardianship. Marion wanted to retain that a while longer. She was upset by the whole matter, and it would oil things if she felt that the situation was still in her control for another year. Charlie agreed, wanting only the tangible, visible child.

Then the question of a governess. Charlie sat in a gloomy agency and talked to a cross Bernaise and to a buxom Breton peasant, neither of whom he could have endured. There were others whom he would see tomorrow.

He lunched with Lincoln Peters at Griffons, trying to keep down his exultation.

"There's nothing quite like your own child," Lincoln said. "But you understand how Marion feels too."

"She's forgotten how hard I worked for seven years there," Charlie said. "She just remembers one night."

"There's another thing." Lincoln hesitated. "While you and Helen were tearing around Europe throwing money away, we were just getting along. I didn't touch any of the prosperity because I never got ahead enough to carry anything but my insurance. I think Marion felt there was some kind of injustice in it — you not even working toward the end, and getting richer and richer."

"It went just as quick as it came," said Charlie.

"Yes, a lot of it stayed in the hands of *chasseurs* and saxophone players and maîtres d'hôtel — well, the big party's over now. I just said that to explain Marion's feeling about those crazy years. If you drop in about six o'clock tonight before Marion's too tired, we'll settle the details on the spot."

Back at his hotel, Charlie found a *pneumatique* that had been redirected from the Ritz bar where Charlie had left his address for the purpose of finding a certain man.

DEAR CHARLIE: You were so strange when we saw you the other day that I wondered if I did something to offend you. If so, I'm not conscious of it. In fact, I have thought about you too much for the last year, and it's always been in the back of my mind that I might see you if I came over here. We *did* have such good times that crazy spring, like the night you and I stole the butcher's tricycle, and the time we tried to call on the president and you had the old derby rim and the wire cane. Everybody seems so old lately, but I don't feel old a bit. Couldn't we get together some time today for old times's sake? I've got a vile hangover for the moment, but will be feeling better this afternoon and will look for you about five in the sweat-shop at the Ritz.

Always devotedly,

LORRAINE.

His first feeling was one of awe that he had actually, in his mature years, stolen a tricycle and pedalled Lorraine all over the Étoile between the small hours and dawn. In retrospect it was a nightmare. Locking out Helen didn't fit in with any other act of his life, but the tricycle incident did — it was one of many. How many weeks or months of dissipation to arrive at that condition of utter irresponsibility?

He tried to picture how Lorraine had appeared to him then — very attractive; Helen was unhappy about it, though she said nothing. Yesterday, in the restaurant, Lorraine had seemed trite, blurred, worn away. He emphatically did not want to see her, and he was glad Alix had not given away his hotel address. It was a relief to think, instead, of Honoria, to think of Sundays spent with her and of saying good morning to her and of knowing she was there in his house at night, drawing her breath in the darkness.

At five he took a taxi and bought presents for all the Peters — a piquant cloth doll, a box of Roman soldiers, flowers for Marion, big linen handkerchiefs for Lincoln.

He saw, when he arrived in the apartment, that Marion had accepted the inevitable. She greeted him now as though he were a recalcitrant member of the family, rather than a menacing outsider. Honoria had been told she was going; Charlie was glad to see that her tact made her conceal her excessive happiness. Only on his lap did she whisper her delight and the question "When?" before she slipped away with the other children.

He and Marion were alone for a minute in the room, and on an impulse he spoke out boldly:

"Family quarrels are bitter things. They don't go according to any rules. They're not like aches or wounds; they're more like splits in the skin that won't heal because there's not enough material. I wish you and I could be on better terms."

"Some things are hard to forget," she answered. "It's a question of confidence." There was no answer to this and presently she asked, "When do you propose to take her?"

"As soon as I can get a governess. I hoped the day after tomorrow."

"That's impossible. I've got to get her things in shape. Not before Saturday."

He yielded. Coming back into the room, Lincoln offered him a drink.

"I'll take my daily whisky," he said.

It was warm here, it was a home, people together by a fire. The children felt very safe and important; the mother and father were serious, watchful. They had things to do for the children more important than his visit here. A spoonful of medicine was, after all, more important than the strained relations between Marion and himself. They were not dull people, but they were very much in the grip of life and circumstances. He wondered if he couldn't do something to get Lincoln out of his rut at the bank.

A long peal at the door-bell; the *bonne de toute faire* passed through and went down the corridor. The door opened upon another long ring, and then voices, and the three in the salon looked up expectantly; Richard moved to bring the corridor within his range of vision, and Marion rose. Then the maid came back along the corridor, closely followed by the voices, which developed under the light into Duncan Schaeffer and Lorraine Quarrles.

They were gay, they were hilarious, they were roaring with laughter. For a moment Charlie was astounded; unable to understand how they ferreted out the Peters' address.

"Ah-h-h!" Duncan wagged his finger roguishly at Charlie. "Ah-h-h!"

They both slid down another cascade of laughter. Anxious and at a loss, Charlie shook hands with them quickly and presented them to Lincoln and Marion. Marion nodded, scarcely speaking. She had drawn back a step toward the fire; her little girl stood beside her, and Marion put an arm about her shoulder.

With growing annoyance at the intrusion, Charlie waited for them to explain themselves. After some concentration Duncan said:

"We came to invite you out to dinner. Lorraine and I insist that all this shishi, cagey business 'bout your address got to stop."

Charlie came closer to them, as if to force them backward down the corridor.

"Sorry, but I can't. Tell me where you'll be and I'll phone you in half an hour."

This made no impression. Lorraine sat down suddenly on the side of a chair, and focussing her eyes on Richard, cried, "Oh, what a nice little boy! Come here, little boy." Richard glanced at his mother, but did not move. With a perceptible shrug of her shoulders, Lorraine turned back to Charlie:

"Come and dine. Sure your cousins won' mine. See you so sel'om. Or solemn."

"I can't," said Charlie sharply. "You two have dinner and I'll phone you."

Her voice became suddenly unpleasant. "All right, we'll go. But I remember once when you hammered on my door at four A.M. I was enough of a good sport to give you a drink. Come on, Dunc."

Still in slow motion, with blurred, angry faces, with uncertain feet, they retired along the corridor.

"Good night," Charlie said.

"Good night!" responded Lorraine emphatically.

When he went back into the salon Marion had not moved, only now her son was standing in the circle of her other arm. Lincoln was still swinging Honoria back and forth like a pendulum from side to side.

"What an outrage!" Charlie broke out. "What an absolute outrage!"

Neither of them answered. Charlie dropped into an armchair, picked up his drink, set it down again and said:

"People I haven't seen for two years having the colossal nerve —"

He broke off. Marion had made the sound "Oh!" in one swift, furious breath, turned her body from him with a jerk and left the room.

Lincoln set down Honoria carefully.

"You children go in and start your soup," he said, and when they obeyed, he said to Charlie:

"Marion's not well and she can't stand shocks. That kind of people make her really physically sick."

"I didn't tell them to come here. They wormed your name out of somebody. They deliberately —"

"Well, it's too bad. It doesn't help matters. Excuse me a minute."

Left alone, Charlie sat tense in his chair. In the next room he could hear the children eating, talking in monosyllables, already oblivious to the scene between their elders. He heard a murmur of conversation from a farther room and then the ticking bell of a telephone receiver picked up, and in a panic he moved to the other side of the room and out of earshot.

In a minute Lincoln came back. "Look here, Charlie. I think we'd better call off dinner for tonight. Marion's in bad shape."

"Is she angry with me?"

"Sort of," he said, almost roughly. "She's not strong and —"

"You mean she's changed her mind about Honoria?"

"She's pretty bitter right now. I don't know. You phone me at the bank tomorrow."

"I wish you'd explain to her I never dreamed these people would come here. I'm just as sore as you are."

"I couldn't explain anything to her now."

Charlie got up. He took his coat and hat and started down the corridor. Then he opened the door of the dining room and said in a strange voice, "Good night, children."

Honoria rose and ran around the table to hug him.

"Good night, sweetheart," he said vaguely, and then trying to make his voice more tender, trying to conciliate something, "Good night, dear children."

v

Charlie went directly to the Ritz bar with the furious idea of finding Lorraine and Duncan, but they were not there, and he realized that in any case there was nothing he could do. He had not touched his drink at the Peters', and now he ordered a whisky-and-soda. Paul came over to say hello.

"It's a great change," he said sadly. "We do about half the business we did. So many fellows I hear about back in the States lost everything, maybe not in the first crash, but then in the second. Your friend George Hardt lost every cent, I hear. Are you back in the States?"

"No, I'm in business in Prague."

"I heard that you lost a lot in the crash."

"I did," and he added grimly, "but I lost everything I wanted in the boom."

"Selling short?"

"Something like that."

Again the memory of those days swept over him like a nightmare — the people they had met travelling; the people who couldn't add a row of figures or speak a coherent sentence. The little man Helen had consented to dance with at the ship's party, who had insulted her ten feet from the table; the women and girls carried screaming with drink or drugs out of public places —

— The men who locked their wives out in the snow, because the snow of twenty-nine wasn't real snow. If you didn't want it to be snow, you just paid some money.

He went to the phone and called the Peters' apartment; Lincoln answered.

"I called up because this thing is on my mind. Has Marion said anything definite?"

"Marion's sick," Lincoln answered shortly. "I know this thing isn't altogether your fault, but I can't have her go to pieces about it. I'm afraid we'll have to let it slide for six months; I can't take the chance of working her up to this state again."

"I see."

"I'm sorry, Charlie."

He went back to his table. His whisky glass was empty, but he shook his head when Alix looked at it questioningly. There wasn't much he could do now except send Honoria some things; he would send her a lot of things tomorrow. He thought rather angrily that this was just money — he had given so many people money. . . .

"No, no more," he said to another waiter. "What do I owe you?"

He would come back some day; they couldn't make him pay forever. But he wanted his child, and nothing was much good now, beside that fact. He wasn't young any more, with a lot of nice thoughts and dreams to have by himself. He was absolutely sure Helen wouldn't have wanted him to be so alone.

CONRAD AIKEN

strange moonlight

I t had been a tremendous week — colossal. Its reverberations around him hardly yet slept — his slightest motion or thought made a vast symphony of them, like a breeze in a forest of bells. In the first place, he had filched a volume of Poe's tales from his mother's bookcase, and had had in consequence a delirious night in inferno. Down, down he had gone with heavy clangs about him, coiling spouts of fire licking dryly at an iron sky, and a strange companion, of protean shape and size, walking and talking beside him. For the most part, this companion seemed to be nothing but a voice and a wing — an enormous jagged black wing, soft and drooping like a bat's; he had noticed veins in it. As for the voice, it had been singularly gentle. If it was mysterious, that was no

"Strange Moonlight" from *The Short Stories of Conrad Aiken* by Conrad Aiken. Reprinted by permission of the publishers, Duell, Sloan and Pearce, Inc. Copyright 1925, 1950 by Conrad Aiken.

doubt because he himself was stupid. Certainly it had sounded placid and reasonable, exactly, in fact, like his father's explaining a problem in mathematics; but, though he had noticed the orderly and logical structure, and felt the inevitable approach toward a vast and beautiful or terrible conclusion, the nature and meaning of the conclusion itself always escaped him. It was as if, always, he had come just too late. When, for example, he had come at last to the black wall that inclosed the infernal city, and seen the arched gate, the voice had certainly said that if he hurried he would see, through the arch, a far, low landscape of extraordinary wonder. He had hurried, but it had been in vain. He had reached the gate, and for the tiniest fraction of an instant he had even glimpsed the wide green of fields and trees, a winding blue ribbon of water, and a gleam of intense light touching to brilliance some far object. But then, before he had time to notice more than that every detail in this fairy landscape seemed to lead toward a single shining solution, a dazzling significance, suddenly the infernal rain, streaked fire and rolling smoke, had swept it away. Then the voice had seemed to become ironic. He had failed, and he felt like crying.

He had still, the next morning, felt that he might, if the opportunity offered, see that vision. It was always just round the corner, just at the head of the stairs, just over the next page. But other adventures had intervened. Prize-day, at school, had come upon him as suddenly as a thunderstorm — the ominous hushed gathering of the entire school into one large room, the tense air of expectancy, the solemn speeches, all had reduced him to a state of acute terror. There was something unintelligible and sinister about it. He had, from first to last, a peculiar physical sensation that something threatened him, and here and there, in the interminable vague speeches, a word seemed to have eyes and to stare at him. His prescience had been correct — abruptly his name had been called, he had walked unsteadily amid applause to the teacher's desk, had received a small black pasteboard box; and then had cowered in his chair again, with the blood in his temples beating like gongs. When it was over, he had literally run away — he didn't stop till he reached the park. There, among the tombstones (the park had once been a graveyard) and trumpet-vines, he sat on the grass and opened the box. He was dazzled. The medal was of gold, and rested on a tiny blue satin cushion. His name was engraved on it — yes, actually cut into the gold; he felt the incisions with his fingernail. It was an experience not wholly to be comprehended. He put the box down in the grass and detached himself from it, lay full length, resting his chin on his wrist, and stared first at a tombstone and then at the small gold object, as if to discover the relation between them. Humming-birds, tombstones, trumpet-vines, and a gold medal. Amazing. He unpinned the medal from its cushion, put the box in his pocket, and walked slowly homeward, carrying the small, live, gleaming thing between fingers and thumb as if it were a bee. This was an experience to be carefully concealed from mother and father. Possibly he would tell Mary and John. . . . Unfortunately, he met his father as he was going in the door, and was thereafter drowned, for a day, in a glory without significance. He felt ashamed, and put the medal away in a drawer, sternly forbidding Mary and John to look at it. Even so, he was horribly conscious of it — its presence there burned him unceasingly. Nothing afforded escape from it, not even sitting under the peach tree and whittling a boat.

II

The oddest thing was the way these and other adventures of the week all seemed to unite, as if they were merely aspects of the same thing. Everywhere lurked that extraordinary hint of the enigma and its shining solution. On Tuesday morning, when it was pouring with rain, and he and Mary and John were conducting gigantic military operations in the back hall, with hundreds of paper soldiers, tents, cannon, battleships, and forts, suddenly through the tall open window, a goldfinch flew in from the rain, beat wildly against a pane of glass, darted several times to and fro above their heads, and finally, finding the open window, flashed out. It flew to the peach tree, rested there for a moment, and then over the outhouse and away. He saw it rising and falling in the rain. This was beautiful — it was like the vision in the infernal city, like the medal in the grass. He found it impossible to go on with the Battle of Gettysburg and abandoned it to Mary and John, who instantly started to quarrel. Escape was necessary, and he went into his own room, shut the door, lay on his bed, and began thinking about Caroline Lee.

John Lee had taken him there to see his new air-gun and a bag

of BB shot. The strange house was dim and exciting. A long winding dark staircase went up from near the front door, a clock was
striking in a far room, a small beautiful statue of a lady, slightly
pinkish, and looking as if it had been dug out of the earth, stood
on a table. The wallpaper beside the staircase was rough and hairy.
Upstairs, in the playroom, they found Caroline, sitting on the floor
with a picture book. She was learning to read, pointing at the
words with her finger. He was struck by the fact that, although
she was extraordinarily strange and beautiful, John Lee did not
seem to be aware of it and treated her as if she were quite an ordinary sort of person. This gave him courage, and after the air-gun
had been examined, and the bag of BB shot emptied of its gleaming
heavy contents and then luxuriously refilled, he told her some of
the words she couldn't make out. "And what's this?" she had said
— he could still hear her say it, quite clearly. She was thin, smaller
than himself, with dark hair and large pale eyes, and her forehead
and hands looked curiously transparent. He particularly noticed
her hands when she brought her five-dollar goldpiece to show him,
opening a little jewel box which had in it also a necklace of yellow
beads from Egypt and a pink shell from Tybee Beach. She gave
him the goldpiece to look at, and while he was looking at it put the
beads round her neck. "Now, I'm an Egyptian!" she said, and
laughed shyly, running her fingers to and fro over the smooth
beads. A fearful temptation came upon him. He coveted the goldpiece, and thought that it would be easy to steal it. He shut his
hand over it and it was gone. If it had been John's, he might have
done so, but, as it was, he opened his hand again and put the goldpiece back in the box. Afterwards, he stayed for a long while, talking with John and Caroline. The house was mysterious and rich,
and he hadn't at all wanted to go out of it, or back to his own hum-
drum existence. Besides, he liked to hear Caroline talking.

But although he had afterwards for many days wanted to go
back to that house, to explore further its dim rich mysteriousness,
and had thought about it a great deal, John hadn't again suggested
a visit, and he himself had felt a curious reluctance about raising
the subject. It had been, apparently, a vision that was not to be
repeated, an incursion into a world that was so beautiful and
strange that one was permitted of it only the briefest of glimpses.
He had, almost, to reassure himself that the house was really there,
and for that reason he made rather a point of walking home from

school with John Lee. Yes, the house was there — he saw John climb the stone steps and open the huge green door. There was never a sign of Caroline, however, nor any mention of her; until one day he heard from another boy that she was ill with scarlet fever, and observed that John had stayed away from school. The news didn't startle or frighten him. On the contrary, it seemed just the sort of romantic privilege in which such fortunate people would indulge. He felt a certain delicacy about approaching the house, however, to see if the red quarantine sign had been affixed by the door, and carefully avoided Gordon Square on his way home from school. Should he write her a letter or send her a present of marbles? For neither action did there seem to be sufficient warrant. But he found it impossible to do nothing, and later in the afternoon, by a very circuitous route which took him past the country jail — where he was thrilled by actually seeing a prisoner looking out between the gray iron bars — he slowly made his way to Gordon Square and from a safe distance, more or less hiding himself behind a palmetto tree, looked for a long while at the wonderful house, and saw, sure enough, the red sign.

Three days later he heard that Caroline Lee was dead. The news stunned him. Surely it could not be possible? He felt stifled, frightened, and incredulous. In a way, it was just what one would expect of Caroline, but none the less he felt outraged. How was it possible for anyone, whom one actually knew, to *die?* Particularly anyone so vividly and beautifully remembered! The indignity, the horror, of death obsessed him. *Had* she actually died? He went again to Gordon Square, not knowing precisely what it was that he expected to find, and saw something white hanging by the green door. But if, as it appeared, it was true that Caroline Lee, somewhere inside the house, lay dead, lay motionless, how did it happen that he, who was so profoundly concerned, had not at all been consulted, had not been invited to come and talk with her, and now found himself so utterly and hopelessly and forever excluded — from the house, as from her? This was a thing which he could not understand. As he walked home, pondering it, he thought of the five-dollar gold-piece. What would become of it? Probably John would get it, and, if so, he would steal it from him. . . . All the same, he was glad he hadn't taken it.

To this reflection he came back many times, as now once more with the Battle of Gettysburg raging in the next room. If he had actually taken it, what a horror it would have been! As it was, the fact that he had resisted the temptation, restored the goldpiece to the box, seemed to have been a tribute to Caroline's beauty and strangeness. Yes, for nobody else would he have made the refusal — nobody on earth. But, for her, it had been quite simple, a momentary pang quickly lost in the pleasure of hearing her voice, watching her pale hands twisting the yellow beads, and helping her with her reading. "And what's this?" she had said, and "Now I'm an Egyptian!" . . . What was death that could put an end to a clear voice saying such things? . . . Mystery was once more about him, the same mystery that had shone in the vision of the infernal city. There was something beautiful which he could not understand. He had felt it while he was lying in the grass among the tombstones, looking at the medal; he had felt it when the goldfinch darted in from the rain and then out again. All these things seemed in some curious way to fit together.

III

The same night, after he had gone to bed, this feeling of enormous and complicated mystery came upon him again with oppressive weight. He lay still, looking from his pillow through the tall window at the moonlight on the white outhouse wall, and again it seemed to him that the explanation for everything was extraordinarily near at hand if he could only find it. The mystery was like the finest of films, like the moonlight on the white wall. Surely, beneath it, there was something solid and simple. He heard someone walk across the yard, with steps that seemed astoundingly far apart and slow. The steps ceased, a door creaked. Then there was a cough. It was old Selena, the Negro cook, going out for wood. He heard the sticks being piled up, then the creak of the door again, and again the slow steps on the hard baked ground of the yard, æons apart. How did the peach tree look in the moonlight? Would its leaves be dark, or shiny? And the chinaberry tree? He thought of the two trees standing there motionless in the moonlight, and at last felt that he must get out of bed and look at them. But when he had reached the hall, he heard his mother's voice from downstairs, and he went and lay on the old sofa in the hall, listen-

ing. Could he have heard aright? His mother had just called his
father "Boy!" Amazing!

"It's two parties *every* week, and sometimes three or four, that's
excessive. You know it is."

"Darling, I *must* have *some* recreation!"

His father laughed in a peculiar angry way that he had never
heard before — as strange, indeed, as his mother's tone had been.

"Recreation's all right," he said, "but you're neglecting your
family. If it goes on, I'll have another child — that's all."

He got off the sofa and went softly down the stairs to the turn
of the railing. He peered over the banisters with infinite caution,
and what he saw filled him with horror. His mother was sitting on
his father's knee, with her arms about his neck. She was kissing
him. How awful! . . . He couldn't look at it. What on earth, he
wondered as he climbed back into bed, was it all about? There was
something curious in the way they were talking, something not at
all like fathers and mothers, but more like children, though he
couldn't in the least understand it. At the same time, it was offensive.

He began to make up a conversation with Caroline Lee. She was
sitting under the peach tree with him, reading her book. What
beautiful hands she had! They were transparent, somehow, like her
forehead, and her dark hair and large pale eyes delighted him. Perhaps she *was* an Egyptian!

"It must be nice to live in your house," he said.

"Yes, it's very nice. And you haven't seen half of it, either."

"No, I haven't. I'd like to see it all. I liked the hairy wallpaper
and the pink statue of the lady on the table. Are there any others
like it?"

"Oh, yes, lots and lots! In the secret room downstairs, where you
heard the silver clock striking, there are fifty other statues, all more
beautiful than that one, and a collection of clocks of every kind."

"Is your father very rich?"

"Yes, he's richer than anybody. He has a special carved ivory
box to keep his collars in."

"What does it feel like to die — were you sorry?"

"Very sorry! But it's really quite easy — you just hold your
breath and shut your eyes."

"Oh!"

"And when you're lying there, after you've died, you're really just pretending. You keep very still, and you have your eyes *almost* shut, but really you know everything! You watch the people and listen to them."

"But don't you want to talk to them, or get out of bed, or out of your coffin?"

"Well, yes, at first you do — but it's nicer than being alive."

"Why?"

"Oh, I don't know! You understand everything so easily!"

"How nice that must be!"

"It is."

"But after they've shut you up in a coffin and sung songs over you and carried you to Bonaventure and buried you in the ground, and you're down there in the dark with all that earth above you — isn't that horrible?"

"Oh, no! . . . As soon as nobody is looking, when they've all gone home to tea, you just get up and walk away. You climb out of the earth just as easily as you'd climb out of bed."

"That's how you're here now, I suppose."

"Of course!"

"Well, it's very nice."

"It's lovely. . . . Don't I look just as well as ever?"

"Yes, you do."

There was a pause, and then Caroline said:

"I know you wanted to steal my goldpiece — I was awfully glad when you put it back. If you had asked me for it, I'd have given it to you."

"I like you very much, Caroline. Can I come to Bonaventure and play with you?"

"I'm afraid not. You'd have to come in the dark."

"But I could bring a lantern."

"Yes, you could do that."

. . . It seemed to him that they were no longer sitting under the peach tree, but walking along the white shell-road to Bonaventure. He held the lantern up beside a chinquapin tree, and Caroline reached up with her pale, small hands and picked two chinquapins. Then they crossed the little bridge, walking carefully between the rails on the sleepers. Mossy trees were all about them; the moss, in long festoons, hung lower and lower, and thicker and thicker, and the wind made a soft, seething sound as it sought a way through the gray ancient forest.

IV

It had been his intention to explore, the next morning, the vault under the mulberry tree in the park — his friend Harry had mentioned that it was open, and that one could go down very dusty steps and see, on the dark floor, a few rotted boards and a bone or two. At breakfast he enlisted Mary and John for the expedition; but then there were unexpected developments. His father and mother had abruptly decided that the whole family would spend the day at Tybee Beach. This was festive and magnificent beyond belief. The kitchen became a turmoil. Selena ran to and fro with sugar sandwiches, pots of deviled ham, cookies, hard-boiled eggs, and a hundred other things; piles of beautiful sandwiches were exquisitely folded up in shining, clean napkins, and the wicker basket was elaborately packed. John and Mary decided to take their pails with them, and stamped up and downstairs, banging the pails with the shovels. He himself was a little uncertain what to take. He stood by his desk wondering. He would like to take Poe's tales, but that was out of the question, for he wasn't supposed to have the book at all. Marbles, also, were dismissed as unsuitable. He finally took his gold medal out of its drawer and put it in his pocket. He would keep it a secret, of course.

All the way to the station he was conscious of the medal burning in his pocket. He closed his fingers over it, and again felt it to be a live thing, as if it were buzzing, beating invisible wings. Would his fingers have a waxy smell, as they did after they'd been holding a June bug, or tying a thread to one of its legs? . . . Father carried the basket, Mary and John clanked their pails, everybody was talking and laughing. They climbed into the funny, undignified little train, which almost immediately was lurching over the wide, green marshes, rattling over red-iron bridges enormously complicated with girders and trusses. Great excitement when they passed the gray stone fort, Fort Pulaski. They'd seen it once from the river, when they were on the steamer going to the cotton islands. His father leaned down beside Mary to tell her about Fort

Pulaski, just as a cloud shadow, crossing it, made it somber. How nice his father's smile was! He had never noticed it before. It made him feel warm and shy. He looked out at the interminable green marshes, the flying clouds of rice-birds, the channels of red water lined with red mud, and listened intently to the strange complex rhythm of the wheels on the rails and the prolonged melancholy wail of the whistle. How curious it all was! His mother was sitting opposite him, very quiet, her gray eyes turned absently toward the window. She wasn't looking at things — she was thinking. If she had been looking at things, her eyes would have moved to and fro, as Mary's were doing.

"Mother," he said, "did you bring our bathing suits?"

"Yes, dear."

The train was rounding a curve and slowing down. They had suddenly left the marshes and were among low sand dunes covered with tall grass. He saw a man, very red-faced, just staggering over the top of one of the dunes and waving a stick. . . . It was hot. They filed slowly off the train and one by one jumped down into the burning sand. How strange it was to walk in! They laughed and shrieked, feeling themselves helpless, ran and jumped, straddled up the steep root-laced sides of dunes and slid down again in slow, warm avalanches of lazy sand. Mother and father, picking their way between the dunes, walked slowly ahead, carrying the basket between them — his father pointed at something. The sunlight came down heavily like sheets of solid brass and they could feel the heat of the sand on their cheeks. Then at last they came out on the enormous white dazzling beach with its millions of shells, its black-and-white-striped lighthouse, and the long, long sea, indolently blue, spreading out slow, soft lines of foam, and making an interminable rushing murmur like trees in a wind.

He felt instantly a desire, in all this space and light, to run for miles and miles. His mother and father sat under a striped parasol. Mary and John, now barefooted, had begun laborious and intense operations in the sand at the water's edge, making occasional sallies into the sliding water. He began walking away along the beach close to the waves, keeping his eye out for any particularly beautiful shell, and taking great care not to step on jellyfish. Suppose a school of flying fish, such as he had seen from the ship, should swim in close to the beach and then, by mistake, fly straight up onto the sand? How delightful that would be! It would be almost as exciting as finding buried treasure, a rotten chest full of gold-pieces and seaweed and sand. He had often dreamt of thrusting his hand into such a sea-chest and feeling the small, hard, beautiful coins mixed with sand and weed. Some people said that Captain Kidd had buried treasure on Tybee Beach. Perhaps he'd better walk a little closer to the dunes, where it was certainly more likely that treasure would have been hidden. . . . He climbed a hot dune, taking hold of the feathery grass, scraping his bare legs on the coarse leaves, and filling his shoes with warm sand. The dune was scooped at the top like a volcano, the hollow all ringed with tall, whistling grass, a natural hiding place, snug and secret. He lay down, made excessively smooth a hand's breadth of sand, then took the medal out of his pocket and placed it there. It blazed beautifully. Was it as nice as the five-dollar goldpiece would have been? He liked especially the tiny links of the little gold chains by which the shield hung from the pin-bar. If only Caroline could see it! Perhaps if he stayed here, hidden from the family, and waited till they had gone back home, Caroline would somehow know where he was and come to him as soon as it was dark. He wasn't quite sure what would be the shortest way from Bonaventure, but Caroline would know — certainly. Then they would spend the night here, talking. He would exchange his medal for the five-dollar goldpiece, and perhaps she would bring, folded in a square of silk, the little pink statue. . . . Thus equipped, their house would be perfect. . . . He would tell her about the goldfinch interrupting the Battle of Gettysburg.

v

The chief event of the afternoon was the burial of his father, who had on his bathing suit. He and Mary and John all excitedly labored at this. When they had got one leg covered, the other would suddenly burst hairily out, or an arm would shatter its mold, and his father would laugh uproariously. Finally they had him wholly buried, all except his head, in a beautiful smooth mound. On top of this they put the two pails, a lot of pink shells in a row, like the buttons of a coat, and a collection of seaweeds. Mother, lying under her parasol, laughed lazily, deliciously. For the first time during the day she seemed to be really happy. She began

pelting small shells at father, laughing in an odd, delightful, teasing
way, as if she was a girl, and father pretended to be furious. How
exactly like a new grave he looked! It was singularly as Caroline
had described it, for there he was all alive in it, and talking, and
able to get up whenever he liked. Mary and John, seeing mother
throw shells, and hearing her teasing laughter, and father's comic
rage, became suddenly excited. They began throwing things wildly
— shells, handfuls of seaweed, and at last sand. At this, father suddenly leapt out of his tomb, terrifying them, scattered his grave
clothes in every direction, and galloped gloriously down the beach
into the sea. The upturned brown soles of his feet followed him
casually into a long, curling green wave, and then his head came
up shaking like a dog's and blowing water, and his strong white
arms flashed slowly over and over in the sunlight as he swam far
out. How magnificent! . . . He would like to be able to do that,
to swim out and out and out, with a sea-gull flying close beside
him, talking.

Later, when they had changed into their clothes again in the
salty-smelling wooden bathhouse, they had supper on the veranda
of the huge hotel. A band played, the colored waiters bowed and
grinned. The sky turned pink, and began to dim; the sea darkened,
making a far sorrowful sound; and twilight deepened slowly, slowly
into night. The moon, which had looked like a white thin shell in
the afternoon, turned now to the brightest silver, and he thought,
as they walked silently toward the train, of which they could see
the long row of yellow windows, that the beach and dunes looked
more beautiful by moonlight than by sunlight. . . . How mysterious
the flooded marshes looked, too, with the cold moon above them!
They reminded him of something, he couldn't remember what. . . .
Mary and John fell asleep in the train; his father and mother were
silent. Someone in the car ahead was playing a concertina, and the
plaintive sound mingled curiously with the clacking of the rails,
the rattle of bridges, the long, lugubrious cry of the whistle. Hoo-o!
Hoo-o! Where was it they were going — was it to anything so
simple as home, the familiar house, the two familiar trees, or were
they, rather, speeding like a fiery comet toward the world's edge,
to plunge out into the unknown and fall down and down forever?

No, certainly it was not to the familiar. . . . Everything was
changed and ghostly. The long street, in the moonlight, was like
a deep river, at the bottom of which they walked, making scattered,

thin sounds on the stones, and listening intently to the whisperings of elms and palmettos. And their house, when at last they stopped before it, how strange it was! The moonlight, falling through the two tall swaying oaks, cast a moving pattern of shadow and light all over its face. Slow swirls and spirals of black and silver, dizzy gallops, quiet pools of light abruptly shattered, all silently followed the swishing of leaves against the moon. It was like a vine of moon-light, which suddenly grew all over the house, smothering every-thing with its multitudinous swift leaves and tendrils of pale silver, and then as suddenly faded out. He stared up at this while his father fitted the key into the lock, feeling the ghostly vine grow strangely over his face and hands. Was it in this, at last, that he would find the explanation of all that bewildered him? Caroline, no doubt, would understand it; she was a sort of moonlight herself. He went slowly up the stairs. But as he took the medal and a small pink shell out of his pocket, and put them on his desk, he realized at last that Caroline was dead.

KATHERINE ANNE PORTER

flowering judas

B raggioni sits heaped upon the edge of a straightbacked chair much too small for him, and sings to Laura in a furry, mournful voice. Laura has begun to find reasons for avoiding her own house until the latest possible moment, for Braggioni is there almost every night. No matter how late she is, he will be sitting there with a surly, waiting expression, pulling at his kinky yellow hair, thumbing the strings of his guitar, snarling a tune under his breath. Lupe the Indian maid meets Laura at the door, and says with a flicker of a glance towards the upper room, "He waits."

Laura wishes to lie down, she is tired of her hairpins and the feel of her long tight sleeves, but she says to him, "Have you a new song for me this evening?" If he says yes, she asks him to sing it. If he says no, she remembers his favorite one, and asks him to sing it again. Lupe brings her a cup of chocolate and a plate of rice, and Laura eats at the small table under the lamp, first inviting Braggioni, whose answer is always the same: "I have eaten, and besides, chocolate thickens the voice."

Laura says, "Sing, then," and Braggioni heaves himself into song. He scratches the guitar familiarly as though it were a pet animal, and sings passionately off key, taking the high notes in a prolonged painful squeal. Laura, who haunts the markets listening to the ballad singers, and stops every day to hear the blind boy playing his reed-flute in Sixteenth of September Street, listens to Braggioni with pitiless courtesy, because she dares not smile at his miserable performance. Nobody dares to smile at him. Braggioni is cruel to everyone, with a kind of specialized insolence, but he is so vain of his talents, and so sensitive to slights, it would require a cruelty and vanity greater than his own to lay a finger on the vast cureless wound of his self-esteem. It would require courage, too, for it is dangerous to offend him, and nobody has this courage.

Braggioni loves himself with such tenderness and amplitude and eternal charity that his followers — for he is a leader of men, a skilled revolutionist, and his skin has been punctured in honorable warfare — warm themselves in the reflected glow, and say to each other: "He has a real nobility, a love of humanity raised above mere personal affections." The excess of this self-love has flowed out, inconveniently for her, over Laura, who, with so many others, owes her comfortable situation and her salary to him. When he is in a very good humor, he tells her, "I am tempted to forgive you for being a *gringa. Gringita!*" and Laura, burning, imagines herself leaning forward suddenly, and with a sound back-handed slap wiping the suety smile from his face. If he notices her eyes at these moments he gives no sign.

She knows what Braggioni would offer her, and she must resist tenaciously without appearing to resist, and if she could avoid it she would not admit even to herself the slow drift of his intention. During these long evenings which have spoiled a long month for her, she sits in her deep chair with an open book on her knees, resting her eyes on the consoling rigidity of the printed page when the sight and sound of Braggioni singing threaten to identify themselves with all her remembered afflictions and to add their weight to her uneasy premonitions of the future. The gluttonous bulk of Braggioni has become a symbol of her many disillusions, for a revolutionist should be lean, animated by heroic faith, a vessel of abstract virtues. This is nonsense, she knows it now and is ashamed of it. Revolution must have leaders, and leadership is a career for energetic men. She is, her comrades tell her, full of romantic error, for what she defines as cynicism in them is merely "a developed sense of reality." She is almost too willing to say, "I am wrong, I suppose I don't really understand the principles," and afterward she makes a secret truce with herself, determined not to surrender her will to such expedient logic. But she cannot help feeling that she has been betrayed irreparably by the disunion between her way of living and her feeling of what life should be, and at times she is almost contented to rest in this sense of grievance as a private store of consolation. Sometimes she wishes to run away, but she stays. Now she longs to fly out of this room, down the narrow stairs, and into the street where the houses lean together like conspirators under a single mottled lamp, and leave Braggioni singing to himself.

Instead she looks at Braggioni, frankly and clearly, like a good child who understands the rules of behavior. Her knees cling together under sound blue serge, and her round white collar is not purposely nunlike. She wears the uniform of an idea, and has renounced vanities. She was born Roman Catholic, and in spite of her fear of being seen by someone who might make a scandal of it, she slips now and again into some crumbling little church, kneels on the chilly stone, and says a Hail Mary on the gold rosary she bought in Tehuantepec. It is no good and she ends by examining the altar with its tinsel flowers and ragged brocades, and feels tender about the battered doll-shape of some male saint whose white, lace-trimmed drawers hang limply around his ankles below the hieratic dignity of his velvet robe. She had encased herself in a set of principles derived from her early training, leaving no detail of gesture or of personal taste untouched, and for this reason she will not wear lace made on machines. This is her private heresy, for in her special group the machine is sacred, and will be the salvation of the workers. She loves fine lace, and there is a tiny edge of fluted cobweb on this collar, which is one of twenty precisely alike, folded in blue tissue paper in the upper drawer of her clothes chest.

Braggioni catches her glance solidly as if he had been waiting for it, leans forward, balancing his paunch between his spread knees, and sings with tremendous emphasis, weighing his words. He has, the song relates, no father and no mother, nor even a friend to console him; lonely as a wave of the sea he comes and goes, lonely as a wave. His mouth opens round and yearns sideways, his balloon cheeks grow oily with the labor of song. He bulges marvelously in his expensive garments. Over his lavender collar, crushed upon a purple necktie, held by a diamond hoop: over his ammunition belt of tooled leather worked in silver, buckled cruelly around his gasping middle: over the tops of his glossy yellow shoes Braggioni swells with ominous ripeness, his mauve silk hose stretched taut, his ankles bound with the stout leather thongs of his shoes.

When he stretches his eyelids at Laura she notes again that his eyes are the true tawny yellow cat's eyes. He is rich, not in money, he tells her, but in power, and this power brings with it the blameless ownership of things, and the right to indulge his love of small luxuries. "I have a taste for the elegant refinements," he said once, flourishing a yellow silk handkerchief before her nose. "Smell that? It is Jockey Club, imported from New York." Nonetheless he is wounded by life. He will say so presently. "It is true everything turns to dust in the hand, to gall on the tongue." He sighs and his leather belt creaks like a saddle girth. "I am disappointed in everything as it comes. Everything." He shakes his head. "You, poor thing, you will be disappointed too. You are born for it. We are more alike than you realize in some things. Wait and see. Some day you will remember what I have told you, you will know that Braggioni was your friend."

Laura feels a slow chill, a purely physical sense of danger, a warning in her blood that violence, mutilation, a shocking death, wait for her with lessening patience. She has translated this fear into something homely, immediate, and sometimes hesitates before crossing the street. "My personal fate is nothing, except as the testimony of a mental attitude," she reminds herself, quoting from some forgotten philosophic primer, and is sensible enough to add, "Anyhow, I shall not be killed by an automobile if I can help it."

"It may be true I am as corrupt, in another way, as Braggioni," she thinks in spite of herself, "as callous, as incomplete," and if this is so, any kind of death seems preferable. Still she sits quietly, she does not run. Where could she go? Uninvited she has promised herself to this place; she can no longer imagine herself as living in another country, and there is no pleasure in remembering her life before she came here.

Precisely what is the nature of this devotion, its true motives, and what are its obligations? Laura cannot say. She spends part of her days in Xochimilco, near by, teaching Indian children to say in English, "The cat is on the mat." When she appears in the classroom they crowd about her with smiles on their wise, innocent, clay-colored faces, crying, "Good morning, my ticher!" in immaculate voices, and they make of her desk a fresh garden of flowers every day.

During her leisure she goes to union meetings and listens to busy important voices quarreling over tactics, methods, internal politics. She visits the prisoners of her own political faith in their cells, where they entertain themselves with counting cockroaches, repenting on their indiscretions, composing their memoirs, writing out manifestoes and plans for their comrades who are still walking about free, hands in pockets, sniffing fresh air. Laura brings them food and cigarettes and a little money, and she brings messages disguised in equivocal phrases from the men outside who dare not set foot in the prison for fear of disappearing into the cells kept empty for them. If the prisoners confuse night and day, and complain, "Dear little Laura, time doesn't pass in this infernal hole, and I won't know when it is time to sleep unless I have a reminder," she brings them their favorite narcotics, and says in a tone that does not wound them with pity, "Tonight will really be night for you," and though her Spanish amuses them, they find her comforting, useful. If they lose patience and all faith, and curse the slowness of their friends in coming to their rescue with money and influence, they trust her not to repeat everything, and if she inquires, "Where do you think we can find money, or influence?" they are certain to answer, "Well, there is Braggioni, why doesn't he do something?"

She smuggles letters from headquarters to men hiding from firing squads in back streets in mildewed houses, where they sit in tumbled beds and talk bitterly as if all Mexico were at their heels, when Laura knows positively they might appear at the band concert in the Alameda on Sunday morning, and no one would notice them. But Braggioni says, "Let them sweat a little. The next time they may be careful. It is very restful to have them out of the way for a while." She is not afraid to knock on any door in any street after midnight, and enter in the darkness, and say to one of these men who is really in danger: "They will be looking for you — seriously

— tomorrow morning after six. Here is some money from Vicente. Go to Vera Cruz and wait."

She borrows money from the Roumanian agitator to give to his bitter enemy the Polish agitator. The favor of Braggioni is their disputed territory, and Braggioni holds the balance nicely, for he can use them both. The Polish agitator talks love to her over café tables, hoping to exploit what he believes is her secret sentimental preference for him, and he gives her misinformation which he begs her to repeat as the solemn truth to certain persons. The Roumanian is more adroit. He is generous with his money in all good causes, and lies to her with an air of ingenuous candor, as if he were her good friend and confidant. She never repeats anything they may say. Braggioni never asks questions. He has other ways to discover all that he wishes to know about them.

Nobody touches her, but all praise her gray eyes, and the soft, round under lip which promises gayety, yet is always grave, nearly always firmly closed: and they cannot understand why she is in Mexico. She walks back and forth on her errands, with puzzled eyebrows, carrying her little folder of drawings and music and school papers. No dancer dances more beautifully than Laura walks, and she inspires some amusing, unexpected ardors, which cause little gossip, because nothing comes of them. A young captain who had been a soldier in Zapata's army attempted, during a horseback ride near Cuernavaca, to express his desire for her with the noble simplicity befitting a rude folk-hero: but gently, because he was gentle. This gentleness was his defeat, for when he alighted, and removed her foot from the stirrup, and essayed to draw her down into his arms, her horse, ordinarily a tame one, shied fiercely, reared and plunged away. The young hero's horse careered blindly after his stable-mate, and the hero did not return to the hotel until rather late that evening. At breakfast he came to her table in full charro dress, gray buckskin jacket and trousers with strings of silver buttons down the leg, and he was in a humorous, careless mood. "May I sit with you?" and "You are a wonderful rider. I was terrified that you might be thrown and dragged. I should never have forgiven myself. But I cannot admire you enough for your riding!"

"I learned to ride in Arizona," said Laura.

"If you will ride with me again this morning, I promise you a horse that will not shy with you," he said. But Laura remembered that she must return to Mexico City at noon.

Next morning the children made a celebration and spent their playtime writing on the blackboard, "We lov ar ticher," and with tinted chalks they drew wreaths of flowers around the words. The young hero wrote her a letter: "I am a very foolish, wasteful, impulsive man. I should have first said I love you, and then you would not have run away. But you shall see me again." Laura thought, "I must send him a box of colored crayons," but she was trying to forgive herself for having spurred her horse at the wrong moment.

A brown, shock-haired youth came and stood in her patio one night and sang like a lost soul for two hours, but Laura could think of nothing to do about it. The moonlight spread a wash of gauzy silver over the clear spaces of the garden, and the shadows were cobalt blue. The scarlet blossoms of the Judas tree were dull purple, and the names of the colors repeated themselves automatically in her mind, while she watched not the boy, but his shadow, fallen like a dark garment across the fountain rim, trailing in the water. Lupe came silently and whispered expert counsel in her ear: "If you will throw him one little flower, he will sing another song or two and go away." Laura threw the flower, and he sang a last song and went away with the flower tucked in the band of his hat. Lupe said, "He is one of the organizers of the Typographers Union, and before that he sold corridos in the Merced market, and before that, he came from Guanajuato, where I was born. I would not trust any man, but I trust least those from Guanajuato."

She did not tell Laura that he would be back again the next night, and the next, nor that he would follow her at a certain fixed distance around the Merced market, through the Zócolo, up Francisco I. Madero Avenue, and so along the Paseo de la Reforma to Chapultepec Park, and into the Philosopher's Footpath, still with that flower withering in his hat, and an indivisible attention in his eyes.

Now Laura is accustomed to him, it means nothing except that he is nineteen years old and is observing a convention with all propriety, as though it were founded on a law of nature, which in the end it might well prove to be. He is beginning to write poems which he prints on a wooden press, and he leaves them stuck like handbills in her door. She is pleasantly disturbed by the abstract, unhurried watchfulness of his black eyes which will in time turn easily towards another object. She tells herself that throwing the flower was a mistake, for she is twenty-two years old and knows better; but she refuses to regret it, and persuades herself that her negation of all external events as they occur is a sign that she is gradually perfecting herself in the stoicism she strives to cultivate against that disaster she fears, though she cannot name it.

She is not at home in the world. Every day she teaches children who remain strangers to her, though she loves their tender round hands and their charming opportunist savagery. She knocks at unfamiliar doors not knowing whether a friend or a stranger shall answer, and even if a known face emerges from the sour gloom of that unknown interior, still it is the face of a stranger. No matter what this stranger says to her, nor what her message to him, the very cells of her flesh reject knowledge and kinship in one monotonous word. No. No. No. She draws her strength from this one holy talismanic word which does not suffer her to be led into evil. Denying everything, she may walk anywhere in safety, she looks at everything without amazement.

No, repeats this firm unchanging voice of her blood; and she looks at Braggioni without amazement. He is a great man, he wishes to impress this simple girl who covers her great round breasts with thick dark cloth, and who hides long, invaluably beautiful legs under a heavy skirt. She is almost thin except for the incomprehensible fullness of her breasts, like a nursing mother's, and Braggioni, who considers himself a judge of women, speculates again on the puzzle of her notorious virginity, and takes the liberty of speech which she permits without a sign of modesty, indeed, without any sort of sign, which is disconcerting.

"You think you are so cold, *gringita!* Wait and see. You will surprise yourself some day! May I be there to advise you!" He stretches his eyelids at her, and his ill-humored cat's eyes waver in a separate glance for the two points of light marking the opposite ends of a smoothly drawn path between the swollen curve of her breasts. He is not put off by that blue serge, nor by her resolutely fixed gaze. There is all the time in the world. His cheeks are bellying with the wind of song. "O girl with the dark eyes," he sings, and reconsiders. "But yours are not dark. I can change all that. O girl with the green eyes, you have stolen my heart away!" then his mind wanders to the song, and Laura feels the weight of his attention being shifted elsewhere. Singing thus, he seems harmless, he is quite harmless, there is nothing to do but sit patiently and say

"No," when the moment comes. She draws a full breath, and her mind wanders also, but not far. She dares not wander too far.

Not for nothing has Braggioni taken pains to be a good revolutionist and a professional lover of humanity. He will never die of it. He has the malice, the cleverness, the wickedness, the sharpness of wit, the hardness of heart, stipulated for loving the world profitably. *He will never die of it.* He will live to see himself kicked out from his feeding trough by other hungry world-saviors. Traditionally he must sing in spite of his life which drives him to bloodshed, he tells Laura, for his father was a Tuscany peasant who drifted to Yucatan and married a Maya woman: a woman of race, an aristocrat. They gave him the love and knowledge of music, thus: and under the rip of his thumbnail, the strings of the instrument complain like exposed nerves.

Once he was called Delgadito by all the girls and married women who ran after him; he was so scrawny all his bones showed under his thin cotton clothing, and he could squeeze his emptiness to the very backbone with his two hands. He was a poet and the revolution was only a dream then; too many women loved him and sapped away his youth, and he could never find enough to eat anywhere, anywhere! Now he is a leader of men, crafty men who whisper in his ear, hungry men who wait for hours outside his office for a word with him, emaciated men with wild faces who waylay him at the street gate with a timid, "Comrade, let me tell you . . ." and they blow the foul breath from their empty stomachs in his face.

He is always sympathetic. He gives them handfuls of small coins from his own pocket, he promises them work, there will be demonstrations, they must join the unions and attend the meetings, above all they must be on the watch for spies. They are closer to him than his own brothers, without them he can do nothing — until tomorrow, comrade!

Until tomorrow. "They are stupid, they are lazy, they are treacherous, they would cut my throat for nothing," he says to Laura. He has good food and abundant drink, he hires an automobile and drives in the Paseo on Sunday morning, and enjoys plenty of sleep in a soft bed beside a wife who dares not disturb him, and he sits pampering his bones in easy billows of fat, singing to Laura, who knows and thinks these things about him. When he was fifteen, he tried to drown himself because he loved a girl, his first love, and she laughed at him. "A thousand women have paid for that," and his tight little mouth turns down at the corners. Now he perfumes his hair with Jockey Club, and confides to Laura: "One woman is really as good as another for me, in the dark. I prefer them all."

His wife organizes unions among the girls in the cigarette factories, and walks in picket lines, and even speaks at meetings in the evening. But she cannot be brought to acknowledge the benefits of true liberty. "I tell her I must have my freedom, net. She does not understand my point of view." Laura has heard this many times. Braggioni scratches the guitar and meditates. "She is an instinctively virtuous woman, pure gold, no doubt of that. If she were not, I should lock her up, and she knows it."

His wife, who works so hard for the good of the factory girls, employs part of her leisure lying on the floor weeping because there are so many women in the world, and only one husband for her, and she never knows where nor when to look for him. He told her: "Unless you can learn to cry when I am not here, I must go away for good." That day he went away and took a room at the Hotel Madrid.

It is this month of separation for the sake of higher principles that has been spoiled not only for Mrs. Braggioni, whose sense of reality is beyond criticism, but for Laura, who feels herself bogged in a nightmare. Tonight Laura envies Mrs. Braggioni, who is alone, and free to weep as much as she pleases about a concrete wrong. Laura has just come from a visit to the prison, and she is waiting for tomorrow with a bitter anxiety as if tomorrow may not come, but time may be caught immovably in this hour, with herself transfixed, Braggioni singing on forever, and Eugenio's body not yet discovered by the guard.

Braggioni says: "Are you going to sleep?" Almost before she can shake her head, he begins telling her about the May-day disturbances coming on in Morelia, for the Catholics hold a festival in honor of the Blessed Virgin, and the Socialists celebrate their martyrs on that day. "There will be two independent processions, starting from either end of town, and they will march until they meet, and the rest depends . . ." He asks her to oil and load his pistols. Standing up, he unbuckles his ammunition belt, and spreads it laden across her knees. Laura sits with the shells slipping through the cleaning cloth dipped in oil, and he says again he cannot understand why she works so hard for the revolutionary idea unless she loves some man who is in it. "Are you not in love with someone?" "No,"

says Laura. "And no one is in love with you?" "No." "Then it is
your own fault. No woman need go begging. Why, what is the
matter with you? The legless beggar woman in the Alameda has a
perfectly faithful lover. Did you know that?"

Laura peers down the pistol barrel and says nothing, but a long,
slow faintness rises and subsides in her; Braggioni curves his swollen fingers around the throat of the guitar and softly smothers the
music out of it, and when she hears him again he seems to have forgotten her, and is speaking in the hypnotic voice he uses when talking in small rooms to a listening, close-gathered crowd. Some day
this world, now seemingly so composed and eternal to the edges of
every sea shall be merely a tangle of gaping trenches, of crashing
walls and broken bodies. Everything must be torn from its accustomed place where it has rotted for centuries, hurled skyward and
distributed, cast down again clean as rain, without separate identity.
Nothing shall survive that the stiffened hands of poverty have
created for the rich and no one shall be left alive except the elect
spirits destined to procreate a new world cleansed of cruelty and injustice, ruled by benevolent anarchy: "Pistols are good, I love them,
cannon are even better, but in the end I pin my faith to good dyna-
mite," he concludes, and strokes the pistol lying in her hands.
"Once I dreamed of destroying this city, in case it offered resistance to General Ortíz, but it fell into his hands like an overripe
pear."

He is made restless by his own words, rises and stands waiting.
Laura holds up the belt to him: "Put that on, and go kill somebody
in Morelia, and you will be happier," she says softly. The presence
of death in the room makes her bold. "Today, I found Eugenio going into a stupor. He refused to allow me to call the prison doctor.
He had taken all the tablets I brought him yesterday. He said he
took them because he was bored."

"He is a fool, and his death is his own business," says Braggioni,
fastening his belt carefully.

"I told him if he had waited only a little while longer, you would
have got him set free," says Laura. "He said he did not want to
wait."

"He is a fool and we are well rid of him," says Braggioni, reaching for his hat.

He goes away. Laura knows his mood has changed, she will not
see him any more for a while. He will send word when he needs

her to go on errands into strange streets, to speak to the strange faces that will appear, like clay masks with the power of human speech, to mutter their thanks to Braggioni for his help. Now she is free, and she thinks, I must run while there is time. But she does not go.

Braggioni enters his own house where for a month his wife has spent many hours every night weeping and tangling her hair upon her pillow. She is weeping now, and she weeps more at the sight of him, the cause of all her sorrows. He looks about the room. Nothing is changed, the smells are good and familiar, he is well acquainted with the woman who comes toward him with no reproach except grief on her face. He says to her tenderly: "You are so good, please don't cry any more, you dear good creature." She says, "Are you tired, my angel? Sit here and I will wash your feet." She brings a bowl of water, and kneeling, unlaces his shoes, and when from her knees she raises her sad eyes under her blackened lids, he is sorry for everything, and bursts into tears. "Ah, yes, I am hungry, I am tired, let us eat something together," he says, between sobs. His wife leans her head on his arm and says, "Forgive me!" and this time he is refreshed by the solemn, endless rain of her tears.

Laura takes off her serge dress and puts on a white linen nightgown and goes to bed. She turns her head a little to one side, and lying still, reminds herself that it is time to sleep. Numbers tick in her brain like little clocks, soundless doors close of themselves around her. If you would sleep, you must not remember anything, the children will say tomorrow, good morning, my teacher, the poor prisoners who come every day bringing flowers to their jailor. 1-2-3-4-5 it is monstrous to confuse love with revolution, night with day, life with death — ah, Eugenio!

The tolling of the midnight bell is a signal, but what does it mean? Get up, Laura, and follow me: come out of your sleep, out of your bed, out of this strange house. What are you doing in this house? Without a word, without fear she rose and reached for Eugenio's hand, but he eluded her with a sharp, sly smile and drifted away. This is not all, you shall see — Murderer, he said, follow me, I will show you a new country, but it is far away and we must hurry. No, said Laura, not unless you take my hand, no; and she clung first to the stair rail, and then to the topmost branch of the Judas tree that bent down slowly and set her upon the earth, and then to the rocky ledge of a cliff, and then to the jagged wave of sea that was not water but a desert of crumbling stone. Where are you taking me, she asked in wonder but without fear. To death, and it is a long way off, and we must hurry, said Eugenio. No, said Laura, not unless you take my hand. Then eat these flowers, poor prisoner, said Eugenio in a voice of pity, take and eat: and from the Judas tree he stripped the warm bleeding flowers, and held them to her lips. She saw that his hand was fleshless, a cluster of small white petrified branches, and his eye sockets were without light, but she ate the flowers greedily for they satisfied both hunger and thirst. Murderer! said Eugenio, and Cannibal! This is my body and my blood. Laura cried No! and at the sound of her own voice, she awoke trembling, and was afraid to sleep again.

JOSEPH CONRAD

the heart of darkness

The *Nellie*, a cruising yawl, swung to her anchor without a flutter of the sails, and was at rest. The flood had made, the wind was nearly calm, and being bound down the river, the only thing for it was to come to and wait for the turn of the tide.

The sea-reach of the Thames stretched before us like the beginning of an interminable waterway. In the offing the sea and the sky were welded together without a joint, and in the luminous space the tanned sails of the barges drifting up with the tide seemed to stand still in red clusters of canvas sharply peaked, with gleams of varnished sprits. A haze rested on the low shores that ran out to sea in vanishing flatness. The air was dark above Gravesend, and farther back still seemed condensed into a mournful gloom, brood-

"The Heart of Darkness" from *Youth; Heart of Darkness; and The End of the Tether* by Joseph Conrad, 1946. Reprinted by permission of J. M. Dent and Sons, Ltd.

ing motionless over the biggest, and the greatest, town on earth.

The Director of Companies was our captain and our host. We four affectionately watched his back as he stood in the bows looking to seaward. On the whole river there was nothing that looked half so nautical. He resembled a pilot, which to a seaman is trustworthiness personified. It was difficult to realize his work was not out there in the luminous estuary, but behind him, within the brooding gloom.

Between us there was, as I have already said somewhere, the bond of the sea. Besides holding our hearts together through long periods of separation, it had the effect of making us tolerant of each other's yarns — and even convictions. The Lawyer — the best of old fellows — had, because of his many years and many virtues, the only cushion on deck, and was lying on the only rug. The Accountant had brought out already a box of dominoes, and was toying architecturally with the bones. Marlow sat cross-legged right aft, leaning against the mizzen-mast. He had sunken cheeks, a yellow complexion, a straight back, and ascetic aspect, and, with his arms dropped, the palms of hands outwards, resembled an idol. The director, satisfied the anchor had good hold, made his way aft and sat down amongst us. We exchanged a few words lazily. Afterwards there was silence on board the yacht. For some reason or other we did not begin that game of dominoes. We felt meditative, and fit for nothing but placid staring. The day was ending in a serenity of still and exquisite brilliance. The water shone pacifically; the sky, without a speck, was a benign immensity of unstained light; the very mist on the Essex marshes was like a gauzy and radiant fabric, hung from the wooded rises inland, and draping the low shores in diaphanous folds. Only the gloom to the west, brooding over the upper reaches, became more somber every minute, as if angered by the approach of the sun.

And at last, in its curved and imperceptible fall, the sun sank low, and from glowing white changed to a dull red without rays and without heat, as if about to go out suddenly, stricken to death by the touch of that gloom brooding over a crowd of men.

Forthwith a change came over the waters, and the serenity became less brilliant but more profound. The old river in its broad reach rested unruffled at the decline of day, after ages of good service done to the race that peopled its banks, spread out in the tranquil dignity of a waterway leading to the uttermost ends of the earth. We looked at the venerable stream not in the vivid flush of a short day that comes and departs forever, but in the august light of abiding memories. And indeed nothing is easier for a man who has, as the phrase goes, "followed the sea" with reverence and affection, than to evoke the great spirit of the past upon the lower reaches of the Thames. The tidal current runs to and fro in its unceasing service, crowded with memories of men and ships it had borne to the rest of home or to the battles of the sea. It had known and served all the men of whom the nation is proud, from Sir Francis Drake to Sir John Franklin, knights all, titled and untitled — the knights-errant of the sea. It had borne all the ships whose names are like jewels flashing in the night of time, from the *Golden Hind* returning with her round flanks full of treasure, to be visited by the Queen's Highness and thus pass out of the gigantic tale, to the *Erebus* and *Terror*, bound on other conquests — and that never returned. It had known the ships and the men. They had sailed from Deptford, from Greenwich, from Erith — the adventurers and the settlers; kings' ships and the ships of men on 'Change; captains, admirals, the dark "interlopers" of the Eastern trade, and the commissioned "generals" of East India fleets. Hunters for gold or pursuers of fame, they all had gone out on that stream, bearing the sword, and often the torch, messengers of the might within the land, bearers of a spark from the sacred fire. What greatness had not floated on the ebb of that river into the mystery of an unknown earth! . . . The dreams of men, the seed of commonwealths, the germs of empires.

The sun set; the dusk fell on the stream, and lights began to appear along the shore. The Chapman lighthouse, a three-legged thing erect on a mud-flat, shone strongly. Lights of ships moved in the fairway — a great stir of lights going up and going down. And farther west on the upper reaches the place of the monstrous town was still marked ominously on the sky, a brooding gloom in sunshine, a lurid glare under the stars.

"And this also," said Marlow suddenly, "has been one of the dark places on the earth."

He was the only man of us who still "followed the sea." The worst that could be said of him was that he did not represent his class. He was a seaman, but he was a wanderer, too, while most seamen lead, if one may so express it, a sedentary life. Their minds are of the stay-at-home order, and their home is always with them

— the ship; and so is their country — the sea. One ship is very much like another, and the sea is always the same. In the immutability of their surroundings the foreign shores, the foreign faces, the changing immensity of life, glide past, veiled not by a sense of mystery but by a slightly disdainful ignorance; for there is nothing mysterious to a seaman unless it be the sea itself, which is the mistress of his existence and as inscrutable as Destiny. For the rest, after his hours of work, a casual stroll or a casual spree on shore suffices to unfold for him the secret of a whole continent, and generally he finds the secret not worth knowing. The yarns of seamen have a direct simplicity, the whole meaning of which lies within the shell of a cracked nut. But Marlow was not typical (if his propensity to spin yarns be excepted), and to him the meaning of an episode was not inside like a kernel but outside, enveloping the tale which brought it out only as a glow brings out a haze, in the likeness of one of these misty halos that sometimes are made visible by the spectral illumination of moonshine.

His remark did not seem at all surprising. It was just like Marlow. It was accepted in silence. No one took the trouble to grunt even; and presently he said, very slow —

"I was thinking of very old times, when the Romans first came here, nineteen hundred years ago — the other day. . . . Light came out of this river since — you say Knights? Yes; but it is like a running blaze on a plain, like a flash of lightning in the clouds. We live in the flicker — may it last as long as the old earth keeps rolling! But darkness was here yesterday. Imagine the feelings of a commander of a fine — what d'ye call 'em? — trireme in the Mediterranean, ordered suddenly to the north; run overland across the Gauls in a hurry; put in charge of one of these craft the legionaries — a wonderful lot of handy men they must have been, too — used to build, apparently by the hundred, in a month or two, if we may believe what we read. Imagine him here — the very end of the world, a sea the color of lead, a sky the color of smoke, a kind of ship about as rigid as a concertina — and going up this river with stores, or orders, or what you like. Sand-banks, marshes, forests, savages, — precious little to eat fit for a civilized man, nothing but Thames water to drink. No Falernian wine here, no going ashore. Here and there a military camp lost in a wilderness, like a needle in a bundle of hay — cold, fog, tempests, disease, exile, and death, — death skulking in the air, in the water, in the bush. They must have been dying like flies here. Oh, yes — he did it. Did it very well, too, no doubt, and without thinking much about it either, except afterwards to brag of what he had gone through in his time, perhaps. They were men enough to face the darkness. And perhaps he was cheered by keeping his eye on a chance of promotion to the fleet at Ravenna by and by, if he had good friends in Rome and survived the awful climate. Or think of a decent young citizen in a toga — perhaps too much dice, you know — coming out here in the train of some prefect, or tax-gatherer, or trader even, to mend his fortunes. Land in a swamp, march through the woods, and in some inland post feel the savagery, the utter savagery, had closed round him, — all that mysterious life of the wilderness that stirs in the forest, in the jungles, in the hearts of wild men. There's no initiation either into such mysteries. He has to live in the midst of the incomprehensible, which is also detestable. And it has a fascination, too, that goes to work upon him. The fascination of the abomination — you know, imagine the growing regrets, the longing to escape, the powerless disgust, the surrender, the hate."

He paused.

"Mind," he began again, lifting one arm from the elbow, the palm of the hand outwards, so that, with his legs folded before him, he had the pose of a Buddha preaching in European clothes and without a lotus-flower — "Mind, none of us would feel exactly like this. What saves us is efficiency — the devotion to efficiency. But these chaps were not much account, really. They were no colonists; their administration was merely a squeeze, and nothing more, I suspect. They were conquerors, and for that you want only brute force — nothing to boast of, when you have it, since your strength is just an accident arising from the weakness of others. They grabbed what they could get for the sake of what was to be got. It was just robbery with violence, aggravated murder on a great scale, and men going at it blind — as is very proper for those who tackle a darkness. The conquest of the earth, which mostly means the taking it away from those who have a different complexion or slightly flatter noses than ourselves, is not a pretty thing when you look into it too much. What redeems it is the idea only. An idea at the back of it; not a sentimental pretense but an idea; and an unselfish belief in the idea — something you can set up, and bow down before, and offer a sacrifice to. . . ."

He broke off. Flames glided in the river, small green flames, red flames, white flames, pursuing, overtaking, joining, crossing each other — then separating slowly or hastily. The traffic of the great city went on in the deepening night upon the sleepless river. We looked on, waiting patiently — there was nothing else to do till the end of the flood; but it was only after a long silence, when he said, in a hesitating voice, "I suppose you fellows remember I did once turn fresh-water sailor for a bit," that we knew we were fated, before the ebb began to run, to hear one of Marlow's inconclusive experiences.

"I don't want to bother you much with what happened to me personally," he began, showing in this remark the weakness of many tellers of tales who seem so often unaware of what their audience would best like to hear; "yet to understand the effect of it on me you ought to know how I got out there, what I saw, how I went up that river to the place where I first met the poor chap. It was the farthest point of navigation and the culminating point of my experience. It seemed somehow to throw a kind of light on everything about me — and into my thoughts. It was somber enough, too — and pitiful — not extraordinary in any way — not very clear either. No, not very clear. And yet it seemed to throw a kind of light.

"I had then, as you remember, just returned to London after a lot of Indian Ocean, Pacific, China Seas — a regular dose of the East — six years or so, and I was loafing about, hindering you fellows in your work and invading your homes, just as though I had got a heavenly mission to civilize you. It was very fine for a time, but after a bit I did get tired of resting. Then I began to look for a ship — I should think the hardest work on earth. But the ships wouldn't even look at me. And I got tired of that game, too.

"Now when I was a little chap I had a passion for maps. I would look for hours at South America, or Africa, or Australia, and lose myself in all the glories of exploration. At that time there were many blank spaces on the earth, and when I saw one that looked particularly inviting on a map (but they all look that) I would put my finger on it and say, 'When I grow up I will go there.' The North Pole was one of these places, I remember. Well, I haven't been there yet, and shall not try now. The glamour's off. Other places were scattered about the Equator, and in every sort of latitude all over the two hemispheres. I have been in some of them, and . . . well, we won't talk about that. But there was one yet — the biggest, the most blank, so to speak — that I had a hankering after.

"True, by this time it was not a blank space any more. It had got filled since my childhood with rivers and lakes and names. It had ceased to be a blank space of delightful mystery — a white patch for a boy to dream gloriously over. It had become a place of darkness. But there was in it one river especially, a mighty big river, that you could see on the map, resembling an immense snake uncoiled, with its head in the sea, its body at rest curving afar over a vast country, and its tail lost in the depths of the land. And as I looked at the map of it in a shop-window, it fascinated me as a snake would a bird — a silly little bird. Then I remembered there was a big concern, a Company for trade on that river. Dash it all! I thought to myself, they can't trade without using some kind of craft on that lot of fresh water — steamboats! Why shouldn't I try to get charge of one? I went on along Fleet Street, but could not shake off the idea. The snake had charmed me.

"You understand it was a Continental concern, that Trading society; but I have a lot of relations living on the Continent, because it's cheap and not so nasty as it looks, they say.

"I am sorry to own I began to worry them. This was already a fresh departure for me. I was not used to getting things that way, you know. I always went my own road and on my own legs where I had a mind to go. I wouldn't have believed it of myself; but, then — you see — I felt somehow I must get there by hook or by crook. So I worried them. The men said 'My dear fellow,' and did nothing. Then — would you believe it? — I tried the women. I, Charlie Marlow, set the women to work — to get a job. Heavens! Well, you see, the notion drove me. I had an aunt, a dear enthusiastic soul. She wrote: 'It will be delightful. I am ready to do anything, anything for you. It is a glorious idea. I know the wife of a very high personage in the Administration, and also a man who has lots of influence with,' etc., etc. She was determined to make no end of fuss to get me appointed skipper of a river steamboat, if such was my fancy.

"I got my appointment — of course; and I got it very quick. It appears the Company had received news that one of their captains had been killed in a scuffle with the natives. This was my chance, and it made me the more anxious to go. It was only months and months afterwards, when I made the attempt to recover what was left of the body, that I heard the original quarrel arose from a mis-

understanding about some hens. Yes, two black hens. Fresleven —
that was the fellow's name, a Dane — thought himself wronged
somehow in the bargain, so he went ashore and started to hammer
the chief of the village with a stick. Oh, it didn't surprise me in the
least to hear this, and at the same time to be told that Fresleven
was the gentlest, quietest creature that ever walked on two legs. No
doubt he was; but he had been a couple of years already out there
engaged in the noble cause, you know, and he probably felt the
need at last of asserting his self-respect in some way. Therefore he
whacked the old nigger mercilessly, while a big crowd of his people watched him, thunderstruck, till some man — I was told the
chief's son — in desperation at hearing the old chap yell, made a
tentative jab with a spear at the white man — and of course it
went quite easy between the shoulder blades. Then the whole population cleared into the forest, expecting all kinds of calamities to
happen, while, on the other hand, the steamer Fresleven commanded
left also in a bad panic, in charge of the engineer, I believe. Afterwards nobody seemed to trouble much about Fresleven's remains,
till I got out and stepped into his shoes. I couldn't let it rest, though;
but when an opportunity offered at last to meet my predecessor, the
grass growing through his ribs was tall enough to hide his bones.
They were all there. The supernatural being had not been touched
after he fell. And the village was deserted, the huts gaped black,
rotting, all askew within the fallen enclosures. A calamity had come
to it, sure enough. The people had vanished. Mad terror had scattered them, men, women, and children, through the bush, and they
had never returned. What became of the hens I don't know either.
I should think the cause of progress got them, anyhow. However,
through this glorious affair I got my appointment, before I had
fairly begun to hope for it.

"I flew around like mad to get ready, and before forty-eight
hours I was crossing the Channel to show myself to my employ-
ers, and sign the contract. In a very few hours I arrived in a city
that always makes me think of a whited sepulcher. Prejudice no
doubt. I had no difficulty in finding the Company's offices. It was
the biggest thing in the town, and everybody I met was full of it.
They were going to run an over-sea empire, and make no end of
coin by trade.

"A narrow and deserted street in deep shadow, high houses, innumerable windows with venetian blinds, a dead silence, grass

sprouting between the stones, imposing carriage archways right and left, immense double doors standing ponderously ajar. I slipped through one of these cracks, went up a swept and ungarnished staircase, as arid as a desert, and opened the first door I came to. Two women, one fat and the other slim, sat on straw-bottomed chairs, knitting black wool. The slim one got up and walked straight at me — still knitting with downcast eyes — and only just as I began to think of getting out of her way, as you would for a somnambulist, stood still, and looked up. Her dress was as plain as an umbrella-cover, and she turned round without a word and preceded me into a waiting-room. I gave my name, and looked about. Deal table in the middle, plain chairs all around the walls, on one end a large shining map, marked with all the colors of a rainbow. There was a vast amount of red — good to see at any time, because one knows that some real work is done in there, a deuce of a lot of blue, a little green, smears of orange, and, on the East Coast, a purple patch, to show where the jolly pioneers of progress drink the jolly lager-beer. However, I wasn't going into any of these. I was going into the yellow. Dead in the center. And the river was there — fascinating — deadly — like a snake. Ough! A door opened, a white-haired secretarial head, but wearing a compassionate expression, appeared, and a skinny forefinger beckoned me into the sanctuary. Its light was dim, and a heavy writing-desk squatted in the middle. From behind that structure came out an impression of pale plumpness in a frock-coat. The great man himself. He was five feet six, I should judge, and had his grip on the handle-end of ever so many millions. He shook hands, I fancy, murmured vaguely, was satisfied with my French. *Bon voyage.*

"In about forty-five seconds I found myself again in the waiting-room with the compassionate secretary, who, full of desolation and sympathy, made me sign some document. I believe I undertook amongst other things not to disclose any trade secrets. Well, I am not going to.

"I began to feel slightly uneasy. You know I am not used to such ceremonies, and there was something ominous in the atmosphere. It was just as though I had been let into some conspiracy — I don't know — something not quite right; and I was glad to get out. In the outer room the two women knitted black wool feverishly. People were arriving, and the younger one was walking back and forth introducing them. The old one sat on her chair. Her flat

cloth slippers were propped up on a foot-warmer, and a cat reposed on her lap. She wore a starched white affair on her head,
had a wart on one cheek, and silver-rimmed spectacles hung on the
tip of her nose. She glanced at me above the glasses. The swift and
indifferent placidity of that look troubled me. Two youths with
foolish and cheery countenances were being piloted over, and she
threw at them the same quick glance of unconcerned wisdom. She
seemed to know all about them and about me, too. An eerie feeling came over me. She seemed uncanny and fateful. Often far
away there I thought of these two, guarding the door of Darkness,
knitting black wool as for a warm pall, one introducing, introducing
continuously to the unknown, the other scrutinizing the cheery and
foolish faces with unconcerned old eyes. *Ave!* Old knitter of black
wool. *Morituri te salutant.* Not many of those she looked at ever
saw her again — not half, by a long way.

"There was yet a visit to the doctor. 'A simple formality,' assured me the secretary, with an air of taking an immense part in all
my sorrows. Accordingly a young chap wearing his hat over the
left eyebrow, some clerk I suppose, — there must have been clerks
in the business, though the house was as still as a house in a city of
the dead — came from somewhere upstairs and led me forth. He
was shabby and careless, with inkstains on the sleeves of his jacket,
and his cravat was large and billowy, under a chin shaped like the
toe of an old boot. It was a little too early for the doctor, so I
proposed a drink, and thereupon he developed a vein of joviality. As
we sat over our vermouths he glorified the Company's business, and
by and by I expressed casually my surprise at him not going out
there. He became very cool and collected all at once. 'I am not
such a fool as I look, quoth Plato to his disciples,' he said senten-
tiously, emptied his glass with great resolution, and we rose.

"The old doctor felt my pulse, evidently thinking of something
else the while. 'Good, good for there,' he mumbled, and then with
a certain eagerness asked me whether I would let him measure my
head. Rather surprised, I said 'Yes,' when he produced a thing like
calipers and got the dimensions back and front and every way,
taking notes carefully. He was an unshaven little man in a thread-
bare coat like a gaberdine, with his feet in slippers, and I thought
him a harmless fool. 'I always ask leave, in the interests of science,
to measure the crania of those going out there,' he said. 'And when
they come back, too?' I asked. 'Oh, I never see them,' he remarked;

'and, moreover, the changes take place inside, you know.' He smiled, as if at some quiet joke. 'So you are going out there. Famous. Interesting, too.' He gave me a searching glance, and made another note. 'Ever any madness in your family?' he asked, in a matter-of-fact tone. I felt very annoyed. 'Is that question in the interests of science, too?' 'It would be,' he said, without taking notice of my irritation, 'interesting for science to watch the mental changes of individuals, on the spot, but . . .' 'Are you an alienist?' I interrupted. 'Every doctor should be — a little,' answered that original, imperturbably. 'I have a little theory which you Messieurs who go out there must help me to prove. This is my share in the advantages my country shall reap from the possession of such a magnificent dependency. The mere wealth I leave to others. Pardon my questions, but you are the first Englishman coming under my observation . . .' I hastened to assure him I was not in the least typical. 'If I were,' said I, 'I wouldn't be talking like this with you.' 'What you say is rather profound, and probably erroneous,' he said, with a laugh. 'Avoid irritation more than exposure to the sun. Adieu. How do you English say, eh? Good-by. Ah! Good-by. Adieu. In the tropics one must before everything keep calm.' . . . He lifted a warning forefinger. . . . '*Du calme, du calme. Adieu.*'

"One thing more remained to do — say good-by to my excellent aunt. I found her triumphant. I had a cup of tea — the last decent cup of tea for many days — and in a room that most soothingly looked just as you would expect a lady's drawing-room to look, we had a long quiet chat by the fireside. In the course of these confidences it became quite plain to me I had been represented to the wife of the high dignitary, and goodness knows to how many more people besides, as an exceptional and gifted creature — a piece of good fortune for the Company — a man you don't get hold of every day. Good heavens! and I was going to take charge of a two-penny-half-penny river-steamboat with a penny whistle attached! It appeared, however, I was also one of the Workers, with a capital — you know. Something like an emissary of light, something like a lower sort of apostle. There had been a lot of such rot let loose in print and talk just about that time, and the excellent woman, living right in the rush of all that humbug, got carried off her feet. She talked about 'weaning those ignorant millions from their horrid ways,' till, upon my word, she made me quite uncomfortable. I ventured to hint that the Company was run for profit.

" 'You forget, dear Charlie, that the laborer is worthy of his hire,' she said, brightly. It's queer how out of touch with truth women are. They live in a world of their own, and there has never been anything like it, and never can be. It is too beautiful altogether, and if they were to set it up it would go to pieces before the first sunset. Some confounded fact we men have been living contentedly with ever since the day of creation would start up and knock the whole thing over.

"After this I got embraced, told to wear flannel, be sure to write often, and so on — and I left. In the street — I don't know why — a queer feeling came to me that I was an impostor. Odd thing that I, who used to clear out for any part of the world at twenty-four hours' notice, with less thought than most men give to the crossing of a street, had a moment — I won't say of hesitation, but of startled pause, before this commonplace affair. The best way I can explain it to you is by saying that, for a second or two, I felt as though, instead of going to the center of a continent, I were about to set off for the center of the earth.

"I left in a French steamer, and she called in every blamed port they have out there, for, as far as I could see, the sole purpose of landing soldiers and custom-house officers. I watched the coast. Watching a coast as it slips by the ship is like thinking about an enigma. There it is before you — smiling, frowning, inviting, grand, mean, insipid, or savage, and always mute with an air of whispering, Come and find out. This one was almost featureless, as if still in the making, with an aspect of monotonous grimness. The edge of a colossal jungle, so dark-green as to be almost black, fringed with white surf, ran straight, like a ruled line, far, far away along a blue sea whose glitter was blurred by a creeping mist. The sun was fierce, the land seemed to glisten and drip with steam. Here and there grayish-whitish specks showed up clustered inside the white surf, with a flag flying above them perhaps. Settlements some centuries old, and still no bigger than pinheads on the untouched expanse of their background. We pounded along, stopped, landed soldiers; went on, landed custom-house clerks to levy toll in what looked like a God-forsaken wilderness, with a tin shed and a flagpole lost in it; landed more soldiers — to take care of the custom-house clerks, presumably. Some, I heard, got drowned in the surf; but whether they did or not, nobody seemed particularly to care. They were just flung out there, and on we went. Every day the coast looked the same, as though we had not moved; but we passed various places — trading places — with names like Gran' Bassam, Little Popo; names that seemed to belong to some sordid farce acted in front of a sinister back-cloth. The idleness of a passenger, my isolation amongst all these men with whom I had no point of contact, the oily and languid sea, the uniform somberness of the coast, seemed to keep me away from the truth of things, within the toil of a mournful and senseless delusion. The voice of the surf heard now and then was a positive pleasure, like the speech of a brother. It was something natural, that had its reason, that had a meaning. Now and then a boat from the shore gave one a momentary contact with reality. It was paddled by black fellows. You could see from afar the white of their eyeballs glistening. They shouted, sang; their bodies streamed with perspiration; they had faces like grotesque masks — these chaps; but they had bone, muscle, a wild vitality, an intense energy of movement, that was as natural and true as the surf along their coast. They wanted no excuse for being there. They were a great comfort to look at. For a time I would feel I belonged still to a world of straightforward facts; but the feeling would not last long. Something would turn up to scare it away. Once, I remember, we came upon a man-of-war anchored off the coast. There wasn't even a shed there, and she was shelling the bush. It appears the French had one of their wars going on thereabouts. Her ensign dropped limp like a rag; the muzzles of the long six-inch guns stuck out all over the low hull; the greasy, slimy swell swung her up lazily and let her down, swaying her thin masts. In the empty immensity of earth, sky, and water, there she was, incomprehensible, firing into a continent. Pop, would go one of the six-inch guns; a small flame would dart and vanish, a little white smoke would disappear, a tiny projectile would give a feeble screech — and nothing happened. Nothing could happen. There was a touch of insanity in the proceeding, a sense of lugubrious drollery in the sight; and it was not dissipated by somebody on board assuring me earnestly there was a camp of natives — he called them enemies! — hidden out of sight somewhere.

"We gave her her letters (I heard the men in that lonely ship were dying of fever at the rate of three a day) and went on. We called at some more places with farcical names, where the merry dance of death and trade goes on in a still and earthy atmosphere as of an overheated catacomb; all along the formless coast bordered

by dangerous surf, as if Nature herself had tried to ward off intruders; in and out of rivers, streams of death in life, whose banks
were rotting into mud, whose waters, thickened into slime, invaded
the contorted mangroves, that seemed to writhe at us in the extremity of an impotent despair. Nowhere did we stop long enough
to get a particularized impression, but the general sense of vague
and oppressive wonder grew upon me. It was like a weary pilgrimage amongst hints for nightmares.

"It was upward of thirty days before I saw the mouth of the
big river. We anchored off the seat of the government. But my
work would not begin till some two hundred miles farther on. So
as soon as I could I made a start for a place thirty miles higher up.

"I had my passage on a little sea-going steamer. Her captain was
a Swede, and knowing me for a seaman, invited me on the bridge.
He was a young man, lean, fair, and morose, with lanky hair and
a shuffling gait. As we left the miserable little wharf, he tossed his
head contemptuously at the shore. 'Been living there?' he asked.
I said, 'Yes.' 'Fine lot these government chaps — are they not?' he
went on, speaking English with great precision and considerable
bitterness. 'It is funny what some people will do for a few francs
a month. I wonder what becomes of that kind when it goes up-
country?' I said to him I expected to see that soon. 'So-o-o!' he exclaimed. He shuffled athwart, keeping one eye ahead vigilantly.
'Don't be too sure,' he continued. 'The other day I took up a man
who hanged himself on the road. He was a Swede, too.' 'Hanged
himself! Why, in God's name?' I cried. He kept on looking out
watchfully. 'Who knows? The sun was too much for him, or the
country perhaps.'

"At last we opened a reach. A rocky cliff appeared, mounds of
turned-up earth by the shore, houses on a hill, others with iron
roofs, amongst a waste of excavations, or hanging to the declivity.
A continuous noise of the rapids above hovered over this scene of
inhabited devastation. A lot of people, mostly black and naked,
moved about like ants. A jetty projected into the river. A blinding
sunlight drowned all this at times in a sudden recrudescence of glare.
'There's your Company's station,' said the Swede, pointing to three
wooden barrack-like structures on the rocky slope. 'I will send
your things up. Four boxes did you say? So. Farewell.'

"I came upon a boiler wallowing in the grass, then found a path
leading up the hill. It turned aside for the boulders, and also for an

undersized railway-truck lying there on its back with its wheels in the air. One was off. The thing looked as dead as the carcass of some animal. I came upon more pieces of decaying machinery, a stack of rusty rails. To the left a clump of trees made a shady spot, where dark things seemed to stir feebly. I blinked, the path was steep. A horn tooted to the right, and I saw the black people run. A heavy and dull detonation shook the ground, a puff of smoke came out of the cliff, and that was all. No change appeared on the face of the rock. They were building a railway. The cliff was not in the way or anything; but this objectless blasting was all the work going on.

"A slight clinking behind me made me turn my head. Six black men advanced in a file, toiling up the path. They walked erect and slow, balancing small baskets full of earth on their heads, and the clink kept time with their footsteps. Black rags were wound round their loins, and the short ends behind waggled to and fro like tails. I could see every rib, the joints of their limbs were like knots in a rope; each had an iron collar on his neck, and all were connected together with a chain whose bights swung between them, rhythmically clinking. Another report from the cliff made me think suddenly of that ship of war I had seen firing into a continent. It was the same kind of ominous voice; but these men could by no stretch of imagination be called enemies. They were called criminals, and the outraged law, like the bursting shells, had come to them, an insoluble mystery from the sea. All their meager breasts panted together, the violently dilated nostrils quivered, the eyes stared stonily up-hill. They passed me within six inches, without a glance, with that complete, deathlike indifference of unhappy savages. Behind this raw matter one of the reclaimed, the product of the new forces at work, strolled despondently, carrying a rifle by its middle. He had a uniform jacket with one button off, and seeing a white man on the path, hoisted his weapon to his shoulder with alacrity. This was simple prudence, white men being so much alike at a distance that he could not tell who I might be. He was speedily reassured, and with a large, white, rascally grin, and a glance at his charge, seemed to take me into partnership in his exalted trust. After all, I also was a part of the great cause of these high and just proceedings.

"Instead of going up, I turned and descended to the left. My idea was to let that chain-gang get out of sight before I climbed the hill. You know I am not particularly tender; I've had to strike and to fend off. I've had to resist and to attack sometimes — that's only one way of resisting — without counting the exact cost, according to the demands of such sort of life as I had blundered into. I've seen the devil of violence, and the devil of greed, and the devil of hot desire; but, by all the stars! these were strong, lusty, red-eyed devils, that swayed and drove men — men, I tell you. But as I stood on this hillside, I foresaw that in the blinding sunshine of that land I would become acquainted with a flabby, pretending, weak-eyed devil of a rapacious and pitiless folly. How insidious he could be, too, I was only to find out several months later and a thousand miles farther. For a moment I stood appalled, as though by a warning. Finally I descended the hill, obliquely, towards the trees I had seen.

"I avoided a vast artificial hole somebody had been digging on the slope, the purpose of which I found it impossible to divine. It wasn't a quarry or a sandpit, anyhow. It was just a hole. It might have been connected with the philanthropic desire of giving the criminals something to do. I don't know. Then I nearly fell into a very narrow ravine, almost no more than a scar in the hillside. I discovered that a lot of imported drainage-pipes for the settlement had been tumbled in there. There wasn't one that was not broken. It was a wanton smash-up. At last I got under the trees. My purpose was to stroll into the shade for a moment; but no sooner within than it seemed to me I had stepped into the gloomy circle of some Inferno. The rapids were near, and an uninterrupted, uniform, headlong, rushing noise filled the mournful stillness of the grove, where not a breath stirred, not a leaf moved, with a mysterious sound — as though the tearing pace of the launched earth had suddenly become audible.

"Black shapes crouched, lay, sat between the trees leaning against the trunks, clinging to the earth, half coming out, half effaced within the dim light, in all the attitudes of pain, abandonment, and despair. Another mine on the cliff went off, followed by a slight shudder of the soil under my feet. The work was going on. The work! And this was the place where some of the helpers had withdrawn to die.

"They were dying slowly — it was very clear. They were not enemies, they were not criminals, they were nothing earthly now, — nothing but black shadows of disease and starvation, lying confusedly in the greenish gloom. Brought from all the recesses of the coast in all the legality of time contracts, lost in uncongenial surroundings, fed on unfamiliar food, they sickened, became inefficient, and were then allowed to crawl away and rest. These moribund shapes were free as air — and nearly as thin. I began to distinguish the gleam of the eyes under the trees. Then, glancing down, I saw a face near my hand. The black bones reclined at full length with one shoulder against the tree, and slowly the eyelids rose and the sunken eyes looked up at me, enormous and vacant, a kind of blind, white flicker in the depths of the orbs, which died out slowly. The man seemed young — almost a boy — but you know with them it's hard to tell. I found nothing else to do but to offer him one of my good Swede's ship's biscuits I had in my pocket. The fingers closed slowly on it and held — there was no other movement and no other glance. He had tied a bit of white worsted round his neck — Why? Where did he get it? Was it a badge — an ornament — a charm — a propitiatory act? Was there any idea at all connected with it? It looked startling round his black neck, this bit of white thread from beyond the seas.

"Near the same tree two more bundles of acute angles sat with their legs drawn up. One, with his chin propped on his knees, stared at nothing, in an intolerable and appalling manner: his brother phantom rested its forehead, as if overcome with a great weariness; and all about others were scattered in every pose of contorted collapse, as in some picture of a massacre or a pestilence. While I stood horror-struck, one of these creatures rose to his hands and knees, and went off on all-fours towards the river to drink. He lapped out of his hand, then sat up in the sunlight, crossing his shins in front of him, and after a time let his wooly head fall on his breastbone.

"I didn't want any more loitering in the shade, and I made haste towards the station. When near the buildings I met a white man, in such an unexpected elegance of get-up that in the first moment I took him for a sort of vision. I saw a high starched collar, white cuffs, a light alpaca jacket, snowy trousers, a clean necktie, and varnished boots. No hat. Hair parted, brushed, oiled, under a green-lined parasol held in a big white hand. He was amazing, and had a penholder behind his ear.

"I shook hands with this miracle, and I learned he was the Company's chief accountant, and that all the bookkeeping was done at this station. He had come out for a moment, he said, 'to get a breath of fresh air.' The expression sounded wonderfully odd, with its suggestion of sedentary desk-life. I wouldn't have mentioned the fellow to you at all, only it was from his lips that I first heard the name of the man who is so indissolubly connected with the memories of that time. Moreover, I respected the fellow. Yes; I respected his collars, his vast cuffs, his brushed hair. His appearance was certainly that of a hair-dresser's dummy; but in the great demoralization of the land he kept up his appearance. That's backbone. His starched collars and got-up shirt-fronts were achievements of character. He had been out nearly three years; and, later, I could not help asking him how he managed to sport such linen. He had just the faintest blush, and said modestly, 'I've been teaching one of the native women about the station. It was difficult. She had a distaste for the work.' Thus this man had verily accomplished something. And he was devoted to his books, which were in apple-pie order.

"Everything else in the station was in a muddle, — heads, things, buildings. Strings of dusty niggers with splay feet arrived and departed; a stream of manufactured goods, rubbishy cottons, beads, and brass-wire set into the depths of darkness, and in return came a precious trickle of ivory.

"I had to wait in the station for ten days — an eternity. I lived in a hut in the yard, but to be out of the chaos I would sometimes get into the accountant's office. It was built of horizontal planks, and so badly put together that, as he bent over his high desk, he was barred from neck to heels with narrow strips of sunlight. There was no need to open the big shutter to see. It was hot there, too; big flies buzzed fiendishly, and did not sting, but stabbed. I sat generally on the floor, while, of faultless appearance (and even slightly scented), perching on a high stool, he wrote, he wrote. Sometimes he stood up for exercise. When a trucklebed with a sick man (some invalid agent from up-country) was put in there, he exhibited a gentle annoyance. 'The groans of this sick person,' he said, 'distract my attention. And without that it is extremely difficult to guard against clerical errors in this climate.'

"One day he remarked, without lifting his head, 'In the interior you will no doubt meet Mr. Kurtz.' On my asking who Mr. Kurtz was, he said he was a first-class agent; and seeing my disappointment at this information, he added slowly, laying down his pen, 'He is a very remarkable person.' Further questions elicited from him that Mr. Kurtz was at present in charge of a trading post, a very important one, in the true ivory-country, at 'the very bottom of there. Sends in as much ivory as all the others put together. . . .' He began to write again. The sick man was too ill to groan. The flies buzzed in a great peace.

"Suddenly there was a growing murmur of voices and a great tramping of feet. A caravan had come in. A violent babble of un-couth sounds burst out on the other side of the planks. All the carriers were speaking together, and in the midst of the uproar the lamentable voice of the chief agent was heard 'giving it up' tearfully for the twentieth time that day. . . He rose slowly. 'What a fright-ful row,' he said. He crossed the room gently to look at the sick man, and returning, said to me, 'He does not hear.' 'What! Dead?' I asked, startled. 'No, not yet,' he answered, with great composure. Then, alluding with a toss of the head to the tumult in the station-yard, 'When one has got to make correct entries, one comes to hate those savages — hate them to the death.' He remained thought-ful for a moment. 'When you see Mr. Kurtz,' he went on, 'tell him for me that everything here' — he glanced at the desk — 'is very satisfactory. I don't like to write to him — with those messengers of ours you never know who may get hold of your letter — at that Central Station.' He stared at me for a moment with his mild, bulg-ing eyes. 'Oh, he will go far, very far,' he began again. 'He will be a somebody in the Administration before long. They, above — the Council in Europe, you know — mean him to be.'

"He turned to his work. The noise outside had ceased, and pres-ently in going out I stopped at the door. In the steady buzz of flies the homeward-bound agent was lying flushed and insensible; the other, bent over his books, was making correct entries of perfectly correct transactions; and fifty feet below the doorstep I could see the still tree-tops of the grove of death.

"Next day I left that station at last, with a caravan of sixty men, for a two-hundred-mile tramp.

"No use telling you much about that. Paths, paths, everywhere; a stamped-in network of paths spreading over the empty land, through long grass, through burnt grass, through thickets, down and up chilly ravines, up and down stony hills ablaze with heat; and a solitude, a solitude, nobody, not a hut. The population had cleared out a long time ago. Well, if a lot of mysterious niggers armed with all kinds of fearful weapons suddenly took to traveling on the road between Deal and Gravesend, catching the yokels right and left to carry heavy loads for them, I fancy every farm and cottage thereabouts would get empty very soon. Only here the dwellings were gone, too. Still I passed through several abandoned villages. There's something pathetically childish in the ruins of grass walls. Day after day, with the stamp and shuffle of sixty pair of bare feet behind me, each pair under a sixty-pound load. Camp, cook, sleep, strike camp, march. Now and then a carrier dead in harness, at rest in the long grass near the path, with an empty water-gourd and his long staff lying by his side. A great silence around and above. Perhaps on some quiet night the tremor of far-off drums, sinking, swelling, a tremor vast, faint; a sound weird, appealing, suggestive, and wild — and perhaps with as profound a meaning as the sound of bells in a Christian country. Once a white man in an unbuttoned uniform, camping on the path with an armed escort of lank Zanzibaris, very hospitable and festive — not to say drunk. Was looking after the upkeep of the road, he declared. Can't say I saw any road or any upkeep, unless the body of a middle-aged Negro, with a bullet-hole in the forehead, upon which I absolutely stumbled three miles farther on, may be considered as a permanent improvement. I had a white companion, too, not a bad chap, but rather too fleshy and with the exasperating habit of fainting on the hot hillsides, miles away from the least bit of shade and water. Annoying, you know, to hold your own coat like a parasol over a man's head while he is coming-to. I couldn't help asking him once what he meant by coming there at all. 'To make money, of course. What do you think?' he said, scornfully. Then he got fever, and had to be carried in a hammock slung under a pole. As he weighed sixteen stone I had no end of rows with the carriers. They jibbed, ran away, sneaked off with their loads in the night — quite a mutiny. So, one evening, I made a speech in English with gestures, not one of which was lost to the sixty pairs of eyes before me, and the next morning I started the hammock off in front all right. An hour afterwards I came upon the whole concern wrecked in a bush — man, hammock, groans, blankets, horrors. The heavy pole had skinned his poor nose. He was very anxious for me to kill somebody, but there wasn't the shadow of a carrier near. I remembered the old doctor — 'It would be interesting for science to watch the mental changes of individuals, on the spot.' I felt I was becoming scientifically interesting. However, all that is to no purpose. On the fifteenth day I came in sight of the big river again, and hobbled into the Central Station. It was on a backwater surrounded by scrub and forest, with a pretty border of smelly mud on one side, and on the three others enclosed by a crazy fence of rushes. A neglected gap was all the gate it had, and the first glance at the place was enough to let you see the flabby devil was running that show. White men with long staves in their hands appeared languidly from amongst the buildings, strolling up to take a look at me, and then retired out of sight somewhere. One of them, a stout, excitable chap with black mustaches, informed me with great volubility and many digressions, as soon as I told him who I was, that my steamer was at the bottom of the river. I was thunderstruck. What, how, why? Oh, it was 'all right.' The 'manager himself' was there. All quite correct. 'Everybody had behaved splendidly! splendidly!' — 'you must,' he said in agitation, 'go and see the general manager at once. He is waiting!'

"I did not see the real significance of that wreck at once. I fancy I see it now, but I am not sure — not at all. Certainly the affair was too stupid — when I think of it — to be altogether natural. Still. . . . But at the moment it presented itself simply as a confounded nuisance. The steamer was sunk. They had started two days before in a sudden hurry up the river with the manager on board, in charge of some volunteer skipper, and before they had been out three hours they tore the bottom out of her on stones, and she sank near the south bank. I asked myself what I was to do there, now my boat was lost. As a matter of fact, I had plenty to do in fishing my command out of the river. I had to set about it the very next day. That, and the repairs when I brought the pieces to the station, took some months.

"My first interview with the manager was curious. He did not ask me to sit down after my twenty-mile walk that morning. He was commonplace in complexion, in feature, in manners, and in voice. He was of middle size and of ordinary build. His eyes, of the usual blue, were perhaps remarkably cold, and he certainly could make his glance fall on one as trenchant and heavy as an ax. But even at these times the rest of his person seemed to disclaim the intention. Otherwise there was only an indefinable, faint expression of his lips, something stealthy — a smile — not a smile — I remember it, but I can't explain. It was unconscious, this smile was, though just after he had said something it got intensified for an instant. It came at the end of his speeches like a seal applied on the words to make the meaning of the commonest phrase appear absolutely inscrutable. He was a common trader, from his youth up employed in these parts — nothing more. He was obeyed, yet he inspired neither love nor fear, nor even respect. He inspired uneasiness. That was it! Uneasiness. Not a definite mistrust — just uneasiness — nothing more. You have no idea how effective such a . . . a . . . faculty can be. He had no genius for organizing, for initiative, or for order even. That was evident in such things as the deplorable state of the station. He had no learning, and no intelligence. His position had come to him — why? Perhaps because he was never ill. . . . He had served three terms of three years out there. . . . Because triumphant health in the general rout of constitutions is a kind of power in itself. When he went home on leave he rioted on a large scale — pompously. Jack ashore — with a difference — in externals only. This one could gather from his casual talk. He originated nothing, he could keep the routine going — that's all. But he was great. He was great by this little thing that it was impossible to tell what could control such a man. He never gave that secret away. Perhaps there was nothing within him. Such a suspicion made one pause — for out there there were no external checks. Once when various tropical diseases had laid low almost every 'agent' in the station, he was heard to say, 'Men who come out here should have no entrails.' He sealed the utterance with that smile of his, as though it had been a door opening into a darkness he had in his keeping. You fancied you had seen things — but the seal was on. When annoyed at meal-times by the constant quarrels of the white men about precedence, he ordered an immense round table to be made, for which a special house had to be built. This was the station's mess-room. Where he sat was the first place — the rest were nowhere. One felt this to be his unalterable conviction. He was neither civil nor uncivil. He was quiet. He allowed his 'boy' — an overfed young Negro from the coast — to treat the white men, under his very eyes, with provoking insolence.

"He began to speak as soon as he saw me. I had been very long on the road. He could not wait. Had to start without me. The up-river stations had to be relieved. There had been so many delays already that he did not know who was dead and who was alive, and how they got on — and so on, and so on. He paid no attention to my explanations, and, playing with a stick of sealing-wax, repeated several times that the situation was 'very grave, very grave.' There were rumors that a very important station was in jeopardy, and its chief, Mr. Kurtz, was ill. Hoped it was not true. Mr. Kurtz was . . . I felt weary and irritable. Hang Kurtz, I thought. I interrupted him by saying I had heard of Mr. Kurtz on the coast. 'Ah! So they talk of him down there,' he murmured to himself. Then he began again, assuring me Mr. Kurtz was the best agent he had, an exceptional man, of the greatest importance to the Company; therefore I could understand his anxiety. He was, he said, 'very, very uneasy.' Certainly he fidgeted on his chair a good deal, exclaimed, 'Ah, Mr. Kurtz!' broke the stick of sealing-wax and seemed dumbfounded by the accident. Next thing he wanted to know 'how long it would take to . . .' I interrupted him again. Being hungry, you know, and kept on my feet too, I was getting savage. 'How can I tell?' I said. 'I haven't even seen the wreck yet — some months, no doubt.' All this talk seemed to me so futile. 'Some months,' he said. 'Well, let us say three months before we can make a start. Yes. That ought to do the affair.' I flung out of his hut (he lived all alone in a clay hut with a sort of veranda) muttering to myself my opinion of him. He was a chattering idiot. Afterwards I took it back when it was borne in upon me startlingly with what extreme nicety he had estimated the time requisite for the 'affair.'

"I went to work the next day, turning, so to speak, my back on that station. In that way only it seemed to me I could keep my hold on the redeeming facts of life. Still, one must look about sometimes; and then I saw this station, these men strolling aimlessly about in the sunshine of the yard. I asked myself sometimes what it all meant. They wandered here and there with their absurd long staves in their hands, like a lot of faithless pilgrims bewitched inside a rotten fence. The word 'ivory' rang in the air, was whispered, was sighed. You would think they were praying to it. A taint of imbecile rapacity blew through it all, like a whiff from some corpse. By Jove! I've never seen anything so unreal in my life. And outside, the silent wilderness surrounding this cleared speck on the earth struck me as something great and invincible, like evil or truth, waiting patiently for the passing away of this fantastic invasion.

"Oh, these months! Well, never mind. Various things happened. One evening a grass shed full of calico, cotton prints, beads, and I don't know what else, burst into a blaze so suddenly that you would have thought the earth had opened to let an avenging fire consume all that trash. I was smoking my pipe quietly by my dismantled steamer, and saw them all cutting capers in the light, with their arms lifted high, when the stout man with mustaches came tearing down to the river, a tin pail in his hand, assured me that everybody was 'behaving splendidly, splendidly,' dipped about a quart of water and tore back again. I noticed there was a hole in the bottom of his pail.

"I strolled up. There was no hurry. You see the thing had gone off like a box of matches. It had been hopeless from the very first. The flame had leaped high, driven everybody back, lighted up everything — and collapsed. The shed was already a heap of embers glowing fiercely. A nigger was being beaten near by. They said he had caused the fire in some way; be that as it may, he was screeching most horribly. I saw him, later, for several days, sitting in a bit of shade looking very sick and trying to recover himself: afterwards he arose and went out — and the wilderness without a sound took him into its bosom again. As I approached the glow from the dark I found myself at the back of two men, talking. I heard the name of Kurtz pronounced, then the words, 'take advantage of this unfortunate accident.' One of the men was the manager. I wished him a good evening. 'Did you ever see anything like it — eh? it is incredible,' he said, and walked off. The other man remained. He was a first-class agent, young, gentlemanly, a bit reserved, with a forked little beard and a hooked nose. He was stand-offish with the other agents, and they on their side said he was the manager's spy upon them. As to me, I had hardly ever spoken to him before. We got into talk, and by and by we strolled away from the hissing ruins. Then he asked me to his room, which was in the main building of the station. He struck a match, and I perceived that this young aristocrat had not only a silver-mounted dressing-case but also a whole candle all to himself. Just at that time the manager was the only man supposed to have any right to candles. Native mats covered the clay walls; a collection of spears, assegais, shields, knives was hung up in trophies. The business intrusted to this fellow was the making of bricks — so I had been informed; but there wasn't a fragment of a brick anywhere in the station, and he had been there more than a year — waiting. It seems he could not make bricks without something, I don't know what — straw, maybe. Anyway, it could not be found there, and as it was not likely to be sent from Europe, it did not appear clear to me what he was waiting for. An act of special creation perhaps. However, they were all waiting — all the sixteen or twenty pilgrims of them — for something; and upon my word it did not seem an uncongenial occupation, from the way they took it, though the only thing that ever came to them was disease — as far as I could see. They beguiled the time by back-biting and intriguing against each other in a foolish kind of way. There was an air of plotting about that station, but nothing came of it, of course. It was as unreal as everything else — as the philanthropic pretense of the whole concern, as their talk, as their government, as their show of work. The only real feeling was a desire to get appointed to a trading-post where ivory was to be had, so that they could earn percentages. They intrigued and slandered and hated each other only on that account, — but as to effectually lifting a little finger — oh, no. By heavens! there is something after all in the world allowing one man to steal a horse while another must not look at a halter. Steal a horse straight out. Very well. He has done it. Perhaps he can ride. But there is a way of looking at a halter that would provoke the most charitable of saints into a kick.

"I had no idea why he wanted to be sociable, but as we chatted in there it suddenly occurred to me the fellow was trying to get at something — in fact, pumping me. He alluded constantly to Europe, to the people I was supposed to know there — putting leading questions as to my acquaintances in the sepulchral city, and so on. His little eyes glittered like mica discs — with curiosity — though he tried to keep up a bit of superciliousness. At first I was astonished, but very soon I became awfully curious to see what he would find out from me. I couldn't possibly imagine what I had in me to make it worth his while. It was very pretty to see how he baffled himself, for in truth my body was full only of chills, and my head had nothing in it but that wretched steamboat business. It was evident he took me for a perfectly shameless prevaricator. At last he got angry, and, to conceal a movement of furious annoyance, he yawned. I rose. Then I noticed a small sketch in oils, on a panel, representing a woman, draped and blindfolded, carrying a lighted torch. The background was somber — almost black. The movement of the woman was stately, and the effect of the torchlight on the face was sinister.

"It arrested me, and he stood by civilly, holding an empty half-

pint champagne bottle (medical comforts) with the candle stuck
in it. To my question he said Mr. Kurtz had painted this — in this
very station more than a year ago — while waiting for means to
go to his trading-post. 'Tell me, pray,' said I, 'who is this Mr.
Kurtz?'

" 'The chief of the Inner Station,' he answered in a short tone,
looking away. 'Much obliged,' I said, laughing. 'And you are the
brickmaker of the Central Station. Everyone knows that.' He was
silent for a while. 'He is a prodigy,' he said at last. 'He is an emissary of pity, and science, and progress, and devil knows what else.
We want,' he began to declaim suddenly, 'for the guidance of the
cause intrusted to us by Europe, so to speak, higher intelligence,
wide sympathies, a singleness of purpose.' 'Who says that?' I asked.
'Lots of them,' he replied. 'Some even write that; and so *he* comes
here, a special being, as you ought to know.' 'Why ought I to
know?' I interrupted, really surprised. He paid no attention. 'Yes.
Today he is chief of the best station, next year he will be assistant-
manager, two years more and . . . but I daresay you know what he
will be in two years' time. You are of the new gang — the gang of
virtue. The same people who sent him specially also recommended
you. Oh, don't say no. I've my own eyes to trust.' Light dawned
upon me. My dear aunt's influential acquaintances were producing
an unexpected effect upon that young man. I nearly burst into a
laugh. 'Do you read the Company's confidential correspondence?'
I asked. He hadn't a word to say. It was great fun. 'When Mr.
Kurtz,' I continued, severely, 'is General Manager, you won't have
the opportunity.'

"He blew the candle out suddenly, and we went outside. The
moon had risen. Black figures strolled about listlessly, pouring
water on the glow, whence proceeded a sound of hissing; steam
ascended in the moonlight, the beaten nigger groaned somewhere.
'What a row the brute makes!' said the indefatigable man with the
mustaches, appearing near us. 'Serve him right. Transgression —
punishment — bang! Pitiless, pitiless. That's the only way. This
will prevent all conflagrations for the future. I was just telling the
manager. . . .' He noticed my companion, and became crestfallen
all at once. 'Not in bed yet,' he said, with a kind of servile heartiness; 'it's so natural. Ha! Danger — agitation.' He vanished. I
went on to the river-side, and the other followed me. I heard a
scathing murmur at my ear, 'Heap of muffs — go to.' The pilgrims

could be seen in knots gesticulating, discussing. Several had still their staves in their hands. I verily believe they took these sticks to bed with them. Beyond the fence the forest stood up spectrally in the moonlight, and through the dim stir, through the faint sounds of that lamentable courtyard, the silence of the land went home to one's very heart — its mystery, its greatness, the amazing reality of its concealed life. The hurt nigger moaned feebly somewhere near by, and then fetched a deep sigh that made me mend my pace away from there. I felt a hand introducing itself under my arm. 'My dear sir,' said the fellow, 'I don't want to be misunderstood, and especially by you, who will see Mr. Kurtz long before I can have that pleasure. I wouldn't like him to get a false idea of my disposition. . . .'

"I let him run on, this papier-mâché Mephistopheles, and it seemed to me that if I tried I could poke my forefinger through him, and would find nothing inside but a little loose dirt, maybe. He, don't you see, had been planning to be assistant-manager by and by under the present man, and I could see that the coming of that Kurtz had upset them both not a little. He talked precipitately, and I did not try to stop him. I had my shoulders against the wreck of my steamer, hauled up on the slope like a carcass of some big river animal. The smell of mud, of primeval mud, by Jove! was in my nostrils, the high stillness of primeval forest was before my eyes; there were shiny patches on the black creek. The moon had spread over everything a thin layer of silver — over the rank grass, over the mud, upon the wall of matted vegetation standing higher than the wall of a temple, over the great river I could see through a somber gap glittering, glittering, as it flowed broadly by without a murmur. All this was great, expectant, mute, while the man jabbered about himself. I wondered whether the stillness on the face of the immensity looking at us two were meant as an appeal or as a menace. What were we who had strayed in here? Could we handle that dumb thing, or would it handle us? I felt how big, how confoundedly big, was that thing that couldn't talk, and perhaps was deaf as well. What was in there? I could see a little ivory coming out from there, and I had heard Mr. Kurtz was in there. I had heard enough about it, too — God knows! Yet somehow it didn't bring any image with it — no more than if I had been told an angel or a fiend was in there. I believed it in the same way one of you might believe there are inhabitants in the planet Mars. I knew once a Scotch sailmaker who was certain, dead sure, there were people in Mars. If you asked him for some idea how they looked and behaved, he would get shy and mutter something about 'walking on all-fours.' If you as much as smiled, he would — though a man of sixty — offer to fight you. I would not have gone so far as to fight for Kurtz, but I went for him near enough to a lie. You know I hate, detest, and can't bear a lie, not because I am straighter than the rest of us, but simply because it appalls me. There is a taint of death, a flavor of mortality in lies — which is exactly what I hate and detest in the world — what I want to forget. It makes me miserable and sick, like biting something rotten would do. Temperament, I suppose. Well, I went near enough to it by letting the young fool there believe anything he liked to imagine as to my influence in Europe. I became in an instant as much of a pretense as the rest of the bewildered pilgrims. This simply because I had a notion it somehow would be of help to that Kurtz whom at the time I did not see — you understand. He was just a word for me. I did not see the man in the name any more than you do. Do you see him? Do you see the story? Do you see anything? It seems to me I am trying to tell you a dream — making a vain attempt, because no relation of a dream can convey the dream-sensation, that commingling of absurdity, surprise, and bewilderment in a tremor of struggling revolt, that notion of being captured by the incredible which is of the very essence of dreams. . . ."

He was silent for a while.

". . . No, it is impossible; it is impossible to convey the life-sensation of any given epoch of one's existence — that which makes its truth, its meaning — its subtle and penetrating essence. It is impossible. We live, as we dream — alone. . . ."

He paused again as if reflecting, then added —

"Of course in this you fellows see more than I could then. You see me, whom you know. . . ."

It had become so pitch dark that we listeners could hardly see one another. For a long time already he, sitting apart, had been no more to us than a voice. There was not a word from anybody. The others might have been asleep, but I was awake. I listened, I listened on the watch for the sentence, for the word, that would give me the clew to the faint uneasiness inspired by this narrative that seemed to shape itself without human lips in the heavy night-air of the river.

"... Yes — I let him run on," Marlow began again, "and think what he pleased about the powers that were behind me. I did! And there was nothing behind me! There was nothing but that wretched, old, mangled steamboat I was leaning against, while he talked fluently about 'the necessity for every man to get on.' 'And when one comes out here, you conceive, it is not to gaze at the moon.' Mr. Kurtz was a 'universal genius,' but even a genius would find it easier to work with 'adequate tools — intelligent men.' He did not make bricks — why, there was a physical impossibility in the way — as I was well aware; and if he did secretarial work for the manager, it was because 'no sensible man rejects wantonly the confidence of his superiors.' Did I see it? I saw it. What more did I want? What I really wanted was rivets, by heaven! Rivets. To get on with the work — to stop the hole. Rivets I wanted. There were cases of them down at the coast — cases — piled up — burst — split! You kicked a loose rivet at every second step in that station yard on the hillside. Rivets had rolled into the grove of death. You could fill your pockets with rivets for the trouble of stooping down — and there wasn't one rivet to be found where it was wanted. We had plates that would do, but nothing to fasten them with. And every week the messenger, a lone Negro, letter-bag on shoulder and staff in hand, left our station for the coast. And several times a week a coast caravan came in with trade goods — ghastly glazed calico that made you shudder only to look at it; glass beads, valued about a penny a quart, confounded spotted cotton handkerchiefs. And no rivets. Three carriers could have brought all that was wanted to set that steamboat afloat.

"He was becoming confidential now, but I fancy my unresponsive attitude must have exasperated him at last, for he judged it necessary to inform me he feared neither God nor devil, let alone any mere man. I said I could see that very well, but what I wanted was a certain quantity of rivets — and rivets were what really Mr. Kurtz wanted, if he had only known it. Now letters went to the coast every week. . . . 'My dear sir,' he cried, 'I write from dictation.' I demanded rivets. There was a way — for an intelligent man. He changed his manner; became very cold, and suddenly began to talk about a hippopotamus; wondered whether sleeping on board the steamer (I stuck to my salvage night and day) I wasn't disturbed. There was an old hippo that had the bad habit of getting out on the bank and roaming at night over the station grounds. The pilgrims used to turn out in a body and empty every rifle they could lay hands on at him. Some even had sat up o' nights for him. All this energy was wasted, though. 'That animal has a charmed life,' he said; 'but you can say this only of brutes in this country. No man — you apprehend me? — no man here bears a charmed life.' He stood there for a moment in the moonlight with his delicate hooked nose set a little askew, and his mica eyes glittering without a wink, then, with a curt good night, he strode off. I could see he was disturbed and considerably puzzled, which made me feel more hopeful than I had been for days. It was a great comfort to turn from that chap to my influential friend, the battered, twisted, ruined, tin-pot steamboat. I clambered on board. She rang under my feet like an empty Huntley & Palmer biscuit-tin kicked along a gutter; she was nothing so solid in make, and rather less pretty in shape, but I had expended enough hard work on her to make me love her. No influential friend would have served me better. She had given me a chance to come out a bit — to find out what I could do. No, I don't like work. I had rather laze about and think of all the fine things that can be done. I don't like work — no man does — but I like what is in the work — the chance to find yourself. Your own reality — for yourself, not for others — what no other man can ever know. They can only see the mere show, and never can tell what it really means.

"I was not surprised to see somebody sitting aft, on the deck, with his legs dangling over the mud. You see I rather chummed with the few mechanics there were in that station, whom the other pilgrims naturally despised — on account of their imperfect manners, I suppose. This was the foreman — a boiler-maker by trade — a good worker. He was a lank, bony, yellow-faced man, with big intense eyes. His aspect was worried, and his head was as bald as the palm of my hand; but his hair in falling seemed to have stuck to his chin, and had prospered in the new locality, for his beard hung down to his waist. He was a widower with six young children (he had left them in charge of a sister of his to come out there), and the passion of his life was pigeon-flying. He was an enthusiast and a connoisseur. He would rave about pigeons. After work hours he used sometimes to come over from his hut for a talk about his children and his pigeons; at work, when he had to crawl in the mud under the bottom of the steamboat, he would tie up that beard of his in a kind of white serviette he brought for the purpose. It had loops to go over his ears. In the evening he could be seen squatted on the bank rinsing that wrapper in the creek with great care, then spreading it solemnly on a bush to dry.

"I slapped him on the back and shouted, 'We shall have rivets!' He scrambled to his feet exclaiming, 'No! Rivets!' as though he couldn't believe his ears. Then in a low voice, 'You . . . eh?' I don't know why we behaved like lunatics. I put my finger to the side of my nose and nodded mysteriously. 'Good for you!' he cried, snapped his fingers above his head, lifting one foot. I tried a jig. We capered on the iron deck. A frightful clatter came out of that hulk, and the virgin forest on the other bank of the creek sent it back in a thundering roll upon the sleeping station. It must have made some of the pilgrims sit up in their hovels. A dark figure obscured the lighted doorway of the manager's hut, vanished, then, a second or so after, the doorway itself vanished, too. We stopped, and the silence driven away by the stamping of our feet flowed back again from the recesses of the land. The great wall of vegetation, an exuberant and entangled mass of trunks, branches, leaves, boughs, festoons, motionless in the moonlight, was like a rioting invasion of soundless life, a rolling wave of plants, piled up, crested, ready to topple over the creek, to sweep every little man of us out of his little existence. And it moved not. A deadened burst of mighty splashes and snorts reached us from afar, as though an ichthyosaurus had been taking a bath of glitter in the great river. 'After all,' said the boiler-maker in a reasonable tone, 'why shouldn't we get the rivets?' Why not, indeed! I did not know of any reason why we shouldn't. 'They'll come in three weeks,' I said, confidently.

"But they didn't. Instead of rivets there came an invasion, an infliction, a visitation. It came in sections during the next three weeks, each section headed by a donkey carrying a white man in new clothes and tan shoes, bowing from that elevation right and left to the impressed pilgrims. A quarrelsome band of footsore sulky niggers trod on the heels of the donkeys; a lot of tents, camp-stools, tin boxes, white cases, brown bales would be shot down in the courtyard, and the air of mystery would deepen a little over the muddle of the station. Five such installments came, with their absurd air of disorderly flight with the loot of innumerable outfit shops and provision stores, that, one would think, they were lugging, after a raid, into the wilderness for equitable division. It was an inextricable mess of things decent in themselves but that human folly made look like the spoils of thieving.

"This devoted band called itself the Eldorado Exploring Expedition, and I believe they were sworn to secrecy. Their talk, however, was the talk of sordid buccaneers: it was reckless without hardihood, greedy without audacity, and cruel without courage; there was not an atom of foresight or of serious intention in the whole batch of them, and they did not seem aware these things are wanted for the work of the world. To tear treasure out of the bowels of the land was their desire, with no more moral purpose at the back of it than there is in burglars breaking into a safe. Who paid the expenses of the whole enterprise I don't know; but the uncle of our manager was leader of that lot.

"In exterior he resembled a butcher in a poor neighborhood, and his eyes had a look of sleepy cunning. He carried his fat paunch with ostentation on his short legs, and during the time his gang infested the station spoke to no one but his nephew. You could see these two roaming about all day long with their heads close together in an everlasting confab.

"I had given up worrying myself about the rivets. One's capacity for that kind of folly is more limited than you would suppose. I said Hang! — and let things slide. I had plenty of time for meditation, and now and then I would give some thought to Kurtz. I wasn't very interested in him. No. Still, I was curious to see whether this man, who had come out equipped with moral ideas of some sort, would climb to the top after all and how he would set about his work when there."

II

"One evening as I was lying flat on the deck of my steamboat, I heard voices approaching — and there were the nephew and the uncle strolling along the bank. I laid my head on my arm again, and had nearly lost myself in a doze, when somebody said in my ear, as it were: 'I am as harmless as a little child, but I don't like to be dictated to. Am I the manager — or am I not? I was ordered to send him there. It's incredible.' . . . I became aware that the two were standing on the shore alongside the forepart of the steamboat, just below my head. I did not move; it did not occur to me to move:

I was sleepy. 'It *is* unpleasant,' grunted the uncle. 'He has asked the Administration to be sent there,' said the other, 'with the idea of showing what he could do; and I was instructed accordingly. Look at the influence that man must have. Is it not frightful?' They both agreed it was frightful, then made several bizarre remarks: 'Make rain and fine weather — one man — the Council — by the nose' — bits of absurd sentences that got the better of my drowsiness, so that I had pretty near the whole of my wits about me when the uncle said, 'The climate may do away with this difficulty for you. Is he alone there?' 'Yes,' answered the manager; 'he sent his assistant down the river with a note to me in these terms: "Clear this poor devil out of the country, and don't bother sending more of that sort. I had rather be alone than have the kind of men you can dispose of with me." It was more than a year ago. Can you imagine such impudence!' 'Anything since then?' asked the other, hoarsely. 'Ivory,' jerked the nephew; 'lots of it — prime sort — lots — most annoying, from him.' 'And with that?' questioned the heavy rumble. 'Invoice,' was the reply fired out, so to speak. Then silence. They had been talking about Kurtz.

"I was broad awake by this time, but, lying perfectly at ease, remained still, having no inducement to change my position. 'How did that ivory come all this way?' growled the elder man, who seemed very vexed. The other explained that it had come with a fleet of canoes in charge of an English half-caste clerk Kurtz had with him; that Kurtz had apparently intended to return himself, the station being by that time bare of goods and stores, but after coming three hundred miles, had suddenly decided to go back, which he started to do alone in a small dugout with four paddlers, leaving the half-caste to continue down the river with the ivory. The two fellows there seemed astounded at anybody attempting such a thing. They were at a loss for an adequate motive. As to me, I seemed to see Kurtz for the first time. It was a distinct glimpse: the dugout, four paddling savages, and the lone white man turning his back suddenly on the headquarters, on relief, on thoughts of home — perhaps; setting his face towards the depths of the wilderness, towards his empty and desolate station. I did not know the motive. Perhaps he was just simply a fine fellow who stuck to his work for its own sake. His name, you understand, had not been pronounced once. He was 'that man.' The half-caste, who, as far as I could see, had conducted a difficult trip with great prudence and pluck, was invariably alluded to as 'that scoundrel.' The 'scoundrel' had reported that the 'man' had been very ill — had recovered imperfectly. . . . The two below me moved away then a few paces, and strolled back and forth at some little distance. I heard: 'Military post — doctor — two hundred miles — quite alone now — unavoidable delays — nine months — no news — strange rumors.' They approached again, just as the manager was saying, 'No one, as far as I know, unless a species of wandering trader — a pestilential fellow, snapping ivory from the natives.' Who was it they were talking about now? I gathered in snatches that this was some man supposed to be in Kurtz's district, and of whom the manager did not approve. 'We will not be free from unfair competition till one of these fellows is hanged for an example,' he said. 'Certainly,' grunted the other; 'get him hanged! Why not? Anything — anything can be done in this country. That's what I say; nobody here, you understand, *here*, can endanger your position. And why? You stand the climate — you outlast them all. The danger is in Europe; but there before I left I took care to — ' They moved off and whispered, then their voices rose again. 'The extraordinary series of delays is not my fault. I did my best.' The fat man sighed. 'Very sad.' 'And the pestiferous absurdity of his talk,' continued the other; 'he bothered me enough when he was here. "Each station should be like a beacon on the road towards better things, a center for trade, of course, but also for humanizing, improving, instructing." Conceive you — that ass! And he wants to be manager! No, it's — ' Here he got choked by excessive indignation, and I lifted my head the least bit. I was surprised to see how near they were — right under me. I could have spat upon their hats. They were looking on the ground, absorbed in thought. The manager was switching his leg with a slender twig: his sagacious relative lifted his head. 'You have been well since you came out this time?' he asked. The other gave a start. 'Who? I? Oh! Like a charm — like a charm. But the rest — oh, my goodness! All sick. They die so quick, too, that I haven't the time to send them out of the country — it's incredible!' 'H'm. Just so,' grunted the uncle. 'Ah! my boy, trust to this — I say, trust to this.' I saw him extend his short flipper of an arm for a gesture that took in the forest, the creek, the mud, the river — seemed to beckon with a dishonoring flourish before the sunlit face of the land a treacherous appeal to the lurking death, to the hidden evil, to the profound darkness of its heart. It was so startling that I leaped to my feet and looked back at the edge of the forest, as though I had expected an answer of some sort to that black display of confidence. You know the foolish notions that come to one sometimes. The high stillness confronted these two figures with its ominous patience, waiting for the passing away of a fantastic invasion.

"They swore aloud together — out of sheer fright, I believe — then pretending not to know anything of my existence, turned back to the station. The sun was low; and leaning forward side by side, they seemed to be tugging painfully uphill their two ridiculous shadows of unequal length, that trailed behind them slowly over the tall grass without bending a single blade.

"In a few days the Eldorado Expedition went into the patient wilderness, that closed upon it as the sea closes over a diver. Long afterwards the news came that all the donkeys were dead. I know nothing as to the fate of the less valuable animals. They, no doubt, like the rest of us, found what they deserved. I did not inquire. I was then rather excited at the prospect of meeting Kurtz very soon. When I say very soon I mean it comparatively. It was just two months from the day we left the creek when we came to the bank below Kurtz's station.

"Going up that river was like traveling back to the earliest beginnings of the world, when vegetation rioted on the earth and the big trees were kings. An empty stream, a great silence, an impenetrable forest. The air was warm, thick, heavy, sluggish. There was no joy in the brilliance of sunshine. The long stretches of the waterway ran on, deserted, into the gloom of overshadowed distances. On silvery sandbanks hippos and alligators sunned themselves side by side. The broadening waters flowed through a mob of wooded islands; you lost your way on that river as you would in a desert, and butted all day long against shoals, trying to find the channel, till you thought yourself bewitched and cut off forever from everything you had known once — somewhere — far away — in another existence perhaps. There were moments when one's past came back to one, as it will sometimes when you have not a moment to spare to yourself; but it came in the shape of an unrestful and noisy dream, remembered with wonder amongst the overwhelming realities of this strange world of plants, and water, and silence. And this stillness of life did not in the least resemble a peace. It was the

stillness of an implacable force brooding over an inscrutable intention. It looked at you with á vengeful aspect. I got used to it afterwards; I did not see it any more; I had no time. I had to keep guess-
ing at the channel; I had to discern, mostly by inspiration, the
signs of hidden banks; I watched for sunken stones; I was learning to
clap my teeth smartly before my heart flew out, when I shaved by
a fluke some infernal sly old snag that would have ripped the life
out of the tin-pot steamboat and drowned all the pilgrims; I had to
keep a lookout for the signs of dead wood we could cut up in the
night for next day's steaming. When you have to attend to things
of that sort, to the mere incidents of the surface, the reality — the
reality, I tell you — fades. The inner truth is hidden — luckily,
luckily. But I felt it all the same; I felt often its mysterious stillness
watching me at my monkey tricks, just as it watches you fellows
performing on your respective tight-ropes for — what is it? half-a-
crown a tumble — "

"Try to be civil, Marlow," growled a voice, and I knew there
was at least one listener awake besides myself.

"I beg your pardon. I forgot the heartache which makes up the
rest of the price. And indeed what does the price matter, if the
trick be well done? You do your tricks very well. And I didn't
do badly either, since I managed not to sink that steamboat on my
first trip. It's a wonder to me yet. Imagine a blindfolded man set
to drive a van over a bad road. I sweated and shivered over that
business considerably, I can tell you. After all, for a seaman, to
scrape the bottom of the thing that's supposed to float all the time
under his care is the unpardonable sin. No one may know of it, but
you never forget the thump — eh? A blow on the very heart. You
remember it, you dream of it, you wake up at night and think of
it — years after — and go hot and cold all over. I don't pretend to
say that steamboat floated all the time. More than once she had to
wade for a bit, with twenty cannibals splashing around and pushing. We had enlisted some of these chaps on the way for a crew.
Fine fellows — cannibals — in their place. They were men one
could work with, and I am grateful to them. And, after all, they did
not eat each other before my face: they had brought along a provision of hippo-meat which went rotten, and made the mystery of
the wilderness stink in my nostrils. Phoo! I can sniff it now. I
had the manager on board and three or four pilgrims with their
staves — all complete. Sometimes we came upon a station close

by the bank, clinging to the skirts of the unknown, and the white
men rushing out of a tumble-down hovel, with great gestures of
joy and surprise and welcome, seemed very strange — had the appearance of being held there captive by a spell. The word ivory
would ring in the air for a while — and on we went again into the
silence, along empty reaches, round the still bends, between the
high walls of our winding way, reverberating in hollow claps the
ponderous beat of the stern-wheel. Trees, trees, millions of trees,
massive, immense, running up high; and at their foot, hugging the
bank against the stream, crept the little begrimed steamboat, like a
sluggish beetle crawling on the floor of a lofty portico. It made you
feel very small, very lost, and yet it was not altogether depressing,
that feeling. After all, if you were small, the grimy beetle crawled
on — which was just what you wanted it to do. Where the pilgrims imagined it crawled to I don't know. To some place where
they expected to get something, I bet! For me it crawled towards
Kurtz — exclusively; but when the steam-pipes started leaking we
crawled very slow. The reaches opened before us and closed behind, as if the forest had stepped leisurely across the water to bar
the way for our return. We penetrated deeper and deeper into the
heart of darkness. It was very quiet there. At night sometimes the
roll of drums behind the curtain of trees would run up the river
and remain sustained faintly, as if hovering in the air high over our
heads, till the first break of day. Whether it meant war, peace, or
prayer we could not tell. The dawns were heralded by the descent
of a chill stillness; the wood-cutters slept, their fires burned low; the
snapping of a twig would make you start. We were wanderers on
a prehistoric earth, on an earth that wore the aspect of an unknown
planet. We could have fancied ourselves the first of men taking
possession of an accursed inheritance, to be subdued at the cost of
profound anguish and of excessive toil. But suddenly, as we struggled round a bend, there would be a glimpse of rush walls, of
peaked grass-roofs, a burst of yells, a whirl of black limbs, a mass
of hands clapping, of feet stamping, of bodies swaying, of eyes
rolling, under the droop of heavy and motionless foliage. The
steamer toiled along slowly on the edge of a black and incomprehensible frenzy. The prehistoric man was cursing us, praying to us,
welcoming us — who could tell? We were cut off from the comprehension of our surroundings; we glided past like phantoms, wondering and secretly appalled, as sane men would be before an

enthusiastic outbreak in a madhouse. We could not understand because we were too far and could not remember, because we were traveling in the night of first ages, of those ages that are gone, leaving hardly a sign — and no memories.

"The earth seemed unearthly. We are accustomed to look upon the shackled form of a conquered monster, but there — there you could look at a thing monstrous and free. It was unearthly, and the men were — No, they were not inhuman. Well, you know, that was the worst of it — this suspicion of their not being inhuman. It would come slowly to one. They howled and leaped, and spun, and made horrid faces; but what thrilled you was just the thought of their humanity — like yours — the thought of your remote kinship with this wild and passionate uproar. Ugly. Yes, it was ugly enough; but if you were man enough you would admit to yourself that there was in you just the faintest trace of a response to the terrible frankness of that noise, a dim suspicion of there being a meaning in it which you — you so remote from the night of first ages — could comprehend. And why not? The mind of man is capable of anything — because everything is in it, all the past as well as all the future. What was there after all? Joy, fear, sorrow, devotion, valor, rage — who can tell? — but truth — truth stripped of its cloak of time. Let the fool gape and shudder — the man knows, and can look on without a wink. But he must at least be as much of a man as these on the shore. He must meet that truth with his own true stuff — with his own inborn strength. Principles won't do. Acquisitions, clothes, pretty rags — rags that would fly off at the first good shake. No; you want a deliberate belief. An appeal to me in this fiendish row — is there? Very well; I hear; I admit, but I have a voice, too, and for good or evil mine is the speech that cannot be silenced. Of course, a fool, what with sheer fright and fine sentiments, is always safe. Who's that grunting? You wonder I didn't go ashore for a howl and a dance? Well, no — I didn't. Fine sentiments, you say? Fine sentiments, be hanged! I had no time. I had to mess about with white-lead and strips of woolen blanket helping to put bandages on those leaky steam-pipes — I tell you. I had to watch the steering, and circumvent those snags, and get the tin-pot along by hook or by crook. There was surface-truth enough in these things to save a wiser man. And between whiles I had to look after the savage who was fireman. He was an improved specimen; he could fire up a vertical boiler. He was there below me, and, upon my word, to look at him was as edifying as seeing a dog in a parody of breeches and a feather hat, walking on his hind-legs. A few months of training had done for that really fine chap. He squinted at the steam-gauge and at the water-gauge with an evident effort of intrepidity — and he had filed teeth, too, the poor devil, and the wool of his pate shaved into queer patterns, and three ornamental scars on each of his cheeks. He ought to have been clapping his hands and stamping his feet on the bank, instead of which he was hard at work, a thrall to strange witchcraft, full of improving knowledge. He was useful because he had been instructed; and what he knew was this — that should the water in that transparent thing disappear, the evil spirit inside the boiler would get angry through the greatness of his thirst, and take a terrible vengeance. So he sweated and fired up and watched the glass fearfully (with an impromptu charm, made of rags, tied to his arm, and a piece of polished bone, as big as a watch, stuck flatways through his lower lip), while the wooden banks slipped past us slowly, the short noise was left behind, the interminable miles of silence — and we crept on, towards Kurtz. But the snags were thick, the water was treacherous and shallow, the boiler seemed indeed to have a sulky devil in it, and thus neither that fireman nor I had any time to peer into our creepy thoughts.

"Some fifty miles below the Inner Station we came upon a hut of reeds, an inclined and melancholy pole, with the unrecognizable tatters of what had been a flag of some sort flying from it, and a neatly stacked woodpile. This was unexpected. We came to the bank, and on the stack of firewood found a flat piece of board with some faded pencil-writing on it. When deciphered it said: 'Wood for you. Hurry up. Approach cautiously.' There was a signature, but it was illegible — not Kurtz — a much longer word. 'Hurry up.' Where? Up the river? 'Approach cautiously.' We had not done so. But the warning could not have been meant for the place where it could be only found after approach. Something was wrong above. But what — and how much? That was the question. We commented adversely upon the imbecility of that telegraphic style. The bush around said nothing, and would not let us look very far, either. A torn curtain of red twill hung in the doorway of the hut, and flapped sadly in our faces. The dwelling was dismantled; but we could see a white man had lived there not very long ago. There remained a rude table — a plank on two posts; a

heap of rubbish reposed in a dark corner, and by the door I picked
up a book. It had lost its covers, and the pages had been thumbed
into a state of extremely dirty softness; but the back had been
lovingly stitched afresh with white cotton thread, which looked
clean yet. It was an extraordinary find. Its title was, *An Inquiry
into some Points of Seamanship*, by a man Towser, Towson —
some such name — Master in his Majesty's Navy. The matter looked
dreary reading enough, with illustrative diagrams and repulsive
tables of figures, and the copy was sixty years old. I handled this
amazing antiquity with the greatest possible tenderness, lest it
should dissolve in my hands. Within, Towson or Towser was inquiring earnestly into the breaking strain of ships' chains and tackle,
and other such matters. Not a very enthralling book; but at the
first glance you could see there a singleness of intention, an honest
concern for the right way of going to work, which made these
humble pages, thought out so many years ago, luminous with another than a professional light. The simple old sailor, with his talk
of chains and purchases, made me forget the jungle and the pilgrims in a delicious sensation of having come upon something un-
mistakably real. Such a book being there was wonderful enough;
but still more astounding were the notes penciled in the margin, and
plainly referring to the text. I couldn't believe my eyes! They
were in cipher! Yes, it looked like cipher. Fancy a man lugging
with him a book of that description into this nowhere and studying
it — and making notes — in cipher at that! It was an extravagant
mystery.

"I had been dimly aware for some time of a worrying noise, and
when I lifted my eyes I saw the woodpile was gone, and the manager, aided by all the pilgrims, was shouting at me from the river-
side. I slipped the book into my pocket. I assure you to leave off
reading was like tearing myself away from the shelter of an old
and solid friendship.

"I started the lame engine ahead. 'It must be this miserable trader
— this intruder,' exclaimed the manager, looking back malevolently
at the place we had left. 'He must be English,' I said. 'It will not
save him from getting into trouble if he is not careful,' muttered
the manager darkly. I observed with assumed innocence that no man
was safe from trouble in this world.

"The current was more rapid now, the steamer seemed at her
last gasp, the stern-wheel flopped languidly, and I caught myself

listening on tiptoe for the next beat of the boat, for in sober truth I expected the wretched thing to give up every moment. It was like watching the last flickers of a life. But still we crawled. Sometimes I would pick out a tree a little way ahead to measure our progress towards Kurtz by, but I lost it invariably before we got abreast. To keep the eyes so long on one thing was too much for human patience. The manager displayed a beautiful resignation. I fretted and fumed and took to arguing with myself whether or no I would talk openly with Kurtz; but before I could come to any conclusion it occurred to me that my speech or my silence, indeed any action of mine, would be a mere futility. What did it matter what anyone knew or ignored? What did it matter who was manager? One gets sometimes such a flash of insight. The essentials of this affair lay deep under the surface, beyond my reach, and beyond my power of meddling.

"Towards the evening of the second day we judged ourselves about eight miles from Kurtz's station. I wanted to push on; but the manager looked grave, and told me the navigation up there was so dangerous that it would be advisable, the sun being very low already, to wait where we were till next morning. Moreover, he pointed out that if the warning to approach cautiously were to be followed, we must approach in daylight — not at dusk, or in the dark. This was sensible enough. Eight miles meant nearly three hours' steaming for us, and I could also see suspicious ripples at the upper end of the reach. Nevertheless, I was annoyed beyond expression at the delay, and most unreasonably, too, since one night more could not matter much after so many months. As we had plenty of wood, and caution was the word, I brought up in the middle of the stream. The reach was narrow, straight, with high sides like a railway cutting. The dusk came gliding into it long before the sun had set. The current ran smooth and swift, but a dumb immobility sat on the banks. The living trees, lashed together by the creepers and every living bush of the undergrowth, might have been changed into stone, even to the slenderest twig, to the lightest leaf. It was not sleep — it seemed unnatural, like a state of trance. Not the faintest sound of any kind could be heard. You looked on amazed, and began to suspect yourself of being deaf — then the night came suddenly, and struck you blind as well. About three in the morning some large fish leaped, and the loud splash made me jump as though a gun had been fired. When the sun rose there was a white fog, very warm and clammy, and more blinding than the night. It did not shift or drive; it was just there, standing all round you like something solid. At eight or nine, perhaps, it lifted as a shutter lifts. We had a glimpse of the towering multitude of trees, of the immense matted jungle, with the blazing little ball of the sun hanging over it — all perfectly still — and then the white shutter came down again, smoothly, as if sliding in greased grooves. I ordered the chain, which we had begun to heave in, to be paid out again. Before it stopped running with a muffled rattle, a cry, a very loud cry, as of infinite desolation, soared slowly in the opaque air. It ceased. A complaining clamor, modulated in savage discords, filled our ears. The sheer unexpectedness of it made my hair stir under my cap. I don't know how it struck the others: to me it seemed as though the mist itself had screamed, so suddenly, and apparently from all sides at once, did this tumultuous and mournful uproar arise. It culminated in a hurried outbreak of almost intolerably excessive shrieking, which stopped short, leaving us stiffened in a variety of silly attitudes, and obstinately listening to the nearly as appalling and excessive silence. 'Good God! What is the meaning —' stammered at my elbow one of the pilgrims, — a little fat man, with sandy hair and red whiskers, who wore side-spring boots, and pink pajamas tucked into his socks. Two others remained open-mouthed a whole minute, then dashed into the little cabin, to rush out incontinently and stand darting scared glances, with Winchesters at 'ready' in their hands. What we could see was just the steamer we were on, her outlines blurred as though she had been on the point of dissolving, and a misty strip of water, perhaps two feet broad, around her — and that was all. The rest of the world was nowhere, as far as our eyes and ears were concerned. Just nowhere. Gone, disappeared; swept off without leaving a whisper or a shadow behind.

"I went forward, and ordered the chain to be hauled in short, so as to be ready to trip the anchor and move the steamboat at once if necessary. 'Will they attack?' whispered an awed voice. 'We will be all butchered in this fog,' murmured another. The faces twitched with the strain, the hands trembled slightly, the eyes forgot to wink. It was very curious to see the contrast of expressions of the white men and of the black fellows of our crew, who were as much strangers to that part of the river as we, though their homes were only eight hundred miles away. The whites, of course, greatly discomposed, had besides a curious look of being painfully shocked by such an outrageous row. The others had an alert, naturally interested expression; but their faces were essentially quiet, even those of the one or two who grinned as they hauled at the chain. Several exchanged short, grunting phrases, which seemed to settle the matter to their satisfaction. Their headman, a young, broad-chested black, severely draped in dark-blue fringed cloths, with fierce nostrils and his hair all done up artfully in oily ringlets, stood near me. 'Aha!' I said, just for good fellowship's sake. 'Catch 'im,' he snapped, with a bloodshot widening of his eyes and a flash of sharp teeth — 'catch 'im. Give 'im to us.' 'To you, eh?' I asked; 'what would you do with them?' 'Eat 'im!' he said, curtly, and, leaning his elbow on the rail, looked out into the fog in a dignified and profoundly pensive attitude. I would no doubt have been properly horrified, had it not occurred to me that he and his chaps must be very hungry: that they must have been growing increasingly hungry for at least this month past. They had been engaged for six months (I don't think a single one of them had any clear idea of time, as we at the end of countless ages have. They still belonged to the beginnings of time — had no inherited experience to teach them as it were), and of course, as long as there was a piece of paper written over in accordance with some farcical law or other made down the river, it didn't enter anybody's head to trouble how they would live. Certainly they had brought with them some rotten hippo-meat, which couldn't have lasted very long, anyway, even if the pilgrims hadn't, in the midst of a shocking hullabaloo, thrown a considerable quantity of it overboard. It looked like a high-handed proceeding; but it was really a case of legitimate self-defense. You can't breathe dead hippo waking, sleeping, and eating, and at the same time keep your precarious grip on existence. Besides that, they had given them every week three pieces of brass wire, each about nine inches long; and the theory was they were to buy their provisions with that currency in riverside villages. You can see how *that* worked. There were either no villages, or the people were hostile, or the director, who like the rest of us fed out of tins, with an occasional old he-goat thrown in, didn't want to stop the steamer for some more or less recondite reason. So, unless they swallowed the wire itself, or made loops of it to snare the fishes with, I don't see what good their extravagant salary could be to them. I must say it was paid with a regularity worthy of a large and honorable trading company. For the rest, the only thing to eat — though it didn't look eatable in the least — I saw in their possession was a few lumps of some stuff like half-cooked dough, of a dirty lavender color, they kept wrapped in leaves, and now and then swallowed a piece of, but so small that it seemed done more for the looks of the thing than for any serious purpose of sustenance. Why in the name of all the gnawing devils of hunger they didn't go for us — they were thirty to five — and have a good tuck-in for once, amazes me now when I think of it. They were big powerful men, with not much capacity to weigh the consequences, with courage, with strength, even yet, though their skins were no longer glossy and their muscles no longer hard. And I saw that something restraining, one of those human secrets that baffle probability, had come into play there. I looked at them with a swift quickening of interest — not because it occurred to me I might be eaten by them before very long, though I own to you that just then I perceived — in a new light, as it were — how unwholesome the pilgrims looked, and I hoped, yes, I positively hoped, that my aspect was not so — what shall I say? — so — unappetizing: a touch of fantastic vanity which fitted well with the dream-sensation that pervaded all my days at that time. Perhaps I had a little fever, too. One can't live with one's finger everlastingly on one's pulse. I had often 'a little fever,' or a little touch of other things — the playful paw-strokes of the wilderness, the preliminary trifling before the more serious onslaught which came in due course. Yes; I looked at them as you would on any human being, with a curiosity of their impulses, motives, capacities, weaknesses, when brought to the test of an inexorable physical necessity. Restraint! What possible restraint? Was it superstition, disgust, patience, fear — or some kind of primitive honor? No fear can stand up to hunger, no patience can wear it out, disgust simply does not exist where hunger is; and as to superstition, beliefs, and what you may call principles, they are less than chaff in a breeze. Don't you know the devilry of lingering starvation, its exasperating torment, its black thoughts, its somber and brooding ferocity? Well, I do. It takes a man all his inborn strength to fight hunger properly. It's really easier to face bereavement, dishonor, and the perdition of one's soul — than this kind of prolonged hunger. Sad, but true. And these chaps, too, had no earthly reason for any kind of scruple. Restraint! I would just as soon have expected restraint from a hyena prowling amongst the corpses of a battlefield. But there was the fact facing me — the fact dazzling, to be seen, like the foam on the depths of the sea, like a ripple on an unfathomable enigma, a mystery greater — when I thought of it — than the curious, inexplicable note of desperate grief in this savage clamor that had swept by us on the river-bank, behind the blind whiteness of the fog.

"Two pilgrims were quarreling in hurried whispers as to which bank. 'Left.' 'No, no; how can you? Right, right, of course.' 'It is very serious,' said the manager's voice behind me; 'I would be desolated if anything should happen to Mr. Kurtz before we came up.' I looked at him, and had not the slightest doubt he was sincere. He was just the kind of man who would wish to preserve appearances. That was his restraint. But when he muttered something about going on at once, I did not even take the trouble to answer him. I knew, and he knew, that it was impossible. Were we to let go our hold of the bottom, we would be absolutely in the air — in space. We wouldn't be able to tell where we were going to — whether up or down stream, or across — till we fetched against one bank or the other, — and then we wouldn't know at first which it was. Of course I made no move. I had no mind for a smash-up. You couldn't imagine a more deadly place for a shipwreck. Whether drowned at once or not, we were sure to perish speedily in one way or another. 'I authorize you to take all the risks,' he said, after a short silence. 'I refuse to take any,' I said, shortly; which was just the answer he expected, though its tone might have surprised him. 'Well, I must defer to your judgment. You are captain,' he said, with marked civility. I turned my shoulder to him in sign of my appreciation, and looked into the fog. How long would it last? It was the most hopeless lookout. The approach to this Kurtz grubbing for ivory in the wretched bush was beset by as many dangers as though he had been an enchanted princess sleeping in a fabulous castle. 'Will they attack, do you think?' asked the manager, in a confidential tone.

"I did not think they would attack, for several obvious reasons. The thick fog was one. If they left the bank in their canoes they would get lost in it, as we would be if we attempted to move. Still, I had also judged the jungle of both banks quite impenetrable — and yet eyes were in it, eyes that had seen us. The river-side bushes were certainly very thick; but the undergrowth behind was evidently penetrable. However, during the short lift I had seen no canoes anywhere in the reach — certainly not abreast of the steamer. But what made the idea of attack inconceivable to me was the nature of the noise — of the cries we had heard. They had not the fierce character boding immediate hostile intention. Unexpected, wild, and violent as they had been, they had given me an irresistible impression of sorrow. The glimpse of the steamboat had for some reason filled those savages with unrestrained grief. The danger, if any, I expounded, was from our proximity to a great human passion let loose. Even extreme grief may ultimately vent itself in violence — but more generally takes the form of apathy. . . .

"You should have seen the pilgrims stare! They had no heart to grin, or even to revile me: but I believe they thought me gone mad — with fright, maybe. I delivered a regular lecture. My dear boys, it was no good bothering. Keep a look-out? Well, you may guess I watched the fog for the signs of lifting as a cat watches a mouse; but for anything else our eyes were of no more use to us than if we had been buried miles deep in a heap of cotton-wool. It felt like it, too — choking, warm, stifling. Besides, all I said, though it sounded extravagant, was absolutely true to fact. What we afterwards alluded to as an attack was really an attempt at repulse. The action was very far from being aggressive — it was not even defensive, in the usual sense: it was undertaken under the stress of desperation, and in its essence was purely protective.

"It developed itself, I should say, two hours after the fog lifted, and its commencement was at a spot, roughly speaking, about a mile and a half below Kurtz's station. We had just floundered and flopped round a bend, when I saw an islet, a mere grassy hummock of bright green, in the middle of the stream. It was the only thing of the kind; but as we opened the reach more, I perceived it was the head of a long sandbank, or rather of a chain of shallow patches stretching down the middle of the river. They were discolored, just awash, and the whole lot was seen just under the water, exactly as a man's backbone is seen running down the middle of his back under the skin. Now, as far as I did see, I could go to the right or to the left of this. I didn't know either channel, of course. The banks looked pretty well alike, the depth appeared the same; but as I had been informed the station was on the west side, I naturally headed for the western passage.

"No sooner had we fairly entered it than I became aware it was much narrower than I had supposed. To the left of us there was the long uninterrupted shoal, and to the right a high, steep bank heavily overgrown with bushes. Above the bush the trees stood in serried ranks. The twigs overhung the current thickly, and from distance to distance a large limb of some tree projected rigidly over the stream. It was then well on in the afternoon, the face of the forest was gloomy, and a broad strip of shadow had already fallen on the water. In this shadow we steamed up — very slowly, as you may imagine. I sheered her well inshore — the water being deepest near the bank, as the sounding-pole informed me.

"One of my hungry and forbearing friends was sounding in the bows just below me. This steamboat was exactly like a decked scow. On the deck, there were two little teak-wood houses, with doors and windows. The boiler was in the fore-end, and the machinery right astern. Over the whole there was a light roof, supported on stanchions. The funnel projected through that roof, and in front of the funnel a small cabin built of light planks served for a pilot-house. It contained a couch, two campstools, a loaded Martini-Henry leaning in one corner, a tiny table, and the steering-wheel. It had a wide door in front and a broad shutter at each side. All these were always thrown open, of course. I spent my days perched up there on the extreme fore-end of that roof, before the door. At night I slept, or tried to, on the couch. An athletic black belonging to some coast tribe, and educated by my poor predecessor, was the helmsman. He sported a pair of brass earrings, wore a blue cloth wrapper from the waist to the ankles, and thought all the world of himself. He was the most unstable kind of fool I had ever seen. He steered with no end of a swagger while you were by; but if he lost sight of you, he became instantly the prey of an abject funk, and would let that cripple of a steamboat get the upper hand of him in a minute.

"I was looking down at the sounding-pole, and feeling much annoyed to see at each try a little more of it stick out of that river, when I saw my poleman give up the business suddenly, and stretch himself flat on the deck, without even taking the trouble to haul his pole in. He kept hold on it though, and it trailed in the water. At the same time the fireman, whom I could also see below me, sat down abruptly before his furnace and ducked his head. I was amazed. Then I had to look at the river mighty quick, because there was a snag in the fairway. Sticks, little sticks, were flying about — thick: they were whizzing before my nose, dropping below me, striking behind me against my pilot-house. All this time the river, the shore, the woods, were very quiet — perfectly quiet. I could only hear the heavy splashing thump of the stern-wheel and the patter of these things. We cleared the snag clumsily. Arrows, by Jove! We were being shot at! I stepped in quickly to close the shutter on the land-side. That fool-helmsman, his hands on the spokes, was lifting his knees high, stamping his feet, champing his mouth, like a reined-in horse. Confound him! And we were staggering within ten feet of the bank. I had to lean right out to swing the heavy shutter, and I saw a face amongst the leaves on the level with my own, looking at me very fierce and steady; and then suddenly, as though a veil had been removed from my eyes, I made out, deep in the tangled gloom, naked breasts, arms, legs, glaring eyes — the bush was swarming with human limbs in movement, glistening, of bronze color. The twigs shook, swayed, and rustled, the arrows flew out of them, and then the shutter came to. 'Steer her straight,' I said to the helmsman. He held his head rigid, face forward; but his eyes rolled, he kept on lifting and setting down his feet gently, his mouth foamed a little. 'Keep quiet!' I said in a fury. I might just as well have ordered a tree not to sway in the wind. I darted out. Below me there was a great scuffle of feet on the iron deck; confused exclamations; a voice screamed, 'Can you turn back?' I caught sight of a V-shaped ripple on the water ahead. What? Another snag! A fusillade burst out under my feet. The pilgrims had opened with their Winchesters, and were simply squirting lead into that bush. A deuce of a lot of smoke came up and drove slowly forward. I swore at it. Now I couldn't see the ripple or the snag either. I stood in the doorway, peering, and the arrows came in swarms. They might have been poisoned, but they looked as though they wouldn't kill a cat. The bush began to howl. Our wood-cutters raised a warlike whoop; the report of a rifle just at my back deafened me. I glanced over my shoulder, and the pilot-house was yet full of noise and smoke when I made a dash at the wheel. The fool-nigger had dropped everything to throw the shutter open and let off that Martini-Henry. He stood before the wide opening, glaring, and I yelled at him to come back, while I straightened the sudden twist out of that steamboat. There was no room to turn even if I had wanted to, the snag was somewhere very near ahead in that confounded smoke, there was no time to lose, so I just crowded her into the bank — right into the bank, where I knew the water was deep.

"We tore slowly along the overhanging bushes in a whirl of broken twigs and flying leaves. The fusillade below stopped short, as I had foreseen it would when the squirts got empty. I threw my head back to a glinting whizz that traversed the pilot-house, in at one shutter-hole and out at the other. Looking past that mad helmsman, who was shaking the empty rifle and yelling at the shore, I saw vague forms of men running bent double, leaping, gliding, distinct, incomplete, evanescent. Something big appeared in the air before the shutter, the rifle went overboard, and the man stepped back swiftly, looked at me over his shoulder in an extraordinary, profound, familiar manner, and fell upon my feet. The side of his head hit the wheel twice, and the end of what appeared a long cane clattered round and knocked over a little campstool. It looked as though after wrenching that thing from somebody ashore he had lost his balance in the effort. The thin smoke had blown away, we were clear of the snag, and looking ahead I could see that in another hundred yards or so I would be free to sheer off, away from the bank; but my feet felt so very warm and wet that I had to look down. The man had rolled on his back and stared straight up at me; both his hands clutched that cane. It was the shaft of a spear that, either thrown or lunged through the opening, had caught him in the side just below the ribs; the blade had gone in out of sight, after making a frightful gash; my shoes were full; a pool of blood lay very still, gleaming dark-red under the wheel; his eyes shone with an amazing luster. The fusillade burst out again. He looked at me anxiously, gripping the spear like something precious, with an air of being afraid I would try to take it away from him. I had to make an effort to free my eyes from his gaze and attend to steering. With one hand I felt above my head for the line of the steamwhistle, and jerked out screech after screech hurriedly. The tumult of angry and warlike yells was checked instantly, and then from the depths of the woods went out such a tremulous and prolonged wail of mournful fear and utter despair as may be imagined to follow the flight of the last hope from the earth. There was a great commotion in the bush; the shower of arrows stopped, a few dropping shots rang out sharply — then silence, in which the languid beat of the stern-wheel came plainly to my ears. I put the helm hard a-starboard at the moment when the pilgrim in pink pajamas, very hot

and agitated, appeared in the doorway. 'The manager sends me — '
he began in an official tone, and stopped short. 'Good God!' he
said, glaring at the wounded man.

"We two whites stood over him, and his lustrous and inquiring
glance enveloped us both. I declare it looked as though he would
presently put to us some question in an understandable language;
but he died without uttering a sound, without moving a limb, without twitching a muscle. Only in the very last moment, as though in
response to some sign we could not see, to some whisper we could
not hear, he frowned heavily, and that frown gave to his black
death-mask an inconceivably somber, brooding, and menacing expression. The luster of inquiring glance faded swiftly into vacant
glassiness. 'Can you steer?' I asked the agent eagerly. He looked
very dubious; but I made a grab at his arm, and he understood at
once I meant him to steer whether or no. To tell you the truth, I
was morbidly anxious to change my shoes and socks. 'He is dead,'
murmured the fellow, immensely impressed. 'No doubt about it,'
said I tugging like mad at the shoe-laces. 'And by the way, I suppose Mr. Kurtz is dead as well by this time.'

"For the moment that was the dominant thought. There was a
sense of extreme disappointment, as though I had found out I had
been striving after something altogether without a substance. I
couldn't have been more disgusted if I had traveled all this way
for the sole purpose of talking with Mr. Kurtz. Talking with . . . I
flung one shoe overboard and became aware that that was exactly
what I had been looking forward to — a talk with Kurtz. I made
the strange discovery that I had never imagined him as doing, you
know, but as discoursing. I didn't say to myself, 'Now I will never
see him,' or 'Now I will never shake him by the hand,' but, 'Now
I will never hear him.' The man presented himself as a voice. Not
of course that I did not connect him with some sort of action.
Hadn't I been told in all the tones of jealousy and admiration that
he had collected, bartered, swindled, or stolen more ivory than all
the other agents together? That was not the point. The point was
in his being a gifted creature, and that of all his gifts the one that
stood out pre-eminently, that carried with it a sense of real presence,
was his ability to talk, his words — the gift of expression, the bewildering, the illuminating, the most exalted and the most con-
temptible, the pulsating stream of light, or the deceitful flow from
the heart of an impenetrable darkness.

"The other shoe went flying unto the devil-god of that river. I thought, by Jove! it's all over. We are too late; he has vanished — the gift has vanished, by means of some spear, arrow, or club. I will never hear that chap speak after all, — and my sorrow had a startling extravagance of emotion, even such as I had noticed in the howling sorrow of these savages in the bush. I couldn't have felt more lonely desolation somehow, had I been robbed of a belief or had missed my destiny in life. . . . Why do you sigh in this beastly way, somebody? Absurd? Well, absurd. Good Lord! mustn't a man ever — Here, give me some tobacco." . . .

There was a pause of profound stillness, then a match flared, and Marlow's lean face appeared, worn, hollow, with downward folds and drooped eyelids, with an aspect of concentrated attention; and as he took vigorous draws at his pipe, it seemed to retreat and advance out of the night in the regular flicker of the tiny flame. The match went out.

"Absurd!" he cried. "This is the worst of trying to tell. . . . Here you all are, each moored with two good addresses, like a hulk with two anchors, a butcher round one corner, a policeman round another, excellent appetites, and temperature normal — you hear — normal from year's end to year's end. And you say, Absurd! Absurd be — exploded! Absurd! My dear boys, what can you expect from a man who out of sheer nervousness had just flung overboard a pair of new shoes! Now I think of it, it is amazing I did not shed tears. I am, upon the whole, proud of my fortitude. I was cut to the quick at the idea of having lost the inestimable privilege of listening to the gifted Kurtz. Of course I was wrong. The privilege was waiting for me. Oh, yes, I heard more than enough. And I was right, too. A voice. He was very little more than a voice. And I heard — him — it — this voice — other voices — all of them were so little more than voices — and the memory of that time itself lingers around me, impalpable, like a dying vibration of one immense jabber, silly, atrocious, sordid, savage, or simply mean, without any kind of sense. Voices, voices — even the girl herself — now — "

He was silent for a long time.

"I laid the ghost of his gifts at last with a lie," he began, suddenly. "Girl! What? Did I mention a girl? Oh, she is out of it — completely. They — the women I mean — are out of it — should be out of it. We must help them to stay in that beautiful world of their own, lest ours gets worse. Oh, she had to be out of it. You should have heard the disinterred body of Mr. Kurtz saying, 'My Intended.' You would have perceived directly then how completely she was out of it. And the lofty frontal bone of Mr. Kurtz! They say the hair goes on growing sometimes, but this — ah — specimen was impressively bald. The wilderness had patted him on the head, and, behold, it was like a ball — an ivory ball; it had caressed him, and — lo! — he had withered; it had taken him, loved him, embraced him, got into his veins, consumed his flesh, and sealed his soul to its own by the inconceivable ceremonies of some devilish initiation. He was its spoiled and pampered favorite. Ivory? I should think so. Heaps of it, stacks of it. The old mud shanty was bursting with it. You would think there was not a single tusk left either above or below the ground in the whole country. 'Mostly fossil,' the manager had remarked, disparagingly. It was no more fossil than I am; but they call it fossil when it is dug up. It appears these niggers do bury the tusks sometimes — but evidently they couldn't bury this parcel deep enough to save the gifted Mr. Kurtz from his fate. We filled the steamboat with it, and had to pile a lot on the deck. Thus he could see and enjoy as long as he could see, because the appreciation of this favor had remained with him to the last. You should have heard him say, 'My ivory.' Oh, yes, I heard him. 'My Intended, my ivory, my station, my river, my —' everything belonged to him. It made me hold my breath in expectation of hearing the wilderness burst into a prodigious peal of laughter that would shake the fixed stars in their places. Everything belonged to him — but that was a trifle. The thing was to know what he belonged to, how many powers of darkness claimed him for their own. That was the reflection that made you creepy all over. It was impossible — it was not good for one either — trying to imagine. He had taken a high seat amongst the devils of the land — I mean literally. You can't understand. How could you? — with solid pavement under your feet, surrounded by kind neighbors ready to cheer you or to fall on you, stepping delicately between the butcher and the policeman, in the holy terror of scandal and gallows and lunatic asylums — how can you imagine what particular region of the first ages a man's untrammeled feet may take him into by the way of solitude — utter solitude without a policeman — by the way of silence — utter silence, where no warning voice of a kind neighbor can be heard whispering of public opinion? These little things make all the great difference. When they are gone you must fall back upon your own innate strength, upon your own capacity for faithfulness. Of course you may be too much of a fool to go wrong — too dull even to know you are being assaulted by the powers of darkness. I take it, no fool ever made a bargain for his soul with the devil: the fool is too much of a fool, or the devil too much of a devil — I don't know which. Or you may be such a thunderingly exalted creature as to be altogether deaf and blind to anything but heavenly sights and sounds. Then the earth for you is only a standing place — and whether to be like this is your loss or your gain I won't pretend to say. But most of us are neither one nor the other. The earth for us is a place to live in, where we must put up with sights, with sounds, with smells, too, by Jove! — breathe dead hippo, so to speak, and not be contaminated. And there, don't you see? your strength comes in, the faith in your ability for the digging of unostentatious holes to bury the stuff in — your power of devotion, not to yourself, but to an obscure, back-breaking business. And that's difficult enough. Mind, I am not trying to excuse or even explain — I am trying to account to myself for — for — Mr. Kurtz — for the shade of Mr. Kurtz. This initiated wraith from the back of Nowhere honored me with its amazing confidence before it vanished altogether. This was because it could speak English to me. The original Kurtz had been educated partly in England, and — as he was good enough to say himself — his sympathies were in the right place. His mother was half-English, his father was half-French. All Europe contributed to the making of Kurtz; and by and by I learned that, most appropriately, the International Society for the Suppression of Savage Customs had intrusted him with the making of a report, for its future guidance. And he had written it, too. I've seen it. I've read it. It was eloquent, vibrating with eloquence, but too high-strung, I think. Seventeen pages of close writing he had found time for! But this must have been before his — let us say — nerves, went wrong, and caused him to preside at certain midnight dances ending with unspeakable rites, which — as far as I reluctantly gathered from what I heard at various times — were offered up to him — do you understand? — to Mr. Kurtz himself. But it was a beautiful piece of writing. The opening paragraph, however, in the light of later information, strikes me now as ominous. He began with the argument that we whites, from the point of development we had arrived at, 'must necessarily appear to them [savages] in the nature of supernatural

beings — we approach them with the might as of a deity,' and so
on, and so on. 'By the simple exercise of our will we can exert a
power for good practically unbounded,' etc., etc. From that point
he soared and took me with him. The peroration was magnificent,
though difficult to remember, you know. It gave me the notion of
an exotic Immensity ruled by an august Benevolence. It made me
tingle with enthusiasm. This was the unbounded power of eloquence — of words — of burning noble words. There were no
practical hints to interrupt the magic current of phrases, unless a
kind of note at the foot of the last page, scrawled evidently much
later, in an unsteady hand, may be regarded as the exposition of a
method. It was very simple, and at the end of that moving appeal
to every altruistic sentiment it blazed at you, luminous and terrifying, like a flash of lightning in a serene sky: 'Exterminate all the
brutes!' The curious part was that he had apparently forgotten all
about that valuable postscriptum, because, later on, when he in a
sense came to himself, he repeatedly entreated me to take good care
of 'my pamphlet' (he called it), as it was sure to have in the future
a good influence upon his career. I had full information about all
these things, and, besides, as it turned out, I was to have the care of
his memory. I've done enough for it to give me the indisputable
right to lay it, if I choose, for an everlasting rest in the dustbin of
progress, amongst all the sweepings and, figuratively speaking, all
the dead cats of civilization. But then, you see, I can't choose. He
won't be forgotten. Whatever he was, he was not common. He
had the power to charm or frighten rudimentary souls into an
aggravated witch-dance in his honor; he could also fill the small
souls of the pilgrims with bitter misgivings: he had one devoted
friend at least, and he had conquered one soul in the world that
was neither rudimentary nor tainted with self-seeking. No; I can't
forget him, though I am not prepared to affirm the fellow was exactly worth the life we lost in getting to him. I missed my late
helmsman awfully, — I missed him even while his body was still
lying in the pilot-house. Perhaps you will think it passing strange
this regret for a savage who was no more account than a grain of
sand in a black Sahara. Well, don't you see, he had done something,
he had steered; for months I had him at my back — a help — an
instrument. It was a kind of partnership. He steered for me — I
had to look after him, I worried about his deficiencies, and thus a
subtle bond had been created, of which I only became aware when

it was suddenly broken. And the intimate profundity of that look he gave me when he received his hurt remains to this day in my memory — like a claim of distant kinship affirmed in a supreme moment.

"Poor fool! If he had only left that shutter alone. He had no restraint, no restraint — just like Kurtz — a tree swayed by the wind. As soon as I had put on a dry pair of slippers, I dragged him out, after first jerking the spear out of his side, which operation I confess I performed with my eyes shut tight. His heels leaped together over the little door-step; his shoulders were pressed to my breast; I hugged him from behind desperately. Oh! he was heavy, heavy; heavier than any man on earth, I should imagine. Then without more ado I tipped him overboard. The current snatched him as though he had been a wisp of grass, and I saw the body roll over twice before I lost sight of it forever. All the pilgrims and the manager were then congregated on the awning-deck about the pilot-house, chattering at each other like a flock of excited magpies, and there was a scandalized murmur at my heartless promptitude. What they wanted to keep that body hanging about for I can't guess. Embalm it, maybe. But I had also heard another, and a very ominous, murmur on the deck below. My friends the wood-cutters were likewise scandalized, and with a better show of reason — though I admit that the reason itself was quite inadmissible. Oh, quite! I had made up my mind that if my late helmsman was to be eaten, the fishes alone should have him. He had been a very second-rate helmsman while alive, but now he was dead he might have become a first-class temptation, and possibly cause some startling trouble. Besides, I was anxious to take the wheel, the man in pink pajamas showing himself a hopeless duffer at the business.

"This I did directly the simple funeral was over. We were going half-speed, keeping right in the middle of the stream, and I listened to the talk about me. They had given up Kurtz, they had given up the station; Kurtz was dead, and the station had been burnt — and so on — and so on. The red-haired pilgrim was beside himself with the thought that at least this poor Kurtz had been properly avenged. 'Say! We must have made a glorious slaughter of them in the bush. Eh? What do you think? Say?' He positively danced, the bloodthirsty little gingery beggar. And he had nearly fainted when he saw the wounded man! I could not help saying, 'You

made a glorious lot of smoke, anyhow.' I had seen, from the way
the tops of the bushes rustled and flew, that almost all the shots had
gone too high. You can't hit anything unless you take aim and fire
from the shoulder; but these chaps fired from the hip with their
eyes shut. The retreat, I maintained — and I was right — was caused
by the screeching of the steam-whistle. Upon this they forgot
Kurtz, and began to howl at me with indignant protests.

"The manager stood by the wheel murmuring confidentially
about the necessity of getting well away down the river before
dark at all events, when I saw in the distance a clearing on the
river-side and the outlines of some sort of building. 'What's this?'
I asked. He clapped his hands in wonder. 'The station!' he cried.
I edged in at once, still going half-speed.

"Through my glasses I saw the slope of a hill interspersed with
rare trees and perfectly free from undergrowth. A long decaying
building on the summit was half buried in the high grass; the large
holes in the peaked roof gaped black from afar; the jungle and the
woods made a background. There was no enclosure or fence of
any kind; but there had been one apparently, for near the house
half-a-dozen slim posts remained in a row, roughly trimmed, and
with their upper ends ornamented with round carved balls. The
rails, or whatever there had been between, had disappeared. Of
course the forest surrounded all that. The river-bank was clear, and
on the water-side I saw a white man under a hat like a cart-wheel
beckoning persistently with his whole arm. Examining the edge
of the forest above and below, I was almost certain I could see
movements — human forms gliding here and there. I steamed past
prudently, then stopped the engines and let her drift down. The
man on the shore began to shout, urging us to land. 'We have been
attacked,' screamed the manager. 'I know — I know. It's all right,'
yelled back the other, as cheerful as you please. 'Come along. It's
all right. I am glad.'

"His aspect reminded me of something I had seen — something
funny I had seen somewhere. As I maneuvered to get alongside, I
was asking myself, 'What does this fellow look like?' Suddenly I
got it. He looked like a harlequin. His clothes had been made of
some stuff that was brown holland probably, but it was covered
with patches all over, with bright patches, blue, red, and yellow,
— patches on the back, patches on the front, patches on elbows, on
knees; colored binding around his jacket, scarlet edging at the bot-

tom of his trousers; and the sunshine made him look extremely gay
and wonderfully neat withal, because you could see how beautifully
all this patching had been done. A beardless, boyish face, very fair,
no features to speak of, nose peeling, little blue eyes, smiles and
frowns chasing each other over that open countenance like sunshine
and shadow on a wind-swept plain. 'Look out, captain!' he cried;
'there's a snag lodged in here last night.' What! Another snag? I
confess I swore shamefully. I had nearly holed my cripple, to finish
off that charming trip. The harlequin on the bank turned his little
pug-nose up to me. 'You English?' he asked, all smiles. 'Are you?'
I shouted from the wheel. The smiles vanished, and he shook his
head as if sorry for my disappointment. Then he brightened up.
'Never mind!' he cried, encouragingly. 'Are we in time?' I asked.
'He is up there,' he replied, with a toss of the head up the hill, and
becoming gloomy all of a sudden. His face was like the autumn
sky, overcast one moment and bright the next.

"When the manager, escorted by the pilgrims, all of them armed
to the teeth, had gone to the house this chap came on board. 'I
say, I don't like this. These natives are in the bush,' I said. He
assured me earnestly it was all right. 'They are simple people,' he
added; 'well, I am glad you came. It took me all my time to keep
them off.' 'But you said it was all right,' I cried. 'Oh, they meant
no harm,' he said; and as I stared he corrected himself, 'Not exactly.' Then vivaciously, 'My faith, your pilot-house wants a clean-
up!' In the next breath he advised me to keep enough steam on the
boiler to blow the whistle in case of any trouble. 'One good screech
will do more for you than all your rifles. They are simple people,'
he repeated. He rattled away at such a rate he quite overwhelmed
me. He seemed to be trying to make up for lots of silence, and
actually hinted, laughing, that such was the case. 'Don't you talk
with Mr. Kurtz?' I said. 'You don't talk with that man — you
listen to him,' he exclaimed with severe exaltation. 'But now — ' He
waved his arm, and in the twinkling of an eye was in the uttermost
depths of despondency. In a moment he came up again with a
jump, possessed himself of both my hands, shook them continuously, while he gabbled: 'Brother sailor . . . honor . . . pleasure . . .
delight . . . introduce myself . . . Russian . . . son of an arch-priest
. . . Government of Tambov. . . . What? Tobacco! English tobacco;
the excellent English tobacco! Now, that's brotherly. Smoke?
Where's a sailor that does not smoke?'

"The pipe soothed him, and gradually I made out he had run away from school, had gone to sea in a Russian ship; ran away again; served some time in English ships; was now reconciled with the arch-priest. He made a point of that. 'But when one is young one must see things, gather experience, ideas; enlarge the mind.' 'Here!' I interrupted. 'You can never tell! Here I met Mr. Kurtz,' he said, youthfully solemn and reproachful. I held my tongue after that. It appears he had persuaded a Dutch trading-house on the coast to fit him out with stores and goods, and had started for the interior with a light heart, and no more idea of what would happen to him than a baby. He had been wandering about that river for nearly two years alone, cut off from everybody and everything. 'I am not so young as I look. I am twenty-five,' he said. 'At first old Van Shuyten would tell me to go to the devil,' he narrated with keen enjoyment; 'but I stuck to him, and talked and talked, till at last he got afraid I would talk the hind-leg off his favorite dog, so he gave me some cheap things and a few guns, and told me he hoped he would never see my face again. Good old Dutchman, Van Shuyten. I've sent him one small lot of ivory a year ago, so that he can't call me a little thief when I get back. I hope he got it. And for the rest I don't care. I had some wood stacked for you. That was my old house. Did you see?'

"I gave him Towson's book. He made as though he would kiss me, but restrained himself. 'The only book I had left, and I thought I had lost it,' he said, looking at it ecstatically. 'So many accidents happen to a man going about alone, you know. Canoes get upset sometimes — and sometimes you've got to clear out so quick when the people get angry.' He thumbed the pages. 'You made notes in Russian?' I asked. He nodded. 'I thought they were written in cipher,' I said. He laughed, then became serious. 'I had lots of trouble to keep these people off,' he said. 'Did they want to kill you?' I asked. 'Oh, no!' he cried, and checked himself. 'Why did they attack us?' I pursued. He hesitated, then said shamefacedly, 'They don't want him to go.' 'Don't they?' I said, curiously. He nodded a nod full of mystery and wisdom. 'I tell you,' he cried, 'this man has enlarged my mind.' He opened his arms wide, staring at me with his little blue eyes that were perfectly round."

III

"I looked at him, lost in astonishment. There he was before me, in motley, as though he had absconded from a troupe of mimes, enthusiastic, fabulous. His very existence was improbable, inexplicable, and altogether bewildering. He was an insoluble problem. It was inconceivable how he had existed, how he had succeeded in getting so far, how he had managed to remain — why he did not instantly disappear. 'I went a little farther,' he said, 'then still a little farther — till I had gone so far that I don't know how I'll ever get back. Never mind. Plenty time. I can manage. You take Kurtz away quick — quick — I tell you.' The glamour of youth enveloped his parti-colored rags, his destitution, his loneliness, the essential desolation of his futile wanderings. For months — for years — his life hadn't been worth a day's purchase; and there he was gallantly, thoughtlessly alive, to all appearance indestructible solely by the virtue of his few years and of his unreflecting audacity. I was seduced into something like admiration — like envy. Glamour urged him on, glamour kept him unscathed. He surely wanted nothing from the wilderness but space to breathe in and to push on through. His need was to exist, and to move onwards at the greatest possible risk, and with a maximum of privation. If the absolutely pure, uncalculating, unpractical spirit of adventure had ever ruled a human being, it ruled this be-patched youth. I almost envied him the possession of this modest and clear flame. It seemed to have consumed all thought of self so completely, that even while he was talking to you, you forgot that it was he — the man before your eyes — who had gone through these things. I did not envy him his devotion to Kurtz, though. He had not meditated over it. It came to him and he accepted it with a sort of eager fatalism. I must say that to me it appeared about the most dangerous thing in every way he had come upon so far.

"They had come together unavoidably, like two ships becalmed near each other, and lay rubbing sides at last. I suppose Kurtz wanted an audience, because on a certain occasion, when encamped in the forest, they had talked all night, or more probably Kurtz had talked. 'We talked of everything,' he said, quite transported at the recollection. 'I forgot there was such a thing as sleep. The night did not seem to last an hour. Everything! Everything! . . . Of love,

too.' 'Ah, he talked to you of love!' I said, much amused. 'It isn't
what you think,' he cried, almost passionately. 'It was in general.
He made me see things — things.'

"He threw his arms up. We were on deck at the time, and
the headman of my wood-cutters, lounging near by, turned upon
him his heavy and glittering eyes. I looked around, and I don't know
why, but I assure you that never, never before, did this land, this
river, this jungle, the very arch of this blazing sky, appear to me
so hopeless and so dark, so impenetrable to human thought, so pitiless to human weakness. 'And, ever since, you have been with him,
of course?' I said.

"On the contrary. It appears their intercourse had been very
much broken by various causes. He had, as he informed me
proudly, managed to nurse Kurtz through two illnesses (he alluded
to it as you would to some risky feat), but as a rule Kurtz wandered alone far in the depths of the forest. 'Very often coming to
this station, I had to wait days and days before he would turn up,'
he said. 'Ah, it was worth waiting for! — sometimes.' 'What was
he doing? exploring or what?' I asked. 'Oh, yes, of course'; he had
discovered lots of villages, a lake, too — he did not know exactly
in what direction; it was dangerous to inquire too much — but
mostly his expeditions had been for ivory. 'But he had no goods
to trade with by that time,' I objected. 'There's a good lot of cartridges left even yet,' he answered, looking away. 'To speak plainly,
he raided the country,' I said. He nodded. 'Not alone, surely!' He
muttered something about the villages round that lake. 'Kurtz got
the tribe to follow him, did he?' I suggested. He fidgeted a little.
'They adored him,' he said. The tone of these words was so extraordinary that I looked at him searchingly. It was curious to see
his mingled eagerness and reluctance to speak of Kurtz. The man
filled his life, occupied his thoughts, swayed his emotions. 'What
can you expect?' he burst out; 'he came to them with thunder and
lightning, you know — and they had never seen anything like it —
and very terrible. He could be very terrible. You can't judge Mr.
Kurtz as you would an ordinary man. No, no, no! Now — just to
give you an idea — I don't mind telling you, he wanted to shoot
me, too, one day — but I don't judge him.' 'Shoot you!' I cried.
'What for?' 'Well, I had a small lot of ivory the chief of that village
near my house gave me. You see I used to shoot game for them.
Well, he wanted it, and wouldn't hear reason. He declared he would

shoot me unless I gave him the ivory and then cleared out of the country, because he could do so, and had a fancy for it, and there was nothing on earth to prevent him killing whom he jolly well pleased. And it was true, too. I gave him the ivory. What did I care! But I didn't clear out. No, no. I couldn't leave him. I had to be careful, of course, till we got friendly again for a time. He had his second illness then. Afterwards I had to keep out of the way; but I didn't mind. He was living for the most part in those villages on the lake. When he came down to the river, sometimes he would take to me, and sometimes it was better for me to be careful. This man suffered too much. He hated all this, and somehow he couldn't get away. When I had a chance I begged him to try and leave while there was time; I offered to go back with him. And he would say yes, and then he would remain; go off on another ivory hunt; disappear for weeks; forget himself amongst these people — forget himself — you know.' 'Why! he's mad,' I said. He protested indignantly. Mr. Kurtz couldn't be mad. If I had heard him talk, only two days ago, I wouldn't dare hint at such a thing. . . . I had taken up my binoculars while we talked, and was looking at the shore, sweeping the limit of the forest at each side and at the back of the house. The consciousness of there being people in that bush, so silent, so quiet — as silent and quiet as the ruined house on the hill — made me uneasy. There was no sign on the face of natur of this amazing tale that was not so much told as suggested to me in desolate exclamations, completed by shrugs, in interrupted phrases, in hints ending in deep sighs. The woods were unmoved, like a mask — heavy, like the closed door of a prison — they looked with their air of hidden knowledge, of patient expectation, of unapproachable silence. The Russian was explaining to me that it was only lately that Mr. Kurtz had come down to the river, bringing along with him all the fighting men of that lake tribe. He had been absent for several months — getting himself adored, I suppose — and had come down unexpectedly, with the intention to all appearance of making a raid either across the river or down stream. Evidently the appetite for more ivory had got the better of the — what shall I say? — less material aspirations. However he had got much worse suddenly. 'I heard he was lying helpless, and so I came up — took my chance,' said the Russian. 'Oh, he is bad, very bad.' I directed my glass to the house. There were no signs of life, but there was the ruined roof, the long mud wall peeping above the grass, with three little square window-holes, no two of the same size; all this brought within reach of my hand, as it were. And then I made a brusque movement, and one of the remaining posts of that vanished fence leaped up in the field of my glass. You remember I told you I had been struck at the distance by certain attempts at ornamentation, rather remarkable in the ruinous aspect of the place. Now I had suddenly a nearer view, and its first result was to make me throw my head back as if before a blow. Then I went carefully from post to post with my glass, and I saw my mistake. These round knobs were not ornamental but symbolic; they were expressive and puzzling, striking and disturbing — food for thought and also for vultures if there had been any looking down from the sky; but at all events for such ants as were industrious enough to ascend the pole. They would have been even more impressive, those heads on the stakes, if their faces had not been turned to the house. Only one, the first I had made out, was facing my way. I was not so shocked as you may think. The start back I had given was really nothing but a movement of surprise. I had expected to see a knob of wood there, you know. I returned deliberately to the first I had seen — and there it was, black, dried, sunken, with closed eyelids, — a head that seemed to sleep at the top of that pole, and with the shrunken dry lips showing a narrow white line of the teeth, was smiling, too, smiling continuously at some endless and jocose dream of that eternal slumber.

"I am not disclosing any trade secrets. In fact, the manager said afterwards that Mr. Kurtz's methods had ruined the district. I have no opinion on that point, but I want you clearly to understand that there was nothing exactly profitable in these heads being there. They only showed that Mr. Kurtz lacked restraint in the gratification of his various lusts, that there was something wanting in him — some small matter which, when the pressing need arose, could not be found under his magnificent eloquence. Whether he knew of this deficiency himself I can't say. I think the knowledge came to him at last — only at the very last. But the wilderness had found him out early, and had taken on him a terrible vengeance for the fantastic invasion. I think it had whispered to him things about himself which he did not know, things of which he had no conception till he took counsel with this great solitude — and the whisper had proved irresistibly fascinating. It echoed loudly within him because he was hollow at the core. . . . I put down the glass, and the head that had appeared near enough to be spoken to seemed at once to have leaped away from me into inaccessible distance.

"The admirer of Mr. Kurtz was a bit crestfallen. In a hurried indistinct voice he began to assure me he had not dared to take these — say, symbols — down. He was not afraid of the natives; they would not stir till Mr. Kurtz gave the word. His ascendancy was extraordinary. The camps of these people surrounded the place, and the chiefs came every day to see him. They would crawl. . . . 'I don't want to know anything of the ceremonies used when approaching Mr. Kurtz,' I shouted. Curious, this feeling that came over me that such details would be more intolerable than those heads drying on the stakes under Mr. Kurtz's windows. After all, that was only a savage sight, while I seemed at one bound to have been transported into some lightless region of subtle horrors, where pure, uncomplicated savagery was a positive relief, being something that had a right to exist — obviously — in the sunshine. The young man looked at me with surprise. I suppose it did not occur to him that Mr. Kurtz was no idol of mine. He forgot I hadn't heard any of these splendid monologues on, what was it? on love, justice, conduct of life — or what not. If it had come to crawling before Mr. Kurtz, he crawled as much as the veriest savage of them all. I had no idea of the conditions, he said: these heads were the heads of rebels. I shocked him excessively by laughing. Rebels! What would be the next definition I was to hear? There had been enemies, criminals, workers — and these were rebels. Those rebellious heads looked very subdued to me on their sticks. 'You don't know how such a life tries a man like Kurtz,' cried Kurtz's last disciple. 'Well, and you?' I said. 'I! I! I am a simple man. I have no great thoughts. I want nothing from anybody. How can you compare me to . . . ?' His feelings were too much for speech, and suddenly he broke down. 'I don't understand,' he groaned. 'I've been doing my best to keep him alive, and that's enough. I had no hand in all this. I have no abilities. There hasn't been a drop of medicine or a mouthful of invalid food for months here. He was shamefully abandoned. A man like this, with such ideas. Shamefully! Shamefully! I — I — haven't slept for the last ten nights. . . .'

"His voice lost itself in the calm of the evening. The long shadows of the forest had slipped downhill while we talked, had gone far beyond the ruined hovel, beyond the symbolic row of stakes. All this was in the gloom, while we down there were yet in the sunshine, and the stretch of the river abreast of the clearing glittered in a still and dazzling splendor, with a murky and over-shadowed bend above and below. Not a living soul was seen on the shore. The bushes did not rustle.

"Suddenly round the corner of the house a group of men appeared, as though they had come up from the ground. They waded waist-deep in the grass, in a compact body, bearing an improvised stretcher in their midst. Instantly, in the emptiness of the land-scape, a cry arose whose shrillness pierced the still air like a sharp arrow flying straight to the very heart of the land; and, as if by enchantment, streams of human beings — of naked human beings — with spears in their hands, with bows, with shields, with wild glances and savage movements, were poured into the clearing by the dark-faced and pensive forest. The bushes shook, the grass swayed for a time, and then everything stood still in attentive im-mobility.

" 'Now, if he does not say the right thing to them we are all done for,' said the Russian at my elbow. The knot of men with the stretcher had stopped, too, halfway to the steamer, as if petrified. I saw the man on the stretcher sit up, lank and with an uplifted arm, above the shoulders of the bearers. 'Let us hope that the man who can talk so well of love in general will find some particular reason to spare us this time,' I said. I resented bitterly the absurd danger of our situation, as if to be at the mercy of that atrocious phantom had been a dishonoring necessity. I could not hear a sound, but through my glasses I saw the thin arm extended commandingly, the lower jaw moving, the eyes of that apparition shining darkly far in its bony head that nodded with grotesque jerks. Kurtz — Kurtz — that means short in German — don't it? Well, the name was as true as everything else in his life — and death. He looked at least seven feet long. His covering had fallen off, and his body emerged from it pitiful and appalling as from a winding-sheet. I could see the cage of his ribs all astir, the bones of his arm waving. It was as though an animated image of death carved out of old ivory had been shaking its hand with menaces at a motionless crowd of men made of dark and glittering bronze. I saw him open his mouth wide — it gave him a weirdly voracious aspect, as though he had wanted to swallow all the air, all the earth, all the men before him. A deep voice reached me faintly. He must have been shouting. He fell back suddenly. The stretcher shook as the bearers staggered forward again, almost at the same time I noticed that the crowd of savages was vanishing without any perceptible movement of retreat, as if the forest that had ejected these beings so suddenly had drawn them in again as the breath is drawn in a long aspiration.

"Some of the pilgrims behind the stretcher carried his arms — two shotguns, a heavy rifle, and a light revolver-carbine — the thunderbolts of that pitiful Jupiter. The manager bent over him murmuring as he walked beside his head. They laid him down in one of the little cabins — just a room for a bedplace and a camp-stool or two, you know. We had brought his belated correspondence, and a lot of torn envelopes and open letters littered his bed. His hand roamed feebly amongst these papers. I was struck by the fire of his eyes and the composed languor of his expression. It was not so much the exhaustion of disease. He did not seem in pain. This shadow looked satiated and calm, as though for the moment it had had its fill of all the emotions.

"He rustled one of the letters, and looking straight in my face said, 'I am glad.' Somebody had been writing to him about me. These special recommendations were turning up again. The volume of tone he emitted without effort, almost without the trouble of moving his lips, amazed me. A voice! a voice! It was grave, profound, vibrating, while the man did not seem capable of a whisper. However, he had enough strength in him — factitious no doubt — to very nearly make an end of us, as you shall hear directly.

"The manager appeared silently in the doorway; I stepped out at once and he drew the curtain after me. The Russian, eyed curiously by the pilgrims, was staring at the shore. I followed the direction of his glance.

"Dark human shapes could be made out in the distance, flitting indistinctly against the gloomy border of the forest, and near the river two bronze figures, leaning on tall spears, stood in the sunlight under fantastic headdresses of spotted skins, warlike and still in statuesque repose. And from right to left along the lighted shore moved a wild and gorgeous apparition of a woman.

"She walked with measured steps, draped in striped and fringed cloths, treading the earth proudly, with a slight jingle and flash of barbarous ornaments. She carried her head high; her hair was done in the shape of a helmet; she had brass leggings to the knee, brass wire gauntlets to the elbow, a crimson spot on her tawny cheek, innumerable necklaces of glass beads on her neck; bizarre things, charms, gifts of witch-men, that hung about her, glittered and trembled at every step. She must have had the value of several elephant tusks upon her. She was savage and superb, wild-eyed and magnificent; there was something ominous and stately in her deliberate progress. And in the hush that had fallen suddenly upon the whole sorrowful land, the immense wilderness, the colossal body of the fecund and mysterious life seemed to look at her, pensive, as though it had been looking at the image of its own tenebrous and passionate soul.

"She came abreast of the steamer, stood still, and faced us. Her long shadow fell to the water's edge. Her face had a tragic and fierce aspect of wild sorrow and of dumb pain mingled with the fear of some struggling, half-shaped resolve. She stood looking at us without a stir, and like the wilderness itself, with an air of brooding over an inscrutable purpose. A whole minute passed, and then she made a step forward. There was a low jingle, a glint of yellow metal, a sway of fringed draperies, and she stopped as if her heart had failed her. The young fellow by my side growled. The pilgrims murmured at my back. She looked at us all as if her life had depended upon the unswerving steadiness of her glance. Suddenly she opened her bared arms and threw them up rigid above her head, as though in an uncontrollable desire to touch the sky, and at the same time the swift shadows darted out on the earth, swept around on the river, gathering the steamer into a shadowy embrace. A formidable silence hung over the scene.

"She turned away slowly, walked on, following the bank, and passed into the bushes to the left. Once only her eyes gleamed back at us in the dusk of the thickets before she disappeared.

" 'If she had offered to come aboard I really think I would have tried to shoot her,' said the man of patches, nervously. 'I have been risking my life every day for the last fortnight to keep her out of the house. She got in one day and kicked up a row about those miserable rags I picked up in the storeroom to mend my clothes with. I wasn't decent. At least it must have been that, for she talked like a fury to Kurtz for an hour, pointing at me now and then. I don't understand the dialect of this tribe. Luckily for me, I fancy Kurtz felt too ill that day to care, or there would have been mischief. I don't understand. . . . No — it's too much for me. Ah, well, it's all over now.'

"At this moment I heard Kurtz's deep voice behind the curtain: 'Save me! — save the ivory, you mean. Don't tell me. Save *me*! Why, I've had to save you. You are interrupting my plans now. Sick! Sick! Not so sick as you would like to believe. Never mind. I'll carry my ideas out yet — I will return. I'll show you what can be done. You with your little peddling notions — you are interfering with me. I will return. I . . .'

"The manager came out. He did me the honor to take me under the arm and lead me aside. 'He is very low, very low,' he said. He considered it necessary to sigh, but neglected to be consistently sorrowful. 'We have done all we could for him — haven't we? But there is no disguising the fact, Mr. Kurtz has done more harm than good to the Company. He did not see the time was not ripe for vigorous action. Cautiously, cautiously — that's my principle. We must be cautious yet. The district is closed to us for a time. Deplorable! Upon the whole, the trade will suffer. I don't deny there is a remarkable quantity of ivory — mostly fossil. We must save it, at all events — but look how precarious the position is — and why? Because the method is unsound.' 'Do you,' said I, looking at the shore, 'call it "unsound method"?' 'Without doubt,' he exclaimed, hotly. 'Don't you?' . . . 'No method at all,' I murmured after a while. 'Exactly,' he exulted. 'I anticipated this. Shows a complete want of judgment. It is my duty to point it out in the proper quarter.' 'Oh,' said I, 'that fellow — what's his name? — the brickmaker, will make a readable report for you.' He appeared confounded for a moment. It seemed to me I had never breathed an atmosphere so vile, and I turned mentally to Kurtz for relief — positively for relief. 'Nevertheless I think Mr. Kurtz is a remarkable man,' I said with emphasis. He started, dropped on me a cold heavy glance, said very quietly, 'he *was*,' and turned his back on me. My hour of favor was over; I found myself lumped along with Kurtz as a partisan of methods for which the time was not ripe: I was unsound! Ah! but it was something to have at least a choice of nightmares.

"I had turned to the wilderness really, not to Mr. Kurtz, who, I was ready to admit, was as good as buried. And for a moment it seemed to me as if I also were buried in a vast grave full of unspeakable secrets. I felt an intolerable weight oppressing my breast, the smell of the damp earth, the unseen presence of victorious corruption, the darkness of an impenetrable night. . . . The Russian tapped me on the shoulder. I heard him mumbling and

stammering something about 'brother seaman — couldn't conceal
— knowledge of matters that would affect Mr. Kurtz's reputation.'
I waited. For him evidently Mr. Kurtz was not in his grave; I suspect that for him Mr. Kurtz was one of the immortals. 'Well!'
said I at last, 'speak out. As it happens, I am Mr. Kurtz's friend —
in a way.'

"He stated with a good deal of formality that had we not been
'of the same profession,' he would have kept the matter to himself without regard to consequences. 'He suspected there was an
active ill will towards him on the part of these white men that — '
'You are right,' I said, remembering a certain conversation I had
overheard. 'The manager thinks you ought to be hanged.' He
showed a concern at this intelligence which amused me at first. 'I
had better get out of the way quietly,' he said, earnestly. 'I can do
no more for Kurtz now, and they would soon find some excuse.
What's to stop them? There's a military post three hundred miles
from here.' 'Well, upon my word,' said I, 'perhaps you had better
go if you have any friends amongst the savages near by.' 'Plenty,'
he said. 'They are simple people — and I want nothing, you know.'
He stood biting his lip, then: 'I don't want any harm to happen to
these whites here, but of course I was thinking of Mr. Kurtz's reputation — but you are a brother seaman and — ' 'All right,' said I,
after a time. 'Mr. Kurtz's reputation is safe with me.' I did not
know how truly I spoke.

"He informed me, lowering his voice, that it was Kurtz who had
ordered the attack to be made on the steamer. 'He hated sometimes
the idea of being taken away — and then again . . . But I don't
understand these matters. I am a simple man. He thought it would
scare you away — that you would give it up, thinking him dead.
I could not stop him. Oh, I had an awful time of it this last month.'
'Very well,' I said. 'He is all right now.' 'Ye-e-es,' he muttered, not
very convinced apparently. 'Thanks,' said I; 'I shall keep my eyes
open.' 'But quiet — eh?' he urged, anxiously. 'It would be awful
for his reputation if anybody here — ' I promised a complete dis-
cretion with great gravity. 'I have a canoe and three black fellows
waiting not very far. I am off. Could you give me a few Martini-
Henry cartridges?' I could, and did, with proper secrecy. He
helped himself, with a wink at me, to a handful of my tobacco. 'Between sailors — you know — good English tobacco.' At the door
of the pilot-house he turned round — 'I say, haven't you a pair of

shoes you could spare?' He raised one leg. 'Look.' The soles were tied with knotted strings sandal-wise under his bare feet. I rooted out an old pair, at which he looked with admiration before tucking them under his left arm. One of his pockets (bright red) was bulging with cartridges, from the other (dark blue) peeped 'Towson's Inquiry,' etc., etc. He seemed to think himself excellently well equipped for a renewed encounter with the wilderness. 'Ah! I'll never, never meet such a man again. You ought to have heard him recite poetry — his own, too, it was, he told me. Poetry!' He rolled his eyes at the recollection of these delights. 'Oh, he enlarged my mind!' 'Good-by,' said I. He shook hands and vanished in the night. Sometimes I ask myself whether I had ever really seen him — whether it was possible to meet such a phenomenon! . . .

"When I woke up shortly after midnight his warning came to my mind with its hint of danger that seemed, in the starred darkness, real enough to make me get up for the purpose of having a look round. On the hill a big fire burned, illuminating fitfully a crooked corner of the station-house. One of the agents with a picket of a few of our blacks, armed for the purpose, was keeping guard over the ivory; but deep within the forest, red gleams that wavered, that seemed to sink and rise from the ground amongst confused columnar shapes of intense blackness, showed the exact position of the camp where Mr. Kurtz's adorers were keeping their uneasy vigil. The monotonous beating of a big drum filled the air with muffled shocks and a lingering vibration. A steady droning sound of many men chanting each to himself some weird incantation came out from the black, flat wall of the woods as the humming of bees comes out of a hive, and had a strange narcotic effect upon my half-awake senses. I believe I dozed off leaning over the rail, till an abrupt burst of yells, an overwhelming outbreak of a pent-up and mysterious frenzy, woke me up in a bewildered wonder. It was cut short all at once, and the low droning went on with an effect of audible and soothing silence. I glanced casually into the little cabin. A light was burning within, but Mr. Kurtz was not there.

"I think I would have raised an outcry if I had believed my eyes. But I didn't believe them at first — the thing seemed so impossible. The fact is I was completely unnerved by a sheer blank fright, pure abstract terror, unconnected with any distinct shape of physical danger. What made this emotion so overpowering was — how shall

I define it? — the moral shock I received, as if something altogether monstrous, intolerable to thought and odious to the soul, had been thrust upon me unexpectedly. This lasted of course the merest fraction of a second, and then the usual sense of commonplace, deadly danger, the possibility of a sudden onslaught and massacre, or something of the kind, which I saw impending, was positively welcome and composing. It pacified me, in fact, so much, that I did not raise an alarm.

"There was an agent buttoned up inside an ulster and sleeping on a chair on deck within three feet of me. The yells had not awakened him; he snored very slightly; I left him to his slumbers and leaped ashore. I did not betray Mr. Kurtz — it was ordered I should never betray him — it was written I should be loyal to the nightmare of my choice. I was anxious to deal with this shadow by myself alone, — and to this day I don't know why I was so jealous of sharing with anyone the peculiar blackness of that experience.

"As soon as I got on the bank I saw a trail — a broad trail through the grass. I remember the exultation with which I said to myself, 'He can't walk — he is crawling on all-fours — I've got him.' The grass was wet with dew. I strode rapidly with clenched fists. I fancy I had some vague notion of falling upon him and giving him a drubbing. I don't know. I had some imbecile thoughts. The knitting old woman with the cat obtruded herself upon my memory as a most improper person to be sitting at the other end of such an affair. I saw a row of pilgrims squirting lead in the air out of Winchesters held to the hip. I thought I would never get back to the steamer, and imagined myself living alone and unarmed in the woods to an advanced age. Such silly things — you know. And I remember I confounded the beat of the drum with the beating of my heart, and was pleased at its calm regularity.

"I kept to the track though — then stopped to listen. The night was very clear; a dark blue space, sparkling with dew and starlight, in which black things stood very still. I thought I could see a kind of motion ahead of me. I was strangely cocksure of everything that night. I actually left the track and ran in a wide semicircle (I verily believe chuckling to myself) so as to get in front of that stir, of that motion I had seen — if indeed I had seen anything. I was circumventing Kurtz as though it had been a boyish game.

"I came upon him, and, if he had not heard me coming, I would have fallen over him, too, but he got up in time. He rose, unsteady, long, pale, indistinct, like a vapor exhaled by the earth, and swayed slightly, misty and silent before me; while at my back the fires loomed between the trees, and the murmur of many voices issued from the forest. I had cut him off cleverly; but when actually confronting him I seemed to come to my senses, I saw the danger in its right proportion. It was by no means over yet. Suppose he began to shout? Though he could hardly stand, there was still plenty of vigor in his voice. 'Go away — hide yourself,' he said, in that profound tone. It was very awful. I glanced back. We were within thirty yards from the nearest fire. A black figure stood up, strode on long black legs, waving long black arms, across the glow. It had horns — antelope horns, I think — on its head. Some sorcerer, some witchman, no doubt: it looked fiend-like enough. 'Do you know what you are doing?' I whispered. 'Perfectly,' he answered, raising his voice for that single word: it sounded to me far off and yet loud, like a hail through a speaking-trumpet. If he makes a row we are lost, I thought to myself. This clearly was not a case for fisticuffs, even apart from the very natural aversion I had to beat that Shadow — this wandering and tormented thing. 'You will be lost,' I said — 'utterly lost.' One gets sometimes such a flash of inspiration, you know. I did say the right thing, though indeed he could not have been more irretrievably lost than he was at this very moment, when the foundations of our intimacy were being laid — to endure — to endure — even to the end — even beyond.

" 'I had immense plans,' he muttered irresolutely. 'Yes,' said I; 'but if you try to shout I'll smash your head with — ' There was not a stick or a stone near. 'I will throttle you for good,' I corrected myself. 'I was on the threshold of great things,' he pleaded, in a voice of longing, with a wistfulness of tone that made my blood run cold. 'And now for this stupid scoundrel — ' 'Your success in Europe is assured in any case,' I affirmed, steadily. I did not want to have the throttling of him, you understand — and indeed it would have been very little use for any practical purpose. I tried to break the spell — the heavy, mute spell of the wilderness — that seemed to draw him to its pitiless breast by the awakening of forgotten and brutal instincts, by the memory of gratified and monstrous passions. This alone, I was convinced, had driven him out to the edge of the forest, to the bush, towards the gleam of fires, the throb of drums, the drone of weird incantations; this alone had beguiled his unlawful soul beyond the bounds of permitted aspirations.

And, don't you see, the terror of the position was not in being knocked on the head — though I had a very lively sense of that danger, too — but in this, that I had to deal with a being to whom I could not appeal in the name of anything high or low. I had, even like the niggers, to invoke him — himself — his own exalted and incredible degradation. There was nothing either above or below him, and I knew it. He had kicked himself loose of the earth. Confound the man! he had kicked the very earth to pieces. He was alone, and I before him did not know whether I stood on the ground or floated in the air. I've been telling you what we said — repeating the phrases we pronounced — but what's the good? They were common everyday words — the familiar, vague sounds exchanged on every waking day of life. But what of that? They had behind them, to my mind, the terrific suggestiveness of words heard in dreams, of phrases spoken in nightmares. Soul! If anybody had ever struggled with a soul, I am the man. And I wasn't arguing with a lunatic either. Believe me or not, his intelligence was perfectly clear — concentrated, it is true, upon himself with horrible intensity, yet clear; and therein was my only chance — barring, of course, the killing him there and then, which wasn't so good, on account of unavoidable noise. But his soul was mad. Being alone in the wilderness, it had looked within itself, and, by heavens! I tell you, it had gone mad. I had — for my sins, I suppose — to go through the ordeal of looking into it myself. No eloquence could have been so withering to one's belief in mankind as his final burst of sincerity. He struggled with himself, too. I saw it, — I heard it. I saw the inconceivable mystery of a soul that knew no restraint, no faith, and no fear, yet struggling blindly with itself. I kept my head pretty well; but when I had him at last stretched on the couch, I wiped my forehead, while my legs shook under me as though I had carried half a ton on my back down that hill. And yet I had only supported him, his bony arm clasped round my neck — and he was not much heavier than a child.

"When next day we left at noon, the crowd, of whose presence behind the curtain of trees I had been acutely conscious all the time, flowed out of the woods again, filled the clearing, covered the slope with a mass of naked, breathing, quivering, bronze bodies. I steamed up a bit, then swung downstream, and two thousand eyes followed the evolutions of the splashing, thumping, fierce river-demon beating the water with its terrible tail and breathing black smoke into the air. In front of the first rank, along the river, three men, plastered with bright red earth from head to foot, strutted to and fro restlessly. When we came abreast again, they faced the river, stamped their feet, nodded their horned heads, swayed their scarlet bodies; they shook towards the fierce river-demon a bunch of black feathers, a mangy skin with a pendent tail — something that looked like a dried gourd; they shouted periodically together strings of amazing words that resembled no sounds of human language; and the deep murmurs of the crowd, interrupted suddenly, were like the responses of some satanic litany.

"We had carried Kurtz into the pilot-house: there was more air there. Lying on the couch, he stared through the open shutter. There was an eddy in the mass of human bodies, and the woman with helmeted head and tawny cheeks rushed out to the very brink of the stream. She put out her hands, shouted something, and all that wild mob took up the shout in a roaring chorus of articulated, rapid, breathless utterance.

" 'Do you understand this?' I asked.

"He kept on looking out past me with fiery, longing eyes, with a mingled expression of wistfulness and hate. He made no answer, but I saw a smile, a smile of indefinable meaning, appear on his colorless lips that a moment after twitched convulsively. 'Do I not?' he said slowly, gasping, as if the words had been torn out of him by a supernatural power.

"I pulled the string of the whistle, and I did this because I saw the pilgrims on deck getting out their rifles with an air of anticipating a jolly lark. At the sudden screech there was a movement of abject terror through that wedged mass of bodies. 'Don't! don't you frighten them away,' cried someone on deck disconsolately. I pulled the string time after time. They broke and ran, they leaped, they crouched, they swerved, they dodged the flying terror of the sound. The three red chaps had fallen flat, face down on the shore, as though they had been shot dead. Only the barbarous and superb woman did not so much as flinch, and stretched tragically her bare arms after us over the somber and glittering river.

"And then that imbecile crowd down on the deck started their little fun, and I could see nothing more for smoke.

"The brown current ran swiftly out of the heart of darkness, bearing us down towards the sea with twice the speed of our upward progress; and Kurtz's life was running swiftly, too, ebbing, ebbing out of his heart into the sea of inexorable time. The manager was very placid, he had no vital anxieties now, he took us both in with a comprehensive and satisfied glance: the 'affair' had come off as well as could be wished. I saw the time approaching when I would be left alone of the party of 'unsound method.' The pilgrims looked upon me with disfavor. I was, so to speak, numbered with the dead. It is strange how I accepted this unforeseen partnership, this choice of nightmares forced upon me in the tenebrous land invaded by these mean and greedy phantoms.

"Kurtz discoursed. A voice! a voice! It rang deep to the very last. It survived his strength to hide in the magnificent folds of eloquence the barren darkness of his heart. Oh, he struggled! he struggled! The wastes of his weary brain were haunted by shadowy images now — images of wealth and fame revolving obsequiously round his unextinguishable gift of noble and lofty expression. My Intended, my station, my career, my ideas — these were the subjects for the occasional utterances of elevated sentiments. The shade of the original Kurtz frequented the bedside of the hollow sham, whose fate it was to be buried presently in the mold of primeval earth. But both the diabolic love and the unearthly hate of the mysteries it had penetrated fought for the possession of that soul satiated with primitive emotions, avid of lying fame, of sham distinction, of all the appearances of success and power.

"Sometimes he was contemptibly childish. He desired to have kings meet him at railway stations on his return from some ghastly Nowhere, where he intended to accomplish great things. 'You show them you have in you something that is really profitable, and then there will be no limits to the recognition of your ability,' he would say. 'Of course you must take care of the motives — right motives — always.' The long reaches that were like one and the same reach, monotonous bends that were exactly alike, slipped past the steamer with their multitude of secular trees looking patiently after this grimy fragment of another world, the forerunner of change, of conquest, of trade, of massacres, of blessings. I looked ahead — piloting. 'Close the shutter,' said Kurtz suddenly one day; 'I can't bear to look at this.' I did so. There was a silence. 'Oh, but I will wring your heart yet!' he cried at the invisible wilderness.

"We broke down — as I had expected — and had to lie up for repairs at the head of an island. This delay was the first thing that shook Kurtz's confidence. One morning he gave me a packet of papers and a photograph — the lot tied together with a shoestring. 'Keep this for me,' he said. 'This noxious fool' (meaning the manager) 'is capable of prying into my boxes when I am not looking.' In the afternoon I saw him. He was lying on his back with closed eyes, and I withdrew quietly, but I heard him mutter, 'Live rightly, die, die. . . .' I listened. There was nothing more. Was he rehearsing some speech in his sleep, or was it a fragment of a phrase from some newspaper article? He had been writing for the papers and meant to do so again, 'for the furthering of my ideas. It's a duty.'

"His was an impenetrable darkness. I looked at him as you peer down at a man who is lying at the bottom of a precipice where the sun never shines. But I had not much time to give him, because I was helping the engine-driver to take to pieces the leaky cylinders, to straighten a bent connecting-rod, and in other such matters. I lived in an infernal mess of rust, filings, nuts, bolts, spanners, hammers, ratchet-drills — things I abominate, because I don't get on with them. I tended the little forge we fortunately had aboard; I toiled wearily in a wretched scrapheap — unless I had the shakes too bad to stand.

"One evening coming in with a candle I was startled to hear him say a little tremulously, 'I am lying here in the dark waiting for death.' The light was within a foot of his eyes. I forced myself to murmur, 'Oh, nonsense!' and stood over him as if transfixed.

"Anything approaching the change that came over his features I have never seen before, and hope never to see again. Oh, I wasn't touched. I was fascinated. It was as though a veil had been rent. I saw on that ivory face the expression of somber pride, of ruthless power, of craven terror — of an intense and hopeless despair. Did he live his life again in every detail of desire, temptation, and surrender during that supreme moment of complete knowledge? He cried in a whisper at some image, at some vision — he cried out twice, a cry that was no more than a breath —

" 'The horror! The horror!'

"I blew the candle out and left the cabin. The pilgrims were dining in the mess-room, and I took my place opposite the manager, who lifted his eyes to give me a questioning glance, which I successfully ignored. He leaned back, serene, with that peculiar smile of his sealing the unexpressed depths of his meanness. A continuous shower of small flies streamed upon the lamp, upon the cloth, upon our hands and faces. Suddenly the manager's boy put his insolent black head in the doorway, and said in a tone of scathing contempt —

" 'Mistah Kurtz — he dead.'

"All the pilgrims rushed out to see. I remained, and went on with my dinner. I believe I was considered brutally callous. However, I did not eat much. There was a lamp in there — light, don't you know — and outside it was so beastly, beastly dark. I went no more near the remarkable man who had pronounced a judgment upon the adventures of his soul on this earth. The voice was gone. What else had been there? But I am of course aware that next day the pilgrims buried something in a muddy hole.

"And then they very nearly buried me.

"However, as you see, I did not go to join Kurtz there and then. I did not. I remained to dream the nightmare out to the end, and to show my loyalty to Kurtz once more. Destiny. My destiny! Droll thing life is — that mysterious arrangement of merciless logic for a futile purpose. The most you can hope from it is some knowledge of yourself — that comes too late — a crop of unextinguishable regrets. I have wrestled with death. It is the most unexciting contest you can imagine. It takes place in an impalpable grayness, with nothing underfoot, with nothing around, without spectators, without clamor, without glory, without the great desire of victory, without the great fear of defeat, in a sickly atmosphere of tepid skepticism, without much belief in your own right, and still less in that of your adversary. If such is the form of ultimate wisdom, then life is a greater riddle than some of us think it to be. I was within a hair's breadth of the last opportunity for pronouncement, and I found with humiliation that probably I would have nothing to say. This is the reason why I affirm that Kurtz was a remarkable man. He had something to say. He said it. Since I had peeped over the edge myself, I understand better the meaning of his stare, that could not see the flame of the candle, but was wide enough to embrace the whole universe, piercing enough to penetrate all the hearts that beat in the darkness. He had summed up — he had judged. 'The horror!' He was a remarkable man. After all, this was the expression of some sort of belief; it had candor, it had conviction, it had a vibrating note of revolt in its whisper, it had the appalling face of a glimpsed truth — the strange commingling of desire and hate. And it is not my own extremity I remember best — a vision of grayness without form filled with physical pain, and a careless contempt for the evanescence of all things — even of this pain itself. No! It is his extremity that I seem to have lived through. True, he had made that last stride, he had stepped over the edge, while I had been permitted to draw back my hesitating foot. And perhaps in this is the whole difference; perhaps all the wisdom, and all truth, and all sincerity, are just compressed into that inappreciable moment of time in which we step over the threshold of the invisible. Perhaps! I like to think my summing-up would not have been a word of careless contempt. Better his cry — much better. It was an affirmation, a moral victory paid for by innumerable defeats, by abominable terrors, by abominable satisfactions. But it was a victory! That is why I have remained loyal to Kurtz to the last, and even beyond, when a long time after I heard once more, not his own voice, but the echo of his magnificent eloquence thrown to me from a soul as translucently pure as a cliff of crystal.

"No, they did not bury me, though there is a period of time which I remember mistily, with a shuddering wonder, like a passage through some inconceivable world that had no hope in it and no desire. I found myself back in the sepulchral city resenting the sight of people hurrying through the streets to filch a little money from each other, to devour their infamous cookery, to gulp their unwholesome beer, to dream their insignificant and silly dreams. They trespassed upon my thoughts. They were intruders whose knowledge of life was to me an irritating pretense, because I felt so sure they could not possibly know the things I knew. Their bearing, which was simply the bearing of commonplace individuals going about their business in the assurance of perfect safety, was offensive to me like the outrageous flauntings of folly in the face of a danger it is unable to comprehend. I had no particular desire to enlighten them, but I had some difficulty in restraining myself from laughing in their faces, so full of stupid importance. I daresay I was not very well at that time. I tottered about the streets — there were various affairs to settle — grinning bitterly at perfectly respectable persons. I admit my behavior was inexcusable, but then my temperature was seldom normal in these days. My dear aunt's endeavors to 'nurse up my strength' seemed altogether beside the mark. It was not my strength that wanted nursing, it was my imagination that wanted soothing. I kept the bundle of papers given me by Kurtz, not knowing exactly what to do with it. His mother

had died lately, watched over, as I was told, by his Intended. A
clean-shaved man, with an official manner and wearing gold-rimmed
spectacles, called on me one day and made inquiries, at first
circuitous, afterwards suavely pressing, about what he was pleased
to denominate certain 'documents.' I was not surprised, because I
had had two rows with the manager on the subject out there. I
had refused to give up the smallest scrap out of that package, and I
took the same attitude with the spectacled man. He became darkly
menacing at last, and with much heat argued that the Company had
the right to every bit of information about its 'territories.' And
said he, 'Mr. Kurtz's knowledge of unexplored regions must have
been necessarily extensive and peculiar — owing to his great abilities and to the deplorable circumstances in which he had been
placed: therefore — ' I assured him Mr. Kurtz's knowledge, however extensive, did not bear upon the problems of commerce or
administration. He invoked then the name of science. 'It would
be an incalculable loss if,' etc., etc. I offered him the report on
the 'Suppression of Savage Customs,' with the postscriptum torn off.
He took it up eagerly, but ended by sniffing at it with an air of
contempt. 'This is not what we had a right to expect,' he remarked.
'Expect nothing else,' I said. 'There are only private letters.' He
withdrew upon some threat of legal proceedings, and I saw him no
more; but another fellow, calling himself Kurtz's cousin, appeared
two days later, and was anxious to hear all the details about his
dear relative's last moments. Incidentally he gave me to understand
that Kurtz had been essentially a great musician. 'There was the
making of an immense success,' said the man, who was an organist,
I believe, with lank gray hair flowing over a greasy coat-collar. I
had no reason to doubt his statement; and to this day I am unable
to say what was Kurtz's profession, whether he ever had any —
which was the greatest of his talents. I had taken him for a painter
who wrote for the papers, or else for a journalist who could paint —
but even the cousin (who took snuff during the interview) could not
tell me what he had been — exactly. He was a universal genius —
on that point I agreed with the old chap, who thereupon blew his
nose noisily into a large cotton handkerchief and withdrew in
senile agitation, bearing off some family letters and memoranda without importance. Ultimately a journalist anxious to know something
of the fate of his 'dear colleague' turned up. This visitor informed
me Kurtz's proper sphere ought to have been politics 'on the popu-

lar side.' He had furry straight eyebrows, bristly hair cropped short, an eye-glass on a broad ribbon, and, becoming expansive, confessed his opinion that Kurtz really couldn't write a bit — 'but heavens! how that man could talk. He electrified large meetings. He had faith — don't you see? — he had the faith. He could get himself to believe anything — anything. He would have been a splendid leader of an extreme party.' 'What party?' I asked. 'Any party,' answered the other. 'He was an — an — extremist.' Did I not think so? I assented. Did I know, he asked, with a sudden flash of curiosity, 'what it was that had induced him to go out there?' 'Yes,' said I, and forthwith handed him the famous Report for publication, if he thought fit. He glanced through it hurriedly, mumbling all the time, judged 'it would do,' and took himself off with this plunder.

"Thus I was left at last with a slim packet of letters and the girl's portrait. She struck me as beautiful — I mean she had a beautiful expression. I know that the sunlight can be made to lie, too, yet one felt that no manipulation of light and pose could have conveyed the delicate shade of truthfulness upon those features. She seemed ready to listen without mental reservation, without suspicion, without a thought for herself. I concluded I would go and give her back her portrait and those letters myself. Curiosity? Yes; and also some other feeling perhaps. All that had been Kurtz's had passed out of my hands: his soul, his body, his station, his plans, his ivory, his career. There remained only his memory and his Intended — and I wanted to give that up, too, to the past, in a way — to surrender personally all that remained of him with me to that oblivion which is the last word of our common fate. I don't defend myself. I had no clear perception of what it was I really wanted. Perhaps it was an impulse of unconscious loyalty, or the fulfillment of one of those ironic necessities that lurk in the facts of human existence. I don't know. I can't tell. But I went.

"I thought his memory was like the other memories of the dead that accumulate in every man's life — a vague impress on the brain of shadows that had fallen on it in their swift and final passage; but before the high and ponderous door, between the tall houses of a street as still and decorous as a well-kept alley in a cemetery, I had a vision of him on the stretcher, opening his mouth voraciously, as if to devour all the earth with all its mankind. He lived then before me; he lived as much as he had ever lived — a shadow insatiable of splendid appearances, of frightful realities; a shadow darker than the shadow of the night, and draped nobly in the folds of a gorgeous eloquence. The vision seemed to enter the house with me — the stretcher, the phantom-bearers, the wild crowd of obedient worshipers, the gloom of the forests, the glitter of the reach between the murky bends, the beat of the drum, regular and muffled like the beating of a heart — the heart of a conquering darkness. It was a moment of triumph for the wilderness, an invading and vengeful rush which, it seemed to me, I would have to keep back alone for the salvation of another soul. And the memory of what I had heard him say afar there, with the horned shapes stirring at my back, in the glow of fires, within the patient woods, those broken phrases came back to me, were heard again in their ominous and terrifying simplicity. I remembered his abject pleading, his abject threats, the colossal scale of his vile desires, the meanness, the torment, the tempestuous anguish of his soul. And later on I seemed to see his collected languid manner, when he said one day, 'This lot of ivory now is really mine. The Company did not pay for it. I collected it myself at a very great personal risk. I am afraid they will try to claim it as theirs though. H'm. It is a difficult case. What do you think I ought to do — resist? Eh? I want no more than justice.' . . . He wanted no more than justice — no more than justice. I rang the bell before a mahogany door on the first floor, and while I waited he seemed to stare at me out of the glassy panel — stare with that wide and immense stare embracing, condemning, loathing all the universe. I seemed to hear the whispered cry, 'The horror! The horror!'

"The dusk was falling. I had to wait in a lofty drawing-room with three long windows from floor to ceiling that were like three luminous and bedraped columns. The bent gilt legs and backs of the furniture shone in indistinct curves. The tall marble fireplace had a cold and monumental whiteness. A grand piano stood massively in a corner; with dark gleams on the flat surfaces like a somber and polished sarcophagus. A high door opened — closed. I rose.

"She came forward, all in black, with a pale head, floating towards me in the dusk. She was in mourning. It was more than a year since his death, more than a year since the news came; she seemed as though she would remember and mourn forever. She took both my hands in hers and murmured, 'I had heard you were coming.' I noticed she was not very young — I mean not girlish. She had a mature capacity for fidelity, for belief, for suffering. The room seemed to have grown darker, as if all the sad light of the cloudy evening had taken refuge on her forehead. This fair hair, this pale visage, this pure brow, seemed surrounded by an ashy halo from which the dark eyes looked out at me. Their glance was guileless, profound, confident, and trustful. She carried her sorrowful head as though she were proud of that sorrow, as though she would say, I — I alone know how to mourn him as he deserves. But while we were still shaking hands, such a look of awful desolation came upon her face that I perceived she was one of those creatures that are not the playthings of Time. For her he had died only yesterday. And, by Jove! the impression was so powerful that for me, too, he seemed to have died only yesterday — nay, this very minute. I saw her and him in the same instant of time — his death and her sorrow — I saw her sorrow in the very moment of his death. Do you understand? I saw them together — I heard them together. She had said, with a deep catch of the breath, 'I have survived' while my strained ears seemed to hear distinctly, mingled with her tone of despairing regret, the summing up whisper of his eternal condemnation. I asked myself what I was doing there, with a sensation of panic in my heart as though I had blundered into a place of cruel and absurd mysteries not fit for a human being to behold. She motioned me to a chair. We sat down. I laid the packet gently on the little table, and she put her hand over it. . . . 'You knew him well,' she murmured, after a moment of mourning silence.

" 'Intimacy grows quickly out there,' I said. 'I knew him as well as it is possible for one man to know another.'

" 'And you admired him,' she said. 'It was impossible to know him and not to admire him. Was it?'

" 'He was a remarkable man,' I said, unsteadily. Then before the appealing fixity of her gaze, that seemed to watch for more words on my lips, I went on, 'It was impossible not to — '

" 'Love him,' she finished eagerly, silencing me into an appalled dumbness. 'How true! how true! But when you think that no one knew him so well as I! I had all his noble confidence. I knew him best.'

" 'You knew him best,' I repeated. And perhaps she did. But with every word spoken the room was growing darker, and only

her forehead, smooth and white, remained illuminated by the unextinguishable light of belief and love.

" 'You were his friend,' she went on. 'His friend,' she repeated,
a little louder. 'You must have been, if he had given you this, and
sent you to me. I feel I can speak to you — and oh! I must speak.
I want you — you have heard his last words — to know I have
been worthy of him. . . . It is not pride. . . . Yes! I am proud to
know I understood him better than anyone on earth — he told me
so himself. And since his mother died I have had no one — no one
— to — to — '

"I listened. The darkness deepened. I was not even sure he had
given me the right bundle. I rather suspect he wanted me to take
care of another batch of his papers which, after his death, I saw
the manager examining under the lamp. And the girl talked, easing
her pain in the certitude of my sympathy; she talked as thirsty
men drink. I had heard that her engagement with Kurtz had been
disapproved by her people. He wasn't rich enough or something.
And indeed I don't know whether he had not been a pauper all his
life. He had given me some reason to infer that it was his impatience of comparative poverty that drove him out there.

" ' . . .Who was not his friend who had heard him speak once?'
she was saying. 'He drew men towards him by what was best in
them.' She looked at me with intensity. 'It is the gift of the
great,' she went on, and the sound of her low voice seemed to have
the accompaniment of all the other sounds, full of mystery, desolation, and sorrow, I had ever heard — the ripple of the river, the
soughing of the trees swayed by the wind, the murmurs of the
crowds, the faint ring of incomprehensible words cried from afar,
the whisper of a voice speaking from beyond the threshold of an
eternal darkness. 'But you have heard him! You know!' she
cried.

" 'Yes, I know,' I said with something like despair in my heart,
but bowing my head before the faith that was in her, before that
great and saving illusion that shone with an unearthly glow in the
darkness, in the triumphant darkness from which I could not have
defended her — from which I could not even defend myself.

" 'What a loss to me — to us!' — she corrected herself with beautiful generosity; then added in a murmur, 'To the world.' By the
last gleams of twilight I could see the glitter of her eyes, full of
tears — of tears that would not fall.

" 'I have been very happy — very fortunate — very proud,' she went on. 'Too fortunate. Too happy for a little while. And now I am unhappy for — for life.'

"She stood up; her fair hair seemed to catch all the remaining light in a glimmer of gold. I rose, too.

" 'And of all this,' she went on, mournfully, 'of all his promise, and of all his greatness, of his generous mind, of his noble heart, nothing remains — nothing but a memory. You and I — '

" 'We shall always remember him,' I said, hastily.

" 'No!' she cried. 'It is impossible that all this should be lost — that such a life should be sacrificed to leave nothing — but sorrow. You know what vast plans he had. I knew of them, too — I could not perhaps understand — but others knew of them. Something must remain. His words, at least, have not died.'

" 'His words will remain,' I said.

" 'And his example,' she whispered to herself. 'Men looked up to him — his goodness shone in every act. His example — '

" 'True,' I said; 'his example, too. Yes, his example. I forgot that.'

" 'But I do not. I cannot — I cannot believe — not yet. I cannot believe that I shall never see him again, that nobody will see him again, never, never, never.'

"She put out her arms as if after a retreating figure, stretching them black and with clasped pale hands across the fading and narrow sheen of the window. Never see him! I saw him clearly enough then. I shall see this eloquent phantom as long as I live, and I shall see her, too, a tragic and familiar Shade, resembling in this gesture another one, tragic also, and bedecked with powerless charms, stretching bare brown arms over the glitter of the infernal stream, the stream of darkness. She said suddenly very low, 'He died as he lived.'

" 'His end,' said I, with dull anger stirring in me, 'was in every way worthy of his life.'

" 'And I was not with him,' she murmured. My anger subsided before a feeling of infinite pity.

" 'Everything that could be done — ' I mumbled.

" 'Ah, but I believed in him more than anyone on earth — more than his own mother, more than — himself. He needed me! Me! I would have treasured every sigh, every word, every sign, every glance.'

"I felt like a chill grip on my chest. 'Don't,' I said, in a muffled voice.

" 'Forgive me. I — I have mourned so long in silence — in silence. . . . You were with him — to the last? I think of his loneliness. Nobody near to understand him as I would have understood. Perhaps no one to hear. . . . '

" 'To the very end,' I said, shakily. 'I heard his very last words. . . . ' I stopped in a fright.

" 'Repeat them,' she murmured in a heart-broken tone. 'I want — I want — something — something — to — live with.'

"I was on the point of crying at her, 'Don't you hear them?' The dusk was repeating them in a persistent whisper all around us, in a whisper that seemed to swell menacingly like the first whisper of a rising wind. 'The horror! The horror!'

" 'His last word to live with,' she insisted. 'Don't you understand I loved him — I loved him — I loved him!'

"I pulled myself together and spoke slowly.

" 'The last word he pronounced was — your name.'

"I heard a light sigh and then my heart stood still, stopped dead short by an exulting and terrible cry, by the cry of inconceivable triumph and of unspeakable pain. 'I knew it — I was sure!' . . . She knew. She was sure. I heard her weeping; she had hidden her face in her hands. It seemed to me that the house would collapse before I could escape, that the heavens would fall upon my head. But nothing happened. The heavens do not fall for such a trifle. Would they have fallen, I wonder, if I had rendered Kurtz that justice which was his due? Hadn't he said he wanted only justice? But I couldn't. I could not tell her. It would have been too dark — too dark altogether. . . . "

Marlow ceased, and sat apart, indistinct and silent, in the pose of a meditating Buddha. Nobody moved for a time. "We have lost the first of the ebb," said the Director, suddenly. I raised my head. The offing was barred by a black bank of clouds, and the tranquil waterway leading to the uttermost ends of the earth flowed somber under an overcast sky — seemed to lead into the heart of an immense darkness.

E. M. FORSTER

the other side of the hedge

My pedometer told me that I was twenty-five; and, though it is a shocking thing to stop walking, I was so tired that I sat down on a milestone to rest. People outstripped me, jeering as they did so, but I was too apathetic to feel resentful, and even when Miss Eliza Dimbleby, the great educationist, swept past, exhorting me to persevere, I only smiled and raised my hat.

At first I thought I was going to be like my brother, whom I had had to leave by the roadside a year or two round the corner. He had wasted his breath on singing, and his strength on helping others. But I had travelled more wisely, and now it was only the monotony of the highway that oppressed me — dust under foot and brown crackling hedges on either side, ever since I could remember.

And I had already dropped several things — indeed, the road behind was strewn with the things we all had dropped; and the white dust was settling down on them, so that already they looked no better than stones. My muscles were so weary that I could not even bear the weight of those things I still carried. I slid off the milestone into the road, and lay there prostrate, with my face to the great parched hedge, praying that I might give up.

A little puff of air revived me. It seemed to come from the hedge; and, when I opened my eyes, there was a glint of light through the tangle of boughs and dead leaves. The hedge could not be as thick as usual. In my weak, morbid state, I longed to force my way in, and see what was on the other side. No one was in sight, or I should not have dared to try. For we of the road do not admit in conversation that there is another side at all.

I yielded to the temptation, saying to myself that I would come back in a minute. The thorns scratched my face, and I had to use my arms as a shield, depending on my feet alone to push me forward. Halfway through I would have gone back, for in the passage all the things I was carrying were scraped off me, and my clothes were torn. But I was so wedged that return was impossible, and I had to wiggle blindly forward, expecting every moment that my strength would fail me, and that I should perish in the undergrowth.

Suddenly cold water closed round my head, and I seemed sinking down for ever. I had fallen out of the hedge into a deep pool. I rose to the surface at last, crying for help, and I heard someone on the opposite bank laugh and say: "Another!" And then I was twitched out and laid panting on the dry ground.

Even when the water was out of my eyes, I was still dazed, for I had never been in so large a space, nor seen such grass and sunshine. The blue sky was no longer a strip, and beneath it the earth had risen grandly into hills — clean, bare buttresses, with beech trees in their folds, and meadows and clear pools at their feet. But the hills were not high, and there was in the landscape a sense of human occupation — so that one might have called it a park, or garden, if the words did not imply a certain triviality and constraint.

As soon as I got my breath, I turned to my rescuer and said:

"Where does this place lead to?"

"Nowhere, thank the Lord!" said he, and laughed. He was a man of fifty or sixty — just the kind of age we mistrust on the road

— but there was no anxiety in his manner, and his voice was that of a boy of eighteen.

"But it must lead somewhere!" I cried, too much surprised at his answer to thank him for saving my life.

"He wants to know where it leads!" he shouted to some men on the hill side, and they laughed back, and waved their caps.

I noticed then that the pool into which I had fallen was really a moat which bent round to the left and to the right, and that the hedge followed it continually. The hedge was green on this side — its roots showed through the clear water, and fish swam about in them — and it was wreathed over with dog-roses and Traveller's Joy. But it was a barrier, and in a moment I lost all pleasure in the grass, the sky, the trees, the happy men and women, and realized that the place was but a prison, for all its beauty and extent.

We moved away from the boundary, and then followed a path almost parallel to it, across the meadows. I found it difficult walking, for I was always trying to out-distance my companion, and there was no advantage in doing this if the place led nowhere. I had never kept step with anyone since I left my brother.

I amused him by stopping suddenly and saying disconsolately, "This is perfectly terrible. One cannot advance: one cannot progress. Now we of the road —— "

"Yes, I know."

"I was going to say, we advance continually."

"I know."

"We are always learning, expanding, developing. Why, even in my short life I have seen a great deal of advance — the Transvaal War, the Fiscal Question, Christian Science, Radium. Here for example — "

I took out my pedometer, but it still marked twenty-five, not a degree more.

"Oh, it's stopped! I meant to show you. It should have registered all the time I was walking with you. But it makes me only twenty-five."

"Many things don't work in here," he said. "One day a man brought in a Lee-Metford, and that wouldn't work."

"The laws of science are universal in their application. It must be the water in the moat that has injured the machinery. In normal conditions everything works. Science and the spirit of emulation — those are the forces that have made us what we are."

I had to break off and acknowledge the pleasant greetings of people whom we passed. Some of them were singing, some talking, some engaged in gardening, hay-making, or other rudimentary industries. They all seemed happy; and I might have been happy too, if I could have forgotten that the place led nowhere.

I was startled by a young man who came sprinting across our path, took a little fence in fine style, and went tearing over a ploughed field till he plunged into a lake, across which he began to swim. Here was true energy, and I exclaimed: "A cross-country race! Where are the others?"

"There are no others," my companion replied; and, later on, when we passed some long grass from which came the voice of a girl singing exquisitely to herself, he said again: "There are no others." I was bewildered at the waste in production, and murmured to myself, "What does it all mean?"

He said: "It means nothing but itself" — and he repeated the words slowly, as if I were a child.

"I understand," I said quietly, "but I do not agree. Every achievement is worthless unless it is a link in the chain of development. And I must not trespass on your kindness any longer. I must get back somehow to the road, and have my pedometer mended."

"First, you must see the gates," he replied, "for we have gates, though we never use them."

I yielded politely, and before long we reached the moat again, at a point where it was spanned by a bridge. Over the bridge was a big gate, as white as ivory, which was fitted into a gap in the boundless hedge. The gate opened outwards, and I exclaimed in amazement, for from it ran a road — just such a road as I had left — dusty under foot, with brown crackling hedges on either side as far as the eye could reach.

"That's my road!" I cried.

He shut the gate and said: "But not your part of the road. It is through this gate that humanity went out countless ages ago, when it was first seized with the desire to walk."

I denied this, observing that the part of the road I myself had left was not more than two miles off. But with the obstinacy of his years he repeated: "It is the same road. This is the beginning, and though it seems to run straight away from us, it doubles so often, that it is never far from our boundary and sometimes touches it." He stooped down by the moat, and traced on its moist

margin an absurd figure like a maze. As we walked back through
the meadows, I tried to convince him of his mistake.

"The road sometimes doubles, to be sure, but that is part of our
discipline. Who can doubt that its general tendency is onward?
To what goal we know not — it may be to some mountain where
we shall touch the sky, it may be over precipices into the sea. But
that it goes forward — who can doubt that? It is the thought of
that that makes us strive to excel, each in his own way, and gives
us an impetus which is lacking with you. Now that man who
passed us — it's true that he ran well, and jumped well, and swam
well; but we have men who can run better, and men who can jump
better, and who can swim better. Specialization has produced re-
sults which would surprise you. Similarly, that girl —— "

Here I interrupted myself to exclaim: "Good gracious me! I
could have sworn it was Miss Eliza Dimbleby over there, with her
feet in the fountain!"

He believed that it was.

"Impossible! I left her on the road, and she is due to lecture this
evening at Tunbridge Wells. Why, her train leaves Cannon Street
in — of course my watch has stopped like everything else. She is
the last person to be here."

"People always are astonished at meeting each other. All kinds
come through the hedge, and some at all times — when they are
drawing ahead in the race, when they are lagging behind, when
they are left for dead. I often stand near the boundary listening to
the sounds of the road — you know what they are — and wonder
if anyone will turn aside. It is my great happiness to help someone
out of the moat, as I helped you. For our country fills up slowly,
though it was meant for all mankind."

"Mankind have other aims," I said gently, for I thought him well-
meaning; "and I must join them." I bade him good evening, for the
sun was declining, and I wished to be on the road by nightfall. To
my alarm, he caught hold of me, crying: "You are not to go yet!"
I tried to shake him off, for we had no interests in common, and his
civility was becoming irksome to me. But for all my struggles the
tiresome old man would not let go; and, as wrestling is not my
speciality, I was obliged to follow him.

It was true that I could have never found alone the place where
I came from, and I hoped that, when I had seen the other sights
about which he was worrying, he would take me back to it. But

I was determined not to sleep in the country, for I mistrusted it, and the people too, for all their friendliness. Hungry though I was, I would not join them in their evening meals of milk and fruit, and, when they gave me flowers, I flung them away as soon as I could do so unobserved. Already they were lying down for the night like cattle — some out on the bare hillside, others in groups under the beeches. In the light of an orange sunset I hurried on with my unwelcome guide, dead tired, faint for want of food, but murmuring indomitably: "Give me life, with its struggles and victories, with its failures and hatreds, with its deep moral meaning and its unknown goal!"

At last we came to a place where the encircling moat was spanned by another bridge, and where another gate interrupted the line of the boundary hedge. It was different from the first gate; for it was half transparent like horn, and opened inwards. But through it, in the waning light, I saw again just such a road as I had left — monotonous, dusty, with brown crackling hedges on either side, as far as the eye could reach.

I was strangely disquieted at the sight, which seemed to deprive me of all self-control. A man was passing us, returning for the night to the hills, with a scythe over his shoulder and a can of some liquid in his hand. I forgot the destiny of our race. I forgot the road that lay before my eyes, and I sprang at him, wrenched the can out of his hand, and began to drink.

It was nothing stronger than beer, but in my exhausted state it overcame me in a moment. As in a dream, I saw the old man shut the gate, and heard him say: "This is where your road ends, and through this gate humanity — all that is left of it — will come in to us."

Though my senses were sinking into oblivion, they seemed to expand ere they reached it. They perceived the magic song of nightingales, and the odour of invisible hay, and stars piercing the fading sky. The man whose beer I had stolen lowered me down gently to sleep off its effects, and, as he did so, I saw that he was my brother.

the celestial omnibus

The boy who resided at Agathox Lodge, 28, Buckingham Park Road, Surbiton, had often been puzzled by the old sign-post that stood almost opposite. He asked his mother about it, and she replied that it was a joke, and not a very nice one, which had been made many years back by some naughty young men, and that the police ought to remove it. For there were two strange things about this sign-post: firstly, it pointed up a blank alley, and, secondly, it had painted on it, in faded characters, the words, "To Heaven."

"What kind of young men were they?" he asked.

"I think your father told me that one of them wrote verses, and was expelled from the University and came to grief in other ways.

"The Celestial Omnibus" reprinted from *The Celestial Omnibus* by E. M. Forster, by permission of Alfred A. Knopf, Inc. Copyright, 1947 by Alfred A. Knopf, Inc.

Still, it was a long time ago. You must ask your father about it. He will say the same as I do, that it was put up as a joke."

"So it doesn't mean anything at all?"

She sent him upstairs to put on his best things, for the Bonses were coming to tea, and he was to hand the cakestand.

It struck him, as he wrenched on his tightening trousers, that he might do worse than ask Mr. Bons about the signpost. His father, though very kind, always laughed at him — shrieked with laughter whenever he or any other child asked a question or spoke. But Mr. Bons was serious as well as kind. He had a beautiful house and lent one books, he was a churchwarden, and a candidate for the County Council; he had donated to the Free Library enormously, he pre-sided over the Literary Society, and had Members of Parliament to stop with him — in short, he was probably the wisest person alive.

Yet even Mr. Bons could only say that the sign-post was a joke — the joke of a person named Shelley.

"Of course!" cried the mother; "I told you so, dear. That was the name."

"Had you never heard of Shelley?" asked Mr. Bons.

"No," said the boy, and hung his head.

"But is there no Shelley in the house?"

"Why, yes!" exclaimed the lady, in much agitation. "Dear Mr. Bons, we aren't such Philistines as that. Two at the least. One a wedding present, and the other, smaller print, in one of the spare rooms."

"I believe we have seven Shelleys," said Mr. Bons, with a slow smile. Then he brushed the cake crumbs off his stomach, and, together with his daughter, rose to go.

The boy, obeying a wink from his mother, saw them all the way to the garden gate, and when they had gone he did not at once re-turn to the house, but gazed for a little up and down Buckingham Park Road.

His parents lived at the right end of it. After No. 39 the quality of the houses dropped very suddenly, and 64 had not even a separate servants' entrance. But at the present moment the whole road looked rather pretty, for the sun had just set in splendour, and the inequalities of rent were drowned in a saffron afterglow. Small birds twittered, and the breadwinners' train shrieked musically down through the cutting — that wonderful cutting which has drawn to itself the whole beauty out of Surbiton, and clad itself, like any Alpine valley, with the glory of the fir and the silver birch and the primrose. It was this cutting that had first stirred desires within the boy — desires for something just a little different, he knew not what, desires that would return whenever things were sunlit, as they were this evening, running up and down inside him, up and down, up and down, till he would feel quite unusual all over, and as likely as not would want to cry. This evening he was even sillier, for he slipped across the road towards the sign-post and began to run up the blank alley.

The alley runs between high walls — the walls of the gardens of "Ivanhoe" and "Bella Vista," respectively. It smells a little all the way, and is scarcely twenty yards long, including the turn at the end. So not unnaturally the boy soon came to a standstill. "I'd like to kick that Shelley," he exclaimed, and glanced idly at a piece of paper which was pasted on the wall. Rather an odd piece of paper, and he read it carefully before he turned back. This is what he read:

S. AND C.R.C.C.

ALTERATION IN SERVICE

Owing to lack of patronage the Company are regretfully compelled to suspend the hourly service, and to retain only the

Sunrise and Sunset Omnibuses,

which will run as usual. It is to be hoped that the public will patronize an arrangement which is intended for their convenience. As an extra inducement, the Company will, for the first time, now issue

Return Tickets!

(available one day only), which may be obtained of the driver. Passengers are again reminded that *no tickets are issued at the other end*, and that no complaints in this connection will receive consideration from the Company. Nor will the Company be responsible for any negligence or stupidity on the part of Passengers, nor for Hailstorms, Lightning, Loss of Tickets, nor for any Act of God.

For the Direction.

Now he had never seen this notice before, nor could he imagine where the omnibus went to. S. of course was for Surbiton, and R.C.C. meant Road Car Company. But what was the meaning of the other C.? Coombe and Malden, perhaps, or possibly "City."

Yet it could not hope to compete with the South-Western. The whole thing, the boy reflected, was run on hopelessly unbusiness-like lines. Why no tickets from the other end? And what an hour to start! Then he realized that unless the notice was a hoax, an omnibus must have been starting just as he was wishing the Bonses good-bye. He peered at the ground through the gathering dusk, and there he saw what might or might not be the marks of wheels. Yet nothing had come out of the alley. And he had never seen an omnibus at any time in the Buckingham Park Road. No: it must be a hoax, like the sign-post, like the fairy tales, like the dreams upon which he would wake suddenly in the night. And with a sigh he stepped from the alley — right into the arms of his father.

Oh, how his father laughed! "Poor, poor Popsey!" he cried, "Diddums! Diddums! Diddums think he'd walky-palky up to Evvink!" And his mother, also convulsed with laughter, appeared on the steps of Agathox Lodge.

"Don't, Bob!" she gasped. "Don't be so naughty! Oh, you'll kill me! Oh, leave the boy alone!"

But all that evening the joke was kept up. The father implored to be taken too. Was it a very tiring walk? Need one wipe one's shoes on the door-mat? And the boy went to bed feeling faint and sore, and thankful for only one thing — that he had not said a word about the omnibus. It was a hoax, yet through his dreams it grew more and more real, and the streets of Surbiton, through which he saw it driving, seemed instead to become hoaxes and shadows. And very early in the morning he woke with a cry, for he had had a glimpse of its destination.

He struck a match, and its light fell not only on his watch but also on his calendar, so that he knew it to be half-an-hour to sunrise. It was pitch dark, for the fog had come down from London in the night, and all Surbiton was wrapped in its embraces. Yet he sprang out and dressed himself, for he was determined to settle once for all which was real: the omnibus or the streets. "I shall be a fool one way or the other," he thought, "until I know." Soon he was shivering in the road under the gas lamp that guarded the entrance to the alley.

To enter the alley itself required some courage. Not only was it horribly dark, but he now realized that it was an impossible ter-minus for an omnibus. If it had not been for a policeman, whom he heard approaching through the fog, he would never have made the attempt. The next moment he had made the attempt and failed. Nothing. Nothing but a blank alley and a very silly boy gaping at its dirty floor. It *was* a hoax. "I'll tell papa and mamma," he decided. "I deserve it. I deserve that they should know. I am too silly to be alive." And he went back to the gate of Agathox Lodge.

There he remembered that his watch was fast. The sun was not risen; it would not rise for two minutes. "Give the bus every chance," he thought cynically, and returned into the alley.

But the omnibus was there.

II

It had two horses, whose sides were still smoking from their journey, and its two great lamps shone through the fog against the alley's walls, changing their cobwebs and moss into tissues of fairyland. The driver was huddled up in a cape. He faced the blank wall, and how he had managed to drive in so neatly and so silently was one of the many things that the boy never discovered. Nor could he imagine how ever he would drive out.

"Please," his voice quavered through the foul brown air, "please, is that an omnibus?"

"Omnibus est," said the driver, without turning round. There was a moment's silence. The policeman passed, coughing, by the entrance of the alley. The boy crouched in the shadow, for he did not want to be found out. He was pretty sure, too, that it was a Pirate; nothing else, he reasoned, would go from such odd places and at such odd hours.

"About when do you start?" He tried to sound nonchalant.

"At sunrise."

"How far do you go?"

"The whole way."

"And can I have a return ticket which will bring me all the way back?"

"You can."

"Do you know, I half think I'll come." The driver made no answer. The sun must have risen, for he unhitched the brake. And scarcely had the boy jumped in before the omnibus was off.

How? Did it turn? There was no room. Did it go forward? There was a blank wall. Yet it was moving — moving at a stately pace through the fog, which had turned from brown to yellow. The thought of warm bed and warmer breakfast made the boy feel faint. He wished he had not come. His parents would not have approved. He would have gone back to them if the weather had not made it impossible. The solitude was terrible; he was the only passenger. And the omnibus, though well-built, was cold and somewhat musty. He drew his coat round him, and in so doing chanced to feel his pocket. It was empty. He had forgotten his purse.

"Stop!" he shouted. "Stop!" And then, being of a polite disposition, he glanced up at the painted notice-board so that he might call the driver by name. "Mr. Browne! stop; oh, do please stop!"

Mr. Browne did not stop, but he opened a little window and looked in at the boy. His face was a surprise, so kind it was and modest.

"Mr. Browne, I've left my purse behind. I've not got a penny. I can't pay for the ticket. Will you take my watch, please? I am in the most awful hole."

"Tickets on this line," said the driver, "whether single or return, can be purchased by coinage from no terrene mint. And a chronometer, though it had solaced the vigils of Charlemagne, or measured the slumbers of Laura, can acquire by no mutation the double-cake that charms the fangless Cerberus of Heaven!" So saying, he handed in the necessary ticket, and, while the boy said "Thank you," continued, "Titular pretensions, I know it well, are vanity. Yet they merit no censure when uttered on a laughing lip, and in an homonymous world are in some sort useful, since they do serve to distinguish one Jack from his fellow. Remember me, therefore, as Sir Thomas Browne."

"Are you a Sir? Oh, sorry!" He had heard of these gentlemen drivers. "It *is* good of you about the ticket. But if you go on at this rate, however does your bus pay?"

"It does not pay. It was not intended to pay. Many are the faults of my equipage; it is compounded too curiously of foreign woods; its cushions tickle erudition rather than promote repose; and my horses are nourished not on the evergreen pastures of the moment, but on the dried bents and clovers of Latinity. But that it pays! — that error at all events was never intended and never attained."

"Sorry again," said the boy rather hopelessly. Sir Thomas looked sad, fearing that, even for a moment, he had been the cause of sadness. He invited the boy to come up and sit beside him on the box, and together they journeyed on through the fog, which was now changing from yellow to white. There were no houses by the road; so it must be either Putney Heath or Wimbledon Common.

"Have you been a driver always?"

"I was a physician once."

"But why did you stop? Weren't you good?"

"As a healer of bodies I had scant success, and several score of my patients preceded me. But as a healer of the spirit I have succeeded beyond my hopes and my deserts. For though my draughts were not better nor subtler than those of other men, yet, by reason of the cunning goblets wherein I offered them, the queasy soul was ofttimes tempted to sip and be refreshed."

"The queasy soul," the boy murmured; "if the sun sets with trees in front of it, and you suddenly come strange all over, is that a queasy soul?"

"Have you felt that?"

"Why, yes."

After a pause he told the boy a little, a very little, about the journey's end. But they did not chatter much, for the boy, when he liked a person, would as soon sit silent in his company as speak, and this, he discovered, was also the mind of Sir Thomas Browne and of many others with whom he was to be acquainted. He heard, however, about the young man Shelley, who was now quite a famous person, with a carriage of his own, and about some of the other drivers who are in the service of the Company. Meanwhile the light grew stronger, though the fog did not disperse. It was now more like mist than fog, and at times would travel quickly across them, as if it was part of a cloud. They had been ascending too, in a most puzzling way; for over two hours the horses had been pulling against the collar, and even if it were Richmond Hill they ought to have been at the top long ago. Perhaps it was Epsom, or even the North Downs; yet the air seemed keener than that which blows on either. And as to the name of their destination, Sir Thomas Browne was silent.

Crash!

"Thunder, by Jove!" said the boy, "and not so far off either. Listen to the echoes! It's more like mountains."

He thought, not very vividly, of his father and mother. He saw them sitting down to sausages and listening to the storm. He saw his own empty place. Then there would be questions, alarms, theories, jokes, consolations. They would expect him back at lunch. To lunch he would not come, nor to tea, but he would be in for dinner, and so his day's truancy would be over. If he had had his purse he would have bought them presents — not that he should have known what to get them.

Crash!

The peal and the lightning came together. The cloud quivered as if it were alive, and torn streamers of mist rushed past. "Are you afraid?" asked Sir Thomas Browne.

"What is there to be afraid of? Is it much farther?"

The horses of the omnibus stopped just as a ball of fire burst up and exploded with a ringing noise that was deafening but clear, like the noise of a blacksmith's forge. All the cloud was shattered.

"Oh, listen, Sir Thomas Browne! No, I mean look; we shall get a view at last. No, I mean listen; that sounds like a rainbow!"

The noise had died into the faintest murmur, beneath which another murmur grew, spreading stealthily, steadily, in a curve that widened but did not vary. And in widening curves a rainbow was spreading from the horses' feet into the dissolving mists.

"But how beautiful! What colours! Where will it stop? It is more like the rainbows you can tread on. More like dreams."

The colour and the sound grew together. The rainbow spanned an enormous gulf. Clouds rushed under it and were pierced by it, and still it grew, reaching forward, conquering the darkness, until it touched something that seemed more solid than a cloud.

The boy stood up. "What is that out there?" he called. "What does it rest on, out at that other end?"

In the morning sunshine a precipice shone forth beyond the gulf. A precipice — or was it a castle? The horses moved. They set their feet upon the rainbow.

"Oh, look!" the boy shouted. "Oh, listen! Those caves — or are they gateways? Oh, look between those cliffs at those ledges. I see people! I see trees!"

"Look also below," whispered Sir Thomas. "Neglect not the diviner Acheron."

The boy looked below, past the flames of the rainbow that licked against their wheels. The gulf also had cleared, and in its depths there flowed an everlasting river. One sunbeam entered and struck a green pool, and as they passed over he saw three maidens rise to the surface of the pool, singing, and playing with something that glistened like a ring.

"You down in the water — " he called.

They answered, "You up on the bridge — " There was a burst of music. "You up on the bridge, good luck to you. Truth in the depth, truth on the height."

"You down in the water, what are you doing?"

Sir Thomas Browne replied: "They sport in the mancipiary possession of their gold"; and the omnibus arrived.

III

The boy was in disgrace. He sat locked up in the nursery of Agathox Lodge, learning poetry for a punishment. His father had said, "My boy! I can pardon anything but untruthfulness," and had caned him, saying at each stroke, "There is *no* omnibus, *no* driver, *no* bridge, *no* mountain; you are a *truant*, a *gutter snipe*, a *liar*." His father could be very stern at times. His mother had begged him to say he was sorry. But he could not say that. It was the greatest day of his life, in spite of the caning and the poetry at the end of it.

He had returned punctually at sunset — driven not by Sir Thomas Browne, but by a maiden lady who was full of quiet fun. They had talked of omnibuses and also of barouche landaus. How far away her gentle voice seemed now! Yet it was scarcely three hours since he had left her up the alley.

His mother called through the door. "Dear, you are to come down and to bring your poetry with you."

He came down, and found that Mr. Bons was in the smoking-room with his father. It had been a dinner party.

"Here is the great traveller!" said his father grimly. "Here is the young gentleman who drives in an omnibus over rainbows, while young ladies sing to him." Pleased with his wit, he laughed.

"After all," said Mr. Bons, smiling, "there is something a little like it in Wagner. It is odd how, in quite illiterate minds, you will find glimmers of Artistic Truth. The case interests me. Let me plead for the culprit. We have all romanced in our time, haven't we?"

"Hear how kind Mr. Bons is," said his mother, while his father said, "Very well. Let him say his Poem, and that will do. He is going away to my sister on Tuesday, and *she* will cure him of this alley-slopering." (Laughter.) "Say your Poem."

The boy began. " 'Standing aloof in giant ignorance.' "

His father laughed again — roared. "One for you, my son! 'Standing aloof in giant ignorance!' I never knew these poets talked sense. Just describes you. Here, Bons, you go in for poetry. Put him through it, will you, while I fetch up the whisky?"

"Yes, give me the Keats," said Mr. Bons. "Let him say his Keats to me."

So for a few moments the wise man and the ignorant boy were left alone in the smoking-room.

" 'Standing aloof in giant ignorance, of thee I dream and of the Cyclades, as one who sits ashore and longs perchance to visit — ' "

"Quite right. To visit what?"

" 'To visit dolphin coral in deep seas,' " said the boy, and burst into tears.

"Come, come! why do you cry?"

"Because — because all these words that only rhymed before, now that I've come back they're me."

Mr. Bons laid the Keats down. The case was more interesting than he had expected. "*You?*" he exclaimed. "This sonnet, *you?*"

"Yes — and look further on: 'Aye, on the shores of darkness there is light, and precipices show untrodden green.' It *is* so, sir. All these things are true."

"I never doubted it," said Mr. Bons, with closed eyes.

"You — then you believe me? You believe in the omnibus and the driver and the storm and that return ticket I got for nothing and — "

"Tut, tut! No more of your yarns, my boy. I meant that I never doubted the essential truth of Poetry. Some day, when you have read more, you will understand what I mean."

"But, Mr. Bons, it *is* so. There *is* light upon the shores of darkness. I have seen it coming. Light and a wind."

"Nonsense," said Mr. Bons.

"If I had stopped! They tempted me. They told me to give up my ticket — for you cannot come back if you lose your ticket. They called from the river for it, and indeed I was tempted, for

The Celestial Omnibus 289

I have never been so happy as among those precipices. But I thought of my mother and father, and that I must fetch them. Yet they will not come, though the road starts opposite our house. It has all happened as the people up there warned me, and Mr. Bons has disbelieved me like everyone else. I have been caned. I shall never see that mountain again."

"What's that about me?" said Mr. Bons, sitting up in his chair very suddenly.

"I told them about you, and how clever you were, and how many books you had, and they said, 'Mr. Bons will certainly disbelieve you.' "

"Stuff and nonsense, my young friend. You grow impertinent. I — well — I will settle the matter. Not a word to your father. I will cure you. Tomorrow evening I will myself call here to take you for a walk, and at sunset we will go up this alley opposite and hunt for your omnibus, you silly little boy."

His face grew serious, for the boy was not disconcerted, but leapt about the room singing, "Joy! joy! I told them you would believe me. We will drive together over the rainbow. I told them that you would come." After all, could there be anything in the story? Wagner? Keats? Shelley? Sir Thomas Browne? Certainly the case was interesting.

And on the morrow evening, though it was pouring with rain, Mr. Bons did not omit to call at Agathox Lodge.

The boy was ready, bubbling with excitement, and skipping about in a way that rather vexed the President of the Literary Society. They took a turn down Buckingham Park Road, and then — having seen that no one was watching them — slipped up the alley. Naturally enough (for the sun was setting) they ran straight against the omnibus.

"Good heavens!" exclaimed Mr. Bons. "Good gracious heavens!"

It was not the omnibus in which the boy had driven first, nor yet that in which he had returned. There were three horses — black, gray, and white, the gray being the finest. The driver, who turned round at the mention of goodness and of heaven, was a sallow man with terrifying jaws and sunken eyes. Mr. Bons, on seeing him, gave a cry as if of recognition, and began to tremble violently.

The boy jumped in.

"Is it possible?" cried Mr. Bons. "Is the impossible possible?"

"Sir; come in, sir. It is such a fine omnibus. Oh, here is his name — Dan someone."

Mr. Bons sprang in too. A blast of wind immediately slammed the omnibus door, and the shock jerked down all the omnibus blinds, which were very weak on their springs.

"Dan . . . Show me. Good gracious heavens! We're moving."

"Hooray!" said the boy.

Mr. Bons became flustered. He had not intended to be kidnapped. He could not find the door-handle nor push up the blinds. The omnibus was quite dark, and by the time he had struck a match, night had come on outside also. They were moving rapidly.

"A strange, a memorable adventure," he said, surveying the interior of the omnibus, which was large, roomy, and constructed with extreme regularity, every part exactly answering to every other part. Over the door (the handle of which was outside) was written, "Lasciate ogni baldanza voi che entrate" — at least, that was what was written, but Mr. Bons said that it was Lashy arty something, and that baldanza was a mistake for speranza. His voice sounded as if he was in church. Meanwhile, the boy called to the cadaverous driver for two return tickets. They were handed in without a word. Mr. Bons covered his face with his hand and again trembled. "Do you know who that is!" he whispered, when the little window had shut upon them. "It is the impossible."

"Well, I don't like him as much as Sir Thomas Browne, though I shouldn't be surprised if he had even more in him."

"More in him?" He stamped irritably. "By accident you have made the greatest discovery of the century, and all you can say is that there is more in this man. Do you remember those vellum books in my library, stamped with red lilies? This — sit still, I bring you stupendous news! — *this is the man who wrote them.*"

The boy sat quite still. "I wonder if we shall see Mrs. Gamp?" he asked, after a civil pause.

"Mrs. — ?"

"Mrs. Gamp and Mrs. Harris. I like Mrs. Harris. I came upon them quite suddenly. Mrs. Gamp's bandboxes have moved over the rainbow so badly. All the bottoms have fallen out, and two of the pippins off her bedstead tumbled into the stream."

"Out there sits the man who wrote my vellum books!" thundered Mr. Bons, "and you talk to me of Dickens and of Mrs. Gamp?"

"I know Mrs. Gamp so well," he apologized. "I could not help being glad to see her. I recognized her voice. She was telling Mrs. Harris about Mrs. Prig."

"Did you spend the whole day in her elevating company?"

"Oh, no. I raced. I met a man who took me out beyond to a race-course. You run, and there are dolphins out at sea."

"Indeed. Do you remember the man's name?"

"Achilles. No; he was later. Tom Jones."

Mr. Bons sighed heavily. "Well, my lad, you have made a miserable mess of it. Think of a cultured person with your opportunities! A cultured person would have known all these characters and known what to have said to each. He would not have wasted his time with a Mrs. Gamp or a Tom Jones. The creations of Homer, of Shakespeare, and of Him who drives us now, would alone have contented him. He would not have raced. He would have asked intelligent questions."

"But, Mr. Bons," said the boy humbly, "you will be a cultured person. I told them so."

"True, true, and I beg you not to disgrace me when we arrive. No gossiping. No running. Keep close to my side, and never speak to these Immortals unless they speak to you. Yes, and give me the return tickets. You will be losing them."

The boy surrendered the tickets, but felt a little sore. After all, he had found the way to this place. It was hard first to be disbelieved and then to be lectured. Meanwhile, the rain had stopped, and moonlight crept into the omnibus through the cracks in the blinds.

"But how is there to be a rainbow?" cried the boy.

"You distract me," snapped Mr. Bons. "I wish to meditate on beauty. I wish to goodness I was with a reverent and sympathetic person."

The lad bit his lip. He made good resolutions. He would imitate Mr. Bons all the visit. He would not laugh, or run, or sing, or do any of the vulgar things that must have disgusted his new friends last time. He would be very careful to pronounce their names properly, and to remember who knew whom. Achilles did not know Tom Jones — at least, so Mr. Bons said. The Duchess of Malfi was older than Mrs. Gamp — at least, so Mr. Bons said. He would be self-conscious, reticent, and prim. He would never say he liked anyone. Yet, when the blind flew up at a chance touch of his head, all these good resolutions went to the winds, for the omnibus had reached the summit of a moonlit hill, and there was the chasm, and there, across it, stood the old precipices, dreaming, with their feet in the everlasting river. He exclaimed, "The mountain! Listen to the new tune in the water! Look at the camp fires in the ravines," and Mr. Bons, after a hasty glance, retorted, "Water? Camp fires? Ridiculous rubbish. Hold your tongue. There is nothing at all."

Yet, under his eyes, a rainbow formed, compounded not of sunlight and storm, but of moonlight and the spray of the river. The three horses put their feet upon it. He thought it the finest rainbow he had seen, but did not dare to say so, since Mr. Bons said that nothing was there. He leant out — the window had opened — and sang the tune that rose from the sleeping waters.

"The prelude of Rhinegold?" said Mr. Bons suddenly. "Who taught you these *leit motifs?*" He, too, looked out of the window. Then he behaved very oddly. He gave a choking cry and fell back onto the omnibus floor. He writhed and kicked. His face was green.

"Does the bridge make you dizzy?" the boy asked.

"Dizzy!" gasped Mr. Bons. "I want to go back. Tell the driver."

But the driver shook his head.

"We are nearly there," said the boy. "They are asleep. Shall I call? They will be so pleased to see you, for I have prepared them."

Mr. Bons moaned. They moved over the lunar rainbow, which ever and ever broke away behind their wheels. How still the night was! Who would be sentry at the Gate?

"I am coming," he shouted, again forgetting the hundred resolutions. "I am returning — I, the boy."

"The boy is returning," cried a voice to other voices, who repeated, "The boy is returning."

"I am bringing Mr. Bons with me."

Silence.

"I should have said Mr. Bons is bringing me with him."

Profound silence.

"Who stands sentry?"

"Achilles."

And on the rocky causeway, close to the springing of the rainbow bridge, he saw a young man who carried a wonderful shield.

"Mr. Bons, it is Achilles, armed."

"I want to go back," said Mr. Bons.

The last fragment of the rainbow melted, the wheels sang upon the living rock, the door of the omnibus burst open. Out leapt the boy — he could not resist — and sprang to meet the warrior, who, stooping suddenly, caught him on his shield.

"Achilles!" he cried, "let me get down, for I am ignorant and vulgar, and I must wait for that Mr. Bons of whom I told you yesterday."

But Achilles raised him aloft. He crouched on the wonderful shield, on heroes and burning cities, on vineyards graven in gold, on every dear passion, every joy, on the entire image of the Mountain that he had discovered, encircled, like it, with an everlasting stream. "No, no," he protested, "I am not worthy. It is Mr. Bons who must be up here."

But Mr. Bons was whimpering, and Achilles trumpeted and cried, "Stand upright upon my shield!"

"Sir, I did not mean to stand! something made me stand. Sir, why do you delay? Here is only the great Achilles, whom you knew."

Mr. Bons screamed, "I see no one. I see nothing. I want to go back." Then he cried to the driver, "Save me! Let me stop in your chariot. I have honoured you. I have quoted you. I have bound you in vellum. Take me back to my world."

The driver replied, "I am the means and not the end. I am the food and not the life. Stand by yourself, as that boy has stood. I cannot save you. For poetry is a spirit; and they that would worship it must worship in spirit and in truth."

Mr. Bons — he could not resist — crawled out of the beautiful omnibus. His face appeared, gaping horribly. His hands followed, one gripping the step, the other beating the air. Now his shoulders emerged, his chest, his stomach. With a shriek of "I see London," he fell — fell against the hard, moonlit rock, fell into it as if it were water, fell through it, vanished, and was seen by the boy no more.

"Where have you fallen to, Mr. Bons? Here is a procession arriving to honour you with music and torches. Here come the men and women whose names you know. The mountain is awake, the river is awake, over the race-course the sea is awaking those dolphins, and it is all for you. They want you — "

There was the touch of fresh leaves on his forehead. Someone
had crowned him.

ΤΕΛΟΣ

◆

From the *Kingston Gazette, Surbiton Times,* and *Raynes Park
Observer.*

The body of Mr. Septimus Bons has been found in a shockingly
mutilated condition in the vicinity of the Bermondsey gas-works.
The deceased's pockets contained a sovereign-purse, a silver cigar-
case, a bijou pronouncing dictionary, and a couple of omnibus
tickets. The unfortunate gentleman had apparently been hurled
from a considerable height. Foul play is suspected, and a thorough
investigation is pending by the authorities.

things

They were true idealists, from New England. But that is some time ago: before the war. Several years before the war, they met and married; he a tall, keen-eyed young man from Connecticut, she a smallish, demure, Puritan-looking young woman from Massachusetts. They both had a little money. Not much, however. Even added together, it didn't make three thousand dollars a year. Still — they were free. Free!

Ah! Freedom! To be free to live one's own life! To be twenty-five and twenty-seven, a pair of true idealists with a mutual love of beauty, and an inclination towards "Indian thought" — meaning, alas, Mrs. Besant — and an income a little under three thousand dollars a year! But what is money? All one wishes to do is to live a full and beautiful life. In Europe, of course, right at the fountain-head of tradition. It might possibly be done in America: in New England, for example. But at a forfeiture of a certain amount of "beauty." True beauty takes a long time to mature. The baroque is only half-beautiful, half-matured. No, the real silver bloom, the real golden-sweet bouquet of beauty had its roots in the Renaissance, not in any later or shallower period.

Therefore the two idealists, who were married in New Haven, sailed at once to Paris: Paris of the old days. They had a studio apartment on the Boulevard Montparnasse, and they became real Parisians, in the old, delightful sense, not in the modern, vulgar. It was the shimmer of the pure impressionists, Monet and his followers, the world seen in terms of pure light, light broken and unbroken. How lovely! How lovely the nights, the river, the mornings in the old streets and by the flower-stalls and the book-stalls, the afternoons up on Montmartre or in the Tuileries, the evenings on the boulevards!

They both painted, but not desperately. Art had not taken them by the throat, and they did not take Art by the throat. They painted: that's all. They knew people — nice people, if possible, though one had to take them mixed. And they were happy.

Yet it seems as if human beings must set their claws in *something*. To be "free," to be "living a full and beautiful life," you must, alas, be attached to something. A "full and beautiful life" means a tight attachment to *something* — at least, it is so for all idealists — or else a certain boredom supervenes; there is a certain waving of loose ends upon the air, like the waving, yearning tendrils of the vine that spread and rotate, seeking something to clutch, something up which to climb towards the necessary sun. Finding nothing, the vine can only trail, half-fulfilled, upon the ground. Such is freedom! — a clutching of the right pole. And human beings are all vines. But especially the idealist. He is a vine, and he needs to clutch and climb. And he despises the man who is a mere *potato,* or turnip, or lump of wood.

Our idealists were frightfully happy, but they were all the time reaching out for something to cotton on to. At first, Paris was enough. They explored Paris *thoroughly*. And they learned French till they almost felt like French people, they could speak it so glibly.

Still, you know, you never talk French with your *soul*. It can't be done. And though it's very thrilling, at first, talking in French to clever Frenchmen — they seem *so* much cleverer than oneself — still, in the long run, it is not satisfying. The endlessly clever *materialism* of the French leaves you cold, in the end, gives a sense of barrenness and incompatibility with true New England depth. So our two idealists felt.

They turned away from France — but ever so gently. France had disappointed them. "We've loved it, and we've got a great deal out of it. But after a while, after a considerable while, several years, in fact, Paris leaves one feeling disappointed. It hasn't quite got what one wants."

"But Paris isn't France."

"No, perhaps not. France is quite different from Paris. And France is lovely — quite lovely. But *to us*, though we love it, it doesn't say a great deal."

So, when the war came, the idealists moved to Italy. And they loved Italy. They found it beautiful, and more poignant than France. It seemed much nearer to the New England conception of beauty: something pure, and full of sympathy, without the *materialism* and the *cynicism* of the French. The two idealists seemed to breathe their own true air in Italy.

And in Italy, much more than in Paris, they felt they could thrill to the teachings of the Buddha. They entered the swelling stream of modern Buddhistic emotion, and they read the books, and they practised meditation, and they deliberately set themselves to eliminate from their own souls greed, pain, and sorrow. They did not realize — yet — that Buddha's very eagerness to free himself from pain and sorrow is in itself a sort of greed. No, they dreamed of a perfect world, from which all greed, and nearly all pain, and a great deal of sorrow, were eliminated.

But America entered the war, so the two idealists had to help. They did hospital work. And though their experience made them realize more than ever that greed, pain, and sorrow *should* be eliminated from the world, nevertheless the Buddhism, or the theosophy, didn't emerge very triumphant from the long crisis. Somehow, somewhere, in some part of themselves, they felt that greed, pain, and sorrow would never be eliminated, because most people don't care about eliminating them, and never will care. Our idealists were far too western to think of abandoning all the world to damnation, while they saved their two selves. They were far too unselfish to sit tight under a bho-tree and reach Nirvana in a mere couple.

It was more than that, though. They simply hadn't enough *Seitzfleisch* to squat under a bho-tree and get to Nirvana by contemplating anything, least of all their own navel. If the whole wide world was not going to be saved, they, personally, were not so very keen on being saved just by themselves. No, it would be so lonesome. They were New Englanders, so it must be all or nothing. Greed, pain, and sorrow must either be eliminated from *all the world,* or else, what was the use of eliminating them from oneself? No use at all! One was just a victim.

And so, although they still *loved* "Indian thought," and felt very tender about it: well, to go back to our metaphor, the pole up which the green and anxious vines had clambered so far now proved dry-rotten. It snapped, and the vines came slowly subsiding to earth again. There was no crack and crash. The vines held themselves up by their own foliage, for a while. But they subsided. The beanstalk of "Indian thought" had given way before Jack and Jill had climbed off the tip of it to a further world.

They subsided with a slow rustle back to earth again. But they made no outcry. They were again "disappointed." But they never admitted it. "Indian thought" had let them down. But they never complained. Even to one another, they never said a word. They were disappointed, faintly but deeply disillusioned, and they both knew it. But the knowledge was tacit.

And they still had so much in their lives. They still had Italy — dear Italy. And they still had freedom, the priceless treasure. And they still had so much "beauty." About the fulness of their lives they were not quite so sure. They had one little boy, whom they loved as parents should love their children, but whom they wisely refrained from fastening upon, to build their lives on him. No, no, they must live their own lives! They still had strength of mind to know that.

But they were now no longer so very young. Twenty-five and twenty-seven had become thirty-five and thirty-seven. And though they had had a very wonderful time in Europe, and though they still loved Italy — dear Italy! — yet: they were disappointed. They had got a lot out of it: oh, a very great deal indeed! Still, it hadn't given them quite, not *quite,* what they had expected. Europe was lovely, but it was dead. Living in Europe, you were living on the past. And Europeans, with all their superficial charm, were not *really* charming. They were materialistic, they had no *real* soul. They just did not understand the inner urge of the spirit, because the inner urge was dead in them, they were all survivals. There, that was the truth about Europeans: they were survivals, with no more getting ahead in them.

It was another bean-pole, another vine-support crumbled under the green life of the vine. And very bitter it was, this time. For up the old tree-trunk of Europe the green vine had been clambering silently for more than ten years, ten hugely important years, the years of real living. The two idealists had *lived* in Europe, lived on Europe and on European life and European things as vines in an everlasting vineyard.

They had made their home here: a home such as you could never make in America. Their watchward had been "beauty." They had rented, the last four years, the second floor of an old Palazzo on the Arno, and here they had all their "things." And they derived a profound, profound satisfaction from their apartment: the lofty, silent, ancient rooms with windows on the river, with glistening dark-red floors, and the beautiful furniture that the idealists had "picked up."

Yes, unknown to themselves, the lives of the idealists had been running with a fierce swiftness horizontally, all the time. They had become tense, fierce hunters of "things" for their home. While their souls were climbing up to the sun of old European culture or old Indian thought, their passions were running horizontally, clutching at "things." Of course they did not buy the things for the things' sakes, but for the sake of "beauty." They looked upon their home as a place entirely furnished by loveliness, not by "things" at all. Valerie had some very lovely curtains at the windows of the long *salotto*, looking on the river: curtains of queer ancient material that looked like finely-knitted silk, most beautifully faded down from vermilion and orange, and gold, and black, down to a sheer soft glow. Valerie hardly ever came into the *salotto* without mentally falling on her knees before the curtains. "Chartres!" she said. "To me they are Chartres!" And Melville never turned and looked at his sixteenth-century Venetian bookcase, with its two or three dozen of choice books, without feeling his marrow stir in his bones. The holy of holies!

The child silently, almost sinisterly, avoided any rude contact with these ancient monuments of furniture, as if they had been nests of sleeping cobras, or that "thing" most perilous to the touch, the Ark of the Covenant. His childish awe was silent and cold, but final.

Still, a couple of New England idealists cannot live merely on the bygone glory of their furniture. At least, one couple could not. They got used to the marvellous Bologna cupboard, they got used to the wonderful Venetian bookcase, and the books, and the Siena curtains and bronzes, and the lovely sofas and side-tables and chairs they had "picked up" in Paris. Oh, they had been picking things up since the first day they landed in Europe. And they were still at it. It is the last interest Europe can offer to an outsider: or to an insider either.

When people came, and were thrilled by the Melville interior, then Valerie and Erasmus felt they had not lived in vain: that they still were living. But in the long mornings, when Erasmus was desultorily working at Renaissance Florentine literature, and Valerie was attending to the apartment: and in the long hours after lunch; and in the long, usually very cold and oppressive evenings in the ancient palazzo: then the halo died from around the furniture, and the things became things, lumps of matter that just stood there or hung there, *ad infinitum*, and said nothing; and Valerie and Erasmus almost hated them. The glow of beauty, like every other glow, dies down unless it is fed. The idealists still dearly loved their things. But they had got them. And the sad fact is, things that glow vividly while you're getting them, go almost quite cold after a year or two. Unless, of course, people envy them very much, and the museums are pining for them. And the Melvilles' "things," though very good, were not quite so good as that.

So, the glow gradually went out of everything, out of Europe, out of Italy — "the Italians are *dears*" — even out of that marvellous apartment on the Arno. "Why, if I had this apartment, I'd never, never even want to go out of doors! It's too lovely and perfect." That was something, of course — to hear that.

And yet Valerie and Erasmus went out of doors: they even went out to get away from its ancient, cold-floored, stone-heavy silence and dead dignity. "We're living on the past, you know, Dick," said Valerie to her husband. She called him Dick.

They were grimly hanging on. They did not like to give in. They did not like to own up that they were through. For twelve

years now, they had been "free" people living a "full and beautiful life." And America for twelve years had been their anathema,
the Sodom and Gomorrah of industrial materialism.

It wasn't easy to own that you were "through." They hated to
admit that they wanted to go back. But at last, reluctantly, they
decided to go, "for the boy's sake." — "We can't *bear* to leave
Europe. But Peter is an American, so he had better look at America
while he's young." The Melvilles had an entirely English accent
and manner; almost; a little Italian and French here and there.

They left Europe behind, but they took as much of it along with
them as possible. Several van-loads, as a matter of fact. All those
adorable and irreplaceable "things." And all arrived in New York,
idealists, child, and the huge bulk of Europe they had lugged along.

Valerie had dreamed of a pleasant apartment, perhaps on River-
side Drive, where it was not so expensive as east of Fifth Avenue,
and where all their wonderful things would look marvellous. She
and Erasmus house-hunted. But alas! their income was quite under
three thousand dollars a year. They found — well, everybody
knows what they found. Two small rooms and a kitchenette, and
don't let us unpack a *thing!*

The chunk of Europe which they had bitten off went into a
warehouse, at fifty dollars a month. And they sat in two small
rooms and a kitchenette, and wondered why they'd done it.

Erasmus, of course, ought to get a job. This was what was written on the wall, and what they both pretended not to see. But it
had been the strange, vague threat that the Statue of Liberty had
always held over them: "Thou shalt get a job!" Erasmus had the
tickets, as they say. A scholastic career was still possible for him.
He had taken his exams brilliantly at Yale, and had kept up his
"researches," all the time he had been in Europe.

But both he and Valerie shuddered. A scholastic career! The
scholastic world! The *American* scholastic world! Shudder upon
shudder! Give up their freedom, their full and beautiful life? Never!
Never! Erasmus would be forty next birthday.

The "things" remained in warehouse. Valerie went to look at
them. It cost her a dollar an hour, and horrid pangs. The "things,"
poor things, looked a bit shabby and wretched, in that warehouse.

However, New York was not all America. There was the great
clean West. So the Melvilles went West, with Peter, but without
the things. They tried living the simple life, in the mountains. But

doing their own chores became almost a nightmare. "Things" are all very well to look at, but it's awful handling them, even when they're beautiful. To be the slave of hideous things, to keep a stove going, cook meals, wash dishes, carry water and clean floors: pure horror of sordid anti-life!

In the cabin on the mountains, Valerie dreamed of Florence, the lost apartment; and her Bologna cupboard and Louis-Quinze chairs, above all, her "Chartres" curtains, stood in New York and costing fifty dollars a month.

A millionaire friend came to the rescue, offering them a cottage on the California coast — California! Where the new soul is to be born in man. With joy the idealists moved a little farther west, catching at new vine-props of hope.

And finding them straws! The millionaire cottage was perfectly equipped. It was perhaps as labour-savingly perfect as is possible: electric heating and cooking, a white-and-pearl enameled kitchen, nothing to make dirt except the human being himself. In an hour or so the idealists had got through their chores. They were "free" — free to hear the great Pacific pounding the coast, and to feel a new soul filling their bodies.

Alas! the Pacific pounded the coast with hideous brutality, brute force itself! And the new soul, instead of sweetly stealing into their bodies, seemed only meanly to gnaw the old soul out of their bodies. To feel you are under the fist of the most blind and crunching brute force: to feel that your cherished idealist's soul is being gnawed out of you, and only irritation left in place of it: well, it isn't good enough.

After about nine months, the idealists departed from the California west. It had been a great experience, they were glad to have had it. But, in the long run, the West was not the place for them, and they knew it. No, the people who wanted new souls had better get them. They, Valerie and Erasmus Melville, would like to develop the old soul a little further. Anyway, they had not felt any influx of new soul, on the California coast. On the contrary.

So, with a slight hole in their material capital, they returned to Massachusetts and paid a visit to Valerie's parents, taking the boy along. The grandparents welcomed the child — poor expatriated boy — and were rather cold to Valerie, but really cold to Erasmus. Valerie's mother definitely said to Valerie, one day, that Erasmus ought to take a job, so that Valerie could live decently. Valerie

haughtily reminded her mother of the beautiful apartment on the
Arno, and the "wonderful" things in store in New York, and of the
"marvellous and satisfying life" she and Erasmus had led. Valerie's
mother said that she didn't think her daughter's life looked so very
marvellous at present: homeless, with a husband idle at the age of
forty, a child to educate, and a dwindling capital: looked the re-
verse of marvellous to *her*. Let Erasmus take some post in one of
the universities.

"What post? What university?" interrupted Valerie.

"That could be found, considering your father's connections and
Erasmus's qualifications," replied Valerie's mother. "And you could
get all your valuable things out of store, and have a really lovely
home, which everybody in America would be proud to visit. As it
is, your furniture is eating up your income, and you are living like
rats in a hole, with nowhere to go to."

This was very true. Valerie was beginning to pine for a home,
with her "things." Of course she could have sold her furniture for
a substantial sum. But nothing would have induced her to. Whatever else passed away, religions, cultures, continents, and hopes,
Valerie would *never* part from the "things" which she and Erasmus
had collected with such passion. To these she was nailed.

But she and Erasmus still would not give up that freedom, that
full and beautiful life they had so believed in. Erasmus cursed
America. He did not *want* to earn a living. He panted for Europe.

Leaving the boy in charge of Valerie's parents, the two idealists
once more set off for Europe. In New York they paid two dollars
and looked for a brief, bitter hour at their "things." They sailed
"student class" — that is, third. Their income now was less than
two thousand dollars, instead of three. And they made straight for
Paris — cheap Paris.

They found Europe, this time, a complete failure. "We have
returned like dogs to our vomit," said Erasmus; "but the vomit has
staled in the meantime." He found he couldn't stand Europe. It
irritated every nerve in his body. He hated America too. But America at least was a darn sight better than this miserable, dirt-eating
continent; which was by no means cheap any more, either.

Valerie, with her heart on her things — she had really burned to
get them out of that warehouse, where they had stood now for
three years, eating up two thousand dollars — wrote to her mother
she thought Erasmus would come back if he could get some suit-

able work in America. Erasmus, in a state of frustration bordering
on rage and insanity, just went round Italy in a poverty-stricken
fashion, his coat-cuffs frayed, hating everything with intensity. And
when a post was found for him in Cleveland University, to teach
French, Italian, and Spanish literature, his eyes grew more beady,
and his long, queer face grew sharper and more rat-like, with utter
baffled fury. He was forty, and the job was upon him.

"I think you'd better accept, dear. You don't care for Europe
any longer. As you say, it's dead and finished. They offer us a
house on the college lot, and mother says there's room in it for all
our things. I think we'd better cable 'Accept'."

He glowered at her like a cornered rat. One almost expected to
see rat's whiskers twitching at the sides of the sharp nose.

"Shall I send the cablegram?" she asked.

"Send it!" he blurted.

And she went out and sent it.

He was a changed man, quieter, much less irritable. A load was
off him. He was inside the cage.

But when he looked at the furnaces of Cleveland, vast and like
the greatest of black forests, with red and white-hot cascades of
gushing metal, and tiny gnomes of men, and terrific noises, gigantic,
he said to Valerie:

"Say what you like, Valerie, this is the biggest thing the modern
world has to show."

And when they were in their up-to-date little house on the college lot of Cleveland University, and that woebegone débris of
Europe, Bologna cupboard, Venice book-shelves, Ravenna bishop's
chair, Louis-Quinze side-tables, "Chartres" curtains, Siena bronze
lamps, all were arrayed, and all looked perfectly out of keeping,
and therefore very impressive; and when the idealists had had a
bunch of gaping people in, and Erasmus had showed off in his best
European manner, but still quite cordial and American; and Valerie
had been most ladylike, but for all that, "we prefer America"; then
Erasmus said, looking at her with queer sharp eyes of a rat:

"Europe's the mayonnaise all right, but America supplies the
good old lobster — what?"

"Every time!" she said, with satisfaction.

And he peered at her. He was in the cage: but it was safe inside.
And she, evidently, was her real self at last. She had got the goods.
Yet round his nose was a queer, evil, scholastic look, of pure scep-
ticism. But he liked lobster.

D. H. LAWRENCE

the rocking-horse winner

There was a woman who was beautiful, who started with all the advantages, yet she had no luck. She married for love, and the love turned to dust. She had bonny children, yet she felt they had been thrust upon her, and she could not love them. They looked at her coldly, as if they were finding fault with her. And hurriedly she felt she must cover up some fault in herself. Yet what it was that she must cover up she never knew. Nevertheless, when her children were present, she always felt the centre of her heart go hard. This troubled her, and in her manner she was all the more gentle and anxious for her children, as if she loved them very much. Only she herself knew that at the centre of her heart was a hard little place that could not feel love, no, not for anybody.

Everybody else said of her: "She is such a good mother. She adores her children." Only she herself, and her children themselves, knew it was not so. They read it in each other's eyes.

There were a boy and two little girls. They lived in a pleasant house, with a garden, and they had discreet servants, and felt themselves superior to anyone in the neighbourhood.

Although they lived in style, they felt always an anxiety in the house. There was never enough money. The mother had a small income, and the father had a small income, but not nearly enough for the social position which they had to keep up. The father went into town to some office. But though he had good prospects, these prospects never materialized. There was always the grinding sense of the shortage of money, though the style was always kept up.

At last the mother said: "I will see if I can't make something." But she did not know where to begin. She racked her brains, and tried this thing and the other, but could not find anything successful. The failure made deep lines come into her face. Her children were growing up, they would have to go to school. There must be more money, there must be more money. The father, who was always very handsome and expensive in his tastes, seemed as if he never would be able to do anything worth doing. And the mother, who had a great belief in herself, did not succeed any better, and her tastes were just as expensive.

And so the house came to be haunted by the unspoken phrase: There must be more money! There must be more money! The children could hear it all the time, though nobody said it aloud. They heard it at Christmas, when the expensive and splendid toys filled the nursery. Behind the shining modern rocking-horse, behind the smart doll's-house, a voice would start whispering: "There must be more money! There must be more money!" And the children would stop playing, to listen for a moment. They would look into each other's eyes, to see if they had all heard. And each one saw in the eyes of the other two that they too had heard. "There must be more money! There must be more money!"

It came whispering from the springs of the still-swaying rocking-horse, and even the horse, bending his wooden, champing head, heard it. The big doll, sitting so pink and smirking in her new pram, could hear it quite plainly, and seemed to be smirking all the more self-consciously because of it. The foolish puppy, too, that took the place of the teddy-bear, he was looking so extraordinarily foolish for no other reason but that he heard the secret whisper all over the house: "There must be more money!"

Yet nobody ever said it aloud. The whisper was everywhere, and therefore no one spoke it. Just as no one ever says: "We are breathing!" in spite of the fact that breath is coming and going all the time.

"Mother," said the boy Paul one day, "why don't we keep a car of our own? Why do we always use uncle's, or else a taxi?"

"Because we're the poor members of the family," said the mother.

"But why are we, mother?"

"Well — I suppose," she said slowly and bitterly, "it's because your father has no luck."

The boy was silent for some time.

"Is luck money, mother?" he asked, rather timidly.

"No, Paul. Not quite. It's what causes you to have money."

"Oh!" said Paul vaguely. "I thought when Uncle Oscar said filthy lucker, it meant money."

"Filthy lucre does mean money," said the mother. "But it's lucre, not luck."

"Oh!" said the boy. "Then what is luck, mother?"

"It's what causes you to have money. If you're lucky you have money. That's why it's better to be born lucky than rich. If you're rich, you may lose your money. But if you're lucky, you will always get more money."

"Oh! Will you? And is father not lucky?"

"Very unlucky, I should say," she said bitterly.

The boy watched her with unsure eyes.

"Why?" he asked.

"I don't know. Nobody ever knows why one person is lucky and another unlucky."

"Don't they? Nobody at all? Does nobody know?"

"Perhaps God. But He never tells."

"He ought to, then. And aren't you lucky either, mother?"

"I can't be, if I married an unlucky husband."

"But by yourself, aren't you?"

"I used to think I was, before I married. Now I think I am very unlucky indeed."

"Why?"

"Well — never mind! Perhaps I'm not really," she said.

The child looked at her, to see if she meant it. But he saw, by the lines of her mouth, that she was only trying to hide something from him.

"Well, anyhow," he said stoutly, "I'm a lucky person."

"Why?" said his mother, with a sudden laugh.

He stared at her. He didn't even know why he had said it.

"God told me," he asserted, brazening it out.

"I hope He did, dear!" she said, again with a laugh, but rather bitter.

"He did, mother!"

"Excellent!" said the mother, using one of her husband's exclamations.

The boy saw she did not believe him; or, rather, that she paid no attention to his assertion. This angered him somewhat, and made him want to compel her attention.

He went off by himself, vaguely, in a childish way, seeking for the clue to "luck." Absorbed, taking no heed of other people, he went about with a sort of stealth, seeking inwardly for luck. He wanted luck, he wanted it, he wanted it. When the two girls were playing dolls in the nursery, he would sit on his big rocking-horse, charging madly into space, with a frenzy that made the little girls peer at him uneasily. Wildly the horse careered, the waving dark hair of the boy tossed, his eyes had a strange glare in them. The little girls dared not speak to him.

When he had ridden to the end of his mad little journey, he climbed down and stood in front of his rocking-horse, staring fixedly into its lowered face. Its red mouth was slightly open, its big eye was wide and glassy-bright.

"Now!" he would silently command the snorting steed. "Now, take me to where there is luck! Now take me!"

And he would slash the horse on the neck with the little whip he had asked Uncle Oscar for. He knew the horse could take him to where there was luck, if only he forced it. So he would mount again, and start on his furious ride, hoping at last to get there. He knew he could get there.

"You'll break your horse, Paul!" said the nurse.

"He's always riding like that! I wish he'd leave off!" said his elder sister Joan.

But he only glared down on them in silence. Nurse gave him up. She could make nothing of him. Anyhow he was growing beyond her.

One day his mother and his Uncle Oscar came in when he was on one of his furious rides. He did not speak to them.

"Hallo, you young jockey! Riding a winner?" said his uncle.

"Aren't you growing too big for a rocking-horse? You're not a very little boy any longer, you know," said his mother.

But Paul only gave a blue glare from his big, rather close-set eyes. He would speak to nobody when he was in full tilt. His mother watched him with an anxious expression on her face.

At last he suddenly stopped forcing his horse into the mechanical gallop, and slid down.

"Well, I got there!" he announced fiercely, his blue eyes still flaring, and his sturdy long legs straddling apart.

"Where did you get to?" asked his mother.

"Where I wanted to go," he flared back at her.

"That's right, son!" said Uncle Oscar. "Don't you stop till you get there. What's the horse's name?"

"He doesn't have a name," said the boy.

"Gets on without all right?" asked the uncle.

"Well, he has different names. He was called Sansovino last week."

"Sansovino, eh? Won the Ascot. How did you know his name?"

"He always talks about horse-races with Bassett," said Joan.

The uncle was delighted to find that his small nephew was posted with all the racing news. Bassett, the young gardener, who had been wounded in the left foot in the war and had got his present job through Oscar Cresswell, whose batman he had been, was a perfect blade of the "turf." He lived in the racing events, and the small boy lived with him.

Oscar Cresswell got it all from Bassett.

"Master Paul comes and asks me, so I can't do more than tell him, sir," said Bassett, his face terribly serious, as if he were speaking of religious matters.

"And does he ever put anything on a horse he fancies?"

"Well — I don't want to give him away — he's a young sport, a fine sport, sir. Would you mind asking him yourself? He sort of takes a pleasure in it, and perhaps he'd feel I was giving him away, sir, if you don't mind."

Bassett was serious as a church.

The uncle went back to his nephew, and took him off for a ride in the car.

"Say, Paul, old man, do you ever put anything on a horse?" the uncle asked.

The boy watched the handsome man closely.

"Why, do you think I oughtn't to?" he parried.

"Not a bit of it! I thought perhaps you might give me a tip for the Lincoln."

The car sped on into the country, going down to Uncle Oscar's place in Hampshire.

"Honour bright?" said the nephew.

"Honour bright, son!" said the uncle.

"Well, then, Daffodil."

"Daffodil! I doubt it, sonny. What about Mirza?"

"I only know the winner," said the boy. "That's Daffodil."

"Daffodil, eh?"

There was a pause. Daffodil was an obscure horse comparatively.

"Uncle!"

"Yes, son?"

"You won't let it go any further, will you? I promised Bassett."

"Bassett be damned, old man! What's he got to do with it?"

"We're partners. We've been partners from the first. Uncle, he lent me my first five shillings, which I lost. I promised him, honour bright, it was only between me and him; only you gave me that ten-shilling note I started winning with, so I thought you were lucky. You won't let it go any further, will you?"

The boy gazed at his uncle from those big, hot, blue eyes, set rather close together. The uncle stirred and laughed uneasily.

"Right you are, son! I'll keep your tip private. Daffodil, eh? How much are you putting on him?"

"All except twenty pounds," said the boy. "I keep that in reserve."

The uncle thought it a good joke.

"You keep twenty pounds in reserve, do you, you young romancer? What are you betting, then?"

"I'm betting three hundred," said the boy gravely. "But it's between you and me, Uncle Oscar! Honour bright?"

The uncle burst into a roar of laughter.

"It's between you and me all right, you young Nat Gould," he said, laughing. "But where's your three hundred?"

"Bassett keeps it for me. We're partners."

"You are, are you! And what is Bassett putting on Daffodil?"

"He won't go quite as high as I do, I expect. Perhaps he'll go a hundred and fifty."

"What, pennies?" laughed the uncle.

"Pounds," said the child, with a surprised look at his uncle. "Bassett keeps a bigger reserve than I do."

Between wonder and amusement Uncle Oscar was silent. He pursued the matter no further, but he determined to take his nephew with him to the Lincoln races.

"Now, son," he said, "I'm putting twenty on Mirza, and I'll put five for you on any horse you fancy. What's your pick?"

"Daffodil, uncle."

"No, not the fiver on Daffodil!"

"I should if it was my own fiver," said the child.

"Good! Good! Right you are! A fiver for me and a fiver for you on Daffodil."

The child had never been to a race-meeting before, and his eyes were blue fire. He pursed his mouth tight, and watched. A Frenchman just in front had put his money on Lancelot. Wild with excitement, he flayed his arms up and down, yelling "Lancelot! Lancelot!" in his French accent.

Daffodil came in first, Lancelot second, Mirza third. The child, flushed and with eyes blazing, was curiously serene. His uncle brought him four five-pound notes, four to one.

"What am I to do with these?" he cried, waving them before the boy's eyes.

"I suppose we'll talk to Bassett," said the boy. "I expect I have fifteen hundred now; and twenty in reserve; and this twenty."

His uncle studied him for some moments.

"Look here, son!" he said. "You're not serious about Bassett and that fifteen hundred, are you?"

"Yes, I am. But it's between you and me, uncle. Honour bright!"

"Honour bright all right, son! But I must talk to Bassett."

"If you'd like to be a partner, uncle, with Bassett and me, we could all be partners. Only, you'd have to promise, honour bright, uncle, not to let it go beyond us three. Bassett and I are lucky, and you must be lucky, because it was your ten shillings I started winning with. . . ."

Uncle Oscar took both Bassett and Paul into Richmond Park for an afternoon, and there they talked.

"It's like this, you see, sir," Bassett said. "Master Paul would get me talking about racing events, spinning yarns, you know, sir. And he was always keen on knowing if I'd made or if I'd lost. It's about a year since, now, that I put five shillings on Blush of Dawn for him — and we lost. Then the luck turned, with that ten shillings he had from you, that we put on Singhalese. And since that time, it's been pretty steady, all things considering. What do you say, Master Paul?"

"We're all right when we're sure," said Paul. "It's when we're not quite sure that we go down."

"Oh, but we're careful then," said Bassett.

"But when are you sure?" smiled Uncle Oscar.

"It's Master Paul, sir," said Bassett, in a secret, religious voice. "It's as if he had it from heaven. Like Daffodil, now, for the Lincoln. That was as sure as eggs."

"Did you put anything on Daffodil?" asked Oscar Cresswell.

"Yes, sir. I made my bit."

"And my nephew?"

Bassett was obstinately silent, looking at Paul.

"I made twelve hundred, didn't I, Bassett? I told uncle I was putting three hundred on Daffodil."

"That's right," said Bassett, nodding.

"But where's the money?" asked the uncle.

"I keep it safe locked up, sir. Master Paul he can have it any minute he likes to ask for it."

"What, fifteen hundred pounds?"

"And twenty! And forty, that is, with the twenty he made on the course."

"It's amazing!" said the uncle.

"If Master Paul offers you to be partners, sir, I would, if I were you; if you'll excuse me," said Bassett.

Oscar Cresswell thought about it.

"I'll see the money," he said.

They drove home again, and sure enough, Bassett came round to the garden-house with fifteen hundred pounds in notes. The twenty pounds reserve was left with Joe Glee, in the Turf Commission deposit.

"You see, it's all right, uncle, when I'm sure! Then we go strong, for all we're worth. Don't we, Bassett?"

"We do that, Master Paul."

"And when are you sure?" said the uncle, laughing.

"Oh, well, sometimes I'm absolutely sure, like about Daffodil," said the boy; "and sometimes I have an idea; and sometimes I haven't even an idea, have I, Bassett? Then we're careful, because we mostly go down."

"You do, do you! And when you're sure, like about Daffodil, what makes you sure, sonny?"

"Oh, well, I don't know," said the boy uneasily. "I'm sure, you know, uncle; that's all."

"It's as if he had it from heaven, sir," Bassett reiterated.

"I should say so!" said the uncle.

But he became a partner. And when the Leger was coming on, Paul was "sure" about Lively Spark, which was a quite inconsiderable horse. The boy insisted on putting a thousand on the horse, Bassett went for five hundred, and Oscar Cresswell two hundred. Lively Spark came in first, and the betting had been ten to one against him. Paul had made ten thousand.

"You see," he said, "I was absolutely sure of him."

Even Oscar Cresswell had cleared two thousand.

"Look here, son," he said, "this sort of thing makes me nervous."

"It needn't, uncle! Perhaps I shan't be sure again for a long time."

"But what are you going to do with your money?" asked the uncle.

"Of course," said the boy, "I started it for mother. She said she had no luck, because father is unlucky, so I thought if I was lucky, it might stop whispering."

"What might stop whispering?"

"Our house. I hate our house for whispering."

"What does it whisper?"

"Why — why" — the boy fidgeted — "why, I don't know. But it's always short of money, you know, uncle."

"I know it, son, I know it."

"You know people send mother writs, don't you, uncle?"

"I'm afraid I do," said the uncle.

"And then the house whispers, like people laughing at you behind your back. It's awful, that is! I thought if I was lucky . . ."

"You might stop it," added the uncle.

The boy watched him with big blue eyes that had an uncanny cold fire in them, and he said never a word.

"Well, then!" said the uncle. "What are we doing?"

"I shouldn't like mother to know I was lucky," said the boy.

"Why not, son?"

"She'd stop me."

"I don't think she would."

"Oh!" — and the boy writhed in an odd way — "I don't want her to know, uncle."

"All right, son! We'll manage it without her knowing."

They managed it very easily. Paul, at the other's suggestion, handed over five thousand pounds to his uncle, who deposited it with the family lawyer, who was then to inform Paul's mother that a relative had put five thousand pounds into his hands, which sum was to be paid out a thousand pounds at a time, on the mother's birthday, for the next five years.

"So she'll have a birthday present of a thousand pounds for five successive years," said Uncle Oscar. "I hope it won't make it all the harder for her later."

Paul's mother had her birthday in November. The house had been "whispering" worse than ever lately, and, even in spite of his luck, Paul could not bear up against it. He was very anxious to see the effect of the birthday letter, telling his mother about the thousand pounds.

When there were no visitors, Paul now took his meals with his parents, as he was beyond the nursery control. His mother went into town nearly every day. She had discovered that she had an odd knack of sketching furs and dress materials, so she worked secretly in the studio of a friend who was the chief "artist" for the leading drapers. She drew the figures of ladies in furs and ladies in silk and sequins for the newspaper advertisements. This young woman artist earned several thousand pounds a year, but Paul's mother only made several hundreds, and she was again dissatisfied. She so wanted to be first in something, and she did not succeed, even in making sketches for drapery advertisements.

She was down to breakfast on the morning of her birthday. Paul watched her face as she read her letters. He knew the lawyer's letter. As his mother read it, her face hardened and became more expressionless. Then a cold, determined look came on her mouth. She hid the letter under the pile of others, and said not a word about it.

"Didn't you have anything nice in the post for your birthday, mother?" said Paul.

"Quite moderately nice," she said, her voice cold and absent.

She went away to town without saying more.

But in the afternoon Uncle Oscar appeared. He said Paul's mother had had a long interview with the lawyer, asking if the whole five thousand could be advanced at once, as she was in debt.

"What do you think, uncle?" said the boy.

"I leave it to you, son."

"Oh, let her have it, then! We can get some more with the other," said the boy.

"A bird in the hand is worth two in the bush, laddie!" said Uncle Oscar.

"But I'm sure to know for the Grand National; or the Lincolnshire; or else the Derby. I'm sure to know for one of them," said Paul.

So Uncle Oscar signed the agreement, and Paul's mother touched the whole five thousand. Then something very curious happened. The voices in the house suddenly went mad, like a chorus of frogs on a spring evening. There were certain new furnishings, and Paul had a tutor. He was really going to Eton, his father's school, in the following autumn. There were flowers in the winter, and a blossoming of the luxury Paul's mother had been used to. And yet the voices in the house, behind the sprays of mimosa and almond blossom, and from under the piles of iridescent cushions, simply trilled and screamed in a sort of ectasy: "There must be more money! Oh-h-h, there must be more money. Oh, now, now-w! Now-w-w — there must be more money! — more than ever! More than ever!"

It frightened Paul terribly. He studied away at his Latin and Greek with his tutors. But his intense hours were spent with Bassett. The Grand National had gone by: he had not "known," and had lost a hundred pounds. Summer was at hand. He was in agony for the Lincoln. But even for the Lincoln he didn't "know" and he lost fifty pounds. He became wild-eyed and strange, as if something were going to explode in him.

"Let it alone, son! Don't you bother about it!" urged Uncle Oscar. But it was as if the boy couldn't really hear what his uncle was saying.

"I've got to know for the Derby! I've got to know for the Derby!" the child reiterated, his big blue eyes blazing with a sort of madness.

His mother noticed how overwrought he was.

"You'd better go to the seaside. Wouldn't you like to go now to the seaside, instead of waiting? I think you'd better," she said, looking down at him anxiously, her heart curiously heavy because of him.

But the child lifted his uncanny blue eyes.

"I couldn't possibly go before the Derby, mother!" he said. "I couldn't possibly!"

"Why not?" she said, her voice becoming heavy when she was opposed. "Why not? You can still go from the seaside to see the Derby with your Uncle Oscar, if that's what you wish. No need for you to wait here. Besides, I think you care too much about these races. It's a bad sign. My family has been a gambling family, and you won't know till you grow up how much damage it has done. But it has done damage. I shall have to send Bassett away, and ask Uncle Oscar not to talk racing to you, unless you promise to be reasonable about it; go away to the seaside and forget it. You're all nerves!"

"I'll do what you like, mother, so long as you don't send me away till after the Derby," the boy said.

"Send you away from where? Just from this house?"

"Yes," he said, gazing at her.

"Why, you curious child, what makes you care about this house so much, suddenly? I never knew you loved it."

He gazed at her without speaking. He had a secret within a secret, something he had not divulged, even to Bassett or to his Uncle Oscar.

But his mother, after standing undecided and a little bit sullen for some moments, said:

"Very well, then! Don't go to the seaside till after the Derby, if you don't wish it. But promise me you won't let your nerves go to pieces. Promise you won't think so much about horse-racing and events, as you call them!"

"Oh, no," said the boy casually. "I won't think much about them, mother. You needn't worry. I wouldn't worry, mother, if I were you."

"If you were me and I were you," said his mother, "I wonder what we should do!"

"But you know you needn't worry, mother, don't you?" the boy repeated.

"I should be awfully glad to know it," she said wearily.

"Oh, well, you can, you know. I mean, you ought to know you needn't worry," he insisted.

"Ought I? Then I'll see about it," she said.

Paul's secret of secrets was his wooden horse, that which had no name. Since he was emancipated from a nurse and a nursery-governess, he had had his rocking-horse removed to his own bed-room at the top of the house.

"Surely, you're too big for a rocking-horse!" his mother had remonstrated.

"Well, you see, mother, till I can have a real horse, I like to have some sort of animal about," had been his quaint answer.

"Do you feel he keeps you company?" she laughed.

"Oh, yes! He's very good, he always keeps me company, when I'm there," said Paul.

So the horse, rather shabby, stood in an arrested prance in the boy's bedroom.

The Derby was drawing near, and the boy grew more and more tense. He hardly heard what was spoken to him, he was very frail, and his eyes were really uncanny. His mother had sudden seizures of uneasiness about him. Sometimes, for half-an-hour, she would feel a sudden anxiety about him that was almost anguish. She wanted to rush to him at once, and know he was safe.

Two nights before the Derby, she was at a big party in town, when one of her rushes of anxiety about her boy, her first-born, gripped her heart till she could hardly speak. She fought with the feeling, might and main, for she believed in common sense. But it was too strong. She had to leave the dance and go down-stairs to telephone to the country. The children's nursery-gover-ness was terribly surprised and startled at being rung up in the night.

"Are the children all right, Miss Wilmot?"

"Oh, yes, they are quite all right."

"Master Paul? Is he all right?"

"He went to bed as right as a trivet. Shall I run up and look at him?"

"No," said Paul's mother reluctantly. "No! Don't trouble. It's all right. Don't sit up. We shall be home fairly soon." She did not want her son's privacy intruded upon.

"Very good," said the governess.

It was about one o'clock when Paul's mother and father drove

up to their house. All was still. Paul's mother went to her room
and slipped off her white fur coat. She had told her maid not to
wait up for her. She heard her husband downstairs, mixing a
whisky-and-soda.

And then, because of the strange anxiety at her heart, she stole
upstairs to her son's room. Noiselessly she went along the upper
corridor. Was there a faint noise? What was it?

She stood, with arrested muscles, outside his door, listening.
There was a strange, heavy, and yet not loud noise. Her heart
stood still. It was a soundless noise, yet rushing and powerful.
Something huge, in violent, hushed motion. What was it? What
in God's name was it? She ought to know. She felt that she knew
the noise. She knew what it was.

Yet she could not place it. She couldn't say what it was. And on
and on it went, like a madness.

Softly, frozen with anxiety and fear, she turned the doorhandle.

The room was dark. Yet in the space near the window, she
heard and saw something plunging to and fro. She gazed in fear
and amazement.

Then suddenly she switched on the light, and saw her son, in his
green pyjamas, madly surging on the rocking-horse. The blaze of
light suddenly lit him up, as he urged the wooden horse, and lit
her up, as she stood, blonde, in her dress of pale green and crystal,
in the doorway.

"Paul!" she cried. "Whatever are you doing?"

"It's Malabar!" he screamed, in a powerful, strange voice. "It's
Malabar."

His eyes blazed at her for one strange and senseless second, as
he ceased urging his wooden horse. Then he fell with a crash to
the ground, and she, all her tormented motherhood flooding upon
her, rushed to gather him up.

But he was unconscious, and unconscious he remained, with some
brain-fever. He talked and tossed, and his mother sat stonily by
his side.

"Malabar! It's Malabar! Bassett, Bassett, I know! It's Malabar!"

So the child cried, trying to get up and urge the rocking-horse
that gave him his inspiration.

"What does he mean by Malabar?" asked the heart-frozen
mother.

"I don't know," said the father stonily.

"What does he mean by Malabar?" she asked her brother Oscar.

"It's one of the horses running for the Derby," was the answer.

And, in spite of himself, Oscar Cresswell spoke to Bassett, and himself put a thousand on Malabar: at fourteen to one.

The third day of the illness was critical: they were waiting for a change. The boy, with his rather long, curly hair, was tossing ceaselessly on the pillow. He neither slept nor regained consciousness, and his eyes were like blue stones. His mother sat, feeling her heart had gone, turned actually into a stone.

In the evening, Oscar Cresswell did not come, but Bassett sent a message, saying could he come up for one moment, just one moment? Paul's mother was very angry at the intrusion, but on second thought she agreed. The boy was the same. Perhaps Bassett might bring him to consciousness.

The gardener, a shortish fellow with a little brown moustache, and sharp little brown eyes, tiptoed into the room, touched his imaginary cap to Paul's mother, and stole to the bedside, staring with glittering, smallish eyes, at the tossing, dying child.

"Master Paul!" he whispered. "Master Paul! Malabar come in first all right, a clean win. I did as you told me. You've made over seventy thousand pounds, you have; you've got over eighty thousand. Malabar came in all right, Master Paul."

"Malabar! Malabar! Did I say Malabar, mother? Did I say Malabar? Do you think I'm lucky, mother? I knew Malabar, didn't I? Over eighty thousand pounds! I call that lucky, don't you, mother? Over eighty thousand pounds! I knew, didn't I know I knew? Malabar came in all right. If I ride my horse till I'm sure, then I tell you, Bassett, you can go as high as you like. Did you go for all you were worth, Bassett?"

"I went a thousand on it, Master Paul."

"I never told you, mother, that if I can ride my horse, and get there, then I'm absolutely sure — oh, absolutely! Mother, did I ever tell you? I am lucky."

"No, you never did," said the mother.

But the boy died in the night.

And even as he lay dead, his mother heard her brother's voice saying to her: "My God, Hester, you're eighty-odd thousand to the good and a poor devil of a son to the bad. But, poor devil, poor devil, he's best gone out of a life where he rides his rocking-horse to find a winner."

EUDORA WELTY

keela, the outcast indian maiden

Oone morning in summertime, when all his sons and daughters were off picking plums and Little Lee Roy was all alone, sitting on the porch and only listening to the screech owls away down in the woods, he had a surprise.

First he heard white men talking. He heard two white men coming up the path from the highway. Little Lee Roy ducked his head and held his breath; then he patted all around back of him for his crutches. The chickens all came out from under the house and waited attentively on the steps.

The men came closer. It was the young man who was doing all of the talking. But when they got through the fence, Max, the older man, interrupted him. He tapped him on the arm and pointed his thumb toward Little Lee Roy.

He said, "Bud? Yonder he is."

But the younger man kept straight on talking, in an explanatory voice.

"Bud?" said Max again. "Look, Bud, yonder's the only little clubfooted nigger man was ever around Cane Springs. Is he the party?"

They came nearer and nearer to Little Lee Roy and then stopped and stood there in the middle of the yard. But the young man was so excited he did not seem to realize that they had arrived anywhere. He was only about twenty years old, very sunburned. He talked constantly, making only one gesture — raising his hand stiffly and then moving it a little to one side.

"They dressed it in a red dress, and it ate chickens alive," he said. "I sold tickets and I thought it was worth a dime, honest. They gimme a piece of paper with the thing wrote off I had to say. That was easy. 'Keela, the Outcast Indian Maiden!' I call it out through a pasteboard megaphone. Then ever' time it was fixin' to eat a live chicken, I blowed the sireen out front."

"Just tell me, Bud," said Max, resting back on the heels of his perforated tan-and-white sport shoes. "Is this nigger the one? Is that him sittin' there?"

Little Lee Roy sat huddled and blinking, a smile on his face. . . . But the young man did not look his way.

"Just took the job that time. I didn't mean to — I mean, I meant to go to Port Arthur because my brother was on a boat," he said. "My name is Steve, mister. But I worked with this show selling tickets for three months, and I never would of knowed it was like that if it hadn't been for that man." He arrested his gesture.

"Yeah, what man?" said Max in a hopeless voice.

Little Lee Roy was looking from one white man to the other, excited almost beyond respectful silence. He trembled all over, and a look of amazement and sudden life came into his eyes.

"Two years ago," Steve was saying impatiently. "And we was travelin' through Texas in those ole trucks. — See, the reason nobody ever come clost to it before was they give it a iron bar this long. And tole it if anybody come near, to shake the bar good at 'em, like this. But it couldn't say nothin'. Turned out they'd tole it it couldn't say nothin' to anybody ever, so it just kind of mumbled and growled, like a animal."

"Hee! hee!" This from Little Lee Roy, softly.

"Tell me again," said Max, and just from his look you could tell that everybody knew old Max. "Somehow I can't get it straight in my mind. Is this the boy? Is this little nigger boy the same as this Keela, the Outcast Indian Maiden?"

Up on the porch, above them, Little Lee Roy gave Max a glance full of hilarity, and then bent the other way to catch Steve's next words.

"Why, if anybody was to even come near it or even bresh their shoulder against the rope it'd growl and take on and shake its iron rod. When it would eat the live chickens it'd growl somethin' awful — you ought to heard it."

"Hee! hee!" It was a soft, almost incredulous laugh that began to escape from Little Lee Roy's tight lips, a little mew of delight.

"They'd throw it this chicken, and it would reach out an' grab it. Would sort of rub over the chicken's neck with its thumb an' press on it good, an' then it would bite its head off."

"O.K.," said Max.

"It skint back the feathers and stuff from the neck and sucked the blood. But ever'body said it was still alive." Steve drew closer to Max and fastened his light-colored, troubled eyes on his face.

"O.K."

"Then it would pull the feathers out easy and neat-like, awful fast, an' growl the whole time, kind of moan, an' then it would commence to eat all the white meat. I'd go in an' look at it. I reckon I seen it a thousand times."

"That was you, boy?" Max demanded of Little Lee Roy unexpectedly.

But Little Lee Roy could only say, "Hee! hee!" The little man at the head of the steps where the chickens sat, one on each step, and the two men facing each other below made a pyramid.

Steve stuck his hand out for silence. "They said — I mean, I said it, out front through the megaphone, I said it myself, that it wouldn't eat nothin' but only live meat. It was supposed to be a Indian woman, see, in this red dress an' stockin's. It didn't have on no shoes, so when it drug its foot ever'body could see. . . . When it come to the chicken's heart, it would eat that too, real fast, and the heart would still be jumpin'."

"Wait a second, Bud," said Max briefly. "Say, boy, is this white man here crazy?"

Little Lee Roy burst into hysterical, deprecatory giggles. He said, "Naw suh, don't think so." He tried to catch Steve's eye, seeking appreciation, crying, "Naw suh, don't think he crazy, mista."

Steve gripped Max's arm. "Wait! Wait!" he cried anxiously. "You ain't listenin'. I want to tell you about it. You didn't catch my name — Steve. You never did hear about that little nigger — all that happened to him? Lived in Cane Springs, Miss'ippi?"

"Bud," said Max, disengaging himself, "I don't hear anything. I got a juke box, see, so I don't have to listen."

"Look — I was really the one," said Steve more patiently, but nervously, as if he had been slowly breaking bad news. He walked up and down the bare-swept ground in front of Little Lee Roy's porch, along the row of princess feathers and snow-on-the-mountain. Little Lee Roy's turning head followed him. "I was the one — that's what I'm tellin' you."

"Suppose I was to listen to what every dope comes in Max's Place got to say, *I'd* be nuts," said Max.

"It's all me, see," said Steve. "I know that. I was the one was the cause for it goin' on an' on an' not bein' found out — such an awful thing. It was me, what I said out front through the megaphone."

He stopped still and stared at Max in despair.

"Look," said Max. He sat on the steps, and the chickens hopped off. "I know I ain't nobody but Max. I got Max's Place. I only run a place, understand, fifty yards down the highway. Liquor buried twenty feet from the premises, and no trouble yet. I ain't ever been up here before. I don't claim to been anywhere. People come to my place. Now. You're the hitchhiker. You're tellin' me, see. You claim a lot of information. If I don't get it I don't get it and I ain't complainin' about it, see. But I think you're nuts, and did from the first. I only come up here with you because I figured you's crazy."

"Maybe you don't believe I remember every word of it even now." Steve was saying gently. "I think about it at night — that an' drums on the midway. You ever hear drums on the midway?" He paused and stared politely at Max and Little Lee Roy.

"Yeh," said Max.

"Don't it make you feel sad. I remember how the drums was goin' and I was yellin', 'Ladies and gents! Do not try to touch Keela, the Outcast Indian Maiden — she will only beat your brains out with her iron rod, and eat them alive!'" Steve waved his arm gently in the air, and Little Lee Roy drew back and squealed. " 'Do not go near her, ladies and gents! I'm warnin' you!' So nobody ever did. Nobody ever come near her. Until that man."

"Sure," said Max. "That fella." He shut his eyes.

"Afterwards when he come up so bold, I remembered seein' him walk up an' buy the ticket an' go in the tent. I'll never forget that man as long as I live. To me he's a sort of — well — "

"Hero," said Max.

"I wish I could remember what he looked like. Seem like he was a tallish man with a sort of white face. Seem like he had bad teeth, but I may be wrong. I remember he frowned a lot. Kept frownin'. Whenever he'd buy a ticket, why, he'd frown."

"Ever seen him since?" asked Max cautiously, still with his eyes closed. "Ever hunt him up?"

"No, never did," said Steve. Then he went on. "He'd frown an' buy a ticket ever' day we was in these two little smelly towns in Texas, sometimes three-four times a day, whether it was fixin' to eat a chicken or not."

"O.K., so he gets in the tent," said Max.

"Well, what the man finally done was, he walked right up to the little stand where it was tied up and laid his hand out open on the planks in the platform. He just laid his hand out open there and said, 'Come here,' real low and quick, that-a-way."

Steve laid his open hand on Little Lee Roy's porch and held it there, frowning in concentration.

"I get it," said Max. "He'd caught on it was a fake."

Steve straightened up. "So ever'body yelled to git away, git away," he continued, his voice rising, "because it was growlin' an' carryin' on an' shakin' its iron bar like they tole it. When I heard all that commotion — boy! I was scared."

"You didn't know it was a fake."

Steve was silent for a moment, and Little Lee Roy held his breath, for fear everything was all over.

"Look," said Steve finally, his voice trembling. "I guess I was supposed to feel bad like this, and you wasn't. I wasn't supposed to ship out on that boat from Port Arthur and all like that. This other had to happen to me — not you all. Feelin' responsible. You'll be O.K., mister, but I won't. I feel awful about it. That poor little old thing."

"Look, you got him right here," said Max quickly. "See him? Use your eyes. He's O.K., ain't he? Looks O.K. to me. It's just you. You're nuts, is all."

"You know — when that man laid out his open hand on the boards, why, it just let go the iron bar," continued Steve, "let it fall down like that — bang — and act like it didn't know what to do. Then it drug itself over to where the fella was standin' an' leaned down an' grabbed holt onto that white man's hand as tight as it could an' cried like a baby. It didn't want to hit him!"

"Hee! hee! hee!"

"No sir, it didn't want to hit him. You know what it wanted?" Max shook his head.

"It wanted him to help it. So the man said, 'Do you wanta get out of this place, whoever you are?' An' it never answered — none of us knowed it could talk — but it just wouldn't let that man's hand a-loose. It hung on, cryin' like a baby. So the man says, 'Well, wait here till I come back.'"

"Uh-huh?" said Max.

"Went off an' come back with the sheriff. Took us all to jail. But just the man owned the show and his son got took to the pen. They said I could go free. I kep' tellin' 'em I didn't know it wouldn't hit me with the iron bar an' kep' tellin' 'em I didn't know it could tell what you was sayin' to it."

"Yeh, guess you told 'em," said Max.

"By that time I felt bad. Been feelin' bad ever since. Can't hold onto a job or stay in one place for nothin' in the world. They made it stay in jail to see if it could talk or not, and the first night it wouldn't say nothin'. Some time it cried. And they undressed it an' found out it wasn't no outcast Indian woman a-tall. It was a little clubfooted nigger man."

"Hee! hee!"

"You mean it was this boy here — yeh. It was him."

"Washed its face, and it was paint all over it made it look red. It all come off. And it could talk — as good as me or you. But they'd tole it not to, so it never did. They'd tole it if anybody was to come near it they was comin' to git it — and for it to hit 'em quick with that iron bar an' growl. So nobody ever come near it —

until that man. I was yellin' outside, tellin' 'em to keep away, keep away. You could see where they'd whup it. They had to whup it some to make it eat all the chickens. It was awful dirty. They let it go back home free, to where they got it in the first place. They made them pay its ticket from Little Oil, Texas, to Cane Springs, Miss'ippi."

"You got a good memory," said Max.

"The way it *started* was," said Steve, in a wondering voice, "the show was just travelin' along in ole trucks through the country, and just seen this little deformed nigger man, sittin' on a fence, and just took it. It couldn't help it."

Little Lee Roy tossed his head back in a frenzy of amusement.

"I found it all out later. I was up on the Ferris wheel with one of the boys — got to talkin' up yonder in the peace an' quiet — an' said they just kind of happened up on it. Like a cyclone happens: it wasn't nothin' it could do. It was just took up." Steve suddenly paled through his sunburn. "An' they found out that back in Miss'-ippi it had it a little bitty pair of crutches an' could just go runnin' on 'em!"

"And there they are," said Max.

Little Lee Roy held up a crutch and turned it about, and then snatched it back like a monkey.

"But if it hadn't been for that man, I wouldn't of knowed it till yet. If it wasn't for him bein' so bold. If he hadn't knowed what he was doin'."

"You remember that man this fella's talkin' about, boy?" asked Max, eying Little Lee Roy.

Little Lee Roy, in reluctance and shyness, shook his head gently.

"Naw suh, I can't say as I remembas that ve'y man, suh," he said softly, looking down where just then a sparrow alighted on his child's toe. He added happily, as if on inspiration, "Now I remembas *this* man."

Steve did not look up, but when Max shook with silent laughter, alarm seemed to seize him like a spasm in his side. He walked painfully over and stood in the shade for a few minutes, leaning his head on a sycamore tree.

"Seemed like that man just studied it out an' knowed it was somethin' wrong," he said presently, his voice coming more remotely than ever. "But I didn't know. I can't look at nothin' an' be sure what it is. Then afterwards I know. Then I see how it was."

"Yeh, but you're nuts," said Max affably.

"You wouldn't of knowed it either!" cried Steve in sudden boyish, defensive anger. Then he came out from under the tree and stood again almost pleadingly in the sun, facing Max where he was sitting below Little Lee Roy on the steps. "You'd of let it go on an' on when they made it do those things — just like I did."

"Bet I could tell a man from a woman and an Indian from a nigger though," said Max.

Steve scuffed the dust into little puffs with his worn shoe. The chickens scattered, alarmed at last.

Little Lee Roy looked from one man to the other radiantly, his hands pressed over his grinning gums.

Then Steve sighed, and as if he did not know what else he could do, he reached out and without any warning hit Max in the jaw with his fist. Max fell off the steps.

Little Lee Roy suddenly sat as still and dark as a statue, looking on.

"Say! Say!" cried Steve. He pulled shyly at Max where he lay on the ground, with his lips pursed up like a whistler, and then stepped back. He looked horrified. "How you feel?"

"Lousy," said Max thoughtfully. "Let me alone." He raised up on one elbow and lay there looking all around, at the cabin, at Little Lee Roy sitting cross-legged on the porch, and at Steve with his hand out. Finally he got up.

"I can't figure out how I could of ever knocked down an athaletic guy like you. I had to do it," said Steve. "But I guess you don't understand. I had to hit you. First you didn't believe me, and then it didn't bother you."

"That's all O.K., only hush," said Max, and added, "Some dope is always giving me the low-down on something, but this is the first time one of 'em ever got away with a thing like this. I got to watch out."

"I hope it don't stay black long," said Steve.

"I got to be going," said Max. But he waited. "What you want to transact with Keela? You come a long way to see him." He stared at Steve with his eyes wide open now, and interested.

"Well, I was goin' to give him some money or somethin', I guess, if I ever found him, only now I ain't got any," said Steve defiantly.

"O.K.," said Max. "Here's some change for you, boy. Just take it. Go on back in the house. Go on."

Little Lee Roy took the money speechlessly, and then fell upon his yellow crutches and hopped with miraculous rapidity away through the door. Max stared after him for a moment.

"As for you" — he brushed himself off, turned to Steve and then said, "When did you eat last?"

"Well, I'll tell you," said Steve.

"Not here," said Max. "I didn't go to ask you a question. Just follow me. We serve eats at Max's Place, and I want to play the juke box. You eat, and I'll listen to the juke box."

"Well . . ." said Steve. "But when it cools off I got to catch a ride some place."

"Today while all you all was gone, and not a soul in de house," said Little Lee Roy at the supper table that night, "two white mens come heah to de house. Wouldn't come in. But talks to me about de ole times when I use to be wid de circus — "

"Hush up, Pappy," said the children.

EUDORA WELTY

a memory

One summer morning when I was a child I lay on the sand
after swimming in the small lake in the park. The sun beat
down — it was almost noon. The water shone like steel, motionless except for the feathery curl behind a distant swimmer. From
my position I was looking at a rectangle brightly lit, actually glaring at me, with sun, sand, water, a little pavilion, a few solitary
people in fixed attitudes, and around it all a border of dark rounded
oak trees, like the engraved thunderclouds surrounding illustrations
in the Bible. Ever since I had begun taking painting lessons, I had
made small frames with my fingers, to look out at everything.

Since this was a weekday morning, the only persons who were
at liberty to be in the park were either children, who had nothing

to occupy them, or those older people whose lives are obscure, irregular, and consciously of no worth to anything: this I put down as my observation at that time. I was at an age when I formed a judgment upon every person and every event which came under my eye, although I was easily frightened. When a person, or a happening, seemed to me not in keeping with my opinion, or even my hope or expectation, I was terrified by a vision of abandonment and wildness which tore my heart with a kind of sorrow. My father and mother, who believed that I saw nothing in the world which was not strictly coaxed into place like a vine on our garden trellis to be presented to my eyes, would have been badly concerned if they had guessed how frequently the weak and inferior and strangely turned examples of what was to come showed themselves to me.

I do not know even now what it was that I was waiting to see; but in those days I was convinced that I almost saw it at every turn. To watch everything about me I regarded grimly and possessively as a *need*. All through this summer I had lain on the sand beside the small lake, with my hands squared over my eyes, finger tips touching, looking out by this device to see everything: which appeared as a kind of projection. It did not matter to me what I looked at; from any observation I would conclude that a secret of life had been nearly revealed to me — for I was obsessed with notions about concealment, and from the smallest gesture of a stranger I would wrest what was to me a communication or a presentiment.

This state of exaltation was heightened, or even brought about, by the fact that I was in love then for the first time: I had identified love at once. The truth is that never since has any passion I have felt remained so hopelessly unexpressed within me or appeared so grotesquely altered in the outward world. It is strange that sometimes, even now, I remember unadulteratedly a certain morning when I touched my friend's wrist (as if by accident, and he pretended not to notice) as we passed on the stairs in school. I must add, and this is not so strange, that the child was not actually my friend. We had never exchanged a word or even a nod of recognition; but it was possible during that entire year for me to think endlessly on this minute and brief encounter which we endured on the stairs, until it would swell with a sudden and overwhelming beauty, like a rose forced into premature bloom for a great occasion.

My love had somehow made me doubly austere in my observations of what went on about me. Through some intensity I had come almost into a dual life, as observer and dreamer. I felt a necessity for absolute conformity to my ideas in any happening I witnessed. As a result, all day long in school I sat perpetually alert, fearing for the untoward to happen. The dreariness and regularity of the school day were a protection for me, but I remember with exact clarity the day in Latin class when the boy I loved (whom I watched constantly) bent suddenly over and brought his handkerchief to his face. I saw red — vermilion — blood flow over the handkerchief and his square-shaped hand; his nose had begun to bleed. I remember the very moment: several of the older girls laughed at the confusion and distraction; the boy rushed from the room; the teacher spoke sharply in warning. But this small happening which had closed in upon my friend was a tremendous shock to me; it was unforeseen, but at the same time dreaded; I recognized it, and suddenly I leaned heavily on my arm and fainted. Does this explain why, even since that day, I have been unable to bear the sight of blood?

I never knew where this boy lived, or who his parents were. This occasioned during the year of my love a constant uneasiness in me. It was unbearable to think that his house might be slovenly and unpainted, hidden by tall trees, that his mother and father might be shabby — dishonest — crippled — dead. I speculated endlessly on the dangers of his home. Sometimes I imagined that his house might catch on fire in the night and that he might die. When he would walk into the schoolroom the next morning, a look of unconcern and even stupidity on his face would dissipate my dream; but my fears were increased through his unconsciousness of them, for I felt a mystery deeper than danger which hung about him. I watched everything he did, trying to learn and translate and verify. I could reproduce for you now the clumsy weave, the exact shade of faded blue in his sweater. I remember how he used to swing his foot as he sat at his desk — softly, barely not touching the floor. Even now it does not seem trivial.

As I lay on the beach that sunny morning, I was thinking of my friend and remembering in a retarded, dilated, timeless fashion the incident of my hand brushing his wrist. It made a very long story. But like a needle going in and out among my thoughts were the children running on the sand, the upthrust oak trees growing over

the clean pointed roof of the white pavilion, and the slowly changing attitudes of the grown-up people who had avoided the city and
were lying prone and laughing on the water's edge. I still would
not care to say which was more real — the dream I could make
blossom at will, or the sight of the bathers. I am presenting them,
you see, only as simultaneous.

I did not notice how the bathers got there, so close to me. Perhaps I actually fell asleep, and they came out then. Sprawled close
to where I was lying, at any rate, appeared a group of loud, squirm-
ing, ill-assorted people who seemed thrown together only by the
most confused accident, and who seemed driven by foolish intent
to insult each other, all of which they enjoyed with a hilarity which
astonished my heart. There were a man, two women, two young
boys. They were brown and roughened, but not foreigners; when
I was a child such people were called "common." They wore old
and faded bathing suits which did not hide either the energy or the
fatigue of their bodies, but showed it exactly.

The boys must have been brothers, because they both had very
white straight hair, which shone like thistles in the red sunlight.
The older boy was greatly overgrown — he protruded from his cos-
tume at every turn. His cheeks were ballooned outward and hid
his eyes, but it was easy for me to follow his darting, sly glances as
he ran clumsily around the others, inflicting pinches, kicks, and
idiotic sounds upon them. The smaller boy was thin and defiant;
his white bangs were plastered down where he had thrown himself
time after time headfirst into the lake when the older child chased
him to persecute him.

Lying in leglike confusion together were the rest of the group, the
man and the two women. The man seemed completely given over
to the heat and glare of the sun; his relaxed eyes sometimes squinted
with faint amusement over the brilliant water and the hot sand. His
arms were flabby and at rest. He lay turned on his side, now and
then scooping sand in a loose pile about the legs of the older
woman.

She herself stared fixedly at his slow, undeliberate movements,
and held her body perfectly still. She was unnaturally white and
fatly aware, in a bathing suit which had no relation to the shape of
her body. Fat hung upon her upper arms like an arrested earthslide
on a hill. With the first motion she might make, I was afraid that
she would slide down upon herself into a terrifying heap. Her

breasts hung heavy and widening like pears into her bathing suit. Her legs lay prone one on the other like shadowed bulwarks, uneven and deserted, upon which, from the man's hand, the sand piled higher like the teasing threat of oblivion. A slow, repetitious sound I had been hearing for a long time unconsciously, I identified as a continuous laugh which came through the motionless open pouched mouth of the woman.

The younger girl, who was lying at the man's feet, was curled tensely upon herself. She wore a bright green bathing suit like a bottle from which she might, I felt, burst in a rage of churning smoke. I could feel the genie-like rage in her narrowed figure as she seemed both to crawl and to lie still, watching the man heap the sand in his careless way about the larger legs of the older woman. The two little boys were running in wobbly ellipses about the others, pinching them indiscriminately and pitching sand into the man's roughened hair as though they were not afraid of him. The woman continued to laugh, almost as she would hum an annoying song. I saw that they were all resigned to each other's daring and ugliness.

There had been no words spoken among these people, but I began to comprehend a progression, a circle of answers, which they were flinging toward one another in their own way, in the confusion of vulgarity and hatred which twined among them all like a wreath of steam rising from the wet sand. I saw the man lift his hand filled with crumbling sand, shaking it as the woman laughed, and pour it down inside her bathing suit between her bulbous descending breasts. There it hung, brown and shapeless, making them all laugh. Even the angry girl laughed, with an insistent hilarity which flung her to her feet and tossed her about the beach, her stiff, cramped legs jumping and tottering. The little boys pointed and howled. The man smiled, the way panting dogs seem to be smiling, and gazed about carelessly at them all and out over the water. He even looked at me, and included me. Looking back, stunned, I wished that they all were dead.

But at that moment the girl in the green bathing suit suddenly whirled all the way around. She reached rigid arms toward the screaming children and joined them in a senseless chase. The small boy dashed headfirst into the water, and the larger boy churned his overgrown body through the blue air onto a little bench, which I had not even known was there! Jeeringly he called to the others, who laughed as he jumped, heavy and ridiculous, over the back of the bench and tumbled exaggeratedly in the sand below. The fat woman leaned over the man to smirk, and the child pointed at her, screaming. The girl in green then came running toward the bench as though she would destroy it, and with a fierceness which took my breath away, she dragged herself through the air and jumped over the bench. But no one seemed to notice, except the smaller boy, who flew out of the water to dig his fingers into her side, in mixed congratulation and derision; she pushed him angrily down into the sand.

I closed my eyes upon them and their struggles but I could see them still, large and almost metallic, with painted smiles, in the sun. I lay there with my eyes pressed shut, listening to their moans and their frantic squeals. It seemed to me that I could hear also the thud and the fat impact of all their ugly bodies upon one another. I tried to withdraw to my most inner dream, that of touching the wrist of the boy I loved on the stair; I felt the shudder of my wish shaking the darkness like leaves where I had closed my eyes; I felt the heavy weight of sweetness which always accompanied this memory; but the memory itself did not come to me.

I lay there, opening and closing my eyes. The brilliance and then the blackness were like some alternate experiences of night and day. The sweetness of my love seemed to bring the dark and to swing me gently in its suspended wind; I sank into familiarity; but the story of my love, the long narrative of the incident on the stairs, had vanished. I did not know, any longer, the meaning of my happiness; it held me unexplained.

Once when I looked up, the fat woman was standing opposite the smiling man. She bent over and in a condescending way pulled down the front of her bathing suit, turning it outward, so that the lumps of mashed and folded sand came emptying out. I felt a peak of horror, as though her breasts themselves had turned to sand, as though they were of no importance at all and she did not care.

When finally I emerged again from the protection of my dream, the undefined austerity of my love, I opened my eyes onto the blur of an empty beach. The group of strangers had gone. Still I lay there, feeling victimized by the sight of the unfinished bulwark where they had piled and shaped the wet sand around their bodies, which changed the appearance of the beach like the ravages of a storm. I looked away, and for the object which met my eye, the small worn white pavilion, I felt pity suddenly overtake me, and I burst into tears.

That was my last morning on the beach. I remember continuing to lie there, squaring my vision with my hands, trying to think ahead to the time of my return to school in winter. I could imagine the boy I loved walking into a classroom, where I would watch him with this hour on the beach accompanying my recovered dream and added to my love. I could even foresee the way he would stare back, speechless and innocent, a medium-sized boy with blond hair, his unconscious eyes looking beyond me and out the window, solitary and unprotected.

JAMES JOYCE

the sisters

There was no hope for him this time: it was the third stroke.
Night after night I had passed the house (it was vacation
time) and studied the lighted square of window: and night after
night I had found it lighted in the same way, faintly and evenly.
If he was dead, I thought, I would see the reflection of candles on
the darkened blind for I knew that two candles must be set at the
head of a corpse. He had often said to me: "I am not long for this
world," and I had thought his words idle. Now I knew they were
true. Every night as I gazed up at the window I said softly to
myself the word paralysis. It had always sounded strangely in my
ears, like the word gnomon in the Euclid and the word simony in
the Catechism. But now it sounded to me like the name of some

maleficent and sinful being. It filled me with fear, and yet I longed to be nearer to it and to look upon its deadly work.

Old Cotter was sitting at the fire, smoking, when I came downstairs to supper. While my aunt was ladling out my stirabout he said, as if returning to some former remark of his:

"No, I wouldn't say he was exactly . . . but there was something queer . . . there was something uncanny about him. I'll tell you my opinion. . . ."

He began to puff at his pipe, no doubt arranging his opinion in his mind. Tiresome old fool! When we knew him first he used to be rather interesting, talking of faints and worms; but I soon grew tired of him and his endless stories about the distillery.

"I have my own theory about it," he said. "I think it was one of those . . . peculiar cases. . . . But it's hard to say. . . ."

He began to puff again at his pipe without giving us his theory. My uncle saw me staring and said to me:

"Well, so your old friend is gone, you'll be sorry to hear."

"Who?" said I.

"Father Flynn."

"Is he dead?"

"Mr. Cotter here has just told us. He was passing by the house."

I knew that I was under observation so I continued eating as if the news had not interested me. My uncle explained to old Cotter.

"The youngster and he were great friends. The old chap taught him a great deal, mind you; and they say he had a great wish for him."

"God have mercy on his soul," said my aunt piously.

Old Cotter looked at me for a while. I felt that his little beady black eyes were examining me but I would not satisfy him by looking up from my plate. He returned to his pipe and finally spat rudely into the grate.

"I wouldn't like children of mine," he said, "to have too much to say to a man like that."

"How do you mean, Mr. Cotter?" asked my aunt.

"What I mean is," said old Cotter, "it's bad for children. My idea is: let a young lad run about and play with young lads of his own age and not be . . . Am I right, Jack?"

"That's my principle, too," said my uncle. "Let him learn to box his corner. That's what I'm always saying to that Rosicrucian there: take exercise. Why, when I was a nipper every morning of my life I had a cold bath, winter and summer. And that's what stands to me now. Education is all very fine and large. . . . Mr. Cotter might take a pick of that leg of mutton," he added to my aunt.

"No, no, not for me," said old Cotter.

My aunt brought the dish from the safe and put it on the table. "But why do you think it's not good for children, Mr. Cotter?" she asked.

"It's bad for children," said old Cotter, "because their minds are so impressionable. When children see things like that, you know, it has an effect. . . . "

I crammed my mouth with stirabout for fear I might give utterance to my anger. Tiresome old red-nosed imbecile!

It was late when I fell asleep. Though I was angry with old Cotter for alluding to me as a child, I puzzled my head to extract meaning from his unfinished sentences. In the dark of my room I imagined that I saw again the heavy grey face of the paralytic. I drew the blankets over my head and tried to think of Christmas. But the grey face still followed me. It murmured; and I understood that it desired to confess something. I felt my soul receding into some pleasant and vicious region; and there again I found it waiting for me. It began to confess to me in a murmuring voice and I wondered why it smiled continually and why the lips were so moist with spittle. But then I remembered that it had died of paralysis and I felt that I too was smiling feebly, as if to absolve the simoniac of his sin.

The next morning after breakfast I went down to look at the little house in Great Britain Street. It was an unassuming shop, registered under the vague name of *Drapery*. The drapery consisted mainly of children's bootees and umbrellas; and on ordinary days a notice used to hang in the window, saying: *Umbrellas Recovered*. No notice was visible now for the shutters were up. A crape bouquet was tied to the door-knocker with ribbon. Two poor women and a telegram boy were reading the card pinned on the crape. I also approached and read:

July 1st, 1895
The Rev. James Flynn (formerly of S. Catherine's Church, Meath Street), aged sixty-five years.
R. I. P.

The reading of the card persuaded me that he was dead and I was disturbed to find myself at check. Had he not been dead I would have gone into the little dark room behind the shop to find him sitting in his arm-chair by the fire, nearly smothered in his great-coat. Perhaps my aunt would have given me a packet of High Toast for him and this present would have roused him from his stupefied doze. It was always I who emptied the packet into his black snuff-box for his hands trembled too much to allow him to do this without spilling half the snuff about the floor. Even as he raised his large trembling hand to his nose little clouds of smoke dribbled through his fingers over the front of his coat. It may have been these constant showers of snuff which gave his ancient priestly garments their green faded look, for the red handkerchief, black-ened, as it always was, with the snuff-stains of a week, with which he tried to brush away the fallen grains, was quite inefficacious.

I wished to go in and look at him but I had not the courage to knock. I walked away slowly along the sunny side of the street, reading all the theatrical advertisements in the shop-windows as I went. I found it strange that neither I nor the day seemed in a mourning mood and I felt even annoyed at discovering in myself a sensation of freedom as if I had been freed from something by his death. I wondered at this for, as my uncle had said the night before, he had taught me a great deal. He had studied in the Irish college in Rome and he had taught me to pronounce Latin properly. He had told me stories about the catacombs and about Napoleon Bona-parte, and he had explained to me the meaning of the different cere-monies of the Mass and of the different vestments worn by the priest. Sometimes he had amused himself by putting difficult ques-tions to me, asking me what one should do in certain circumstances or whether such and such sins were mortal or venial or only imper-fections. His questions showed me how complex and mysterious were certain institutions of the Church which I had always regarded as the simplest acts. The duties of the priest towards the Eucharist and towards the secrecy of the confessional seemed so grave to me that I wondered how anybody had ever found in himself the courage to undertake them; and I was not surprised when he told me that the fathers of the Church had written books as thick as the *Post Office Directory* and as closely printed as the law notices in the newspaper, elucidating all these intricate questions. Often when I thought of this I could make no answer or only a very foolish and halting one upon which he used to smile and nod his head twice or thrice. Sometimes he used to put me through the responses of the Mass which he had made me learn by heart; and, as I pattered, he used to smile pensively and nod his head, now and then pushing huge pinches of snuff up each nostril alternately. When he smiled he used to uncover his big discoloured teeth and let his tongue lie upon his lower lip — a habit which had made me feel uneasy in the beginning of our acquaintance before I knew him well.

As I walked along in the sun I remembered old Cotter's words and tried to remember what had happened afterwards in the dream. I remembered that I had noticed long velvet curtains and a swinging lamp of antique fashion. I felt that I had been very far away, in some land where the customs were strange — in Persia, I thought. . . . But I could not remember the end of the dream.

In the evening my aunt took me with her to visit the house of mourning. It was after sunset; but the window-panes of the houses that looked to the west reflected the tawny gold of a great bank of clouds. Nannie received us in the hall; and, as it would have been unseemly to have shouted at her, my aunt shook hands with her for all. The old woman pointed upwards interrogatively and, on my aunt's nodding, proceeded to toil up the narrow staircase before us, her bowed head being scarcely above the level of the banister-rail. At the first landing she stopped and beckoned us forward encouragingly towards the open door of the dead-room. My aunt went in and the old woman, seeing that I hesitated to enter, began to beckon me again repeatedly with her hand.

I went in on tiptoe. The room through the lace end of the blind was suffused with dusky golden light amid which the candles looked like pale thin flames. He had been coffined. Nannie gave the lead and we three knelt down at the foot of the bed. I pretended to pray but I could not gather my thoughts because the old woman's mutterings distracted me. I noticed how clumsily her skirt was hooked at the back and how the heels of her cloth boots were trodden down all to one side. The fancy came to me that the old priest was smiling as he lay there in his coffin.

But no. When we rose and went up to the head of the bed I saw that he was not smiling. There he lay, solemn and copious, vested as for the altar, his large hands loosely retaining a chalice. His face was very truculent, grey and massive, with black cavernous nostrils and circled by a scanty white fur. There was a heavy odour in the room — the flowers.

We crossed ourselves and came away. In the little room downstairs we found Eliza seated in his arm-chair in state. I groped my way towards my usual chair in the corner while Nannie went to the sideboard and brought out a decanter of sherry and some wineglasses. She set these on the table and invited us to take a little glass of wine. Then, at her sister's bidding, she filled out the sherry into the glasses and passed them to us. She pressed me to take some cream crackers also but I declined because I thought I would make too much noise eating them. She seemed to be somewhat disappointed at my refusal and went over quietly to the sofa where she sat down behind her sister. No one spoke: we all gazed at the empty fireplace.

My aunt waited until Eliza sighed and then said:

"Ah, well, he's gone to a better world."

Eliza sighed again and bowed her head in assent. My aunt fingered the stem of her wine-glass before sipping a little.

"Did he . . . peacefully?" she asked.

"Oh, quite peacefully, ma'am," said Eliza. "You couldn't tell when the breath went out of him. He had a beautiful death, God be praised."

"And everything . . . ?"

"Father O'Rourke was in with him a Tuesday and anointed him and prepared him and all."

"He knew then?"

"He was quite resigned."

"He looks quite resigned," said my aunt.

"That's what the woman we had in to wash him said. She said he just looked as if he was asleep, he looked that peaceful and resigned. No one would think he'd make such a beautiful corpse."

"Yes, indeed," said my aunt.

She sipped a little more from her glass and said:

"Well, Miss Flynn, at any rate it must be a great comfort for you to know that you did all you could for him. You were both very kind to him, I must say."

Eliza smoothed her dress over her knees.

"Ah, poor James!" she said. "God knows we done all we could, as poor as we are — we wouldn't see him want anything while he was in it."

Nannie had leaned her head against the sofa-pillow and seemed about to fall asleep.

"There's poor Nannie," said Eliza, looking at her, "she's wore out. All the work we had, she and me, getting in the woman to wash him and then laying him out and then the coffin and then arranging about the Mass in the chapel. Only for Father O'Rourke I don't know what we'd done at all. It was him brought us all them flowers and them two candlesticks out of the chapel and wrote out the notice for the *Freeman's General* and took charge of all the papers for the cemetery and poor James's insurance."

"Wasn't that good of him?" said my aunt.

Eliza closed her eyes and shook her head slowly.

"Ah, there's no friends like the old friends," she said, "when all is said and done, no friends that a body can trust."

"Indeed, that's true," said my aunt. "And I'm sure now that he's gone to his eternal reward he won't forget you and all your kindness to him."

"Ah, poor James!" said Eliza. "He was no great trouble to us. You wouldn't hear him in the house any more than now. Still, I know he's gone and all to that. . . ."

"It's when it's over that you'll miss him," said my aunt.

"I know that," said Eliza. "I won't be bringing him in his cup of beef-tea any more, nor you, ma'am, sending him his snuff. Ah, poor James!"

She stopped, as if she were communing with the past and then said shrewdly:

"Mind you, I noticed there was something queer coming over him latterly. Whenever I'd bring in his soup to him I'd find him with his breviary fallen to the floor, lying back in the chair and his mouth open."

She laid a finger against her nose and frowned: then she continued:

"But still and all he kept on saying that before the summer was over he'd go out for a drive one fine day just to see the old house again where we were all born down in Irishtown and take me and Nannie with him. If we could only get one of them new-fangled carriages that makes no noise that Father O'Rourke told him about, them with the rheumatic wheels, for the day cheap — he said, at Johnny Rush's over the way there and drive out the three of us together of a Sunday evening. He had his mind set on that. . . . Poor James!"

"The Lord have mercy on his soul!" said my aunt.

Eliza took out her handkerchief and wiped her eyes with it. Then she put it back again in her pocket and gazed into the empty grate for some time without speaking.

"He was too scrupulous always," she said. "The duties of the priesthood was too much for him. And then his life was, you might say, crossed."

"Yes," said my aunt. "He was a disappointed man. You could see that."

A silence took possession of the little room and, under cover of it, I approached the table and tasted my sherry and then returned quietly to my chair in the corner. Eliza seemed to have fallen into a deep revery. We waited respectfully for her to break the silence: and after a long pause she said slowly:

"It was that chalice he broke. . . . That was the beginning of it. Of course, they say it was all right, that it contained nothing, I mean. But still. . . . They say it was the boy's fault. But poor James was so nervous, God be merciful to him!"

"And was that it?" said my aunt. "I heard something. . . ."

Eliza nodded.

"That affected his mind," she said. "After that he began to mope by himself, talking to no one and wandering about by himself. So one night he was wanted for to go on a call and they couldn't find him anywhere. They looked high up and low down; and still they couldn't see a sight of him anywhere. So then the clerk suggested to try the chapel. So then they got the keys and opened the chapel and the clerk and Father O'Rourke and another priest that was there brought in a light for to look for him. . . . And what do you think but there he was, sitting up by himself in the dark in his confession-box, wide-awake and laughing-like softly to himself?"

She stopped suddenly as if to listen. I too listened; but there was no sound in the house; and I knew that the old priest was lying still in his coffin as we had seen him, solemn and truculent in death, an idle chalice on his breast.

Eliza resumed:

"Wide-awake and laughing-like to himself. . . . So then, of course, when they saw that, that made them think that there was something gone wrong with him. . . ."

JAMES JOYCE

the dead

Lily, the caretaker's daughter, was literally run off her feet.
Hardly had she brought one gentleman into the little pantry
behind the office on the ground floor and helped him off with his
overcoat than the wheezy hall-door bell clanged again and she had
to scamper along the bare hallway to let in another guest. It was
well for her she had not to attend to the ladies also. But Miss Kate
and Miss Julia had thought of that and had converted the bathroom
upstairs into a ladies' dressing-room. Miss Kate and Miss Julia were
there, gossiping and laughing and fussing, walking after each other
to the head of the stairs, peering down over the banisters and calling
down to Lily to ask her who had come.

It was always a great affair, the Misses Morkan's annual dance.

Everybody who knew them came to it, members of the family, old friends of the family, the members of Julia's choir, any of Kate's pupils that were grown up enough, and even some of Mary Jane's pupils too. Never once had it fallen flat. For years and years it had gone off in splendid style, as long as anyone could remember; ever since Kate and Julia, after the death of their brother Pat, had left the house in Stoney Batter and taken Mary Jane, their only niece, to live with them in the dark, gaunt house on Usher's Island, the upper part of which they had rented from Mr. Fulham, the corn-factor on the ground floor. That was a good thirty years ago if it was a day. Mary Jane, who was then a little girl in short clothes, was now the main prop of the household, for she had the organ in Haddington Road. She had been through the Academy and gave a pupils' concert every year in the upper room of the Antient Concert Rooms. Many of her pupils belonged to the better-class families on the Kingstown and Dalkey line. Old as they were, her aunts also did their share. Julia, though she was quite grey, was still the leading soprano in Adam and Eve's, and Kate, being too feeble to go about much, gave music lessons to beginners on the old square piano in the back room. Lily, the caretaker's daughter, did housemaid's work for them. Though their life was modest, they believed in eating well; the best of everything: diamond-bone sirloins, three-shilling tea and the best bottled stout. But Lily seldom made a mistake in the orders, so that she got on well with her three mistresses. They were fussy, that was all. But the only thing they would not stand was back answers.

Of course, they had good reason to be fussy on such a night. And then it was long after ten o'clock and yet there was no sign of Gabriel and his wife. Besides they were dreadfully afraid that Freddy Malins might turn up screwed. They would not wish for worlds that any of Mary Jane's pupils should see him under the influence; and when he was like that it was sometimes very hard to manage him. Freddy Malins always came late, but they wondered what could be keeping Gabriel: and that was what brought them every two minutes to the banisters to ask Lily had Gabriel or Freddy come.

"O, Mr. Conroy," said Lily to Gabriel when she opened the door for him, "Miss Kate and Miss Julia thought you were never coming. Goodnight, Mrs. Conroy."

"I'll engage they did," said Gabriel, "but they forget that my wife here takes three mortal hours to dress herself."

He stood on the mat, scraping the snow from his goloshes, while Lily led his wife to the foot of the stairs and called out:

"Miss Kate, here's Mrs. Conroy."

Kate and Julia came toddling down the dark stairs at once. Both of them kissed Gabriel's wife, said she must be perished alive, and asked was Gabriel with her.

"Here I am as right as the mail, Aunt Kate! Go on up. I'll follow," called Gabriel from the dark.

He continued scraping his feet vigorously while the three women went upstairs, laughing, to the ladies' dressing-room. A light fringe of snow lay like a cape on the shoulders of his overcoat and like toecaps on the toes of his goloshes; and, as the buttons of his overcoat slipped with a squeaking noise through the snow-stiffened frieze, a cold, fragrant air from out-of-doors escaped from crevices and folds.

"Is it snowing again, Mr. Conroy?" asked Lily.

She had preceded him into the pantry to help him off with his overcoat. Gabriel smiled at the three syllables she had given his surname and glanced at her. She was a slim, growing girl, pale in complexion and with hay-coloured hair. The gas in the pantry made her look still paler. Gabriel had known her when she was a child and used to sit on the lowest step nursing a rag doll.

"Yes, Lily," he answered, "and I think we're in for a night of it."

He looked up at the pantry ceiling, which was shaking with the stamping and shuffling of feet on the floor above, listened for a moment to the piano and then glanced at the girl, who was folding his overcoat carefully at the end of a shelf.

"Tell me, Lily," he said in a friendly tone, "do you still go to school?"

"O no, sir," she answered. "I'm done schooling this year and more."

"O, then," said Gabriel gaily, "I suppose we'll be going to your wedding one of these fine days with your young man, eh?"

The girl glanced back at him over her shoulder and said with great bitterness:

"The men that is now is only all palaver and what they can get out of you."

Gabriel coloured, as if he felt he had made a mistake and, without looking at her, kicked off his goloshes and flicked actively with his muffler at his patent-leather shoes.

He was a stout, tallish young man. The high colour of his cheeks pushed upwards even to his forehead, where it scattered itself in a few formless patches of pale red; and on his hairless face there scintillated restlessly the polished lenses and the bright gilt rims of the glasses which screened his delicate and restless eyes. His glossy black hair was parted in the middle and brushed in a long curve behind his ears where it curled slightly beneath the groove left by his hat.

When he had flicked lustre into his shoes he stood up and pulled his waistcoat down more tightly on his plump body. Then he took a coin rapidly from his pocket.

"O Lily," he said, thrusting it into her hands, "it's Christmas-time, isn't it? Just . . . here's a little. . . . "

He walked rapidly towards the door.

"O no, sir!" cried the girl, following him. "Really, sir, I wouldn't take it."

"Christmas-time! Christmas-time!" said Gabriel, almost trotting to the stairs and waving his hand to her in deprecation.

The girl, seeing that he had gained the stairs, called out after him:

"Well, thank you, sir."

He waited outside the drawing-room door until the waltz should finish, listening to the skirts that swept against it and to the shuffling of feet. He was still discomposed by the girl's bitter and sudden retort. It had cast a gloom over him which he tried to dispel by arranging his cuffs and the bows of his tie. He then took from his waistcoat pocket a little paper and glanced at the headings he had made for his speech. He was undecided about the lines from Robert Browning, for he feared they would be above the heads of his hearers. Some quotation that they would recognise from Shakespeare or from the Melodies would be better. The indelicate clacking of the men's heels and the shuffling of their soles reminded him that their grade of culture differed from his. He would only make himself ridiculous by quoting poetry to them which they could not understand. They would think that he was airing his superior education. He would fail with them just as he had failed with the girl in the pantry. He had taken up a wrong tone. His whole speech was a mistake from first to last, an utter failure.

Just then his aunts and his wife came out of the ladies' dressing-room. His aunts were two small, plainly dressed old women. Aunt

Julia was an inch or so the taller. Her hair, drawn low over the
tops of her ears, was grey; and grey also, with darker shadows,
was her large flaccid face. Though she was stout in build and stood
erect, her slow eyes and parted lips gave her the appearance of a
woman who did not know where she was or where she was going.
Aunt Kate was more vivacious. Her face, healthier than her sister's,
was all puckers and creases, like a shrivelled red apple, and her hair,
braided in the same old-fashioned way, had not lost its ripe nut
colour.

They both kissed Gabriel frankly. He was their favourite
nephew, the son of their dead elder sister, Ellen, who had married
T. J. Conroy of the Port and Docks.

"Gretta tells me you're not going to take a cab back to Monkstown to-night, Gabriel," said Aunt Kate.

"No," said Gabriel, turning to his wife, "we had quite enough
of that last year, hadn't we? Don't you remember, Aunt Kate,
what a cold Gretta got out of it? Cab windows rattling all the way,
and the east wind blowing in after we passed Merrion. Very jolly
it was. Gretta caught a dreadful cold."

Aunt Kate frowned severely and nodded her head at every word.

"Quite right, Gabriel, quite right," she said. "You can't be too
careful."

"But as for Gretta there," said Gabriel, "she'd walk home in the
snow if she were let."

Mrs. Conroy laughed.

"Don't mind him, Aunt Kate," she said. "He's really an awful
bother, what with green shades for Tom's eyes at night and making
him do the dumb-bells, and forcing Eva to eat the stirabout. The
poor child! And she simply hates the sight of it! . . . O, but you'll
never guess what he makes me wear now!"

She broke out into a peal of laughter and glanced at her husband, whose admiring and happy eyes had been wandering from
her dress to her face and hair. The two aunts laughed heartily, too,
for Gabriel's solicitude was a standing joke with them.

"Goloshes!" said Mrs. Conroy. "That's the latest. Whenever it's
wet underfoot I must put on my goloshes. To-night even, he
wanted me to put them on, but I wouldn't. The next thing he'll
buy me will be a diving suit."

Gabriel laughed nervously and patted his tie reassuringly, while

Aunt Kate nearly doubled herself, so heartily did she enjoy the joke. The smile soon faded from Aunt Julia's face and her mirthless eyes were directed towards her nephew's face. After a pause she asked:

"And what are goloshes, Gabriel?"

"Goloshes, Julia!" exclaimed her sister. "Goodness me, don't you know what goloshes are? You wear them over your . . . over your boots, Gretta, isn't it?"

"Yes," said Mrs. Conroy. "Guttapercha things. We both have a pair now. Gabriel says everyone wears them on the continent."

"O, on the continent," murmured Aunt Julia, nodding her head slowly.

Gabriel knitted his brows and said, as if he were slightly angered:

"It's nothing very wonderful, but Gretta thinks it very funny because she says the word reminds her of Christy Minstrels."

"But tell me, Gabriel," said Aunt Kate, with brisk tact. "Of course, you've seen about the room. Gretta was saying . . ."

"O, the room is all right," replied Gabriel. "I've taken one in the Gresham."

"To be sure," said Aunt Kate, "by far the best thing to do. And the children, Gretta, you're not anxious about them?"

"O, for one night," said Mrs. Conroy. "Besides, Bessie will look after them."

"To be sure," said Aunt Kate again. "What a comfort it is to have a girl like that, one you can depend on! There's that Lily, I'm sure I don't know what has come over her lately. She's not the girl she was at all."

Gabriel was about to ask his aunt some questions on this point, but she broke off suddenly to gaze after her sister, who had wandered down the stairs and was craning her neck over the banisters.

"Now, I ask you," she said almost testily, "where is Julia going? Julia! Julia! Where are you going?"

Julia, who had gone half way down one flight, came back and announced blandly:

"Here's Freddy."

At the same moment a clapping of hands and a final flourish of the pianist told that the waltz had ended. The drawing-room door was opened from within and some couples came out. Aunt Kate drew Gabriel aside hurriedly and whispered into his ear:

"Slip down, Gabriel, like a good fellow and see if he's all right, and don't let him up if he's screwed. I'm sure he's screwed. I'm sure he is."

Gabriel went to the stairs and listened over the banisters. He could hear two persons talking in the pantry. Then he recognised Freddy Malins' laugh. He went down the stairs noisily.

"It's such a relief," said Aunt Kate to Mrs. Conroy, "that Gabriel is here. I always feel easier in my mind when he's here. . . . Julia, there's Miss Daly and Miss Power will take some refreshment. Thanks for your beautiful waltz, Miss Daly. It made lovely time."

A tall wizen-faced man, with a stiff grizzled moustache and swarthy skin, who was passing out with his partner, said:

"And may we have some refreshment, too, Miss Morkan?"

"Julia," said Aunt Kate summarily, "and here's Mr. Browne and Miss Furlong. Take them in, Julia, with Miss Daly and Miss Power."

"I'm the man for the ladies," said Mr. Browne, pursing his lips until his moustache bristled and smiling in all his wrinkles. "You know, Miss Morkan, the reason they are so fond of me is —— "

He did not finish his sentence, but, seeing that Aunt Kate was out of earshot, at once led the three young ladies into the back room. The middle of the room was occupied by two square tables placed end to end, and on these Aunt Julia and the caretaker were straightening and smoothing a large cloth. On the sideboard were arrayed dishes and plates, and glasses and bundles of knives and forks and spoons. The top of the closed square piano served also as a sideboard for viands and sweets. At a smaller sideboard in one corner two young men were standing, drinking hop-bitters.

Mr. Browne led his charges thither and invited them all, in jest, to some ladies' punch, hot, strong and sweet. As they said they never took anything strong, he opened three bottles of lemonade for them. Then he asked one of the young men to move aside, and, taking hold of the decanter, filled out for himself a goodly measure of whisky. The young men eyed him respectfully while he took a trial sip.

"God help me," he said, smiling, "it's the doctor's orders."

His wizened face broke into a broader smile, and the three young ladies laughed in musical echo to his pleasantry, swaying their bodies to and fro, with nervous jerks of their shoulders. The boldest said:

"O, now, Mr. Browne, I'm sure the doctor never ordered anything of the kind."

Mr. Browne took another sip of his whisky and said, with sidling mimicry:

"Well, you see, I'm like the famous Mrs. Cassidy, who is reported to have said: 'Now, Mary Grimes, if I don't take it, make me take it, for I feel I want it.' "

His hot face had leaned forward a little too confidentially and he had assumed a very low Dublin accent so that the young ladies, with one instinct, received his speech in silence. Miss Furlong, who was one of Mary Jane's pupils, asked Miss Daly what was the name of the pretty waltz she had played; and Mr. Browne, seeing that he was ignored, turned promptly to the two young men who were more appreciative.

A red-faced young woman, dressed in pansy, came into the room, excitedly clapping her hands and crying:

"Quadrilles! Quadrilles!"

Close on her heels came Aunt Kate, crying:

"Two gentlemen and three ladies, Mary Jane!"

"O, here's Mr. Bergin and Mr. Kerrigan," said Mary Jane. "Mr. Kerrigan, will you take Miss Power? Miss Furlong, may I get you a partner, Mr. Bergin. O, that'll just do now."

"Three ladies, Mary Jane," said Aunt Kate.

The two young gentlemen asked the ladies if they might have the pleasure, and Mary Jane turned to Miss Daly.

"O, Miss Daly, you're really awfully good, after playing for the last two dances, but really we're so short of ladies to-night."

"I don't mind in the least, Miss Morkan."

"But I've a nice partner for you, Mr. Bartell D'Arcy, the tenor. I'll get him to sing later on. All Dublin is raving about him."

"Lovely voice, lovely voice!" said Aunt Kate.

As the piano had twice begun the prelude to the first figure Mary Jane led her recruits quickly from the room. They had hardly gone when Aunt Julia wandered slowly into the room, looking behind her at something.

"What is the matter, Julia?" asked Aunt Kate anxiously. "Who is it?"

Julia, who was carrying in a column of table-napkins, turned to her sister and said, simply, as if the question had surprised her:

"It's only Freddy, Kate, and Gabriel with him."

In fact right behind her Gabriel could be seen piloting Freddy Malins across the landing. The latter, a young man of about forty, was of Gabriel's size and build, with very round shoulders. His face was fleshy and pallid, touched with colour only at the thick hanging lobes of his ears and at the wide wings of his nose. He had coarse features, a blunt nose, a convex and receding brow, tumid and protruded lips. His heavy-lidded eyes and the disorder of his scanty hair made him look sleepy. He was laughing heartily in a high key at a story which he had been telling Gabriel on the stairs and at the same time rubbing the knuckles of his left fist backwards and forwards into his left eye.

"Good-evening, Freddy," said Aunt Julia.

Freddy Malins bade the Misses Morkan good-evening in what seemed an offhand fashion by reason of the habitual catch in his voice and then, seeing that Mr. Browne was grinning at him from the sideboard, crossed the room on rather shaky legs and began to repeat in an undertone the story he had just told to Gabriel.

"He's not so bad, is he?" said Aunt Kate to Gabriel.

Gabriel's brows were dark but he raised them quickly and answered:

"Oh, no, hardly noticeable."

"Now, isn't he a terrible fellow!" she said. "And his poor mother made him take the pledge on New Year's Eve. But come on, Gabriel, into the drawing-room."

Before leaving the room with Gabriel she signalled to Mr. Browne by frowning and shaking her forefinger in warning to and fro. Mr. Browne nodded in answer and, when she had gone, said to Freddy Malins:

"Now, then, Teddy, I'm going to fill you out a good glass of lemonade just to buck you up."

Freddy Malins, who was nearing the climax of his story, waved the offer aside impatiently but Mr. Browne, having first called Freddy Malins' attention to a disarray in his dress, filled out and handed him a full glass of lemonade. Freddy Malins' left hand accepted the glass mechanically, his right hand being engaged in the mechanical readjustment of his dress. Mr. Browne, whose face was once more wrinkling with mirth, poured out for himself a glass of whisky while Freddy Malins exploded, before he had well reached the climax of his story, in a kink of high-pitched bronchitic laughter and, setting down his untasted and overflowing glass, began to rub the knuckles of his left fist backwards and forwards into his left eye, repeating words of his last phrase as well as his fit of laughter would allow him.

*   *   *

Gabriel could not listen while Mary Jane was playing her Academy piece, full of runs and difficult passages, to the hushed drawing-room. He liked music but the piece she was playing had no melody for him and he doubted whether it had any melody for the other listeners, though they had begged Mary Jane to play something. Four young men, who had come from the refreshment-room to stand in the doorway at the sound of the piano, had gone away quietly in couples after a few minutes. The only persons who seemed to follow the music were Mary Jane herself, her hands racing along the key-board or lifted from it at the pauses like those of a priestess in momentary imprecation, and Aunt Kate standing at her elbow to turn the page.

Gabriel's eyes, irritated by the floor, which glittered with beeswax under the heavy chandelier, wandered to the wall above the piano. A picture of the balcony scene in *Romeo and Juliet* hung there and beside it was a picture of the two murdered princes in the Tower which Aunt Julia had worked in red, blue and brown wools when she was a girl. Probably in the school they had gone to as girls that kind of work had been taught for one year. His mother had worked for him as a birthday present a waistcoat of purple tabinet, with little foxes' heads upon it, lined with brown satin and having round mulberry buttons. It was strange that his mother had had no musical talent though Aunt Kate used to call her the brains carrier of the Morkan family. Both she and Julia had always seemed a little proud of their serious and matronly sister. Her photograph stood before the pierglass. She held an open book on her knees and was pointing out something in it to Constantine who, dressed in a man-o'-war suit, lay at her feet. It was she who had chosen the names of her sons for she was very sensible of the dignity of family life. Thanks to her, Constantine was now senior curate in Balbriggan and, thanks to her, Gabriel himself had taken his degree in the Royal University. A shadow passed over his face as he remembered her sullen opposition to his marriage. Some slighting phrases she had used still rankled in his memory; she had once spoken of Gretta as being country cute and that was not true of Gretta at all. It was Gretta who had nursed her during all her last long illness in their house at Monkstown.

He knew that Mary Jane must be near the end of her piece for she was playing again the opening melody with runs of scales after every bar and, while he waited for the end the resentment died down in his heart. The piece ended with a trill of octaves in the treble and a final deep octave in the bass. Great applause greeted Mary Jane as, blushing and rolling up her music nervously, she escaped from the room. The most vigorous clapping came from the four young men in the doorway who had gone away to the refreshment-room at the beginning of the piece but had come back when the piano had stopped.

Lancers were arranged. Gabriel found himself partnered with Miss Ivors. She was a frank-mannered talkative young lady, with a freckled face and prominent brown eyes. She did not wear a low-cut bodice and the large brooch which was fixed in the front of her collar bore on it an Irish device and motto.

When they had taken their places she said abruptly:

"I have a crow to pluck with you."

"With me?" said Gabriel.

She nodded her head gravely.

"What is it?" asked Gabriel, smiling at her solemn manner.

"Who is G.C.?" answered Miss Ivors, turning her eyes upon him.

Gabriel coloured and was about to knit his brows, as if he did not understand, when she said bluntly:

"O, innocent Amy! I have found out that you write for *The Daily Express*. Now, aren't you ashamed of yourself?"

"Why should I be ashamed of myself?" asked Gabriel, blinking his eyes and trying to smile.

"Well, I'm ashamed of you," said Miss Ivors frankly. "To say you'd write for a paper like that. I didn't think you were a West Briton."

A look of perplexity appeared on Gabriel's face. It was true that he wrote a literary column every Wednesday in *The Daily Express*, for which he was paid fifteen shillings. But that did not make him a West Briton surely. The books he received for review were almost more welcome than the paltry cheque. He loved to feel the covers and turn over the pages of newly printed books. Nearly every day when his teaching in the college was ended he used to wander down the quays to the second-hand booksellers, to Hickey's on Bachelor's Walk, to Webb's or Massey's on Aston's Quay, or to O'Clohissy's in the by-street. He did not know how to meet her charge. He wanted to say that literature was above politics. But they were friends of many years' standing and their careers had been parallel, first at the University and then as teachers: he could not risk a grandiose phrase with her. He continued blinking his eyes and trying to smile and murmured lamely that he saw nothing political in writing reviews of books.

When their turn to cross had come he was still perplexed and inattentive. Miss Ivors promptly took his hand in a warm grasp and said in a soft friendly tone:

"Of course, I was only joking. Come, we cross now."

When they were together again she spoke of the University question and Gabriel felt more at ease. A friend of hers had shown her his review of Browning's poems. That was how she had found out the secret: but she liked the review immensely. Then she said suddenly:

"O, Mr. Conroy, will you come for an excursion to the Aran Isles this summer? We're going to stay there a whole month. It will be splendid out in the Atlantic. You ought to come. Mr. Clancy is coming, and Mr. Kilkelly and Kathleen Kearney. It would be splendid for Gretta too if she'd come. She's from Connacht, isn't she?"

"Her people are," said Gabriel shortly.

"But you will come, won't you?" said Miss Ivors, laying her warm hand eagerly on his arm.

"The fact is," said Gabriel, "I have just arranged to go —— "

"Go where?" asked Miss Ivors.

"Well, you know, every year I go for a cycling tour with some fellows and so —— "

"But where?" asked Miss Ivors.

"Well, we usually go to France or Belgium or perhaps Germany," said Gabriel awkwardly.

"And why do you go to France and Belgium," said Miss Ivors, "instead of visiting your own land?"

"Well," said Gabriel, "it's partly to keep in touch with the languages and partly for a change."

"And haven't you your own language to keep in touch with — Irish?" asked Miss Ivors.

"Well," said Gabriel, "if it comes to that, you know, Irish is not my language."

Their neighbours had turned to listen to the cross-examination. Gabriel glanced right and left nervously and tried to keep his good humour under the ordeal which was making a blush invade his forehead.

"And haven't you your own land to visit," continued Miss Ivors, "that you know nothing of, your own people, and your own country?"

"O, to tell you the truth," retorted Gabriel suddenly, "I'm sick of my own country, sick of it!"

"Why?" asked Miss Ivors.

Gabriel did not answer for his retort had heated him.

"Why?" repeated Miss Ivors.

They had to go visiting together and, as he had not answered her, Miss Ivors said warmly:

"Of course, you've no answer."

Gabriel tried to cover his agitation by taking part in the dance with great energy. He avoided her eyes for he had seen a sour expression on her face. But when they met in the long chain he was surprised to feel his hand firmly pressed. She looked at him from under her brows for a moment quizzically until he smiled. Then, just as the chain was about to start again, she stood on tiptoe and whispered into his ear:

"West Briton!"

When the lancers were over Gabriel went away to a remote corner of the room where Freddy Malins' mother was sitting. She was a stout feeble old woman with white hair. Her voice had a catch in it like her son's and she stuttered slightly. She had been told that Freddy had come and that he was nearly all right. Gabriel asked her whether she had had a good crossing. She lived with her married daughter in Glasgow and came to Dublin on a visit once a year. She answered placidly that she had had a beautiful crossing and that the captain had been most attentive to her. She spoke also of the beautiful house her daughter kept in Glasgow, and of all the friends they had there. While her tongue rambled on Gabriel tried to banish from his mind all memory of the unpleasant incident with Miss Ivors. Of course the girl, or woman, or whatever she was, was an enthusiast, but there was a time for all things. Perhaps he ought not to have answered her like that. But she had no right to call him a West Briton before people, even in joke. She had tried to make him ridiculous before people, heckling him and staring at him with her rabbit's eyes.

He saw his wife making her way towards him through the waltzing couples. When she reached him she said into his ear:

"Gabriel, Aunt Kate wants to know won't you carve the goose as usual. Miss Daly will carve the ham and I'll do the pudding."

"All right," said Gabriel.

"She's sending in the younger ones first as soon as this waltz is over so that we'll have the table to ourselves."

"Were you dancing?" asked Gabriel.

"Of course I was. Didn't you see me? What row had you with Molly Ivors?"

"No row. Why? Did she say so?"

"Something like that. I'm trying to get that Mr. D'Arcy to sing. He's full of conceit, I think."

"There was no row," said Gabriel moodily, "only she wanted me to go for a trip to the west of Ireland and I said I wouldn't."

His wife clasped her hands excitedly and gave a little jump.

"O, do go, Gabriel," she cried. "I'd love to see Galway again."

"You can go if you like," said Gabriel coldly.

She looked at him for a moment, then turned to Mrs. Malins and said:

"There's a nice husband for you, Mrs. Malins."

While she was threading her way back across the room Mrs. Malins, without adverting to the interruption, went on to tell Gabriel what beautiful places there were in Scotland and beautiful scenery. Her son-in-law brought them every year to the lakes and they used to go fishing. Her son-in-law was a splendid fisher. One day he caught a beautiful big fish and the man in the hotel cooked it for their dinner.

Gabriel hardly heard what she said. Now that supper was coming near he began to think again about his speech and about the quotation. When he saw Freddy Malins coming across the room to visit his mother Gabriel left the chair free for him and retired into the embrasure of the window. The room had already cleared and from the back room came the clatter of plates and knives. Those who still remained in the drawing-room seemed tired of dancing and were conversing quietly in little groups. Gabriel's warm trembling fingers tapped the cold pane of the window. How

cool it must be outside! How pleasant it would be to walk out
alone, first along by the river and then through the park! The snow
would be lying on the branches of the trees and forming a bright
cap on the top of the Wellington Monument. How much more
pleasant it would be there than at the supper-table!

.He ran over the headings of his speech: Irish hospitality, sad
memories, the Three Graces, Paris, the quotation from Browning.
He repeated to himself a phrase he had written in his review: "One
feels that one is listening to a thought-tormented music." Miss
Ivors had praised the review. Was she sincere? Had she really any
life of her own behind all her propagandism? There had never been
any ill-feeling between them until that night. It unnerved him to
think that she would be at the supper-table, looking up at him
while he spoke with her critical quizzing eyes. Perhaps she would
not be sorry to see him fail in his speech. An idea came into his
mind and gave him courage. He would say, alluding to Aunt Kate
and Aunt Julia: "Ladies and Gentlemen, the generation which is
now on the wane among us may have had its faults, but for my part
I think it had certain qualities of hospitality, of humour, of humanity, which the new and very serious and hypereducated generation
that is growing up around us seems to me to lack." Very good:
that was one for Miss Ivors. What did he care that his aunts were
only two ignorant old women?

A murmur in the room attracted his attention. Mr. Browne was
advancing from the door, gallantly escorting Aunt Julia, who
leaned upon his arm, smiling and hanging her head. An irregular
musketry of applause escorted her also as far as the piano and then,
as Mary Jane seated herself on the stool, and Aunt Julia, no longer
smiling, half turned so as to pitch her voice fairly into the room,
gradually ceased. Gabriel recognized the prelude. It was that of
an old song of Aunt Julia's — *Arrayed for the Bridal.* Her voice,
strong and clear in tone, attacked with great spirit the runs which
embellish the air and though she sang very rapidly she did not miss
even the smallest of the grace notes. To follow the voice, without
looking at the singer's face, was to feel and share the excitement of
swift and secure flight. Gabriel applauded loudly with all the others
at the close of the song and loud applause was borne in from the
invisible supper-table. It sounded so genuine that a little colour
struggled into Aunt Julia's face as she bent to replace in the music-
stand the old leather-bound song-book that had her initials on the

cover. Freddy Malins, who had listened with his head perched sideways to hear her better, was still applauding when everyone else had ceased and talking animatedly to his mother who nodded her head gravely and slowly in acquiescence. At last, when he could clap no more, he stood up suddenly and hurried across the room to Aunt Julia whose hand he seized and held in both his hands, shaking it when words failed him or the catch in his voice proved too much for him.

"I was just telling my mother," he said, "I never heard you sing so well, never. No, I never heard your voice so good as it is to-night. Now! Would you believe that now? That's the truth. Upon my word and honour that's the truth. I never heard your voice sound so fresh and so . . . so clear and fresh, never."

Aunt Julia smiled broadly and murmured something about compliments as she released her hand from his grasp. Mr. Browne extended his open hand towards her and said to those who were near him in the manner of a showman introducing a prodigy to an audience:

"Miss Julia Morkan, my latest discovery!"

He was laughing very heartily at this himself when Freddy Malins turned to him and said:

"Well, Browne, if you're serious you might make a worse discovery. All I can say is I never heard her sing half so well as long as I am coming here. And that's the honest truth."

"Neither did I," said Mr. Browne. "I think her voice has greatly improved."

Aunt Julia shrugged her shoulders and said with meek pride:

"Thirty years ago I hadn't a bad voice as voices go."

"I often told Julia," said Aunt Kate emphatically, "that she was simply thrown away in that choir. But she never would be said by me."

She turned as if to appeal to the good sense of the others against a refractory child while Aunt Julia gazed in front of her, a vague smile of reminiscence playing on her face.

"No," continued Aunt Kate, "she wouldn't be said or led by anyone, slaving there in that choir night and day, night and day. Six o'clock on Christmas morning! And all for what?"

"Well, isn't it for the honour of God, Aunt Kate?" asked Mary Jane, twisting round on the piano-stool and smiling.

Aunt Kate turned fiercely on her niece and said:

"I know all about the honour of God, Mary Jane, but I think it's not at all honourable for the pope to turn out the women out of the choirs that have slaved there all their lives and put little whipper-snappers of boys over their heads. I suppose it is for the good of the Church if the pope does it. But it's not just, Mary Jane, and it's not right."

She had worked herself into a passion and would have continued in defence of her sister for it was a sore subject with her, but Mary Jane, seeing that all the dancers had come back, intervened pacifically:

"Now, Aunt Kate, you're giving scandal to Mr. Browne who is of the other persuasion."

Aunt Kate turned to Mr. Browne, who was grinning at this allusion to his religion, and said hastily:

"O, I don't question the pope's being right. I'm only a stupid old woman and I wouldn't presume to do such a thing. But there's such a thing as common everyday politeness and gratitude. And if I were in Julia's place I'd tell that Father Healey straight up to his face . . ."

"And besides, Aunt Kate," said Mary Jane, "we really are all hungry and when we are hungry we are all very quarrelsome."

"And when we are thirsty we are also quarrelsome," added Mr. Browne.

"So that we had better go to supper," said Mary Jane, "and finish the discussion afterwards."

On the landing outside the drawing-room Gabriel found his wife and Mary Jane trying to persuade Miss Ivors to stay for supper. But Miss Ivors, who had put on her hat and was buttoning her cloak, would not stay. She did not feel in the least hungry and she had already overstayed her time.

"But only for ten minutes, Molly," said Mrs. Conroy. "That won't delay you."

"To take a pick itself," said Mary Jane, "after all your dancing."

"I really couldn't," said Miss Ivors.

"I am afraid you didn't enjoy yourself at all," said Mary Jane hopelessly.

"Ever so much, I assure you," said Miss Ivors, "but you really must let me run off now."

"But how can you get home?" asked Mrs. Conroy.

"O, it's only two steps up the quay."

Gabriel hesitated a moment and said:

"If you will allow me, Miss Ivors, I'll see you home if you are really obliged to go."

But Miss Ivors broke away from them.

"I won't hear of it," she cried. "For goodness' sake go in to your suppers and don't mind me. I'm quite well able to take care of myself."

"Well, you're the comical girl, Molly," said Mrs. Conroy frankly.

"*Beannacht libh*," cried Miss Ivors, with a laugh, as she ran down the staircase.

Mary Jane gazed after her, a moody puzzled expression on her face, while Mrs. Conroy leaned over the banisters to listen for the hall-door. Gabriel asked himself was he the cause of her abrupt departure. But she did not seem to be in ill humour: she had gone away laughing. He stared blankly down the staircase.

At the moment Aunt Kate came toddling out of the supper-room, almost wringing her hands in despair.

"Where is Gabriel?" she cried. "Where on earth is Gabriel? There's everyone waiting in there, stage to let, and nobody to carve the goose!"

"Here I am, Aunt Kate!" cried Gabriel, with sudden animation, "ready to carve a flock of geese, if necessary."

A fat brown goose lay at one end of the table, and at the other end, on a bed of creased paper strewn with sprigs of parsley, lay a great ham, stripped of its outer skin and peppered over with crust crumbs, a neat paper frill round its shin, and beside this was a round of spiced beef. Between these rival ends ran parallel lines of side-dishes: two little minsters of jelly, red and yellow; a shallow dish full of blocks of blancmange and red jam, a large green leaf-shaped dish with a stalk-shaped handle, on which lay bunches of purple raisins and peeled almonds, a companion dish on which lay a solid rectangle of Smyrna figs, a dish of custard topped with grated nutmeg, a small bowl full of chocolates and sweets wrapped in gold and silver papers and a glass vase in which stood some tall celery stalks. In the centre of the table there stood, as sentries to a fruit-stand which upheld a pyramid of oranges and American apples, two squat old-fashioned decanters of cut glass, one containing port and the other dark sherry. On the closed square piano a pudding in a huge yellow dish lay in waiting and behind it were three squads of bottles of stout and ale and minerals, drawn up according to the colours of their uniforms, the first two black, with brown and red labels, the third and smallest squad white, with transverse green sashes.

Gabriel took his seat boldly at the head of the table and, having looked to the edge of the carver, plunged his fork firmly into the goose. He felt quite at ease now for he was an expert carver and liked nothing better than to find himself at the head of a well-laden table.

"Miss Furlong, what shall I send you?" he asked. "A wing or a slice of the breast?"

"Just a small slice of the breast."

"Miss Higgins, what for you?"

"O, anything at all, Mr. Conroy."

While Gabriel and Miss Daly exchanged plates of goose and plates of ham and spiced beef, Lily went from guest to guest with a dish of hot floury potatoes wrapped in a white napkin. This was Mary Jane's idea and she had also suggested apple sauce for the goose, but Aunt Kate had said that plain roast goose without any apple sauce had always been good enough for her and she hoped she might never eat worse. Mary Jane waited on her pupils and saw that they got the best slices, and Aunt Kate and Aunt Julia opened and carried across from the piano bottles of stout and ale for the gentlemen and bottles of minerals for the ladies. There was a great deal of confusion and laughter and noise, the noise of orders and counter-orders, of knives and forks, of corks and glass-stoppers. Gabriel began to carve second helpings as soon as he had finished the first round without serving himself. Everyone protested loudly so that he compromised by taking a long draught of stout, for he had found the carving hot work. Mary Jane settled down quietly to her supper but Aunt Kate and Aunt Julia were still toddling round the table, walking on each other's heels, getting in each other's way and giving each other unheeded orders. Mr. Browne begged of them to sit down and eat their suppers and so did Gabriel, but they said there was time enough, so that, at last, Freddy Malins stood up and, capturing Aunt Kate, plumped her down on her chair amid general laughter.

When everyone had been well served Gabriel said, smiling:

"Now, if anyone wants a little more of what vulgar people call stuffing let him or her speak."

A chorus of voices invited him to begin his own supper and Lily came forward with three potatoes which she had reserved for him.

"Very well," said Gabriel amiably, as he took another preparatory draught, "kindly forget my existence, ladies and gentlemen, for a few minutes."

He set to his supper and took no part in the conversation with which the table covered Lily's removal of the plates. The subject of talk was the opera company which was then at the Theatre Royal. Mr. Bartell D'Arcy, the tenor, a dark-complexioned young man with a smart moustache, praised very highly the leading contralto of the company but Miss Furlong thought she had a rather vulgar style of production. Freddy Malins said there was a negro chieftain singing in the second part of the Gaiety pantomime who had one of the finest tenor voices he had ever heard.

"Have you heard him?" he asked Mr. Bartell D'Arcy across the table.

"No," answered Mr. Bartell D'Arcy carelessly.

"Because," Freddy Malins explained, "now I'd be curious to hear your opinion of him. I think he has a grand voice."

"It takes Teddy to find out the really good things," said Mr. Browne familiarly to the table.

"And why couldn't he have a voice too?" asked Freddy Malins sharply. "Is it because he's only a black?"

Nobody answered this question and Mary Jane led the table back to the legitimate opera. One of her pupils had given her a pass for *Mignon.* Of course it was very fine, she said, but it made her think of poor Georgina Burns. Mr. Browne could go back farther still, to the old Italian companies that used to come to Dublin — Tietjens, Ilma de Murzka, Campanini, the great Trebelli Giuglini, Ravelli, Aramburo. Those were the days, he said, when there was something like singing to be heard in Dublin. He told too of how the top gallery of the old Royal used to be packed night after night, of how one night an Italian tenor had sung five encores to *Let me like a Soldier fall*, introducing a high C every time and of how the gallery boys would sometimes in their enthusiasm unyoke the horses from the carriage of some great *prima donna* and pull her themselves through the streets to her hotel. Why did they never play the grand old operas now, he asked, *Dinorah, Lucrezia Borgia?* Because they could not get the voices to sing them: that was why.

"O, well," said Mr. Bartell D'Arcy, "I presume there are as good singers to-day as there were then."

"Where are they?" asked Mr. Browne defiantly.

"In London, Paris, Milan," said Mr. Bartell D'Arcy warmly. "I suppose Caruso, for example, is quite as good, if not better than any of the men you have mentioned."

"Maybe so," said Mr. Browne. "But I may tell you I doubt it strongly."

"O, I'd give anything to hear Caruso sing," said Mary Jane.

"For me," said Aunt Kate, who had been picking a bone, "there was only one tenor. To please me, I mean. But I suppose none of you ever heard of him."

"Who was he, Miss Morkan?" asked Mr. Bartell D'Arcy politely.

"His name," said Aunt Kate, "was Parkinson. I heard him when he was in his prime and I think he had then the purest tenor voice that was ever put into a man's throat."

"Strange," said Mr. Bartell D'Arcy. "I never even heard of him."

"Yes, yes, Miss Morkan is right," said Mr. Browne. "I remember hearing of old Parkinson but he's too far back for me."

"A beautiful, pure, sweet, mellow English tenor," said Aunt Kate with enthusiasm.

Gabriel having finished, the huge pudding was transferred to the table. The clatter of forks and spoons began again. Gabriel's wife served out spoonfuls of the pudding and passed the plates down the table. Midway down they were held up by Mary Jane, who replenished them with raspberry or orange jelly or with blancmange and jam. The pudding was of Aunt Julia's making and she received praises for it from all quarters. She herself said that it was not quite brown enough.

"Well, I hope, Miss Morkan," said Mr. Browne, "that I'm brown enough for you because, you know, I'm all brown."

All the gentlemen, except Gabriel, ate some of the pudding out of compliment to Aunt Julia. As Gabriel never ate sweets the celery had been left for him. Freddy Malins also took a stalk of celery and ate it with his pudding. He had been told that celery was a capital thing for the blood and he was just then under doctor's care. Mrs. Malins, who had been silent all through the supper, said that her son was going down to Mount Melleray in a week or so. The table then spoke of Mount Melleray, how bracing the air was down there, how hospitable the monks were and how they never asked for a penny-piece from their guests.

"And do you mean to say," asked Mr. Browne incredulously, "that a chap can go down there and put up there as if it were a hotel and live on the fat of the land and then come away without paying anything?"

"O, most people give some donation to the monastery when they leave," said Mary Jane.

"I wish we had an institution like that in our Church," said Mr. Browne candidly.

He was astonished to hear that the monks never spoke, got up at two in the morning and slept in their coffins. He asked what they did it for.

"That's the rule of the order," said Aunt Kate firmly.

"Yes, but why?" asked Mr. Browne.

Aunt Kate repeated that it was the rule, that was all. Mr. Browne still seemed not to understand. Freddy Malins explained to him, as best he could, that the monks were trying to make up for the sins committed by all the sinners in the outside world. The explanation was not very clear for Mr. Browne grinned and said:

"I like that idea very much but wouldn't a comfortable spring bed do them as well as a coffin?"

"The coffin," said Mary Jane, "is to remind them of their last end."

As the subject had grown lugubrious it was buried in a silence of the table during which Mrs. Malins could be heard saying to her neighbour in an indistinct undertone:

"They are very good men, the monks, very pious men."

The raisins and almonds and figs and apples and oranges and chocolates and sweets were now passed about the table, and Aunt Julia invited all the guests to have either port or sherry. At first Mr. Bartell D'Arcy refused to take either, but one of his neighbours nudged him and whispered something to him upon which he allowed his glass to be filled. Gradually as the last glasses were being filled the conversation ceased. A pause followed, broken only by the noise of the wine and by unsettlings of chairs. The Misses Morkan, all three, looked down at the tablecloth. Someone coughed once or twice and then a few gentlemen patted the table gently as a signal for silence. The silence came and Gabriel pushed back his chair and stood up.

The patting at once grew louder in encouragement and then ceased altogether. Gabriel leaned his ten trembling fingers on the

tablecloth and smiled nervously at the company. Meeting a row of
upturned faces he raised his eyes to the chandelier. The piano was
playing a waltz tune and he could hear the skirts sweeping against
the drawing-room door. People, perhaps, were standing in the
snow on the quay outside, gazing up at the lighted windows and
listening to the waltz music. The air was pure there. In the distance lay the park where the trees were weighted with snow. The
Wellington Monument wore a gleaming cap of snow that flashed
westward over the white field of Fifteen Acres.

He began:

"Ladies and Gentlemen,

"It has fallen to my lot this evening, as in years past, to perform a very pleasing task, but a task for which I am afraid my poor
powers as a speaker are all too inadequate."

"No, no!" said Mr. Browne.

"But, however that may be, I can only ask you to-night to take
the will for the deed, and to lend me your attention for a few moments while I endeavour to express to you in words what my feelings are on this occasion.

"Ladies and Gentlemen, it is not the first time that we have
gathered together under this hospitable roof, around this hospitable
board. It is not the first time that we have been the recipients — or
perhaps, I had better say, the victims — of the hospitality of certain
good ladies."

He made a circle in the air with his arm and paused. Everyone
laughed or smiled at Aunt Kate and Aunt Julia and Mary Jane who
all turned crimson with pleasure. Gabriel went on more boldly:

"I feel more strongly with every recurring year that our country
has no tradition which does it so much honour and which it should
guard so jealously as that of its hospitality. It is a tradition that is
unique as far as my experience goes (and I have visited not a few
places abroad) among the modern nations. Some would say, perhaps, that with us it is rather a failing than anything to be boasted
of. But granted even that, it is, to my mind, a princely failing, and
one that I trust will long be cultivated among us. Of one thing, at
least, I am sure. As long as this one roof shelters the good ladies
aforesaid — and I wish from my heart it may do so for many and
many a long year to come — the tradition of genuine warm-hearted
courteous Irish hospitality, which our forefathers have handed

down to us and which we in turn must hand down to our descendants, is still alive among us."

A hearty murmur of assent ran round the table. It shot through Gabriel's mind that Miss Ivors was not there and that she had gone away discourteously: and he said with confidence in himself:

"Ladies and Gentlemen,

"A new generation is growing up in our midst, a generation actuated by new ideas and new principles. It is serious and enthusiastic for these new ideas, and its enthusiasm, even when it is misdirected, is, I believe, in the main sincere. But we are living in a sceptical and, if I may use the phrase, a thought-tormented age: and sometimes I fear that this new generation, educated or hypereducated as it is, will lack those qualities of humanity, of hospitality, of kindly humour which belonged to an older day. Listening tonight to the names of all those great singers of the past it seemed to me, I must confess, that we were living in a less spacious age. Those days might, without exaggeration, be called spacious days: and if they are gone beyond recall let us hope, at least, that in gatherings such as this we shall still speak of them with pride and affection, still cherish in our hearts the memory of those dead and gone great ones whose fame the world will not willingly let die."

"Hear, hear!" said Mr. Browne loudly.

"But yet," continued Gabriel, his voice falling into a softer inflection, "there are always in gatherings such as this sadder thoughts that will recur to our minds: thoughts of the past, of youth, of changes, of absent faces that we miss here to-night. Our path through life is strewn with many such sad memories: and were we to brood upon them always we could not find the heart to go on bravely with our work among the living. We have all of us living duties and living affections which claim, and rightly claim, our strenuous endeavours.

"Therefore, I will not linger on the past. I will not let any gloomy moralising intrude upon us here to-night. Here we are gathered together for a brief moment from the bustle and rush of our everyday routine. We are met here as friends, in the spirit of good-fellowship, as colleagues, also to a certain extent, in the true spirit of *camaraderie*, and as the guests of — what shall I call them? — the Three Graces of the Dublin musical world."

The table burst into applause and laughter at this allusion. Aunt

Julia vainly asked each of her neighbours in turn to tell her what Gabriel had said.

"He says we are the Three Graces, Aunt Julia," said Mary Jane.

Aunt Julia did not understand but she looked up, smiling, at Gabriel, who continued in the same vein:

"Ladies and Gentlemen,

"I will not attempt to play to-night the part that Paris played on another occasion. I will not attempt to choose between them. The task would be an invidious one and one beyond my poor powers. For when I view them in turn, whether it be our chief hostess herself, whose good heart, whose too good heart, has become a byword with all who know her, or her sister, who seems to be gifted with perennial youth and whose singing must have been a surprise and a revelation to us all to-night, or, last but not least, when I consider our youngest hostess, talented, cheerful, hard-working and the best of nieces, I confess, Ladies and Gentlemen, that I do not know to which of them I should award the prize."

Gabriel glanced down at his aunts and, seeing the large smile on Aunt Julia's face and the tears which had risen to Aunt Kate's eyes, hastened to his close. He raised his glass of port gallantly, while every member of the company fingered a glass expectantly, and said loudly:

"Let us toast them all three together. Let us drink to their health, wealth, long life, happiness and prosperity and may they long continue to hold the proud and self-won position which they hold in their profession and the position of honour and affection which they hold in our hearts."

All the guests stood up, glass in hand, and turning towards the three seated ladies, sang in unison, with Mr. Browne as leader:

"For they are jolly gay fellows,
For they are jolly gay fellows,
For they are jolly gay fellows,
Which nobody can deny."

Aunt Kate was making frank use of her handkerchief and even Aunt Julia seemed moved. Freddy Malins beat time with his pudding-fork and the singers turned towards one another, as if in melodious conference, while they sang with emphasis:

"Unless he tells a lie,
Unless he tells a lie,"

Then, turning once more towards their hostesses, they sang:

> "For they are jolly gay fellows,
> For they are jolly gay fellows,
> For they are jolly gay fellows,
> Which nobody can deny."

The acclamation which followed was taken up beyond the door of the supper-room by many of the other guests and renewed time after time, Freddy Malins acting as officer with his fork on high.

* * *

The piercing morning air came into the hall where they were standing so that Aunt Kate said:

"Close the door, somebody. Mrs. Malins will get her death of cold."

"Browne is out there, Aunt Kate," said Mary Jane.

"Browne is everywhere," said Aunt Kate, lowering her voice.

Mary Jane laughed at her tone.

"Really," she said archly, "he is very attentive."

"He has been laid on here like the gas," said Aunt Kate in the same tone, "all during the Christmas."

She laughed herself this time good-humouredly and then added quickly:

"But tell him to come in, Mary Jane, and close the door. I hope to goodness he didn't hear me."

At that moment the hall-door was opened and Mr. Browne came in from the doorstep, laughing as if his heart would break. He was dressed in a long green overcoat with mock astrakhan cuffs and collar and wore on his head an oval fur cap. He pointed down the snow-covered quay from where the sound of shrill prolonged whistling was borne in.

"Teddy will have all the cabs in Dublin out," he said.

Gabriel advanced from the little pantry behind the office, struggling into his overcoat and, looking round the hall, said:

"Gretta not down yet?"

"She's getting on her things, Gabriel," said Aunt Kate.

"Who's playing up there?" asked Gabriel.

"Nobody. They're all gone."

"O no, Aunt Kate," said Mary Jane. "Bartell D'Arcy and Miss O'Callaghan aren't gone yet."

"Someone is fooling at the piano anyhow," said Gabriel.

Mary Jane glanced at Gabriel and Mr. Browne and said with a shiver:

"It makes me feel cold to look at you two gentlemen muffled up like that. I wouldn't like to face your journey home at this hour."

"I'd like nothing better this minute," said Mr. Browne stoutly, "than a rattling fine walk in the country or a fast drive with a good spanking goer between the shafts."

"We used to have a very good horse and trap at home," said Aunt Julia sadly.

"The never-to-be-forgotten Johnny," said Mary Jane, laughing.

Aunt Kate and Gabriel laughed too.

"Why, what was wonderful about Johnny?" asked Mr. Browne.

"The late lamented Patrick Morkan, our grandfather, that is," explained Gabriel, "commonly known in his later years as the old gentleman, was a glue-boiler."

"O, now, Gabriel," said Aunt Kate, laughing, "he had a starch mill."

"Well, glue or starch," said Gabriel, "the old gentleman had a horse by the name of Johnny. And Johnny used to work in the old gentleman's mill, walking round and round in order to drive the mill. That was all very well; but now comes the tragic part about Johnny. One fine day the old gentleman thought he'd like to drive out with the quality to a military review in the park."

"The Lord have mercy on his soul," said Aunt Kate compassionately.

"Amen," said Gabriel. "So the old gentleman, as I said, harnessed Johnny and put on his very best tall hat and his very best stock collar and drove out in grand style from his ancestral mansion somewhere near Back Lane, I think."

Everyone laughed, even Mrs. Malins, at Gabriel's manner and Aunt Kate said:

"O, now, Gabriel, he didn't live in Back Lane, really. Only the mill was there."

"Out from the mansion of his forefathers," continued Gabriel, "he drove with Johnny. And everything went on beautifully until Johnny came in sight of King Billy's statue: and whether he fell in love with the horse King Billy sits on or whether he thought he was back again in the mill, anyhow he began to walk round the statue."

Gabriel paced in a circle round the hall in his goloshes amid the laughter of the others.

"Round and round he went," said Gabriel, "and the old gentleman, who was a very pompous old gentleman, was highly indignant. 'Go on, sir! What do you mean, sir? Johnny! Johnny! Most extraordinary conduct! Can't understand the horse!'"

The peals of laughter which followed Gabriel's imitation of the incident was interrupted by a resounding knock at the hall door. Mary Jane ran to open it and let in Freddy Malins. Freddy Malins, with his hat well back on his head and his shoulders humped with cold, was puffing and steaming after his exertions

"I could only get one cab," he said.

"O, we'll find another along the quay," said Gabriel.

"Yes," said Aunt Kate. "Better not keep Mrs. Malins standing in the draught."

Mrs. Malins was helped down the front steps by her son and Mr. Browne and, after many manoeuvres, hoisted into the cab. Freddy Malins clambered in after her and spent a long time settling her on the seat, Mr. Browne helping him with advice. At last she was settled comfortably and Freddy Malins invited Mr. Browne into the cab. There was a good deal of confused talk, and then Mr. Browne got into the cab. The cabman settled his rug over his knees, and bent down for the address. The confusion grew greater and the cabman was directed differently by Freddy Malins and Mr. Browne, each of whom had his head out through a window of the cab. The difficulty was to know where to drop Mr. Browne along the route, and Aunt Kate, Aunt Julia and Mary Jane helped the discussion from the doorstep with cross-directions and contradictions and abundance of laughter. As for Freddy Malins he was speechless with laughter. He popped his head in and out of the window every moment to the great danger of his hat, and told his mother how the discussion was progressing, till at last Mr. Browne shouted to the bewildered cabman above the din of everybody's laughter:

"Do you know Trinity College?"

"Yes, sir," said the cabman.

"Well, drive bang up against Trinity College gates," said Mr. Browne, "and then we'll tell you where to go. You understand now?"

"Yes, sir," said the cabman.

"Make like a bird for Trinity College."

"Right, sir," said the cabman.

The horse was whipped up and the cab rattled off along the quay amid a chorus of laughter and adieus.

Gabriel had not gone to the door with the others. He was in a dark part of the hall gazing up the staircase. A woman was standing near the top of the first flight, in the shadow also. He could not see her face but he could see the terra-cotta and salmon-pink panels of her skirt which the shadow made appear black and white. It was his wife. She was leaning on the banisters, listening to something. Gabriel was surprised at her stillness and strained his ear to listen also. But he could hear little save the noise of laughter and dispute on the front steps, a few chords struck on the piano and a few notes of a man's voice singing.

He stood still in the gloom of the hall, trying to catch the air that the voice was singing and gazing up at his wife. There was grace and mystery in her attitude as if she were a symbol of something. He asked himself what is a woman standing on the stairs in the shadow, listening to distant music, a symbol of. If he were a painter he would paint her in that attitude. Her blue felt hat would show off the bronze of her hair against the darkness and the dark panels of her skirt would show off the light ones. *Distant Music* he would call the picture if he were a painter.

The hall-door was closed; and Aunt Kate, Aunt Julia and Mary Jane came down the hall, still laughing.

"Well, isn't Freddy terrible?" said Mary Jane. "He's really terrible."

Gabriel said nothing but pointed up the stairs towards where his wife was standing. Now that the hall-door was closed the voice and the piano could be heard more clearly. Gabriel held up his hand for them to be silent. The song seemed to be in the old Irish tonality and the singer seemed uncertain both of his words and of his voice. The voice, made plaintive by distance and by the singer's hoarseness, faintly illuminated the cadence of the air with words expressing grief:

> "O, the rain falls on my heavy locks
> And the dew wets my skin,
> My babe lies cold . . ."

"O," exclaimed Mary Jane. "It's Bartell D'Arcy singing and he wouldn't sing all the night. O, I'll get him to sing a song before he goes."

"O, do, Mary Jane," said Aunt Kate.

Mary Jane brushed past the others and ran to the staircase, but before she reached it the singing stopped and the piano was closed abruptly.

"O, what a pity!" she cried. "Is he coming down, Gretta?"

Gabriel heard his wife answer yes and saw her come down towards them. A few steps behind her were Mr. Bartell D'Arcy and Miss O'Callaghan.

"O, Mr. D'Arcy," cried Mary Jane, "it's downright mean of you to break off like that when we were all in raptures listening to you."

"I have been at him all the evening," said Miss O'Callaghan, "and Mrs. Conroy, too, and he told us he had a dreadful cold and couldn't sing."

"O, Mr. D'Arcy," said Aunt Kate, "now that was a great fib to tell."

"Can't you see that I'm as hoarse as a crow?" said Mr. D'Arcy roughly.

He went into the pantry hastily and put on his overcoat. The others, taken aback by his rude speech, could find nothing to say. Aunt Kate wrinkled her brows and made signs to the others to drop the subject. Mr. D'Arcy stood swathing his neck carefully and frowning.

"It's the weather," said Aunt Julia, after a pause.

"Yes, everybody has colds," said Aunt Kate readily, "everybody."

"They say," said Mary Jane, "we haven't had snow like it for thirty years; and I read this morning in the newspapers that the snow is general all over Ireland."

"I love the look of snow," said Aunt Julia sadly.

"So do I," said Miss O'Callaghan. "I think Christmas is never really Christmas unless we have the snow on the ground."

"But poor Mr. D'Arcy doesn't like the snow," said Aunt Kate, smiling.

Mr. D'Arcy came from the pantry, fully swathed and buttoned, and in a repentant tone told them the history of his cold. Everyone gave him advice and said it was a great pity and urged him to be very careful of his throat in the night air. Gabriel watched his wife, who did not join in the conversation. She was standing right under the dusty fanlight and the flame of the gas lit up the rich bronze of her hair, which he had seen her drying at the fire a few days before. She was in the same attitude and seemed unaware of the talk about her. At last she turned towards them and Gabriel saw that there was colour on her cheeks and that her eyes were shining. A sudden tide of joy went leaping out of his heart.

"Mr. D'Arcy," she said, "what is the name of that song you were singing?"

"It's called *The Lass of Aughrim*," said Mr. D'Arcy, "but I couldn't remember it properly. Why? Do you know it?"

"*The Lass of Aughrim*," she repeated. "I couldn't think of the name."

"It's a very nice air," said Mary Jane. "I'm sorry you were not in voice to-night."

"Now, Mary Jane," said Aunt Kate, "don't annoy Mr. D'Arcy. I won't have him annoyed."

Seeing that all were ready to start she shepherded them to the door, where good-night was said:

"Well, good-night, Aunt Kate, and thanks for the pleasant evening."

"Good-night, Gabriel. Good-night, Gretta!"

"Good-night, Aunt Kate, and thanks ever so much. Good-night, Aunt Julia."

"O, good-night, Gretta, I didn't see you."

"Good-night, Mr. D'Arcy. Good-night, Miss O'Callaghan."

"Good-night, Miss Morkan."

"Good-night, again."

"Good-night, all. Safe home."

"Good-night. Good-night."

The morning was still dark. A dull, yellow light brooded over the houses and the river; and the sky seemed to be descending. It was slushy underfoot; and only streaks and patches of snow lay on the roofs, on the parapets of the quay and on the area railings. The lamps were still burning redly in the murky air and, across the river, the palace of the Four Courts stood out menacingly against the heavy sky.

She was walking on before him with Mr. Bartell D'Arcy, her shoes in a brown parcel tucked under one arm and her hands holding her skirt up from the slush. She had no longer any grace of attitude, but Gabriel's eyes were still bright with happiness. The blood went bounding along his veins; and the thoughts went rioting through his brain, proud, joyful, tender, valorous.

She was walking on before him so lightly and so erect that he longed to run after her noiselessly, catch her by the shoulders and say something foolish and affectionate into her ear. She seemed to him so frail that he longed to defend her against something and then to be alone with her. Moments of their secret life together burst like stars upon his memory. A heliotrope envelope was lying beside his breakfast-cup and he was caressing it with his hand. Birds were twittering in the ivy and the sunny web of the curtain was shimmering along the floor: he could not eat for happiness. They were standing on the crowded platform and he was placing a ticket inside the warm palm of her glove. He was standing with her in the cold, looking in through a grated window at a man making bottles in a roaring furnace. It was very cold. Her face, fragrant in the cold air, was quite close to his; and suddenly he called out to the man at the furnace:

"Is the fire hot, sir?"

But the man could not hear with the noise of the furnace. It was just as well. He might have answered rudely.

A wave of yet more tender joy escaped from his heart and went coursing in warm flood along his arteries. Like the tender fire of stars moments of their life together, that no one knew of or would ever know of, broke upon and illumined his memory. He longed to recall to her those moments, to make her forget the years of their dull existence together and remember only their moments of ecstasy. For the years, he felt, had not quenched his soul or hers. Their children, his writing, her household cares had not quenched all their souls' tender fire. In one letter that he had written to her then he had said: "Why is it that words like these seem to me so dull and cold? Is it because there is no word tender enough to be your name?"

Like distant music these words that he had written years before were borne towards him from the past. He longed to be alone with her. When the others had gone away, when he and she were in the room in the hotel, then they would be alone together. He would call her softly:

"Gretta!"

Perhaps she would not hear at once: she would be undressing. Then something in his voice would strike her. She would turn and look at him. . . .

At the corner of Winetavern Street they met a cab. He was glad of its rattling noise as it saved him from conversation. She was looking out of the window and seemed tired. The others spoke only a few words, pointing out some building or street. The horse galloped along wearily under the murky morning sky, dragging his old rattling box after his heels, and Gabriel was again in a cab with her, galloping to catch the boat, galloping to their honeymoon.

As the cab drove across O'Connell Bridge Miss O'Callaghan said:

"They say you never cross O'Connell Bridge without seeing a white horse."

"I see a white man this time," said Gabriel.

"Where?" asked Mr. Bartell D'Arcy.

Gabriel pointed to the statue, on which lay patches of snow. Then he nodded familiarly to it and waved his hand.

"Good-night, Dan," he said gaily.

When the cab drew up before the hotel, Gabriel jumped out and, in spite of Mr. Bartell D'Arcy's protest, paid the driver. He gave the man a shilling over his fare. The man saluted and said:

"A prosperous New Year to you, sir."

"The same to you," said Gabriel cordially.

She leaned for a moment on his arm in getting out of the cab and while standing at the curbstone, bidding the others good-night. She leaned lightly on his arm, as lightly as when she had danced with him a few hours before. He had felt proud and happy then, happy that she was his, proud of her grace and wifely carriage. But now, after the kindling again of so many memories, the first touch of her body, musical and strange and perfumed, sent through him a keen pang of lust. Under cover of her silence he pressed her arm closely to his side; and, as they stood at the hotel door, he felt that they had escaped from their lives and duties, escaped from home and friends and run away together with wild and radiant hearts to a new adventure.

An old man was dozing in a great hooded chair in the hall. He lit a candle in the office and went before them to the stairs. They followed him in silence, their feet falling in soft thuds on the thickly carpeted stairs. She mounted the stairs behind the porter, her head bowed in the ascent, her frail shoulders curved as with a burden, her skirt girt tightly about her. He could have flung his arms about her hips and held her still, for his arms were trembling with desire to seize her and only the stress of his nails against the palms of his hands held the wild impulse of his body in check. The porter halted on the stairs to settle his guttering candle. They halted, too, on the steps below him. In the silence Gabriel could hear the falling of the molten wax into the tray and the thumping of his own heart against his ribs.

The porter led them along a corridor and opened a door. Then he set his unstable candle down on a toilet-table and asked at what hour they were to be called in the morning.

"Eight," said Gabriel.

The porter pointed to the tap of the electric-light and began a muttered apology, but Gabriel cut him short.

"We don't want any light. We have light enough from the street. And I say," he added, pointing to the candle, "you might remove that handsome article, like a good man."

The porter took up his candle again, but slowly, for he was surprised by such a novel idea. Then he mumbled good-night and went out. Gabriel shot the lock to.

A ghastly light from the street lamp lay in a long shaft from one window to the door. Gabriel threw his overcoat and hat on a couch and crossed the room towards the window. He looked down into the street in order that his emotion might calm a little. Then he turned and leaned against a chest of drawers with his back to the light. She had taken off her hat and cloak and was standing before a large swinging mirror, unhooking her waist. Gabriel paused for a few moments, watching her, and then said:

"Gretta!"

She turned away from the mirror slowly and walked along the shaft of light towards him. Her face looked so serious and weary that the words would not pass Gabriel's lips. No, it was not the moment yet.

"You looked tired," he said.

"I am a little," she answered.

"You don't feel ill or weak?"

"No, tired: that's all."

She went on to the window and stood there, looking out. Gabriel waited again and then fearing that diffidence was about to conquer him, he said abruptly:

"By the way, Gretta!"

"What is it?"

"You know that poor fellow Malins?" he said quickly.

"Yes. What about him?"

"Well, poor fellow, he's a decent sort of chap, after all," continued Gabriel in a false voice. "He gave me back that sovereign I lent him, and I didn't expect it, really. It's a pity he wouldn't keep away from that Browne, because he's not a bad fellow, really."

He was trembling now with annoyance. Why did she seem so abstracted? He did not know how he could begin. Was she annoyed, too, about something? If she would only turn to him or come to him of her own accord! To take her as she was would be brutal. No, he must see some ardour in her eyes first. He longed to be master of her strange mood.

"When did you lend him the pound?" she asked, after a pause.

Gabriel strove to restrain himself from breaking out into brutal language about the sottish Malins and his pound. He longed to cry to her from his soul, to crush her body against his, to overmaster her. But he said:

"O, at Christmas, when he opened that little Christmas-card shop in Henry Street."

He was in such a fever of rage and desire that he did not hear her come from the window. She stood before him for an instant, looking at him strangely. Then, suddenly raising herself on tiptoe and resting her hands lightly on his shoulders, she kissed him.

"You are a very generous person, Gabriel," she said.

Gabriel, trembling with delight at her sudden kiss and at the quaintness of her phrase, put his hands on her hair and began smoothing it back, scarcely touching it with his fingers. The washing had made it fine and brilliant. His heart was brimming over with happiness. Just when he was wishing for it she had come to him of her own accord. Perhaps her thoughts had been running with his. Perhaps she had felt the impetuous desire that was in him, and then the yielding mood had come upon her. Now that she had fallen to him so easily, he wondered why he had been so diffident.

He stood, holding her head between his hands. Then, slipping one arm swiftly about her body and drawing her towards him, he said softly:

"Gretta, dear, what are you thinking about?"

She did not answer nor yield wholly to his arm. He said again, softly:

"Tell me what it is, Gretta. I think I know what is the matter. Do I know?"

She did not answer at once. Then she said in an outburst of tears:

"O, I am thinking about that song, *The Lass of Aughrim.*"

She broke loose from him and ran to the bed and, throwing her arms across the bed-rail, hid her face. Gabriel stood stock-still for a moment in astonishment and then followed her. As he passed in the way of the cheval-glass he caught sight of himself in full length, his broad, well-filled shirt-front, the face whose expression always puzzled him when he saw it in a mirror, and his glimmering gilt-rimmed eyeglasses. He halted a few paces from her and said:

"What about the song? Why does that make you cry?"

She raised her head from her arms and dried her eyes with the back of her hand like a child. A kinder note than he had intended went into his voice.

"Why, Gretta?" he asked.

"I am thinking about a person long ago who used to sing that song."

"And who was the person long ago?" asked Gabriel, smiling.

"It was a person I used to know in Galway when I was living with my grandmother," she said.

The smile passed away from Gabriel's face. A dull anger began to gather again at the back of his mind and the dull fires of his lust began to glow angrily in his veins.

"Someone you were in love with?" he asked ironically.

"It was a young boy I used to know," she answered, "named Michael Furey. He used to sing that song, *The Lass of Aughrim.* He was very delicate."

Gabriel was silent. He did not wish her to think that he was interested in this delicate boy.

"I can see him so plainly," she said, after a moment. "Such eyes as he had: big, dark eyes! And such an expression in them — an expression!"

"O, then, you are in love with him?" said Gabriel.

"I used to go out walking with him," she said, "when I was in Galway."

A thought flew across Gabriel's mind.

"Perhaps that was why you wanted to go to Galway with that Ivors girl?" he said coldly.

She looked at him and asked in surprise:

"What for?"

Her eyes made Gabriel feel awkward. He shrugged his shoulders and said:

"How do I know? To see him, perhaps."

She looked away from him along the shaft of light towards the window in silence.

"He is dead," she said at length. "He died when he was only seventeen. Isn't it a terrible thing to die so young as that?"

"What was he?" asked Gabriel, still ironically.

"He was in the gasworks," she said.

Gabriel felt humiliated by the failure of his irony and by the evocation of this figure from the dead, a boy in the gasworks. While he had been full of memories of their secret life together, full of tenderness and joy and desire, she had been comparing him in her mind with another. A shameful consciousness of his own person assailed him. He saw himself as a ludicrous figure, acting as a pennyboy for his aunts, a nervous, well-meaning sentimentalist, orating to vulgarians and idealising his own clownish lusts, the pitiable fatuous fellow he had caught a glimpse of in the mirror. Instinctively he turned his back more to the light lest she might see the shame that burned upon his forehead.

He tried to keep up his tone of cold interrogation, but his voice when he spoke was humble and indifferent.

"I suppose you were in love with this Michael Furey, Gretta," he said.

"I was great with him at that time," she said.

Her voice was veiled and sad. Gabriel, feeling now how vain it would be to try to lead her whither he had purposed, caressed one of her hands and said, also sadly:

"And what did he die of so young, Gretta? Consumption, was it?"

"I think he died for me," she answered.

A vague terror seized Gabriel at this answer, as if, at that hour when he had hoped to triumph, some impalpable and vindictive being was coming against him, gathering forces against him in its vague world. But he shook himself free of it with an effort of reason and continued to caress her hand. He did not question her again, for he felt that she would tell him of herself. Her hand was warm and moist: it did not respond to his touch, but he continued to caress it just as he had caressed her first letter to him that spring morning.

"It was in the winter," she said, "about the beginning of the winter when I was going to leave my grandmother's and come up here to the convent. And he was ill at the time in his lodgings in Galway and wouldn't be let out, and his people in Oughterard were written to. He was in decline, they said, or something like that. I never knew rightly."

She paused for a moment and sighed.

"Poor fellow," she said. "He was very fond of me and he was such a gentle boy. We used to go out together, walking, you know, Gabriel, like the way they do in the country. He was going to study singing only for his health. He had a very good voice, poor Michael Furey."

"Well; and then?" asked Gabriel.

"And then when it came to the time for me to leave Galway and come up to the convent he was much worse and I wouldn't be let see him so I wrote him a letter saying I was going up to Dublin and would be back in the summer, and hoping he would be better then."

She paused for a moment to get her voice under control, and then went on:

"Then the night before I left, I was in my grandmother's house in Nuns' Island, packing up, and I heard gravel thrown up against the window. The window was so wet I couldn't see, so I ran downstairs as I was and slipped out the back into the garden and there was the poor fellow at the end of the garden, shivering."

"And did you not tell him to go back?" asked Gabriel.

"I implored of him to go home at once and told him he would get his death in the rain. But he said he did not want to live. I can see his eyes as well as well! He was standing at the end of the wall where there was a tree."

"And did he go home?" asked Gabriel.

"Yes, he went home. And when I was only a week in the convent he died and he was buried in Oughterard, where his people came from. O, the day I heard that, that he was dead!"

She stopped, choking with sobs, and, overcome by emotion, flung herself face downward on the bed, sobbing in the quilt. Gabriel held her hand for a moment longer, irresolutely, and then, shy of intruding on her grief, let it fall gently and walked quietly to the window.

She was fast asleep.

Gabriel, leaning on his elbow, looked for a few moments unresentfully on her tangled hair and half-open mouth, listening to her deep-drawn breath. So she had had that romance in her life: a man had died for her sake. It hardly pained him now to think how poor a part he, her husband, had played in her life. He watched her while she slept, as though he and she had never lived together as man and wife. His curious eyes rested long upon her face and on her hair: and, as he thought of what she must have been then, in that time of her first girlish beauty, a strange, friendly pity for her entered his soul. He did not like to say even to himself that her face was no longer beautiful, but he knew that it was no longer the face for which Michael Furey had braved death.

Perhaps she had not told him all the story. His eyes moved to the chair over which she had thrown some of her clothes. A petticoat string dangled to the floor. One boot stood upright, its limp upper fallen down: the fellow of it lay upon its side. He wondered at his riot of emotions of an hour before. From what had it proceeded? From his aunt's supper, from his own foolish speech, from the wine and dancing, the merrymaking when saying good-night in the hall, the pleasure of the walk along the river in the snow. Poor Aunt Julia! She, too, would soon be a shade with the shade of Patrick Morkan and his horse. He had caught that haggard look upon her face for a moment when she was singing *Arrayed for the Bridal*. Soon, perhaps, he would be sitting in that same drawing-room, dressed in black, his silk hat on his knees. The blinds would be drawn down and Aunt Kate would be sitting beside him, crying and blowing her nose and telling him how Julia had died. He would cast about in his mind for some words that might console her, and would find only lame and useless ones. Yes, yes: that would happen very soon.

The air of the room chilled his shoulders. He stretched himself cautiously along under the sheets and lay down beside his wife. One by one, they were all becoming shades. Better pass boldly into that other world, in the full glory of some passion, than fade and wither dismally with age. He thought of how she who lay beside him had locked in her heart for so many years that image of her lover's eyes when he had told her that he did not wish to live.

Generous tears filled Gabriel's eyes. He had never felt like that himself towards any woman, but he knew that such a feeling must be love. The tears gathered more thickly in his eyes and in the partial darkness he imagined he saw the form of a young man standing under a dripping tree. Other forms were near. His soul had approached that region where dwell the vast hosts of the dead. He was conscious of, but could not apprehend, their wayward and flickering existence. His own identity was fading out into a grey impalpable world: the solid world itself, which these dead had one time reared and lived in, was dissolving and dwindling.

A few light taps upon the pane made him turn to the window. It had begun to snow again. He watched sleepily the flakes, silver and dark, falling obliquely against the lamplight. The time had come for him to set out on his journey westward. Yes, the newspapers were right, snow was general all over Ireland. It was falling on every part of the dark central plain, on the treeless hills, falling softly upon the Bog of Allen and, farther westward, softly falling into the dark mutinous Shannon waves. It was falling, too, upon every part of the lonely churchyard on the hill where Michael Furey lay buried. It lay thickly drifted on the crooked crosses and headstones, on the spears of the little gate, on the barren thorns. His soul swooned slowly as he heard the snow falling faintly through the universe and faintly falling, like the descent of their last end, upon all the living and the dead.

JAMES JOYCE'S

dubliners

> My intention was to write a chapter of the moral history of
> my country and I chose Dublin for the scene because the city
> seemed to me the centre of paralysis.
>
> James Joyce on *Dubliners*.

> The soul is born . . . first in those moments I told you of. It
> has a slow and dark birth, more mysterious than the birth of
> the body. When the soul of a man is born in this country
> there are nets flung at it to hold it back from flight. You talk
> to me of nationality, language, religion. I shall try to fly by
> those nets.
>
> Stephen Dedalus, in
> *A Portrait of the Artist as a Young Man.*

FROM THE FIRST PAGES OF *Dubliners*, WHERE, GAZING UP AT THE WIN-
dow of the dying Father Flynn, a boy softly mouths the word
"paralysis," to the last, where, looking out the window at the faintly
falling snow, an aging "boy," Gabriel Conroy, thinks of the final end
of the freezing paralysis, death, Joyce is lamenting the fall of feeling, the fall of intellect, the fall of the imagination. Captured, fet-
tered, and paralyzed by the nets, feeling has become sentimentality,
intellect has become slogan and cliché, imagination has become lie
and romantic illusion. All the stories in *Dubliners* dramatize this
theme of paralysis in the situations of characters who, unlike
Stephen Dedalus, either fail to recognize the nets or, if they do
recognize them, tragically fail to escape them. To the boy of
the first story, "The Sisters," paralysis is more than a word: "Now
it sounded to me like the name of some maleficent and sinful being.
It filled me with fear, and yet I longed to be nearer to it and to
look upon its deadly work" (page 337). Thus it was with Joyce too:
in *Dubliners* Joyce — perhaps filled with a fear which underlies the
serious, ironic and humorous tonalities — looks steadily at the deadly
work of paralysis, as he did later in all his other major works, the
Portrait, Exiles, Ulysses, and *Finnegans Wake.*

In "The Sisters," the boy's soul, under the guidance of Father Flynn, is undergoing the "slow and dark birth" mentioned by Stephen, awakening to ritual, tradition, things of the intellect and the imagination. But the birth takes place in the presence of the "nets." Like a fearful and expectant Orpheus entering Hades, the boy has discovered the realm of the imagination (a "pleasant and vicious region") where nothing is simple and unambiguous. In the real world itself nothing fits the ready-made categories of the sentimental, generalizing adults — not even death itself: the death of Father Flynn comes with none of the expected reactions: "I found it strange that neither I nor the day seemed in a mourning mood" (page 339).

The "nets" themselves do not lack ambiguity: recognized, they contribute to the development of the critical faculty and so to the growth of the soul. The boy's sensitivity blossoms in the environment of stupid anti-intellectualism and Achaean athleticism. Mr. Cotter, now a vicious and "tiresome old fool," once appealed to the boy's curiosity: "When we knew him first he used to be rather interesting, talking of faints and worms; but I soon grew tired of him and his endless stories about the distillery" (page 337).

Cotter's tiresomeness proceeds in part from his attitude toward intellectual activity. Learning, even if it is from priests, was "bad for children," he says, and the boy's uncle is in substantial agreement. " 'That's what I'm always saying to that Rosicrucian here: take exercise. Why, when I was a nipper every morning of my life I had a cold bath, winter and summer. And that's what stands to me now. Education is all very fine and large. . . . ' " (pages 337–8).

Aware of the dark world of paralysis where everything is "faded," "blackened," "grey," or "gloomy," the boy looks to the natural world or to his imagination for escape. The experience with death made him wish to walk "slowly along the sunny side of the street, reading all the theatrical advertisements in the shop-windows as I went" (page 339). He covers his head with a blanket and tries "to think of Christmas" (page 338) when Cotter's implications, his "unfinished sentences," bring to mind "the heavy grey face of the paralytic," Father Flynn. But the world is not to be denied — Joyce sums everything up in the visit to the Sisters Flynn. There the mood and the mystery of death are on the boy who declines "cream crackers . . . because I thought I would make too much noise eating them" (page 341); there he hears the cold, loud, ugly comments of the literal, superficial adults reporting on how the body looked while it was being laid out and what "the woman we had in to wash him said" (page 341). Joyce has retired; the boy's point of view having been established, the boy takes over. All that the reader must keep in mind is that the boy who thinks Cotter a "tiresome old red-nosed imbecile!", the boy who declines the cream crackers, is the listener to the dialogue which follows. Thus Eliza: " 'Ah, there's no friends like the old friends,' she said, 'when all is said and done, no friends that a body can trust' " (page 342).

The paralyzing nets seen surrounding the boy in "The Sisters" reappear — in different forms, stronger and more extensive — in the other *Dubliners* stories. Organically arranged, the stories color one another, adding complexities through the reiteration of situations, themes, and feelings. It is as though the succeeding images, superimposed on those which preceded — with a technique similar to movie montage — retrace the outlines of the nets, making the strands darker and clearer, building through the repetition of situations, a pity and compassion for those caught by the nets.

The arrangement of the stories, as Joyce pointed out in a letter to his publisher, follows a plan of "childhood, adolescence, maturity and public life." The central characters of the stories which follow "The Sisters" are older than the boy, and, though there are many differences in the details of their stories, the total effect is always the dramatization of isolation, frustration, defeat — trap and entanglement in the nets of Ireland. These stories are of two kinds, involving two kinds of characters and two kinds of situation: the first, like "The Sisters" ("Araby," "A Little Cloud," "A Painful Case," "The Dead"), has a central character who is more or less aware of what is going on; the second (all the other stories in the book), has characters who are either unaware or at best merely partially aware of the nature of the world around them and its effect upon them.

In the first group, one may follow the boy of "The Sisters" through successive stages of sensitivity: in "Araby" his daydreams symbolize his actual isolation ("I imagined that I bore my chalice safely through a throng of foes"); in "A Little Cloud," "A Painful Case," and "The Dead," the central character's awareness of his own situation becomes more and more clear. In these stories the main characters are artists-and-intellectuals-writ-small — Little Chandler, Mr. Duffy, Gabriel Conroy — who reach the conclusion of Stephen Dedalus in the *Portrait*; but their ability to analyze situations and reach conclusions does not mean that decisive action follows — as it does in the case of Stephen. For instance, Little Chandler discovers: "There was no doubt about it: if you wanted to succeed you had to go away. You could do nothing in Dublin." In "A Painful Case," Mr. Duffy finds himself more and more cut off from love, intellectual stimulation and spiritual contentment: "He heard the strange impersonal voice which he recognized as his own, insisting on the soul's incurable loneliness. We cannot give ourselves, it said: we are our own."

These characters are the heroes of twentieth century tragedies, where the hero — though decidedly unheroic by Aristotelian standards — suffers total defeat, paralyzed by the nets from which it is too late for him to fly. Little Chandler, who reveals a sensitivity to poetry, discovers too late that "he was a prisoner for life." Mr. Duffy finds that "he was an outcast from life's feast."

The most important event in each of the stories is the central character's *epiphany* (i.e., an occurrence which reveals to the character and/or the reader the full meaning of that character's life and identity). In *Dubliners* the character in the first group recognizes his inadequacy and his defeat through the epiphany; Joyce shows the reader the effect of paralysis on unheroic heroes, men of intellect and sensibility defeated by their uncomprehending, generalizing world.

In the second group of stories, Joyce's main purpose is to discover ugliness and show its effects on people of different talents and different levels of comprehension. In these stories the situations divide themselves into two smaller groups: in one, like "Clay," the central character (Maria) is almost totally unaware of the cruelty and ugliness around her; in the other, like "The Boarding House," "Two Gallants," "Eveline," the character's partial awareness leads him to wish for escape; but, like the more sensitive characters of a higher cultural level (Little Chandler and Mr. Duffy), he finds himself trapped. Here the epiphany comes from the failure of some small pleasure to materialize, like Maria's losing the cake in "Clay," and the boy's finding in "An Encounter" not the adventure he seeks but the ugliness of an aged pervert. Or it comes from the realization that a moment of triumph has obliterated the future, such as Farrington's telling his boss off in "Counterparts," losing his job, and returning home to take out all his frustrations on his screaming, praying little boy; or in "A Mother," Mrs. Kearney's triumph over the concert committee which ends in the ruin of her daughter. In the other stories the important thing is the photograph of ugliness: in "After the Race" the burgher values of Jimmy's father; in "Ivy Day in the Committee Room" the political bankruptcy of Ireland; in "Grace" the spiritual paucity of Ireland's businessmen.

Gabriel Conroy, in "The Dead," the aptly named coda to *Dub-*

liners, is a later, totally defeated version of the young boy of "The Sisters." Like his prototypes, Chandler and Duffy, he has *not* flown the nets of Ireland. If Stephen Dedalus had remained in Ireland till he was Gabriel Conroy's age, he might have been Gabriel Conroy; for Gabriel is Stephen . . . less hope, less courage, less heroic Dedalean stature. Where Stephen's discovery of the nets leads to an affirmation of life, a determination to journey eastward to the continent the nationalists despise, Gabriel's discovery leads to a readying for "the journey westward," for his "final end."

The snow that Gabriel watches at the end of the book is the snow that is introduced into Dublin town with him. At first it seems to be no more than a symbol of escape, a symbol of the world outside the pettiness and the ugliness of the "Misses Morkan's annual dance." The things Gabriel wishes to escape from form the microcosm of the Ireland Stephen Dedalus *did* fly from, the nets from which his soul escaped. Stephen had no illusions about the world in which he found himself. Opposition he met head on, whether it was from friend, foe, family, or female. Only in this way are the nets evaded. Gabriel, on the other hand, keeps insisting to himself, in his vapid illusions and romantic imaginings, that the nets are but gossamer webs. Unlike Stephen, he attempts to temporize, to assume the attitudes of the different members of the different cultural levels meeting in the home of his aunts. But nothing works: he has an unpleasant encounter with the rude maid, Lily, when he — unseeing — attempts casual conversation in order to communicate with somebody — anybody — at the party. Loud, corny, self-styled humorists like the Protestant Browne (" 'I hope, Miss Morkan . . . that I am brown enough for you because, you know, I'm all brown.' "), ignorant, quarreling drunks like the "aesthetically-involved" Freddy Malins (" 'And why couldn't he have a voice too?' asked Freddy Malins sharply. 'Is it because he's only a black?' "), tremendous architectural bores like Mrs. Malins ("Her son-in-law was a splendid fisher. One day he caught a beautiful big fish and the man in the hotel cooked it for their dinner."), prudish fanatics like Miss Ivors ("She did not wear a low-cut bodice and the large brooch which was fixed in the front of her collar bore on it an Irish device and motto."), are much more successful at the party than the sensitive intellectual, Gabriel. They all have levels on which they can communicate with someone — he none. The unpleasantness which follows his encounter with each of the members of the different levels induces in Gabriel a desire to escape; the symbols of snow and cold, which are introduced into the story with Gabriel's entrance into the house of the Misses Morkan, become more and more meaningful till they are fully understood at the very end of the story.

The first description of Gabriel contains other details which later assume larger meaning. "A light fringe of snow lay like a cape on the shoulders of his overcoat and like toe-caps on the toes of his goloshes; and, as the buttons of his overcoat slipped with a squeaking noise through the snow-stiffened frieze, a cold, fragrant air from out-of-doors escaped from crevices and folds" (page 346). The reappearance of snow and cold mark the successive stages of Gabriel's failure of communication. After the rude answer from Lily, after he has assumed the failure with Lily to portend the inevitable failure of his speech, after the slight unpleasantness with his aunt over the "continent" (the incident of the goloshes), after being revealed as a nervous, ill-at-ease man who frets over his children and his wife, after his tiff with Miss Ivors and gruffness with Gretta, Gabriel returns to thoughts of the cold, snow-covered outside. Inside is isolation, outside solitude:

Gabriel's warm trembling fingers tapped the cold pane of the window. How cool it must be outside! How pleasant it would be to walk out alone, first along by the river and then through the park! The snow would be lying on the branches of the trees and forming a bright cap on the top of the Wellington Monument. How much more pleasant it would be there than at the supper-table! (Pages 357–8).

The symbols begin to take on added meaning. After the faked heartiness of the carving rites, just before beginning the much worried-over speech, Gabriel once more returns to thoughts of escape, again symbolized by the world of snow and cold: "People, perhaps, were standing in the snow on the quay outside, gazing up at the lighted windows and listening to the waltz music. The air was pure there. In the distance lay the park where the trees were weighted with snow. The Wellington Monument wore a gleaming cap of snow that flashed westward over the white field of Fifteen Acres" (page 366).

Away from the party, his speech over, Gabriel reacts to the cold and the snow; even though the surroundings are anything but what his illusions are fixed on, he feels liberated, happy, ready for anything. The movement away from the party is treated with a sudden change of pace and the diction is foreboding, dwelling on all the unpleasantness of the winter scene:

The morning was still dark. A dull, yellow light brooded over the houses and the river; and the sky seemed to be descending. It was slushy underfoot; and the only streaks and patches of snow lay on the roofs, on the parapets of the quay and on the area railings. The lamps were still burning redly in the murky air and, across the river, the palace of the Four Courts stood out menacingly against the heavy sky. (Page 374)

However, Gabriel is unconscious of these surroundings; only Gretta means anything to him now: "Gabriel's eyes were still bright with happiness. The blood went bounding along his veins; and the thoughts went rioting through his brain, proud, joyful, tender, valorous" (page 375). His gaiety is a new mood and the tone of the section that follows is new to the story. But Joyce does not forget the meaning of the symbols of snow and cold: even in his gaiety, when he waves at the statue of Daniel O'Connell — another dead hero like Wellington, and another symbol of snow-covered greatness — "on which lay patches of snow," and when he tips the cabman handsomely, Gabriel is moving toward the epiphany in which the full meaning of all the symbols becomes clear.

Gabriel believes he has escaped, that he and Gretta have flown the world of ugliness, that they will "run away together with wild and radiant hearts to a new adventure" (page 376); in sentimental language he recalls their days of happiness together, when "Birds were twittering in the ivy." But once alone with Gretta, once in the hotel room where, like Lochinvar finding an unattended Guinevere, he locks the door in readiness for his great moment of love, all his diffidence returns. "He longed to cry to her from his soul, to crush her body against his, to overmaster her" (page 378), but what he says is dull, prosaic, inspiring neither lust nor love in Gretta.

His patient wait for her to come to him as he wishes her to is destroyed by the tale she tells of Michael Furey. Gabriel finds that Gretta — and Michael — were capable of a kind of love he can conceive of only dimly. His defeat is completed. In the epiphany which follows, all his temporizing, all his illusions, all his sentimental nostalgia, appear to him for what they are. He sees himself whole, giving up in the act the possibility of a future with meaning:

A shameful consciousness of his own person assailed him. He saw himself a ludicrous figure, acting as a pennyboy for his aunts, a nervous, well-meaning sentimentalist, orating to vulgarians and idealising his own clownish lusts, the pitiable fatuous fellow he had caught a glimpse of in the mirror. (Page 380)

The tableau of the sobbing Gretta and the inadequate Gabriel dramatizes his complete isolation: "Gabriel held her hand for a moment longer, irresolutely, and then, shy of intruding on her grief, let it fall gently and walked quietly to the window" (pages 381–2). The act of dropping Gretta's hand is the act of recognition: Gabriel now knows that his last hope of achieving identification — for all his other attempts have been failures just as his acts at the party ended in failure — is gone: "His own identity was fading out into the grey impalpable world: the solid world itself, which these dead had one time reared and lived in, was dissolving and dwindling" (page 383).

It is here that the careful reader must recall other details which previously appeared in the story. Recalling the description of Gabriel on his entrance into the house, he will see that the details are substantially the same as those which describe the snow-covered statues of the departed great, Wellington and O'Connell. He will see that by connecting Gabriel with the statues, Joyce is saying that Gabriel is without life, inanimate, made of stone, a paralytic after his final stroke, like Father Flynn of "The Sisters." Now he will recall that the description of Gabriel was that of a harbinger of death ("a cold, fragrant air from out-of-doors escaped from crevices and folds"); now he will recall Gabriel's fixation with the dead past (and past dead) and the story of Johnny the horse: "Poor Aunt Julia! She, too, would soon be a shade with the shade of Patrick Morkan and his horse." Now the reader will recall that Gabriel's mother was very conscious of the dignity of names, naming the son who became a "senior curate in Balbriggan," Constantine, after the famous emperor and Christian, and the son who tells of the "final end," the one with the task of singing a requiem, Gabriel.

Now it is seen that there is nothing of romantic escape about the symbols of snow and cold: Gabriel's escape is the escape into death. The snow that formed a cape on his overcoat, the snow that formed a bright cap on the Wellington Monument, the snow that covered Daniel O'Connell's statue in patches, snow like this is beginning to blanket all, "falling faintly through the universe and faintly falling, like the descent of their last end, upon all the living and the dead" (page 383). Snow, as Mary Jane reported and Gabriel now recalls in the coda to the volume, is "general all over Ireland." Paralysis is general all over Ireland. Death is general all over Ireland. For his own death Gabriel now waits. He merges with the dead of the past and the dead of the present, watching the snow — the death of all — "falling faintly . . . upon all the living and the dead."

JACK BARRY LUDWIG

THREE

a second generation

ELIZABETH TAYLOR

the first death of her life

Suddenly, tears poured from Lucy's eyes. She rested her forehead against her mother's hand and let the tears soak into the counterpane.

Dear Mr. Wilcox, she began, for her mind was always composing letters, I shall not be at the shop for the next four days, as my mother has passed away and I shall not be available until after the funeral. My mother passed away very peacefully. . . .

The nurse came in. She took her patient's wrist for a moment, replaced it on the bed, removed a jar of white lilac from the table, as if this were no longer necessary, and went out again.

The girl kneeling by the bed had looked up, but Dear Mr. Wilcox, she resumed, her eyes returning to the counterpane, My mother has died. I shall come back to work the day after tomorrow. Yours sincerely, Lucy Mayhew.

Her father was late. She imagined him hurrying from work, bicycling through the darkening streets, dogged, hunched up, slush thrown up by his wheels. Her mother did not move. Lucy stroked her mother's hand, with its loose gold ring, the calloused palm, the fine, long fingers. Then she stood up stiffly, her knees bruised from the waxed floor, and went to the window.

Snowflakes turned idly, drifting down over the hospital gardens. It was four o'clock in the afternoon and already the day seemed over. So few sounds came from this muffled and discolored world. In the hospital itself, there was a deep silence.

Her thoughts came to her in words, as if her mind spoke them first, understood them later. She tried to think of her childhood — little scenes she selected to prove how she and her mother had loved one another. Other scenes, especially last week's quarrel, she chose to forget, not knowing that in this moment she sent them away forever. Only loving-kindness remained. But, all the same, intolerable pictures broke through — her mother at the sink; her mother ironing; her mother standing between the lace curtains, staring out at the dreary street with a wounded look in her eyes; her mother tying the same lace curtains with yellow ribbons; attempts at lightness, gaiety, which came to nothing; her mother gathering her huge black cat to her, burying her face in its fur while a great, shivering sigh — of despair, of boredom — escaped her.

Her mother no longer sighed. She lay very still and sometimes took a little sip of air. Her arms were neatly at her side. Her eyes, which all day long had been turned to the white lilacs, were closed. Her cheekbones rose sharply from her bruised, exhausted face. She smelled faintly of wine. A small lilac flower floated on a glass of champagne, now discarded on the table at her side.

The champagne, with which they hoped to stretch out the thread of her life minute by minute, the lilac, the room of her own, all came to her at the end of a life of drabness and denial, just as, all along the mean street of the small English town where they lived, the dying and the dead were able to claim a lifetime's savings from the bereaved.

She is no longer there, Lucy thought, standing beside the bed. All day, her mother had stared at the white lilac; now she had sunk away. Outside, beyond the hospital gardens, mist settled over the town, blurred the street lamps.

The nurse returned with the matron. Lucy tautened, ready to be on her best behavior. In her heart, she trusted her mother to die without frightening her, and when the matron, deftly drawing Lucy's head to rest on her own shoulder, said in her calm voice, "She has gone," Lucy felt she had met this happening halfway.

A little bustle began, quick footsteps along the empty passages, and for a moment she was left alone with her dead mother. She laid her hand timidly on the soft, dark hair, so often touched, played with, when she was a child, standing on a stool behind her mother's chair while she sewed.

There were still the smell of wine and the hospital smell. It was growing dark in the room. She went to the dressing table and took her mother's handbag, very worn and shiny, and a book, a library book that she had chosen carefully, believing her mother would read it. Then she had a quick sip from the glass on the table, a mouthful of champagne, which she had never tasted before, and, looking wounded and aloof, walked down the middle of the corridor, feeling nurses falling away to left and right. Opening the glass doors onto the snowy gardens, she thought that it was like the end of a film. But no music rose up and engulfed her. Instead, there was her father turning in at the gates. He propped his bicycle against the wall and began to run clumsily across the wet gravel.

JEAN STAFFORD

the nemesis

Sue Ledbetter and Ramona Dunn became friends through the commonplace accident of their sitting side by side in a philosophy lecture three afternoons a week. There were many other American students at Heidelberg University that winter — the last before the war — but neither Sue nor Ramona had taken up with them. Ramona had not because she scorned them; in her opinion, they were Philistines, concerned only with drinking beer, singing German songs, and making spectacles of themselves on their bicycles and in their little rented cars. And Sue had not because she was self-conscious and introverted and did not make friends easily. In Ramona's presence, she pretended to deplore her compatriots' escapades, which actually she envied desperately. Sometimes on Saturday nights she lay on her bed unable to read or daydream and in an agony of frustration as she listened to her fellow-lodgers at the Pension Kirchenheim laughing and teasing and sometimes bursting into song as they played bridge and Monopoly in the cozy veranda café downstairs.

Soon after the semester opened in October, the two girls fell into the habit of drinking their afternoon coffee together on the days they met in class. Neither of them especially enjoyed the other's company, but in their different ways they were lonely, and as Ramona once remarked, in her highfalutin way, "From time to time, I need a rest from the exercitation of my intellect." She was very vain of her intellect, which she had directed to the study of philology, to the exclusion of almost everything else in the world. Sue, while she had always taken her work seriously, longed also for beaux and parties, and conversation about them, and she was often bored by Ramona's talk, obscurely gossipy, of the vagaries of certain Old High Franconian verbs when they encountered the High German consonant shift, or of the variant readings of passages in Layamon's "Brut," or the linguistic influence Eleanor of Aquitaine had exerted on the English court. But because she was well-mannered she listened politely and even appeared to follow Ramona's exuberant elucidation of Sanskrit "a"-stem declensions and her ardent plan to write a monograph on the word "ahoy." They drank their coffee in the Konditorei Luitpold, a very noisy café on a street bent like an elbow, down behind the cathedral. The din of its two small rooms was aggravated by the peripheral racket that came from the kitchen and from the outer shop, where the cakes were kept. The waiters, all of whom looked cross, hustled about at a great rate, slamming down trays and glasses and cups any which way before the many customers, who grabbed and rattled newspapers and pounded on the table for more of something. Over all the to-do was the blare of the radio, with its dial set permanently at a station that played nothing but stormy choruses from "Wilhelm Tell." Ramona, an invincible expositor, had to shout, but shout she did as she traced words like "rope" and "calf" through dozens of languages back to their Indo-Germanic source. Sometimes Sue, somewhat befuddled by the uproar, wanted by turns to laugh and to cry with disappointment, for this was not at all the way she had imagined that she would live in Europe. Half incredulously and half irritably, she would stare at Ramona as if in some way she were to blame.

Ramona Dunn was fat to the point of parody. Her obesity fitted her badly, like extra clothing put on in the wintertime, for her embedded bones were very small and she was very short, and she had a foolish gait, which, however, was swift, as if she were a mechanical doll whose engine raced. Her face was rather pretty, but its features were so small that it was all but lost in its billowing surroundings, and it was covered by a thin, fair skin that was subject to disfiguring affections, now hives, now eczema, now impetigo, and the whole was framed by fine, pale hair that was abused once a week by a *Friseur* who baked it with an iron into dozens of horrid little snails. She habitually wore a crimson tam-o'-shanter with a sportive spray of artificial edelweiss pinned to the very top of it. For so determined a bluestocking, her eccentric and extensive wardrobe was a surprise; nothing was ever completely clean or completely whole, and nothing ever matched anything else, but it was apparent that all these odd and often ugly clothes had been expensive. She had a long, fur-lined cape, and men's tweed jackets with leather patches on the elbows, and flannel shirts designed for hunters in the State of Maine, and high-necked jerseys, and a waistcoat made of unborn gazelle, dyed Kelly green. She attended particularly to the dressing of her tiny hands and feet, and she had gloves and mittens of every color and every material, and innumerable pairs of extraordinary shoes, made for her by a Roman bootmaker. She always carried a pair of field glasses, in a brassbound leather case that hung over her shoulder by a plaited strap of rawhide; she looked through the wrong end of them, liking, for some reason that she did not disclose, to diminish the world she surveyed. Wherever she went, she took a locked pigskin satchel, in which she carried her grammars and lexicons and the many drafts of the many articles she was writing in the hope that they would be published in learned journals. One day in the café, soon after the girls became acquainted, she opened up the satchel, and Sue was shocked at the helter-skelter arrangement of the papers, all mussed and frayed, and stained with coffee and ink. But, even more, she was dumfounded to see a clear-green all-day sucker stuck like a bookmark between the pages of a glossary to "Beowulf."

Sue knew that Ramona was rich, and that for the last ten years her family had lived in Italy, and that before that they had lived in New York. But this was all she knew about her friend; she did not even know where she lived in Heidelberg. She believed that

Ramona, in her boundless erudition, was truly consecrated to her studies and that she truly had no other desire than to impress the subscribers to *Speculum* and the *Publications of the Modern Language Association*. She was the sort of person who seemed, at twenty-one, to have fought all her battles and survived to enjoy the quiet of her unendangered ivory tower. She did not seem to mind at all that she was so absurd to look at, and Sue, who was afire with ambitions and sick with conflict, admired her arrogant self-possession.

The two girls had been going to the Konditorei Luitpold three times a week for a month or more, and all these meetings had been alike; Ramona had talked and Sue had contributed expressions of surprise (who would have dreamed that "bolster" and "poltroon" derived from the same parent?), or murmurs of acquiescence (she agreed there might be something in the discreet rumor that the Gothic language had been made up by nineteenth-century scholars to answer riddles that could not otherwise be solved), or laughter, when it seemed becoming. The meetings were neither rewarding nor entirely uninteresting to Sue, and she came to look upon them as a part of the week's schedule, like the philosophy lectures and the seminar in Schiller.

And then, one afternoon, just as the weary, mean-mouthed waiter set their cake down before them, the radio departed from its custom and over it came the "Minuet in G," so neat and winning and surprising that for a moment there was a general lull in the café, and even the misanthropic waiter paid the girls the honor, in his short-lived delight, of not slopping their coffee. As if they all shared the same memories that the little sentimental piece of music awoke in her, Sue glanced around smiling at her fellows and tried to believe that all of them — even the old men with Hindenburg mustaches and palsied wattles, and even the Brown Shirts fiercely playing chess — had been children like herself and had stumbled in buckled pumps through the simple steps of the minuet at the military command of a dancing teacher, Miss Conklin, who had bared her sinewy legs to the thigh. In some public presentation of Miss Conklin's class, Sue had worn a yellow bodice with a lacing of black velvet ribbon, a bouffant skirt of chintz covered all over with daffodils, and a cotton-batting wig that smelled of stale talcum powder. Even though her partner had been a sissy boy with nastily damp hands and white eyelashes, and though she had been grave with stagefright, she had had moments of most thrilling expectation, as if this were only the dress rehearsal of the grown-up ball to come.

If she had expected all the strangers in the café to be transported by the "Minuet" to a sweet and distant time, she had not expected Ramona Dunn to be, and she was astonished and oddly frightened to see the fat girl gazing with a sad, reflective smile into her water glass. When the music stopped and the familiar hullabaloo was reëstablished in the room, Ramona said, "Oh, I don't know of anything that makes me more nostalgic than that tinny little tune! It makes me think of Valentine parties before my sister Martha died."

It took Sue a minute to rearrange her family portrait of the Dunns, which heretofore had included, besides Ramona, only a mother and a father and three brothers. Because this was by far the simplest way, she had seen them in her mind's eye as five stout, scholarly extensions of Ramona, grouped together against the background of Vesuvius. She had imagined that they spent their time examining papyri and writing Latin verses, and she regretted admitting sorrow into their lives, as she had to do when she saw Ramona's eyes grow vague and saw her, quite unlike her naturally greedy self, push her cake aside, untouched. For a moment or two, the fat girl was still and blank, as if she were waiting for a pain to go away, and then she poured the milk into her coffee, replaced her cake, and began to talk about her family, who, it seemed, were not in the least as Sue had pictured them.

Ramona said that she alone of them was fat and ill-favored, and the worst of it was that Martha, the most beautiful girl who ever lived, had been her twin. Sue could not imagine, she declared, how frightfully good-looking all the Dunns were — except herself, of course: tall and dark-eyed and oval-faced, and tanned from the hours they spent on their father's boat, the San Filippo. And they were terribly gay and venturesome; they were the despair of the croupiers at the tables on the Riviera, the envy of the skiers at San Bernardino and of the yachtsmen on the Mediterranean. Their balls and their musicales and their dinner parties were famous. All the brothers had unusual artistic gifts, and there was so much money in the family that they did not have to do anything but work for their own pleasure in their studios. They were forever involved in scandals with their mistresses, who were either married noble-women or notorious dancing girls, and forever turning over a new leaf and getting themselves engaged to lovely, convent-bred princesses, whom, however, they did not marry; the young ladies were too submissively Catholic, or too stupid, or their taste in painting was vulgar.

Of all this charming, carefree brood, Martha, five years dead, had been the most splendid, Ramona said, a creature so light and delicate that one wanted to put her under a glass bell to protect her. Painters were captivated by the elegant shape of her head, around which she wore her chestnut hair in a coronet, and there were a dozen portraits of her, and hundreds of drawings hanging in the big bedroom where she had died and which now had been made into a sort of shrine for her. If the Dunns were odd in any way, it was in this devotion to their dead darling; twice a year Mrs. Dunn changed the nibs in Martha's pens, and in one garden there grew nothing but anemones, Martha's favorite flower. She had ailed from birth, pursued malevolently by the disease that had melted her away to the wick finally when she was sixteen. The family had come to Italy in the beginning of her mortal languor in the hope that the warmth and novelty would revive her, and for a while it did, but the wasting poison continued to devour her slowly, and for years she lay, a touching invalid, on a balcony overlooking the Bay of Naples. She lay on a blond satin chaise longue, in a quaint peignoir made of leaf-green velvet, and sometimes, as she regarded her prospect of sloops and valiant skiffs on the turbulent waves, the cypress trees, white villas in the midst of olive groves, and the intransigent smoldering of Vesuvius, she sang old English airs and Irish songs as she accompanied herself on a lute. If, in the erratic course of her illness, she got a little stronger, she asked for extra cushions at her back and half sat up at a small easel to paint in water colors, liking the volcano as a subject, trite as it was, and the comic tourist boats that romped over the bay from Naples to Capri. If she was very unwell, she simply lay smiling while her parents and her sister and her brothers attended her, trying to seduce her back to health with their futile offerings of plums and tangerines and gilt-stemmed glasses of Rhine wine and nosegays bought from the urchins who bargained on the carriage roads.

When Martha died, Ramona's own grief was despair, because the death of a twin is a foretaste of one's own death, and for months she had been harried with premonitions and prophetic dreams, and often she awoke to find that she had strayed from her bed, for what awful purpose she did not know, and was walking barefoot, like a pilgrim, down the pitch-black road. But the acute phase of her mourning had passed, and now, although sorrow was always with her, like an alter ego, she had got over the worst of it.

She paused in her narrative and unexpectedly laughed. "What a gloom I'm being!" she said, and resumed her monologue at once but in a lighter tone, this time to recount the drubbing her brother Justin had given someone when he was defending the honor of a dishonorable soprano, and to suggest, in tantalizing innuendoes, that her parents were not faithful to each other.

Sue, whose dead father had been an upright, pessimistic clergyman and whose mother had never given voice to an impure thought, was bewitched by every word Ramona said. It occurred to her once to wonder why Ramona so frowned upon the frolics of the other American students when her beloved relatives were so worldly, but then she realized that the manners of the *haut monde* were one thing and those of undergraduates another. How queer, Sue thought, must seem this freakish bookworm in the midst of it all! And yet such was the ease with which Ramona talked, so exquisitely placed were her fillips of French, so intimate and casual her allusions to the rich and celebrated figures of international society, that Ramona changed before Sue's eyes; from the envelope of fat emerged a personality as *spirituelle* and knowing as any practicing sophisticate's. When, in the course of describing a distiller from Milan who was probably her mother's lover, she broke off and pressingly issued Sue an invitation to go with her a month from then, at the Christmas holiday, to San Bernardino to meet her brothers for a fortnight of skiing, Sue accepted immediately, not stopping to think, in the heady pleasure of the moment, that the proposal was unduly sudden, considering the sketchy nature of their friendship. "My brothers will adore you," she said, giving Sue a look of calm appraisal. "They are eclectic and they'll find your red hair and brown eyes irresistibly naïve." As if the plan had long been in her mind, Ramona named the date they would leave Heidelberg; she begged permission, in the most gracious and the subtlest possible way, to let Sue be her guest, even to the extent of supplying her with ski equipment. When the details were settled — a little urgently, she made Sue promise "on her word of honor" that she would not default — she again took up her report on Signor da Gama, the distiller, who was related by blood to the Pope and had other distinctions of breeding as well to recommend him to her mother, who was, she confessed, something of a snob. "Mama," she said, accenting the ultima, "thinks it is unnecessary for anyone to be badly born."

The Konditorei Luitpold was frequented by teachers from the Translators' Institute, and usually Ramona rejoiced in listening to them chattering and expostulating, in half a dozen European languages, for she prided herself on her gift of tongues. But today her heart was in Sorrento, and she paid no attention to them, not even to two vociferous young Russians at a table nearby. She disposed of the roué from Milan (Sue had read Catullus? Signor da Gama had a cottage at Sirmio not far from his reputed grave) and seemed to be on the point of disclosing her father's delinquencies when she was checked by a new mood, which made her lower her head, flush, and, through the long moment of silence, study the greasy hoops the rancid milk had made on the surface of her coffee.

Sue felt as if she had inadvertently stumbled upon a scene of deepest privacy, which, if she were not careful, she would violate, and, pretending that she had not observed the hiatus at all, she asked, conversationally, the names of Ramona's brothers besides Justin.

The two others were called Daniel and Robert, but it was not of them, or of her parents, or of Martha, that Ramona now wanted to speak but of herself, and haltingly she said that the "Minuet in G" had deranged her poise because it had made her think of the days of her childhood in New York, when she had been no bigger than her twin and they had danced the minuet together, Ramona taking the dandy's part. A friend of the family had predicted that though they were then almost identical, Ramona was going to be the prettier of the two. Now Sue was shocked, for she had thought that Ramona must always have been fat, and she was nearly moved to tears to know that the poor girl had been changed from a swan into an ugly duckling and that it was improbable, from the looks of her, that she would ever be changed back again. But Sue was so young and so badly equipped to console someone so beset that she could not utter a word, and she wished she could go home.

Ramona summoned the waiter and ordered her third piece of cake, saying nervously, after she had done so, "I'm sorry. When I get upset, I have to eat to calm myself. I'm awful! I ought to kill myself for eating so much." She began to devour the cake obsessively, and when she had finished it down to the last crumb and the last fragment of frosting, she said, with shimmering eyes, "Please let me tell you what it is that makes me the unhappiest girl in the world, and maybe you can help me." Did Sue have any idea what it was like to be ruled by food and half driven out of one's mind until one dreamed of it and had at last no other ambition but to eat incessantly with an appetite that grew and grew until one saw oneself, in nightmares, as nothing but an enormous mouth and a tongue, trembling lasciviously? Did she know the terror and the remorse that followed on the heels of it when one slyly sneaked the lion's share of buttered toast at tea? Had she ever desired the whole of a pudding meant for twelve and hated with all her heart the others at the dinner table? Sue could not hide her blushing face or put her fingers in her ears or close her eyes against the tortured countenance of that wretched butterball, who declared that she had often come within an ace of doing away with herself because she looked so grotesque.

Leaning across the table, almost whispering, Ramona went on, "I didn't come to Heidelberg for its philologists — they don't know any more than I do. I have exiled myself. I would not any longer offend that long-suffering family of mine with the sight of me." It had been her aim to fast throughout this year, she continued, and return to them transformed, and she had hoped to be thinner by many pounds when she joined her brothers at Christmastime. But she had at once run into difficulties, because, since she was not altogether well (she did not specify her illness and Sue would not have asked its name for anything), she had to be under the supervision of a doctor. And the doctor in Heidelberg, like the doctor in Naples, would not take her seriously when she said her fatness was ruining her life; they had both gone so far as to say that she was *meant* to be like this and that it would be imprudent of her to diet. Who was bold enough to fly in the face of medical authority? Not she, certainly.

It appeared, did it not, to be a dilemma past solution, Ramona asked. And yet this afternoon she had begun to see a way out, if Sue would pledge herself to help. Sue did not reply at once, sensing an involvement, but then she thought of Ramona's brothers, whom she was going to please, and she said she would do what she could.

"You're not just saying that? You are my friend? You

know, of course, that you'll be repaid a hundredfold." Ramona
subjected Sue's sincerity to some minutes of investigation and then
outlined her plan, which seemed very tame to Sue after all these
preparations, for it consisted only of Ramona's defying Dr. Freudenburg and of Sue's becoming a sort of unofficial censor and confessor. Sue was to have lunch with her each day, at Ramona's expense, and was to remind her, by a nudge or a word now and
again, not to eat more than was really necessary to keep alive.
If at any time Sue suspected that she was eating between meals or
late at night, she was to come out flatly with an accusation and so
shame Ramona that it would never happen again. The weekends
were particularly difficult, since there were no lectures to go to
and it was tempting not to stir out of her room at all but to gorge
throughout the day on delicacies out of tins and boxes that she had
sent to herself from shops in Strasbourg and Berlin. And since, in
addition to fasting, she needed exercise, she hoped that Sue would
agree to go walking with her on Saturdays and Sundays, a routine
that could be varied from time to time by a weekend trip to some
neighboring town of interest.

When Sue protested mildly that Ramona had contradicted her
earlier assertion that she would not dare dispute her doctor's word,
Ramona grinned roguishly and said only, "Don't be nosy."

Ramona had found an old ladies' home, called the Gerstnerheim,
which, being always in need of funds, welcomed paying guests at
the midday meal, whom they fed for an unimaginably low price.
Ramona did not patronize it out of miserliness, however, but because the food was nearly inedible. And it was here that the girls
daily took their Spartan lunch. It was quite the worst that Sue
had ever eaten anywhere, for it was cooked to pallor and flaccidity
and then was seasoned with unheard-of condiments, which sometimes made her sick. The bread was sour and the soup was full of
pasty clots; the potatoes were waterlogged and the old red cab-
bage was boiled until it was blue. The dessert was always a basin
of molded farina with a sauce of gray jelly that had a gray taste.
The aged ladies sat at one enormously long table, preserving an in-
stitutional silence until the farina was handed around, and, as if this
were an alarm, all the withered lips began to move simultaneously
and from them issued high squawks of protest against the dreary
lot of being old and homeless and underfed. Sue could not help
admiring Ramona, who ate her plate of eel and celeriac as if she

really preferred it to tuna roasted with black olives and who talked all the while of things quite other than food — of Walther von der Vogelweide's eccentric syntax, of a new French novel that had come in the mail that morning, and of their trip to Switzerland.

Justin and Daniel and Robert were delighted that Sue was coming, Ramona said, and arrangements were being made in a voluminous correspondence through the air over the Alps. Sue had never been on skis in her life, but she did not allow this to deflate her high hopes. She thought only of evenings of lieder (needless to say, the accomplished Dunns sang splendidly) and hot spiced wine before a dancing fire, of late breakfasts in the white sun and brilliant conversation. And of what was coming afterward! The later holidays (Ramona called them *villeggiatura*), spent in Sorrento! The countesses' garden parties in Amalfi and the cruises on the Aegean Sea, the visits to Greece, the balls in the princely houses of Naples! Ramona could not decide which of her brothers Sue would elect to marry. Probably Robert, she thought, since he was the youngest and the most affectionate.

It was true that Sue did not quite believe all she was told, but she knew that the ways of the rich are strange, and while she did not allow her fantasies to invade the hours assigned to classes and study, she did not rebuff them when they came at moments of leisure. From time to time, she suddenly remembered that she was required to give something in return for Ramona's largess, and then she would say how proud she was of her friend's self-discipline or would ask her, like a frank and compassionate doctor, if she had strayed at all from her intention (she always had; she always immediately admitted it and Sue always put on a show of disappointment), and once in a while she said that Ramona was looking much thinner, although this was absolutely untrue. Sometimes they took the electric tram to Neckargemünd, where they split a bottle of sweet Greek wine. Occasionally they went to Mannheim, to the opera, but they never stayed for a full performance; Ramona said that later in the year Signor da Gama would invite them to his house in Milan and then they could go to the Scala every night. Once they went for a weekend to Rothenburg, where Ramona, in an uncontrollable holiday mood, ate twelve cherry tarts in a single day. She was tearful for a week afterward, and to show Sue how sorry she was, she ground out a cigarette on one of her downy wrists. This dreadful incident took place in the Luitpold and was witnessed by several patrons, who could not conceal their alarm. Sue thought to herself, Maybe she's cuckoo, and while she did not relinquish any of her daydreams of the festivities in Italy, she began to observe Ramona more closely.

She could feel the turmoil in her when they went past bakeshop windows full of cream puffs and cheesecake and petits fours. Ramona, furtively glancing at the goodies out of the corner of her eye, would begin a passionate and long-winded speech on the present-day use of Latin in Iceland. When, on a special occasion, they dined together at the Ritterhalle, she did not even look at the menu but lionheartedly ordered a single dropped egg and a cup of tea and resolutely kept her eyes away from Sue's boiled beef and fritters. When drinking cocktails in the American bar at the Europäischer Hof, she shook her head as the waiter passed a tray of canapés made of caviar, anchovy, lobster, foie gras, and Camembert, ranged fanwise around a little bowl of ivory almonds. But sometimes she did capitulate, with a piteous rationalization — that she had not eaten any breakfast or that she had barely touched her soup at the Gerstnerheim and that therefore there would be nothing wrong in her having two or perhaps three or four of these tiny little sandwiches. One time Sue saw her take several more than she had said she would and hide them under the rim of her plate.

As the date set for their departure for Switzerland drew nearer, Ramona grew unaccountable. Several times she failed to appear at lunch, and when Sue, in a friendly way, asked for an explanation, she snapped, "None of your business. What do you think you are? My nurse?" She was full of peevishness, complaining of the smell of senility in the Gerstnerheim, of students who sucked the shells of pistachio nuts in the library, of her landlady's young son, who she was sure rummaged through her bureau drawers when she was not at home. Once she and Sue had a fearful row when Sue, keeping up her end of the bargain, although she really did not care a pin, told her not to buy a bag of chestnuts from a vender on a street corner. Ramona shouted, for all the world to hear, "You are sadly mistaken, Miss Ledbetter, if you think you know more than Dr. Augustus Freudenburg, of the Otto-Ludwigs Clinic!" And a little after that she acquired the notion that people were staring at her, and she carried an umbrella, rain or shine, to hide herself from them. But oddest of all, when the skis and boots and poles that she had ordered for Sue arrived, and Sue thanked her for them, she said, "I can't think what use they'll be. Obviously there never is any snow in this ghastly, godforsaken place."

There was an awful afternoon when Ramona was convinced that the waiter at the Luitpold had impugned her German, and Sue found herself in the unhappy role of intermediary in a preposterous altercation so bitter that it stopped just short of a bodily engagement. When the girls left the café — at the insistence of the management — they were silent all the way to the cathedral, which was the place where they usually took leave of each other to go their separate ways home. They paused a moment there in the growing dark, and suddenly Ramona said, "Look at me!" Sue looked at her. "I say!" said Ramona. "In this light you look exactly like my sister. How astonishing! Turn a little to the left, there's a dear." And when Sue had turned as she directed, a whole minute — but it seemed an hour to Sue — passed before Ramona broke from her trance to cry, "How blind I've been! My brothers would be shocked to death if they should see you. It would kill them!"

She put out her hands, on which she wore white leather mittens, and held Sue's face between them and studied it, half closing her eyes and murmuring her amazement, her delight, her perplexity at her failure until now to see this marvellous resemblance. Once, as her brown eyes nimbly catechized the face before her, she took off her right mitten and ran her index finger down Sue's nose, as if she had even learned her sister's bones by heart, while Sue, unable to speak, could only think in panic, *What does she mean if they should see me?*

Ramona carried on as if she were moon-struck, making fresh discoveries until not only were Sue's and Martha's faces identical but so were their voices and their carriage and the shape of their hands and feet. She said, "You must come to my room and see a picture of Martha right now. It's desperately weird."

Fascinated, Sue nodded, and they moved on through the quiet street. Ramona paused to look at her each time they went under a street light, touched her hair, begged leave to take her arm, and called her Martha, Sister, Twin, and sometimes caught her breath in an abortive sob. They went past the lighted windows of the *Bierstuben*, where the shadows of young men loomed and waved, and then turned at the Kornmarkt and began to climb the steep, moss-slick steps that led to the castle garden. As they went through the avenue of trees that lay between the casino and the castle,

Ramona, peering at Sue through the spooky mist, said, "They would have been much quicker to see it than I," so Sue knew, miserably and for sure, that something had gone wrong with their plans to go to San Bernardino. And then Ramona laughed and broke away and took off her tam-o'-shanter, which she hurled toward the hedge of yew, where it rested tipsily.

"I could vomit," she said, standing absolutely still.

There was a long pause. Finally, Sue could no longer bear the suspense, and she asked Ramona if her brothers knew that she and Ramona were not coming.

"Of course they know. They've known for two weeks, but you're crazy if you think the reason we're not going is that you look like Martha. How beastly vain you are!" She was so angry and she trembled so with her rage that Sue did not dare say another word. "It was Freudenburg who said I couldn't go," she howled. "He has found out that I have lost ten pounds."

Sue had no conscious motive in asking her, idly and not really caring, where Dr. Freudenburg's office was; she had meant the guileless question to be no more than a bit of noncommittal and courteous interest, and she was badly frightened when, in reply, Ramona turned on her and slapped her hard on either cheek, and then opened her mouth to emit one hideous, protracted scream. Sue started instinctively to run away, but Ramona seized and held her arms, and began to talk in a lunatic, fast monotone, threatening her with lawsuits and public exposure if she ever mentioned the name Freudenburg again *or* her brothers *or* her mother and father *or* Martha, that ghastly, puling, pampered hypochondriac who had totally wrecked her life.

Sue felt that the racket of her heart and her hot, prancing brain would drown out Ramona's voice, but it did nothing of the kind, and they stood there, rocking in their absurd attitude, while the fit continued. Sue was sure that the police and the townsfolk would come running at any moment and an alarm would be sounded and they would be arrested for disturbing the peace. But if anyone heard them, it was only the shades of the princes in the castle.

It was difficult for Sue to sort out the heroes and the villains in this diatribe. Sometimes it appeared that Ramona's brothers and her parents hated her, sometimes she thought they had been glad when Martha died; sometimes Dr. Freudenburg seemed to be the cause of everything. She had the impression that he was an alienist, and she wondered if now he would send his patient to an institution; at other times she thought the Doctor did not exist at all. She did not know whom to hate or whom to trust, for the characters in this *Walpurgisnacht* changed shape by the minute and not a one was left out — not Signor da Gama or the ballet girls in Naples or the old ladies at the Gerstnerheim or the prehistoric figures of a sadistic nurse, a base German governess, and a nefarious boy cousin who had invited Ramona to misbehave when she was barely eight years old. Once she said that to escape Dr. Freudenburg she meant to order her father to take her cruising on the San Filippo; a minute later she said that that loathsome fool Justin had wrecked the boat on the coast of Yugoslavia. She would go home to the villa in Sorrento and be comforted by her brothers, who had always preferred her to everyone else in the world — except that they hadn't! They had always despised her. Freudenburg would write to her father and he would come to fetch her back to that vulgar, parvenu house, and there, in spite of all her efforts to outwit them, they would make her eat and eat until she was the laughing stock of the entire world. What *were* they after? Did they want to indenture her to a sideshow?

She stopped, trailed off, turned loose Sue's arm, and stood crestfallen, like a child who realizes that no one is listening to his tantrum. Tears, terribly silent, streamed down her round cheeks.

Then, "It isn't true, you know. They aren't like that, they're good and kind. The only thing that's true is that I eat all the time," and softly, to herself, she repeated, "All the time." In a mixture of self-hatred and abstracted bravado, she said that she had supplemented all her lunches at the Gerstnerheim and had nibbled constantly, alone in her room; that Dr. Freudenburg's recommendation had been just the opposite of what she had been saying all along.

Unconsolable, Ramona moved on along the path, and Sue followed, honoring her tragedy but struck dumb by it. On the way through the courtyard and down the street, Ramona told her, in a restrained and rational voice, that her father was coming the next day to take her back to Italy, since the experiment of her being here alone had not worked. Her parents, at the counsel of Dr. Freudenburg, were prepared to take drastic measures, involving, if need be, a hospital, the very thought of which made her blood run cold. "Forgive me for that scene back there," she said. "You grow wild in loneliness like mine. It would have been lovely if it had all worked out the way I wanted and we had gone to Switzerland."

"Oh, that's all right," said Sue, whose heart was broken. "I don't know how to ski anyway."

"Really? What crust! I'd never have bought you all that gear if I had known." Ramona laughed lightly. They approached the garden gate of a tall yellow house, and she said, "This is where I live. Want to come in and have a glass of kirsch?"

Sue did not want the kirsch and she knew she should be on her way home if she were to get anything hot for supper, but she was curious to see the photograph of Martha, and since Ramona seemed herself again, she followed her down the path. Ramona had two little rooms, as clean and orderly as cells. In the one where she studied, there was no furniture except a long desk with deep drawers and a straight varnished chair and a listing bookcase. She had very few books, really, for one so learned — not more than fifty altogether — and every one of them was dull: grammars, dictionaries, readers, monographs reprinted from scholarly journals, and treatises on semantics, etymology, and phonetics. Her pens and pencils lay straight in a lacquered tray, and a pile of notebooks sat neatly at the right of the blotter, and at the left there was a book open to a homily in Anglo-Saxon which, evidently, she had been translating. As soon as they had taken off their coats, Ramona went into the bedroom and closed the door; from beyond it Sue could hear drawers being opened and quickly closed, metal clashing, and paper rustling, and she imagined that the bureaus were stocked with contraband — with sweets and sausages and cheese. For the last time, she thought of Daniel and Justin and Robert, of whom she was to be forever deprived because their sister could not curb her brutish appetite.

She wandered around the room and presently her eye fell on a photograph in a silver frame standing in a half-empty shelf of the bookcase. It could only be Martha. The dead girl did not look in the least like Sue but was certainly as pretty as she had been described, and as Sue looked at the pensive eyes and the thoughtful lips, she was visited by a fugitive feeling that this was really Ramona's face at which she looked and that it had been refined and made immaculate by an artful photographer who did not scruple to help his clients deceive themselves. For Martha wore a look of lovely wonder and remoteness, as if she were all disconnected spirit, and it was the same as a look that sometimes came to Ramona's eyes and lips just as she lifted her binoculars to contemplate the world through the belittling lenses.

Sue turned the photograph around, and on the back she read the penned inscription "Martha Ramona Dunn at sixteen, Sorrento." She looked at that ethereal face again, and this time had no doubt that it had once belonged to Ramona. No wonder the loss of it had left her heartbroken! She sighed to think of her friend's desperate fabrication. In a sense, she supposed the Martha side of Ramona Dunn *was* dead, dead and buried under layers and layers of fat. Just as she returned it guiltily to its place, the door to the bedroom opened and Ramona, grandly gesturing toward her dressing table, cried, "Come in! Come in! Enter the banquet hall!" She had emptied the drawers of all their forbidden fruits, and arrayed on the dressing table, in front of her bottles of cologne and medicine, were cheeses and tinned fish and pickles and pressed meat and cakes, candies, nuts, olives, sausages, buns, apples, raisins, figs, prunes, dates, and jars of pâté and glasses of jelly and little pots of caviar, as black as ink. "Don't stint!" she shouted, and she bounded forward and began to eat as if she had not had a meal in weeks.

"All evidence must be removed by morning! What a close shave! What if my father had come without telling me and had found it all!" Shamelessly, she ranged up and down the table, cropping and lowing like a cow in a pasture. There were droplets of sweat on her forehead and her hands were shaking, but nothing else about her showed that she had gone to pieces earlier or that she was deep, deeper by far than anyone else Sue had ever known.

Sucking a rind of citron, Ramona said, "You must realize that our friendship is over, but not through any fault of yours. When I went off and turned on you that way, it had nothing to do with you at all, for of course you don't look any more like Martha than the man in the moon."

"It's all right, Ramona," said Sue politely. She stayed close to the door, although the food looked very good. "I'll still be your friend."

"Oh, no, no, there would be nothing in it for you," Ramona said, and her eyes narrowed ever so slightly. "Thank you just the same. I am exceptionally ill." She spoke with pride, as if she were really saying "I am exceptionally talented" or "I am exceptionally attractive."

"I didn't know you were," said Sue. "I'm sorry."

"*I'm* not sorry. It is for yourself that you should be sorry. You have such a trivial little life, poor girl. It's not your fault. Most people do."

"I'd better go," said Sue.

"Go! Go!" cried Ramona, with a gesture of grand benediction. "I weep not."

Sue's hand was on the knob of the outer door, but she hesitated to leave a scene so inconclusive. Ramona watched her as she lingered; her mouth was so full that her cheeks were stretched out as if in mumps, and through the food and through a devilish, mad grin she said, "Of *course* you could never know the divine joy of being twins, provincial one! Do you know what he said the last night when my name was Martha? The night he came into that room where the anemones were? He pretended that he was looking for a sheet of music. Specifically for a sonata for the harpsichord by Wilhelm Friedrich Bach."

But Sue did not wait to hear what he, whoever he was, had said; she ran down the brown-smelling stairs and out into the cold street with the feeling that Ramona was still standing there before the food, as if she were serving herself at an altar, still talking, though there was no one to listen. She wondered if she ought to summon Dr. Freudenburg, and then decided that, in the end, it was none of her business. She caught a trolley that took her near her pension, and was just in time to get some hot soup and a plate of cold meats and salad before the kitchen closed. But when the food came, she found that she had no appetite at all. "What's the matter?" asked Herr Sachs, the fresh young waiter. "Are you afraid to get fat?" And he looked absolutely flabbergasted when, at this, she fled from the café without a word.

BRYAN MACMAHON

the corn was springing

T he boy heard the young footsteps behind and beneath him.
Then he heard the tittering like tearing paper. When the
footsteps stopped he dared not turn round though he was aware
that the eyes behind and beneath him were gimleting holes in his
shoulder-blades. As he turned, a fistful of spalls was thrown in his
face: a sharp stone caught him on the cheek bone. He blinked his
eyes protectively. When he opened them again he had a memory
of two dresses whisking beneath his little scaffold and vanishing
through the chapel door. He heard the inner glass door swish open.
Within the chapel the first footsteps of his attackers were excited
and irreverent. The door was a long while closing, as it was con-
trolled by an apparatus designed to prevent it slamming. Then he
heard the footsteps within grow reverent and meek and innocent.

"The Corn Was Springing" taken from *The Lion-Tamer and Other Stories*, by
Bryan MacMahon, published by E. P. Dutton and Company, Inc., New York.

The boy put the back of his hand to his cheek where the spall had nicked him; when he withdrew it there was a small sign of blood on the point of the knuckle. He resumed his carving on the hood moulding around the doorway. As he worked he hummed menacingly through his teeth:

> I'm sitting on the stile, Mary, where we sat, side by side,
> On a bright May morning long ago when first you were
>   my bride.
> The corn was springing fresh and green . . .

Through the song and the noise of the mallet his ears were most alert.

The convent, with the chapel to the right of it and the schools to the left, was wonderfully clear in the pure air of the May morning. The three buildings formed a quadrangle with an open side or mouth. This mouth was turned to the south: thus the sunlight of the young summer was trapped in the garden beds before the convent door. In the middle of the beds was a statue of Our Lady. Around the base of the statue was a bed of tulips, already alight with vivid blooms which leaped up from a carpet of forget-me-nots. The façade of the convent proper was scrawled over by the angry cords of Virginia creeper which in autumn whooshed the sober building into a red-gold blaze. The high convent peeped over the ivied wall into the village, the single street of which fell downhill to peter out in a mutter of thatched cottages at the base of the hill.

The planks on which the boy was seated were supported by two six-foot trestles. The youngster appeared to be about seventeen years of age. He was wearing a soiled white coat. A pair of goggles was pushed high up on his forehead. He had an open, even a merry face. Soon his anger ebbed in him and he began to forget that he was waiting for his assailants to emerge. He focused his attention on the mallet and chisel. This was the first time the foreman had entrusted him with important work of this nature and it behoved him to be careful. He continued to sing softly, but the malice had now vanished from his song; "The lark's loud song is in my ear and the corn is green again." The mallet wasn't a whit too heavy for his hand: it was accurate, obedient, and kind, going where he asked it to go. Funny to listen to the old stone-cutters talking of mallets. Holly was good, American hickory better, but neither the one nor the other could hold candlelight to the wood of the female crabtree. The old fellows on the job were a study. Matthews was so accurate that the others said jokingly that he could carve faces on the shoulders of a lemonade bottle; Flanagan was peerless at lettering a tombstone. But they had their faults: Matthews was deplorable at foliage and Flanagan was hopeless at the angle-cut to get shadows. The foreman, Finucane, was the best all-round man in the province but he was unpredictable in mood, and if he were ill-tempered he couldn't carve soap. They were all superstitious to an extraordinary degree, and if a mallet fell from a scaffold every man on the job watched to see if its handle pointed to the gateway, for if it did there was trouble ahead. Their conversation was invariably trade-proud and esoteric; to a man they were contemptuous of tailors.

The boy again heard the footsteps behind him. Crunching on the limestone spalls. He knew immediately it was the foreman. The man stayed watching him for a moment before he spoke gruffly. His cap hid his eyes.

"Well, how're you doing?" The foreman was as lean as a mustang. He had a small brown moustache.

"Fine, sir."

"That's it! Go on, go on! What are you afraid of? You're working on the freeway." Finucane put his hand in behind one of the trestles and with his fingers caressed the foliage carved on one of the terminal bosses. This was his own work. On the boss were the letters I. H. S. on a bed of leaves. The caressing appeared to afford him keen satisfaction. Coming out in front of the doorway again he kicked the spalls away. "Keep the path clean underneath you and don't let people be dragging that stuff up the middle of the chapel," he said. Then he gave a grunt indicative of a grudged satisfaction of the boy's work.

As the foreman turned to go away he spoke with a half-smile. "Mother Xavier is in the garden — she's gathering more leaves." He turned down the short cement pathway that led to the road. As he walked away he kicked more of the spalls aside.

Finucane must have heard the nun coming, for scarcely had he gone than Mother Xavier came round the corner of the chapel with a great ado of hissing and trundling. She was a gigantic woman with an enormous, bespectacled face. It was almost impossible to determine her expression, as she had a trick of sealing up her eyes by reflecting the sunlight on the lenses of her spectacles. Her face was pale and the mouth indeterminate. The tremendous girth of her body made playthings of her rosary and girdle. Through the creakings of her approach the boy made a last effort to sift the noises that he fancied were coming from within the chapel. His effort was unavailing, for no sound could be heard above the clacking of the nun's rosary and the great rustle of her moving garments. The boy looked down into the twin circles of reflected sunlight that hid her eyes. Then he saw that the old nun was carrying a handful of leaves.

"Aha, young man!" Mother Xavier wheezed. The boy stopped working, and as a mark of respect dipped his goggled forehead towards his mallet-head.

"Well, did you find out what kind of leaves they were?"

"I did, ma'am — I think they're hop leaves."

"Hop leaves?" she complained. Grumbling, she moved to one side and peered through the stilts of the trestles at the foliage carved on the terminal boss. Then, "They don't look like hop leaves to me. I don't know much about hop leaves. Why didn't he put vine leaves or some other kind of leaves on them?"

"I couldn't exactly say, ma'am."

"Tck-tck! Well, maybe he knows his own business. And maybe he doesn't! Now isn't that a nice leaf?" She was handing him up a sycamore leaf that was splendid in its young green leaf and red stem. The boy took it gravely and, catching it by the stem, revolved it appraisingly between his thumb and forefinger.

"That's a lovely leaf, ma'am."

"And that?" She handed up another leaf.

"That's a grand leaf, too, ma'am."

"And that? — and that? — and that?"

The boy said they were all beautiful leaves.

"And will you tell me why he didn't put those leaves on the boss instead of his old hop leaves?"

The young stone-cutter said he couldn't exactly say.

Suddenly the great nun became conscious of the boy as a boy. Her face grew a shade softer.

"What's your name, sonny?" she asked.

"Jamesy Dunphy, ma'am."

"And where are you from?"

He told her that. Also his age. That his father and mother were alive. That he was the eldest of six. That his mother had had an operation for gall-stones. That the baby was as good as gold, except the time that he had the whooping-cough, when he got up any amount of phlegm. That he had an aunt a radiologist in an hospital in Lancaster. That his father had bound him to a stonemason. That he pulled the goggles down on his eyes when he was working on a certain class of stone.

This information received, the old nun delivered judgment. "God bless you, Jamesy, but you're a great boy altogether. Your father and mother should be proud of you!"

The boy had no reply to this, except to attempt a faint smile. This smile was killed decisively as he heard a low squeak from the chapel door. His sudden tautness communicated itself to the old nun, who immediately moved herself to a position where she could peer in the doorway. She continued to look in suspiciously. Just as she was about to investigate the squeak further two other nuns came walking out of the pathway that wandered through the flower-beds. One was a tall, graceful nun of thirty-five or so, who had the accurate features of statuary allied to the capital complexion of rude health. Her companion was a tiny old nun with a bright scarlet face so pointed that it instantly reminded one of a small song-bird. On catching sight of Mother Xavier this small old nun sprang to the attack. She turned her face to the tall nun beside her.

"There she is now, Reverend Mother, pestering the poor little boy," said tiny Mother Catherine.

Mother Xavier gathered herself for attack. Herself and Mother Catherine were old friends who played being old foes. For many years they had taken every second term at being Reverend Mother. At last they had been successful in their pleadings for a younger nun in command. They were now testing the new Reverend Mother, playing at being enemies in her presence, simulating contrariness and even dotage; not infrequently taking refuge behind barriers of obtuseness in order to witness her reactions of perplexity. It was all a game, and the new Reverend Mother thoroughly understood the rules. She knew that the two old nuns were probing her for that kernel of royalty that must of necessity be present in every woman who seeks to rule a community of women.

So Mother Xavier, playing according to the rules of the game, bridled in the midst of her fat. She employed her old subterfuge of taking refuge behind the light-laden lenses of her spectacles. She tucked her leaves up her capacious sleeves, and mock-fumed at the venom of the little woman's onslaught.

"The Lord give me patience!" she breathed.

The young Reverend Mother extended her arms in a wholly delightful gesture. "Hush, mothers, hush!" she chided. The boy was tapping softly, one eye on the newcomers so as to be ready with his salute if they addressed him.

Then two traitorous leaves began to sneak down out of Mother Xavier's sleeves. They were buoyant and took a long time to fall to the ground. Mother Xavier saw their treachery reflected faithfully on Mother Catherine's face. Mother Catherine opened her mouth and made the preparatory noises of a song-bird who hears singing afar. Her opponent pursed her mouth as a prelude to retaliation. The young Reverend Mother took them by the arms and drew them softly away. "Something I wish to ask you both . . ." she said. She guided them as a dancer moves a partner. They seemed unwilling to part company with their anger. As the three nuns moved among the flower-beds the boy watched them curiously. In his own mind he compared them to a hillock of black serge on the move. He heard the two old voices clash on one another; then the oil of the young nun's speech was poured between.

When they had gone, the girls came out of the chapel.

One, a black-haired girl of fifteen or so, scurried skittishly out from beneath the scaffold and rushed to the doorway that led to the road. The other, a tall girl of about seventeen, with ripe-corn hair bushing on her shoulder blades, walked out slowly. She was obviously a disdainful but graceful minx. Despite the apparent valour of her carriage, the indefinable impression of unsureness in calves and ankles was unmistakable.

James Dunphy lowered his hammer and eyed her fully and severely. Watching her move away from him he said nothing, for he was shrewd enough to know that if he stayed motionless the girl would turn round. She did so, a good deal sooner than he had expected. Finding herself fully apprehended, she faced him as bold as brass. The boy ran his hand down the moulding in the direction of the terminal boss, thereby subtly implying that the carving of the foliage was his unaided work. The tall girl was still staring. Their glances were locked for a little while.

"D'you see me?" asked Jamesy. The words of themselves seemed harsh, but the intonation was soft.

"I do."

"You'll know me again when you see me."

More than a hint of her tongue appeared. "A cat can look at a queen," she said.

"Can a cat fire stones at a queen?"

She looked around at the light spalls. "Stones!" she said contemptuously.

A pause. The boy over-earnestly returned to his work. Again the sound of young footsteps behind him, picking their way among the spalls.

"What are you doing?" she asked.

"Can't you see what I'm doing?"

She was about four yards from him now. She was peering at the boss on the left-hand side of the doorway. "Did you do that?"

"Huh-huh!"

"You did in your eye!"

The boy said evenly, "And who do you think did it so?"

"You didn't do it — that's one sure thing!"

A pause. Then the boy spoke out of the corner of his mouth.

"Run away, little girl, and do your lessons!"

"Lessons? I'm in Intermediate!"

The boy's face creased in its film of powder. He said a curious thing. "Trace the character of Banquo."

Her eyebrows lifted in genuine amazement. "Did you do Inter.?"

"Uh-huh!"

"An' what are you doing picking old stones if you did Intermediate?"

The boy gave her a look of concentrated scorn.

"Here, buzz off!" he said.

"I'll buzz off if I like."

There was a sudden agitated whisper from the doorway at the roadway. "Kitty! Kitty Kavanagh! Reverend Mother is over in the playground. She's watching you!"

A momentary wiggle of fear came into Kitty's eyes. She looked across the flower-beds and saw Reverend Mother walking up and down on the nearer edge of the school playground. She stepped backwards and placed the head of a bush in the line of vision between herself and the nun. "Ah, she can't see me at all." She threw the defiant words across her shoulder.

"She's after looking over at you, Kitty," wailed the dark girl. Then in terror and uprighteousness, "I'm going away."

"Who's stopping you, cowardly-cat?"

But the young Reverend Mother had seen the girl. The speed of her gait increased as she debated within herself whether or not she should reprove Kitty Kavanagh for her forwardness. She found it difficult to reach a decision, for her own memory was harrying her without respite. Then, as now, it was a bright May morning. The slow, soft effervescence of the apple-blossom was foaming in the vat of the orchard; Bernard had come striding through the trees, his head every now and again was bending engagingly. She was picking rust off the garden seat with her finger-nail. Bernard came nearer and nearer, bringing with him the treasures of his carriage and eyes and hair. Again and again the vision sprang out from the ambush of the years. The young Reverend Mother groped for her beads and ran them through her fingers as she walked.

The Great Parlour was on the second story of the convent. The lower half of the windows had been raised to their full extent so as to let in the May air. Within, the two old nuns were seated behind the table watching the young Reverend Mother and Kitty Kavanagh. Mechanical impulses of their lips compelled them to call the girl "Baggage! Minx! Madcap! Hussy!" but their imprecations had no validity. They continued to watch, with such immobility that they might have been sleepers. They were independent of eagerness and anger and surprise. Their souls were beyond invasion. Long ago they had made a truce with life, and life had respected the terms of the bargain. Now they were two old gentlewomen of God who were superior to the memories of tulle and music and huzzas. From their holy stupor they continued to watch as they had watched the village below them for more than fifty years. They knew themselves for what they were — two old leaks by which the tremendous confidences of tormented wives had been vented. They continued to watch, with such an extraordinary concentration as almost passed muster for obtuseness. But they were not obtuse. They had seen too many novices with smiling distances in their eyes, and finger-tips for ever seeking their ear-lobes. They had seen too many ringleted cherubs grow up and meet seduction, too many angular imps enlarge and become country empresses. They had strong precedents to guide them: they themselves had distilled lamplight on far hills and the litmus bloom of rhododen-

drons to inadequate drops in the eye-corners. They had recognized
themselves in everyone with whom they came in contact, until personal pain was lessened by division and subdivision. A shot in the
boundary elms would have startled them; a rat gnawing in the partition would have terrified them. But the remoter phenomenon of
people's emotions they perfectly understood.

Mother Xavier had now no sunlight to gild her glasses, and there
behind the lenses was discovered the reason why she herself had
been selected Reverend Mother. Now more than ever was Mother
Catherine a bird of God. But what kind of bird was she? She was
neither His falcon nor His magpie nor even His beloved black hen.
Age had granted her the boon of interpreting aright the authenticity
of curious hallelujahs. A slow, sad smile slitted her beak. She continued to regard Kitty Kavanagh, and, as she watched, she saw the
girl's dead mother and dead grandmother stand behind, directly behind, the flirting child. Just so they had coquetted and pirouetted
and flirted. And had they been the worse for it all? No, a thousand
times no. (The soft silver gongs of first love were ringing through
the sunny convent and were strangely welcome.)

The two old nuns continued to watch in stubby pattern; their
etiolated faces framed in the black passe-portout of their veils and
their facial bones thrown into relief by the light reflected from the
inverted fans of their gamps. Their amazing power of self-identification was now being exerted to the full.

Just then the foreman stole past the dark-haired sentry at the
gateway and took in the situation at a glance. He saw the boy and
girl, the nuns behind the open window and the striding Reverend
Mother. His decision was swift. "Hey, come off it!" he roared at
the boy.

The girl stood, a cool spectator, enjoying the youngster's shame.
The foreman did not intimidate her. Her sense of amusement
heightened as the boy went round the corner of the chapel, to work
on large rough stones lying beside the gooseberry bushes. As he
went he had the wit to hum to himself, "And I'll not forget you,
darling, in the land I'm going to. . . . "

A breeze came up out of the good green fields. It prinked and
pranced like a flighty filly. Suddenly it stood stock-still, and instantly the bright May morning was motionless. The young Reverend Mother moved up through the tulip beds on her way to the

main door. Her face had the lustre of prayer-book gilt. The old nuns remained regardant until such time as the approaching nun was out of sight beneath them. Then each awoke to find that her mind had been a box within a box within a box.

WILLIAM SANSOM

on stony ground

One moment with eyes blinking into the shade of that department store, one moment entering it and with head bowed thinking how I must insist on a particular seed and on no account be persuaded otherwise, and indeed seeing already the bright-coloured flowers grown up and wrestling in heady luxuriance — and the next moment standing in front of her who seemed then unquestionably the most beautiful of all, her in the pale khaki smock among the green-handled tools and bark benches of the garden accessory department.

At length I managed:

— Carnations . . . and pansies, Hoffman's Giant.

— Seedlings? Plants?

"On Stony Ground" by William Sansom reprinted from *The Penguin New Writing* #36. Penguin Books, Harmondsworth, Middlesex, England. Used by permission of the author.

— No. That is, seeds.

— Giant Chabaud carnations we have. But we're out of Hoffman's. Wouldn't Scrutton's Mammoth do you? They're warranted tested.

— Certainly, certainly. By all means. Scrutton's will do fine.

She handed me then quite simply the little coloured packets.

— Will there be anything else?

I looked round at the pigeon-cots and lawn-mowers and the green artificial grass. It never occurred to me then that I might just go on buying more and more seed. Perhaps there was an instinct stronger than the wish to stay, an urgency to withdraw from the brilliant danger? I could not bear to look into her eyes. Only when her head, her dark healthy hairy head was bent down over the little pad which she held so delicately to her breast and upon which she wrote out my bill — only then did I dare again look fearfully at her.

— Would you please pay at the cash-desk?

Dry words of parting, they were said with no emotion — with a staged softening of the corners of her mouth, a substitute smile. I took the little slip — taking it carefully at its very edge with the tips of my fingers to avoid touching hers, the pale varnished tips — and threaded my lonely way through the hoes and pergolas to where the bright light of the cashier's cottage shone, a depressive light of destination, homecoming, severance from adventure. Thus the distance uncoiling its cruel tape between us: but then as the cashier stamped the three separate parts of the bill — I realized there was a slip I must take back to her . . . the journey was not over! Walking at first quickly, but more slowly as I drew near, I returned and held out my slip. Already she was engaged with another customer, a rugged-necked macintoshed man buying a hose-whirler, a purchase that can be discussed at length. I stood there for some time before she turned and handed me my seed. But when she said 'Thank you,' she had already turned back to the hose-whirler. I stuttered my 'good afternoon' and left, receiving no reply nor another look.

*   *   *

For the rest of the day, on and off, I saw her face. Why that particular face persuades me so I can't say — it is certainly a pretty face, but so are many others. There is the belief that every man is in love with one woman all his life, a forgotten face that once peered down at him in childhood and whose presence coincided with some stage of early excitation. Perhaps it was so with the face of the woman in the garden accessories. It held significances incomparable with other faces, it was adored as soon as seen; it was also remote and untouchable. Round wide-open eyes, crescented beneath with deep shadows like bruises, and of a pale colour that asked sympathy for her great unguarded helplessness. Dark hair, dressed in the ordinary style of to-day. A mouth full and sculpted, but bloodless, almost white. A shape of face oval, perfectly regular and of a helpless strength that suggested the plastic features of classic sculpture. Generally — it can be said at this remove — an anaemic face, but in its pale flesh crying for the manly protections.

The next day I was back buying seed.

And on each day following. I have no garden — only two window-boxes. For these I have an affection, and I love a garden too — but having none, and no gardener's knowledge, the atmosphere of such an accessory department was dry, dry and in many ways fearful. None of the things there had any relation to the earth, they were new and shining and weatherless. Tools in real gardens are rusted and caked with earth, summer-houses and sheds are paled and softened by rain and sun and lichen, wooden sticks turn grey and even the black eel of hose takes on the softer, weathered look of old water. But here on the clean soaped floor such rustic sheds stood yellow and gummy with bright varnish, tools of steel were painted postal scarlet and locomotive green, and everywhere there flashed the white of unsoiled wood — sticks, axe-handles, fresh rakes. Stiff sacks of bone-meal stood with big tins of blight control and liquid manure — even the dark steel of spades had been stuck over with bright paper labels. For a place dedicated to the fruits of the earth, a place packed with fertilizers, it smelled only sterile. It smelled of wood, machine oil and fish-glue.

Yet there against the false green grass, against a rotating summer-cot and a tin of creosote, there stood my pale woman in her khaki smock — and there too was life. At first I bought only seeds. The gay packets of hardy annuals began to mount on my mantelpiece at home. But after a while I progressed — I could scarcely afford a garden roller, nor did I want one, but I made careful inquiries. Together we wheeled the green-painted rollers over her polished floor. Together we discussed the endurance of dove-cots. At length

I bought a long brass pest-syringe. Practical considerations were remembered — the syringe would come in for watering my window-boxes and in winter for moth-spray.

Slowly we grew to know one another. I kept a most reserved distance. I bought my seeds and went quickly away — scarcely noticing her, scarcely giving her the usual words of polite encounter. In this I hoped to be 'different': my adoration told me that day after day this woman was pestered by men trying to get her to meet them after hours — and I would be different. I would be sincere. I was not one for idle flirtation but instead he who recognized the flame of her great soul, her worth. I kept my distance — until the day when I judged sincerity to be established and consulted her upon the roller. From then on our acquaintance grew. But not apace. It may sound as if all this were coldly and carefully calculated — but nothing of the sort. My simple hopes were the companions of unbearable terror, of failures of strength and sudden exits, of tentative pleasantries that smothered me as I stammered them — it was then like balancing on some impelling precipice — and I was dogged by an overwhelming distaste for the falsehoods I had to tell. I had, for instance, to invent a garden. But gradually we grew to know each other.

And there were aspects of great charm in our development. When, for instance, I noticed how in her very words she began to change towards me. At first she had spoken to me only in the aloof, impersonal vernacular of gardens. When I inquired how to use an insecticide — I was told that I must 'broadcast among the plants.' About a carton of lime — this must be dusted along the rows of peas to 'hasten pod-filling.' But as time went on and ease overcame her, it was 'just scatter it everywhere' — and 'pod-filling' became 'the peas come quicker.'

There were setbacks. Though these derived from circumstances more than from her. Once, for instance, I thought I would alter the quality of our discussion, seek in fact the more pleasurable atmosphere of striped summer garden cushions and steel-sprung hammocks. I thought this more congenial for a proposal I promised myself the courage to make. But it proved only a step back — I had to be handed over to a male attendant, a hardened specialist in garden comfort, and with him was squandered a whole day's advance. Then again — on another day she was not there at all! It was her afternoon off — in that store they had some system of special afternoons. I never went on a Wednesday again.

But how, finally, to make this proposal? What words? Every phrase I invented took to itself a leer, the most innocent words suggested not only sin but underhand, slimy, disreputable sin. Several times I was on the point of speaking. But always a pre-resonance of the phrase in my own ears stopped me. At length, quite casually, for no more reason perhaps than that she was feeling fit and tolerant, she herself made the breach. We had been speaking of bonemeal. Suddenly she said:

— You ought to take me to see this garden of yours one day. I'm getting quite to know it!

She was smiling — and in a way that comes to those placid faces where one least expects it, her eyes flashed. For once confounding the consequences — for I had no garden — I took my plunge.

— But of course you must! Could you — could you spare one of your Wednesdays? And come to tea? We — we could drive down.

— Well!

Her face had fixed suddenly stiff and pressed. She fixed me with a hard astonished eye — as outraged as her voice. I started to stammer my apology — and then the coldness was as instantly gone, she broke out laughing, she had been playing.

— Well that's very nice of you I'm sure! As it is — I don't see that I'm doing anything on the Wednesday, no nothing Wednesday. . . .

— Then Wednesday it is! Here? Where?

— I don't know that I ought, really.

— Oh come on — it would be fun.

— Fun would it be? Fun for who? You I expect.

— I mean, you'll enjoy seeing the garden.

— Well . . . ye-es . . .

— You will really.

And after much more of this — frightening, trivial, painfully so pleasant — she agreed to meet me at three o'clock on the following Wednesday. I made a point of not coming in the next day — to show I was not too eager — but of coming in on each alternate day — to show that I was still the customer. I remember that week particularly buying Sweet Brandenburg Dianthus — and a pack of hybrid pinks called after their breeder 'Robinsonii'.

*   *   *

Wednesday came round. At three o'clock she was there, standing by the last of the long row of plate-glass windows. At first I was unsure, I had been looking for a khaki apron. But of course she was dressed in other clothes, a hat and a coat which I noted with disappointment and apprehension. On no count of bad quality — they were well-chosen and, as I saw later, they suited her: but at first they made her less attainable, reducing instantly the intimacy to which I had grown accustomed — and also they revealed her suddenly as a girl with a life of her own. Thus the cool ministress of impersonal equipment was gone, and in her place there came a confusing vista of flat and kitchen and relations and friends, of a district and shops and recreations and habits. However — through all this her old attraction shone.

I came up to her flustered.

— How do you do? Am I late?

— Oh, how do *you* do? No, not at all.

She was more assured — the clothes — and she smiled capably. She turned a little and said:

— All my own work!

I looked at her hat and searched for some definitive compliment — then simply stammered how well it looked. In fact she was referring to the window by which we stood, and which was filled with a new garden scene from her department. A pink wax man in white flannels mowed a false lawn, paper doves hung in ghostly flight round a thatched pedestal, implements of all kinds were scattered about separately like giant insects — it was called 'Spring Offensive'. The sight of it put me again at ease. I said:

— I say, I've got terrible news. I'd have got here this morning to tell you, but I couldn't. I'm afraid — the car's packed up.

— Oh!

— *I've tried everything.* But not a murmur out of her.

— Then what are we going to do?

— I — don't really know. Perhaps — couldn't we have tea here in town, go to a movie . . . or what you like?

— *Well.* Well, I don't suppose there's anything else for it.

That was the beginning. 'There wasn't anything else for it.' Placidly — never tartly said. We went to a film, had tea, and I saw her on her bus.

*　　*　　*

'There wasn't anything else for it.' As I grew to know her better, I found those words to be the bone of her character. If I said: 'Wouldn't it be pleasant to be in the Scillies — now, with all the spring flowers out?' — the answer would come: 'Why? We'll have our own spring flowers soon.' Or if, thinking for a subject to amuse her, I would grumble at the rations, she would reply in her pale way: 'Well, after all we must make do.' Making do, in fact. And from so serene and lovely a face, a face as slow as a statue. It is difficult to convey these placidities. She was neither dull nor dumb. Nor was she disinterested, nor bored. She spoke neither from humility, nor from resignation — but more from an absolute acceptance of events. A difficult manner to criticise — no ranting cheeriness to set one on edge, no lassitude to provoke one's energies. But of course it was at times uneasy. The temperate voice spoke and stopped. And there it was. Another conversation complete, another topic gone.

Yet for me — a magic outweighed such difficulties of communion. And on occasions there sparked from the placid face an energy of spirit and understanding that both startled and proved its constant, if unexercised, capacity within her. I first saw such a spark after we had been out together several times. We did not always meet on the Wednesdays: I had work to do, and could not often get off — so we met sometimes in the evenings. But already the evenings were growing lighter, and that fictitious car could not remain much longer in the workshops. In the end I took the plunge, I confessed there was no car, no garden, and that even my visits to the store were false. Such involved dissimulation was, when you considered it, of course a compliment: it had been taken so far that it could no longer be thought of as a means to a fickle end. But at least I expected some show of consternation, some little fuss, a period of reprimand. Whatever the reason, it is never flattering to find oneself deceived. However, Desirée — Desirée Griffiths — simply sat quiet for a second, her eyes widening and her mind placidating, until she said in a voice of unusual tenderness:

— How very, *very* sweet of you.

But there was one subject that did always animate her. This was the mention of a certain circle of her friends. At the sound of their names, and she pronounced them often, she brightened and became more affirmative. She used to repeat what they said fer-

vently, as though she might have wished such views herself — yet
was thankful she could express them at least at second-hand thus
from the mouths of those she trusted. I knew none of these
strangers looming somewhere within the strange citadel of her
home-life. They had names that grew huge in significance; yet they
themselves remained formless. I could see no faces, imagine neither
appearance nor manner. George. Kay. Norbert. I grew stonily en-
vious of them. But because I could not see them, such envy remained remote and cold, I felt markedly indifferent to them, they
were labelled the least important people alive.

We were at the Ideal Home Exhibition, pressing through the
crowd in the kitchen section, pressing against the ropes guarding
those setpiece kitchens — those that so rack the nerves, as though
they belonged to someone else, and one had intruded — and she
looked suddenly serious:

— You know, George is a simply wonderful cook. It's funny in
a man, isn't it? He's quite the professional. You never tasted anything like George's scrambled eggs. I suppose it's a kind of touch.
Yes.

I said nothing but took care to glance long and longingly at her
profile, it reassured me to look at her.

We went to a film. It was a back-stage affair, the heroine
wanted to sing in a Broadway musical and so became an usherette
in a night-club in order to faint at the feet of the tall, curly-haired
bandleader. Afterwards, Desirée leant across to me and whispered
in great confidence:

— She's the spitting image of Kay, Kay's just like that. Honour
bright — Kay'll get an idea into her head, any crazy idea — and go
off and do it there and then! You can't say a word! Once it was
farm-work — and now she's put her name down for Spanish at
the Polly. Spanish! You can't stop Kay. Yes.

I never felt quite so indifferent to Kay as to the others, she was a
girl. She may have monopolized too much of my Desirée's worship
— but she was still a girl. There was nothing of the slaphappy
virile George. Nor of Norbert, who became perhaps the most sinister
of the three. One suspected Norbert of having the worst appeal —
an indefinable appeal. Something slow and unseen. Of Norbert she
said:

— He's the quiet type. You can't fathom Norbert. But when he

gets going — look out! It's always the same with the quiet ones,
isn't it? Do you know — he's read all sorts of books. *All sorts.*
Yes.

George. Kay. Norbert. They assumed the legendary but remarkably real qualities of historical characters. Her descriptions de-
fintd them as the drawings in history books define kings: fabulous
figures yet possible, one believes in them but sees them only in
imaginative outline. Had she shown me photographs — as often
chance acquaintances will reach for their wallets and pull forth the
tired likenesses of families and friends — I would have seen George,
Kay and Norbert in humble monochrome, small, remote in time,
exposed in the nudity of group and grin, no longer of significance.
But she showed me no such monochrome emetic. And the shapes
of these three still glittered in giant and treacherous colours of the
imagination.

*   *   *

But finally I met them.

Desirée and I had been seeing each other for three or four weeks.
Once, even, we had met on a Sunday. Sunday was her special day
for meeting these three and this one was granted only because
George and Kay and Norbert were away on a day trip, something on a steamer — and Desirée had desisted for lack of a love for
water. Not for lack of love for them, nor love for me. I suppose
I was for her a convenient sort of companion. There was — at that
time — neither flirtation nor passion. A few frightened compliments from me — and from her a placid acceptance. I knew this
could not last for long — if it did, it would develop into a con-
firmed 'friendly' companionship, the requiem that begins 'dear old
Clifford' and lasts for ever. But I was determined to move carefully; moreover I was enchanted and wanted to act sincerely; moreover I was scared.

Then one Wednesday she invited me to tea on the Sunday:

— You must meet George and Kay. And Norbert.

A contraction of the stomach, the doom-seizure before the den-
tist. Sunday tea, the special hour, George's and Kay's and Norbert's! I began to stutter my refusals; but her look of surprise —
as if anyone could refuse such an opportunity! — and my own
curiosity decided the affair. That evening, as we said good-night,
I leaned forward and kissed her on the cheek. It was the first time.

I think it was because I wanted to affirm some personal bond between us, some degree of possession with which I could defend myself when we met those three.

Sunday came. At four o'clock I knocked on Desirée's front door.
Her room was upstairs, on the first floor. Not until we were up
the stairs, not until I had puffed up my awkward courage on the
dark landing, did she say so brightly:

— No one's here yet. You'll just have to talk to this child.

A large room, a sunny afternoon — the sun made a gentility
of the fawn wallpaper, the daffodils, the tea-cups.

On the sideboard plates of sandwiches, crustless little triangles
threading a line of pink paste: rock cakes as big as large buttons:
a bright yellow square of plain cut cake: green tea-cups: five paper
napkins. Desirée was much brighter than usual. I remember saying:

— Do you mind if I smoke?

Quick as a dart came the response from that dear round face,
palely animated:

— I don't mind if you burst into flame.

When I was almost again calmed, the ring came on the bell. The
springs of the divan echoed as up Desirée jumped. She was off
downstairs — the room around me grew quiet and restless as the
door below opened and a shouting and laughing as of many people crowded up with a dreadful clattering of feet. I remember
standing up, then sitting down again. In they came.

To me, shaking hands with each, they loomed as large and pres-
enceful as I had foreseen. But then as we sat down, as the first high
talking lowered and slowed, as the blood cleared and the room
moved into clearer focus — those three took on fresh definition.
In three distinct stages. First, there had been the large looming of
introduction. Then the shock of realizing that though recognizable
in manner, in physical shape each of them was very different from
what I had imagined. George I had seen as square-faced and crisp-
haired: instead he was all circular, a circular face, with other inner
circles made by a cherub mouth and hummock-round cheeks and
circular eyebrows high above round surprised eyes. Kay should
have been keen-faced and inquisitive — instead she turned out
Scots-speaking and firm-jawed, wearing a bow in her hair and
trousers: she had the appearance of a grimly serious girl playing the
kind of true-blue young housewife one sees in advertisements for
soapflakes. Above her right breast she wore a brooch in the form

of a telephone dial, with the inscription DIAL LOV. Norbert I had only imagined as a pair of spectacles. He had none. He was bloodless, with a yellow skin — his black hair grew and had been clipped far down the neck, smearing it with a shadow like dark cycle grease. He wore at least the impression of spectacles, he kept his eyes down and withdrawn, he concerned himself secretly with the carpet by his shoes.

However — they retained their presence, for me their mastery. But as tea was eaten and variously we talked, the third stage occurred. It was as if physically they were shrinking. One by one they came into sharper focus — the large blur lensed into the smaller clearer figures. I found in fact that they were all as nervous as I was: their impregnability had been my own projection. As I caught the eye of one or the other they acted always in either of two ways — they were whipped to a quick brightness, or slowed into a surly cage of nonchalance: thus they would either chatter too brightly, or turn away purposively to show that one did not exist. They began to show, too, small individual faults. George, a lively one, enjoyed too much his own jokes — while he never laughed at them, he looked round every time for approval. I remember, for instance, how he asked for more cake:

— Desirée! Desirée, I desire you — to chuck me noch ein rock cake —

And while at this sally Desirée was still slowly smiling, quick Kay chipped in:

— Coming over, one R.C.

Kay was a tomboy, a boy-girl; though she never rejected her femininity she liked to be 'one of the chaps'. When from his superior shadow, during a pause, Norbert enunciated with a sly smile:

— Angels passing overhead. Or is it twenty-five to?

Then Kay came in with:

— Angels or no angels, says I, what's the dirt?

— Dirt, did you say? Did I hear her say the 'dirt'?

— Come on, chaps — George, what offers?

— Me? We-e-ll. Now if I was to say, to say that I do hear, I *do* hear how a certain party — no names — was observed at ten pip emma entering the portals of one public house not a hundred miles from one institution to wit the Polly in the company of . . .

— George!

— Kay?

— Objection overruled.

— Thank you, Norbert. In the company, as I was saying, of none other than the *Spanish instructor* —

— George, that's hitting a chap below the belt! Come on, wherever did you hear such a thing, out with it —

— At my mother's knee — or some other low joint. . . .

Peals of laughter. And then I remember Kay, pretending to be outraged, turned on Norbert:

— Well it's a poor story, isn't it, Nor?

And slowly Norbert answered, after a pause long enough to wrinkle up his forehead; a pause for pronouncement:

— Mauvais in parts, like the reverend ovoid.

Norbert, more than the others, could never say anything quite straight, his ponderous facetions leered themselves out like the editorials of cycling magazines or the weighty patter of a Lancashire comedian. Often, in fact, he assumed a Lancashire accent. With Norbert, a lie was never anything else but a 'terminological inexactitude'. Yet he was plainly considered the brains of the party — his reading, I think, came valiantly from the shorter manuals on biology, engineering, even philosophy. He could only express himself in phrases spoken it seemed in capital letters, dogma of the short road. But most often he fell below even this standard. I remember him standing up, tea-cup in one hand, another hand napoleonic under his lapel:

— Notwithstanding sundry setbacks on the part of persons present that we shall refrain from naming — san faryan and honi-soit-qui-mal-y-pense — it is my deep pleasure to announce as a vote of heartfelt thanks to our esteemed hostess is deemed advisible by one and all. . . .

Thus, again, George, Kay and Norbert. It was not until many days later, days after that inaugural tea-party, that a fourth development in our relationship occurred: a fourth I could never have foreseen.

But meanwhile that tea-party proceeded. Not much can be said of it. At one point the wireless was switched on and we were cheered by the violins of a Winter Garden on the South Coast. A silver band from the North took over, and was switched off. Then began a period of longer reminiscence — the first battling of tongues was over — and while George and Kay talked of their lives we nodded and smiled and smoked. I remember going over to

the window. Small spring flies hurried their folded wings about
the pane. I stood there for a long time looking down at the neat
Sunday street. The only open shop was a tea-shop, a home-cooked
establishment, its name angled in tall plastic green capitals on a black
background: in the window, daffodils and saffron-yellow cakes:
one could imagine, beyond the plate-glass window, on the little
black chairs, the sipping of clear, violet-coloured tea. And George
spoke on behind about his camping holiday near Dunoon:

— . . . smashing site we found, nice and sheltered, nice and dry.
Everything in the garden was lovely. And best of all, nice and
smooth — a lovely spot of turf for your groundsheet. Well. Well,
then lights out. But comes the dawn and we wake up — and blimey-
old-Riley you should have heard! Moans and groans. Groans and
moans. You'd have thought an earthquake'd come in the night,
the bumps there were! Right underneath our sheets, bumps like
Mount Everest. Know what it was? Moles. I'm not telling a lie.
Moles. . . .

All the time I was conscious of the nearness of my Desirée — delighted, pale, serene. She seldom said more than 'Yes' —
but that to everything. A tender, understanding sigh of a 'Yes'
modulating through two long, downward caressive notes. Even
when she herself did say something she ended it with the same
'yes'. Nothing disturbed her. Placid, infinitely affirmative, for me
she held the room. Whatever I said, to whomsoever — I said it to
her. I felt her near me — and sometimes looking out of the window,
or just into the corner beneath the thin table legs, I forgot about
George and Kay and Norbert and imagined her again in her khaki
smock among the bright green rollers.

Later, as the ash mounted and our mouths dried, we grew quiet.
At seven we hurried out to the pub.

*   *   *

Some nights later Desirée and I were walking back from the
cinema. It was nearly eleven o'clock, dark. Her room lay off the
main street and we had to cross a long square of gardens — there
were few street-lamps, I remember only one, distant and speckled
among the early leaves. Part of an iron railing still held a telephone box, the green of a cabshelter showed in the light and there
were no cabs. With curtained windows on one side and on the

other the dark trees and shrubbery, the pavements lay empty —
shuffling with night, forlorn and fresh.

Since that Sunday I had seen her twice — on both occasions we
had kissed good-night, it had become easily and passionlessly a
routine. A routine breeds upon itself; again there was the danger
of 'dear old Clifford.' So, that night, leaving the cabshelter behind
and facing then the long dark pavement to the end of the gardens,
I took my heart from my boots and decided to kiss her there and
then.

We were walking arm in arm — joined and marching forward.
To bring this to a halt, to stop, would be startling: over-alert, I
even imagined that such a sudden halt might bowl her over. Also —
she was talking. Without emphasis she was picking to pieces a film
star we had seen that evening — and then carefully and consider-
ately reassembling her on a consoling note: 'Still — she does as well
as she can.' It seemed rude to interrupt this. Furthermore I was
carrying on my left arm an umbrella and in the hand a small parcel.

The distance to the lighted streets grew less, it was then or never.
Then, to my surprise, when I was giving up hope, the parcel came
to my aid. Its loop was strung too tightly round my finger: I found
myself stopping, disengaging my arm from hers, and fiddling the
loop looser. And there we were — surprisingly — standing about
in the dark! The phrase goes: 'I woke up to the fact.' So I did, it
was exactly like waking up. The tension relaxed, the night around
rose darkly into shape. I remember thinking: 'Had the string been
hurting all the time?' — before turning suddenly round on her and
taking her shoulders and pressing down my face to hers.

She had been talking, I ate with my lips her last words. And
she — she made no resisting move at all. One moment she had been
talking and at the next she was being kissed. She accepted the
change as though it were no change at all. And thus for some
seconds, with no word passing, we kissed.

No words passed — much else came to try us. It was an awkward, fumbling business. My hand with the parcel embraced her
neck, the parcel swung against her back. The umbrella stuck out
at an absurd angle — its handle pressed a tourniquet round my fore-
arm and the ferrule was caught between the railings. Her turned-up
collar edged between our lips, my free hand clutched half parcel
and half the folds of her coat and little of her. But such little em-

barrassments were mitigated by the magic — I was kissing her! She was patient in my arms! Patient. Not, indeed, responsive. But that was her way.

And that was well enough. But not for long. Passion accumulates. After that first long kiss, I suddenly struggled my left arm free and dropped the umbrella and the parcel on the pavement.

That was the end. She stiffened. All the time she must have been conscious of some safety in those impedimenta. Now smoothly she turned down her head, made a rigid little fence of her arms. There came no declamatory refusal, no dramatic 'No!' — instead, in the same second, her cool voice said most reasonably:

— Clifford! You'll muss me all up.

We hurried home.

Two days later we were to meet again — but a stroke of ill luck befell me. It had happened before, it will happen again. The spring weather was treacherous. For days it had been hot: then before midday the temperature fell abruptly, the wind rose and hurried clouds over and the rain began. I was out of town, visiting a new branch thirty miles out. And foolishly I had left off my wool kidney-band. By mid morning the chill had got me. I was in for the old trouble. It was impossible to get home before late afternoon. I had to send Desirée a note and go to bed. I was there for a fortnight.

As soon as I was up I went round to Desirée's store. It was mid morning, a grey day. But the garden accessories department bloomed brightly in the glaze of its own summer. Electric lights drew a fine glistening from the varnished summer-houses and dove-cots, the glossed green paint on rollers and mowers. Aluminium fertilizer tins winked. The sacks of hoof-meal and nicotine dust themselves sat drier and more comfortably, safe on a polished floor, safe in their own weather. But Desirée was not there. However — it was eleven o'clock, I knew she would be out for her mid-morning coffee. So I waited for some time by the ornamental sections, quietly enjoying the dear dry smells.

When she had not returned by half-past eleven I went over to the man in the hammocks and sunbeds and asked whether the lady would soon be back. He smiled. He was evidently pleased at this. He said:

— Back? Not likely. Not our Miss Griffiths.

I remember a little tooth sticking coyly from his upper lip, and the erosion it had made in the lip beneath. In the false interior summer a false cloud seemed to pass, the electric light grew dark. He looked at me wittily, storing up his riddle, pleased that I had to stammer:

— Why . . . what . . . isn't she . . . ?

He sucked in his tooth with a sigh of great perseverance — then as quickly perked it out again and never stopping jigged it up and down with words that fell damply as rain.

— Miss Griffiths, eh? Miss Griffiths's gone. Gone to be engaged. Gone and got herself married by now at the rate those two're going. Didn't you know? You didn't?

A pause while he peered forward his astonishment.

— Bless you, only a week ago it was when the young fellow comes in and goes to her seed counter there and whisks her off pronto to a social the very same a'tnoon. Next morning she comes in — Miss Easy-Come-Easy-Go — and says she's off. Off! Quick on his pins that lad, I'll say that much I will.

He sucked in again a whalish breath — peremptory, final, a breath that washed his hands of it all — and then, while the room was closing down on me and the future began to unreel its weary road, he added in a more reflective tone, both tender and sad:

— Nice set-up lad too. Got a lovely rose garden. Out on the North Circular, she says. Lovely roses, she said.

*   *   *

I never saw her again. It took some pains to avoid this, for I began to see a lot of George and Kay and Norbert. George I had already met again once after that Sunday tea-party. He himself had telephoned me — of his own accord! — and we had taken a drink together. It was then, as early as then, that the fourth stage in my relationship with those three began. First they had been too perfect, then perfect, then imperfect: now, through these last imperfections, there formed with familiarity a more settled knowledge of them and with it a liking. As I knew them better, they became rounded and lovable. Familiarity bred no contempt — it was otherwise, strangeness and fear had bred the contempt. As we grew more intimate, our imperfections bred affection — we became people of no mould, unpredictable always beyond a few superficial mannerisms.

They told me about Desirée. She was happily settled and Arthur the husband was a very decent fellow, a metallurgical chemist. I liked to think of Desirée going about their evening meal, the smell of cooked meat drifting out over the garden and mingling its promise with the other succulence of the roses. He, in his sober suit, his fingers just not touching a rose, experiencing for charmed evening minutes the poetic exaltation — full and visionary as any artist's — that comes to a man who has grown his plant. And she, aproned among the clean white dishes, her eyes on the figure pursuing its soundless progress through the garden. I avoided them for fear, as with the others, of growing too much to like the bastard.

the white rooster

There were two disturbances in Mrs. Marcy Samuels' life that were worrying her nearly insane. First, it was, and had been for two years now, Grandpa Samuels, who should have long ago been dead but kept wheeling around her house in his wheel chair, alive as ever. The first year he came to live with them it was plain that he was in good health and would probably live long. But during the middle of the second year he fell thin and coughing and after that there were some weeks when Mrs. Samuels and her husband, Watson, were sure on Monday that he would die and relieve them of him before Saturday. Yet he wheeled on and on, not ever dying at all.

The second thing that was about to drive Marcy Samuels crazy was a recent disturbance which grew and grew until it became a terror. It was a stray white rooster that crowed at her window all day long and, worst of all, in the early mornings. No one knew where he came from, but there he was, crowing to all the other roosters far and near — and they answering back in a whole choir of crowings. His shrieking was bad enough, but then he had to outrage her further by digging in her pansy bed. Since he first appeared to harass her, Mrs. Samuels had spent most of her day chasing him out of the flowers or throwing objects at him where he was, under her window, his neck stretched and strained in a perfectly blatant crow. After a week of this, she was almost frantic, as she told her many friends on the telephone or in town or from her back yard.

It seemed that Mrs. Samuels had been cursed with problems all her life and everyone said she had the unluckiest time of it. That a woman sociable and busy as Marcy Samuels should have her father-in-law, helpless in a wheel chair, in her house to keep and take care of was just a shame. And Watson, her husband, was no help at all, even though it was his very father who was so much trouble. He was a slow, patient little man, not easily ruffled. Marcy Samuels was certain that he was not aware that her life was so hard and full of trouble.

She could not stand at her stove, for instance, but what Grandpa Samuels was there, asking what was in the pot and smelling of it. She could not even have several of the women over without him riding in and out among them, weak as he was, as they chatted in confidence about this or that town happening, and making bright or ugly remarks about women and what they said, their own affairs. Marcy, as she often told Watson, simply could not stop Grandpa's mouth, could not stop his wheels, could not get him out of her way. And she was busy. If she was hurrying across a room to get some washing in the sink or to get the broom, Grandpa Samuels would make a surprise run out at her from the hall or some door and streak across in front of her, laughing fiendishly or shouting boo! and then she would leap as high as her bulbous ankles would lift her and scream, for she was a nervous woman and had so many things on her mind. Grandpa had a way of sneaking into things Marcy did, as a weevil slips into a bin of meal and bores around in it. He had a way of objecting to Marcy, which she sensed everywhere. He haunted her, pestered her. If she would be bending down to find a thing in her cupboard, she would suddenly sense some shadow over her and then it would be Grandpa Samuels, he would be there, touch her like a ghost in the ribs and frighten her so that she would bounce up and let out a scream. Then he would just sit and grin at her with an owlish face. All these things he did, added to the trouble it was for her to keep him, made Marcy Samuels sometimes want to kill Grandpa Samuels. He was everywhere upon her, like an evil spirit following her; and indeed there was a thing in him which scared her often, as if he was losing his mind or trying to kill her.

As for Grandpa, it was hard to tell whether he really had a wicked face or was deliberately trying to look mean, to keep Marcy troubled and to pay her back for the way she treated him. It may have been that his days were dull and he wanted something to happen, or that he remembered how he heard her fight with his son, her husband, at night in their room because Watson would not put him in a Home and get the house and Marcy free of him. "You work all day and you're not here with him like I am," she would whine. "And you're not man enough to put him where he belongs." He had been wicked in his day, as men are wicked, had drunk always and in all drinking places, had gambled and had got mixed up in some scrapes. But that was because he had been young and ready. He had never had a household, and the wife he finally got had long since faded away so that she might have been only a shadow from which this son, Watson, emerged, parentless. Then Grandpa had become an old wanderer, lo here lo there, until it all ended in this chair in which he was still a wanderer through the rooms of this house. He had a face which, although mischievous lines were scratched upon it and gave it a kind of devilish look, showed that somewhere there was abundant untouched kindness in him, a life which his life had never been able to use.

Marcy could not make her husband see that this house was cursed and tormented; and then to have a scarecrow rooster annoying her the length of the day and half the early morning was too much for Marcy Samuels. She had nuisances in her house and nuisances in her yard.

It was on a certain morning that Mrs. Samuels first looked out her kitchen window to see this gaunt rooster strutting white on the ground. It took her only a second to know that this was the rooster that crowed and scratched in her flowers and so the whole thing started. The first thing she did was to poke her blowsy head out her window and puff her lips into a ring and wheeze shooooooo! through it, fiercely. The white rooster simply did a pert leap, erected his flamboyantly combed head sharp into the air, chopped it about for a moment, and then started scratching vigorously in the lush bed of pansies, his comb slapping like a girl's pigtails.

Since her hands were wet in the morning sink full of dishes, Mrs. Samuels stopped to dry them imperfectly and then hurried out the back door, still drying her hands in her apron. Now she would get him, she would utterly destroy him if she could get her hands on him. She flounced out the door and down the steps and threw her great self wildly in the direction of the pansy bed, screaming shoo! shoo! go 'way! go 'way! and then cursed the rooster. Marcy Samuels must have been a terrible sight to any barnyard creature, her hair like a big bush and her terrible bosom heaving and falling, her hands thrashing the air. But the white rooster was not dismayed at all. Again he did a small quick hop, struck his beak into the air, and stood firmly on his ground, his yellow claw spread over the face of a purple pansy and holding it to the ground imprisoned as a cat holds down a mouse. And then a sound, a clear melodious measure, which Mrs. Samuels thought was the most awful noise in the world, burst from his straggly throat.

He was plainly a poorly rooster, thin as some sparrow, his white feathers drooping and without lustre, his comb of extravagant growth but pale and flaccid, hanging like a wrinkled glove over his eye. It was clear that he had been run from many a yard and that in fleeing he had torn his feathers and so tired himself that whatever he found to eat in random places was not enough to keep any flesh on his carcass. He would not be a good eating chicken, Mrs. Samuels thought, running at him, for he has no meat on him at all. Anyway, he was not like a chicken but like some nightmare rooster from Hades sent to trouble her. Yet he was most vividly alive in some courageous way.

She threw a stone at him and at this he leaped and screamed in fright and hurdled the shrubbery into a vacant lot. Mrs. Samuels dashed to her violated pansy bed and began throwing up loose dirt about the stems, making reparations. This was no ordinary rooster in her mind. Since she had a very good imagination and was, actually, a little afraid of roosters anyway, the white rooster took on a shape of terror in her mind. This was because he was so indestructible. Something seemed to protect him. He seemed to dare her to capture him, and if she threw a shoe out her window at him, he was not challenged, but just let out another startling crow at her. And in the early morning in a snug bed, such a crowing is like the cry of fire! or an explosion in the brain.

It was around noon of that day that Mrs. Samuels, at her clothesline, sighted Mrs. Doran across the hedge, at her line, her long fingers fluttering over the clothespins like butterflies trying to light there.

"That your rooster that's been in my pansy bed and crows all the time, Mrs. Doran?"

"Marcy, it must be. You know we had two of them intending to eat them for Christmas, but they both broke out of the coop and went running away into the neighborhood. My husband Carl just gave them up because he says he's not going to be chasing any chickens like some farmer."

"Well then I tell you we can't have him here disturbing us. If I catch him do you want him back?"

"Heavens no, honey. If you catch him, do what you want to with him, we don't want him any more. Lord knows where the other one is." And then she unfolded from her tub a long limp outing gown and pinned it to the line by its shoulders to let it hang down like an effigy of herself.

Mrs. Samuels noticed that Mrs. Doran was as casual about the whole affair as she was the day she brought back her water pitcher in several pieces, borrowed for a party and broken by the cat. It made her even madder with the white rooster. This simply means killing that white rooster, she told herself as she went from her line. It means wringing his neck until it is twisted clean from his breastbone — if we can catch him; and I'll try — catch him and throw him in the chickenyard and hold him there until Watson comes home from work and then Watson will do the wringing, not me. When she came in the back door she was already preparing herself in her mind for the killing of the white rooster, how she would catch him and then wait for Watson to wring his neck — if Watson actually could get up enough courage to do anything at all for her.

In the afternoon around two, just as she was resting, she heard a cawing and it was the rooster back again. Marcy bounded from her bed and raced to the window. "Now I will get him," she said severely.

She moved herself quietly to a bush and concealed herself behind it, her full-blown buttocks protruding like a monstrous flower
in bud. Around the bush in a smiling innocent circle were the
pansies, all purple and yellow faces, bright in the wind. When he
comes scratching here, she told herself, and when he gets all interested in the dirt, I'll leap upon him and catch him sure.

Behind the bush she waited; her eyes watched the white rooster
moving towards the pansy bed, pecking here and there in the grass
at whatever was there and might be eaten. As she prepared herself to leap, Mrs. Samuels noticed the white hated face of Grandpa
at the window. He had rolled his wheel chair there to watch the
maneuvers in the yard. She knew at a glance that he was against her
catching the white rooster. But because she hated him, she did not
care what he thought. In fact she secretly suspected Grandpa and
the rooster to be partners in a plot to worry her out of her mind,
one in the house, the other in the yard, tantalizing her outside and
inside; she wouldn't put it past them. And if she could destroy the
rooster that was a terror in the yard she had a feeling that she would
be in a way destroying a part of Grandpa that was a trouble in her
house. She wished she were hiding behind a bush to leap out upon
him to wring *his* neck. He would not die, only wheel through her
house day after day, asking for this and that, meddling in everything she did.

The rooster came to the pansy bed so serene, even in rags of
feathers, like a beggar-saint, sure in his head of something, something unalterable, although food was unsure, even life. He came
as if he knew suffering and terror, as if he were all alone in the
world of fowls, far away from his flock, alien and far away from
any golden grain thrown by caring hands, stealing a wretched
worm or cricket from a foreign yard. What made him so alive,
what did he know? Perhaps as he thrust the horned nails of his
toes in the easy earth of the flower bed he dreamed of the fields on
a May morning, the jeweled dew upon their grasses and the sun
coming up like the yolk of an egg swimming in an albuminous sky.
And the roseate freshness of his mouth when he was a tight-fleshed
slender-thighed cockerel, alert on his hill and the pristine morning
breaking all around him. To greet it with cascading trills of crowings, tremulous in his throat, was to quiver his thin red tongue in
trebles. What a joy he felt to be of the world of wordless creatures, where crowing or whirring of wings or the brush of legs

together said everything, said praise, we live. To be of the grassy world where things blow and bend and rustle; of the insect world so close to it that it was known when the most insignificant mite would turn in its minute course or an ant haul an imperceptible grain of sand from its tiny cave.

And to wonder at the world and to be able to articulate the fowl-wonder in the sweetest song. He knew time as the seasons know it, being of time. He was tuned to the mechanism of dusk and dawn, it may have been in his mind as simple as the dropping of a curtain to close out the light or the lifting of it to let light in upon a place. All he knew, perhaps, was that there is a going round, and first light comes ever so tinily and speck-like, as through the opening of a stalk, when it is time. Yet the thing that is light breaking on the world is morning breaking open, unfolding within him and he feels it and it makes him chime, like a clock, at his hour. And this is daybreak for him and he feels the daybreak in his throat, and tells of it, rhapsodically, not knowing a single word to say.

And once he knew the delight of wearing red-blooded wattles hanging folded from his throat and a comb climbing up his forehead all in crimson horns to rise from him as a star, pointed. To be rooster was to have a beak hard and brittle as shell, formed just as he would have chosen a thing for fowls to pick grain or insect from their place. To be bird was to be of feathers and shuffle and preen them and to carry wings and arch and fold them, or float them on the wind, to be wafted, to be moved a space by them.

But Marcy Samuels was behind the bush, waiting, and while she waited her mind said over and over, "If he would die!" If he would die, by himself. How I could leap upon him, choke the life out of him. The rooster moved toward the pansies, tail feathers drooped and frayed. If he would die, she thought, clenching her fists. If I could leap upon him and twist his old wrinkled throat and keep out the breath.

At the window, Grandpa Samuels knew something terrible was about to happen. He watched silently. He saw the formidable figure of Mrs. Samuels crouching behind the bush, waiting to pounce upon the rooster.

In a great bounce-like movement, Mrs. Samuels suddenly fell upon the rooster, screaming, "If he would die!" And caught him. The rooster did not struggle, although he cawed out for a second and then meekly gave himself up to Mrs. Samuels. She ran with

him to the chickenyard and stopped at the fence. But before throwing him over, she first tightened her strong hands around his neck
and gritted her teeth, just to stop the breathing for a moment, to
crush the crowing part of him, as if it were a little waxen whistle
she could smash. Then she threw him over the fence. The white
rooster lay over on his back, very tired and dazed, his yellow legs
straight in the air, his claws clenched like fists and not moving, only
trembling a little. The Samuels' own splendid golden cock approached the shape of feathers to see what this was, what had come
over into his domain, and thought surely it was dead. He leaped
upon the limp fuss of feathers and drove his fine spurs into the
white rooster just to be sure he was dead. And all the fat pampered
hens stood around gazing and casual in a kind of fowlish elegance,
not really disturbed, only a bit curious, while the golden cock
bristled his fine feathers and, feeling in himself what a thing of
price and intrepidity he was, posed for a second like a statue imitat-
ing some splendid ancestor cock in his memory, to comment upon
this intrusion and to show himself unquestionable master, his beady
eyes all crimson as glass hat pins. It was apparent that his hens
were proud of him and that in their eyes he had lost none of his
prowess by not having himself captured the rooster, instead of Mrs.
Samuels. And Marcy Samuels, so relieved, stood by the fence a
minute showing something of the same thing in her that the hens
showed, very viciously proud. Then she brushed her hands clean
of the white rooster and marched victoriously to the house.

Grandpa Samuels was waiting for her at the door, a dare in his
face, and said, "Did you get him?"

"He's in the yard waiting until Watson comes home to kill him.
I mashed the breath out of the scoundrel and he may be dead the
way he's lying on his back in the chickenyard. No more crowing
at my window, no more scratching in my pansy bed, I'll tell you.
I've got one thing off my mind."

"Marcy," Grandpa said calmly and with power, "that rooster's
not dead that easily. Don't you know there's something in a rooster
that won't be downed? Don't you know there's some creatures
won't be dead easily?" And wheeled into the living room.

But Mrs. Samuels yelled back from the kitchen,

"All you have to do is wring their necks."

All afternoon the big wire wheels of Grandpa Samuels' chair
whirled through room and room. Sometimes Mrs. Samuels thought

she would pull out her mass of wiry hair, she got so nervous with the cracking of the floor under the wheels. The wheels whirled around in her head just as the crow of the rooster had burst in her brain all week. And then Grandpa's coughing: he would, in a siege of cough, dig away down in his throat for something troubling him there, and, finally, seizing it as if the cough were a little hand reaching for it, catch it and bring it up, the old man's phlegm, and spit it quivering into a can which rode around with him on the chair's footrest.

"This is as bad as the crowing of the white rooster," Mrs. Samuels said to herself as she tried to rest. "This is driving me crazy." And just when she was dozing off, she heard a horrid gurgling sound from the front bedroom where Grandpa was. She ran there and found him blue in his face and gasping.

"I'm choking to death with a cough, get me some water, quick!" he murmured hoarsely. As she ran to the kitchen faucet, Marcy had the picture of the white rooster in her mind, lying breathless on his back in the chickenyard, his thin yellow legs in the air and his claws closed and drooped like a wilted flower. "If he would die," she thought. "If he would strangle to death."

When she poured the water down his throat, Marcy Samuels put her fat hand there and pressed it quite desperately as if the breath were a little bellows and she could perhaps stop it still just for a moment. Grandpa was unconscious and breathing laboriously. She heaved him out of his chair and to his bed, where he lay crumpled and exhausted. Then was when she went to the telephone and called Watson, her husband.

"Grandpa is very sick and unconscious and the stray rooster is caught and in the chickenyard to be killed by you," she told him. "Hurry home, for everything is just terrible."

When Marcy went back to Grandpa's room with her hopeful heart already giving him extreme unction, she had the shock of her life to find him not dying at all but sitting up in his bed with a face like a caught rabbit, pitiful yet daredevilish.

"I'm all right now, Marcy, you don't have to worry about *me*. You couldn't *kill* an old crippled man like me," he said firmly.

Marcy was absolutely spellbound and speechless, but when she looked out Grandpa's window to see the white rooster walking in the leaves, like a resurrection, she thought she would faint with astonishment. Everything was suddenly like a haunted house; there was death and then a bringing to life again all around her and she felt so superstitious that she couldn't trust anything or anybody. Just when she was sure she was going to lose her breath in a fainting spell, Watson arrived home. Marcy looked wild. Instead of asking about Grandpa, whether he was dead, he said, "There's no stray rooster in my chickenyard like you said, because I just looked." And when he looked to see Grandpa all right and perfectly conscious he was in a quandary and said they were playing a trick on a worried man.

"This place is haunted, I tell you," Marcy said, terrorized, "and you've got to do something for once in your life." She took him in the back room where she laid out the horror and the strangeness of the day before him. Watson, who was always calm and a little underspoken, said, "All right, pet, all right. There's only one thing to do. That's lay a trap. Then kill him. Leave it to me, and calm your nerves." And then he went to Grandpa's room and sat and talked to him to find out if he was all right.

For an hour, at dusk, Watson Samuels was scrambling in a lumber pile in the garage like a possum trying to dig out. Several times Mrs. Samuels inquired through the window by signs what he was about. She also warned him, by signs, of her fruit-jars stored on a shelf behind the lumber pile and to be careful. But at a certain time during the hour of building, as she was hectically frying supper, she heard a crash of glass and knew it was her Mason jars all over the ground, and cursed Watson.

When finally Mr. Samuels came in, with the air of having done something grand in the yard, they ate supper. There was the sense of having something special waiting afterwards, like a fancy dessert.

"I'll take you out in awhile and show you the good trap I built," Watson said. "That'll catch anything."

Grandpa, who had been silent and eating sadly as an old man eats (always as if remembering something heartbreaking), felt sure how glad they would be if they could catch *him* in the trap.

"Going to kill that white rooster, son?" he asked.

"It's the only thing to do to keep from making a crazy woman out of Marcy."

"Can't you put him in the yard with the rest of the chickens when you catch him?" He asked this mercifully. "That white rooster won't hurt anybody."

"You've seen we can't keep him in there, Papa. Anyway, he's probably sick or got some disease."

"His legs are scaly. I saw that," Mrs. Samuels put in.

"And then he'd give it to my good chickens," said Mr. Samuels. "Only thing for an old tramp like that is to wring his neck and throw him away for something useless and troublesome."

When supper was eaten, Watson and Marcy Samuels hurried out to look at the trap. Grandpa rolled to the window and watched through the curtain. He watched how the trap lay in the moonlight, a small dark object like a box with one end open for something to run in, something seeking a thing needed, like food or a cup of gold beyond a rainbow, and hoping to find it here within this cornered space. "It's just a box with one side kicked out," he said to himself. "But it is a trap and built to snare and to hold." It looked lethal under the moon; it cast a shadow longer than itself and the open end was like a big mouth, open to swallow down. He saw his son and his son's wife — how they moved about the trap, his son making terrifying gestures to show how it would work, how the guillotine end would slide down fast when the cord was released from inside the house, and close in the white rooster, close him in and lock him there, to wait to have his neck wrung off. He was afraid, for Mrs. Samuels looked strong as a lion in the night, and how cunning his son seemed! He could not hear what they spoke, only see their gestures. But he heard when Mrs. Samuels pulled the string once, trying out the trap, and the top came sliding down with a swift clap when she let go. And then he knew how adroitly they could kill a thing and with what craftiness. He was sure he was no longer safe in this house, for after the rooster then certainly he would be trapped.

The next morning early the white rooster was there, crowing in a glittering scale. Grandpa heard Marcy screaming at him, threatening, throwing little objects through the window at him. His son Watson did not seem disturbed at all; always it was Marcy. But still the rooster crowed. Grandpa went cold and trembling in his bed. He had not slept.

It was a rainy day, ashen and cold. By eight o'clock it had settled down to a steady gray pour. Mrs. Samuels did not bother with the morning dishes. She told Grandpa to answer all phone calls and tell them she was out in town. She took her place at the window and held the cord in her hand.

Grandpa was so quiet. He rolled himself about ever so gently and tried not to cough, frozen in his throat with fear and a feeling of havoc. All through the house, in every room, there was darkness and doom, the air of horror, slaughter and utter finish. He was so full of terror he could not breathe, only gasp, and he sat leaden in his terror. He thought he heard footsteps creeping upon him to choke his life out, or a hand to release some cord that would close down a heavy door before him and lock him out of his life forever. But he would not keep his eyes off Marcy. He sat in the doorway, half obscured, and peeked at her; he watched her like a hawk.

Mrs. Samuels sat by the window in a kind of ecstatic readiness. Everywhere in her was the urge to release the cord — even before the time to let it go, she was so passionately anxious. Sometimes she thought she could not trust her wrist, her fingers, they were so ready to let go, and then she changed the cord to the other hand. But her hands were so charged with their mission that they could have easily thrust a blade into a heart to kill it, or brought down mightily a hammer upon a head to shatter the skull in. Her hands had well and wantonly learned slaughter from her heart, had been thoroughly taught by it, as the heart whispers to its agents — hands, tongue, eyes — to do their action in their turn.

Once Grandpa saw her body start and tighten. She was poised like a huge cat, watching. He looked, mortified, through the window. It was a bird on the ground in the slate rain. Another time, because a dog ran across the yard, Mrs. Samuels jerked herself straight and thought, something comes, it is time.

And then it seemed there was a soft ringing in Grandpa's ears, almost like a delicate little jingle of bells or of thin glasses struck, and some secret thing told him in his heart that it was time. He saw Mrs. Samuels sure and powerful as a great beast, making certain, making ready without flinching. The white rooster was coming upon the grass.

He strode upon the watered grass all dripping with the rain, a tinkling sound all about him, the rain twinkling upon his feathers, forlorn and tortured. Yet even now there was a blaze of courage about him. He was meager and bedraggled. But he had a splendor in him. For now his glory came by being alone and lustreless in a beggar's world, and there is a time for every species to know lack-lustre and loneliness where there was brightness and a flocking to-gether, since there is a change in the way creatures must go to find their ultimate station, whether they fall old and lose blitheness, ragged and lose elegance, lonely and lose love; and since there is a shifting in the levels of understanding. But there is something in each level for all creatures, pain or wisdom or despair, and never nothing. The white rooster was coming upon the grass.

Grandpa wheeled so slowly and so smoothly towards Mrs. Samuels that she could not tell he was moving, that not one board cracked in the floor. And the white rooster moved toward the trap, closer and closer he moved. When he saw the open door leading to a dry place strewn with grain, he went straight for it, a haven suddenly thrown up before his eye, a warm dry place with grain. When he got to the threshold of the trap and lifted his yellow claw to make the final step, Grandpa Samuels was so close to Mrs. Samuels that he could hear her passionate breath drawn in a kind of lust-panting. And when her heart must have said, "Let go!" to her fingers, and they tightened spasmodically so that the veins stood turgid blue in her arm, Grandpa Samuels struck at the top of her spine where the head flares down into the neck and there is a little stalk of bone, with a hunting knife he had kept for many years. There was no sound, only the sudden sliding of the cord as it made a dip and hung loose in Marcy Samuels' limp hand. Then Grandpa heard the quick clap of the door hitting the wooden floor of the trap outside, and a faint crumpling sound as of a dress dropped to the floor when Mrs. Samuels' blowsy head fell limp on her breast. Through the window Grandpa Samuels saw the white rooster leap pertly back from the trap when the door came down, a little frightened. And then he let out a peal of crowings in the rain and went away.

Grandpa sat silent for a moment and then said to Mrs. Samuels, "You will never die any other way, Marcy Samuels, my son's wife, you are meant to be done away with like this. With a hunting knife."

And then he wheeled wildly away through the rooms of Marcy Samuels' house, feeling a madness all within him, being liberated, running free. He howled with laughter and rumbled like a run-away carriage through room and room, sometimes coughing in paroxysms. He rolled here and there in every room, destroying everything he could reach, he threw up pots and pans in the kitchen, was in the flour and sugar like a whirlwind, overturned chairs and ripped the upholstery in the living room until the stuffing flew in the air; and covered with straw and flour, white like a demented ghost, he flayed the bedroom wallpaper into hanging shreds; coughing and howling, he lashed and wrecked and razed until he thought he was bringing the very house down upon himself.

When Watson came home some minutes later to check on the success of his engine to trap the rooster and fully expecting to have to wring his neck, he saw at one look his house in such devastation that he thought a tornado had struck and demolished it inside, or that robbers had broken in. "Marcy! Marcy!" he called.

He found out why she did not call back when he discovered her by the window, cord in hand as though she had fallen asleep fishing.

"Papa! Papa!" he called.

But there was no calling back. In Grandpa's room Watson found the wheel chair with his father's wild dead body in it, his life stopped by some desperate struggle. There had obviously been a fierce spasm of coughing, for the big artery in his neck had burst and was still bubbling blood like a little red spring.

Then the neighbors all started coming in, having heard the uproar and gathered in the yard; and there was a dumbfoundedness in all their faces when they saw the ruins in Watson Samuels' house, and Watson Samuels standing there in the ruins unable to say a word to any of them to explain what had happened.

ANGUS WILSON

mummy to the rescue

Nurse Ramsay was an incongruous figure in her friend Marjorie's dainty little room. Her muscular, almost masculine, arms and legs seemed to emerge uneasily from the cosy chintz-covered chair, her broad, thick-fingered hands moved cumbrously among the Venetian glass swans and crocheted silk table mats. Tonight she seemed even more like an Amazon at rest. She was half asleep after a tiring and difficult day with her charge, yet the knowledge that she must get up from her hostess's cheerful fireside and make her way home along the deserted village street through torrents of rain and against a bitter gale forced her into painful, bad-tempered wakefulness. Her huge brow was puckered with lines of resentment, her lips set tight with envy of her friend's independence. It was easy enough to be dainty and sweet if you had a place of your own, but a nurse's position — neither servant nor companion — was a very different matter. She bit almost savagely into the chocolate biscuits, arranged so prettily by Marjorie in the little silver dish, and her glass of warm lemonade seemed only to add to the sourness of her mood.

"Of course, if they weren't so wealthy," she said, "they'd have to send her away, granddaughter or no granddaughter. She's got completely out of hand."

"I suppose the old people like to have her with them," said Marjorie in her jolly, refined voice. She licked the chocolate from her fingers, each in turn, holding them out in a babyish, captivating way of which, however, Nurse Ramsay was too cross to take any notice. "But she *does* sound a holy terror. Poor old Joey," for so she called Nurse Ramsay, "you must have a time with her. They've spoilt her, that's the trouble."

Nurse Ramsay drew her legs apart, and the heavy woollen skirt hitched above her knees, displaying the thick grey of her winter knickers, allowing a suspender to glint in the firelight.

"Spoilt," she said in her deep voice with its Australian twang. "I should think *so* if you *can* spoil a cracked pot. I've had many tiresome ones, but our dear Celia takes the biscuit. The tempers, the sulking you wouldn't believe, and violent, too, sometimes; of course she doesn't know her own strength. So selfish with her toys — that's Mrs. Hartley's fault. 'Whatever she wants, Nurse,' she told me, 'we must give her. It's the least we can do.' Well! I ask you — of course the old lady's getting a bit queer herself, that's the trouble, and the old gentleman's not much better. 'You're asking for trouble,' I told her, but you might as well talk to a stone wall. You should have heard the fuss the other day just because I couldn't find an old doll. 'If other little girls bit and scratched when they lost their dolls,' I said."

Marjorie gave a little scream of laughter. Nurse Ramsay scowled. She was always suspicious of ridicule.

"What's funny about that?" she asked. "Oh, nothing, I s'pose," said Marjorie, "if you're used to it, but better you than me."

"I should think so," said Nurse Ramsay. "Why, Doctor Lardner said to me only the other day, 'Nobody but you would stand it, Nurse, you must have nerves of steel.' I suppose I am unusually . . ."

But Marjorie had closed her ears to a familiar story. She was busy wiping a chocolate stain from her pretty blue crepe-de-Chine frock, liberally soaking her little lace-bordered hanky with spittle to perform the task. Really Joey was always full of moans nowadays.

It was so very dark in the little bed and if you turned one way you would fall out and if you turned the other it was wall and you were shut in. Celia held her doll very tightly to her. She was shaking all over with fright. Nanny had pushed and scratched so because she wanted Mummy in bed with her. Nanny always tried to stop her having Mummy, because she was jealous. But you had to be careful, you had to watch your time, because however much you bit, squelching and driving the teeth into the arm-flesh, cracking the bone, they could always tie you in, as they had done before, and then even Granny didn't help you. So she had pretended to Nanny that she was beaten, that she would do without Mummy. But Nanny did not know — Mummy was in bed. Celia pushed back the clothes and looked at the familiar blue wool by the light of the moonbeam from the window-shutter. "It's all right when Mummy's with you, darling." So long ago she had said that, before she went on the ship, leaving her with Granny. "I shall be back with you before you can say Jack Robinson," she had said, as Celia sat on the edge of the cabin trunk and wrapped her doll in the old blue cardigan. She did not come and she did not come and then she was there all the time in the blue cardigan and if she was with you it was all right. But you had to be very careful not to let them part you from Mummy's protection — they could do it by force, but only for a little because Granny wouldn't allow it; but the worst was when they tricked you into losing. Nanny had done that once and they searched and searched, at least all of them had except Nanny, and she pretended to, but all the time you could tell from her eyes that she was wishing they would never find. The look in Nanny's eyes had enraged Celia and she had scratched until the blood ran. That had meant a bad time following, with Granny angry and Granddad's voice loud and stern, and being held into bed and little white pills. No, it was important never to be separated — so Celia took Mummy and very carefully passing the arms round her neck, she knotted them to the bedpost behind her. It was very difficult to do, but at last she was satisfied that Nanny could not separate them. Then she lay back and watched the yellow moonlight from the window. Yellow was the middle light, and as they drove behind Goddard in the car — Goddard who gave the barley-sugar — with Granny smelling of flowers, they would say yellow that was the middle light, and green we move, and red we must stop, and green we move, and yellow was the middle light, and red we stop. . . .

"It's simply a question of the money not being there," said old Mr. Hartley, and his voice was cracked and irritable. He didn't like the business any more than his wife, and yet her refusal to comprehend financial dealings — thirty-five years before he would have found it feminine, charming — was putting him into the role of advocate, of cruel realist. He had already succumbed to a glass of port in his agitation at the whole idea, and the thought of to-morrow's gout was a further irritant.

"Well, you know best, dear, of course," his wife answered in that calm, pacifying voice which had vexed him over so many years. "But you've often said we ought to change our lawyers, that Mr. Cartwright was a terrible old woman . . ."

"Yes, yes, I know," Mr. Hartley broke in. "Cartwright's an old fool, but he isn't responsible for taxation and this damned government. The truth is, my dear, we're living on very diminished capital and we just can't afford it."

"Well, I do my best to economize," said Mrs. Hartley, "but prices . . ."

"I know, I know," Mr. Hartley broke in again. "But it isn't a question of cheeseparing here and there. We've got to change our whole way of living. In the first place we've got to find somewhere cheaper and smaller to live."

"Well, I don't know how you think we're all going to fit into a smaller house," said his wife.

"That's just the point," he replied. "I don't." He pulled his upper lip over the lower and stared into the fire, then he looked up at his wife as though he expected her to be waiting for him to say more. But she had no thought for his continuing, only a deep abhorrence and refusal of the proposal he had implied. She folded her embroidery and, getting up, she moved the pot of cyclamens from the little table by the window. "You've been letting Nurse Ramsay get at you," she said.

"Letting Nurse Ramsay get at me," echoed the old man savagely.

"What nonsense you do talk, dear. Anyone would think I was a child who couldn't think for myself."

"We're neither of us young, dear," Mrs. Hartley said drily. "Old people *are* a bit childish, you know."

Such flashes of realism in the even dullness of his wife's thought only irritated Mr. Hartley more.

"One thing is clear to me," he said sharply, "on this subject you'll never see sense. Celia gets worse and worse in her behaviour. Nurse Ramsay won't put up with it much longer and we'll never get another nurse nowadays."

Mrs. Hartley set out the patience cards on the little table. "Celia's always very sweet with me," she said. "I don't see what Nurse has to grumble at."

"My dear," Mr. Hartley said and his tone was tender and soothing, "be reasonable. It can't be very pleasant you know — all those rages and the difficulty with feeding, and really she's less able to be clean in her habits than two years ago."

The coarseness of the old man's allusion made Mrs. Hartley's hand tremble. She said nothing, however, but "red on black." Her silence encouraged her husband.

"I want your help, Alice, over this, can't you see that? Don't force me to act alone. Come over with me and see this place at Dagmere. You're so much better at judging these things than I am."

Mrs. Hartley was silent for a few minutes, then, "Very well," she said, "we'll drive over to-morrow." But her daughter's voice was in her ears. "I'm leaving her with you, Mother. I know she'll be in good hands."

Celia was on the deck of the ship. The sun shone brightly, the gongs beat, the whistles blew and her pink hair ribbons were flying in the wind. All the stair rails were painted bright red, pillar box red like blood, and that was Celia's favourite colour. Red meant we must stop, so Celia stopped. The gentleman in the postman's suit came up to her. "Go on," he said, "don't stand there gaping like a sawney." She wanted to tell him that it was red and that she couldn't go, but the whistles and the gongs made such a noise that he couldn't hear her. "Go on," he cried, and he clapped his hands over her head. Such a wind blew when he clapped his hands that her hair ribbons blew off. Celia began to cry. "A nice thing if every little girl cried when her ribbons blew away," said Nurse Ramsay. She hoped to make Celia run after them, although it was red and that meant we must stop. But there was Granny beckoning to her and there were the hair ribbons dancing in the sunshine a little way ahead — they were two little pink dolls. So Celia ran, although it was red. And now the side of the ship had gone and great waves came up to pull her down, green and grey. "Mummy, Mummy," she cried, but the waves were folding over her. Mummy would not come, and suddenly there was Mummy holding out her arms to save her — Mummy all in blue. Celia ran into her mother's arms and she sobbed on her mother's bosom. She would not be lonely now, now she was safe. But Celia's Mummy's arms folded tight round her neck, tighter and tighter. "Don't, Mummy, don't. You're hurting me," Celia cried, and she looked up to see her Mummy's eyes cruel and hard like Nurse Ramsay's. Celia began to scream and to fight, but her Mummy's hands closed more and more tightly around her neck, crushing and pulping.

Nurse Ramsay heard the screams as she came up the dark drive. The battery in her torch had given out and she was feeling her way beside the wet bushes. The screams penetrated slowly into her consciousness, for she was oppressed by the memory of that humiliating scene at the Flannel Hop when Ivy had made such a fool of her in front of Ronnie Armitage. Really, it's getting impossible, she thought at first; you can't leave her alone for half an hour now without trouble. Then suddenly something in the screams made her quicken her pace, and now she was running in panic, the branches of the rhododendron and laurel bushes catching at her like long spiky arms.

When she reached Celia's bedroom, it was already too late. No efforts of poor old Mr. Hartley or even of Goddard could bring life back to those flushed, purple cheeks, that swollen black neck. Dr. Lardner, who came shortly after, said that death was due as much to failure of the heart as to strangulation. "She must have woken herself in struggling to free her neck from the woollen jacket," he said, "and the fright acted upon an already weakened heart." It was easy to believe as one surveyed the body: the wreck of a great Britannia blonde, thirteen stone at least — she had put on weight ever since her twenty-fifth year — the round blue eyes might have fascinated had they not stared in childish idiocy, the masses of golden hair won praise had they not sprouted in tufts on the great pink cheeks, allying the poor lunatic to the animal world, marking her off from normal men and women.

Nurse Ramsay said the whole thing was a judgment. "If they hadn't been so obstinate and had agreed to send her to a proper home she'd have been alive to-day," she added. But Mrs. Hartley, who was a religious woman, offered thanks to God that night that Death had come in time to prevent her being taken away. It's almost as though her mother had come to help her when she was in trouble, she thought.

lions, harts, leaping does

Thirty-ninth pope. Anastasius, a Roman, appointed that while the Gospel was reading they should stand and not sit. He exempted from the ministry those that were lame, impotent, or diseased persons, and slept with his forefathers in peace, being a confessor.' "

"Anno?"

" 'Anno 404.' "

They sat there in the late afternoon, the two old men grown gray in the brown robes of the Order. Angular winter daylight forsook the small room, almost a cell in the primitive sense, and passed through the window into the outside world. The distant horizon, which it sought to join, was still bright and strong against approaching night. The old Franciscans, one priest, one brother, were left among the shadows in the room.

"Can't you see to read one more, Titus?" the priest Didymus asked. "Number fourteen." He did not cease staring out the window at day becoming night on the horizon. The thirty-ninth pope said Titus might not be a priest. Did Titus, reading, understand? He could never really tell about Titus, who said nothing now. There was only silence, then a dry whispering of pages turning. "Number fourteen," Didymus said. "That's Zephyrinus. I always like the old heretic on that one, Titus."

According to one bibliographer, Bishop Bale's *Pageant of Popes Contayninge the Lyves of all the Bishops of Rome, from the Beginninge of them to the Year of Grace 1555* was a denunciation of every pope from Peter to Paul IV. However inviting to readers that might sound, it was in sober fact a lie. The first popes, persecuted and mostly martyred, wholly escaped the author's remarkable spleen and even enjoyed his crusty approbation. Father Didymus, his aged appetite for biography jaded by the orthodox lives, found the work fascinating. He usually referred to it as "Bishop Bale's funny book" and to the Bishop as a heretic.

Titus squinted at the yellowed page. He snapped a glance at the light hovering at the window. Then he closed his eyes and with great feeling recited:

" 'O how joyous and how delectable is it to see religious men devout and fervent in the love of God, well-mannered — ' "

"Titus," Didymus interrupted softly.

" ' — and well taught in ghostly learning.' "

"Titus, read." Didymus placed the words in their context. The First Book of *The Imitation* and Chapter, if he was not mistaken, XXV. The trick was no longer in finding the source of Titus's quotations; it was putting them in their exact context. It had become an unconfessed contest between them, and it gratified Didymus to think he had been able to place the fragment. Titus knew two books by heart, *The Imitation* and *The Little Flowers of St. Francis*. Lately, unfortunately, he had begun to learn another. He was more and more quoting from Bishop Bale. Didymus reminded himself he must not let Titus read past the point where the martyred popes left off. What Bale had to say about Peter's later successors sounded incongruous — "unmete" in the old heretic's own phrase — coming from a Franciscan brother. Two fathers had already inquired of Didymus concerning Titus. One had noted the antique style of his words and had ventured to wonder if Brother Titus, Christ preserve us, might be slightly possessed. He cited the case of the illiterate Missouri farmer who cursed the Church in a forgotten Aramaic tongue.

"Read, Titus."

Titus squinted at the page once more and read in his fine dead voice.

" 'Fourteenth pope, Zephyrinus. Zephyrinus was a Roman born, a man as writers do testify, more addicted with all endeavor to the service of God than to the cure of any worldly affairs. Whereas before his time the wine in the celebrating the communion was ministered in a cup of wood, he first did alter that, and instead thereof brought in cups or chalices of glass. And yet he did not this upon any superstition, as thinking wood to be unlawful, or glass to be more holy for that use, but because the one is more comely and seemly, as by experience it appeareth than the other. And yet some wooden dolts do dream that the wooden cups were changed by him because that part of the wine, or as they thought, the royal blood of Christ, did soak into the wood, and so it can not be in glass. Surely sooner may wine soak into any wood than any wit into those winey heads that thus both deceive themselves and slander this Godly martyr.' "

"Anno?"

Titus squinted at the page again. " 'Anno 222,' " he read.

They were quiet for a moment which ended with the clock in the tower booming once for the half hour. Didymus got up and stood so close to the window his breath became visible. Noticing it, he inhaled deeply and then, exhaling, he sent a gust of smoke churning against the freezing pane, clouding it. Some old unmelted snow in tree crotches lay dirty and white in the gathering dark.

"It's cold out today," Didymus said.

He stepped away from the window and over to Titus, whose face was relaxed in open-eyed sleep. He took Bishop Bale's funny book unnoticed from Titus's hands.

"Thank you, Titus," he said.

Titus blinked his eyes slowly once, then several times quickly. His body gave a shudder, as if coming to life.

"Yes, Father?" he was asking.

"I said thanks for reading. You are a great friend to me."

"Yes, Father."

"I know you'd rather read other authors." Didymus moved to the window, stood there gazing through the tops of trees, their limbs black and bleak against the sky. He rubbed his hands. "I'm going for a walk before vespers. Is it too cold for you, Titus?"

" 'A good religious man that is fervent in his religion taketh all things well, and doth gladly all that he is commanded to do.' "

Didymus, walking across the room, stopped and looked at Titus just in time to see him open his eyes. He was quoting again: *The Imitation* and still in Chapter XXV. Why had he said that? To himself Didymus repeated the words and decided Titus, his mind moving intelligently but so pathetically largo, was documenting the act of reading Bishop Bale when there were other books he preferred.

"I'm going out for a walk," Didymus said.

Titus rose and pulled down the full sleeves of his brown robe in anticipation of the cold.

"I think it is too cold for you, Titus," Didymus said.

Titus faced him undaunted, arms folded and hands muffled in his sleeves, eyes twinkling incredulously. He was ready to go. Didymus got the idea Titus knew himself to be the healthier of the two. Didymus was vaguely annoyed at this manifestation of the truth. *Vanitas.*

"Won't they need you in the kitchen now?" he inquired.

Immediately he regretted having said that. And the way he had said it, with some malice, as though labor *per se* were important and the intention not so. *Vanitas* in a friar, and at his age too. Confronting Titus with a distinction his simple mind could never master and which, if it could, his great soul would never recognize. Titus only knew all that was necessary, that a friar did what he was best at in the community. And no matter the nature of his toil, the variety of the means at hand, the end was the same for all friars. Or indeed for all men, if they cared to know. Titus worked in the kitchen and garden. Was Didymus wrong in teaching geometry out of personal preference and perhaps — if this was so he was — out of pride? Had the spiritual worth of his labor been vitiated because of that? He did not think so, no. No, he taught geometry because it was useful and eternally true, like his theology, and though of a lower order of truth it escaped the common fate of theology and the humanities, perverted through the ages in the mouths of dunderheads and fools. From that point of view, his work came to the same thing as Titus's. The vineyard was everywhere; they were in it, and that was essential.

Didymus, consciously humble, held open the door for Titus. Sandals scraping familiarly, they passed through dark corridors until they came to the stairway. Lights from floors above and below spangled through the carven apertures of the winding stair and fell in confusion upon the worn oaken steps.

At the outside door they were ambushed. An old friar stepped out of the shadows to intercept them. Standing with Didymus and Titus, however, made him appear younger. Or possibly it was the tenseness of him.

"Good evening, Father," he said to Didymus. "And Titus."

Didymus nodded in salutation and Titus said deliberately, as though he were the first one ever to put words in such conjunction: "Good evening, Father Rector."

The Rector watched Didymus expectantly. Didymus studied the man's face. It told him nothing but curiosity — a luxury which could verge on vice in the cloister. Didymus frowned his incomprehension. He was about to speak. He decided against it, turning to Titus:

"Come on, Titus, we've got a walk to take before vespers."

The Rector was left standing.

They began to circle the monastery grounds. Away from the buildings it was brighter. With a sudden shudder, Didymus felt the freezing air bite into his body all over. Instinctively he drew up his cowl. That was a little better. Not much. It was too cold for him to relax, breathe deeply, and stride freely. It had not looked this cold from his window. He fell into Titus's gait. The steps were longer, but there was an illusion of warmth about moving in unison. Bit by bit he found himself duplicating every aspect of Titus in motion. Heads down, eyes just ahead of the next step, undeviating, they seemed peripatetic figures in a Gothic frieze. The stones of the walk were trampled over with frozen footsteps. Titus's feet were gray and bare in their open sandals. Pieces of ice, the thin edges of ruts, cracked off under foot, skittering sharply away. A crystal fragment lit between Titus's toes and did not melt there. He did not seem to notice it. This made Didymus lift his eyes.

A fine Franciscan! Didymus snorted, causing a flurry of vapors.

He had the despicable caution of the comfortable who move mountains, if need be, to stay that way. Here he was, cowl up and
heavy woolen socks on, and regretting the weather because it ex-
ceeded his anticipations. Painfully he stubbed his toe on purpose
and at once accused himself of exhibitionism. Then he damned the
expression for its modernity. He asked himself wherein lay the
renunciation of the world, the flesh and the devil, the whole point
of following after St. Francis today. Poverty, Chastity, Obedience
— the three vows. There was nothing of suffering in the poverty
of the friar nowadays: he was penniless, but materially rich compared to — what was the phrase he used to hear? — "one third of
the nation." A beggar, a homeless mendicant by very definition,
he knew nothing — except as it affected others "less fortunate" —
of the miseries of begging in the streets. Verily, it was no heavy
cross, this vow of Poverty, so construed and practiced, in the
modern world. Begging had become unfashionable. Somewhere
along the line the meaning had been lost; they had become too
"fortunate." Official agencies, to whom it was a nasty but necessary
business, dispensed Charity without mercy or grace. He recalled
with wry amusement Frederick Barbarossa's appeal to fellow princes
when opposed by the might of the medieval Church: "We have a
clean conscience, and it tells us that God is with us. Ever have we
striven to bring back priests and, in especial, those of the topmost
rank, to the condition of the first Christian Church. In those days
the clergy raised their eyes to the angels, shone through miracles,
made whole the sick, raised the dead, made Kings and Princes subject to them, not with arms but with their holiness. But now they
are smothered in delights. To withdraw from them the harmful
riches which burden them to their own undoing is a labor of love
in which all Princes should eagerly participate."

And Chastity, what of that? Well, that was all over for him —
a battle he had fought and won many years ago. A sin whose temp-
tations had prevailed undiminished through the centuries, but withal
for him, an old man, a dead issue, a young man's trial. Only Obedience remained, and that, too, was no longer difficult for him. There
was something — much as he disliked the term — to be said for
"conditioning." He had to smile at himself: why should he bristle
so at using the word? It was only contemporary slang for a theory
the Church had always known. "Psychiatry," so called, and all the
ghastly superstition that attended its practice, the deification of

its high priests in the secular schools, made him ill. But it would pass. Just look how alchemy had flourished, and where was it today?

Clearly an abecedarian observance of the vows did not promise perfection. Stemmed in divine wisdom, they were branches meant to flower forth, but requiring of the friar the water and sunlight of sacrifice. The letter led nowhere. It was the spirit of the vows which opened the way and revealed to the soul, no matter the flux of circumstance, the means of salvation.

He had picked his way through the welter of familiar factors again — again to the same bitter conclusion. He had come to the key and core of his trouble anew. When he received the letter from Seraphin asking him to come to St. Louis, saying his years prohibited unnecessary travel and endowed his request with a certain prerogative — No, he had written back, it's simply impossible, not saying why. God help him, as a natural man, he had the desire, perhaps the inordinate desire, to see his brother again. He should not have to prove that. One of them must die soon. But as a friar, he remembered: "Unless a man be clearly delivered from the love of all creatures, he may not fully tend to his Creator." Therein, he thought, the keeping of the vows having become an easy habit for him, was his opportunity — he thought! It was plain and there was sacrifice and it would be hard. So he had not gone.

Now it was plain that he had been all wrong. Seraphin was an old man with little left to warm him in the world. Didymus asked himself — recoiling at the answer before the question was out — if his had been the only sacrifice. Rather, had he not been too intent on denying himself at the time to notice that he was denying Seraphin also? Harshly Didymus told himself he had used his brother for a hair shirt. This must be the truth, he thought; it hurts so.

The flesh just above his knees felt frozen. They were drawing near the entrance again. His face, too, felt the same way, like a slab of pasteboard, stiffest at the tip of his nose. When he wrinkled his brow and puffed out his cheeks to blow hot air up to his nose, his skin seemed to crackle like old parchment. His eyes watered from the wind. He pressed a hand, warm from his sleeve, to his exposed neck. Frozen, like his face. It would be chapped tomorrow.

Titus, white hair awry in the wind, looked just the same.

They entered the monastery door. The Rector stopped them. It was almost as before, except that Didymus was occupied with feeling his face and patting it back to life.

"Ah, Didymus! It must be cold indeed!" The Rector smiled at Titus and returned his gaze to Didymus. He made it appear that they were allied in being amused at Didymus's face. Didymus touched his nose tenderly. Assured it would stand the operation, he blew it lustily. He stuffed the handkerchief up his sleeve. The Rector, misinterpreting all this ceremony, obviously was afraid of being ignored.

"The telegram, Didymus. I'm sorry; I thought it might have been important."

"I received no telegram."

They faced each other, waiting, experiencing a hanging moment of uneasiness.

Then, having employed the deductive method, they both looked at Titus. Although he had not been listening, rather had been studying the naked toes in his sandals, he sensed their eyes questioning him.

"Yes, Father Rector?" he answered.

"The telegram for Father Didymus, Titus?" the Rector demanded. "Where is it?" Titus started momentarily out of willingness to be of service, but ended, his mind refusing to click, impassive before them. The Rector shook his head in faint exasperation and reached his hand down into the folds of Titus's cowl. He brought forth two envelopes. One, the telegram, he gave to Didymus. The other, a letter, he handed back to Titus.

"I gave you this letter this morning, Titus. It's for Father Anthony." Intently Titus stared unremembering at the letter. "I wish you would see that Father Anthony gets it right away, Titus. I think it's a bill."

Titus held the envelope tightly to his breast and said, "Father Anthony."

Then his eyes were attracted by the sound of Didymus tearing open the telegram. While Didymus read the telegram, Titus's expression showed he at last understood his failure to deliver it. He was perturbed, mounting inner distress moving his lips silently.

Didymus looked up from the telegram. He saw the grief in Titus's face and said, astonished, "How did you know, Titus?"

Titus's eyes were both fixed and lowered in sorrow. It seemed to Didymus that Titus knew the meaning of the telegram. Didymus was suddenly weak, as before a miracle. His eyes went to the Rector to see how he was taking it. Then it occurred to him the Rector could not know what had happened.

As though nothing much had, the Rector laid an absolving hand lightly upon Titus's shoulder.

"Didymus, he can't forgive himself for not delivering the telegram now that he remembers it. That's all."

Didymus was relieved. Seeing the telegram in his hand, he folded it quickly and stuffed it back in the envelope. He handed it to the Rector. Calmly, in a voice quite drained of feeling, he said, "My brother, Father Seraphin, died last night in St. Louis."

"Father Seraphin *from Rome?*"

"Yes," Didymus said, "in St. Louis. He was my brother. Appointed a confessor in Rome, a privilege for a foreigner. He was ninety-two."

"I know that, Didymus, an honor for the Order. I had no idea he was in this country. Ninety-two! God rest his soul!"

"I had a letter from him only recently."

"You did?"

"He wanted me to come to St. Louis. I hadn't seen him for twenty-five years at least."

"Twenty-five years?"

"It was impossible for me to visit him."

"But if he was in this country, Didymus . . ."

The Rector waited for Didymus to explain.

Didymus opened his mouth to speak, heard the clock in the tower sound the quarter hour, and said nothing, listening, lips parted, to the last of the strokes die away.

"Why, Didymus, it could easily have been arranged," the Rector persisted.

Didymus turned abruptly to Titus, who, standing in a dream, had been inattentive since the clock struck.

"Come, Titus, we'll be late."

He hastened down the corridor with Titus. "No," he said in agitation, causing Titus to look at him in surprise. "I told him no. It was simply impossible." He was conscious of Titus's attention. "To visit him, Seraphin, who is dead." That had come naturally enough, for being the first time in his thoughts that Seraphin was dead. Was there not some merit in his dispassionate acceptance of the fact?

They entered the chapel for vespers and knelt down.

The clock struck. One, two . . . two. Two? No, there must have been one or two strokes before. He had gone to sleep. It was three. At least three, probably four. Or five. He waited. It could not be two: he remembered the brothers filing darkly into the chapel at that hour. Disturbing the shadows for matins and lauds. If it was five — he listened for faint noises in the building — it would only be a few minutes. They would come in, the earliest birds, to say their Masses. There were no noises. He looked toward the windows on the St. Joseph side of the chapel. He might be able to see a light from a room across the court. That was not certain even if it was five. It would have to come through the stained glass. Was that possible? It was still night. Was there a moon? He looked round the chapel. If there was, it might shine on a window. There was no moon. Or it was overhead. Or powerless against the glass. He yawned. It could not be five. His knees were numb from kneeling. He shifted on them. His back ached. Straightening it, he gasped for breath. He saw the sanctuary light. The only light, red. Then it came back to him. Seraphin was dead. He tried to pray. No words. Why words? Meditation in the Presence. The perfect prayer. He fell asleep . . .

. . . Spiraling brown coil on coil under the golden sun the river slithered across the blue and flower-flecked land. On an eminence they held identical hands over their eyes for visors and mistook it with pleasure for an endless murmuring serpent. They considered unafraid the prospect of its turning in its course and standing on tail to swallow them gurgling alive. They sensed it was in them to command this also by a wish. Their visor hands vanished before their eyes and became instead the symbol of brotherhood clasped between them. This they wished. Smiling the same smile back and forth they began laughing: "Jonah!" And were walking murkily up and down the brown belly of the river in mock distress. Above them, foolishly triumphant, rippling in contentment, mewed the waves. Below swam an occasional large fish, absorbed in ignoring them, and the mass of crustacea, eagerly seething, too numerous on the bottom to pretend exclusiveness. "Jonah indeed!" the brothers said, surprised to see the bubbles they birthed. They strolled then for hours this way. The novelty wearing off (without regret, else they would have wished themselves elsewhere), they began to talk and say ordinary things. Their mother had died, their father too, and how old did that make them? It was the afternoon of the funerals, which they had managed, transcending time, to have held jointly. She had seemed older and for some reason he otherwise. How, they wondered, should it be with them, *memento mori* clicking simultaneously within them, lackaday. The sound of dirt descending six feet to clatter on the coffins was memorable but unmentionable. Their own lives, well . . . only half curious (something to do) they halted to kick testingly a waterlogged rowboat resting on the bottom, the crustacea complaining and olive-green silt rising to speckle the surface with dark stars . . . well, what *had* they been doing? A crayfish pursued them, clad in sable armor, dearly desiring to do battle, brandishing hinged swords. Well, for one thing, working for the canonization of Fra Bartolomeo, had got two cardinals interested, was hot after those remaining who were at all possible, a slow business. Yes, one would judge so in the light of past canonizations, though being stationed in Rome had its advantages. Me, the same old grind, teaching, pounding away, giving Pythagoras no rest in his grave . . . They made an irresolute pass at the crayfish, who had caught up with them. More about Fra Bartolomeo, what else is there? Except, you will laugh or have me excommunicated for wanton presumption, though it's only faith in a faithless age, making a vow not to die until he's made a saint, recognized rather — he is one, convinced of it, Didymus (never can get used to calling you that), a saint sure as I'm alive, having known him, no doubt of it, something wrong with your knee? Knees then! The crayfish, he's got hold of you there, another at your back. If you like, we'll leave — only I do like it here. Well, go ahead then, you never did like St. Louis, isn't that what you used to say? Alone, in pain, he rose to the surface, parting the silt stars. The sun like molten gold squirted him in the eye. Numb now, unable to remember, and too blind to refurnish his memory by observation, he waited for this limbo to clear away. . . .

Awake now, he was face to face with a flame, blinding him. He avoided it. A dead weight bore him down, his aching back. Slowly, like ink in a blotter, his consciousness spread. The supports beneath him were kneeling limbs, his, the veined hands, bracing him, pressing flat, his own. His body, it seemed, left off there; the rest was something else, floor. He raised his head to the flame again and tried to determine what kept it suspended even with his face. He shook his head, blinking dumbly, a four-legged beast. He could see nothing, only his knees and hands, which he felt rather, and the flame floating unaccountably in the darkness. That part alone was a mystery. And then there came a pressure and pull on his shoulders, urging him up. Fingers, a hand, a rustling related to its action, then the rustling in rhythm with the folds of a brown curtain, a robe naturally, ergo a friar, holding a candle, trying to raise him up, Titus. The clock began striking.

"Put out the candle," Didymus said.

Titus closed his palm slowly around the flame, unflinching, snuffing it. The odor of burning string. Titus pinched the wick deliberately. He waited a moment, the clock falling silent, and said, "Father Rector expects you will say a Mass for the Dead at five o'clock."

"Yes, I know." He yawned deliciously. "I told him *that*." He bit his lips at the memory of the disgusting yawn. Titus had found him asleep. Shame overwhelmed him, and he searched his mind for justification. He found none.

"It is five now," Titus said.

It was maddening. "I don't see anyone else if it's five," he snapped. Immediately he was aware of a light burning in the sacristy. He blushed and grew pale. Had someone besides Titus seen him sleeping? But, listening, he heard nothing. No one else was up yet. He was no longer pale and was only blushing now. He saw it all hopefully. He was saved. Titus had gone to the sacristy to prepare for Mass. He must have come out to light the candles on the main altar. Then he had seen the bereaved keeping vigil on all fours, asleep, snoring even. What did Titus think of that? It withered him to remember, but he was comforted some that the only witness had been Titus. Had the sleeping apostles in Gethsemane been glad it was Christ?

Wrong! Hopelessly wrong! For there had come a noise after all. Someone else was in the sacristy. He stiffened and walked palely toward it. He must go there and get ready to say his Mass. A few steps he took only, his back buckling out, humping, his knees sinking to the floor, his hands last. The floor, with fingers smelling of dust and genesis, reached up and held him. The fingers were really spikes and they were dusty from holding him this way all his life.

For a radiant instant, which had something of eternity about it, he saw the justice of his position. Then there was nothing.

A little snow had fallen in the night, enough to powder the dead grass and soften the impression the leafless trees etched in the sky. Grayly the sky promised more snow, but now, at the end of the day following his collapse in the chapel, it was melting. Didymus, bundled around by blankets, sat in a wheel chair at the window, unsleepy. Only the landscape wearied him. Dead and unmoving though it must be — of that he was sure — it conspired to make him see everything in it as living, moving, something to be watched, each visible tuft of grass, each cluster of snow. The influence of the snow perhaps? For the ground, ordinarily uniform in texture and drabness, had split up into individual patches. They appeared to be involved in a struggle of some kind, possibly to overlap each other, constantly shifting. But whether it was equally one against one, or one against all, he could not make out. He reminded himself he did not believe it was actually happening. It was confusing and he closed his eyes. After a time this confused and tired him in the same way. The background of darkness became a field of vari-colored factions, warring, and, worse than the landscape, things like worms and comets wriggled and exploded before his closed eyes. Finally, as though to orchestrate their motions, they carried with them a bewildering noise or music which grew louder and caco-phonous. The effect was cumulative, inevitably unbearable, and Didymus would have to open his eyes again. The intervals of peace became gradually rarer on the landscape. Likewise when he shut his eyes to it the restful darkness dissolved sooner than before into riot.

The door of his room opened, mercifully dispelling his illusions, and that, because there had been no knock, could only be Titus. Unable to move in his chair, Didymus listened to Titus moving about the room at his back. The tinkle of a glass once, the squeak of the bookcase indicating a book taken out or replaced — they were sounds Didymus could recognize. But that first tap-tap and the consequent click of metal on metal, irregular and scarcely aud-ible, was disconcertingly unfamiliar. His curiosity, centering on it, raised it to a delicious mystery. He kept down the urge to shout at Titus. But he attempted to fish from memory the precise character of the corner from which the sound came with harrowing repetition. The sound stopped then, as though to thwart him on the brink of revelation. Titus's footsteps scraped across the room. The door opened and closed. For a few steps, Didymus heard Titus going down the corridor. He asked himself not to be moved by idle curiosity, a thing of the senses. He would not be tempted now.

A moment later the keystone of his good intention crumbled, and the whole edifice of his detachment with it. More shakily than quickly, Didymus moved his hands to the wheels of the chair. He would roll over to the corner and investigate the sound. . . . He would? His hands lay limply on the wheels, ready to propel him to his mind's destination, but, weak, white, powerless to grip the wheels or anything. He regarded them with contempt. He had known they would fail him; he had been foolish to give them another chance. Disdainful of his hands, he looked out the window. He could still do that, couldn't he? It was raining some now. The landscape started to move, rearing and reeling crazily, as though drunken with the rain. In horror, Didymus damned his eyes. He realized this trouble was probably going to be chronic. He turned his gaze in despair to the trees, to the branches level with his eyes and nearer than the insane ground. Hesitating warily, fearful the gentle boughs under scrutiny would turn into hideous waving tentacles, he looked. With a thrill, he knew he was seeing clearly.

Gauzily rain descended in a fine spray, hanging in fat berries from the wet black branches where leaves had been and buds would be, cold crystal drops. They fell now and then ripely of their own weight, or shaken by the intermittent wind they spilled before their time. Promptly they appeared again, pendulous.

Watching the raindrops prove gravity, he was grateful for nature's, rather than his, return to reason. Still, though he professed faith in his faculties, he would not look away from the trees and down at the ground, nor close his eyes. Gratefully he savored the cosmic truth in the falling drops and the mildly trembling branches. There was order, he thought, which in justice and science ought to include the treacherous landscape. Risking all, he ventured a glance at the ground. All was still there. He smiled. He was going to close his eyes (to make it universal and conclusive), when the door opened again.

Didymus strained to catch the meaning of Titus's movements.

Would the clicking sound begin? Titus did go to that corner of the room again. Then it came, louder than before, but only once this time.

Titus came behind his chair, turned it, and wheeled him over to the corner.

On a hook which Titus had screwed into the wall hung a bird cage covered with black cloth.

"What's all this?" Didymus asked.

Titus tapped the covered cage expectantly.

A bird chirped once.

"The bird," Titus explained in excitement, "is inside."

Didymus almost laughed. He sensed in time, however, the necessity of seeming befuddled and severe. Titus expected it.

"I don't believe it," Didymus snapped.

Titus smiled wisely and tapped the cage again.

"There!" he exclaimed when the bird chirped.

Didymus shook his head in mock anger. "You made that beastly noise, Titus, you mountebank!"

Titus, profoundly amused by such skepticism, removed the black cover.

The bird, a canary, flicked its head sidewise in interest, looking them up and down. Then it turned its darting attention to the room. It chirped once in curt acceptance of the new surroundings. Didymus and Titus came under its black dot of an eye once more, this time for closer analysis. The canary chirped twice, perhaps that they were welcome, even pleasing, and stood on one leg to show them what a gay bird it was. It then returned to the business of pecking a piece of apple.

"I see you've given him something to eat," Didymus said, and felt that Titus, though he seemed content to watch the canary, waited for him to say something more. "I am very happy, Titus, to have this canary," he went on. "I suppose he will come in handy now that I must spend my days in this infernal chair."

Titus did not look at him while he said, "He is a good bird, Father. He is one of the Saint's own good birds."

Through the window Didymus watched the days and nights come and go. For the first time, though his life as a friar had been copiously annotated with significant references, he got a good idea of eternity. Monotony, of course, was one word for it, but like all the others, as well as the allegories worked up by imaginative retreat masters, it was empty beside the experience itself, untranslatable. He would doze and wonder if by some quirk he had been cast out of the world into eternity, but since it was neither heaven nor exactly purgatory or hell, as he understood them, he concluded it must be an uncharted isle subscribing to the mother forms only in the matter of time. And having thought this, he was faintly annoyed at his ponderous whimsy. Titus, like certain of the hours, came periodically. He would read or simply sit with him in silence. The canary was there always, but except as it showed signs of sleepiness at twilight and spirit at dawn, Didymus regarded it as a subtle device, like the days and nights and bells, to give the lie to the vulgar error that time flies. The cage was small and the canary would not sing. Time, hanging in the room like a jealous fog, possessed him and voided everything except it. It seemed impossible each time Titus came that he should be able to escape the room.

" 'After him,' " Titus read from Bishop Bale one day, " 'came Fabius, a Roman born, who (as Eusebius witnesseth) as he was returning home out of the field, and with his countrymen present to elect a new bishop, there was a pigeon seen standing on his head and suddenly he was created pastor of the Church, which he looked not for.' "

They smiled at having the same thought and both looked up at the canary. Since Didymus sat by the window most of the day now, he had asked Titus to put a hook there for the cage. He had to admit to himself he did this to let Titus know he appreciated the canary. Also, as a secondary motive, he reasoned, it enabled the canary to look out the window. What a little yellow bird could see to interest it in the frozen scene was a mystery, but that, Didymus sighed, was a two-edged sword. And he took to watching the canary more.

So far as he was able to detect the moods of the canary he participated in them. In the morning the canary, bright and clownish, flitted back and forth between the two perches in the cage, hanging from the sides and cocking its little tufted head at Didymus querulously. During these acrobatics Didymus would twitch his hands in quick imitation of the canary's stunts. He asked Titus to construct a tiny swing, such as he had seen, which the canary might learn to use, since it appeared to be an intelligent and daring sort. Titus got the swing, the canary did master it, but there seemed to

be nothing Didymus could do with his hands that was like swinging. In fact, after he had been watching awhile, it was as though
the canary were fixed to a pendulum, inanimate, a piece of machinery, a yellow blur — ticking, for the swing made a little sound, and
Didymus went to sleep, and often when he woke the canary was
still going, like a clock. Didymus had no idea how long he slept
at these times, maybe a minute, maybe hours. Gradually the canary
got bored with the swing and used it less and less. In the same
way, Didymus suspected, he himself had wearied of looking out
the window. The first meager satisfaction had worn off. The dead
trees, the sleeping snow, like the swing for the canary, were sources
of diversion which soon grew stale. They were captives, he and the
canary, and the only thing they craved was escape. Didymus slowly
considered the problem. There was nothing, obviously, for him
to do. He could pray, which he did, but he was not sure the only
thing wrong with him was the fact he could not walk and that to
devote his prayer to that end was justifiable. Inevitably it occurred
to him his plight might well be an act of God. Why this punishment, though, he asked himself, and immediately supplied the answer. He had, for one thing, gloried too much in having it in him
to turn down Seraphin's request to come to St. Louis. The intention — that was all important, and he, he feared, had done the right
thing for the wrong reason. He had noticed something of the faker
in himself before. But it was not clear if he had erred. There was
a certain consolation, at bottom dismal, in this doubt. It was true
there appeared to be a nice justice in being stricken a cripple if he
had been wrong in refusing to travel to see Seraphin, if human love
was all he was fitted for, if he was incapable of renunciation for
the right reason, if the mystic counsels were too strong for him, if
he was still too pedestrian after all these years of prayer and contemplation, if . . .

The canary was swinging, the first time in several days.

The reality of his position was insupportable. There were two
ways of regarding it and he could not make up his mind. Humbly
he wished to get well and to be able to walk. But if this was a punishment, was not prayer to lift it declining to see the divine point?
He did wish to get well; that would settle it. Otherwise his pre-
dicament could only be resolved through means more serious than
he dared cope with. It would be like refusing to see Seraphin all
over again. By some mistake, he protested, he had at last been placed

in a position vital with meaning and precedents inescapably Christian. But was he the man for it? Unsure of himself, he was afraid to go on trial. It would be no minor trial, so construed, but one in which the greatest values were involved — a human soul and the means of its salvation or damnation. Not watered down suburban precautions and routine pious exercises, but Faith such as saints and martyrs had, and Despair such as only they had been tempted by. No, he was not the man for it. He was unworthy. He simply desired to walk and in a few years to die a normal, uninspired death. He did not wish to see (what was apparent) the greatest significance in his affliction. He preferred to think in terms of physical betterment. He was so sure he was not a saint that he did not consider this easier road beneath him, though attracted by the higher one. That was the rub. Humbly, then, he wanted to be able to walk, but he wondered if there was not presumption in such humility.

Thus he decided to pray for health and count the divine hand not there. Decided. A clean decision — not distinction — no mean feat in the light of all the moral theology he had swallowed. The canary, all its rocking come to naught once more, slept motionless in the swing. Despite the manifest prudence of the course he had settled upon, Didymus dozed off ill at ease in his wheel chair by the window. Distastefully, the last thing he remembered was that "prudence" is a virtue more celebrated in the modern Church.

At his request in the days following a doctor visited him. The Rector came along, too. When Didymus tried to find out the nature of his illness, the doctor looked solemn and pronounced it to be one of those things. Didymus received this with a look of mystification. So the doctor went on to say there was no telling about it. Time alone would tell. Didymus asked the doctor to recommend some books dealing with cases like his. They might have one of them in the monastery library. Titus could read to him in the meantime. For, though he disliked being troublesome, "one of those things" as a diagnosis meant very little to an unscientific beggar like him. The phrase had a philosophic ring to it, but to his knowledge neither the Early Fathers nor the Scholastics seemed to have dealt with it. The Rector smiled. The doctor, annoyed, replied drily:

"Is that a fact?"

Impatiently Didymus said, "I know how old I am, if that's it."

Nothing was lost of the communion he kept with the canary. He still watched its antics and his fingers in his lap followed them clumsily. He did not forget about himself, that he must pray for health, that it was best that way — "prudence" dictated it — but he did think more of the canary's share of their captivity. A canary in a cage, he reasoned, is like a bud which never blooms.

He asked Titus to get a book on canaries, but nothing came of it and he did not mention it again.

Some days later Titus read:

" 'Twenty-ninth pope, Marcellus, a Roman, was pastor of the Church, feeding it with wisdom and doctrine. And (as I may say with the Prophet) a man according to God's heart and full of Christian works. This man admonished Maximianus the Emperor and endeavored to remove him from persecuting the saints —— ' "

"Stop a moment, Titus," Didymus interrupted.

Steadily, since Titus began to read, the canary had been jumping from the swing to the bottom of the cage and back again. Now it was quietly standing on one foot in the swing. Suddenly it flew at the side of the cage nearest them and hung there, its ugly little claws, like bent wire, hooked to the slender bars. It observed them intently, first Titus and then Didymus, at whom it continued to stare. Didymus's hands were tense in his lap.

"Go ahead, read," Didymus said, relaxing his hands.

" 'But the Emperor being more hardened, commanded Marcellus to be beaten with cudgels and to be driven out of the city, wherefore he entered into the house of one Lucina, a widow, and there kept the congregation secretly, which the tyrant hearing, made a stable for cattle of the same house and committed the keeping of it to the bishop Marcellus. After that he governed the Church by writing Epistles, without any other kind of teaching, being condemned to such a vile service. And being thus daily tormented with strife and noisomeness, at length gave up the ghost. Anno 308.' "

"Very good, Titus. I wonder how we missed that one before."

The canary, still hanging on the side of the cage, had not moved, its head turned sidewise, its eye as before fixed on Didymus.

"Would you bring me a glass of water, Titus?"

Titus got up and looked in the cage. The canary hung there, as though waiting, not a feather stirring.

"The bird has water here," Titus said, pointing to the small cup fastened to the cage.

"For me, Titus, the water's for me. Don't you think I know you look after the canary? You don't forget us, though I don't see why you don't."

Titus left the room with a glass.

Didymus's hands were tense again. Eyes on the canary's eye, he got up from his wheel chair, his face strained and white with the impossible effort, and, his fingers somehow managing it, he opened the cage. The canary darted out and circled the room chirping. Before it lit, though it seemed about to make its perch triumphantly the top of the cage, Didymus fell over on his face and lay prone on the floor.

In bed that night, unsuffering and barely alive, he saw at will everything revealed in his past. Events long forgotten happened again before his eyes. Clearly, sensitively, he saw Seraphin and himself, just as they had always been — himself, never quite sure. He heard all that he had ever said, and that anyone had said to him. He had talked too much, too. The past mingled with the present. In the same moment and scene he made his first Communion, was ordained, and confessed his sins for the last time.

The canary perched in the dark atop the cage, head warm under wing, already, it seemed to Didymus, without memory of its captivity, dreaming of a former freedom, an ancestral summer day with flowers and trees. Outside it was snowing.

The Rector, followed by others, came into the room and administered the last sacrament. Didymus heard them all gathered prayerfully around his bed thinking (they thought) secretly: this sacrament often strengthens the dying, tip-of-the-tongue wisdom indigenous to the priesthood, Henry the Eighth had six wives. He saw the same hackneyed smile, designed to cheer, pass bravely among them, and marveled at the crudity of it. They went away then, all except Titus, their individual footsteps sounding (for him) the character of each friar. He might have been Francis himself for what he knew then of the little brothers and the cure of souls. He heard them thinking their expectation to be called from bed before daybreak to return to his room and say the office of the dead over his body, become the body, and whispering hopefully to the contrary. Death was now an unwelcome guest in the cloister.

He wanted nothing in the world for himself at last. This may have been the first time he found his will amenable to the Divine. He had never been less himself and more the saint. Yet now, so close to sublimity, or perhaps only tempted to believe so (the Devil is most wily at the deathbed), he was beset by the grossest distractions. They were to be expected, he knew, as indelible in the order of things: the bingo game going on under the Cross for the seamless garment of the Son of Man: everywhere the sign of the contradiction, and always. When would he cease to be surprised by it? Incidents repeated themselves, twined, parted, faded away, came back clear, and would not be prayed out of mind. He watched himself mounting the pulpit of a metropolitan church, heralded by the pastor as the renowed Franciscan father sent by God in His goodness to preach this novena — like to say a little prayer to test the microphone, Father? — and later reading through the petitions to Our Blessed Mother, cynically tabulating the pleas for a Catholic boy friend, drunkenness banished, the sale of real estate and coming furiously upon one: "that I'm not pregnant." And at the same church on Good Friday carrying the crucifix along the communion rail for the people to kiss, giving them the indulgence, and afterwards in the sacristy wiping the lipstick of the faithful from the image of Christ crucified.

"Take down a book, any book, Titus, and read. Begin anywhere."

Roused by his voice, the canary fluttered, looked sharply about and buried its head once more in the warmth of its wing.

" 'By the lions,' " Titus read, " 'are understood the acrimonies and impetuosities of the irascible faculty, which faculty is as bold and daring in its acts as are the lions. By the harts and the leaping does is understood the other faculty of the soul, which is the concupiscible — that is ——' "

"Skip the exegesis," Didymus broke in weakly. "I can do without that now. Read the verse."

Titus read: " 'Birds of swift wing, lions, harts, leaping does, mountains, valleys, banks, waters, breezes, heats and terrors that keep watch by night, by the pleasant lyres and by the siren's song, I conjure you, cease your wrath and touch not the wall . . .' "

"Turn off the light, Titus."

Titus went over to the switch. There was a brief period of darkness during which Didymus's eyes became accustomed to a different shade, a glow rather, which possessed the room slowly. Then he saw the full moon had let down a ladder of light through the window. He could see the snow, strangely blue, falling outside. So sensitive was his mind and eye (because his body, now faint, no longer blurred his vision?) he could count the snowflakes, all of them separately, before they drifted, winding, below the sill.

With the same wonderful clarity, he saw what he had made of his life. He saw himself tied down, caged, stunted in his apostolate, seeking the crumbs, the little pleasure, neglecting the source, always knowing death changes nothing, only immortalizes . . . and still ever lukewarm. In trivial attachments, in love of things, was death, no matter the appearance of life. In the highest attachment only, no matter the appearance of death, was life. He had always known this truth, but now he was feeling it. Unable to move his hand, only his lips, and hardly breathing, was it too late to act?

"Open the window, Titus," he whispered.

And suddenly he could pray. *Hail Mary . . . Holy Mary, Mother of God, pray for us sinners now and at the hour of our death . . .* finally the time to say, *pray for* me *now — the hour of* my *death, amen.* Lest he deceive himself at the very end that this was the answer to a lifetime of praying for a happy death, happy because painless, he tried to turn his thoughts from himself, to join them to God, thinking how at last he did — didn't he *now?* — prefer God above all else. But ashamedly not sure he did, perhaps only fearing hell, with an uneasy sense of justice he put himself foremost among the wise in their own generation, the perennials seeking after God when doctor, lawyer, and bank fails. If he wronged himself, he did so out of humility — a holy error. He ended, to make certain he had not fallen under the same old presumption disguised as the face of humility, by flooding his mind with maledictions. He suffered the piercing white voice of the Apocalypse to echo in his soul: *But because thou art lukewarm, and neither cold, nor hot, I will begin to vomit thee out of my mouth.* And St. Bernard, fiery-eyed in a white habit, thundered at him from the twelfth century: "Hell is paved with the bald pates of priests!"

There was a soft flutter, the canary flew to the window sill, paused, and tilted into the snow. Titus stepped too late to the window and stood gazing dumbly after it. He raised a trembling old hand, fingers bent in awe and sorrow, to his forehead, and turned stealthily to Didymus.

Didymus closed his eyes. He let a long moment pass before he opened them. Titus, seeing him awake then, fussed with the window latch and held a hand down to feel the draught, nodding anxiously as though it were the only evil abroad in the world, all the time straining his old eyes for a glimpse of the canary somewhere in the trees.

Didymus said nothing, letting Titus keep his secret. With his whole will he tried to lose himself in the sight of God, and failed. He was not in the least transported. Even now he could find no divine sign within himself. He knew he still had to look outside, to Titus. God still chose to manifest Himself most in sanctity.

Titus, nervous under his stare, and to account for staying at the window so long, felt for the draught again, frowned, and kept his eye hunting among the trees.

The thought of being the cause of such elaborate dissimulation in so simple a soul made Didymus want to smile — or cry, he did not know which . . . and could do neither. Titus persisted. How long would it be, Didymus wondered faintly, before Titus ungrievingly gave the canary up for lost in the snowy arms of God? The snowflakes whirled at the window, for a moment for all their bright blue beauty as though struck still by lightning, and Didymus closed his eyes, only to find them there also, but darkly falling.

PAUL BOWLES

under the sky

Inland from the sea on the dry coastal plain lay the town, open, spread out under the huge high sky. People who lived outside in the country, and even some of the more educated town-dwellers, called the town "the Inferno" because nowhere in the region was the heat so intense. No other place around was quite so shadowless and so dusty; it seemed that the clouds above shrank upwards to their farthest possible positions. Many miles above, and to all sides, they hung there in their massive patterns, remote and motionless. In the spring, during the nights, the lightning constantly jumped from one cloud to another, revealing unexpected distances between them. Then, if anyone ever looked at the sky, he was surprised to see how each flash revealed a seemingly more distant portion of the heavens to which still more clouds had receded. But people in the town seldom turned their heads upward. They knew at what time of the year the rains would come, and it was unnecessary to scan those vast regions in order to say what day that would be. When the wind had blown hard for two weeks so that the dust filled the wide empty streets, and the lightning grew brighter each night until finally there was a little thunder, they could be sure the water would soon fall.

Once a year when the lightning was in the sky Jacinto left his village in the mountains and walked down to the town, carrying with him all the things his family had made since his last trip. There were two days of walking in the sierra where it was cool; the third day the road was through the hot lands, and this was the day he preferred, because the road was flat and he could walk faster and leave the others behind. He was taller and prouder than they, and he refused to bend over in order to be able to trot uphill and downhill as they did. In the mountains he labored to keep up with them, but on the plain he strode powerfully ahead and sometimes arrived at the market before sunset.

Now he stood in the public square with a small paper parcel in his hand. He had arrived the day before. Instead of sitting in the sidestreet near the fountain and discussing the sales with the others from his village, he walked into the municipal garden and sat down on a concrete bench marked "1936." He looked up and down the walk. No one paid him any attention. He was barefoot, so the shoeshine boys passed him by.

Tearing open the paper packet he emptied the dried leaves into his left hand. With his right he picked out all the little round, black berries and tossed them away. Then he crushed the leaves and slowly rolled them into five thin cigarettes. This took all his attention for a half hour.

A voice beside him said: "That's pretty."

He looked up. It was a town-dweller; he had never seen him before, so he did not answer.

"All for you?" said the other in the silken town voice that Jacinto had learned to distrust.

"I bought it. I made them," said Jacinto.

"But I like *grifas* too," smiled the stranger. He was poorly dressed and had black teeth.

Jacinto covered the cigarettes completely with one big hand

which he placed on the seat of the bench. The stranger pointed to a soldier sleeping on another bench near the iron bandstand.

"He wants one and I want one. You should be more careful. It's three months now for possessing marijuana. Don't you know?"

"No," said Jacinto. "I don't know." Then he slowly handed over two of the cigarettes. The man took them.

"So long," he said.

Jacinto stood up full of fury, and with the other three cigarettes still in his hand, he walked out into the plaza and down the long street that led to the station. It was nearly time for the daily train from the north. Sometimes crazy people got off, who would give a man enough money for two good meals, just for carrying a bundle into the town for them. There was a cemetery behind the roundhouse where some of the railroad employees went to smoke the weed. He remembered it from the preceding year; he had met an inspector there who had taken him to see a girl. She had proved to be ugly — one side of her face was mottled with blue and purple.

At the station the train had already arrived. The people trying to get on were fighting with those who were trying to get off. He wondered why with all those open windows everyone insisted on going through the two little doors at the ends of the cars. It would have been very simple the other way, but these people were too stupid to think of it. His defeat at the hands of the townsman still bothered him; he wanted to have a gun so he could pull it out and shout: "I am the father of all of you!" But it was not likely that he ever would have a gun.

Without approaching the platform where so many people were moving about, he stood and impassively watched the confusion. From the crowd three strange-looking people suddenly emerged. They all had very white skin and yellow hair. He knew, of course, that they were from a faraway place because everyone knows that when people look as strange as that they are from the capital or even farther. There were two women and one man, and as they approached him, he noticed that they were speaking a language which only they could understand. Each one carried a leather bag covered with small squares of colored paper stuck on at different angles. He stepped back, keeping his eyes on the face of the younger woman. He could not be sure whether he found her beautiful or revolting. Still he continued to look at her as she passed, holding on to the man's arm. The other woman noticed him, and smiled faintly as she went by.

He turned angrily and walked toward the tracks. He was angry at her stupidity — for thinking he could have enough money to pay her as much as she would surely want. He walked on until he came to the cemetery. It was empty save for the gray lizards that scurried from the path at his feet. In the farthest corner there was a small square building with a white stone woman on top. He sat in the shade of the little building and took out his cigarettes.

The train whistled; it was starting on its trip to the sea where the people eat nothing but fish and travel on top of the water. He drew in the first few breaths very slowly and deliberately, holding the smoke in his lungs until he felt it burning the edges of his soul. After a few minutes the feeling began to take shape. From the back of his head it moved down to his shoulders. It was as if he were wearing a tight metal garment. At that instant he looked at the sky and saw far above him the tiny black dots that were vultures, moving ever so slowly in circles as they surveyed the plain in the afternoon sunlight. Beyond them stood the clouds, deep and monumental. "Ay!" he sighed, shutting his eyes, and it occurred to him that this was what the dead people, who were lying on all sides of him, looked at day after day. This was all they could see — the clouds, and the vultures, which they did not need to fear, hidden safely as they were, deep in holy ground.

He continued to smoke, going deeper and deeper into delight. Finally he lay back and murmured: "Now I am dead too." When he opened his eyes it was still the same day, and the sun was very low in the sky. Some men were talking nearby. He listened; they were trainmen come to smoke, discussing wages and prices of meals. He did not believe any of the figures they so casually mentioned. They were lying to impress one another, and they did not even believe each other. He smoked half of the second cigarette, rose, stretched, and jumped over the cemetery wall, going back to the station by a roundabout path in order not to have to speak to the trainmen. Those people, when they smoked, always wanted more and more company; they would never let a fellow smoker go quietly on his way.

He went to the cantina by the station, and standing in the street, watched the railway employees playing billiards inside. As night approached, the lightning became increasingly visible. He walked up the long street toward the center of town. Men were playing marimbas in the doorways and in front of the houses — three or four together, and sometimes only one, indolently. The marimbas and the marijuana were the only good things in the town, reflected Jacinto. The women were ugly and dirty, and the men were all thieves and drunkards. He remembered the three people at the station. They would be in the hotel opposite the plaza. He walked a little faster, and his eyes, bloodshot from lack of sleep and too much of the drug, opened a bit wider.

After he had eaten heartily in the market sitting by the edge of the fountain, he felt very well. By the side wall of the cathedral were all the families from the mountains, some already asleep, the others preparing for the night. Almost all the stalls in the market were dark; a few figures still stood in front of the cold fruit-juice stand. Jacinto felt in his pocket for the stub and the whole cigarette, and keeping his fingers around them, walked across to the park. The celestial fireworks were very bright, but there was no thunder. Throughout the town sounded the clink and purr of the marimbas, some near and some far away. A soft breeze stirred the branches of the few lemon trees in the park. He walked along thoughtfully until he came to a bench directly opposite the entrance of the hotel, and there he sat down and brazenly began to smoke his stub. After a few minutes it was easier for him to believe that one of the two yellow-haired women would come out. He flicked away the butt, leaned back and stared straight at the hotel. The manager had put a square loudspeaker over the entrance door, and out of it came a great crackling and hissing that covered the sound of the marimbas. Occasionally a few loud notes of band music rose above the chaos, and from time to time there seemed to be a man's voice speaking behind the noise. Jacinto was annoyed: the women would want to stay inside where they could hear the sound better.

A long time went by. The radio was silenced. The few voices in the park disappeared down the streets. By the cathedral everyone was asleep. Even the marimbas seemed to have stopped, but when the breeze occasionally grew more active, it brought with it, swelling and dying, long marimba trills from a distant part of the town.

It grew very late. There was no sound but the lemon leaves rubbing together and the jet of water splashing in the basin in the center of the market. Jacinto was used to waiting. And halfway through the night a woman stepped out of the hotel, stood for a moment looking at the sky, and walked across the street to the park. From his bench in the dark he watched her as she approached. In the lightning he saw that it was not the younger one. He was disappointed. She looked upward again before moving into the shade of the lemon trees, and in a moment she sat down on the next bench and lighted a cigarette. He waited a few minutes. Then he said: "Señorita."

The yellow-haired woman cried: "Oh!" She had not seen him. She jumped up and stood still, peering toward his bench.

He moved to the end of the seat and calmly repeated the word. "Señorita."

She walked uncertainly toward him, still peering. He knew this was a ruse. She could see him quite clearly each second or so, whenever the sky lighted up. When she was near enough to the bench, he motioned for her to sit down beside him. As he had suspected, she spoke his tongue.

"What is it?" she asked. The talk in the strange language at the station had only been for show, after all.

"Sit down, señorita."

"Why?"

"Because I tell you to."

She laughed and threw away her cigarette.

"That's not a reason," she said, sitting down at the other end of the bench. "What are you doing here so late?" She spoke carefully and correctly, like a priest. He answered this by saying: "And you, what are you looking for?"

"Nothing."

"Yes. You are looking for something," he said solemnly.

"I was not sleeping. It is very hot."

"No. It is not hot," said Jacinto. He was feeling increasingly sure of himself, and he drew out the last cigarette and began to smoke it. "What are you doing here in this town?" he asked her after a moment.

"Passing on my way south to the border," she said, and she told him how she was traveling with two friends, a husband and wife, and how she often took a walk when they had gone to bed.

Jacinto listened as he drew in the smoke and breathed it out. Suddenly he jumped up. Touching her arm, he said: "Come to the market."

She arose, asking: "Why?" and walked with him across the park. When they were in the street, he took her wrist fiercely and pressing it, said between his teeth: "Look at the sky."

She looked up wonderingly, a little fearfully. He went on in a low, intense voice: "As God is my witness, I am going into the hotel and kill the man who came here with you."

Her eyes grew large. She tried to wrest her arm away, but he would not let it go, and he thrust his face into hers. "I have a pistol in my pocket and I am going to kill that man."

"But why?" she whispered weakly, looking up and down the empty street.

"I want his wife."

The woman said: "It is not possible. She would scream."

"I know the proprietor," said Jacinto, rolling his eyes and grinning. The woman seemed to believe him. Now he felt that a great thing was about to happen.

"And you," he said, twisting her arm brutally, "you do not scream."

"No."

Again he pointed to the sky.

"God is my witness. You can save the life of your friend. Come with me."

She was trembling violently, but as they stumbled through the street and he let go of her an instant, she began to run. With one bound he had overtaken her, and he made her stop and look at the sky again as he went through his threats once more. She saw his wide, red-veined eyes in a bright flash of lightning, and his utterly empty face. Mechanically she allowed him to push her along through the streets. He did not let go of her again.

"You are saving your friend's life," he said. "God will reward you."

She was sobbing as she went along. No one passed them as they moved unsteadily on toward the station. When they were nearly there they made a great detour past the edge of town, and finally came to the cemetery.

"This is a holy place," he murmured, swiftly crossing himself. "Here you are going to save your friend's life."

He took off his shirt, laid it on the stony ground, and pushed her down. There was nothing but the insistent, silent flashing in the sky. She kept her eyes shut, but she shuddered at each flash, even with her lids closed. The wind blew harder, and the smell of the dust was in her nostrils.

He took her back as far as the park and there he let go of her. Then he said: "Good night, señorita," and walked away very quickly. He was happy because she had not asked for any money.

The next year when he came down to the town he waited at the station four afternoons to see the train come in. The last afternoon he went to the cemetery and sat near the small square building that had the stone woman on top of it. On the ground the dust blew past. The enormous clouds hung in the sky and the vultures were there high above him. As he smoked he recalled the yellow-haired woman. After a time he began to weep, and rolled over onto the earth, clutching the pebbles as he sobbed. An old woman of the town, who came every day to her son's grave, passed near to him. Seeing him, she shook her head and murmured to herself: "He has lost his mother."

PAUL BOWLES'S

under the sky

AT THE VERY END OF THE STORY, A YEAR AFTER THE CENTRAL EPISODE, Bowles confronts the reader with a new character; we are told nothing about her except that she is an "old woman of the town who came every day to her son's grave." In such a story as J. F. Powers's "Lions, Hearts, Leaping Does," where nearly all of the characters are richly developed, the intrusion of a stranger might have disrupted the tonality and focus of the story. Yet it is entirely consistent with the purposes of "Under the Sky" to have as the final speaker a nameless citizen of the town. For the town is a major figure in the story, and its personality is active both in the obtrusive effect of the setting and in the impressions of ugliness which it stimulates in Jacinto. In his mind, the town and all the people in it are nameless; he cannot identify them for us because he is isolated from them, and he knows them only pictorially, as embodying the features of repulsiveness.

In the movement or form of the story, we begin with a description of the town. Its atmosphere is aboriginal and antediluvian: the promise of a great rain, the gray lizards that scurry across Jacinto's path, the heat and aridity, all provide a kind of backdrop which makes the violence of the story seem a consequence as much of situation as of character. The town is "open" on the plain; it has neither mountains around it nor the sea; in contact only with the sky, it is naked before the savagery of the elements. But even the sky seems fearful and suspicious of the town: the clouds "shrank upward . . . receded" (page 487). Given the immensity and malevolence of the surroundings, it is both pathetic and ironic that Jacinto, when we first see him, is "taller" and "prouder" than the others on the road, refusing to bend, as they do, while climbing the mountain. He is defiant of what "the more educated town-dwellers" aptly call the "Inferno" (page 487).

Once he has completed his business, Jacinto tries desperately to blot out the malignance of the "Inferno," and in so doing he unconsciously gives symbolic significance to two other elements of the setting, the railroad station and the cemetery. Because of his terribly self-conscious isolation from the town, Jacinto finds in the railroad station a possibility of romantic escape. Before going to the cemetery he stops at the station to see and perhaps meet the "strange people" who arrive from "far away" places. Failing at the station to make contact with life from outside the "Inferno," he turns to the cemetery and an escape through an unconsciousness akin to death. But even as Jacinto begins to smoke, the train whistle excites him to a vision of vital and pleasurable life, of a place far off "where the people eat nothing but fish and travel on top of the water" (page 490). That Bowles has intentionally juxtaposed his symbols is indicated by his having carefully placed "a cemetery behind the roundhouse" (page 489). Jacinto moves among these places — the "Inferno," the railroad station, and the cemetery — like a man on pilgrimage, but he is always isolated, never content with any one of them, and initially condemned, as the simplicity, poverty, and incredible innocence of his conversational style suggest, to the primitiveness and wildness characteristic of the town itself.

In his personal relationships Jacinto has a vast almost comic distrust of everyone, even of "the others from his village" who have entered the town with him: "The marimbas and the marijuana were the only good things in the town, reflected Jacinto. The women were ugly and dirty, and the men were all thieves and drunkards" (page 491). The sound of the marimbas coming from the doorways allows Jacinto a contact which is for him ideally distant and impersonal; marijuana is a means by which he escapes from the antagonistic world of the living into the world of the dead. But Jacinto's addiction is not the reason for his isolation; rather, he is an addict because he is so lonely and lost. Superficially, he may be identified with the "town-dweller" whom he meets in the park and whose "silken town voice" he distrusts. That we are to make distinctions between the motivations of the two characters is clear, however, from the structure of the story. The central episode which ends with Jacinto's bidding good night to the *señorita* opens with one act of blackmail and develops into another: Jacinto is forced to give cigarettes to the town-dweller; the yellow-haired woman is forced by the most desperate threats to surrender to Jacinto. By extorting the cigarettes from Jacinto, the town-dweller hopes to escape through marijuana into a state like death; by his clumsy intimidation of the woman, Jacinto hopes to escape from an overwhelming sense of death through contact with life and the life-giving sexual act.

Because of the structural balance of the story, Jacinto's rape of the yellow-haired woman is made a natural result of the frustrating experiences which precede it. In this way violence is necessary to the theme; it is neither accidental nor shocking. Throughout the first half of the story, Bowles puts continual emphasis on the isolation of Jacinto — from his fellow travellers, from the "stupid people" on the train, from the trainmen in the cemetery, from the billiard players. Since this isolation is partly a consequence of Jacinto's arrogance, Bowles avoids sentimentality even when this arrogance arises, as it often does, from Jacinto's sense of his own personal inadequacy. Out of his pride, on the one hand, and his feelings of incompleteness, on the other, comes his belief that all human contact, like his contact with the town-dweller, is brought about by intimidation or violence. Frustrated by his defeat in the park, and angered by the foreign activity of the train passengers, Jacinto imagines himself drawing a pistol and shouting, "I am the father of all of you" (page 489). Even when they are not merely imagined, Jacinto's gestures of power and authority are pathetically clumsy. In using them it is always his unconscious intention to integrate himself with those from outside the "Inferno," with life rather than with death. In his actions, however, the customary associations of life and death are ironically transposed: as he tries to enter the normal processes of life, he is violent, savage, and destructive; as he approaches death, he is calm, placid, and "delighted." Just as Jacinto asserts with an imaginary pistol his claim to being "the father of all of you," so God, the actual "father," is viewed as asserting himself through lightning. The violence in the "Inferno" is given an apparent sanction by the violence in the heavens. Thus, Jacinto forces the woman to look at the lightning, and with almost comic simplicity calls upon God to be divine witness to an act of violation carried out on holy ground.

The significance of the scene of the rape, and consequently of the three scenes in the cemetery, is largely responsible for the structural unity and dramatic compactness of the story. When we first see Jacinto under the stone statue, it is as if he himself were in the grave. He is almost completely absorbed by death: death is in the earth, death is in the sky with the vultures, death is in Jacinto's soul whose "edges" are burned by the marijuana smoke. Having failed at the railway station to make contact with anyone in life, he finds delight in identifying himself with the dead: "He continued to smoke, going deeper and deeper into delight. Finally he lay back and murmured: 'Now I am dead too'" (page 490). In this first episode, Jacinto takes pleasure in life which is indistinguishable from death; in the last episode, although in the same state of death-like intoxication, he weeps out of an anguished sense that life is inaccessible to him. The change has been brought about by the second episode in the cemetery. His experience with the yellow-haired woman who, though not young and perhaps not beautiful, represents the vitality of the world outside and is in sharp contrast to the one woman he has met in the "Inferno": "She had proved to be ugly — one side of her face was mottled with blue and purple" (page 489).

The old woman in the final scene may believe that Jacinto is grieving the death of his mother, but the reader knows that Jacinto is not grieving the loss of the dead, but the loss of the living. The stone statue of the woman may well represent in his mind the cold and inanimate world of death which has replaced the world of violent life which he once experienced with the yellow-haired woman. In place of her body, he now grasps at the pebbles and at a world of such hardness that marijuana is no longer a sufficient comfort. It is likely, however, that Bowles wishes us to go further and to find in the statement of the old woman an ambiguity which has elements of truth. Jacinto, whose pretensions to being a giver of life we may recall — "I am the father of all of you" — is in the end pathetically viewed as being cut off from the very source of his own life, his mother. Though she mistakes the person he has lost, the old woman does define the nature of his loss. Out of her mistake, Bowles has made a rich symbolic statement.

W. RICHARD POIRIER

notes on the authors

Goldsmith, Oliver (1728–1774). British poet, novelist, and dramatist. Best known for his play *She Stoops to Conquer* and his novel *The Vicar of Wakefield*.

Hardy, Thomas (1840–1928). British novelist and poet. Hardy is another writer, like Melville and Hawthorne, who is more popular today than he was at the time he was writing his novels and short stories. Among his best-known works are *Tess of the D'Urbervilles*, *Jude the Obscure*, *The Mayor of Casterbridge*, and *The Return of the Native*.

Hawthorne, Nathaniel (1804–1864). American novelist and short-story writer who, with Melville and Henry James, constitutes the strongest claim that there is an American literature. Hawthorne is best known for his many short stories and novels such as *The Scarlet Letter*, *The Marble Faun*, and *The Blithedale Romance*.

Melville, Herman (1819–1891). American novelist, poet, and short-story writer. Melville's art is truly a discovery of the twentieth century, which has given books like *Moby Dick, Billy Budd, Pierre,* and Melville's poetry and stories the recognition they lacked in Melville's own time.

Anderson, Sherwood (1876–1941). American short-story writer. Anderson is one of the most important figures in the history of the American short story, more because of his influence than because of the greatness of his stories. Helped by Dreiser at the beginning of his career, he in turn was influential in the writing careers of a host of writers during the twenties and thirties; his best-known work is *Winesburg, Ohio.*

Faulkner, William (b. 1897). American novelist and short-story writer. A native of Mississippi, William Faulkner is the outstanding American writer of the past twenty years or so. His *Absalom, Absalom,* his *The Sound and the Fury,* his *Light in August, As I Lay Dying,* and *Requiem for a Nun,* are major works by a major writer. "Spotted Horses" is an example of Faulkner at his most humorous. Faulkner, like other modern writers — Joyce, Katherine Anne Porter, E. M. Forster, and Eudora Welty — has (contrary to a common belief about modern literature) a great deal of humor in all his writings. However, like the others mentioned, his humor is always at the service of some other larger artistic purpose — as in "Spotted Horses."

Clark, Walter Van Tilburg (b. 1909). American novelist and short-story writer. Born in Maine, Clark attended school and college in Nevada, and now lives in New Mexico. He has, both in his best-known novel, *The Ox-Bow Incident,* and in "The Wind and Snow of Winter," been able to use the stock materials of "Westerns" to dramatize some very meaningful and complex human experience. His other novels are *The City of Trembling Leaves* and *The Track of the Cat.*

Hemingway, Ernest (b. 1898). American novelist and short-story writer. Hemingway, very popular, is the central figure in the school of "bullet-biting writers." The style is spare and the ideas harmonize with the style. His best-known works are *The Sun Also Rises, A Farewell to Arms, For Whom the Bell Tolls,* and the recent *Old Man and the Sea.*

Trilling, Lionel (b. 1905). American critic, who has written a novel, *The Middle of the Journey,* and two well-known short stories, "The

Other Margaret," and "Of This Time, Of That Place." Mr. Trilling
is one of the leading critics in America today and, besides his two
treatments of major authors, *Matthew Arnold* and *E. M. Forster*, he
has collected his perceptive and influential essays in a recent volume,
The Liberal Imagination.

Bowen, Elizabeth (b. 1899). Irish short-story writer and novelist. Elizabeth Bowen has been interested in the lessons the modern writer may
learn from a study of the movies and the detective story. The reader
of a story like "The Cat Jumps," will see how suspense follows the
pictorial technique of the movies, how animisms suggest the mental
state of characters, as in the movies. Her novels include *To the North*
and *The Heat of the Day.* Her collections of short stories include
Look at All Those Roses and *Ivy Gripped the Steps.*

Fitzgerald, F. Scott (1896–1940). American novelist and short-story
writer, whose life is fast assuming mythic proportions which threaten
to eclipse his stature as writer. Fitzgerald has been embraced by the
social historians of the 1920's and 1930's, and his novels — notably
The Far Side of Paradise, Tender is the Night, and *The Great Gatsby*
— have been treated as journalistic records of a time, rather than as
the sensitive, artistic dramatizations of loneliness which they are.

Aiken, Conrad (b. 1889). American short-story writer, poet, and novelist, whose recognition was marked in 1952 through the eulogy
afforded him in Seymour Lawrence's Aiken volume of *Wake.* Aiken
has lived as a writer writing, bypassing the usual literary soirées,
writers' conferences, and speeches to clubs. Mr. Aiken's *Collected
Stories* contains some of the best writing of the twentieth century.
His stories are marked by a poetic, symbolic texture, to be found elsewhere only in the best stories of Eudora Welty.

Porter, Katherine Anne (b. 1894). American short-story writer. Katherine Anne Porter has undoubtedly helped more writers in her generation than any other person now writing; her influence at this time
is even greater than was Sherwood Anderson's when he was a force
in American writing. Among those who have been encouraged by
Miss Porter one must include Eudora Welty, J. F. Powers, Peter
Taylor, and William Goyen. Her volumes of short stories include
*Flowering Judas and Other Stories; Pale Horse, Pale Rider; The
Leaning Tower.*

Conrad, Joseph (1857–1924). British-Pole who wrote stories and novels, many of which have the sea as a setting. According to Conrad, one is to take "The Heart of Darkness" as an autobiographical account of what happened on one of his many voyages while a fairly young sailor — this one a voyage into the Belgian Congo. Conrad's work suffered the misunderstanding Melville suffered until recently: his stories were taken for nothing more than the sea and adventure tales they obviously were on the surface. However, Conrad is one of the writers most influential in making the novel and the story serious vehicles for serious ideas and moral questions. Conrad wrote a tremendous amount, but among his best works are *Youth*, *Victory*, *Nostromo*, *The Nigger of the Narcissus*, *Under Western Eyes*, and *The Shadow Line*.

Forster, E. M. (b. 1879). British short-story writer, novelist and essayist, who sometimes uses fantasy to deal with serious themes of twentieth century attitudes toward life and art. In his novels, in his stories, and in his criticism, Forster is an exponent of a humanistic tradition which derives from both classical and eastern sources. His stories have been gathered in *The Collected Tales of E. M. Forster*. His critical volumes include *Aspects of the Novel* and *Two Cheers for Democracy*, while his best-known novels are *The Longest Journey*, *A Room with a View*, *Howard's End*, and *A Passage to India*.

Lawrence, D. H. (1885–1930). British novelist and short-story writer. Lawrence exists as a legend in somewhat the same way Fitzgerald does. His personal way of life influenced a whole generation of individualists, few of whom had either Lawrence's artistic genius or his passionate involvement in what he was doing. His stories are all gigantic metaphors of love and sexuality. He also wrote some poetry, but a glance at his work is enough to convince a reader that Lawrence is a short-story writer and a novelist. His novels include *Sons and Lovers*, *The Rainbow*, and *Lady Chatterley's Lover*.

Welty, Eudora (b. 1909). American short-story writer. Eudora Welty, born in Mississippi, has spent most of her life in her native state. She has worked in publicity and advertising, has written feature stories and radio scripts, and has even taken publicity photographs — but now devotes all her time to writing. Her stories have appeared in *The Atlantic Monthly*, *Harper's*, *The Southern Review*, and *The New Yorker*. In 1942 and 1943 Miss Welty received the O. Henry Memorial prize for the short story. In May, 1944, she was given an award of $1000 by the American Academy of Arts and Letters "in recognition of her skill in the short story and her artistry in the subtle portrayal of character." She is the author of two novels, *The*

Robber Bridegroom (1942) and *Delta Wedding* (1946), and many of her stories have been gathered together in three volumes, *A Curtain of Green* (1941), *The Wide Net* (1943), and *The Golden Apples* (1949).

Joyce, James (1882–1941). Irish novelist, short-story writer, and poet, who was aptly referred to by Delmore Schwartz — speaking for serious artists of the twentieth century — as "our dead king" (an expression used by one of Joyce's own characters referring to Parnell). Joyce is the greatest writer the twentieth century has so far produced, and his four major works, *Dubliners* (short stories), *A Portrait of the Artist as a Young Man* (novel), *Ulysses* (stream-of-consciousness novel), and *Finnegans Wake* (stream-of-unconsciousness "novel") constitute among themselves a history of the development of complexity in fiction in the twentieth century — although no writer so far has attempted to follow Joyce along the strange new paths opened up by *Finnegans Wake*. Joyce's influence on twentieth-century writing is enormous — both on the style of writers and on their serious attitudes toward their art.

Taylor, Elizabeth (b. 1912). English short-story writer and novelist, born in Reading, Berkshire, England. She attended Abbey School and in 1930 moved to her present home near High Wycombe. There she worked as a governess to young children. As she herself puts it: "When these had reached the age for learning fractions (which I do not know how to do) I took a job as librarian in the local Books Library thinking that a liking for books would be useful." Mrs. Taylor moved from the liking of books to the writing of them. She writes very slowly, she claims, and rewrites a great deal. In recent years American readers have become familiar with her stories through *The New Yorker*, in which a number of them have appeared.

Stafford, Jean (b. 1915). American short-story writer and novelist, born in Covina, California, and reared and educated in Colorado. After a life which took her to all parts of the United States and to Germany, Miss Stafford settled down in Connecticut, where she now resides. Her short stories, usually cast in the form of reminiscences of some bizarre event (this is especially true of those which have been printed in *The New Yorker*) have appeared in the leading magazines of the United States — *Harper's*, *The Atlantic Monthly*, *The New Yorker*, *The Kenyon Review*, and *The Partisan Review*. In addition, Miss Stafford has written three novels: *Boston Adventure* (1944), *The Mountain Lion* (1947), and *The Catherine Wheel* (1952).

MacMahon, Bryan (b. 1909). Irish short-story writer, poet, and novelist. MacMahon is one of the new Irish writers whose stories are really tales out of the bardic and folk traditions of Ireland, set in a modern world, carrying themes that concern this modern world. Mr. MacMahon's *The Lion Tamer and Other Stories*, from which "The Corn is Springing" is taken, reveals a large range of subject matter and technique, from stories that could be sung in ballads to those that are as complicated as Eudora Welty's; from those about Irish pub-crawlers to those about characters in a seminary. Mr. MacMahon's stories have appeared in *The Partisan Review* in this country. Among his other publications is a novel, *Children of the Rainbow*.

Sansom, William (b. 1912). English short-story writer and novelist. In the opinion of the editors, William Sansom is the leading young writer in England at the present time. His short stories are varied, mingling humor with tragedy, treating all social levels, both in and out of England. Mr. Sansom is able to use the most colloquial and the most literary styles — sometimes, for special effects, within the same story. His stories have appeared in the United States in many leading magazines and he has published a great number in the now defunct English magazine, *Penguin New Writing*, and in *The Cornhill Magazine*. In 1946 and 1947 he was awarded literary scholarships by the Society of Authors in London. Mr. Sansom has published many volumes of short stories: *Fireman Flower* (1944), *Three* (1946), *Something Terrible, Something Lovely* (1948), *The Passionate North* (1950), and *A Touch of the Sun* (1952). In addition he has written two novels, *The Body* (1949) and *The Face of Innocence* (1952).

Goyen, William (b. 1918). American novelist and short-story writer, born in East Texas, William Goyen grew up in Houston where he attended Rice Institute. He received his B.A. in 1937 and his M.A. in Literature in 1939. After his graduation from Rice he taught at the University of Houston until the war, during which he served in the United States Navy for four years. His stories have appeared in *Horizon, Accent, Partisan Review,* and *Penguin New Writing*. In 1948 he was awarded a *Southwest Review* Fellowship in Creative Writing for work on *The House of Breath*, his first novel, which was published in 1950. For his second book, *Ghost and Flesh*, published in 1952, Mr. Goyen has written a group of eight stories, many of which, like "The White Rooster," had been published previously in magazines.

Wilson, Angus (b. 1914). British short-story writer and novelist. Angus

Wilson, though born in England, spent much of his later childhood in South Africa. His adolescent years as a day boy at Westminster School were lived in private hotels. He then moved on to Oxford, where he was during the 1930's. After two years spent in many and strange employments (including waiting in a teashop and judging displays of folk-dancing), he achieved one of his ambitions by joining the staff of the British Museum Library. He worked for the Foreign Office during the war and has now returned to the British Museum Library staff, engaged in a large project — replacing 200,000 volumes destroyed by bombing. Angus Wilson's first volume of short stories, *The Wrong Set*, brought him critical recognition, as did his following publications, *Such Darling Dodos* (short stories, containing "Mummy to the Rescue"), *Emile Zola* (criticism), and *Hemlock and After* (his first novel).

Powers, J. F. (b. 1917). American short-story writer. J. F. Powers was born in Jacksonville, Illinois, and from there moved to Minnesota. He received his high-school education from Franciscan friars, and has taught at St. John's Benedictine Monastery in Minnesota and at Marquette University. He began writing while working for book firms in Chicago and though he has not published a large number of stories, his *Prince of Darkness and Other Stories* (1947), contains some of the best writing of the younger generation of American artists. Mr. Powers has received several prizes and distinctions, including a Guggenheim Fellowship in 1948.

Bowles, Paul (b. 1911). American short-story writer, poet, novelist, and composer. Born in New York City, Paul Bowles, after starting his college education at the University of Virginia, ran off to Paris. He toured Europe, then returned to study composition with Aaron Copeland. The next few years of his life were devoted to travel in South and North Africa, the West Indies, and South America — with time out to write scores for Hollywood films and Orson Welles' Mercury Theatre Radio Productions. Mr. Bowles began writing short stories in 1945. These were collected in *The Delicate Prey* (1950), from which "Under the Sky" is taken. In 1949 he published his first novel, *The Sheltering Sky*, and in 1952, another novel, *Let It Come Down*. For the last year or two, Mr. Bowles has been living in Ceylon.

Date Due

7-28-58		
8-18-		
8-19- 9:00 A.M.		
8-20-58		
FEB 1 6 1961		
3/19/62		
MAR 1 6 1963		
MAY 1 5 1963		
APR 2 8 1964		
MAY 1 9 1964		
JAN 5 1965		
Apr 16 '66		
May 2 '66		
Mar 12 6 8		
APR. 26. 1979		